TWILIGHT DESCENDING

GW00505582

James E Quick

PEPPER PRESS
Dublin

First published in Ireland in 1996 by
Pepper Press
29 Upper Mount Street
Dublin 2

ISBN 1 85594 198 8

The moral right of James E Quick to be identified as the Author of this Work is asserted.

Cover design: Mick O'Dwyer
Origination: Pepper Press
Printing: The Guernsey Press Co. Ltd

DEDICATION

To William Dominick Quick and Margaret Flaherty, my great-grandparents, who started it all.

PREFACE

This is the story of the Aran Islander, Tadhg O'Cuirc, who set out from his home on Inishmór on what he thought would be a short trip and a short visit to County Clare on the mainland.

A great wind, however, altered his course to cross that of James II, deposed king of England; William III, James's successor; Louis XIV of France, his Most Christian Majesty; the Duke of Tyrconnell, General Ginkel, General Lauzun, General St Ruth, Patrick Sarsfield and many others who fought, plotted, loved, strutted and bled among the highways and boreens of life at the closing of the seventeenth century.

Since we will travel with Tadhg through all four provinces of Ireland and even to France, we will encounter many persons. Some we will meet frequently, others but briefly. Some will be familiar, others will not. Caught in the flow of history, Tadhg is carried from Connaucht to Ulster, to Leinster, to Munster, to France then back to Ireland.

The story is comprised of six parts. For the convenience of those who choose to accompany Tadhg on his travels, each part will list the characters as we meet them.

PART I

Connaught

Cast of Characters

Dónal Óg O'Devaney, a youth of Moyrus Parish in the Barony of Ballyinahinch, Connemara

Connor O'Donnell, a young and recent recruit to the band of Cathal O'Flaherty's Rapparees

Tadhg O'Cuirc, a fisherman from Inishmór, the Aran Islands

Cathal O'Flaherty, a member of an ancient Connemara family, chief of the Rapparees

Donough O'Flaherty, his younger brother

Dermot O'Lee, also a member of an old Iar-Chonnacht family, hereditary physicians to the O'Flahertys

Sir Thomas Montgomery, a judge from Dublin, the bastion of English authority in Ireland

John Montgomery, his son, a notorious dandy and duellest

Lady Margaret FitzGerald, a descendant of the Geraldines who played so great a role in the history of Ireland

Mary Casey, her maidservant

Mortagh Blake, a poor farmer from Moyrus Parish

Máire Blake, his wife, and sister to Conor O'Donnell

Donough O'Kerrigan, the trusted friend of the O'Flahertys, and a member of the band of Rapparees

Tomas Nugent, a member of an old Westmeath family, also a Rapparee

Sir John Ferguson, a former officer in Cromwell's Army, now a propietor of huge estates in the Barony of Ballynahinch

Father Maurice O'Conlon, the 'hedge priest' of the Parish of Moyrus

CHAPTER I

The Curragh

It was Dónal Óg who first saw the curragh from his watchpoint high on the cliff overlooking Kiltiernan Bay.

"Tis a curragh making its way towards the strand,' he shouted. 'May the Son of God be guiding them on this day,' he added reverently to himself, his words nearly smothered by the shrieking of the wild wind and savage roar of the surf below.

Conor O'Donnell climbed quickly from the rough camp in the spinney of ancient oaks, sheltered in the corrie behind the cliffs where it was protected from the fury of the wind, to join Dónal Óg at his observation post. Squinting into the wind he could see the dark outline of the curragh, riding the crest of one of the raging mountainous seas which swept in relentlessly, row after row from the open ocean to roar across the rocky strand with deafening thunder before spending their force on the wild shore of Connemara.

'They are fools or strangers, or both fools and strangers,' he muttered anxiously, more to himself than to his companion, 'to think they can gain sanctuary safely here in the angry face of this great storm. For them to hit yon small cove is like Blind Séamus trying to thread a needle.' He turned to Dónal, his eyes worried. 'Can you make out how many persons there are in the curragh?'

Dónal Óg shaded his eyes with his left hand to stop the flutter of his eyelashes in the violent wind, staring intently at the small craft on the broad bosom of the hostile sea, buffeted and tossed as the great walls of angry green water lifted it high, only to drop it again in the seemingly bottomless troughs, sinking from sight as if lost forever, then miraculously appearing again on the crest of the next monstrous roller.

'It's three men I see,' he said.

'How far out is the curragh?'

Dónal hesitated, estimating the distance. 'About half a mile,' he said.

Conor contemplated the situation briefly, then instructed Dónal. 'You stay here and keep watching while I get help and go below to the strand.'

Dónal Óg nodded happily. It was grand to be considered of help to the bold Rapparees, even though he was but a stripling of sixteen. Conor descended to the Rapparee camp where a score of men was gathered around a stone fireplace and smoke-blackened chimney, the only remains of what had once been a cabin.

Cathal O'Flaherty, the leader of the Rapparees, was munching hungrily a piece of a large brown oatcake, freshly baked in the turf fire, and was stirring, with a stick broken from a dead oak branch, a potato roasting among the glowing embers.

The burly Rapparee chief was dressed in a blue, open-fronted jerkin from under which peeped a rough linen shirt, and blue trousers which reached halfway down his shins. His long, wavy brown hair streamed down to his shoulders under a tight-fitting bonnet. A heavy cloak was thrown over his shoulders. He was shod in heavy-soled buskins.

In sharp contrast was the slender lithe form of Conor, who wore a shapeless coat made of goatskin, a cap with long ear flaps of the same material, and frieze knee-breeches with flaps fore and aft. His legs were bare, and his feet were thrust into shoes of unseasoned leather with wooden soles and no heels. He appeared to be about twenty years of age. Bright blue eyes, now showing concern, looked steadfastly at Cathal from under a lock of golden hair.

'A curragh with three men in it is making for the strand,' he told Cathal. 'Do you think we ought to go below to offer help?'

The Rapparee chief crammed the last portion of oatcake into his mouth, rubbed his fingers together to flick off the crumbs, then slowly stroked his brown beard and moustache. 'Are you sure that it is a curragh, and not a longboat with Sassanach soldiers,' he asked Conor, his voice resonant and cultured, contrasting with his rough garments and wild surroundings.

'Dónal Óg, who has sharper eyes than I, says that it is indeed a curragh.'

Cathal shook his head. 'They will be three dead men if they persist in trying to make shore in this storm,' he said gloomily. 'It would take St Brendan the Navigator himself to guide that curragh through the reef. What do you think, Donough?'

His question was directed to a small figure seated by the fire. Respect for Donough's opinion was indicated in Cathal's tone. He was bareheaded, and his dark brown hair cascaded down his back. Large grey eyes set in a well-shaped head, a firm, full mouth in a face freshly shaven, and well-tailored clothes with cuffs, fine shirt with ruffles, hose and finished leather shoes with bright buckles, set Donough apart from his companions. Among the tall Rapparees his short stature seemed childlike unless one noticed that, under the *bainín* he wore, he was a hunchback.

Donough's voice, when he replied, was similar in tone to that of his brother, but his Irish was spoken carefully and precisely, with a hint of reaching for words long unused. 'It depends,' he said, 'on what type of vessel it is, and the skill of the crewmen. If they are men of Connemara, and exceptional curragh men, then they have a fighting chance.'

Cathal looked fondly at his brother, then turned to a short, dark-haired man standing at his side. 'Seamus, you stay here and guard the camp. Take a musket. If we hear firing, we will know that Ferguson's men are near. The rest of us will go down to the strand to see if we can substitute for the holy St Brendan.'

All the Rapparees but Séamus O'Callaghan, who took a position at the narrow defile that led to the corrie, followed Cathal down the tortuous, twisted path to the shore below. Puffins and gulls protested their invasion with wild cries, sweeping and turning in the air above them while the men scrambled as best they could in the face of the boisterous February wind which tried in vain to blow them off the cliffside as it whipped their clothes about their bodies, keening like the *beansí* all the while.

Then suddenly, as they made a wide turn near the base of the cliff, the shrieking wind was muted and a small, almost quiet cove lay before them. This comparatively safe haven was created by Patrick's Point, a massive rocky headland thrust into the sea where, it was said, the venerated saint had prayed at sunset. Now it offered some protection against the fierce gales which swept in from the broad Atlantic.

Out about a stone's throw, the great, grey-green combers broke over the rock-studded reef, driving long fingers of hissing water tumbling and boiling and surging up to the shore where Cathal stood with his men, peering out into the open sea, watching for the curragh.

High on the edge of the cliff above them stood Dónal. The curragh had come closer to the shore and the youth could now see that it held three figures; two were motionless and only the third, seated in the bow of the boat, was rowing. His companions were slumped in their seats, and only the rhythmic sweep of the lone rower's oars kept Dónal from thinking it was a ship with a ghostly crew.

While he watched anxiously, the sun shone momentarily through a gap in the dark, scudding clouds, and was reflected from the flashing oars. It illuminated the solitary oarsman, showing him half-turned on his seat so that he could see ahead of the curragh as well as behind. Occasionally he would strive mightily to drive his craft ahead on the crest of a great wave, then again he would seem to make hardly any progress at all, staying nearly stationary, his oars dipping lightly in the water. Ahead of him the vast, white-crested monstrous waves rolled thunderously towards the distant reefs, completely submerging the dangerous, denticulated rocks.

Down on the strand, Cathal edged his way, taking a vantage point where he could watch the curragh cautiously approach the reef. After three titanic waves had seemingly engulfed the frail vessel, a slight lull set in, as if the storm had stopped to catch its breath after so vigorous an effort. When Cathal next saw the curragh, the oarsman had reversed its position so that he could scan the reef and the long line of crashing breakers better.

As Cathal watched apprehensively, a gigantic wave, larger than any that had gone before, loomed out of the grey sea, relentless and menacing. 'Oh Mary, Mother of God,' he cried aloud, 'warn him to look and be prepared!'

The howling wind tore the warning from his lips, hurling salt spume in his face, but the lonely curraghman seemed to sense disaster. Half-turning in his seat, with a single powerful stroke of his right oar he swung the boat's bow directly into the path of the threatening wave.

On the shore the fearful watchers groaned as the massive wall of water appeared to overwhelm the tiny craft, like the whale swallowing Jonah, and rising and rising, blotted out the grey sky, charging towards the shore as if it would wash away all of Ireland, until it finally spent itself on the bleak rocks, leaving behind it pools of foamy water and masses of oily kelp where all had been dry before.

As the waters receded, rushing and hissing back to the sea from whence they had come, a joyful shout arose from the throats of Cathal and his men as they saw the curragh, still unvanquished, bobbing like a Spanish wine cork on the vast, troubled, surging surface of the sea.

'That brave lad will make his move soon,' Cathal predicted to Donough standing by him. 'When he turned his curragh a while ago, he was getting prepared. He knows it's high tide and intends to take full advantage of the high water over the reef. Look,' and Cathal pointed to the centre of the reef, 'there's little white water where the waves roll over it. That indicates a gap in the rocks. An expert curraghman can read his water like Father O'Conlon can his breviary, and if I'm right, he will try to bring his boat through the gap.'

'But in the name of God,' said Donough, anguish in his voice, 'why don't the other men help him row? They sit there like they are dead men.'

Cathal, who had a better view, answered somberly, 'They sit there like dead men, Donough Beag, most likely because they are dead men. Yon curragh men is handling the boat all alone. I have watched carefully, yet neither other man has stirred or moved an oar.'

The curraghman moved his craft out into the open sea again. He maneouvered the curragh until a trio of menacing waves had rolled past' then, in the lull that followed, he set it in forward motion again towards the distant shore. Around the watchers the air was filled with the booming of the waves. The shore shook with their fury, and the wind seemed to increase in force and ferocity as it flung spindrift in their anxious faces while the lonely curraghman fought for survival against the sea.

With oars flashing, the curragh was edged closer to the white, foaming, wild water of the reef. When it rode high on the crest of a wave, the viewers could see its curving bow and the glistening sides of the wet cowhide, but when it dropped down into a trough for what seemed an eternity, it was gone from the surface of the earth, and despair gripped them until the boat reappeared on the rim of the next giant comber.

As the curragh approached the strand the men crossed themselves, praying for the brave man and his fragile craft in their unequal duel with the more powerful foe. 'Let St Brendan be your guide, and St Christopher your passenger, and let the good God give strength to both your arms, for if you ever needed strength and divine assistance, you need it now,' Cathal prayed.

Three curragh-lengths from the perfidious and deadly submerged rocks of the reef, the boatman halted his forward movement. It was the crucial moment. It would be next to impossible to go out to sea again safely. He would have to come in. The curraghman kept the boat nearly stationary, dipping his oars right and left to keep it steady, and Cathal knew he was waiting for the next trio of great waves to come sweeping in from the vast expanse of the ocean, hoping to ride one of them high and safe over the fanged foe waiting to rip the belly out of his boat.

The first of a trinity of huge waves came roaring relentlessly towards the shore, with the oarsman riding it easily forward for a boat-length. Then, as the second comber approached, he leaned against his oars, powerful muscles tightening, sinews of back and shoulder flexed, until the wave lifted the curragh, and plying his oars with mighty strokes, he sent the skin-sheathed vessel flying forward as if wedded to the wave, like a seagull. The great wave thundered on and on, bearing its tiny burden until, in an immense mass of roiling white water, it crashed over the lurking rocks, foaming and frothing, losing much of its force and momentum, yet carrying sufficient impetus to dash angry little wavelets right up to the shore where Cathal stood.

When the curragh disappeared from their sight in the wall of cascading sea water, the assembled Rapparees groaned in unison, realising that only a miracle could keep the frail craft afloat and upright. Fearfully they watched as the spent wave receded, reluctantly returning to its mother, the sea, and there - Mother of God be praised! - was the curragh driving boldly into the churning shallow waters. A dozen men dashed into the sea to drag it to safety.

They guided the craft speedily to a sheltered area away from the greedy, clutching fingers of the sea. All three oarsmen were now slumped forward in their seats. They were lashed securely with stout *súgán* to stop them from going overboard. All three were similarly clad: Galway blue shirts, tight-fitting and of hand-woven wool, and knitted seamen's caps with tassels, untanned cowhide trousers, and *pampooties*, also made of cowhide, attached to their feet with leather thongs.

The curragh was a typical West Coast craft of sallyrod frame over which was stretched sewn cowhide. About twenty feet in length, its sloping high bow helped it ride like a sea-bird over the great waves. It was light, buoyant and extremely seaworthy. Attached to the bowstem, on the inside of the boat, was the usual small flask of holy water to keep the boatmen safe. The flask was of glass, apparently the product of a Florentine craftsman, and salvaged from the sea.

As the Rapparees hurriedly cut the *súgán* thongs with their *sceana* - long sharp knives - they discovered why the man in the middle and the man in the stern had not helped to bring in the curragh. They were both dead. Conor O'Donnell and Cathal O'Flaherty struggled to lift the surviving crew member from the curragh. After much exertion they deposited him, a giant of a man, on a dry and level place on the strand. His clothes were sodden and encrusted with salt. Other Rapparees solicitously lifted the bodies of the two dead men from the boat, reverently laying them on the opposite side, away from the living man.

Dermot O'Lee, ruddy-faced, of medium height, gentle of mien and bearing, put his hand inside the big man's shirt, feeling for a heartbeat. After a few moments he raised his head to the anxious Cathal. 'He is still alive, but barely. Quick, someone, let me have a *bainín* to cover him. And you, Conor, get back to the camp for hot bonnyclabber and oatcakes!'

It was Donough O'Flaherty who whipped off his white *bainín* to cover the boatman, disclosing his own big torso but short legs. While they waited for Conor's return, the Rapparees admired the huge proportions of the unconscious curraghman, and Donough went to examine the curragh, returning with a long, flat, cowhide case.

'It was tied to the boat with rope,' he said. He fumbled with the thongs at one end, loosening a flap, and drew forth a magnificent sword.

It was a rapier. To most of the Rapparees, familiar only with the huge claymore, it seemed a delicate, almost fragile weapon. Donough examined it thoroughly, from oval pommel to ricasso, turning it in his hands the better to see its cup hilt, curving knuckle bows, quillons and *pas d'ane*, all silver-filigreed. Then, holding the sword aloft, he read slowly, 'Pedro de Toro, Toledo, 1651.'

'He's a Spaniard?' Cathal asked incredulously.

Donough smiled. 'No. The sword is Spanish-made, not yon Islander. But hark to this, for there is more.' Squinting slightly, he read slowly, '*Sacada solo en defensa del honor.*'

'A noble sentiment,' said Dermot O'Lee, one of the few present who understood Spanish. 'Drawn only in defence of honour, I hope he follows his weapon's motto, for a man as big as he would need draw it for no other reason.'

Conor, returning with oatcakes and a wooden mug of bonnyclabber, a hot-milk mixture laced liberally with butter, squatted at the side of the still unconscious boatman, anxiously examining his features, Warmed by the *bainín*, colour was

13

returning to the curraghman's face. As Conor watched, the black eyelashes fluttered, and fierce, deep-blue eyes looked with sudden alarm at the rough, armed men standing beside him. Instantly, the young giant bounded to his feet, throwing off Donough's *bainín*, seized his sword from the hands of a startled Cathal, and with one lithe leap, was free of the surprised group facing him.

'Put down your weapon, lad,' Cathal said coolly, 'we mean you no harm.'

'What place is this, and who are these men?' the curraghman asked fiercely, still grasping his weapon.

'I am Cathal O'Flaherty, leader of this band of Gaels sworn to resist the tyrannical government of Dublin Castle. We are labelled Tories, Rapparees, thieves, scoundrels, patriots - take your choice. The place is Moyrus parish on Kilkieran Bay. While you were unconscious we lifted you from your curragh. Your two companions, I regret to say, are dead, apparently from hunger and exposure. Their bodies lie yonder. Right now I think it best if you would take the bonnyclabber and oatcakes Conor is holding for you.'

The young giant, putting his left hand to his chin, pondered briefly. Then, putting down his sword, he ate the proffered food wolfishly, washing down the cakes with great quaffs of hot milk. Then he dropped to his knees, earnestly offering a prayer to God for having saved him from the sea, and for the souls of his dead companions.

Rising, he addressed the Rapparees. 'God and Mary bless you, especially Donough, for your good, warm coat, and you, Conor, for this food which is the first I have eaten in three days.'

'There is more. You are welcome to it,' Conor declared. 'And now tell us what name is on you, and from whence you come?'

'I am Tadhg O'Cuirc from Inishmór. I left on Monday with Somhairle O'Conchubhair and Peadar Laidír in Peadar's curragh. Because I was the best curraghman, I had the bow seat despite the fact that I have had but twenty birthdays.'

The speaker paused, apparently embarrassed to be the centre of attraction. 'The sea was calm when we left the strand in the morning,' he continued. 'We intended to go to Ballyvaughan on the Clare side, where Peadar was to visit his older brother who is ill nigh unto death - God have mercy on his soul! We were but a short time gone when the wind picked up, blowing with such force off the land that we could no longer make headway, and to avoid being cast up on the rocks of Inishmán, we passed through Gregory's Sound.'

'I remember that wind,' Conor interrupted. 'It blew so mightily, I thought surely it would uproot these oaks. It was as if the Abbot of Hell himself was puffing and blowing.'

'We were blown so far out to sea,' the curraghman continued, 'we though we would surely be spending the night, if not the rest of our lives, in Hy Brasil. On the second day, we ran out of food. Rain gave us water for which we thanked God. We were wet and chilled, and during the night the cold crept into our bones. On Wednesday we saw a *pucán* off in the distance, its sails straining in the wind, but despite our frantic waving, the crew didn't see us. Then we truly despaired. Oh, the great loneliness of that vast sea! Nothing but wind and water, and water and wind.'

He paused, and then, with a shudder, brought himself back to the present. 'Some time after, the off-shore wind changed, and a great calm settled over the sea, just like the Widow Molly's duckpond at Kilmurvy. Then the sky in the west grew black and fearsome, and a great storm that had been brewing churned the sea all around us, the waves growing bigger and bigger. We were happy at first since the wind was blowing us the right way, back towards Inishmór and home, although we were as weak as babies.'

Tadhg paused, then made the Sign of the Cross. 'Late yesterday, just before dusk, Peadar shouted out that he could see a curragh approaching from the east with two men in it, one in the stern and one in the middle. Then Somhairle Mór said he could see it also. This seemed strange to me, for all I could see were the green waves, with not even a gull or other living creature. I asked Peadar where the curragh was, and he said it was abreast of us. Then he hailed the craft, which I couldn't see, asking who they were and whither they were bound. When there was no answer, I asked Peadar about it. He had a wild look in his eyes. He said that the men had not replied, and that now the curragh had disappeared into the gathering darkness.'

Once more the narrator hesitated before continuing his tale. 'Although I strained my eyes, I couldn't see any curragh, and when Peadar asked Somhairle Mór in a strange tone if the two men in the canoe didn't look exactly like the pair of them, and when Somhairle Mór solemnly agreed, I thought I was going mad. They were convinced that the spectral canoe was an omen, and that they were doomed to die. They shipped their oars, refusing to row any longer, despite my entreaties, since they were destined to die. I lashed them to the boat to save them from the water.

'All night I rowed, trying to keep the curragh steady before the wind and the following sea. I made good time with the wind at my back, and then this morning I saw the shore again for the first time in three days. Ah, 'twas a grand feeling entirely!'

'Did you know where you were?' asked Cathal O'Flaherty.

Tadhg shook his head. 'No. It was a strange shore. Although I have been to Inverin and Costello, I have never been here. As I was getting weaker by the hour, I knew that I would soon have to risk the surf trying to land or I would be taking the empty seat in the ghost curragh.'

'The angels were guiding you,' said Donough O'Kerrigan, making the Sign of the Cross, 'otherwise you too would have seen the ghost canoe.'

Donough O'Flaherty spoke up sharply. 'That is pagan nonsense,' he snapped. 'Your companions were out of their heads from fatigue and hunger. Don't put any stock in those old superstitious tales.'

Tadhg looked at Donough respectfully, recognising in the hunchback's authoritative manner and his speech that he differed from the other Rapparees. 'That may be, *a dhuine uasail*, for it did seem that Peadar and Somhairle were speaking wildly. Be that as it may, as I approached the shore I watched the waves breaking over the reef, noting that at one place there seemed to be much less white water. God was by me then. The next that I remember was finding myself on the shore with all of you staring at me.'

'I have known many great curragh men,' said Cathal admiringly, 'but never have I witnessed a feat such as yours. 'Twas little hope we held for you indeed. But let us return to the comfort of our camp.' He turned to his men. 'Carry the bodies of Peadar Laidir and Somhairle Mór up above,' he ordered. 'We must arrange for their burial.'

When the party reached the safety of the corrie, Cathal sent Conor O'Donnell to relive Dónal Óg at the observation point, and Eoghan MacDeeris to relieve Séamus O'Callaghan at the entrance to the defile leading to the protected area of the Rapparees' camp. Dónal Óg he then dispatched to get Father O'Conlon, a hedge priest who was staying at a nearby farm.

'This stand of oaks was planted by my grandfather, Eoghan O'Flaherty, more than sixty years ago,' Cathal told Tadhg. 'It is one of the few places in all of the Ballinahinch region where you will find their likes, for 'tis rare indeed to find even a potato that hasn't been stolen by Sir John Ferguson, who now occupies these lands that were once the O'Flaherty's.'

'And how did he get them?' Tadhg asked, his curiosity stimulated.

'How did he get them? He got them the way the Sasanaigh get all their lands in Ireland, by theft and murder! When Cromwell - may he burn forever in hell - was ravaging Ireland in 1649, his lieutenant in Connemara was this same John Ferguson, then a young officer. For ruthless killing of men, women and children, burning, pillaging and destroying, this lackey of Cromwell was only excelled by his master. As his reward he was given large grants of land here in Iar-Chonnacht that had once belonged to my father, Murrough O'Flaherty.'

Tadhg's brow furrowed, his eyes glared, and he spoke with anger 'How can this be? When Cromwell died, Charles should have restored your father's land. For wasn't it Cromwell who murdered the king's father?'

'Be not so naive,' Cathal told him pityingly. 'The king made great promises but kept few. Instead, he rewarded the regicides, the rebels, his sworn enemies, his persecutors. And to the faithful Catholic Irish he gave the back of his hand.'

'If Charles had rewarded those who had supported him,' Séamus O'Callaghan said bitterly, 'there would be no band of Rapparees here today, for we would be home on our own lands.'

'Aye,' Cathal agreed. 'The O'Flahertys suffered cruelly. By Cromwell's Act of 1652, Morrough ne Moyer O'Flaherty and Tadhg O'Flaherty were specifically excluded from any pardon, and their estates confiscated. Morrough left Ireland for France where he joined the young Charles in exile. Oh, great was that prince's reward for loyal service, for all Morrough ever received was the king's thanks in the Act of Settlement. Neither Morrough nor his heirs ever got their lands back.'

'Was that your father?' Tadhg asked.

'No. My father was a cousin to this other Morrough, who was The O'Flaherty,' Cathal explained. 'Our holdings and those of others of the clan were much smaller than his.'

Tadhg shook his head in bewilderment. 'It sounds unbelievable that King Charles would not have restored the lands of those who were loyal to them.'

Cathal turned to Donough. 'Tell him what happened when our

Uncle Rory appeared in Dublin in 1693 at the Court of Claims to regain the ancestral lands for the family of his murdered brother, Morrough.'

Donough seated himself near the fire, his eyes smouldering with the recollection of injustice. 'I was about fourteen years of age as I accompanied my uncle. He was one of the last of more than a thousand claimants to appear before the August deadline. At that, he was lucky, for more than seven thousand claimants failed to get a hearing at all! He presented his evidence to the court to show that our family had held the lands since about 1300, when they arrived here from the area east of Loch Corrib. Then came a witness, one John Hampton, who swore that my father was the leader of a band of Irish who burned the Protestant church at Moycullen in November 1641, with a hundred and fifty persons in it. In vain did Rory protest that he and my father had been in London on that date, that the church couldn't hold more than fifty people because it was so small. He even produced the former pastor of the church, who told the court that the church burned down due to the carelessness of the caretaker, and it was in the small hours of the morning with nary a person in it. He also pointed out that the so-called eye-witness was within a year of being born when the alleged offence occurred.'

'And what happened to your claim?' Tadhg asked.

Donough laughed derisively. What do you think happened? King Charles had promised protection, justice and favour to the Irish Catholics who had supported his father with their fortunes and their lives. He promised faithfully to reinstate those twenty thousand Irish who had fought with, and for, him during his exile. But when Sir John Ferguson presented his claims to Charles's Court of Claims, based upon his service to the Usurper, the vile Cromwell, and although Ferguson had been in possession of the lands for only nine years, the Earl of Limerick persuaded his fellow commissioners to find for Fergusons instead of the O'Flahertys, the rightful owners. Oh, 'twas a fine farce, especially when the court, in affirming that our father had been a loyal supporter of the king's father, granted his heirs five acres of the rockiest, most miserable, barren land in all of the barony of Ballinahinch as reward for his faithful service.'

'It pays to have friends in high places,' Cathal said bitterly. 'This same Captain Ferguson who was so highly rewarded was once dismissed from the army for drunkenness and gambling, but was reinstated by Cromwell upon the intercession of Ferguson's cousin Henry, a sort of army agent and important person at Whitehall.'

Passionately Tadhg exclaimed, 'All will be different now that King James is on the throne. He will see that justice is done.'

Cathal grimaced. 'And will he now? What has King James done for the Irish who were loyal to his father? He has reigned for three years, dutifully imitating his brother in following the advice of Lord Clarendon: 'Be good to your enemies; your friends will love you without it.' Because he has been no different from his brother, my men and I are still Tories - wanted men - living in the hills, while James's enemies occupy out ancestral lands. That is why these men ' Cathal's gesture included the men gathered around the fire - 'are on their keeping. That is why they have rallied to my standard of rebellion, each one a victim of the folly of the Stuarts, the father and his two sons.'

Cathal paused and looked at Tadhg sardonically. 'Is that enough or do you need more? Dónal Óg you know who got the cream, and who got the leavings of the churn? Why, none other than Lords Colony and Kingston, a parcel of earls and lesser nobility, all of whom were in open rebellion against the first Charles. And has your friend King James taken steps to evict and punish the murderers of his father, and reward his faithful Irish subjects instead? Not by the beard of Paddy the Piper!'

Tadhg lowered his head. 'I suppose I should know better,' he acknowledged. 'My father's family, the O'Cuircs, were driven from their lands in Tipperary by Cromwell because they were Irish Catholics. Their holdings were small,' he said apologetically, 'nothing like those of the O'Flahertys, but they dwelled there for centuries. They fled to County Clare, when my father was but a youth, where they settled in a Godforsaken spot along the seashore near the territory of the MacGormans. Even though my father was very poor, and had naught to offer but a strong back and a faithful heart, my mother, bless her, took him as husband. He tried hard to get along with the MacGormans, but when my mother's brother called him a lazy *spailpín*, he felled him with one stout blow, borrowed a curragh and fled with my mother to Inishmór where I was born, the eldest of three children.'

'Cromwell has caused more blood to flow and more tears to be shed than all the previous tyrants in Ireland together,' said Cathal, gnashing his teeth in rage. 'The crags of Connaught are red with the blood of the Gael. The bogs are littered with their bones since the accursed Cromwell gave the Irish their choice of ' To hell or to Connaught'. They crept here by the thousands from Ulster, Leinster and Munster to try to live in a land where the chief crop is death, where even the ponies have to scrounge for their miserable existence, where the winds shriek and only the Sasanaigh live off the little fat this bleak land has to offer.'

'Aye,' Donough agreed, 'and it wasn't only the Gael that was forced out, for Norman-Irish and English-Irish, who were also Catholics, fled alike from the death and destruction unleashed by Cromwell and his men. Even a grandson of Edmund Spenser, the Sassanach poet who had been granted rich Irish lands in the County Cork by the virago queen Elizabeth, was forced to flee from his modern-day cousins seeking the same kind of ill-gotten handouts of Irish land, and he crawled into Connaught with the others. No, Tadhg, it isn't idly said of Connaught: 'Not enough wood to hang a man, water enough to drown him nor earth enough to bury him'!'

'And it isn't only the Sasanaigh who dislike the Rapparees,' Cathal added grimly. 'There are others, like some of the Catholic bishops, who object also. We 'stir up the people', they complain, making the government take drastic steps against Ireland. Would you believe that the Provisional Synod held in 1670 by the Bishop Oliver Plunkett and Dr Brendan of Cashel, ordered the priests not to aid what they referred to as 'the lawless bandits called Tories'? That's us. And do you know what happened to the noble Catholic, Plunkett? Eight years ago he was taken by the Sasanaigh to the Tower of London, falsely accused, illegally convicted, and basely hanged, drawn and quartered. And who did this to him? The lawless bandits? No, his Dublin Castle friends!'

Cathal looked around at the fierce faces of his colleagues. 'What do you say, Fergus Dillon, you who are a descendant of the old Norman Dillons who fled here from the County Meath? And you, Donough O'Kerrigan of the old stock from Mayo? And Eamon O'Folan of Sligo? And Séamus O'Callaghan of North Cork? And you, O'Carroll, of Louth? And you, O'Doherty of Donegal? And MacNamara of Limerick? And my old friend O'Lee, of Connemara? And all the rest of you?'

Dónal's arrival with the Franciscan priest O'Hanlon halted any replies. Because of the condition of the bodies, the service for the dead was quickly consecrated and the mortal remains of Peadar Láidir and Somhairle Mór consigned to hastily dug graves in the sand, far above the highest high-water mark.

With heavy heart Tadhg had followed the bodies of his two comrades to their final resting place. There were no loved ones to keen for their dead - only the soft cadence of the priest, the howl of the wind, the sad cries of the gulls.

'Slán leat go deo,' Tadhg murmured sadly as the bodies were committed to the grave.

Later, after a meal of potatoes and fresh salmon, poached from a nearby stream, together with a generous portion of buttermilk and *arán* - a coarse bread made from ground peas, barley and oats - the O'Flaherty brothers joined Tadhg by the warm turf fire.

'What plans are you after making now?' asked Cathal kindly. 'Will you be going back to Inishmór soon? If so, we will be glad to take you to a place where there will be a curragh to take you home.'

Tadhg had an image of his parents, his brother and sister, gathered around the table for the evening meal, and for the first time since he had left, felt an overwhelming wave of homesickness. Tears sprung unbidden to his eyes, his throat felt choked, and he was unable to answer.

Noting Tadhg's emotion, Cathal lighted his pipe from a glowing coal, puffing vigorously to get it drawing. Donough glanced at his brother questioningly, then addressed Tadhg. 'I recently returned from France, Tadhg, where I have been for the last twenty-five years, to start a school here for the children of this parish. You are aware that there are no schools here for the Catholics, for both schools and schoolmasters are forbidden unless they are conducted by the Church of England. When I sailed from France there was a rumour prevalent that King Louis was raising a great army to help his cousin, King James. Most likely regiments will be raised here in Connaught. If you are of a mind, you could join one.

As Donough had hoped, his plan altered Tadhg's sombre mood. Turning to Cathal, Tadhg blurted, 'It's joining your band I'd rather be. It would make me happier than being a soldier for King James.'

Cathal looked at Tadhg, compassion in his steadfast grey eyes. he shook his head sadly. 'We are all men with a price on our heads. All except Donough, Conor and young Dónal. Each of us,' and he pointed his pipe at the other men in the gathering darkness, 'have been attainted, or outlawed, or are on the run because we tried to retain or reclaim that which was rightfully ours. We must eat what and when we can, we must move from place to place, having no

21

fixed abode, we see our kin when we can risk it, the sky is our roof, the stars our candles, the cold ground our beds. We dwell in the past because for us there is no future. We are a rare collection of rebels all gathered here in Connemara trying to restore that what was, and which we know in our hearts can never be again. We like to believe we are striking mortal blows at Dublin Castle, but in truth we are but gnats, buzzing futilely. It is only the charity of the poor people who also remember the old days that keeps us alive as they feed, clothe and warn us of the approach of the enemy - a sort of voluntary tax. But it is warming to an old heart, to an ageing lonely man, that they love and revere us still, despite our illusions. You are young, Tadhg, your life is still ahead of you. There are better ways and places to spend it than hiding in these hills. And so, although I would welcome your sword at my side, I must firmly say 'no' to your request.'

'You had better return to your family, who are probably grieving for you, believing you dead,' Donough added. 'You are fortunate enough still to have loving parents, a roof over your head, a warm hearth and a soft bed to sleep in.'

'Speaking of beds,' Cathal said, rising to his feet, 'I had better post some guards for the night. That old devil Ferguson probably knows we're here. He has informers everywhere.'

Dónal Óg, always eager to help, went to the fire where he covered the embers with ashes while he recited this prayer: 'I preserve this fire as God preserves me.'

Soon the camp was silent save for the snores of the sleeping men. After kneeling and saying the Rosary, Tadhg found a place for himself between two Rapparees, covering himself with the loose ends of their coats. But slumber was long in coming. His thoughts were mostly of his family and of Somhairle Mór and Peadar Láidir, now sleeping in the cold ground far from their homes on Inishmór. Finally he slept.

CHAPTER II

The Rescue

When Tadhg awoke, the sun was shining brightly, with just a few scattered clouds remaining from the storm. Cathal O'Flaherty and five of his men were mounted on their horses, all girded with swords, *sceana* and *pící*, or short pikes, from which the Rapparees had gained their name. Only Séamus O'Callaghan, a barrel-chested grey-haired man with a hearty laugh and ready smile, carried a musket. On a word from Cathal, they trotted out of the corrie.

'They are out to forage a little, and perhaps singe Sir John Ferguson's beard,' commented Donough O'Flaherty, who was seated at the fire watching Tadhg from his deep-set blue eyes. A long frieze coat covered his misshapen body so that only his big head at one end and his shoes at the other were visible.

Tadhg stretched, loosening his muscles which were aching from his hard bed. He felt cold despite the pleasant warmth of the sun. It would take some time to overcome the chill of the night on the cold ground.

'There's warm bread and bonnyclabber,' Donough said, pointing towards the fire. 'It's the best we have to offer.'

While Tadhg was waiting, a shout came from Dónal Óg on his observation point in the cliff. 'A ship, a ship,' he yelled, pointing out to sea. As on the previous day, it was Conor O'Donnell who scrambled up the hill to join Dónal. After a few minutes he descended to the camp-site, addressing Donough. 'It appears to be the wreckage of a ship, drifting towards Inishfuipíni, the Island of the Young Puffins. If we get out to it, we might find something of value.'

'It's my curragh we can use,' Tadhg volunteered. 'Are any of you boatmen? Will you go out in the curragh with me?'

'Ach!' said Conor indignantly. "Tis many the time I have taken my place in a curragh.'

'And me,' said Dónal Óg, his face eager.

'The surf is still strong,' Tadhg said. "Tis no place for one so young as you.' Then, noting Dónal's crest-fallen countenance, he looked closer, observing the well-muscled frame in the tattered old tunic and torn goatskin trousers, the broad, bare feet unadorned by even the poorest of brogues, the pleading look in the grey-green eyes. 'All right,' he assented, 'you can come with us. But we will have to have help launching the curragh.'

Donough O'Flaherty spoke. 'I'll take Dónal's watch on the cliff. The rest of you help Tadhg.'

With Tadhg leading and the other Rapparees following, they descended the twisting path to where the curragh was beached. With the change in the weather, the cliffs above them were alive with sea-birds alarmed at their coming. Dwarfed trees and shrubs, fighting bravely for existence, leaned to the east like devoted mullahs in prayer to Mecca.

Lifting the curragh aloft, the Rapparees walked down and into the sea knee-deep before launching it. Then Tadhg leaped into the bow, Dónal Óg into the centre, and Conor into the stern. Setting the thin-bladed oars to their openings, they awaited the signal from Tadhg, who was examining the height of the grey waves still rolling in from the storm. Finally he waved his hand, the men in the water gave the curragh a shove, and they rowed out towards the reef which they would have to pass.

Although the storm had blown itself out and the wind had subsided, big waves still rolled in from the broad Atlantic, hurling themselves angrily and frothily on the rocky reef, flinging spray high in the air.

Tadhg guided the canoe close to the reef expertly, keeping an alert eye on the jagged rocks as he searched for the gap which he had traversed the previous day. When he had located it, carefully noting the width between the rocks on both sides, he waited for the ebb of a big wave which had passed to return its wall of water to the sea, offsetting the force of the lesser waves rolling shoreward. Then, in the relative calm, he and his crew threaded their way quickly and skilfully through the gap.

Once free of the reef, with oars moving rhythmically, they set course for Inishfuipíni, where Dónal Óg had seen the wreckage heading. This was a small, rocky island, several leagues southeast of St MacDara's Island, uninhabited by humans, but a favourite nesting ground for thousands of birds, especially the puffins for which it was named.

As the approached the island they could see a large section of a sailing ship riding low in the water, drifting sluggishly with the long rollers towards the shore.

'Faith, it will be smashed to smithereens when it hits yonder,' Conor remarked, 'and anything valuable will go down to benefit

Manannan MacLir himself. 'Only splinters to light the fire will be left for us.'

'It will be a while yet before it hits,' said Tadhg, 'for it moves slowly. There's plenty of time to get aboard.'

Three strong backs bent as one, and the canoe quickly ate up the distance until they came close to the drifting hulk. Waves were breaking lazily over the jagged timbers, and the oarsmen could see that it was the stern section of what had been a fine ship. Apparently the storm had broken it in two. Separated from its fore section, and drifting at the caprices of wind, wave and tide, it was headed for the wild and rocky coast of Inishfuipíni. One the deck, still firmly lashed, was the ship's cargo of lumber, keeping the wreckage afloat when otherwise it would have long since plunged to the bottom of the sea.

The stump of a mast, about ten feet in length, still protruded from the ship's bottom, pointing its ragged tip towards the clear blue sky, and moving pendulum-like with the rhythmic toll of the waves. As it swayed, the rays of the sun lighted some object near the base of the mast, and Conor jokingly remarked that the ship had a cargo of gold.

'Holy Mary, Mother of God,' Tadhg exclaimed, making the Sign of the Cross. 'Gold it is, but it is on someone's head, someone who is tied to the mast.'

'Yerra,' Dónal exclaimed excitedly, 'you're right. I can see what looks like someone's body!'

'It looks like a patch of golden wheat,' added Conor.

'Let's get the curragh as close as possible,' Tadhg directed. 'I'll try to get aboard.'

Carefully they brought the curragh up to the side of the stricken ship. After several aborted starts, Tadhg leaped lithely to the fender strip, clambered aboard the wreck and made his way carefully across the littered deck. Meanwhile, Conor and Dónal eased the curragh to safety. Tadhg could see pieces of torn, soggy sail-cloth, lengths of rope, the now useless wheel spinning idly with the roll of the ship, and large masses of oily kelp which was playing host to limpets, sea snails and small green crabs which scuttled wildly out of his way as he approached the shattered mast.

Then, as he raised his eyes from the deck, he was suddenly face to face with a golden vision, so lovely and so out of place here on the wild and lonely sea that he sank to his knees, awed and reverent by the apparition, and made the Sign of the Cross. His

25

unbelieving eyes stared at a pale face with a halo of golden hair around its head, and a pair of green eyes, wide with terror, staring at him.

'Surely 'tis Deirdre of the Sorrows come back to life,' he whispered.

The vision was trembling so violently that Tadhg thought she assuredly would have fallen had she not been so securely lashed to the mast. The young woman's tresses streamed down her back like a golden waterfall. She was elegantly garbed in a style unfamiliar to Tadhg, who knew only the rough garb of the countrywomen and not the silks and satins of the gentry. The girl wore a black cape over a full-flowing pink gown. A hood, with a gaily decorated broad collar, trailed down the back of the cape. Her feet were hidden by the length and fullness of the gown.

Never, thought Tadhg, had he seen anything so beautiful, and he knelt spellbound, oblivious of everything but the lovely vision before him.

The girl implored him; Tadhg had no English but intuitively understood her appeal, and drawing his *scian*, cut the ropes that bound her. She sagged and Tadhg caught her, gazing into her face, the full lips now purple, the delicate skin pale from the long, cold ordeal, and the eyes now closed in a merciful faint. Her clothes were wet with sea water, and Tadhg realised that she would need warmth and food. As he moved to carry her, her green eyes opened and she stared into Tadhg's compassionate face. Then, impulsively wrapping her arms around his neck, she began to sob wildly.

'There now, *mo chailín bán*, no need to cry like that,' he comforted her, 'you're safe now. We will take you to shore and safety.'

He made his way cautiously across the sloping deck and the piled lumber to the ship's side where he gestured to the pair in the curragh to approach. 'It's a girl! I'll have to lower her with a piece of rope,' he shouted.

Tadhg tried to make her understand what he intended to do, but she clung tightly to him, weeping as if her heart would break. Finally he was forced to tear her grip loose. Making a loop in a piece of rope, he draped it under her arms, and although she struggled, he lowered her into the curragh below, where Conor received her, depositing her safely on the craft's floor. She tried to rise, pointing at the wreckage, shouting to Tadhg.

Conor, who understood English, yelled to him. 'She says that

26

there are more people up there, probably in the cabin.'

Tadhg quickly estimated the distance between the wreckage and the shore, and figuring that there was still time, crossed the deck and mounted some steps to the remains of the cabin. A splintered section of a massive spar blocked the door. Tadhg wrested it aside and pried open the door. When his eyes became adjusted to the gloom of the dark cabin, he saw three figures securely tied to the framework. Two were men, one old and one young, the latter several years older than Tadhg, probably in his mid-twenties. The third person was a woman about the same age as the younger man.

The older man exclaimed loudly and imperiously in English. In Irish Tadhg apologised that he spoke no English. The other man glared, then said in halting Irish, 'Cut us loose at once, you bog-trotting savage.'

Ignoring the insult, Tadhg drew his *scian*, cutting the ropes that bound the trio. Easing himself to the cabin floor, the older man sat a while, rubbing his wrists vigorously to restore the circulation. The younger man stood erect, stretching his muscles like a cat after a nap, and then, hand on sword, watched Tadhg warily.

The older man wore a loose-flowing coat with full sleeves reaching down past the elbows, disclosing ribbon-tied white shirtsleeves. He wore no hat. His sword was carried in a richly ornamented baldric. The younger man was garbed in the latest London fashion. His coat was fitted close to his slim body, with a braided front, the fringed ends held by buttons running the full length of the coat. His fine waistcoat was cut the same length as the coat. His knee-length breeches buttoned up the side of the legs. A hat, low of crown but broad of brim, with a gay yellow ribbon tied with a big bow running around it, sat jauntily on his head. He too carried his sword in a gaily decorated baldric. But whereas the older man's shoes were tied with strings, the younger's had bright buckles high on the instep. Neither man wore a periwig. Perhaps they had been removed when the storm began.

From the plainness of her clothes, the young woman was evidently of the servant class. Her pleasant face, broad and ruddy of hue, peeped out from under a wide-brimmed hat. She had moved to the back of the group and was clutching the folds of the brown cloak that fell to her feet.

Tadhg noticed a strong resemblance between the two men. Although the elder's face was lined, they were both long of forehead, the eyes of such a dark brown that in the dim light of the cabin they appeared black, and both had thin lips set under finely chiselled noses. The older of the pair had coarse black hair, streaked with grey, while the younger had luxuriant brown hair tied with a narrow ribbon at the nape of the neck.

After a moment, the silent tableau sprung to life. The younger man helped the older to his feet, the woman spoke anxiously to them in English, and the older man turned to Tadhg, asking in his poor Irish if he had seen anything of another woman on the ship.

Tadhg nodded. 'Yes,' he said, 'a young woman. We have her safely in the curragh.'

'Thanks to a merciful God,' the woman said fervently, raising her hand instinctively to her forehead as if she was about to make the Sign of the Cross, then hurriedly lowered her hand as the two men looked sharply at her.

The older man addressed himself to Tadhg. 'Where are we, and how did you happen to find us?'

'This is Kilkieran Bay, Moyrus parish, Ballinahinch Barony, Iar-Chonnacht. We saw the wreckage of the ship from the cliff, and came out to examine it.'

'Looking for loot, no doubt,' the older man sneered.

Tadhg disregarded the insult. 'For anything of value,' he corrected. 'We who live by the sea accept its gifts, no matter what source.'

The two men then conversed in English, the older one finally asking Tadhg if he was alone. 'No,' Tadhg replied, 'there are two more of us in the curragh. Because the sea is still rough we couldn't tie the curragh to the ship for fear of damage. But this is no time for talking. We must leave quickly before the wreckage drifts on to the rocks.'

The younger man motioned for Tadhg to go first. Proceeding cautiously, they made their perilous way from the cabin, down the steps, and across the slippery, sloping deck to the side of the ship. Tadhg was angered to see that both men left the woman to fend for herself, neither offering a helping hand.

Conor and Dónal, worrying about Tadhg because the wreck was moving dangerously close to the rocky shore of the island, were relieved to see him appear at the side of the ship. They brought the curragh as close as safety would allow, while the girl waved happily to her three companions and they waved and shouted gaily to her in return.

Tadhg told the older man in Irish that he would lower the woman to the curragh below with the aid of a length of rope. Appraising Tadhg's massive frame, and the great muscled shoulders and arms, he spoke to the woman in English. Without fuss, she allowed Tadhg to draw the rope into a loop under her shoulders, and to be dangled over the side while Tadhg carefully lowered her, waiting for the curragh to be directly below. When she was safely aboard, the two men and Tadhg climbed over the side, and when the curragh was on a crest of a wave, stepped nimbly into the craft.

Tadhg quickly took his seat in the bow, and picking up his oars, started to row. They were now so close to the shore that they could see the puffins nesting on the heights. The backlash of the waves recoiling from the rocky shore now met the new waves rolling in from the open sea, creating a dangerous turbulence as the heavily laden curragh fought against the waves, wind and tide to be free.

With Tadhg pulling powerfully, their drift towards the rocks was reversed, and slowly the craft was brought under control and headed for land. When Tadhg could take his eyes from the sea, they were invariably directed to the girl sitting at his feet. As the sun glinted on her golden hair, Tadhg was reminded again of her resemblance to the fabled Deirdre of the Sorrows, for this girl had the same golden hair and green eyes. He hoped that the similarity would end there, for Deirdre's fate was too sad to contemplate.

In turn, the girl eyed Tadhg surreptitiously as he rowed, his powerful shoulders bent to the oars. Her glance rested fleetingly on the clefted, determined chin, the black wavy hair tossed by the wind, the intense blue eyes constantly scanning the surface of the sea. Tadhg was unaware of her scrutiny, for his concern was for the boat and its passengers, but the younger man had noticed, and his dark eyes were hostile with jealousy.

With careful manoeuvring, they safely negotiated the passage of the reef, crossing the inlet to the shore where the waiting Rapparees waded into the water to steady the curragh. Tadhg shipped his oars, leaped into the water, and extended his arms to lift the girl from the boat. With an oath the younger man jumped into the water beside him, roughly pushing Tadhg aside. The startled girl looked from one to the other, then judiciously allowed her ship companion to carry her to shore. Tadhg shrugged, and graciously reached out his arms to the other woman, who smilingly accepted his offer.

When all four were ashore, and the curragh carried to its resting place, Donough stepped forward to greet them. 'I am Donough O'Flaherty,' he said in English, bowing to the ladies, 'and I welcome you to Iar-Chonnacht, the land of the O'Flaherty. Let us go speedily to the clifftop where there is a warm fire and food and drink. The ladies must have suffered greatly in your misadventure.'

The older man eyed Donough's misshapen body and the wild, unkempt appearance of the silent Rapparees with distaste, then declared haughtily, 'My name is Henry Thompson. I am a merchant from Dublin. This is my son John. The young lady is Margaret FitzGerald, who is affianced to my son. The older woman is Mary Casey, her servant. We sailed from Galway two days ago, bound for Dublin on the ship '*Protector*', but ran into a storm the first day out. Late yesterday the ship struck a reef, broke in half, leaving us to drift at the mercy of the storm. Without food or water or warmth, it was a nightmare for all of us.'

'All the more reason to hasten above,' said Donough sympathetically.

'I would like to talk to my son and the ladies first,' Thompson said.

The quartet drew to one side, with the elder Thompson doing all the talking, the others listening attentively. Then they returned to the waiting Rapparees. 'We are now ready,' Thompson said.

As they ascended the steep hillside, with the younger Thompson assisting the Lady FitzGerald, Tadhg followed with mixed emotions. It was with shock and disappointment he intuitively realised the relationship between the pair. Why should he be jealous, he thought angrily, when the possibility of his playing Naoise to this Deirdre was as impossible as his becoming Pope at Rome? This was just a chance encounter between a great lady from Dublin and an ignorant fisherman from a remote and bleak island. Their worlds couldn't be further apart.

While the guests consumed a meal of brown oatcakes baked on the hearth, served with *cáis buí* and generous amounts of buttermilk, a rough fare unsuited to their social status but wholly satisfying to the demands of their stomachs, Donough drew Tadhg aside and asked him about the rescue, the ship's cargo and whether he had brought back anything of value.

'Only the gold on yon *cailín*'s head,' said Tadhg, 'and a length of rope which I used to lower the ladies into the curragh.

'What was the cargo?' Donough asked.

'Fortunately for those people, there was a shipment of lumber. It was lashed to the deck, which kept the ship from sinking. The rest of it was awash in the water, and there was no way of knowing. Probably some oats, barley, and maybe some hides. Perhaps we can go out again tomorrow when the sea is calmer. The wreckage should supply some planking and lumber, and if we're lucky, copper fitting and other valuables.'

After the guests were finished with their meal, the elder Thompson further described the horrors of the night as they drifted into the wild, tossing seas. He told of the incessant scream of the wind, the buffeting by the great waves, the terrifying hours in the darkness of the cabin before dawn, their aching muscles, the thirst and hunger, and the pervading fear of being cast up on the rocky shore. But through their fears ran the thread of hope of rescue which sustained them. God answered their prayers for suddenly the young fisherman had appeared.

'Why were you tied?' Donough asked. 'I would think that you would have been better off if you were free.'

Thompson smiled grimly. 'We had no choice. When the ship broke in twain, the captain and most of the crew were in the forward half, and we never saw them again. Soon, one of the seamen, a surly brute, came into the cabin. At pistol-point he forced us to give up our money and valuables. He even took the ladies' rings. Then he tied up my son, Mary Casey and myself. He forced Lady Margaret to go with him. We didn't know of her fate until we were rescued.'

The Lady Margaret, with her hair plaited by her maid, and with colour restored to her cheeks, was looked at expectantly by the interested audience. So she took up the tale. Speaking only in English, her story was understood by few of the Irish, so Donough interpreted each successive portion into the Gaelic.

'This sailor,' she related vivaciously, 'forced me to go down to the deck where several other members of the crew were readying a lifeboat. They had piled everything of value they would find into it, including a cask of water and some food. When I sought to go back to the cabin, the ringleader tied me to the stump of mast so I wouldn't be in the way. He informed me I would bring a high price on the Barbary coast because of my colouring. He said he knew of a ship that would be leaving Galway soon for Africa, and the captain would be most happy to have me. When they finally launched the lifeboat, this man came back for me. I can still see his evil face as he climbed over the lumber on the deck. At that moment the ship lurched, and a tremendous wave crashed over the ship, carrying him away and upsetting the lifeboat. I thought we were going to capsize, but at the last moment the ship righted itself. If I hadn't been tied, I too would have gone overboard.'

She paused, smiled at Tadhg, then continued with her story. 'When this young man appeared suddenly out of nowhere, I thought at first he was one of the crew come back to get me. It wasn't until I looked into his kindly face that I realised he had come to save me.'

'St Christopher must have been watching over you,' said Fergus Dillon, who spoke English. 'It was a miracle, surely, that you all survived that great storm.'

'It was a double miracle,' Donough observed, 'for this young man who saved you was himself miraculously saved yesterday when St Brendan guided his curragh through that treacherous reef.'

'But Tadhg helped himself to make his own miracle,' said Dermot O'Lee.

'He is a remarkable young man,' said the Lady Margaret, again bestowing a radiant smile on him, 'and I owe my life to him.'

Although Tadhg didn't understand her words, that smile was reward enough. He smiled back at her, and for a moment the green eyes and the blue were caught, and it was only the arrival of Cathal and his Rapparees that broke it.

They had a successful foray. The horses were heavily loaded with flagons of wine, haunches of beef, sacks of meal, and even a squealing pig. Several of the men were armed with newly acquired muskets, indicating a raid on one of Ferguson's armed farmhouses.

'What have we here?' inquired Cathal, frowning.

'A shipwrecked party,' Donough explained. 'This is the Lady Máiread FitzGerald, and her servant, Mary Casey. The gentlemen are Henry Thompson, a merchant of Dublin, and his son John. Tadhg, Dónal and Conor plucked them from the sea.'

Cathal's frown faded. 'We have nothing fancy here, but you are welcome to what hospitality we have to offer,' he said graciously.

'Are there horses or a carriage available,' the elder Thompson asked anxiously. 'We would like to get to Galway as soon as possible.'

'It's a full day's journey to Galway from here,' Cathal said. 'We are in a remote spot in wild Connemara. No carriage is available, but we do have our horses. You could start early in the morning.'

'Is there an inn hereabouts where we could stay? The ladies are sadly in need of a good night's lodging.'

'I sympathise with them.' Cathal answered, 'but there is no inn nearby. We can make them reasonably comfortable with beds of furze, covered with my mens' warm coats. We have plenty of good food, as you can see.'

'It's not what we would prefer, but under the circumstances we will accept your kind offer. If we can get an early start tomorrow, we can find better lodgings in Galway tomorrow night.'

Gilleduff O'Fallon, who had been on the raid, approached Cathal, asking to speak with him in private. They withdrew.

'Well,' asked Cathal, 'what is it?'

'That man over there who calls himself a Dublin merchant is no more Thompson than I am Oliver Cromwell. He is Sir Thomas Montgomery, a cousin of Hugh Montgomery, Lord Mount Alexander. Often it is that I have seen him in Dublin. Hang-Draw-and-Quarter Thomas has sent more Westmeath and Roscommon men to their deaths than any other judge in Ireland.'

Cathal's face became purple with rage. 'Are you positive he is Justice Montgomery?' he thundered.

'I have seen him too often not to recognise him, even without his wig and cloak of office. That high forehead, that long, lean nose, those deadly dark eyes filled with hate of everything Irish ... yes, Cathal, if I am sure of anything, I am sure that it is he.'

Cathal looked doubtful.

'The younger one is obviously his son,' O'Fallon continued. 'I know he has one who was educated in England. The women are apparently who they are supposed to be, lady and servant. There are Dublin offshoots of Clann nGearailt, some of them Protestants.'

Cathal stood silent and looked off into the distance, remembering how he had returned to the castle on the island in Loch Corrib with his father's brother Rory O'Flaherty. There they had found the castle sacked by Cromwell's soldiers, under the command of Captain John Ferguson, and the entire garrison put to the sword. Thus had perished his mother, father, a brother, three sisters, uncles, aunts, cousins and family retainers - a hundred and fifty persons. Although the atrocity was nearly two score years past, Cathal trembled with rage as he recalled the heads of his father, kin and friends impaled on spikes on the castle walls, and the insolent flag of Cromwell and the red pennant of Captain

Ferguson fluttering from the battlements.

'At last Jehovah has delivered him into my hands,' Cathal exulted. 'Vengeance is mine, saith the Lord.'

'What is that you say,' said the startled O'Fallon.

'You will learn in due time. Now let us return to our Mr Thompson,' Cathal replied grimly.

The guests were conversing amicably with Dermot O'Lee when Cathal and Gilleduff strode up and stood beside them. 'Sir Thomas Montgomery, be ready to meet your God,' Cathal thundered, his hand on his sword.

Both Thompsons, now unmasked as Montgomerys, spun about and quickly drew their swords, standing with their backs to the blackened fireplace. All the Rapparees, aware that the situation had drastically changed, formed a ring about the contestants, blocking any possibility of escape.

Donough O'Flaherty forced his way through the circle to his brother's side. Staring at the strangers, he quietly asked, 'Is this Ensign Montgomery?'

Cathal nodded, his eyes fierce.

Donough continued in a calm tone. 'If this is indeed the Ensign Montgomery, now Sir Thomas Montgomery, then we must be just and give him a fair trial. That is the least that our good sovereign, King James, who appointed him to the bench, would expect of us.'

'Run him through with your sword, Cathal,' a Rapparee shouted, 'and his spawn as well!'

'To the sword!' the others joined in chorus.

Cathal stood transfixed, his eyes intent on his ancient enemy; then, exhaling lengthily, he said resignedly, 'Donough is right. We must give him a fair trial.'

'A fair trial?' sneered John Montgomery. 'I can see you barbarous Irish giving my father a fair trial. And for what is he being tried? For his sentences against murderous riffraff like yourselves?'

'On the grounds of murder, of pillage, of wanton cruelty,' Donough said.

'And who will defend him? Yon beardless youth?' He pointed at Dónal. 'Or that savage in the filthy goatskins?' pointing at Dermot O'Lee. 'Or that learned counsel, the curraghman?'

'That savage is a physician. He has been educated in France and in Spain. His ancestors, for hundreds of years, have been physicians. His people were educated when your ancestors ran

34

around the forests of England, daubed with clay and painted blue, and with nary a goatskin to wear. And who will be your father's defender? Why you, sir!'

Donough turned to his brother. 'With your permission, Cathal, the judge will be Fergus Dillon, who has had some experience with the law. Prosecutor will be Dermot O'Lee, who is familiar with the crimes. John Montgomery will defend. You and I will be the witnesses. The remaining Rapparees will comprise the jury.'

Sir Thomas Montgomery spoke for the first time. 'As an officer of your lawful king James, I demand that this charade be stopped, and I be freed instantly. Because some of your band have saved my life, and those of my party, I will seek leniency for you. If you persist in going through with this farce, I will personally see that you are all hanged.'

'Hanged, drawn and quartered,' someone shouted.

Donough held up his hand for silence. 'Members of the jury, restrain yourselves. You will have your chance to render a verdict after you have heard the evidence, not before. And since Sir Thomas is in haste to have us all incarcerated, let us not delay his trial. Let the accused and his counsel take their places at my left. Judge Dillon, will you please be seated at the hearth - and not too close to the fire. We want to rule with cool justice, not heated posterior. Dermot O'Lee, the prosecutor, take your place at my right. The jurors will be seated to the rear. Are we all ready?'

The two women stood disdainfully to one side. Father and son conferred while the prosecutor waited courteously. When they had finished, Dermot O'Lee stepped up to the hearth.

'In 1649 an army under the leadership of Oliver Cromwell, a leading light in the beheading of his sovereign, Charles, and in the usurping of the authority of the King of England, arrived in Ireland to subdue what he in his dementia considered rebellious subjects. His army was composed of religious fanatics, mercenaries, released criminals, and opportunistic but poor adventurers with a sharp eye for acquiring quick fortunes.

'Cromwell's foul deeds are too well known to need repeating here, and he is not on trial. We are concerned only with the acts of one of his lieutenants, a young ensign named Thomas Montgomery, who was in charge of a platoon of troops under the command of Captain John Ferguson, who is none other than the man now known as Sir John Ferguson, our esteemed landlord. They arrived with Cromwell in 1649, but it was not until 1652, when Galway was taken by Sir Charles Coote, that they arrived on the west coast. Both took part in the sack of Galway where the wealth of the old city was plundered, the churches burned and twelve hundred townspeople, including three score priests of God and the parents of our good friend, Murtagh Blake, were sent to the Barbados as slaves. Young Ensign Montgomery marched north and west from Galway at the head of his men, robbing, killing and burning as they went, all in the name of God and the Protector.'

O'Lee paused, and turning to Sir Thomas Montgomery, asked, 'Do you remember this place, Sir Thomas?'

When the accused haughtily disdained to answer, O'Lee again turned to address his remarks to Judge Dillon. 'Here stood the cabin of the grandparents of Dónal Óg O'Devaney. They were not armed, they were not in rebellion. They offered no danger. They were simple folk gleaning a precarious living from the meagre soil. Angered when they could find no loot, the band, under Ensign Montgomery, slew the parents and the children who were at home, and to cover their foul deed, they burned the little cabin. Now only the naked hearth and the memory of their dark deeds are left. Dónal Óg's father, then a young man and gone for the day, found the smoking embers and charred bodies upon his return at nightfall.

O'Lee turned to gaze at the old fireplace, a mute witness of death and destruction and desecration, now standing stark and stern in silent accusation. A low and angry murmur rose from the throats of the Rapparees. The two women looked expectantly at Sir Thomas, waiting to hear him deny the brutal charges, but he said nothing as he stared off into the distance, remembering that day thirty-six years before.

Then O'Lee resumed his presentation. 'Ensign Montgomery and his band rode north until they came to the territory of Murrough O'Flaherty. Falling in with one Seán Mac Annraoí, called by the Sassanaigh John MacHenry, of a family near Moycullen who thought he should be paramount chief of the region instead of The O'Flaherty, the raiders devised a stratagem to conquer the castle on its island in Lough Corrib. Treachery, bribery and deceit have always been favourite weapons of the Sassanaigh in their attempts to conquer our blessed island; yea, ever since Strongbow allied himself with the traitorous Dermot MacMurrough when they first set their feet on Ireland.

'While Ensign Montgomery conferred with Mac Annraoí, the

main body of troops under Captain Ferguson joined them, having marched up from Galway. Between them they hatched a plot whereby Mac Annraoí would lead a small group after dark, and secrete themselves in the ruin of an old monastery on the island. When this was done, Mac Annraoí, as a friend of the family, gained admittance to the castle where he told Murrough O'Flaherty that a small band of Cromwell's men was camped on the mainland, and that they could easily be defeated by the Irish. Believing the treacherous Mac Annraoí, O'Flaherty left the castle the next morning with his men. Instead of the small force described, he and his men were overwhelmed and decimated by the superior forces of Captain Ferguson. Back on the island, Ensign Montgomery had little difficulty in wresting the castle from the small force left behind. I am now going to call upon an eyewitness to the carnage. Séamus Rua O'Callacháin, would you please come forward?'

O'Callanan was the oldest of the Rapparees. His long hair and beard, although grey, still showed traces of the red that had given him his name. His usually pleasant blue eyes were cold and remote in his lined face as he stepped to O'Lee. He looked with compassion at Cathal and Donough, then with cold contempt at Sir Thomas. The latter stared at the old man curiously, wondering what he could possibly tell.

'I was one of those left in the castle,' the old man began in a low voice. 'There was a mist on the lake, and over the island. None of us dreamed that there were any Sassanaigh about. Suddenly they appeared out of the reek, firing at the men on the walls. I watched them as they brought up a petard, not knowing what it was. It looked like a cooking pot, and harmless. But it had been filled with several pounds of powder, more than enough to blast the big gate open. They charged into the castle, and in a short fight, took possession. I was early felled with a ball from a musket. Cathal O'Connell, who was fighting beside me, was almost cut in two by a Sassanach with a huge claymore, and as his life's blood welled from his grievous wound I was covered with it. The Sasanaigh stormed wildly through the castle, indiscriminately killing man, woman and child. The O'Flaherty women and children were in the chapel with the priest, praying before the holy altar, when the fiends from hell found them. And there, in the House of God, they were spitted on the soldiers' swords as these noble Defenders of the Faith gleefully murdered them in cold blood.'

Seamus Rua raised his icy blue eyes to Sir Thomas

Montgomery and, lifting his arm, pointed his long bony forefinger at the accused and thundered in a voice like Jehovah's: 'And that man, Ensign Montgomery, was the worst of all. I had regained consciousness and could see the blasphemous spectacle through the open doors of the chapel. Murrough's wife, Gobnait, begged for her life and for that of her children, imploring the monster to spare her. He laughed, and tearing a crucifix from the wall, flung it at her, saying, 'Save yourself with this, Papist,' and ran his sword through her breast.'

The witness paused, shaking his head as if he still couldn't believe the atrocity he had seen. Only the gentle sighing of the wind' through the oak trees disturbed the absolute quiet as all present seemed to stand breathless on his words.

Once more he resumed his tale. 'In the orgy of killing that followed, the old rooms of the castle ran red with the blood of the innocent. Above the shouting of the kill-crazed soldiers suddenly arose the shrill wail of an infant. It was little Donough O'Flaherty, who had been overlooked, being in his bed. Ensign Montgomery heard his cries, and found him in his room. Holding the child by his feet, he emerged from the room, and then, seeing a companion some distance away, shouted, 'Here, have a little Papist,' and threw the baby to him. The companion, however, had just found a bottle of wine, and was more interested in it than a baby, so he calmly stepped aside, and the child, Donough, fell with a sickening crash to the stone floor.'

The old man turned sadly to Donough. 'Until that moment you were a normal child, with no blemish. Your little frame was as straight as a pikepole. And while the drunken soldiers caroused, you and I lay among the dead, saved by a strange Providence.

'Captain Ferguson arrived with his men to help celebrate their victory. The wine flowed as freely as the blood had flowed earlier. Seán Mac Annraoí, may he burn in hell forever, swaggered and shouted with the rest of them. But when he began to talk about 'my castle' and 'my lands', Captain Ferguson called him to him. 'John,' said he, 'you deserve a reward for your help. How would you like this fine sword?' Seán covetously eyed the weapon, inlaid with gold and silver and precious stones, and said, 'It's a noble sword. I would be most happy to have it.' Captain Ferguson smiled grimly, then said, 'Have it you shall, John,' and plunged the sword through Seán's stomach.

'Night fell, and the drinking and debauchery continued until the small hours when the last drunken soldier finally toppled on his face and slept. It was bitterly cold. and Donough and I lay there among the dead. Finally, when all was quiet, I crept to Donough's small body, thanking God to find that he was still alive. I made my way over the bodies of the slain, past the sleeping Cromwellians, and fleeing the castle, took a boat to the shore. I travelled north to the country of the O'Malleys, where they took poor Donough and miraculously saved his life. Later he was restored to the O'Flahertys.

Sir Thomas Montgomery showed consternation. The two women were obviously horrified. Lady Margaret had covered her eyes with her hands. Young Montgomery was truculent and defiant.

O'Lee then said gently, 'Thank you, Séamus Rua. We will now hear from Cathal O'Flaherty.'

Cathal moved to the place vacated by Séamus Rua. He bowed to the judge, glared at Sir Thomas, and began. 'I was only ten years old at the time of the assault on the castle. I had been visiting my uncle Rory's family for some time, and was happy to be going home again to my father and mother. It was the day after the attack, and word of it hadn't yet spread. We came upon the bodies of those slain in the ambush, including the beheaded corpse of my father. It was horrible and sickening. But the full horror wasn't apparent until we came to the point of land opposite the castle, and beheld the hated flag of Cromwell flying over the battlements, and the bloody heads of my kin impaled on spikes. We were only a small party, lightly armed, so Rory made us leave quickly, going north as fast as our horses could carry us. After a few days, Séamus Rua arrived at Rory's stronghold from the country of the O'Malleys to relate how Ensign Montgomery and his men had slaughtered my mother and her children, and to tell us Donough had survived, though he was badly hurt. I prayed to God that some day the monster, Montgomery, would be delivered into my hands. And today my prayers are answered.'

Dermot O'Lee turned to Donough. 'Is there anything to add?'

Donough smiled a sad smile. 'I was too young to know what happened,' he said. 'All I can offer as evidence is my hump.'

With a courteous gesture, O'Lee turned to young Montgomery. 'It's your turn now to present your case.'

With a sneer on his handsome face, the accused man's son turned his back to the judge, and faced the Rapparees. 'My case is simple. It's merely truth versus falsehood. This witless old man's pratings are a vicious pack of slanderous lies. My father was never in this area before in his life. And so he cannot be guilty of the crimes with which he is charged.' He faced his father, asking, 'Is this man's story true? Did you participate in the conquest of the castle?'

Sir Thomas had recovered his composure. Arrogantly he answered, 'Absolutely not! His story is an invention, and utterly preposterous. Now, for the last time, I demand that you set us free. I will remind you again that I am an officer of King James's government in Ireland.'

'To the devil with King James!' a Rapparee shouted.

Judge Dillon raised his hand. He faced the jury. 'You have heard the evidence from both sides. What is your verdict?'

'Guilty,' they replied in unison.

'And what will be the punishment?'

'Hang and quarter him like he has killed and mutilated so many innocent Gaels,' Eoghan MacDeeris cried passionately.

'We seek only justice, not revenge,' the judge remonstrated. 'We are not barbarians. We are not Sassanaigh. Hanged he will be. But there will be no butchery.'

'Don't be an old woman, Fergus,' Sean O'Carroll shouted. 'It's an eye for an eye, a tooth for a tooth ...'

Cathal O'Flaherty raised his hands. When the clamour subsided, he said, 'I speak as one of the aggrieved. Hate has run like fire through my veins for these many years. I exulted when this man was delivered to me. I would have been the first to advocate having him hanged, drawn and quartered. Now, strangely, the fire of vengeance has cooled. I can now look upon this man before me, this Thomas Montgomery of foulest memory, with cool detachment. That he is a monster in the guise of a man, there is no doubt. That he is the same instrument of the devil who slew innocent women and children in my father's house, there is no doubt. That he is the same magistrate who has condemned to death so many of our countrymen, there is no doubt. That he must die for his crimes, there is no doubt. He cannot be freed to condemn more innocent victims to the gallows. Like any vicious, mad dog, he must be destroyed. But let us not succumb to the same poison. I appeal to you to let Judge Dillon's verdict stand.'

Donough moved to his brother's side. 'Fellow Gaels, savage reprisal will not remove my hump. It will not restore that which is gone. I stand with Cathal and Fergus. Let us not demean ourselves.'

The Rapparees remained silent. Apparently they would abide by the O'Flaherty brothers' decision, disappointing though it might be.

John Montgomery faced the Rapparees. 'Wait!' he shouted. 'You Irish like to claim that the English defeat you only by superior numbers, better weapons, or by treachery, as it was charged here today. You like to boast of being great warriors. You like the sporting chance. I hereby challenge any one of you to face me singly in a fight with swords. If I lose, you have killed one more hated Sassanach. If I win, then you must let my father go free!'

First of the assemblage to react was Cathal O'Flaherty. Drawing his sword, he angrily charged the slender Englishman. But Gilleduff O'Fallon quickly stepped between them, and drew the enraged Rapparee chief to one side. 'Restrain yourself,' he begged. 'This is just another Sassanach trick. That man has the reputation of being one of the best swordsmen in London. He has already slain several skilled opponents in duels. He is gambling on our Irish sense of honour. If he wins, and be sure that he will, another Irishman dies at the hand of a Montgomery, and his father goes free. Refuse the challenge. Let the verdict be the rope.

Cathal's heavy breathing subsided and his rage diminished. He replaced his sword in its scabbard. 'You're right, Gilleduff,' he admitted, 'I almost fell into his trap.' Cathal then addressed the assembly. 'There will be no duel. Sir Thomas Montgomery must hang.'

'Cowards!' sneered John Montgomery. He raised his voice. 'Is there no man here who is willing to fight for the honour of Ireland? How about you, Cuchulainn?' he asked, turning to Tadhg, who had been a deeply interested observer.

'No, John, you can't do that,' Lady Margaret cried. 'This youth saved your life this morning and now you would kill him in a duel!'

Tadhg has bristled at the insolence and contempt in the man's tone. A fierce resentment against Montgomery Óg grew in him until he could bear it no longer. He turned sharply on his heel, and walking to the area where he had slept, returned with his sword and scabbard.

Young Montgomery spoke heatedly to the girl. 'This is not an affair for women. Please keep your opinions to yourself.' He turned again to Tadhg. 'Are you afraid, Cuchulainn,' he taunted. 'You carry a fancy sword. Do you use it to fight with or to shave with? Or are you but a boy, not old enough to shave? Or do you use your sword for cutting onions? Do you wish to hide behind the skirts of a woman? She entreats me not to kill you.'

'Yes, Sassanach, I will fight you!' Tadhg roared.

Cathal was both surprised and dismayed, but he responded quickly. 'Tadhg,' he shouted authoritatively, 'come here.'

The habit of obedience to his elders was so deeply ingrained in Tadhg that despite his great passion he stepped to Cathal's side, where the two of them began a low-toned but vehement discussion.

A buzz of excitement swept through the ranks. All eyes were on the two men. At first it was Cathal who did the talking, then it was Tadhg, with Cathal listening quietly, occasionally nodding his head in agreement, a contemplative look replacing his previously dismayed expression. When Tadhg stopped speaking, the Rapparee chief smiled, embraced him, then turned and faced the expectant group.

He raised his hand as if calling for silence. First in English, then in Irish, he announced in ringing tones: 'For the honour of Ireland, Tadhg accepts the challenge.'

After a moment of quiet, the furious Rapparees howled at Cathal. 'Don't be cheating us of our vengeance!' 'You're sending him to his death!' 'Have you lost your wits entirely?' 'Remember what the Sassanach did to your own dear mother!'

Young Montgomery, who had hurled the challenge in desperation without much hope that it would be taken up, smiled at his father, exultation on his lean face. The old man smiled back confidently, feeling for the first time since the trial that he might still save his neck.

The Lady Margaret covered her eyes, then dashed forward to young Montgomery, where she dropped to her knees and wrapped her arms around his legs. 'Don't do this, John,' she implored him. 'He saved your life. And the rest of us. He is not a soldier, skilled in the use of arms. He is just a simple fisherman. If you fight him it will be plain murder. For my sake, John, challenge another of these hateful men.'

Young Montgomery savagely thrust her away. 'It is settled!' he exclaimed furiously. 'O'Flaherty and the curraghman have agreed

42

to the terms. This is no affair for a woman. Go back to your serving maid and be silent!' He unbuckled his belt, taking his sword from its scabbard. It was a stout cut-and-thrust double-edged blade, reaching from his waist to his toes. The hilt was of bronze, with sharply curved quillons, and a broad knuckle-bow attached to the oval pommel; its *pas d'ane*, the side ring and the twin-shell guard were ornate but sturdy.

Tadhg carefully scrutinised the weapon. Apparently it was not his foe's duelling sword, for Tadhg could not conceive of a skilled duellist using it against competent foes. It was a soldier's blade, but a good one, and in the hands of a master swordsman it could more than adequately serve its purpose.

Observing the well-protected hilt, Tadhg realised that he would have to concentrate on body thrusts, being aware that his own hilt offered less protection for his hand. And he prayed that the master craftsman in Toledo who had forged his sword was the expert that Senor de Alvarez claimed.

The Rapparees had formed a ring around the combatants. Both the women stood to one side with Sir Thomas Montgomery near the smoke-blackened old chimney. The two grim contestants faced each other warily.

Tadhg was acutely aware of the mocking face of his opponent, his own rapidly beating heart, and the realisation that this might be his last day on earth. He was fighting to avenge unknown men, women and children who had been dead long before he was born. He was fighting for a vague and illusory abstraction that men called honour.

Carrying his sheathed sword in his hands in the Irish fashion, Tadhg drew the weapon from its scarred, cowhide scabbard, which he tossed aside. Kicking off his brogues, he dug his toes into the earth as if to get the feel of it. He stood stiff-legged and awkward, brandishing the weapon aloft.

His opponent, after one swift, surprised look at the quality of Tadhg's weapon, glanced at his father confidently. He pointed his sword at Tadhg's middle and, advancing quickly, cut the distance between them in half. When he was two sword-lengths away, he abruptly turned his lithe body to minimise the target and, with right leg bent slightly forward, engaged the blade of Tadhg's sword, applying pressure to wrest if from Tadhg's hand or to force it aside.

Tadhg moved his bare right foot quickly while he adjusted his left foot so that it was almost at right angles to its mate but about a cubit behind. He, too, turned his body with his right shoulder out, but because of his girth he still presented a massive target for Montgomery's blade.

As his foe moved in expertly and confidently, Tadhg lowered his blade. He extended his sword arm, keeping his elbow close to his body, and balancing his weight evenly on both legs, awaited his enemy's next move, ready to move forwards or backwards as circumstances demanded.

Tadhg's sudden switch from awkward amateur to the position of the swordsman disconcerted his opponent, who had thought he had an inexperienced peasant to deal with. Momentarily he fell back, parrying Tadhg's weapon. Then, assuming that Tadhg had merely copied his own stance, he confidently pressed forward again. Engaging Tadhg's blade, he hacked away with his own heavier weapon, steel against steel, as if in ferocity alone he would vanquish his foe.

When Tadhg made no effort to attack, Montgomery prepared to close with him, and in a series off rapid advances, executed with expert and agile footwork, forced Tadhg back. Never having participated in a duel with an opponent whose purpose was to kill him, Tadhg desperately tried to remember all the advice Alvarez had given him in his training on Inishmór. He recalled that a heavier weapon in itself is not an insurmountable advantage, and that a parry, using the theory of applied leverage, could offset the advantage of a foe's heavier weapon. Using his strong wrist and powerful arm muscles, Tadhg thus turned his opponent's sword time and time again, always watching Montgomery's every move.

As the two men fought, there was a varied reaction among the tense spectators. The Rapparees, who had thought that Cathal's decision was a death sentence for Tadhg, now watched with hope and admiration as their champion skilfully evaded the thrusts of the English swordsman. Sir Thomas Montgomery observed every movement through narrowed eyes, painfully aware that the Irish bogtrotter showed some knowledge of the fine use of the sword.

And Lady Margaret now became fearful for the life of her betrothed. Mary Casey stood apparently impassive.

The Englishman's vast experience in duelling stood him in good stead, but Tadhg's great height, his longer sword arm, tremendous physical strength, youth and the fine craftsmanship of the Toledo swordmaker all helped to offset the other's initial advantage.

When Montgomery would move aggressively forward, hacking and thrusting and readying himself for the death-dealing fatal lunge, Tadhg would give way before him. In the split second that Montgomery would take to extend his rear leg, moving his right foot slightly off the ground to set it forward a length or two, Tadhg would parry and counter with a thrust of his own, forcing his foe to fall back on guard and lose the distance gained. On one such exchange, Montgomery succeeded in slashing Tadhg's hand, which became covered in blood, causing the Rapparees to groan in dismay and the ladies to blanch.

All was quiet but for the laboured breathing of the antagonists and the clash of steel. Tadhg's sword handle became slippery with blood, but he grasped the weapon more firmly, awaiting Montgomery's error in judgement.

Montgomery's cocky assurance increased as he noted with satisfaction the blood dripping from Tadhg's sword hand, and he returned with renewed fury to the attack.

Content to play a defensive role, Tadhg had carefully studied his foe's style, observing that when Montgomery prepared for a decisive lunge he invariably moved his right foot slightly in anticipation of the following movement of the rear leg, and he watched closely until this telltale sign should occur again.

After one furious and prolonged attack in which Montgomery drove Tadhg back several lengths, coming perilously close to ending the fight, he suddenly drew back into a defensive position, thoughtfully analysing the ground where Tadhg awaited him. Apparently having made a decision, he advanced again vigorously in the attack, right arm extended and deadly blade pointed, hacking and thrusting. These thrusts Tadhg parried skilfully.

Montgomery's right foot moved. Anticipating the lunge that was to follow, Tadhg moved quickly with the lithe grace of a huge cat, and while his foe was slightly off balance in that brief and fatal unguarded moment, thrust his blade through his opponent's body.

Montgomery's unbelieving eyes looked briefly into Tadhg's. his sword dropped from his hand, and he sank slowly to the ground, clutching at his chest as a fountain of red welled from his wound. A sharp sigh escaped the watchers.

With an agonised cry, Lady Margaret ran to the body of her betrothed, cradling his head in her lap, crying repeatedly, 'Oh, God, John, he has killed you!'

Tadhg stood undecided, watching the golden head bent over

his former foe. Then he turned abruptly, moving off to the protective cover of the oaks. The exultant Rapparees pounded each other happily on the back and jumped up and down at Tadhg's victory. The older Montgomery stood dazed, gazing mutely at the still form of his son whose life's blood was seeping into the packed earth where once had stood the cabin of Dónal Óg O'Devaney's grandparents before he and his men had shed their blood in the same soil so many years before. Was this divine retribution? Was it God's will that brought him back to the scene of a brutal and senseless crime to pay with the life of his only son?

'We need a rope,' shouted Denis O'Doherty.

'There's one below. We brought it from the wreck,' Conor O'Donnell said.

'I'll fetch it,' Dónal Óg volunteered, darting to the path that led to the beach below.

In a short time a breathless Dónal returned with the rope. A hangman's knot was quickly fashioned and the loop placed around the unresisting Sir Thomas Montgomery's elegant neck. He was led away to the tallest of the oaks where the rope end was thrown over a stout limb. Cathal's horse was brought up and Sir Thomas forced to mount him.

Dermot O'Lee then addressed the prisoner. 'Is there anything you would like to say before sentence of death is carried out?'

Sir Thomas bent his bare head as best he could with the rope next to his right ear, facing the two O'Flahertys who were standing at the horse's right flank. A sneer showed on the long face and the dark eyes were vicious. 'It's too bad that I didn't know you were at the edge of the lake the morning after the taking of the castle,' he said to Cathal, 'for you wouldn't be here today.' Then, contemptuously to Dónal, 'And you, ugly dwarf. I should have bashed your head against your crib.'

Cathal's eyes grew fierce, his mouth tightened into a thin line, and he slapped the horse sharply on its flank. The surprised horse bolted, leaving Sir Thomas Montgomery suspended in the air, his head cocked at a grotesque angle as if listening for sounds he would never hear, his body swaying to and fro like a giant pendulum, with the last rays of the setting sun glinting from the silver buckle on his coat.

Watching from amongst the oaks at the edge of the field - to be known henceforward as Gortnacraghig, the field of the hanging - Tadhg witnessed the final violent act in the drama.

Nature's cruelties and complexities were accepted by Tadhg without question. Death was a part of life. It was God's will. After his great rage had given way to sadness and his momentary elation to melancholy, he felt sick in both stomach and soul at the defeat of young Montgomery. Self-loathing had seized him at the realisation that he had taken a human life. Suddenly the tears came - tears for himself, as well as his fallen foe. With the tears came a surge of self-pity, washing away his feelings of guilt. It was then not difficult to convince himself that it was either his life or the Englishman's he had merely killed in self-defence.

But what about the Lady Mairéad? What about this strange obsession which gripped him that he would never be the same again since he had lifted her into his arms, gazed into that exquisite face, felt her frail form against his, watched those dainty feet tread the path to the cliff? It was as if a capricious fate had placed a *geasa* on him - like Diarmid with Grainne, and Naoise with Deirdre. His future was inextricably bound to hers.

It's time, Sir Tadhg, he told himself, to rejoin your companions.

Sir Thomas Montgomery's body had been removed from the oak tree. With macabre humour, the Rapparees had deposited it in a nearby ravine which was about twelve feet deep, the length of a legal hanging rope, where it had been covered with a thin layer of rocks and sand. The grave was left unmarked. His son, however, had been buried near the graves of Somhairle Mór and Peadar Laidir, and a rude cross erected, giving his name and date of death. He had died an honourable death, and deserved an honourable grave.

Lady Mairéad, weeping and distraught, was being comforted by her maid when Tadhg returned to the vicinity of the fireplace where stood both the O'Flahertys, Dermot O'Lee and several others.

None made reference to his absence. Cathal, crooking his forefinger, beckoned to him and addressed him in a low voice. 'I think it would be best if the two ladies were taken to the house of Conor O'Donnell's sister for the night. There is too much around here to remind Lady FitzGerald of her bereavement. You and Conor and Dónal Óg who rescued them will escort them. In the morning take them as close to Galway as you can without serious risk. Take five horses, one for each of you. And go safely.

'Have you told them,' said Tadhg, gesturing to the weeping

47

women.

Cathal nodded. His eyes were haggard, sad.

The horses were led up by Dónal Óg, and with some effort the Lady Mairéad was put aboard a gentle mare. There were no saddles, in the Irish custom, so Tadhg walked next to her horse, ready to catch her if she fell. Conor led the way, followed by Dónal, leading Tadhg's horse, then came Mary Casey and Tadhg and Lady Mairéad bringing up the rear. Tadhg felt an overwhelming desire to comfort the weeping girl as she crouched forlornly on her mount, but wisely refrained. Vagrant breezes playfully ruffled the golden hair as the sun highlighted the bent head. It's the colour of the bog-fir in summer, Tadhg thought.

At a broad glen where a narrow, muddy road meandered among brown bog and small cultivated plots of poor land, each enclosed by walls of stones, Dónal Óg halted and dismounted.

'I'll just stroll ahead to see if all is safe at the Blakes,' he said.

'Tadhg,' Conor asked as they waited, 'just where did you learn to handle a sword like you did back there?' All of us expected that the English man would cut you up in pieces for his dinner.'

'One Pedro de Alvarez, a Spanish captain of a ship, was cast up on Inishmór by a storm. He was the only survivor. Because of the authorities who knew of the wrecked ship, we kept him hidden in our village. When he subsequently learned from Spain that he was being blamed for the loss of the ship, he stayed with different families on the island, doing odd jobs for his keep, for about five years, before he felt it was safe to return home. In that time he taught me how to use a sword, all the tricks of footwork, of arm position, use of the wrist, how to parry and feint, and how to analyse an opponent's style.'

Tadhg pointed to his sword in its rough scabbard. 'When he felt that I was ready, he gave me his sword which he said had been made by one of the finest swordsmiths in Toleldo. But, *a chara*, I never used it before on anybody. And I assure you, it is entirely different to fight with a man who is trying to kill you than one merely demonstrating its use. If it wasn't for the great anger that young Montgomery provoked in me, I never would have had the courage to fight him, surely. To give him his due, he was a fine swordsman. If he hadn't had such contempt for me, he probably would have killed me because he had more experience. That is one of the important things that Don Pedro taught me: never underestimate you opponent. And I'm riding with you this day

48

because the Sassanach didn't learn that lesson very well.'

'But how did you convince Cahill to let you face him?'

'I told him I had a good chance because of my training. Also because I was bigger and stronger. Even de Alvarez used to say that I was quick as a cat despite my size, and quickness is a major asset in sword fighting. In addition, I told Cahill that my sword was better than the Sassanach's. Don Pedro always did speak dispairingly of English steel.'

Just then a hooded crow flew close to the Lady Mairéad's horse. The animal reared, and Tadhg grabbed the girl to keep her from being thrown. 'Don't touch me, you murderer,' she exclaimed vehemently, glaring at him in loathing. Despite his lack of English, Tadhg flinched under her hostility. Mary Casey turned her horse, flinging a reviling *'Gommach'* at Tadhg, then said soothingly, 'There, Mairéad *a stóir*, don't be fearful, everything will be all right.'

Conor looked at Tadhg with a sly twinkle in his eye. 'Watch out, *gommach*, two angry *cailíns* are more than a match for even a Fionn MacCool like yourself.'

A bedevilled Tadhg was spared the problem of reply by the return of Dónal Óg. 'The *bean an tí* bids you welcome,' he said. Lady Mairéad looked questioningly at Mary Casey, who, for the first time acknowledged that she understood Irish by explaining to her mistress that the 'woman of the house' welcomed them.

With Dónal Óg leading, they soon arrived at the small, whitewashed cabin nestling against a hill where dwelt Conor's oldest sister Máire, with her husband, Mortagh Blake, and their four children. Máire, whose jet-black hair was threaded was grey, greeted her brother with a warm embrace. Then, turning to the two women, she smiled and said, 'God be with you.'

With a quick, questioning look at her mistress, Mary gave the traditional reply in the Gaelic, 'God and Mary with you.'

Like a mother hen protecting her chick, Mary Casey guided Lady Mairéad into the warm cabin. Conor, Tadhg and Dónal Óg followed.

At the far end of the room was a massive fireplace in which a turf fire was blazing cheerfully. The walls were built of rough-shaped stones, mortared with mud. Thatched rushes made the roof. Near the fireplace, and benefiting from its warmth, was the bedchamber - separated from the rest of the room by long, hanging mats woven from rushes. Furnishings were simple - a big wooden table with long benches on each side, a crude chest of drawers, another wide bench against the opposite wall which could also serve as a bed, and a crucifix on the wall near the door. Opposite was another door, not closed against the wind. The floor was of well-trodden earth.

At the lower end of the room, a cow, brought in for the night, was noisily munching hay. Several chickens scratched listlessly in the dirt, and a ewe with two lambs lay with quiet dignity. Here the ground sloped down to a drainage ditch for sanitation.

Dónal Óg had apparently informed Murtagh and Máire of the circumstances which brought the visitors to their home. Although Máire was not accustomed to entertaining the aristocracy, especially Protestants, her solicitude for the young woman soon dispelled any awkwardness. Mortagh was even more taciturn than usual. The Protestant Ascendancy, which had grown greatly in property and power after the Cromwellian conquest, was still his prime hate. But the remarkable beauty of this representative of the ruling class, and her great sorrow and distress, kept him quiet in his seat by the hearth as he smoked his old *duidín* surrounded by his wide-eyed children.

Máire led her guests to the table, setting out a *troander* for them. Made of sour milk, mixed with some sweet milk from the cow added, it was served in a *meddar*, a square wooden vessel carved all of one piece. Mary Casey consumed hers with gusto, but Lady Mairéad, either repelled by the aroma of sour milk, or too sick at heart to take food, gently refused her share. She thought longingly of the syllabub she was accustomed to drinking in Dublin. She addressed her maid in English, and Mary Casey informed Máire in Irish that her mistress was weary and would like to retire.

At a word from Máire, the eldest child, Eithne, went to the bedchamber where she spread rushes on the floor to the depth of half a cubit. Over this went a linen sheet, called a *breadeen*, taken from the chest of drawers, and evidently reserved for great occasions like this. Dusk having fallen, dip candles made of seal fat were lit while the family and their guests made ready for bed. The women retired while Mortagh, temporarily dispossessed, helped his two sons spread rushes in the main room. Then the Blakes, and Conor, Dónal Óg and Tadhg, lay down to sleep.

CHAPTER III

The Departure

Despite his strange surroundings, Tadhg slept well on his bed of rushes. He awoke to the clucking of the chickens and the restless movements of the livestock. As he adjusted himself to his whereabouts, he saw two wraithlike forms issuing from the bedchamber, and Máire and Eithne proceed to the big room to prepare the household for the day.

Eithne gently removed the ashes from the seed of the fire, laying on fresh sods of turf, and with the aid of the bellows, soon the fire blazed merrily. Her mother had lit the dip candles in the large sea-shells, then started breakfast. Because of the strong, unpleasant odour of the burning seal fat, the candles were placed as close as possible to the fireplace so that the draught would whisk most of the smell up the chimney. Soon the pungent aroma of the turf fire, the biting fumes of the candles, the acrid odours of livestock dung and urine blended to form a heady perfume that might easily turn the stomach of a sensitive soul unused to the bucolic life of a poor farmer like Murtagh.

To Tadhg it was all normal, but it was new and unusual to awaken in a strange bed. He had never been away from home overnight. Now each dawn seemed to find him in a new place.

Máire had finished dusting the powdery ash of the fire from the kitchen table with a goose wing, and sweeping the hearth with a besom. Then setting out the querns, two flat circular stones with holes in the middle, she ground some oats into meal. Adding water, she made a batter into which she mixed butter. When stirred to the right consistency, she poured it on a griddle set on a tripod among the blazing sods of turf. The result was a tasty, thin panbread. With hope in her heart and a prayer on her lips, Máire reached into the poreen, a square hole built into the chimney, and sure enough, there was a fresh egg! This was to be for the Lady Mairéad. In the meanwhile, Eithne had put a supply of potatoes to bake in the fire. She prepared some stirabout, which was a porridge of oatmeal in hot milk, then mixed a large portion of buttermilk with oatmeal added for the morning beverage.

When the potatoes were done, the oatcake cut into farls, the stirabout thoroughly cooked, and the solitary egg boiled, the Blake family and their guests filled the benches to overflowing. Wooden noggins and bowls were the dishes, and sea-shells were used for spoons. There were no forks, and the men used their *sceana* to cut with.

The Lady Mairéad was much improved with a good night's rest. Colour had returned to her cheeks, and only her eyes showed the sadness on her. Her golden hair had been combed by Mary Casey until it shone in the flickering light of the candles. When the egg was served to her, she observed that it was the only one, and protested, but Máire said that all the others wanted her to have it so she graciously accepted.

Tadhg sat at the far end of the table, at the opposite side, but whenever his eyes met hers she immediately looked away. Apparently the death of Montgomery far outweighed Tadhg's having saved her from the sea. He was as deep in despair as he had been high in hope.

With a downcast Tadhg, a taciturn Murtagh, a saddened Lady Mairéad, and awed children, the burden of the conversation was carried by Máire, with assistance from Mary Casey and Conor. The maid, seemingly happy to be speaking the despised Irish again, related how the two Montgomerys, her mistress and herself, had left Dublin for Galway in a coach which had become mired in the impassable roads. They were forced to continue their journey on horseback, carrying their luggage on pack-horses. It was such a rough trip that the judge decided to take the more comfortable voyage by sea on their return to the capital, although it would be longer in time and distance.

"Twas an odd time for such a trip,' Murtagh remarked, frowning. 'The judge must have had a compelling reason to bring him here to Connemara in the cold and the wet.'

Mary Casey glanced quickly at her mistress who was listening but could not understand, and continued in the Irish. 'Oh, the judge was mighty mulvathered when King James sent over Richard Talbot to Ireland, and especially when the old viceroy, the Earl of Clarendon, was recalled, and Talbot was made viceroy and Earl of Tyrconnell. But his rage new no bounds when the new victory started putting Catholics in charge of the army. He decided he would sell his property, including that in Connemara, retire from the bench and return to England.

Murtagh puffed slowly at his *duidín*. Looking at Tadhg and Conor, he asked, 'Do you know how he got those lands?'

They shook their heads. 'After the rebellion against Cromwell collapsed,' he explained, 'many of the old families' estates were declared forfeit. In other times the lands were sold, and the soldiers paid from the sales, but this time the soldiers of Cromwell were to be paid with the lands themselves. The idea was twofold: first, it was a way of paying the soldiery, and second, a way of having a permanent, inexpensive, anti-Irish garrison in Ireland.'

Murtagh jabbed his pipestem at his listeners as his anger grew in recollection. 'All the forfeited lands were surveyed and divided. Then each soldier's account was added up, and the total amount due him was certified. To keep the old comrades-in-arms together, the various regiments were assigned to different districts, all chosen by lot. The lands were valued at a certain rate, with each soldier getting as much value in land as he had coming in pay.'

'The dirty devils!' Dónal exclaimed. 'All at the expense of the Irish.'

Murtagh nodded. 'But it wasn't the average soldier who benefited. Many of them wanted cash, not land; others needed money badly; some just didn't want to live in Ireland. So they sold their debentures at great losses. Their greedy officers, and the speculators, got them for one-fifth or two-fifths of their value. Ensign Montgomery was one of those who obtained big estates in this way.'

'And to think that the Lady Mairéad almost married into that family,' Mary Casey said, her brown eyes angry.

Dawn was breaking when the party said their thanks and goodbyes. 'God bless you and send you safe,' Máire said, tears in her eyes as she gave the Lady Mairéad a squeeze. They mounted their horses, again led by Dónal Óg, followed in turn by the maid, then Lady Mairéad and Tadhg and Conor, who kept a watchful eye on the road behind. A cold rain fell as they plodded down the narrow path. Their route led through an area dominated by grey rock and heather, with occasional bogs and cleared areas where the remains of abandoned cabins indicated that human beings had once dwelled there.

By noon the party had negotiated the hardest, slowest part of the journey. Their path now lay southeast with the Mountains of Beola behind them, and a better road ahead. Conor halted in a glade where the horses could drink and eat. He produced some oatcakes and jackdaw cheese which Máire had packed. They ate it ravenously, with even the Lady Mairéad enjoying her share.

'This is probably the time to discuss our future conduct on the

53

road,' Conor declared. 'We will soon be meeting other travellers along the road, and if you choose, you can scream and point us out as Rapparees responsible for hanging Sir Thomas Montgomery. In that case, we will be obliged to flee, leaving you at the mercy of the road. And I assure you that there are worse people about than Rapparees and Papist peasants. Our obligation of safe passage will have been abrogated. Rather than abandon you, we would much prefer a truce, an understanding that nothing will be said except that we rescued you from your shipwrecked vessel. The fate of the others will not be mentioned. Can we rely on you?'

After an awkward silence, Margaret FitzGerald spoke. 'We are grateful to you for saving our lives. We also thank you for your many kindness and courtesies.' Tears filled her eyes, and her voice faltered. Then, regaining her composure, she continued, 'However, I find it difficult to accept that barbarous hanging of the judge just because of ancient grievances. The death of his son is a personal matter. I know that he goaded that young giant into the fight, and on that score Tadhg is perhaps blameless. But I cannot forget that he was to be my husband and that he has been taken from me. No matter the cause, I cannot think kindly of you for that.' Wiping tears from her eyes, she said, 'I will accept your conditions for the truce, but you must realise that we will have to tell the true story to the authorities at Galway. Your sins and crimes are on your own head.'

Conor bowed. 'Thank you, it will make it much easier this way.'

Late in the afternoon, several leagues from Galway, a squad of soldiers came trotting down the road. The young ensign in command rode up to intercept the party. 'Tell him that we Irish speak no English,' Conor whispered to the Lady Mairéad.

'I am Lady Margaret FitzGerald of Dublin, and this is my maid,' she haughtily greeted the officer. 'These men,' and she pointed to the three apprehensive Irishmen whose fate lay in her next words, 'saved our lives when we were shipwrecked on the way to Dublin from Galway. They are guiding us.'

'Ensign Henry Greene, of the Shropshire Horse, at your service, milady,' he said, staring suspiciously at Tadhg, Conor and Dónal. They eyed him coolly in return. Noting their crude brogues, their rough clothing, their lack of weapons but their *sceana*, he arrogantly dismissed them from further consideration.

Conor addressed Mary Casey in Irish. 'Ask your mistress if she will request this officer to escort you the rest of the way to

Galway. Have her tell him that we should return quickly to our work. And also tell him that the two horses you are riding belong to Sir John Ferguson, and must be returned to him.'

'What did he say?' the ensign asked, turning to glare at Conor.

Ignoring him, Mary Casey spoke directly to her mistress, repeating in English what Conor had asked. Lady Mairéad spoke in turn to the ensign. 'He wants to know if you will take us to Galway. They would like to return home.' She looked at Conor sardonically. 'Oh yes, they must return these two horses to Sir John Ferguson.'

Ensign Greene was more than happy to escort such a beautiful young woman, but tried to hide his eagerness. He wrinkled his forehead in thought. 'We are supposed to be on patrol to investigate rumours that O'Flaherty's Rapparees are in the vicinity, but I have seen no evidence of it.' He sat for a while, flapping his elegant gloves against his thigh. Then he smiled, trying to charm the ladies. 'But FitzGeralds take precedence over O'Flahertys every time,' he said carefully, trying to hide his west-of-England accent. 'And what better way to compensate for this Godforsaken countryside than to travel with you to Galway?'

Curtly he ordered two of his troopers to dismount and assist the ladies onto their horses. This done, the men each rode with a companion.

Conor had shown no sign he understood the ensign's English, but sat waiting. When Mary Casey informed him in Irish of the decision, he and Tadhg took the reins of the two horses, and trotted sedately down the road without a backwards glance. When they passed the first turn, however, he said, 'We had better take to the hills for a while, for there is no way of knowing how long the lady will keep her promise. Besides, I didn't like the way he was eyeing our horses.'

They scrambled up a rocky hill to a ridge and crossed several valleys before coming to another road that led to the northwest and Iar-Chonnacht.

They were received effusively by Murtagh and Máire, who had been concerned when they hadn't returned promptly. Neither Conor nor Dónal were Rapparees but did assist them at times. This was probably known to informers. Tadhg, of course, was new to the area, but the story of his duel with the young Montgomery had been widely spread.

'You must be famished,' Máire said, 'Wash yourselves and the meal will be ready.'

When they were seated, Máire gave the prayer which she had refrained from offering the night before in deference to her Protestant guests, not being too sure of their religious customs: 'May the blessings of the five loaves and the two fishes which Our Lord divided amongst the multitude be ours, and may the Good Lord who divided the food give us good fortune in our portion, Amen.'

'Gilleduff O'Fallon stopped by today,' Máire informed them as they started to eat, 'to say that Cathal and his men have moved to the region of Ballyconeely Bay for a while. Cathal thinks that Kilkieran will be swarming with soldiers once word of the hanging is known at Galway.'

'All the Irish hereabouts know of it already,' Murtagh said with quiet satisfaction. 'In many a cabin there has been celebrating, and many a drop of *uisce beatha* taken in drinking the health of Cathal O'Flaherty and his Rapparees. They are curious about the young giant who slew young Montgomery in a great duel. 'Tis famous you are, Tadhg. 'Twas a great day indeed when that servant from hell was returned to his master.'

Eithne, whose large, expressive eyes had been watching Tadhg with satisfaction, turned to her mother. 'Is it forgetting you are what Donough O'Flaherty spoke to you about?'

'I saved that for the last because it is the best. Donough stopped by the cabin, too. We've had more visitors in the last two days than we usually have in two months. Donough wants to start a school for the children of the parish. Poor things,' and she glanced fondly at her own brood, 'they're growing up without knowledge of reading or writing. 'Tis a sad pity!'

'And a fine idea it is,' said Conor. 'It's time that somebody other than the Protestants started a school because they will not admit Catholics unless they renounce their own faith. 'Tis a cruel, despicable way to make converts.'

Murtagh nodded in agreement. 'I've been told that several families in the Moycullen area have quit the Church so that the children can be educated. 'Tis a hard decision surely, but I'd rather have mine know the right way to heaven than the right road to London.'

'Donough should be a good teacher,' Conor said enthusiastically. 'He has been studying in France and Spain these many years. And 'tis said that he has even gone to Rome and seen the Pope himself. Ah, he's the clever one. He can teach Latin and Greek and arithmetic.'

The talk of a school excited Tadhg. The image of Sir Thomas Montgomery aboard the wreck came to his mind. He could see the judge's contemptuous look and hear the arrogant voice saying, 'Cut us loose, you bogtrotting savage.' He suddenly heard himself blurt, 'I would like to go to school too.'

'Haven't you any schooling?' Máire asked sympathetically.

'I spent a year at the priest's school on Inishmór,' he replied, 'but I didn't learn any of those grand thing Conor mentioned.'

'Can your parents pay Donough for your schooling?' Murtagh asked. 'He is attainted and has no money of his own. The parents of the pupils will have to help maintain the school and the poor schoolmaster.'

'My father is a poor fisherman. He has no money.'

'We have no money either,' said Máire. 'We will have to pay Donough by feeding him, and making his clothes from the wool of our few sheep. That is the way most of the parents around here will pay him.'

'I could fish,' Tadhg offered eagerly.

Máire smiled gently. 'But if you fished all day, there would be no time for school.'

Murtagh looked at the downcast Tadhg and then at Máire. 'Perhaps the lads could make a small garden of rocks, and the Good Lord knows we have enough of those. With some hard work, it might yield enough potatoes and corn to feed the three of them.'

Máire beamed affectionately at the solid man. She turned to her brother. 'What do you say, Conor, and you, Dónal? Would you be willing to break your backs to help your friend to go to school?'

Conor pondered the question. Would he help Tadhg? Gladly! But why not help himself and go to school too? His schooling, like Tadhg's, had been limited. He nodded his head. 'I'll not only help Tadhg with the garden, but I will go to school as well, and help him with his lessons.'

Dónal, who worshipped the giant islander, enthusiastically promised to do his share, and he, too, would go to school.

For the next ten days the trio laboured from early morn until dusk in the small rocky patch behind the cabin. It was completely barren of any soil. Using a heavy iron sledgehammer borrowed from a neighbour, Tadhg smashed the loose boulders of heavy quartzite into pieces small enough for Conor and Dónal to carry to the edge of the patch, where they slowly became a wall to protect the new garden from hungry and undiscriminating animals. When the area was cleared and levelled, they borrowed a cart from Murtagh and a Connemara pony from Conor's brother Séan, and hauled coarse sand from the strand.

The storm which had brought Tadhg to Kilkieran had also cast generous amounts of seaweed on the shore, but not enough to the critical eye of Murtagh, who was their adviser and goad. So Tadhg spent hours in the cold sea, cutting more kelp loose with his knife and carrying it to shore, where it was put into the cart. Eithne and young Tomás helped, carrying sand and weed in panniers made of sallyrods, trudging sturdily up the steep hillsides and along the winding boreen to the new garden.

Murtagh supervised the operation carefully so that only the good coarse sand was used, and none of the fine unproductive 'dead sand' that predominated on the beach. When the sand and the seaweed were blended properly and a satisfactory level reached, Máire and the girls planted the seed potatoes. It was now an 'if' garden. If the seaweed decayed rapidly and thoroughly, if the seed potatoes sprouted, if the rains came just right - not too much or too little - and if spring and summer should bring adequate sunshine, there might be a crop first year.

CHAPTER IV

The School

Rain was falling softly when Tadhg, Conor and Dónal, and Eithne and Tomás Blake set off for the start of Donough's school at the nearby farm of Kevin O'Devaney, a cousin of Dónal's. About twenty children were already gathered near the old cabin, which was to be used as a schoolhouse, when they arrived.

Donough had replaced his French clothing with the homespun woollen tunic and trousers of his Connemara neighbours. He was shaved, his hair cut short, and he greeted the newcomers warmly, especially Tadhg, saying that he was extremely gratified that the islander could attend. The walls of the cabin were newly limed. An old rickety table, piled high with Donough's books and materials, stood at the far end of the room.

Finally, when all the pupils were present and seated on a variety of benches scrounged from the neighbours, Donough took his place behind the table and raised his hand for silence. It took several minutes for the clamour to subside, with repeated admonitions from the schoolmaster, since most of the children had never been to school before, and the only time they were ever collectively silent was at Mass.

'I am Donough O'Flaherty,' the teacher began in ringing tones, his deep-set eyes agleam with fervour, 'an old friend of most of your fathers and mothers. We have long dreamed of establishing a school here in Moyrus parish, so that you will not grow up in ignorance such as the present rulers of this country want, for they know that people steeped in ignorance are easier kept in subjugation. I will speak and teach in Irish, except when I conduct the English-language class for some of you, especially the older ones. We will start with the essentials, which will be reading, writing and arithmetic. When we have progressed in these basic studies, we will take up history, geography, literature, music and other advanced subjects. Now, before we begin, are there any questions?'

Conor arose, obviously embarrassed among his fellow pupils, most of whom hardly stood up to his chest. 'Some of us,' he said, clearing his throat, 'have already had some schooling. What are you going to do with us?'

'I will speak to each of you students to learn how far you have progressed. After a review of the basic subjects, I will set a course of study for each, depending on your aptitude and desire. You, Conor, are the oldest in the school, and talking to your sister, Máire, I learned that you are the most advanced. Tadhg, Dónal Óg and Eithne all have had some schooling, and they too will be placed in the advanced class. All the rest,' and he looked at the bright eyes - and some open mouths - 'will start from scratch. You may be seated, Conor.'

While Donough was speaking, Tomás Blake, seeing a boody crawling in the collar of his seatmate, Eoghan MacConeely, struck so hard at the louse that was about to disappear into Eoghan's long hair that he knocked the poor lad off the seat. With fire in his eyes, Eoghan turned on Tomás, and in a moment, the whole class was in an uproar.

'Don't try your sly tricks on me,' Eoghan shouted furiously, rushing at Tomás and swinging his fists furiously.

The surprised Tomás shielded his face with his hands while Donough, with a speed and agility unsuspected in one with such short legs, dashed out from behind the table and grabbed the protesting Eoghan. Conor held his nephew, who struggled furiously to be freed.

When order was finally restored, and the two combatants assigned new seats far apart, Donough faced the class, his countenance grim.

'There will be no fighting or interruptions in my classroom. You have been sent by your parents to get an education, and an education is what you are going to get. I am the master here. Any one of you who chooses to dispute that will be sent packing. Is that clearly understood?'

He glared at the rows of solemn faces, then, noticing tears forming in the eyes of some of the younger children, he suddenly smiled at them, transforming his face from that of a forbidding ogre to that of a gently saint. Then the smile was gone and he assumed his usual benign demeanour.

'You may have wondered why I returned to my native land,' he began, 'when I could have remained in France were there are a great many schools. But while I stayed there, I began to feel the obligation to return some of this knowledge to Ireland, where today there is so much darkness - this in a land where from time immemorial there have been many schools and scholars, even in the days when our forefathers were pagans.

'In Eire there have always been many who have been anxious to learn and to teach. Before St Patrick converted our ancestors from paganism, teaching was in the hands of the Druids, who were the priests in those days, and the Filí, the poets. With the advent of the St Patrick, however, the Druids lost their powers, teaching being in the hands of the great scholars. Soon buildings were erected to house students, who had learned in the open, under the sky. Tadhg, here, comes from Inishmór where many of those schools can still be seen. Because of the hundreds of pious scholars in St Enda's school the islands became known as 'Ara of the Saints'. After the schools became permanent, they were followed by other teachers from Europe, bringing the learning and wisdom of centuries. And in Ireland, these teachers found the Gaels thirsting for knowledge. Their schools flourished; peace was on the land.

Donough paused and his face became sad. 'Meanwhile, evil days had fallen on Europe. Barbaric heathens - Huns, Vandals, Goths and Visigoths - swept down in great hordes from the east, north and west, killing, pillaging and destroying. They moved through the land like voracious locusts through a grainfield, leaving little but destruction. Schools were burned, also precious manuscripts that could never be replaced, teachers and scholars were put to the sword. Slowly the light of knowledge flickered and went out.

'But all was not lost. Some of the best teachers and scholars of Europe fled to Ireland. They brought with them Greek and Latin, mathematics and the sciences, so enriching that our little island became the University of the western world. Then, as the savage hordes retreated, or were decimated by war and disease or absorption, the old desire of knowledge reasserted itself. Men hungry for learning looked about them, and far to the west, in 'insula sanctorum et doctorum', in the Island of the Saints, the light of learning was still burning brightly.

'By the scores and then by the hundreds they left their native lands - from Italy and France, from the far-flung lands of the Holy Roman Empire, from the lowlands and the mountains, from the farms and the cities, they travelled as best they could to Banba, our green island, to the light that beckoned there. Many stayed and their bones are buried here, but many returned to their native lands, anxious to establish new schools there. During this time many Irish scholars, too, left for the Continent, zealously helping to dispel the darkness, founding schools wherever there were eager pupils. At long last the gift of knowledge was again available to those who sought it.'

The young children sat spellbound and quiet. The older students were enthralled. He was expressing in words the exhilaration they felt.

Again Donough's expression turned to sadness. 'Eventually it was our turn to suffer the deprecations of the heathens. From their cold, mist-ridden and forbidding lands came the Fionnghaill, the fair strangers called the Norse, and then the Dubhghaill called Danes, in their longboats to attack for plunder, isolated schools, monasteries, churches and communities. It was the same savage, senseless destruction which had been inflicted on Europe. Churches were looted and priests slain, schools destroyed and priceless manuscripts lost forever.'

Donough sighed heavily. 'Some of these barbarians founded settlements along our shores such as Waterford and Wexford. Through savagery and deceit, and alas, through the treachery of some of the Irish chiefs who sought advantages over other Irish, these invaders kept a knife at the throat of Eire until defeated by the great Brian Boru in the year 1014 at Clontarf.

Donough paused again. 'After a hundred years of freedom from invasion, Banba faced a new attack. This time it was the Normans who had conquered England fifty years after Brian put down the Danes. They too cast their covetous eyes on Eire. Using traitors like Dermot MacMurrough, they established themselves along the coast and built fortified castles. Then, by continual warfare against the Irish, by intermarriage with native families, they gained control of large parts of our land for England. And to make themselves more secure, they ordered that the Irish tongue should not be spoken or taught, and that all schools for Irish children be forbidden. They might just as well have demanded that the rain cease to fall.

'New attempts were always being made to stifle learning for the Gael. For example, in 1367, the Anglo-Normans under Prince Lionel, son of King Edward the Third of England, ordered that a special Parliament be held at Kilkenny. These tyrannical *spailpíns* then enacted a series of restrictions against the native Irish. One of these was that education of the Irish was forbidden and no colleges or seminaries were permitted to enrol them. Equally tyrannical and futile was the order that only English be spoken in the land, and that no subject of the king be known by any but an English name.

Now, just to show you how ridiculous that was, I ask that all of you who speak no Irish raise your right hand.'

Not a hand was raised. The pupils all looked at each other solemnly. Then a titter went through the classroom, growing into loud laughter as they realised their teacher's point.

'Some years ago, Archbishop Ussher of Dublin was a member of a commission to eliminate all teaching that was not Protestant. So the commission came to Galway where they found a school of a thousand scholars so well taught that they answered the commissioner's questions in Latin. Now do you think that these students were rewarded for their diligence and scholarship? On the contrary. The school was immediately closed - because their master, Sean Lynch, was a Catholic.

'Because I, too, am a Catholic, this little school, hidden behind the hedge, is forbidden. At any time it could be raided, your schoolmaster seized, the students dispelled, the cabin razed and your parents jailed for sending you here. I need not remind you that the law against an Irishman attending a college or seminary is still in force. That is why I had to go to France for my education. That is why many young men slip away in the dead of night, surreptitiously boarding a ship for France or Spain so that he will not be deprived of the education he is forbidden in his own native land. Oh, yes, the Sassanach will allow you to go to the Protestant school if you will give up your Catholic faith. But thank God few of the Gaeltacht are so destitute of honour that they will sink that low.'

Donough stopped and looked out at the distant hills through the open door. Then, bringing his attention back to his audience, he said, 'I suppose that you are wondering why I came back to my native Iar-Chonnacht. It happened one day when I was visiting one of the sites of some of those old schools founded by Irishmen in France many hundreds of years ago. This one was founded by St Fiacre at Breuil, not far from Paris. Several months ago, when I was there, I seemed to see St Fiacre frowning at me and saying, 'Donough O'Flaherty, what are you doing here when in your native land are many children who have no schooling or hopes of schooling. You have been given a great gift. Go now and share it!'

'I wrote to my brother Cathal immediately telling him that I would like to come home and establish a school somewhere in the Barony of Ballinahinch. He replied that I should do it, and he and his men would offer what protection they could. He said that with

Richard Talbot, a Catholic, as Viceroy in Dublin Castle, conditions might be more favourable than in the past. I arranged for passage, and as I crossed the sea to Ireland, I thanked God for the rare privilege He had granted me, that of returning the torch of knowledge again to the Island of the Saints. I was fulfilling the prophecy of a wise man named Solomon many centuries ago, who said, 'Cast thy bread upon the waters, for thou shalt find it after many days."

As Donough concluded, his voice faltered with his emotion, his eyes were bright with his vision, and Tadhg offered a silent prayer to Jesus: Please, Iosa, let me become learned like little Donough so that I, too, can cast my bread upon the waters.

CHAPTER VI

James Flees

The pleasant autumn days passed. On the hillside tillock where the new garden had been planted, a fairly good crop was maturing in the thin soil. Tadhg spent many back-breaking hours helping Murtagh remove huge rocks from his fields to repay him for the food and shelter he provided. Although Murtagh was fond of the strong young giant, he remained adamant in his stand against any possible match with Eithne. He was appreciative of Tadhg's labours, admitting to himself that he was probably getting the best of the bargain, for Tadhg was the equal of two ordinary men when it came to heavy work.

After school, when the weather permitted, Tadhg, Dónal and Conor went fishing in the curragh. A supply of glashan, the coalfish, was set out to dry on the roof of the cabin, while bream, rockfish, pollock, whiting, plaice and sole helped to vary the diet and fill the plates at dinnertime. In addition there were limpets, mussels, cockles and an occasional salmon or trout poached by one of the trio.

When Tadhg was in the curragh, he was reminded of his home and family. At times he could see the islands low on the distant ocean. He was torn between his desire to be reunited with his family, and his passion for learning. But he dreaded meeting Peadar's old mother, and the widowed Una O'Conchubhair and her three children.

Some months after he had come to the Blake cabin, Tadhg was persuaded by Conor and Máire to walk to a distant small village where lived fishermen who sailed to the Aran Islands, but the three days he stayed in the village a storm raged, and no curragh left port. Finally he despaired of finding a curraghman who would brave the weather, so he left a message for his family, and one for his dead friends' bereaved kin, and walking all night, arrived in time for school.

Occasionally when the Rapparees sallied forth from their hills on a foray, Cathal would stop to visit Donough. One morning Donough sent word he would be late, and that Conor should conduct the class. Knowing Tadhg's talent for mimicry, Conor called on him to imitate Donough, and tell a story to keep the students occupied until Donough should arrive.

'Today we will study the Greeks and the Romans,' Tadhg began, his tone and inflections so like Donough's that the younger children looked curiously about to see where their teacher was. 'Before the birth of our Lord Jesus, the ancient peoples worshipped different gods. The Greeks had a fine lad, called Poseidon Mac Kronos, who was their god of the sea, while the Romans, not to be outdone, had one named Neptune Mac Saturn.'

Tadhg paused, trying to suppress a grin. Winking at the smiling Conor, he continued. 'One day after Mass, when both of these bold lads were out with their favourite *cailíns* for a spin in their chariots, which were drawn by seahorses, they chanced upon another in the great Italian Sea. 'Faith,' says Neptune, angrily tugging the reins, 'and what is the likes of you doing in my sea?'

"Your sea?' says Poseidon, stomping his pampooties in rage, 'I'll give you the back of your hand, you Italian sardine, if you don't go back immediately to your subjects, those slimy eels and loathsome crabs of the Pontine marshes.'

'With a loud war cry, the pair hurled their tridents at each other. Then, suddenly, appeared in their midst a great boiling and surging, and sure if it wasn't our own Irish Manannan MacLir himself, out for a stroll. And just as the two tridents were about to pass each other in flight, didn't he leap up and grab them with one hand to use to pick his teeth with.

'What's the reason for this pillalew of yours?' he roared, showing a big oak cudgel he had cut fresh in the Wood of Shillelagh in the Wicklow Mountains that very morning. 'It's spoiling the clams you are. And you,' he says in his very best Greek to Poseidon Mac Kronos, 'get back to your underseas cavern before I make crab bait out of you.' Then, turning to Neptune MacSaturn, and in his voice hoarse from too much *uisce beatha*, grunted in his choicest Latin, with just a trace of a Connemara accent, 'And you, cousin to a mackerel, head for Italy before I give you a good Irish boot.'

'Now both those bold lads were gods in their own right, but there was no use in talking back to Mannanan MacLir, and they knew it, so using their whips on their seahorses, and with a furious ruction and shaking of their fists, they departed as fast as they could go.'

Cathal and Dermot O'Lee walked into the schoolroom, looking about in a bewildered fashion and then beckoned to Conor. 'Where is Donough?' Cathal asked. 'I'd like to speak with him.'

'He hasn't arrived yet, but we expect him at any minute,' Conor said.

Cathal frowned. 'He must be here,' he insisted. 'I just heard him talking to the class.'

Conor shook his head. 'No. That wasn't Donough. That was Tadhg.' The corners of Conor's mouth twitched slightly as he tried to refrain from laughing, and turning to Tadhg, said, 'Speak to your brother, Donough.'

Tadhg grinned. 'Good morning, brother dear, and what's the news you bring from the north?'

Cathal shook his head with amazement. 'I wouldn't have believed it if I hadn't seen it with my own eyes and heard it with my own ears. This young man has more talents than my old dog has fleas. But where did you learn that story? From Donough?'

'No,' replied Tadhg. 'Donough wouldn't waste his time with such nonsense. He feels that each moment is too precious to be wasted. We learn only the best from him.'

'Thank you, Tadhg,' the real Donough's voice came from the doorway. 'Apparently I missed a good story. But what is it that you want, Cathal?'

'Just to talk to you for a while. Could we speak outside?'

Donough nodded. Addressing Conor, he said, 'Take over the class until I return.'

Tadhg followed the others from the room, for he was always interested in the news of the outside world that Cathal brought to Donough. When they were out of earshot of the pupils, Cathal, looking worried, said, 'When we were near Castlebar yesterday, Donough Beag, we met a party of travellers, including a Protestant minister. After they had made their involuntary contribution to aid the starving Rapparees of Iar-Chonnacht, the minister angrily informed me that the situation in Ireland will soon be different, and all the lawless Irish hanged. When asked what change he alluded to, he told us that a large force was being raised in the Lowlands under William of Orange to invade England and expel James. And when this was accomplished, Ireland's turn would be next, with all the Catholics driven from the country.'

'Do you think he was telling the truth?' Donough asked gravely.

Cathal shrugged. 'From his vehemence, he seemed to believe it.'

'What would it mean if it were true?'

The Rapparee chief sighed heavily. 'It means hard times again for the Catholics, both in England and here. And it means further trouble for the Gael. The Sassanaigh have been restive here of late in Ireland. Only the fact that James is a Catholic has kept them from further punitive measures against us Irish Catholics. If James is driven from his throne, it certainly would encourage Sir John Ferguson, who has long been threatening to lead an expedition to wipe out me and my Rapparees. One way he could strike at me would be to turn out all the native Irish farmers whom he suspects of supplying us with food and shelter. He would use the situation to gleek us, I'm sure. I expected a massive retaliation after the Montgomerys were slain, but nothing happened, probably because the new Viceroy has been appointing Catholics as governors of the fortified cities like Cork, Galway, Athlone, Limerick and the like. Watch for trouble, Donough, and keep an eye on the hills.'

'You will try to signal with fire or smoke?'

'Yes, smoke by day, fire by night.'

After Cathal and Dermot departed, Tadhg asked Donough about the signals.

'The O'Flahertys have used the system for many years, *a chara*, to warn of approaching enemies. Men are posted on the hills to start a fire if hostile forces are coming. We had plenty of clansmen in the old days, but today many of the O'Flahertys are on the side of the government, or give it lip service since they have no grievances. It is only our branch of the family, with Cathal and me as survivors, that is contumacious.'

Donough continued. 'You know, Tadhg, Cathal's band of Rapparees is unique. Among his score or so of men, there are at least a dozen representing old Irish, or Norman-Irish, families from all four provinces. They have all been attainted, their lands seized. Cathal takes great pride in leading and representing them. He feels that he heads more than what the Sassanaigh call a band of robbers and knaves.'

'Conor MacNessa would have been proud to have Cathal and his men as members of the Red Branch,' Tadhg protested, 'but I can't understand why the other O'Flahertys are not doing anything to help you and Cathal.'

Donough shrugged, and peered up at Tadhg. 'What could they do?' he asked. 'Fight King James's government in Ireland? Storm Dublin Castle? Join the Rapparees? No, *a chara*, they would only be jeopardising their own lives and families. It is best the way if is. Cathal leads his Red Branch Knights, and I teach school. We both think we are doing something for Ireland, each in our own way.'

While the O'Flaherty brothers went about their own pursuits, momentous news reached the lonely cabins in January of 1689. King James had fled to France, and his son-in-law, the Prince of Orange, with Mary, his queen, were reigning in the palace of St James. What had been rumour was now fact.

Resistance in England had collapsed with the flight of the king. Scotland, already Protestant and with but a small Catholic minority, fell easily. Most of the Catholic lords of England and Scotland were with James in France. Thirty Scots lords and four score gentry assembled in the Palace of St James and obediently acquiesced to the demands of William.

A different climate, however, prevailed in Ireland. Because of the activities of the Lord-Lieutenant in Dublin Castle, Catholics had recently been placed in command of key elements of the army in Ireland. With the exception of some of the fortified cities of Ulster, the governors of the force were Catholics, some of them Irish. Many Protestants were fleeing the smaller towns and rural areas, some going to the cities, some to England. When Clarendon had been replaced by Richard Talbot, about 1,500 Dublin Protestants left for England with him. For the first time in many years, native Irish and English settlers, joined by the band of their Catholicism, were united.

The noble families, Irish, Norman and English, began recruiting troops, much of the expense borne by themselves as the promised monies from Louis XIV in France, failed to materialise. Around Galway, a regiment was being raised by Colonel John Burke, Lord Boffin, and when word of it arrived, Tadhg was sorely tempted to join. The flame of his patriotism, however, burned not nearly as strongly as his flame for knowledge. He was making rapid strides in his studies, and becoming fluent in English, which he practised with Donough and others, such as Conor, who spoke the tongue of the Sassanaigh.

He decided to stay in school.

CHAPTER VII

The Pooka

One unusually warm and sunny afternoon in March, Tadhg decided to get a fresh salmon for the morrow's meal to which Father O'Hanlon was to be the guest after Mass, since it was the Blakes' turn to provide the place for the service, and to feed the pastor.

He climbed the high hill behind the farmhouse to where a silvery stream tumbled down from the hills as it coursed its merry way to the sea. Here the wily salmon came to lurk in the deep pools. As usual, he walked quietly, both to keep his presence unknown to the fish or to any of the agents of Sir John Ferguson who might be skulking nearby to catch poachers. At Atha Dara, called Ford of the Oaks by the English, he crawled cautiously to the ground which could alert the fish in their lairs under the overhanging banks. If he was fortunate, a fine salmon would be finning in the gentle current, awaiting titbits carried down the stream. It was his intention to immerse his arm quietly, gently stroke his quarry's white belly until, with a lightning grab at the unsuspecting fish's gills, he would have it flopping safely on the bank.

As Tadhg peered into the water's depths, adjusting his eyes, he heard a thrashing in a big pool downstream. At first he thought it was a deer, or even a thirsty horse, and he was irked because the disturbance could put down the fish. At the thought that it might be a garron, he became fearful, for then it might be a kelpie, a water spirit that took the form of a horse, and drowned people. He drew back, suddenly alarmed.

Then he saw what appeared to burnished copper against a milk-white background, and with a start he realised it was Eithne, bathing herself happily, unaware that a spectator had intruded on her bath. While the abashed but curious Tadhg watched, she turned and waded to the shore, a picture of youthful innocence and loveliness, stretching forth her arms as if in supplication to the sun god Bal as she stood in the warm and comforting rays to dry.

Tadhg had seen nursing mothers give their breasts to their babies, but never had he gazed upon a naked nymph, her young breasts upthrust, her gently curving hips and thighs, with the water dripping from her slender white body, and the long coppery hair clinging like tendrils about her head and slim shoulders. He though of the old tale of the young bride, famed for her purity and beauty, who had been deserted by Manannan Mac Lir, god of the sea. She was named Fand - the tear that passes over the pupil of the eye, clear and pure. Here was Fand, Tadhg thought, in the mortal form of Eithne.

At that moment the girl turned, and her startled gaze met Tadhg's admiring eyes upon her. She clasped her arms to her body in an attempt to cover her nakedness. Realising the futility of it, she darted to where her clothes lay. She pulled her shift hastily over her head.

'Och,' Tadhg exclaimed lamely, 'I didn't come here to spy on you, *cailín rua*. I came only to catch a salmon for the priest's dinner tomorrow.'

'But you stayed. And stared,' she said, her eyes furious.

'You were so beautiful standing there in the water, Eithne *a rún*, that you reminded me of Fand.'

'Halt your slewthering tongue. 'Tis a poor excuse at best for your shameful ogling of me. To be sure, it's not Mannanan Mac Lir you are but an overgrown *spailpín* who has nothing better to do than to watch a girl at her bath.'

'Arrah, 'tis true I'm not Manannan, for if I were I would have fled from you like he did from Fand after they were married. But stop your bellyragging. No harm is done.'

She lowered her eyes demurely for a moment, then raised them artlessly, and looking up at Tadhg, said softly, 'Ah, that may be, but what will my father say when I tell him?'

Tadhg blanched. 'You wouldn't tell him!' he said, aghast at the possibility.

'And why not? Would you have me keep it a secret from him? And what will he say when I tell him that you want to keep it a secret?'

'Eithne, you wouldn't,' he implored. 'I meant no harm.'

She slipped her dress on over her shift, digging her feet into her brogues. She looked at him archly. 'I'll consider it. Now tie the thongs, please.'

Tadhg bent over, tying the leather thongs that bound the shoes to her feet. Eithne ran her fingers through his long, dark curling locks. 'I wish that my hair curled like yours,' she said wistfully.

When the laces were secured, Tadhg stood erect, aware that Eithne's clear hazel eyes were gazing at him with a strange tenderness which belied the words she had spoken previously. He looked down at her from his great height. She laid her wet head on his chest, putting her arms around him tightly, her youthful body pressed to his. Tadhg gently disengaged her arms and lifted her so that the level of their eyes met, the hazel and the blue, and as they gazed in wonder at each other, each gripped by a new and overpowering emotion, their heads moved closer together until their lips met.

After a while, she moved her mouth from his, looked at him with a triumphant smile, and said, 'I have wanted you to kiss me ever since I first saw you. But you have always been so busy, or with others. Or my father and mother were around.'

'Your father has other plans for you, *a grá*, than for you to wed a poor islander with no silver in his pocket, no livestock, and no prospects.'

Eithne laughed gaily, snuggled closer, and putting her arms around his neck, she put her lips to his ear, saying, 'I care not what Father wants. He would pick anyone with property, no matter what age, or size, or shape. It's you I want, Tadhg, and no other.'

'Easier said than done. There is the matter of the dowry and the priest. Without your father's consent, there can be no marriage.'

Eithne's answer was to kiss him again, long and lovingly. 'If you resist, I will put a spell on you like Deirdre did on Naoise.'

Tadhg shook his head. He was now worried. 'Yes, and Deirdre's wilfulness and the spell she placed on Naoise led to their deaths. Would you have it so with us?'

Sighing contentedly, she declared, 'Just kiss me and squeeze me, Tadhg *a rún*. Save the arguments for after we're married.'

But Eithne's mention of Deirdre evoked the image of the Lady Mairéad. The enchantment was broken. He looked sadly at the girl. 'Eithne, your father's mind and heart are set on making a good match for you. You must forget about me, for as long as your father lives, he will not consider a man with nothing but a strong back. Would you break his heart?'

'Better to break his than mine,' she said passionately. 'I will marry you or none!'

He gently pushed her from him, holding her at arm's length. 'That's a mighty final decision to be making for one so young.'

She faced him fiercely. 'Is it my father's opinion that makes you so obstinate, or has a spell been placed on you by that grand Dublin lady you rescued from the sea? Do you think there is any less chance for me to have you for a husband against my father's wishes than for you to have her for a wife?'

Tadhg coloured. 'It's nonsense you talk,' he said angrily. 'What if the soldiers were to catch me for slaying young Montgomery? A fine young widow you would be with a long, lonely life ahead of you.'

'Better a few months of happiness with you than a lifetime of discontent with another,' she cried. 'I want more of life than drudgery and misery in a lonely mud cabin. What value will my schooling have with such a fate? I already know how to cook and spin and sew and milk the cow. The great lady from Dublin has a maid, finery and a gay life. Did the good Lord intend it for her and not for Eithne Blake?'

'If it's the gay life in Dublin you desire, *mo ghrá*, you had better cast your spell on someone else. I have nothing but the clothes on my back. My family is poorer than yours. And my education has just begun.'

'But I want you, Tadhg, just as you are,' she said, beginning to sob.

'Please don't cry, Eithne *a chroí*,' Tadhg implored. 'Here, let me kiss away your tears.'

She clung to him as he kissed her tenderly, but the tears continued to course down her cheeks. 'Take me, Tadhg, and let us flee together. We can be far beyond the parish before we're missed.'

Tadhg was helpless; he didn't want to hurt her. Trapped between his better judgement and his sentiment, he cast about for an answer. There was a sudden rustling of the leaves, and the sound of a body moving among the shrubs and dwarf trees. Eithne's tears ceased abruptly as she looked at Tadhg apprehensively.

'Come out of there,' Tadhg called. 'We know you're there.'

The noise stopped. All was silent. Tadhg beckoned to Eithne to stand behind him. 'Come out, you blackguard,' Tadhg shouted, 'or I'll take a cudgel to you.'

'Maybe it's the *síoga*,' Eithne whispered fearfully.

Tadhg crossed himself. He recalled all the stories he had heard about the fairies. The hair at the back of his neck seemed to be standing erect.

'We had better run down the boreen,' he said, bending his head to the frightened girl, 'before it gets any closer.'

73

Another sound, this time nearer, caused them to freeze in their tracks. Tadhg stared in that direction through the branches. 'My soul to God,' he exclaimed fearfully, 'it must be the Pooka. I can see its horns.'

Eithne closed her eyes tightly as if by doing so the apparition would vanish. She reached out blindly, grasping Tadhg firmly about the waist. 'Save me, Tadhg,' she whimpered, 'please save me from the Pooka.'

Then the Pooka raised its head, its horns pushing aside the branches, its big eyes peering at the frightened pair. It bellowed plaintively.

Eithne opened her eyes wide in surprise. 'Why, it's the brown cow,' she cried, clapping her hands with joy, tears of laughter streaming down her cheeks.

'We had better lead her home,' Tadhg said, chagrined at his fear, but glad that it happened because it had broken the mood Eithne had evoked. He picked up a broken branch, and brandishing it, drove the cow along the boreen.

It was dusk when they got home. Murtagh was absent, but Máire was waiting anxiously at the half-door. 'Is it you, Eithne *a stóir*?' she called. 'And who is it with you? Ah, it's Tadhg and the brown cow.'

'Not the brown cow, Mother,' Eithne called gaily. 'It's the Pooka. Tadhg captured it, horns and all.'

The Blakes enjoyed the story of the Pooka immensely. Even Tadhg, who still felt foolish at his fear, laughed at the telling. Máire noticed Eithne's damp tresses, and remembered that she had gone to bathe in the pool, but wisely said nothing of it. She could question her daughter later. Then she saw how animated Eithne appeared, and thought there was more to the excitement than merely the fright caused by the cow. Nor did her daughter's story explain her affectionate and knowing glances towards Tadhg.

'Stir the potatoes in the fire, Eithne,' she directed, 'and we will eat as soon as your father comes home.'

Eithne was glad of the opportunity to bend over the fire and dry her hair, reliving the afternoon. She felt no shame that Tadhg had seen her naked. She was head over heels in love with him, and was glad that the incident had occurred because of what had transpired. She was determined to marry the young islander despite her father. In most things she was obedient, but in this, the choice of her mate, she was adamant. In this trait she resembled Murtagh whose stubbornness was well known in the parish. 'He will do what he believes to be right even if it kills him,' Máire often told the neighbours.

When he finally arrived he was so worried and preoccupied with his own problem that the story of the Pooka aroused no question in him as to what the pair had been doing at the pool so late in the day. Máire did not question him; she knew that he would tell her in his own way in his own good time. After dinner, when the children had gone to bed - Sheila, the child of cradle age; Phelim, the child crawling on the floor; Tomás, the child of school age; and Eithne, the child well grown - he unburdened himself.

'I met Morton, Sir John Ferguson's agent, on the road today. He told me our rent was going to be raised again. When I informed him that it is already more than I can pay, he said that there are plenty of others who would be happy to have it at the increased rate.'

Máire was aghast. 'Oh God, Murtagh *mo chroí*, what can we do?'

Murtagh sighed heavily. He reached out to the fire for a glowing ember to light his pipe, took a few deep draws, then blowing the smoke towards the rafters, he said, pointing to his pipe, 'I could give up smoking and save a few pence. Better yet, if Eithne were to get married, we would have one less to feed and clothe. Or perhaps I could appeal to Sir John.'

'Indeed! You might just as well appeal to the Devil himself - God save us from the dirty beast - for all the good that would do.'

'We have worked so hard to make this farm a better place to live,' he said, his pale eyes sad.

'I know, Murtagh. But it is late. Perhaps tomorrow we will find a solution.

CHAPTER VIII

Donough Disappears

Tadhg was awakened by the red rooster in the far corner as it arose from its bed in the straw, stretched its wings, strutted proudly, raised its comb, inflated its chest, and greeted the new day with exuberant crowing. It was Sunday morning.

Raising himself on one elbow, Tadhg glanced around the room. Murtagh and the two boys were still asleep, their breathing deep and regular. A movement at the far end of the room attracted his attention. He saw a dark form, either Máire or Eithne, bending over the fire, laying fresh sods of turf over the smouldering embers. Then the form fitted back to the bedchamber where the women and girls had slept since Tadhg, Conor and Dónal had moved in.

Tadhg stretched, arose and walked to the door. It was still dark, but dawn was beckoning in the east over the bay. As he stood in the half-door, the darkness slowly dissolved, disclosing the familiar sights before the cabin. When the beehive-shaped outbuilding where the farm tools were stored emerged from the obscurity that had hidden it, Tadhg took a *goulogue*, a wooden, homemade digging fork, and went up to the little vegetable patch he and his friends had established a year before.

The day was cold and raw. Tadhg shivered. He needed a coat, a *bainín*, but where he could acquire one was left to the will of God. As he dug vigorously, turning the thin soil, he noted more manuring would be needed before the next crop was planted.

After a half-hour of brisk work, he returned to the house. Máire was preparing breakfast. Eithne was busy at the churn, keeping it moving vigorously as she sang in her sweet young voice the old love song 'Eileen A Rún'.

Tadhg watched her at her work. She would make a good wife, he thought. She was competent, cheerful and pretty with her copper tresses, her bright eyes, quick smile, and rich red lips, so sweet for kisses. But as she sang plaintively, 'Céad míle fáilte romhat, Eileen a rún,' he sang quietly 'Mairéad a rún'.

He felt foolish, and a little guilty, linking himself with the unattainable while the girl who loved him, and who was ready to defy her father, sat a few paces away, smiling at him tenderly. It's a cruel world, he told himself, where people love others who do not reciprocate. An endless and futile chain: Eithne loved Tadhg, Tadhg loved Mairéad, and Mairéad had loved young Montgomery.

With the Blakes playing host for the church services, and Father O'Conlon as a guest for dinner, the day passed quickly. What with the general clamour and excitement, Máire didn't mention to Murtagh her concern over Eithne. He had enough worries, she told herself sternly, without adding to them, especially when they were merely suspicions. She noted how Eithne managed to seat herself next to Tadhg, both at Mass and at the meal, and the fond and admiring way she looked at him. He's a fine strapping lad, she thought, and would make an excellent husband if only he had something to bring to the marriage. She knew how Murtagh had set his heart on getting the best match for the girl. She would just have to keep an eye on Eithne.

On Monday, the children and the older students returned to school. When they arrived at the little schoolhouse on Kevin O'Devaney's farm, they found the pupils having a good time, running about and shouting. This was unusual, for Donough was strict with them.

The Blake group walked into the room, where Conor took charge as he did in Donough's occasional absence, dividing the classwork between himself and Eithne. Tadhg and Dónal, uneasy over Donough's prolonged absence, waited outside. Finally Tadhg told Dónal to run up to the cabin and ask his aunt if she knew where the schoolmaster might be.

Dónal returned shortly, a perplexed look on his usually carefree face. 'The *bean an tí* says he left for Mass at the Blakes' yesterday, but didn't return. She thought he stayed overnight at the Blakes'.'

'He didn't attend Mass,' Tadhg said, frowning, 'for I would have seen him. I think we had better search for him along the boreen between here and Murtagh's.' But despite their careful search along the path and adjacent area, no trace of the schoolmaster was found.

Now very much concerned, the trio spoke to Máire. 'You had better go to the field and fetch Murtagh,' she advised. 'Perhaps he can think of something.'

When Murtagh had listened to their story and was assured that a thorough search had been made of the area, he suggested that Tadhg find Cathal and tell him. 'Perhaps Donough decided to visit his brother. At any rate, go and inform him.'

Cathal and his Rapparees were operating in the Maamturk Mountains. Conor, who knew the area, volunteered to go instead of Tadhg. He set off immediately. It would take him half a day to get there.

Shortly after he left, Cathal and Dermot O'Lee arrived on horseback. 'How did you get here so quickly?' a dumbfounded Tadhg asked.

'What do you mean?'

'Conor left but a while ago to tell you about Donough.'

Cathal looked at him askance. 'What about Donough?'

'He didn't appear for class this morning. And he didn't attend Mass yesterday. No one has seen him for some time.'

Cathal's eyes sought Dermot's. The latter turned to Tadhg. 'Have you looked for him?'

Tadhg nodded. 'Yes. We searched the whole area between Kevin O'Devaney's and Murtagh Blake's. He isn't there.'

Cathal wheeled about on his horse. 'Follow me to the short road above Kevin's place where it crosses the boreen,' he shouted, digging his heels into the heaving flanks of his steed. Dermot O'Lee, followed by the others on foot, took off after Cathal. When they arrived at the designated spot, Cathal had dismounted, and was searching among the withered furze and brambles, crying out in anguished tones, 'Donough! Donough, are you there?'

The others joined him, shouting for Donough. Finally Dónal Óg cried out, 'Here's something,' holding aloft a dark oblong object.

Cathal blanched. He reached out and took the book. Quickly he flipped it open. 'This is Donough's prayer book,' he said. 'See, here on the flyleaf. He brought it from Paris.'

'He must have dropped it,' Murtagh said.

'It looks more like it was thrown down violently,' Tadhg pointed out. 'Look how dirty it is. And the pages are greatly scuffed.'

'I think you're right, Tadhg,' Cathal agreed, turning the pages with trembling fingers. 'But let us look further, Donough might have fallen and hurt himself so that he cannot hear us calling.'

Tadhg walked down the winding boreen, eyes alert. In a small corrie, some distance from the path, he noticed fresh horse dropping. He called to Cathal. 'Look, *a thiarna*, horses have been here recently.'

'Yes, and from the signs there were at least a dozen. And they were shod.'

'What does that mean?'

'That they were ridden by Sassanaigh, because few Irish horses hereabouts have shoes.'

Dermot O'Lee, Murtagh and Dónal joined them, and Cathal turned to his old friend. 'Apparently a party of English, maybe a troop of horse, was hiding here,' he said heavily, 'and they have seized Donough.'

Murtagh frowned. 'But why would Donough have been so far from the direct path from Kevin's place to mine? And why would a troop of horse be so far from the main roads?'

Cathal sighed. 'I told Donough when I saw him last that I would meet him here on the boreen before Mass on Sunday. A messenger with the latest news from England was due at my camp on Saturday. Both Donough and I were worried about the whereabouts of my son, Hugh, who is an officer with some of the Irish troops recently sent into England by the Viceroy at Dublin Castle to help King James. I have been informed that William of Orange is already in England, and many of the country's most powerful leaders have joined him, including James's other daughter, Anne, and her husband the Prince of Denmark. James and his family have fled to France, while the fate of Hugh and his men is still unknown. The messenger from Dublin was delayed a whole day - he didn't arrive until early this morning - so Dermot and I left immediately thereafter, expecting to find Donough at his school.'

'Yes, *a thiarna*,' said Murtagh, 'that explains why Donough was here, but why the Sassanaigh?'

'I don't know,' Cathal replied. 'But they have Donough, and I must rescue him. Dermot,' he said, turning to his friend, 'we'd better return to the hills and get the other Rapparees.'

Tadhg respectfully addressed himself to Cathal. '*A thiarna*, I am but a youth and should not be offering counsel to a chief like you, but it appears to me that you are about to do just what the Sassanaigh expect.'

'What do you mean?' he asked. 'Speak freely.'

'I am a fisherman,' Tadhg began, 'and when I want to catch a big fish, I use a little fish for bait. I think that the Sassanaigh are using Donough Beag as bait to catch you. They are waiting for you to come to his rescue. Then - snap - the hook is set and they've got you!'

Cathal stared at him. 'For a youth,' he began, 'you have the wisdom of an old man.' He gazed speculatively at the distant hills. 'I will return to the Maamturks by a roundabout way to avoid capture,' he said. 'Then, with my men, we can devise a safe method to get Donough back.'

'I want to go with you,' Tadhg said, 'if you will wait until I can get my sword.'

'I would welcome your strong right arm, God knows,' Cathal told Tadhg, 'but if you come with me you will be outlawed along with the rest of us. Your education will end - it will mean no more school. You will be on the keeping, living in the hills among the crags with hunger often the only thing in your belly, and a hard, cold bed for your poor tired limbs. Each day could be your last. So, Tadhg, you must decide.'

'Donough Beag is part of my heart, *a thiarna*,' Tadhg said simply. 'What kind of a heart can it be when part of it is missing? I must go and find it.'

'Where Tadhg goes, I go,' Dónal Óg added.

Cathal looked at him fondly. 'I will thank you, not for myself, but for Donough. He has taught you something that isn't in the school-books. But have you horses? It's a rough trip when we have to hurry.'

'We don't customarily have horses to ride,' Tadhg replied deferentially. So we will have to use the steeds that God gave us.' He slapped his thigh.

Skirting the bogs, hugging the hills, skulking in the shadows, by-passing the lonely cabins, the party travelled the roundabout way to the Maamturks, hoping to avoid detection by curious or unfriendly eyes. While they watered the horses, Tadhg questioned Cathal about the details of the rendezvous he had arranged with Donough.

'It seems strange to me, *a thiarna*,' he said, 'that the Sassanaigh would go to that out-of-the-way place. How could they know they would find Donough there?'

Cathal turned worried eyes to Tadhg. 'That has been bothering me also, *a mhic*.'

'If it wasn't by accident, then it must have been by design,' Dermot said. 'And that indicates they knew Donough would be there.'

Tadhg nodded. 'And Cathal as well. It was only the lateness of the messenger from Dublin that kept him from being there at the appointed time. And further,' he added, 'from the signs in the corrie, they must have waited there quite a while.'

Cathal pondered. 'What you are hinting at,' he said finally, 'is that the English knew I was going to be meeting Donough. And they waited as long as they could before deciding I wasn't coming. If this is accurate, somebody must have informed them of my meeting. But who?'

'Who knew of the meeting?' Tadhg asked.

Cathal shrugged. 'Only Donough and some of my men.'

Dermot O'Lee counted on his fingers. 'Let's see who was at the camp and would have known. There were Fergus Dillon, Morris Breen, Tomás Nugent, Séamus O'Callanan, Pierce MacNamara, Sean O'Carroll and myself. All the rest were away.'

Cathal shook his head. 'Each of these men I would trust with my life. I can't believe that any one of them would betray me - or Donough.'

'You are too trusting, Cathal,' said Dermot.

'Undoubtedly you are right,' Cathal replied gloomily. 'We had better return to camp, and find out who the Judas is.'

'*A thiarna*,' Tadhg interjected, 'I have been giving much thought to this whole affair. If, as we suppose, the Sassanaigh have taken Donough prisoner to trap you, then they are expecting you to do this. And if they are expecting you to attack them, then they must feel confident that their forces are superior to yours. Where do you think they could have taken Donough?'

'Either to Galway or to Ferguson's stronghold in our old castle on Brúgh na h-Inse, the Isle of the Fort. More than likely the latter because it is in the area, and I would be more likely to attack it than the fortified town of Galway. Also, Galway now has a Catholic commanding the garrison.'

'Do you think that your Rapparees could successfully storm the castle?' Tadhg asked.

Cathal shook his head. 'No. We have no cannon to breach the walls.'

'So,' Tadhg pursued his subject, 'if the English are trying to set a trap for you, they know it is unlikely you could take the castle without cannon, and that you would have to use some other method to gain entry to the castle?'

'I suppose so.'

'Well, then, if we can't get in, why don't we get them to come out?'

'What do you mean?' Cathal gazed speculatively at Tadhg.

'Donough told us in school about the Greeks and the Trojans, and how the Greeks hid in a wooden horse and got into Troy. The English will be expecting you to try some kind of a trick. But if they're wondering why you did not appear at the rendezvous yesterday ... ' and quickly he outlined his plan.

Cathal was sceptical, but the others saw the advantages and convinced him that it would work. It was risky, it was dangerous, but they had no other option. Eventually he conceded to Tadhg's plan.

'Tadhg,' he ordered, 'when you reach the camp you will remain there, watching Dillon, Breen, O'Carroll, MacNamara and Nugent, and anyone else who might excite your suspicions.'

'What about O'Callanan?' said Tadhg.

'Seamus would never expose me or Donough,' Cathal replied. 'He has been with us since we were small children. It was he who saved Donough when he was injured as a baby. No, Sassanach silver would never buy Séamus. I would as soon suspect Dermot.'

The news came like a thunderbolt to the camp.

Donough O'Flaherty was abducted.

Cathal O'Flaherty was dead.

Most of them men cried openly and unashamedly, some of them prostrating themselves on the ground, tearing at their long hair and crying out their lamentations. Tadhg became as affected as the others, tears streaming down his face. Some of the men, notably O'Kerrigan and O'Doherty, remained dry-eyed, keeping their emotions in check but inwardly seething with grief. Tadhg watched each of the suspected men, but there was no way to tell whose grief was spurious and whose genuine.

Finally, when the emotional outburst had subsided, Dermot O'Lee called them all together. 'Rapparees, companions, friends,' he said, 'perhaps it was fitting that I was the bearer of these tidings, since I have been a personal friend of Cathal and Donough for many years and have known them in happier days. Now death has ended my obligation. We do not know Donough's fate, but if he is in the hands of the Sassanaigh, we can but pray for mercy on his soul. I am sure that Cathal would like to have you, his loyal followers, attend his last trip through his beloved land to his final resting place. I must leave now to go to St Malachi's to make arrangements for the funeral. In my absence Donough O'Kerrigan will be in charge. Will you stay here until we can attend the wake together?'

'Yes, yes,' the shout went up.

After Dermot O'Lee left the camp, the men crowded around Tadhg, welcoming him back to their ranks, inquiring about his progress at school and asking the details about Cathal's death and Donough's disappearance.

'Donough didn't appear at school this morning,' he began, 'so after a while some of us older students inquired as to what was the matter with him. We learned that nobody had seen him since yesterday. Conor was sent to the camp to fetch Cathal.'

The men nodded; Conor had arrived and having been told that Cathal had already gone, had departed for home.

'While we were looking in the neighbourhood for Donough,' Tadhg resumed, 'Dermot O'Lee arrived to inform Donough that his brother had been killed in a fall. We traded our sad news of Donough for his sad news of Cathal. Dermot was so overcome with grief that I accompanied him back to the camp. Dónal Óg will return with Conor tomorrow.

'How did the accident happen?' Tomás Nugent asked. 'Cathal was a good horseman.'

'I don't know,' Tadhg answered with some truth. 'Dermot was so broken up by the death of Cathal that I couldn't learn much from him. It seems that Cathal was supposed to have met Donough before Mass yesterday to impart some news or other. But Cathal was a day late, and in a great hurry. He pushed his horse too fast and the brute stumbled and threw him, breaking his neck so that he died instantly.'

'I thought I heard the *beansí* wail last night,' Gilleduff O'Fallon said, crossing himself, 'but not knowing that Cathal was dead, I thought it was an animal crying.'

'I see you have your sword with you, Tadhg,' Sean O'Carroll commented. 'Have you slain any more Englishmen lately?'

Tadhg looked closely at O'Carroll. But the man's grey eyes were friendly and innocent. 'No,' Tadhg replied shortly, 'I have not used it.'

'I thought that the Sassanaigh would try to catch you for the death of Montgomery,' Pierce MacNamara commented. 'I'm surprised they didn't.'

Maybe they didn't believe you, Tadhg thought. Didn't he sound convincing enough? It was natural to ask questions, but it was peculiar that the five suspects were the most curious about details. Is it you, MacNamara, that is the traitor? Or O'Carroll? Or Nugent? Dillon? Or Breen, who heard the *beansí* cry?'

In the afternoon of the next day, word arrived in the camp that Cathal's body was ready for viewing at St Malachi's. The saddened, solemn band, now under the leadership of O'Kerrigan, left the glen where they had been encamped and descended to the narrow road leading to the church. Those who had horses were mounted. Tadhg, joined by Conor and Dónal, and a few of the men who were without horses, walked behind. Each of the men was armed with his *rapaire*. Some had swords, some pistols, some muskets, and each had his *scian*. Tadhg had his sword and *rapaire*; Conor and Dónal Óg also had pikes. It was a motley but formidable band, going to pay their last respects to their leader.

St Malachi's, a small church, was packed with mourners, with scores standing outside, unable to get in. News of the death of an O'Flaherty brought the people from miles around. Old and young, native Irish and usurper English, genuine mourners and mere morbid, Catholic and Protestant, friend and foe, all stood elbow to elbow, jostling and talking and gaping.

Above the murmur of the gathering rose the piercing cry, the *caoine*, the ancient rite performed by the women. It was led by Nora Connealy, who had come all the way from Ballyconneely in the parish of Omey. She was a large, gaunt woman of great age, with dark brooding eyes, and a voice of great power. She sang the death song which she extemporised. The other women provided the *ologón*, the burden of the chorus.'

'She sounds like the *beansí*,' Dónal said, his eyes bright with fear.

After a while the keening ceased. Dermot O'Lee appeared in front of the church, beckoning to O'Kerrigan to lead his men inside. Leaning their pikes against the church wall, but retaining their other weapons, the Rapparees entered the church. They walked softly and reverently down the aisle to the altar, where a coffin was set. There were a few flowers, purloined no doubt from a 'Big House' where they had been carefully nurtured and protected from the cold. Candles flickered and guttered, making it difficult to see in the dark, gloomy recesses of the building. One by one the Rapparees paused and genuflected at the coffin, making the Sign of the Cross before being shepherded along by the impatient Dermot.

When Tadhg's turn came, he stared wonderingly at the still form and waxen face. Cathal's beard and moustache had been neatly trimmed. A large cuirass, much too big for him, covered his chest.

When all the Rapparees were back outside, Dermot O'Lee addressed them briefly. 'The funeral Mass will be tomorrow morning. I hope you will all be here to pay your last respects to Cathal.' They were dismissed.

Tadhg was to watch MacNamara. Murtagh Blake had Tomás Nugent, Conor had O'Carroll. Dónal Óg had Dillon, and Séamus O'Callanan had Breen. As they gathered to talk excitedly, each of the five stayed near the man he was assigned to watch. Most of the Rapparees chose to spend some time at the church, talking to friends and kin. As the mourners left the scene, others arrived to take their places. The keening had begun again.

MacNamara was one of the first to leave. He mounted his grey horse, and without a word to anyone, set off on a canter down the road. Tadhg followed as quickly as he could without making obvious what he was doing; he was hard put to keep within watching distance of his quarry. With mounting excitement, he followed MacNamara down the road past the church in the direction opposite the Rapparees' camp. His heart pounding, Tadhg doggedly kept on MacNamara's trail. Despite his vigilance, however, he almost missed MacNamara when the latter abruptly turned into a narrow boreen. Tadhg paused, stopping behind on the road, wondering what the other man was up to. MacNamara, now dismounted, stepped out to the road, peering to right and left. Not seeing Tadhg, and seeming satisfied, he scrambled through a rowan thicket and disappeared.

Tadhg waited a few minutes longer, then cautiously emerged from his hiding place. He found MacNamara's horse standing quietly where his rider had left him in a protected area among the huge boulders. Taking the same route as the other, he crawled on hands and knees until he heard voices from the craggy hillside.

'I didn't expect you today,' a voice, strange to Tadhg, was saying.

Then came MacNamara's voice. 'Is everything ready?'

'All set,' said the other. 'You haven't told any of the Rapparees, have you?'

'Do you think I'm a *gomáile*?' MacNamara responded contemptuously.

The other man laughed nervously. 'No, but we are both in this up to our necks. And if we are caught at it, it will mean our necks.'

'You worry too much,' MacNamara said.

'I know, I know. It's only the money that keeps me in it.'

'Do you have my share?' MacNamara asked.

Rage mounted in Tadhg. The blackguard! The scoundrel! He

put his hand on his sword.

'Don't worry about your money, you'll get it,' the stranger said. 'But why not sample a little? I'm sure it's ready.'

Silence for a minute. Then a deep breath of satisfaction. 'By my soul, Edmund, that tickles the palate. Fill my cup again.'

A loud and distinct smack was followed by MacNamara saying, 'Fill it up again. Such *uisce beatha* I haven't had for a long, long time.'

'You know how to make a fine still,' Edmund said with admiration.

'And you, my friend, are a master distiller. Such clarity, such flavour, such smoothness, such impact, such *such*!' MacNamara laughed. 'Yes, especially the such such. Fill my cup again, my tongue insists.'

Edmund tittered. 'You'll be drinking up all our profits.'

'It is better to die happy and poor than sad and rich. Look, my cup is empty. It must have evaporated. To tell you the truth, *a chara*, this *uisce beatha* is not going into my stomach. It is going into my heart which is broken to smithereens since Cathal is dead and Donough gone. Woe is me! The weight of the world is on me. Fill up my cup again. Perhaps it can drown my sorrow.'

Tadhg felt a wave of shame to think he had suspected MacNamara of treachery. He moved a little higher, and through an aperture could see MacNamara and a heavy-set, swarthy man with long hair and whiskers, seated around a still. A peat fire, in a small, iron egg-shaped stove was sending lazy waves of bluish smoke skyward. The sweet mash being heated emitted its own perfume. Tubes ran from the mash container to two stout casks standing precariously side by side on their three wooden legs. Out of the further one pale golden liquid dripped into an earthen jug. Both men were so rapt in their contemplation of distillation that they didn't notice Tadhg.

I must tell MacNamara that his still is poorly hidden, Tadhg thought. Then, as he gazed upon the pair before him, he decided that he would tell them some other time. He backed slowly and quietly down the hill and in a few minutes was back in the churchyard. Most of the Rapparees were gone, only Dónal keeping close to Fergus Dillon as agreed. When Dillon saw Tadhg he asked him where he had been. Tadhg said that he had gone for a stroll among the hills. Then Dillon suggested going back to camp. The three of them climbed the hills to the bivouac area of the

Rapparees. Séamus O'Callanan and Breen were there, as were Conor and O'Carroll, munching on oatcakes and quaffing bonnyclabber.

Seamus beckoned to Tadhg and the two went off to one side. 'What happened to MacNamara? Did you lose him?' His eyes were alight with anxiety.

'He is quietly getting drunk on *poitín*,' Tadhg said and described the scene.

Seamus nodded. 'He's a wizard at building stills. He pretends that it is to make him some pocket money, but I'm of the opinion he likes *poitín* more than gold.'

'His partner was concerned that he was going to drink up all the profits.'

'I'm glad he wasn't the whoreson who informed on Donough. I always liked him. What did you think of our corpse?'

'He looked so dead that I will worry until I see him actually alive again,' Tadhg said fervently.

'At dusk the mourners will be sent from the church so that Cathal will be able to leave the casket for a while. Do you think the plan will work?'

Tadhg shrugged his massive shoulders. 'I don't know. The attack can't be made unless Sir John Ferguson knows for sure that Cathal is dead and leaves his castle with his men. Only Tomás Nugent of the five suspects isn't here. If he, too, is innocent, then our plan will fail. Or perhaps the traitor decided not to go and inform Ferguson this time. Or he might have made contact with an agent right there at the church.'

Seamus nodded again. 'How did Cathal appear so dead?' he asked. 'He seemed to have not a breath of life in him.'

'Dermot O'Lee,' Tadhg said, 'has not forgotten all the doctoring he learned in France and Spain. Herbs, he said, can slow the heartbeat and the breathing. And the cuirass masked any sign of his chest moving.'

The Rapparees drifted in, singley and in groups, until all of them were back, including Tomás Nugent. But Murtagh Blake, who had followed him, was not to be seen. Tadhg pondered. Had Murtagh gone back to his own farm to get his family for the funeral? Had he stayed down in the valley with friends rather than mingle with the Rapparees so that he wouldn't be considered an outlaw by the authorities? Had he become tired, and was resting elsewhere?

When darkness came, Tadhg joined Conor and Dónal. Some Rapparee had lent Conor a *bainín* and the three huddled together with the coat over them. It didn't cover much of Tadhg's big body, and he slept fitfully as the cold crept into his bones.

Some hours later he was awakened by someone tugging at him. 'Tadhg, wake up! Tadhg, wake up!'

He sat upright, shrugging the sleep from him and rubbing his eyes. 'It's Murtagh,' the dark shape whispered. 'I must talk to you privately.'

Tadhg shuddered from the cold. He stood upright, rubbing his arms and hands to restore the circulation as Murtagh drew him away from the sleeping men.

'I have sad news,' he blurted. 'Donough is dead.'

Tadhg whirled about. 'What's that? Donough dead?'

Murtagh nodded in the darkness. 'Yes. His headless body is mounted on the castle walls.'

'At Sir John Ferguson's?' Tadhg spat the name. 'But what were you doing at the castle? You were supposed to be watching Nugent.'

'That I did,' Murtagh said. 'I followed him down the road several miles to the farmhouse of Jeremiah Morton, the brother of Thomas Morton, Sir John's land agent. He went inside, then after a few minutes got back on his horse and headed towards camp. I thought it best to let him go and watch what would happen after. Shortly, Jeremiah Morton saddled his horse and headed for Brúgh na h-Inse. He had such a head start I couldn't keep up with him, but guessing that he was going to the castle I took that road. I got there just before dusk. It was a clear evening and across the water I could plainly see the battlements of the castle. And there, mounted on the wall, was the body of Donough.'

'Are you sure it was Donough,' Tadhg demanded furiously.

'You couldn't mistake poor Donough's twisted body.' Murtagh choked back a sob.

'Donough, little gentle Donough,' Tadhg cried through clenched teeth. 'Oh God, how could You do this to him? How could You let such a thing happen?' Tadhg stood, arms outstretched, glaring at the dark sky above him as if he expected an answer. After a while he lowered his arms disconsolately, and embracing the weeping Murtagh, said, 'We must go at once to Cathal. But first let me warn Conor so that he can watch Nugent, that devil's offspring.'

After a brief whispered conversation, Conor arose, and with

bleak countenance and angry eyes, seated himself where he could observe the traitorous Nugent, who slept soundly, untroubled by conscience. Tadhg and Murtagh descended in the cold night to the valley below to find the home of Dermot's sister.

Why should they kill Donough? What threat did this gentle teacher pose to authority? Tadhg was numbed.

Dermot's sister lived about a league from St Malachi's, in a small cabin huddled against a hillside. Murtagh, who knew the way, led Tadhg along a lonely, winding path that approached the cottage from the east. All was dark in the cabin. As they came close, there was a loud shout from the darkness, and two figures hurled themselves upon them, knocking them down with the surprise and suddenness of the onslaught. Despite his opponent's initial advantage, Tadhg's great strength soon reversed the situation, and sitting astride his assailant, wrested the *scian* from his hand.

'My soul to the Devil,' the other exclaimed, 'it's Tadhg Mór! And who is this with you?'

'Murtagh Blake,' Tadhg replied, recognising the voice of Dermot O'Lee.

The wild thrashing of the two other men ceased and they separated. Dermot's nephew, Peregrine O'Flaherty, said ruefully, 'Oro, that was a murderous blow you gave me.'

'You deserved it,' Murtagh said, brushing himself. 'What do you mean leaping on us like that?'

'You were lucky, Peregrine, that you didn't pick this big one. He's as strong as Fionn MacCool. But what brings you here at this time of night?'

'We bear dreadful news, Dermot. We must see Cathal at once.'

Dermot looked at Tadhg, started to say something, then checked himself. He hooked his forefinger, beckoning them to follow. Dermot led them to the entrance of a small cave in the hillside, hidden by a thicket of *saileog*. Bending low, they entered. Dermot strode to the dark form huddled in sleep on the floor of the cave, and gently shook it. 'Cathal, wake up. Tadhg is here with a message for you.'

Cathal sat up, staring through the darkness at his visitors until Dermot lit a lamp. 'What is it, Tadhg, that brings you here? Bad tidings, surely, from your face.'

Tadhg hesitated. 'It is so sad, *a thiarna*, that I cannot find the words.'

'It is Donough, isn't it *a mhic*? Something has happened to Donough.;

'He is dead,' Tadhg said.

Cathal lowered his head, covering his face with his hands. The others stood in awkward silence. The world could never be the same again without Donough. He had brought hope, friendliness, promise; he had been a light shining in the darkness; he had been a bright star on which Tadhg had set a new course.

Cathal took his hands from his face, and turning tear-stained eyes on Tadhg, asked him how it had happened. Tadhg looked at Murtagh, who repeated his story.

'I cannot say this comes as a great surprise,' Cathal said dully. 'I tried to keep Donough from returning to Ireland. But it was to no avail. He wanted to open his school. I feared that the authorities would prevent it. When he was not at the place of appointment on Sunday, I dreaded the outcome. May he rest in peace.'

'But what of Nugent,' Tadhg demanded.

Cathal arose, buckled his sword about his waist. 'I will take care of that Judas,' he said, his face grim. 'He will get little pleasure from his thirty pieces of silver.'

Leaving Peregrine O'Flaherty at the church to make sure that no early mourners would view the empty coffin, the grim party ascended the hills to the camp of the Rapparees. All were asleep except Conor, who lay a few feet from Nugent, watching. Cathal stood a while observing the sleeping man, whose chest rose and fell rhythmically with his breathing, his auburn head resting on his arm.

Cathal drew his sword and with its point prodded the sleeper in the ribs. Nugent sprang up with a strong oath, reaching for his *scian*. Then, in the dim light of the misty dawn he recognised the man before him. He cowered, his eyes staring and unbelieving. Quickly he made the sign of the cross. 'Cathal O'Flaherty?' he croaked. 'Arisen from the dead?'

'Cathal O'Flaherty to whom you swore fealty!'

'But you are dead! I saw you in your coffin. I saw you with my own eyes! Go back to the church, Cathal, go back before I go mad!'

Cathal advanced, his sword poised. Nugent retreated. 'You saw me in the church, Tomás Judas, then went to the Sassanaigh with the news!'

Nugent looked fearfully about him, seeing the ring of men

hemming him in. 'That is a lie,' he said boldly.

Murtagh Blake spoke up. 'It was I who followed you to Jeremiah Morton's house. It was I who followed Jeremiah to Ferguson. It was these eyes that saw Donough O'Flaherty's body on the castle wall. Do you call me a liar?'

Nugent's eyes met Murtagh's, held them for a moment, then faltered. Again he looked around the circle of grim Rapparees. He saw nothing but loathing and hatred. The air was heavy with it.

He shrugged his slender shoulders, his big handsome face defiant. 'Your day is over, Cathal, be you alive or dead. And all the rest of you,' he added to the other men. 'The Prince of Orange has driven James from the throne. The new government will not tolerate the laxity that has existed in Ireland since James was crowned. There will be more oppression, more confiscation, more elimination of the influence of the Catholic Church. Make your terms with the Sassanaigh while you can. You will not only save your lives, but you may even get some of your property restored.'

'You would sell your country, your religion, your friends, for your property? Is that your thirty pieces of silver, Tomás Judas?' Cathal's eyes were blazing.

'My noble kinsman Christopher wears fine broadcloth, not goatskins,' Tomás said, fingering his coarse garment. 'He sleeps in a soft, warm bed at night, not cold and wet in the furze. He has tasty viands and red meats, not coarse foods and 'white meat' from an udder. Yes, it was longing for these comforts that made me reconcile myself with the Sassanaigh.

Cathal shook his head sadly. 'Tomás, you have a short memory. You know what Sir William Skeffington did to Christopher Parese when Parese betrayed the interests of Lord Offaly to the English. Skeffington knew he couldn't trust a man who would betray another, so as Parese's reward Skeffington had him executed.'

Nugent looked back at his accuser, his face drained of all colour. His eyes were bleak. 'Have you no mercy for me, Cathal?' he pleaded. 'Long have we been friends. Many a foray have we ridden together. Many a camp-fire have we shared. I didn't know that they would kill Donough. They promised not to.'

'Any man stupid enough to believe Sassanaigh promises deserves to die. Any man who betrays another deserves to die. Any man who would be a traitor to his country deserves to die. I might have had pity if the betrayal involved only me, for after all there is a price on my head. But I cannot condone your betrayal of

Donough Beag, who wore no sword, who robbed no one, who endangered no man. He had a broken, twisted back, but he stood taller than you. He risked his life to teach the children of Gaels who could get no education. Donough Beag of the gentle heart.'

'You can't kill me in cold blood, Cathal. Let me have my sword.'

Cathal unbuckled his sword, dropping it on the earth. He drew his *scian*. 'We are now on equal terms,' he said quietly. The two adversaries circled each other, knives at the ready. Cathal moved in slowly, doggedly, his eyes alert, watching every move of the younger man. The Rapparees, including some newly awakened by the younger man, incredulous to find their dead chieftain, watched with fascination. Cathal feinted, slashed, missed and stepped back. Nugent, who knew he was doomed to die, either at Cathal's hands or those of the other Rapparees, fought desperately. He was graceful, his feet dancing as he evaded the thrusts of the invincible foe. Dawn had come, cold and clear, lighting up the mountain as Cathal and Tomás fought. At last, as Tomás made a thrust at his foe, Cathal's free hand quickly reached out to grasp the wrist that held the knife, bending it up and back out of harm's way. Then Cathal's *scian* plunged into his foe's bowels, and with one long sigh the life of Tomás Nugent fled his body.

A loud cheer went up from the Rapparees, waking those who had slept through the fight. They converged on their leader, embracing him, grasping his hands, crying out a hundred questions. They shook their heads in disbelief, for hadn't they seen him in his coffin? And what was the cause for the fight with Nugent? What about Donough? Was it true that he was dead? Was there to be an expedition to force Old Ferguson from his stronghold? These, and many more, until at last Cathal raised his hand for silence.

'My beloved companions,' he began, 'I owe you an explanation and an apology. When I found that Donough had been seized at a spot where I was to meet him, and that a band of riders had spent considerable time there, I conferred with Dermot, Murtagh and young Tadhg here. They convinced me that we had been betrayed, most likely by a member of my own band.'

A murmur of indignation arose among the men. 'I agree with you. It was a repugnant thought, but not an impossible one. We decided to bait a trap for the guilty one. So we concocted my false death and wake, wanting to convince Sir John Ferguson and his agent that I was truly dead. Men I knew were faithful were assigned to watch the suspected men. To these innocent men I now apologise. I will not give names. No one will ever know.' He told the shocked men of Nugent's betrayal, of how Murtagh had followed him, and seen the body o.ᶜ Donough on the castle walls.

'But why should they kill Donough and expose his body that way,' Fergus Dillon asked. 'What had they to gain?'

'What had they to lose?' Cathal answered. 'It was a warning to the native Irish. It was a chance of revenge against me. It completed what they had done when Donough was an infant. If I was dead, as rumour had it, I could not avenge myself on them. If I wasn't dead - and they had no confirmation until after they had killed Donough - then it would goad me to a blind and stupid attack on the castle, leading me into a trap they had prepared. No, they had nothing to lose.'

Again a murmur swept through the ranks of the Rapparees. 'What do we do now,' MacNamara shouted. 'Do we avenge Donough,' cried O'Doherty. 'Death before dishonour!' shouted Dillon.

Cathal raised his hand and the murmur subsided. 'You forget, gentlemen, that today is the day of my funeral,' and he smiled wryly. 'Do you want to disappoint all those people from far and near who are planning to attend - especially Sir John Ferguson, who will want to see it with his own eyes? No, I know you don't. Listen closely, for this is what we are going to do.'

He outlined his plan. Occasionally a question was asked. Some had doubts that the Sassanaigh would come. Some though he might force his way into the church.

'We don't know if he will come,' Cathal conceded. We think that he will. He will want to know for sure that Cathal O'Flaherty is dead. It is a reasonable certainty that he will appear at the church in time for the coffin to be carried to the graveyard. Our success will depend on our timing. Those of you assigned to block the road with the heavy chain must be sure that you can lift it and attach it securely. And now, in farewell, long life to you - and death in Ireland.'

CHAPTER IX

The Ambush

Quickly the Rapparees scattered to their appointed tasks. Dermot, Cathal, Tadhg, Conor and Dónal Óg, with the body of Tomás Nugent lashed to a horse, returned to the church where Cathal was to be hidden until the funeral began. Plumes of bluish smoke rose lazily from the cabins as they passed. If anyone saw them, no sign was given.

Many of the mourners arrived early, filling the small church to overflowing. Some of the more agile latecomers clambered up on to the roof where they could hear, but not see, the services. When the rites began, even the area in front of the church was filled. There was scarcely a dry eye when the priest began. He spoke of the deceased as a member of an old family. He referred to the rough life in the hills of the men on our keeping. He deprecated the outlaw role of the departed. But his oration was disappointing to those who had expected him to praise the virtues of the O'Flahertys, to dwell upon the extinction of the great Gaelic families, or to praise the generosity of a fallen chief. Some were curious, some uneasy over the omission.

As the casket emerged from the church to the sound of lamentation, Dermot O'Lee, receiving a signal from Dónal Óg perched high on the hillside, imperatively shouted for all the people to disperse from the front of the church. 'Sir John Ferguson's soldiers will be here in a moment and there may be trouble.' The mourners scattered like leaves in an autumn gale. At the same time church doors were closed and Father Mulvaney implored the people to stay inside. After some muttering and indecision, they reluctantly complied.

Down the pass came the clatter of approaching horses, and about fifty mounted men, armed with muskets, pistols and swords, swept around the bend in the road. At their head, mounted on a magnificent white horse gaily caparisoned, was an erect, well-built man in his sixties. He sat his horse imperiously. He wore a dark blue cuirass, a morion to match, tight black knee-breeches and long leather gauntlets. His restless icy-grey eyes swept the area as he advanced.

Several cubits from the coffin, he stopped. The pall-bearers stopped. His armed men stopped. All was silent.

'You, there,' he directed his words to Murtagh Blake, 'open that coffin so I may pay my last respects to my old friend Cathal O'Flaherty,'

Murtagh Blake, confronted by a man who represented everything he despised, stood immobile.

'I said open that coffin.'

Murtagh's eyes flashed with anger. 'It would be a desecration. I will not do it.'

The mounted man looked at him coldly. He drew a pistol, cocked it, and pointing it at Murtagh's head, repeated the order.

'I'll need something to prise the lid with,' Murtagh said sullenly.

Sir John turned to several of his soldiers who were crowded about him, the better to view the sport. 'Dismount and lend them your bayonets,' he ordered.

The men looked questioningly at him, but obeyed. Murtagh and Peregrine grasped the unfamiliar muskets gingerly. They prised at the coffin lid and worked it loose. Sir John leaned from his horse, but being unable to see inside the coffin, he cautiously dismounted. Leading his horse, he walked to the coffin and peered within.

He recoiled as if stung by a hornet.

Tomas Nugent stared back at him from sightless eyes.

At the same moment, Cathal O'Flaherty appeared in the church doorway. 'A dead giveaway, eh, Sir John?' he said, his hand on his sword.

Rapparees, their pikes extended, charged down the slopes from their hiding places. Other Rapparees, with muskets and pistols, opened fire on the massed horsemen. Men cursed, horses screamed, animals and men went down in a *melée* of flailing hooves and dying men. Half of Sir John's force fell on the first charge. Those at the rear of the column wheeled frantically and dashed down the road, but a huge chain had been placed across their path and only a few fortunate ones whose horses jumped and cleared the barrier were able to escape. Hidden Rapparees in the hills picked off a dozen more with pistols and muskets as the Sassanaigh milled in wild confusion.

Sir John Ferguson, seeing his forces decimated, turned to Cathal, who was advancing towards him. He drew his sword.

'I have waited many years for this opportunity,' Cathal said grimly. 'We are matched evenly now for the first time, weapon for weapon, man for man. I think God that I have lived long enough to see you pay for your many crimes.'

Tadhg had brought down three of the Sassanaigh with his pike as he fought his way towards Cathal. The latter, intent on Sir John, failed to see Thomas Morton raise his pistol, point it at the Rapparee chief and fire at close range. Cathal staggered and fell, blood spurting from the wound. Seeing Cathal fall, Murtagh Blake, still holding the musket he had used as a pry, roared with rage and grief and with a quick thrust drove the bayonet through the land agent's chest. His pistol still smoking, Morton swayed in the saddle, then plunged heavily to the ground where Cathal lay dying. Morton's brother Jeremiah spurred forward and, with one mighty stroke, brought his sabre down on Murtagh's head, cleaving his skull. Instantly, Peregrine O'Flannery jabbed with his bayonet and Murtagh's assailant joined his brother on the bloody earth.

The four deaths had occurred so fast that Tadhg stood still, completely overwhelmed by the shock of seeing Cathal and Murtagh dying at his feet. Then, dropping his *rapaire*, he drew his sword. Sir John Ferguson stood there, weapon in hand, calmly looking about him. Tadhg stared at him, at the haughty face, the determined mouth, the cold searching eyes.

As he stood and contemplated the man who had ruined the lives of so many O'Flahertys, Tadhg felt as if ice water was running in his veins. As he advanced on the older man, Tadhg thought only of killing this man for his dark deeds. Sir John saw only a big young man in countryman's clothing, armed with a sword. Coolly and expertly he thrust at Tadhg, who nimbly evaded him. He continued to advance, sword extended. After a few more thrusts, which were easily parried, Sir John realised that his adversary was a skilled swordsman. Only then did he recall the story of the young Irishman who had slain John Montgomery the previous year. He knew now that he was in great danger. None of his men was within fifteen paces.

Tadhg looked with calm detachment at his opponent. He could see the rivets of the cuirass and the stitching in the gauntlets. With ease he broke through Sir John's defence and cut a deep gash through the fancy breeches, bright blood rushing down the unprotected right leg. Sir John looked down with dismay. 'That was for Cathal O'Flaherty,' Tadhg said grimly.

Advancing bravely despite the wounded leg, Sir John thrust and slashed at the big target before him. Tadhg avoided each thrust skilfully, then deliberately slashed his opponent's left thigh. Again bright blood ran crimson. 'That was for Murtagh Blake,' Tadhg said.

As the blood poured down his legs, Sir John realised that his life was running out. 'Damn you,' he cried in frustration as he thrust futilely at the dancing will-o'-the-wisp before him. He felt his legs tottering beneath him. When he wavered momentarily, Tadhg drove the tip of his blade through his enemy's throat. Down went Sir John's weapon as the red blood gushed over the blue cuirass. His icy eyes turned on Tadhg, an expression of bafflement and wonder on his ashen face.

'And that thrust, Sir John, was to avenge Donough O'Flaherty. And now may you burn in hell until Judgement Day.'

With the death of their leader, the few surviving members of the Ferguson forces asked for quarter. A great silence settled momentarily over the area as the sound of battle ceased, then a great cry burst from the throats of the people who had come to attend Cathal O'Flaherty's funeral, only to see his death instead. Above the clamour arose the high-voiced keening of Nora Connealy, giving vent to her emotions. Quickly the other women joined her in the *ólogón*. Tadhg shivered at the eerie primitive wail.

Dermot O'Lee was the first to rush to Tadhg, embracing him and congratulating him on his victory. Then came O'Kerrigan and others, bloodstained, dirty and wet-eyed, as Tadhg stood over the body of Cathal. Conor O'Donnell was seeking to comfort his sister, Máire Blake, who was seated in the dusty road beside Murtagh, his bloody head in her lap, and weeping inconsolably.

Father Mulvaney went among the dying, friend and foe alike, giving them the last rites of the Church. Several of the Sassanaigh, although non-Catholics, appeared grateful for his ministrations, touching the hem of his robe as he walked amongst them, his gentle voice rising and falling in the cadence of Latin.

Of the eighteen Rapparees, eight were dead, including Cathal. Several who were wounded were being tended by Dermot O'Lee. Tadhg was happy to see Conor and Dónal Óg, apparently unscathed, among the survivors. Five of Ferguson's men had surrendered, about three or four had escaped, and the rest of the half a hundred of armed men who had ridden confidently into the pass a short time before were dead.

Several of the Rapparees assisted Tadhg in laying aside the bodies of the slain, the Irish on one side of the road, the Sassanaigh on the other. Weapons, armour and valuables were gathered and Dónal Óg placed guard over them. The remaining horses, among them the beautiful white stallion that had been ridden by Sir John, were gathered and tethered, with Tadhg laying claim to the stallion by right of conquest.

Gobnait O'Flannery, with a group of women, began the task of preparing the Irish dead for burial. Tomas O'Fuldeny and Peregrine O'Flannery conferred on the problem of acquiring enough coffins for the eight Rapparees and Murtagh Blake.

After some semblance of order was restored, O'Kerrigan, who had been wounded in the fighting but was able to be up and about, called all the available Rapparees together. Answering to the roll call were Fergus Dillon, Séamus O'Callanan, Séan O'Carroll, Dermot O'Lee, Finín O'Regan and Lawrence O'Toole. Gilleduff O'Fallon and Phelim MacTully were seriously wounded but would recover.

Cathal O'Flaherty had been joined among the fallen by Morris Breen, Sean MacGibbon, Séamus O'Callaghan, Denis O'Doherty, Padraic O'Scully, Eamon O'Bolan and Pierce MacNamara.

'I know that you are saddened and shocked by the death of our chief and comrades,' O'Kerrigan began, and you are bone-weary from the fighting, but we have one final task to accomplish, the recovery of Donough O'Flaherty's body so that he can be buried with Cathal here at St Malachi's.

O'Carroll looked dubious. 'How do you expect this small band to take the castle and get Donough's body? Wouldn't it be better to wait until we get reinforcements?'

O'Kerrigan's voice was grim. 'By the time that we arrive there they will know from those who escaped that all is not well with Sir John's force. And we have the body to prove that their leader has fallen. They might resist, but I think I know these Sassanaigh vassals well enough to say that they will do anything to save their own skins.'

'I agree with O'Kerrigan,' Tadhg declared. 'This is what Cathal would want us to do. Let us strike while the iron is still hot!'

O'Kerrigan nodded his head in approval. 'Hark to the man who has slain our hated enemy, Sir John Ferguson,' he said.

Tadhg's words carried conviction and the Rapparees, who had grown to respect him greatly, especially since his conquest of the Sassanach chief, eagerly selected horses and weapons. Hearing no further protests, O'Kerrigan ordered that the body of Sir John be lashed to the saddle of the big stallion. Soon the Rapparees, mounted and armed with pistols, swords, muskets and their half-pikes, some wearing armour and the trappings of their fallen foe, clattered up the road. Dónal Óg, riding proudly at the head of the column, led the horse bearing the body of its late rider.

Several hours of hard galloping brought them to the western shores of Lough Corrib, where they turned southward. They finally halted on a high spot overlooking the lake. Dark clouds scudded overhead, drifting towards the distant Twelve Bens, driven by the strong February winds. Below them the lake was dark and sullen, and the ancient castle of the O'Flahertys on its small island some distance from the shore stood stark against the forbidding background of lake and headlands.

Tadhg drew a deep breath. The castle, not large but formidable because of its insular position, dominated the island. It had four walled sides with turrets at each corner. The keep was off to the left. Blue pennons of Sir John's design waved briskly from the walls, whipped about by the boisterous breezes. They were the only sign of movement on the island.

Tadhg's heart began to pump furiously when he discovered a small, dark shape, in sharp contrast to the grey stone of the castle, spreadeagled on a bastion near the centre. Above the body, on a spike driven into the wall, was the head of Donough O'Flaherty.

Never before and never again would Tadhg be so affected as he was by the sad, cruel, flaunting of the poor broken body of the gentle schoolmaster. He remembered Donough's kindly eyes, his low, resonant voice, the beauty of his smile, the long conversations, his advice and counsel, his burning zeal to teach the children, his pride in his little school.

All the men but O'Kerrigan wept openly and unashamedly. O'Kerrigan sat his horse impassively, but Dermot O'Lee, who knew him well, was aware that he felt the savage, senseless slaying of Donough O'Flaherty as keenly as the others.

When their tears had run their course and the heavy sobbing had subsided, O'Kerrigan called for Finín O'Regan, who had once served in the French army, to blow a call on the trumpet seized at the rout of the troops of Sir John. O'Regan rolled his tongue around his mouth to wet it, then set the trumpet to his lips and blew a mighty blast that shattered the quiet of the lonely lake. When no one showed on the walls opposite, O'Kerrigan ordered another blast of the horn. Again Finín sent the challenging sound across the lake. This time several men appeared on the walls, gazing defiantly at the little band of Rapparees.

O'Kerrigan gestured to Dónal Óg to come forward with the body-laden white horse. Then, cupping his hands to his mouth, he shouted, 'We bring you the body of your lord and master!'

After much gesticulating and conferring, one of the group shouted back, 'We do not believe you. It is just another Irish trick. Sir John Ferguson would never fall before the likes of you.'

Again O'Kerrigan shouted across the waters. 'Sir John and most of his men are dead. Let one of you come and identify the body.'

After much consultation and argument, one of the men disappeared. In a few minutes a castle gate slowly opened and a figure emerged. Getting into a small boat tied to a wharf on the island, the man rowed to the shore where the Rapparees waited. He was a small, thin man, clad in dark, sombre clothing, and wore no armour or weapon. Watching warily, he approached the big stallion, and bending slightly at the waist, he carefully examined the body and features of the corpse of Sir John.

Apparently satisfied with the identification, he raised his eyes to O'Kerrigan. 'Yes, it is the body of Colonel Ferguson.' He gazed at the dead man for a short time, then, turning again to the Rapparees, said, 'What terms are you asking?'

'Surrender of the castle, all its garrisons and contents, and the return of the body of Donough O'Flaherty.'

'Let me introduce myself,' the Englishman said. 'I am James Henderson, a merchant of Bristol, visiting my sister, who is the wife - or widow - of Sir John. I have full authority to represent her here.'

'I am Donough O'Kerrigan of the County Mayo, and being dispossessed of my lands by English thieves, am now merely an Irish patriot.' Pointing to the other Rapparees, he added, 'With their consent, I am authorised to represent this band of patriots in these negotiations in the interest of the surviving son of Cathal O'Flaherty.'

Henderson nodded politely to the forbidding-looking 'patriots'.

When their fangs are pulled, these snakes are charming, O'Kerrigan thought cynically to himself. I wonder if he would be as polite if the shoe were on the other foot? Then aloud he said, 'The terms are the unconditional surrender of the castle and departure of all now in it by nightfall. They can take their clothes and personal belonging, and that it all.'

'These are severe terms,' Henderson protested. 'Some of these people have resided here for nearly forty years. They just can't pull stakes and leave on short notice with night coming on. Besides, the women will need carriages of some sort.'

'Would you prefer the terms the O'Flahertys received when John Ferguson took their castle?' O'Kerrigan thundered, his eyes angry. 'They were slaughtered in their ancestral home, man, woman and child!

Henderson recoiled, and raised a restraining hand. 'I appreciate your consideration. But I must report back to the others. What will they say when I tell them that your forces consist of just nine men and a half-grown boy? Do you think that you can take that stronghold with such a motley crew?'

O'Kerrigan smiled grimly. 'This motley crew plus just ten more cut down and destroyed Sir John and his fifty horse troops. You are not so ignorant as not to know that King James's adherents are in control of most of Ireland now. Do you think that you can wait for King Billy for succour? If you choose resistance rather than capitulation, then let it be your choice. But then the terms will be death to the entire garrison and all its inhabitants. There will be no mercy. Take your choice.'

'It's a poor choice,' said Henderson wryly.

'When you return and inform them that their protector, Sir John, and the bulk of his armed forces are all dead, they will be far less pugnacious.'

Henderson pondered. 'I will communicate your terms to Lady Ferguson,' he said. 'Can I take the body with me?'

O'Kerrigan shook his head. 'No. The body will be delivered to you when you depart. Tell Lady Ferguson that three horses, with saddles, will be made available. I feel that I am being more than generous. Séamus O'Callanan there was at the castle on the day of the massacre. He was the one who took the badly injured Donough O'Flaherty to his kin. Would you like to have him tell you what Sir John and his men did to the O'Flaherty family?'

'No, no,' Henderson replied quickly. 'It will not be necessary. I will try to persuade my sister to leave as quickly as possible.'

While the emissary rowed back to the island, Dermot O'Lee, whose horse was next to that of Tadhg, commented sadly, 'To think on this momentous day for the O'Flahertys, nether Cathal nor Donough are here to rejoice in the defeat of their enemy and to return to their family castle.'

'Donough is here,' Tadhg replied grimly, pointing to the castle wall.

Dermot nodded assent. 'Yes, that's true.' He turned to Tadhg. 'But fate does play strange tricks. You, a young stranger, played a major role in the apprehension and deaths of both Thomas Montgomery and John Ferguson, the men mainly responsible for the tragedy of Murrough O'Flaherty and his family.' He shook his head in wonder.

Tadhg drew his sword from his scabbard, reading aloud the Spanish inscription. 'Draw me only in defence of honour.' He returned the weapon. 'Not until I left Inishmór did I know at first hand the wrongs done to the Irish. And each of the Rapparees was living evidence of injustices. Now I would like to devote the rest of my life to helping right these wrongs.'

'If there were more like you, Tadhg, and fewer like Tomas Nugent, Ireland would be a happier land. It's our great curse, the number of traitors we breed!'

Suddenly there was great activity on the island. The gate was opened and a stream of men, women and children poured forth, each with a burden of some sort. Men appeared on the walls to remove the pennants. Finally, when the boats had shuttled back and forth to the mainland, the entire party had left the castle.

While the group glared with open hostility at the Irish, James Henderson climbed the hill to where the Rapparees waited.

'We are leaving now,' he said, 'to gain as much daylight as there is left on this sad day. With your kind permission, I would now like to take the horses that you promised and the body of Colonel Ferguson.'

O'Kerrigan pointed to Dónal Óg, O'Toole and MacDeeris. Grumbling, the trio dismounted, and with ill grace handed the reins to the Englishmen. Tadhg transferred the body to the horse that he had ridden, keeping the big white stallion for himself. Henderson thanked O'Kerrigan courteously, and leading the four animals, rejoined the dispirited party on the lake shore. Several older ladies were helped into the saddles, with younger ones seating themselves behind them. One, a tall, stately woman with a grief-ravaged face, who was receiving the special solicitude of Henderson, was apparently the widow. Most of the men appeared to be family retainers and servants, and several wore livery. Only four or five of the men wore cuirasses and were armed. These were most likely the remnants of Sir John's troops who had escaped.

About a score were children of varying ages, most of whom were crying. With armed men in the vanguard and at the rear, the party shuffled off to the north.

'Where do you think they will go?' Conor asked O'Kerrigan.

He shrugged. 'Probably to Derry or Enniskillen. I have heard that rebels are gathering in those places.'

'As much as I hate the Sassanaigh,' Tadhg said, watching the departing column, 'I find it depressing that those poor women and children must travel the long hard road this day.'

'Don't waste your tears on them,' O'Toole said bitterly. 'It's harsh medicine, surely, but maybe it will help cure them of the disease of taking Irish property. We didn't invite them here.'

When the former occupants of the castle disappeared from view, O'Kerrigan turned to the Rapparees. 'You, Finín, Sean and Lawrence, stay here and watch that the English don't return. Blow a blast on the trumpet if there is an alarm. The rest of you leave your horses and come with me.'

Tadhg and the others followed O'Kerrigan to the boats. Tadhg looked with curiosity at the wooden boat in which he took the rower's seat, observing the wide-bladed oars and the oarlocks. The vessel seemed heavy and sluggish in comparison with the lightness and manoeuvrability of his curragh. They tied the boat at the wharf, and then with awe walked through the gaping gates of the castle, through the outer yard, and through a stone arch doorway into the castle proper. Still faintly visible in the stone, despite its long exposure to weather and time, was the ancient coat-of-arms of the O'Flahertys, with its two lions supporting a hand between them, and below a boat with eight oars, indicating the maritime activities of a family whose territory reached to the edge of the wild Atlantic.

Seamus O'Callachán, a triumphant expression on his withered old face, led the party up a narrow, winding tower to the bastion with Donough's body. The wind was noticeably stronger on the top of the wall, and fortunately blowing away from the castle, permitting the hushed group to approach the body, which, having been exposed to the weather for several days, was beginning to decompose. After they had halted and gazed in silent reverence for some time, O'Kerrigan in a choked voice, said, 'Since it was Séamus O'Callachán who carried Donough from this, his home, as a baby, it should be his privilege to carry him on this, his last journey. And Tadhg, who loved him so, and who slew his foul

103

murderer, will carry the head.'

Eager hands helped Séamus disengage the body from the wall and wrap the pitiful remains in a blanket. With much trepidation, yet rejoicing at the honour bestowed on him, Tadhg approached Donough's head. Birds had pecked at his sightless eyes. As Tadhg tenderly removed it from the spike, a wave of emotion for the poor slain schoolmaster swept over him and he clutched the relic to his breast, his tears falling freely while he murmured over and over, 'Oh Donough, what have they done to you?'

His companions watched with compassion, their hearts heavy with sorrow, until Tadhg, who finally, drained of all emotion, moved away with his burden and followed Séamus down the winding stairs as the old man carried the slight form of Donough grasped reverently and firmly in his arms.

When they reached the bottom and moved out into the hall, Séamus stood uncertainly for a moment, then pointed to a door. 'That room is the chapel,' he said. Conor pushed open the massive wooden door, whose panels were carved with holy scenes of the Nativity, and the solemn party entered. But alas, the ancient chapel of the O'Flahertys had been converted to a nursery, and where the holy altar had once stood was a cradle with beautiful curved rockers made of some exotic wood. Tadhg, Conor and Dónal Óg gaped with wonder at the rich furniture of the room, the colourful fabrics, the high-beamed ceilings. They had never seen such splendour before, but most of the other Rapparees, coming from the noble Irish families, saw little now except that this was the place where Cathal's mother and others of the family had been slain many years before.

'It's getting too late in the day to take Donough back to St Malachi's,' O'Kerrigan observed, 'so we will stay here for the night. Join together what the Sassanaigh put asunder,' he instructed Tadhg and Séamus Rua. Gently they deposited their burdens on a satin sheet on the floor, the head back with the body again.

Leaving Donough alone in the former chapel, they followed Séamus Rua to a large hall. A long, heavy table with more than a dozen chairs around it dominated the room. The table was set with numerous dishes, and from an adjoining kitchen drifted the savoury aroma of cooking food. Suddenly realising that they hadn't eaten all day, they trooped after the smell. In a huge fireplace, pots and kettles of various sizes were steaming, and a haunch of venison was being turned on a spit by a ragged young boy of about ten years old. With fear in his eyes, he stared at the wild-looking Rapparees, yet dutifully kept turning the spit.

'Who are you?' O'Kerrigan asked. 'And why didn't you go with the rest?'

'I am Thomas, the scullion,' the lad replied, hardly audibly.

'Why didn't you go with the others?' O'Kerrigan repeated.

The boy grinned vacantly, showing large buck teeth. 'Because they didn't want me,' he said simply.

O'Kerrigan glanced at him impatiently. 'Where are your parents?'

Again the boy grinned. 'I don't have any. I'm a love-child.'

One of the Rapparees guffawed, and then they all laughed, including the boy. With the laughter, for the first time in several days their tensions were released and the heavy oppression of the day seemed magically lifted. They drifted around the kitchen, peering into the pots, sniffing at the cooking meat, poking into pantries, and making nuisances of themselves until O'Kerrigan ordered several of them to help young Thomas with the meal.

When Fergus Dillon found several pipes of wine and poured them into a jorum of exquisitely cut glass on the big table, the gaiety began to mount. They talked, sang, danced, and in the grasp of Bacchus, swore eternal fealty to each other.

Never had Tadhg eaten, or even dreamed of eating, as he did that night, of the meal intended for Sir John Ferguson, his family and guests. There was the venison, of course, and a shoulder of mutton, buttered carrots, artichokes, peas, choice young pullets, eggs flavoured with clary, dark treacle bread, jelly made of the mountain blackberry, cabbage, and then to top it off, a delicious venison pie.

After dinner they roamed the castle, admiring the lofty rooms, the ancient tapestries, the elaborate furniture and fittings. Sir John had done magnificently in the barren land of Connaught, squeezing a rich living from the poor peasants like the Blakes, who scrimped and scraped to pay the exorbitant rents demanded of them by their master.

The Rapparees helped themselves to the wardrobe left by the late occupants. Even Tadhg, to his great surprise, found some clothes that fit him, albeit a little tightly. Despite their snugness, he donned shirt and breeches, jerkin and gay hat with a jaunty feather, stockings and boots. True, he had to slash the leather in strategic places to get them on, but any fool knew that fresh air was good for the feet. They preened and pranced in their new costumes, admiring each other and themselves.

Soothed by the wine, stuffed with the tasty viands, Tadhg slept in a magnificent bed with clean white linen sheets and warm blankets. He was so exhausted, both physically and emotionally, that he slept like a dead man, and even the restless boodies, who never seemed to sleep, troubled him not a whit. About midnight he was shaken awake by a grinning O'Toole, whose lonely guard post he was to take. While the newcomer gratefully crawled into Tadhg's warm bed, Tadhg rowed across to the headland, shivering in the raw night air, to spend the rest of the night standing watch over the road leading to Brúgh na h-Inse. It was an uneventful night, with only an occasional hare scampering along the roadside to relieve the quiet.

As dawn crept reluctantly from out of the east, lighting up the lonely lake and disclosing the misty outlines of the old castle, Conor returned with O'Regan and Dónal Óg, who were to relieve them at their posts. Tadhg and Conor went eagerly to the kitchen where young Thomas was heating fresh milk over the fire. When it was heated properly, he poured it into a meddar containing buttermilk, making a big dish of curds. Into this mixture he put a pound weight of butter, and then offered a mug of the steaming drink to the half-frozen youths, who downed it eagerly in great gulps. Warmed and restored to good spirits, they sat down to a meal of boiled eggs, the leftovers of last night's mutton, boxty bread with blackberry preserves, all washed down with Sir John's best ale.

'This is the life for me, *a chara*,' said Conor, wiping his mouth and patting his stomach. 'I never really realised how nice it was to be one of the gentry.'

'Indeed,' Tadhg exclaimed. 'Just imagine having two kinds of meat and fowl at the same meal!'

'Imagine having just one kind of meat at the same meal,' Conor replied, smacking his lips. 'It's been so long since I had red meat that I forgot what it tasted like.'

'Better enjoy it while you can,' said a voice behind them, 'for it might be a long time before you have red meat again.' O'Kerrigan had come into the room, accompanied by Dermot O'Lee.

'What do you mean,' Conor asked in mock indignation, 'aren't we going to stay in this well-stocked place for ever?' He winked at Tadhg. 'Didn't Tadhg win this castle along with Sir John's horse?'

106

'If his name is Tadhg O'Flaherty, he can have it surely,' O'Lee said drily. 'And O'Flaherty is what we came to talk about. Someone has to ride to Aughananure to notify the O'Flahertys there of the death of Sir John and of our being in possession of the castle. And someone has to ride to Dublin to seek word at the Castle of Captain Hugh O'Flaherty, who was last heard of in England in the service of King James, to notify him that his father and uncle are dead, and that the family lands are free of the Sassanaigh.'

Conor slapped his forehead. 'My soul to the Devil,' he exclaimed. 'I had completely forgotten that Murtagh is dead and that Máire needs me.' He rose hurriedly.

'I was about to talk to you about that,' O'Kerrigan remarked. 'You can see that our little band will have to split up, perhaps for ever. Séamus O'Callanan and Dermot here, as old friends, will accompany Donough's body. O'Regan will ride to Aughananure. Conor must go to his sister's and I, along with O'Carroll, Dillon, MacDeeris and O'Toole will try to hold the castle until relief comes from The O'Flaherty. That leaves you, Tadhg, and Dónal Óg if you want him, to go to Dublin. Do you think you have enough English to make out there?'

'I'll try. I still have the little book I was studying from at Donough's school.'

'He can do it,' Conor affirmed. 'He soaked up that language faster than O'Toole soaked up the wine last night.'

'In that event, he must be quite fluent,' O'Kerrigan said. 'Good. You will go right to the Castle of Dublin, to the Lord-Lieutenant, and seek information about Captain Hugh O'Flaherty. The last word Cathal had of him was shortly before King James fled the country, when he was the cathedral city of Coventry company of the King's Fusiliers under Lord Dumbarton. God knows whether he's alive or dead.'

'Do you think he might have escaped to Dublin?' Tadhg asked.

O'Kerrigan shook his head. 'I don't know, Tadhg. But if there is knowledge of him anywhere in Ireland, it should be in Dublin. It was the Lord-Lieutenant who ordered him along with other Irish troops to England last year. There is must activity in Dublin. It is said that throughout Ireland the great lords are raising regiments for King James. And that his cousin, King Louis, is forming a huge army in France for James, who is supposed to arrive soon in Ireland.' He shrugged his shoulders, adding, 'But there are so many stories circulating these days it is difficult to say what is true and what is not.'

And so it was that the farewells were said. Conor promised to come to Dublin to seek out Tadhg and Dónal as soon as he could leave his widowed sister, for the trio had decided to join King James's army after they had finished their business in Dublin. At the suggestion of Dermot O'Lee, who knew the capital well, they were to meet at the Brazen Head, an old inn near the quays on the River Liffey.

Within the hour, Tadhg on the big white stallion, and Dónal Óg on a frisky bay, rode southwards on the road to Galway, Dublin-bound. They were accompanied for a part of the way by Finín O'Regan, before they separated at Oughterard. After his mission was completed, Finín was heading back to Cork, his home.

PART II

Ulster

Cast of Characters

*Cornet Edmond Butler, of Kilcop, an officer in the Earl of Tyrconnell's Regiment

Sergeant Cavanaugh, a quartermaster in the Earl of Tyrconnell's Regiment

*De Rosen, a mercenary from Livonia, commanding general of King James' Army at Derry

Lieutenant De Vimeny, a French expert on codes and ciphers

Henry FitzGerald, uncle of Lady Margaret Fitzgerald

*Henry FitzJames, Duke of Berwick, bastard son of James II and Arabella Churchill

Sergeant Cahir Gallagher,, of Tyrconnell's Regiment

*Reverand James Gordon, the original firebrand minister who exhorted the apprentices of Derry to close the gates

Richard Hamilton, a general in James' Army in Ulster

Robert Holmes, a deserter from King James' Army

*General Kirk, commander of the Rebels' relief ships at Derry

Jacques Le Berge, a French Hugenot refugee, a Dublin weaver and boarder at Cáit O'Reilly's

Rory MacAuley, orphaned son of a creaght family from Fermanagh

Sergeant MacGillivray, a Scot in the services of William III

Meg Murray, an Ulster woman who befriends Tadhg at Derry

*Major Robert Nangle, of Tyrconnell's Regiment

Siobhan O'Coffey, a widow of Aughrim, County Galway

*Richard Talbot, Viceroy of Ireland

Francis Murphy

(* denotes historical figures)

CHAPTER I

On To Dublin

Their road led through country where the chief crops appeared to be rocks - rocks of all sizes and shapes. Some were scattered helter-skelter where they had been left on Creation Day. Some, too big to be moved, still jutted from cultivated fields. Some were piled neatly into walls demarking the farmers' small fields.

They had not ridden far before a heavy rain began pelting them from a sullen, grey sky, making them rue the impulse that caused them to discard their own woollen water-repellent clothes for their newly confiscated rament. Sodden and cold, they plodded south-ward across lonely bogland and desolate hills, populated only by flocks of ghostly sheep.

Near Oughterard they crossed a small river where still stood the crumbling remains of an O'Flaherty castle, battered into ruins by Cromwell's cannon. At Gortachalla Lough they paused briefly to rest their horses. Then, passing Ballycuirce Lough on their left, they came to the narrowing where Lough Corrib ceases. Travelling southeast now, they arrived at the outskirts of *Cathair na Gaillimhe* - the City of Galway - where, stopping on the crest of a hill, they gazed with awe at the tall towers, churches, ships at the quays, and the numerous people strolling about.

Reasoning that it would be safest to by-pass the city, they forded the river above it. Swinging eastward, they discovered to their pleasure the nature of the countryside changing. Fewer bogs, fewer rocks, gently rolling hills, herds of cattle - all combined to present a wonderland to the two weary travellers. Here and there stood stacks of turf which the inhabitants had dug from the seemingly bottomless bogs.

Reluctant to approach a dwelling too close to Galway, they slept in a dry ditch that night, behind a thick hedge. At the first light of day they mounted, turning their horses towards Athenry, on the road to Ballinasloe. At Athenry a score of simple cabins clustered around the ruins of several big stone houses and an ancient castle, now mercifully covered with a mantle of ivy to hide its scars. Here they purchased a meal from a surly and suspicious large woman with one of the coins acquired in the battle with Sir John Ferguson. The old woman, whose feet were as big as a man's, stood at the half-door, glowering at them until they disappeared around the bend.

'*Yon caileach na cosamhóra* probably thinks we're robbers,' Dónal exclaimed indignantly between mouthfuls of bread and cold mutton.

Tadhg chuckled. 'You aptly called her the old woman with the big feet, and not the old woman with the big heart. But after all, that coin we gave her didn't come from the priest.'

'True,' Dónal acknowledged, 'but we merely took back what the Sassanaigh stole from us.'

Tadhg peered quizzically at Dónal. 'Stole from us?' he echoed. 'I don't recall ever having any money of my own that the English could steal. And stealing is never justified, as Donough Beag always preached to us.'

'Poor Donough Beag, God rest his soul,' Dónal said. 'He surely will be missed.'

And none will miss him more than I, Tadhg thought, a melancholy wave sweeping away the light mood of the moment before. From Donough his thoughts drifted to the Lady Mairéad. He realised that she was all too frequently on his mind. He knew he would have no peace until he could banish her from his memory.

In talking to a farmer who was repairing his rock wall, the travellers learned that an armed body of men had been seen the night before at Kilconnel. No, he didn't know if they were English or Irish. Yes, there was recruiting for King James's army in the district. Many young men had already left for Drogheda where General Hamilton was reportedly assembling an Irish army. Who was General Hamilton? He was a Catholic officer now serving King James. Of course, a Hamilton could be a Catholic even though his family had come from Scotland to Ireland in the sixteenth century. Besides, wasn't he a Tipperary man, from Nenagh, not too many miles distant?

Handsome and witty young John Hamilton, in France with other Irishmen in the service of Louis XIV, had captured the heart of the Princess di Conti, a natural daughter of the Emperor himself, but unfortunately for Hamilton, she already had a husband. When the King learned of the affair, he angrily informed the brash young Hamilton to cease and desist!

With the choice of the Bastille or banishment, he wisely chose the latter. He returned to England, but quickly decided that he had a better future back in his native country.

Richard Talbot, widely known as 'Lying Dick', who earlier attatched himself to the future James II, was now the Earl of Tyrconnell, and the Viceroy of Ireland. As the Irish Army burgeoned, the Viceroy commissioned John Hamilton as brigadier general and commander of the Irish Army.

A new flag flew defiantly over Dublin Castle, proudly proclaiming in gold letters, 'Now or Never! Now and Forever'. For the first time in the country's history, practically all the Catholics - native Irish, Norman Irish and English Irish - were united in their common cause against the enemy. There were O'Briens, MacCarthys and O'Donnells; Fitzgeralds, Burkes and Powers; Luttrells, Purcells and Blakes. Yes, even Hugolin Spenser, grandson of Edmund Spenser (who had hated all things Irish) was serving as a lieutenant in Lord Kilmallock's regiment. None other than the great Brian Ború, in rallying the Irish in conquest of the Danes way back in 1014, had been faced with Catholic Irish in the ranks of the foe! In all the abortive risings against the authority of England for five centuries, the native families had been divided, more concerned with avenging ancient wrongs, real or imagined, than with opposing the common foe for the glory and unification of their country. Now, thanks to God, this was all changed.

CHAPTER II

The Poet

To avoid trouble, if indeed the armed party of men at Kilconnell were Protestants, Tadhg and Dónal changed their course, taking a narrow, rutted road leading to a little hamlet called Aughrim. Here, late in the afternoon, they rested and watered their mounts near the ruins of an old castle. It started to rain as they were about to ride on. Tadhg looked questioningly at Dónal, and Dónal looked at Tadhg.

'It's little desire I have for getting wet again for the short time left to us this day,' said Tadhg. 'We have covered twenty miles since dawn, and my bones are aching. What say we stay here for the night?'

Inasmuch as Dónal worshipped Tadhg, agreeing whole-heartedly with everything he proposed, he quickly nodded assent. A small cabin, from which peat smoke curled cheerfully from the hole in the roof which served as a chimney, huddled close by. The half-door was invitingly open. A red-haired woman, with pock-marked face, responded to their 'Bless all here' with 'And yourself, likewise'.

Her engaging blue eyes appraised with approval Tadhg's huge form, and an impish smile came over her face when she noticed the tight fit of his clothes. 'You have been in the rain too long, *mo bhuachaillín dhubh*, your clothes are beginning to shrink.' Seeing Tadhg discomfited, she added, 'But come in, come in before they shrink right up to your neck and choke you to death.'

As they followed her into the cabin, Tadhg observed two burned embers, fashioned in the form of a cross for protection against fire, stuck into the thatch overhead. The cabin was small and simple, but a cheerful fire blazed in a circle of rocks in the centre of the room. Tadhg looked curiously about, then asked. 'Where is the *fear-an-tí*?'

'The man of the house? Och, he is dead, God rest his soul.' She dabbed at her eyes. 'I'm a poor widow, all alone in the world. Sure and it's a hard life for the poor widow O'Coffey. But tell me, what are you bold lads doing at this lonely crossroads on the road to nowhere?'

'We're on our way to Dublin,' Tadhg explained. 'We have little money to spend on meals and lodging at the inn.'

'The inn,' she said, a curl of humorous contempt on her full lips. 'That's the last thing you'll be finding at this Godforsaken spot.' Her shrewd eyes observed the fine quality of their clothes; she had already appraised their horses, weapons and trappings. Yet from their speech they were obviously not of the gentry. Her first impression was that they were robbers, and had stolen the clothes and horses. She became apprehensive at her impetuous generosity in inviting them into the house. But as they conversed further, she became convinced that they were but young country lads who would do her no harm. The big one, now; wasn't he an armful? And handsome too, with his dark hair and curling eyelashes. That broad back, and the big-muscled arms, could be capable of performing a lot of hard work on her small farm. And the Good Lord knew it needed a man now that O'Coffey had gone to his grave.

'There's a byre in the back,' she offered. 'You'd better be putting your horses out of the cold and the rain while I get a hot meal going.'

'Will they be safe there?' Tadhg inquired worriedly.

The widow laughed heartily, her blue eyes crinkling at the corners. 'Safe? Nothing ever happens at Aughrim, Tadhg *a stóir*. Nobody not daft would ever come here. We're so poor, and so remote that even the thieves avoid us, it would be the stupid robber who would be looking into Siobhan O'Coffey's byre. Everyone knows that the poor widow is no richer than a church mouse.'

'Speaking of church mice,' Dónal said, 'I should be going to my duty for tomorrow is Sunday.'

Again the widow laughed heartily. 'You'll have to save your sins for a while, Dónal. We have no church here. The priest says Mass in Piers O'Madden's house down the boreen. Once every four weeks he arrives early for those who need to go to confession. There is no church, there is no inn, for Aughrim is at the end of the world where each dull day has been the same from the beginning, and will be the same until Judgement Day. But go put away your horses or morn will be here before we eat.'

When they returned after stabling their mounts, the widow had potatoes cooking, along with cabbage and peas, and the delicious aroma of rabbit stew permeated the small room. She ground oats on a quern, added water and butter, then baked oatcakes on the fire. Because she seldom entertained guests any more, she had to dig deep among her linens to find several hidden pewter plates.

After they had finished their meal, Tadhg produced a shilling which he put on the table in front of their hostess. 'I'm not a *spailín fánach*,' he stated firmly, 'trying to cheat a poor widow, so here is payment for our food and a night's lodging in the byre.'

Siobhan pushed away the proffered coin indignantly, exclaiming, 'And I'll not be charging hungry wayfarers while God still provides food for me to eat. 'Tis not an inn I'm running.'

Tadhg was apologetic. 'I didn't intend to make you angry, Siobhan, but I don't want to take advantage of a poor widow.'

'So you wouldn't be taking advantage of a poor widow, would you now?' She glanced at him archly, then added, 'More's the pity!' She eyed the coin, still lying on the table. Och, and it's a chill, wet night. The fire will be warming our outsides, but not our insides, and it's not a drop of anything that I have in the house. Let me take this shilling, now, and get a bottle of poteen from one of the neighbours to be a-warming our insides.

Throwing a shawl over her shoulders, she left the cabin, returning in a few minutes triumphantly carrying a bottle of a clear liquid, which she set on the table. 'Mind you now, be careful with that bottle,' she warned, 'they're hard to come by, and it will cost us another shilling if we break it.'

She carefully poured the poitín into a mether, and when it was almost brim-full, passed it to Tadhg. Not sure of the proper etiquette in such as situation, never having sat drinking poitín with a comely widow in such cosy circumstances, Tadhg raised the wooden cup in a toast.

'Health and life to you,
The man of your choice to you,
Land without rent to you,
And death in Ireland.'

He gulped a generous portion. The fiery liquid, probably still fresh from its illicit birth, burned its passage down his throat to his stomach, where indeed it began to warm him even as he blinked his eyes and gasped for breath.

He handed the cup to Siobhan, who, with a gay '*Sláinte!*' tossed down several swallows imperturbably, smacking her lips in enjoyment. Dónal Óg was next. Although he had sampled similar *uisce beatha* before, he had never had it offered without the preliminary admonition, 'Go easy now, remember that you're just a boy'. having observed Tadhg's reaction to the great swig he had taken, Dónal drank cautiously in gentle sips.

The gaiety increased as the contents of the bottle decreased. Overhead, the rain beat on the thatch, leaking - drip, drip, drip - on to the earthen floor below. But who minded a little rain on a joyous night like this? And was there ever finer company anywhere? They talked and they sang, with Siobhan's sweet voice blending well with Tadhg's bass and Dónal's tenor. Siobhan hadn't enjoyed herself so much since before her husband's death. Her eyes sparkled; she was witty and jolly; her animation made her a carefree young woman again.

While Dónal Óg was in the midst of telling the hostess it was the nicest party he had ever attended, he suddenly paused, his face turning from its normal rosy hue to a bilious green, and he clutched his hands to his stomach. He gulped, his eyes wide and solemn. Siobhan arose quickly, opened the door to the pelting rain, motioning to Tadhg to bring Dónal to the doorway. The unhappy youth made it just in time - the evening's pleasure and his dinner all went out together.

'Och, the poor lad,' Siobhan murmured sympathetically, 'it must have been the rabbit stew that didn't set too well with him.' She rummaged around in a wooden chest, producing a blanket. 'Here, take this, he'll probably feel better if he lies down.'

Tadhg eyed the victim thoughtfully while trying to focus his eyes, which were acting strangely. Dónal was still bent over the half-door, retching and moaning. 'Perhaps I had better put him in the straw in the byre,' Tadhg suggested. 'He looks like he will be sick for some time yet.'

Siobhan nodded.

'Come, Dónal,' said Tadhg gently. 'I'll put you to bed.' He lifted his companion to his shoulder, almost falling, and suddenly realising that the poitín was affecting his balance. He felt light-hearted and giddy, and walking carefully, giggling as he went, got Dónal safely bedded in the byre. Hearing the lad retch as he returned to the cabin, his conscience bothered him briefly for leaving him alone, but, he told himself - and he didn't take much convincing - there was little he could do to help Dónal anyway.

Adding a few sods of turf to the fire, Siobhan returned to the table where she filled the cup with the last of the poitín, while humming in a low tone. 'Tadhg, *a stóir*,' she began, finally voicing the thought that she had been entertaining for some time, 'why don't you stay on the farm here with me instead of traipsing off to Dublin? Spring will arrive soon, and there's much work to be done.

117

This farm needs a man, for there's too much heavy work for a poor, weak woman. I have a cow, a horse, some sheep and chickens. Between us, we could make this a prosperous farm, for the soil is good.'

Tadhg shook his head sadly. ''Tis a fine offer, Siobhan, and I thank you kindly, but it's important to find Cathal's son to tell him that his father and uncle are dead, and the O'Flaherty lands are free of Sir John Ferguson.'

'Is that more important that helping a poor widow? Why can't Dónal Óg go to Dublin to deliver the message?'

He shook his head. 'No. I have an obligation.' Looking into Siobhan's sad eyes, Tadhg poured out the entire story of his meeting and his association with the O'Flaherty brothers, including the rescue of Lady Mairéad and the subsequent deaths. The widow listened quietly as Tadhg talked, a veritable deluge of words pouring from him.

When he finally stopped, Siobhán asked him his age.

'I'm nearly twenty-one,' he said.

'How old is it you think I am?' she asked, peering at him intently.

Tadhg floundered. Focusing his eyes carefully, he stared into her face. Despite the pockmarks, the skin was still youthful and firm, her lips full and red, her eyes a bright blue, her red hair wavy under her kerchief. 'Thirty?' he hazarded.

'I should have know better than to have asked,' she replied, her eyes filling with tears. Then she added bitterly, 'It's only twenty-five I am, just five years older than yourself.'

Taking Tadhg's hand, she touched his fingertips to her face. 'It's the pocks that make me look older - that, and the hard work of keeping up this place. Sure, and I was a pretty *cailín* when I married Rísteard, the prettiest in the entire parish, it was said. I had my pick of the eligible men, a rare chance for a girl. And Rísteard was my choice, he was fair where you are dark. Although he was strong and muscular, his feet were the lightest of all in the dance. He was a great one for fun, but he also knew the need and value of hard work. He had a cow, a horse and some fowl, and 'twas many an anxious father wanting him to pick his daughter.'

She smiled for a moment through her tears. 'I had nothing to give but myself, for my mother was a widow, and there was no dowry. Rísteard turned down many a tempting offer for acquiring more livestock along with a wife. And I turned down many a fine lad with more worldly goods that Rísteard. In the short time we were married, we were not blessed with any children.' She shrugged. 'Perhaps it was God's will, for now they would be fatherless. It was on Shrove Tuesday, nearly a year ago, that smallpox hit Aughrim. Rísteard died; I lived. With my face, once so bonny, like this. Many the time I've wished that I too was in the cold cold earth.'

Tadhg felt her tears dropping on his hand. He was filled with compassion for the poor woman. Crying girls or women always affected him deeply. 'Come, *a ghrá*,' he murmured, his voice tender as he impulsively took her in his arms. She flung her arms around him, burying her head on his chest, sobbing wildly, her tears an unrestrained torrent. He caressed her hair, running his fingers through the long locks, talking softly all the while, imploring her not to worry, that merciful God would bring her another husband in due time. He was reminded of Eithne, who had similarly cried on his chest not too long before.

'Perhaps I will be getting another husband,' she sobbed, 'but only the good God knows how long I will have to wait. Och, the terrible loneliness of it! Many a man who courted me when I was a pretty young girl now scurries by when he sees me as if I had the plague. Sure, there are some who would marry me for my property, but they are old or decrepit or drunkards. And isn't it my pillow that's wet with my years on many a night as I have been so long without a man lying next to me in my bed. It's now I need one, Tadhg *a stóir*, not next month or next year.'

She raised her head, her blue eyes staring into his intently. 'Do you know what it is for a loving woman to be without a man? Do you know that a woman needs a man to provide her with other things than food for the table, clothes for her back and a roof over her head? Oh, Tadhg, I hunger for a man's loving caresses like the parched earth hungers for the rain.'

Suddenly she pressed her warm, eager lips against his, snuggling her body against him. His usual cautious and restrained attitude towards women dulled by the whiskey, Tadhg yielded to a strange recklessness, and he responded to her kisses with equal fervour. In the dim light of the cabin, her pockmarks were indistinguishable - she was again the prettiest girl in the parish, a loving woman, vibrant with life, aglow with emotion.

'Hold me tight, *mo ghrá*, and never let go of me,' she sighed ecstatically. 'And sure if it's my ribs you cave in, I'll not be

119

complaining. 'Tis heaven that sent you this way this night. Och, your muscles are so hard, yet your lips are soft as velvet. I could die happy just being smothered by your kisses!'

It was awkward in the chair, so Tadhg lifted her carefully and carried her to the bed. Siobhán clung tightly to him as if afraid that he was going to leave her. He put her down gently, then stretched his big frame alongside her. She breathed an audible sigh of contentment, then leaned her head over his, her long hair falling about his face as she kissed him long and lovingly.

When he awakened in the morning, he sat bolt upright in the bed, trying to recall where he was. Then he saw Siobhan's well-rounded figure, dressed in her shift, silhouetted against the faint light of the fire as she nursed the seed with a fresh turf among the glowing coals. When she heard him stirring she came quickly to the side of the bed, kissing him gently on the lips.

'Stay where you are, I have a couple of eggs on to boil. They will be ready as soon as the fire catches. You just lie there like the *fear an tí* until they are ready.'

Tadhg was alarmed. 'But what about Dónal Óg?' he whispered.

She nodded. 'You're right. Perhaps it would be better if you got up.'

He was embarrassed as she watched him candidly as he flung back the linen sheet, hurriedly thrusting his bare legs into his tight breeches. She handed him his shirt and helped him into his boots. When he stood up, running his fingers through his thoroughly tousled hair, she stood expectantly on tiptoes, and pulling his head down to hers, kissed him repeatedly.

'Come, Siobhán *a stór,*' he said nervously as he glanced at the door, 'Dónal Óg might appear at any moment.'

She released him reluctantly, her eyes filling with tears.

'Now what brings this on?' he asked gruffly, wiping them away with his knuckles.

'Because I know I'll never see you again.' She sighed heavily. 'You will ride down the road to Athlone and out of my life just as you rode into it last night. I know in my heart I was foolish to think I could keep you here, but we have to live in hope, don't we? There isn't much more than hope, especially for a lonely widow woman living in a dull village like Aughrim.'

Tadhg felt a great sadness, his heart went out to her, but he knew that he must leave. He lifted her so that her face was close to his. 'Listen, Siobhán *mavourneen*,' he said gently, 'those pockmarks are all on the outside. Don't let them scar your soul as well. In your eyes there is brightness and laughter; on your lips there is sweetness and song; in your heart is affection and love. God has been generous in His gifts to you. These are the things I will remember of Siobhán O'Coffey as long as I live.'

It was his manifest sincerity, more than the words themselves, that moved her. A radiant smile suddenly transformed her face. Then her expressive, large blue eyes assumed a roguish twinkle, and she kissed him, saying, 'Och, macushla, it's no fisherman you are but the *gean-canach*, the fairy love-talker, come here to delude the poor widow.'

'No, Siobhán, 'tis the truth, all of it. I could not say it if I didn't mean it. Some day a man will come down the boreen. You will know he is the one.'

She looked at him, her eyes tender. 'I believe you, and I thank you for it. But now I better get those eggs off the fire or they will be harder than the landlord's heart.'

While she prepared the breakfast, Tadhg went to the byre to get Dónal. He was still asleep, his youthful mouth agape, the blanket clutched tightly around him. Tadhg gently shook him awake. Dónal slowly opened his eyes, shook his head, grimaced, closed his eyes tightly again and then, putting both hands to his forehead, exclaimed mournfully, 'Oh, what *spalpín* has been beating my poor head? Did I only dream that the smith had it on his anvil, pounding it with his big hammer? But if it was a dream the pain would be gone now.' He groaned, turned over on his stomach and pulled the blanket over his head again.

Turning him over, right side up, Tadhg lifted the woebegone youth to his unsteady feet. 'Breakfast is near ready and we must be on our way to Dublin. Come now, *a chara*, get yourself cleaned up, for the sun will soon be rising.'

Groaning and protesting, Dónal allowed himself to be led to the cow's drinking trough where Tadhg doused him liberally with cold water. Later, after Siobhán served him a good breakfast, Dónal reluctantly agreed that he might survive, although he didn't think it was worth it, the way his poor head was pounding and his stomach was churning.

When the horses were saddled and brought around, Siobhán was waiting to say goodbye. Tadhg leaned from the saddle, put his arm around her slim waist and, lifting her off the ground, placed her on the horse with him.

'Tadhg, *a stór*,' she said in a low tone so that Dónal could not hear, 'I want you to know that I am not the kind of woman who takes up with every wandering *spailpín* who comes to my door. You are the first and the only one since my husband died. It is unlikely there will ever be another.' She looked at him, her eyes pleading. 'It was my loneliness and despair which made me so desperate, and it was the *uisce beatha* which made me so bold. And you were so big, so handsome and so understanding. I feel like a different woman today.'

His eyes were gentle and smiling as he kissed her softly on the lips. 'I know,' he said, 'you seem different now. If I helped to make you happy, I will treasure the night for ever.' He deposited her gently back on the soggy earth.

'*Beannacht Dé leat*,' she responded, her eyes shining with a beauty that transcended the ravages of the pock-marked face.

'The blessing of God on your soul too,' he replied, adding '*Slan leat*, Siobhán *mavourneen, but not slan leat go deo.*'

They set off down the muddy road towards Athlone, the widow waving her kerchief as long as she could see them. Dónal Óg turned to Tadhg, his eyes questioning. 'That was quite a touching farewell,' he said laconically. 'Since you made it such a point to say goodbye, but not goodbye for ever, it is planning you are to see her again some day?'

Tadhg shrugged. 'Only God has that answer, Dónal. She's a poor lonely woman. If it softened the leave-taking, what harm could it do?'

At any other time, Dónal might have pursued the subject, but his thoughts turned to himself. 'Och, my poor head,' he muttered, 'I promise never to touch another drop if it does that to me! Never shall it touch my lips again.'

'Better be careful what you promise,' Tadhg warned him. 'Old Félim of our village made such a promise to the priest in a weak moment. Now he has to pour his whiskey directly down his throat so that none of it will touch his lips. Of course, he can drink it faster that way.'

'I wish I could drink like you,' Dónal said admiringly. 'It didn't affect you at all, did it?'

Tadhg hesitated, and evaded the question by saying, 'I'm so much bigger than you that there's more room for it to soak in.'

They rode in silence, each busy with his own problems. By the time the sun was high in the sky, they had covered the three miles to Ballinalsoe where they crossed the wide stone bridge that separated Galway from Roscommon.

Occasionally they met travellers on the road, some armed, some not. Tadhg greeted them in Irish; if he received a blank or surly response, he tried out his English on them. In this manner they learned of the condition of the roads, the best route to Dublin, places to stop for rest or meals, and even local news and events. Among the native Irish there was a strong current of optimism and hope, largely because of the recruiting by the Catholic lords of men to fight for King James. The few Protestants they encountered showed fear, truculence or indifference, depending upon their assessment of their future.

A few miles beyond Balllinasloe they heard loud and angry voices from a field beside the road, a group of men was trying to hold a struggling figure so that another man with a pistol could bring it to aim. Unwilling to see murder committed while he stood idly by, especially in the light of the uneven odds against the intended victim, Tadhg slapped his horse, which he had named Cúchulainn, smartly and galloped to the spot.

Taking advantage of his surprise onslaught, he burst into the milling throng to wrest the pistol from the hand of the amazed holder. His face aflame with anger and frustration, the man glared up at Tadhg astride his horse, then demanded wrathfully that his weapon be returned. Stocky of build, he wore a blue cloak which revealed a shirt beneath his jerkin. His trouser legs were thrust into calf-high boots, and his style of dress indicated that he was a man of substance, probably a prosperous farmer. The others were dressed in the crude, rough clothes of farm labourers. They were shod with brogues of unseasoned leather.

As Tadhg glared back angrily, the farmer again demanded the return of his gun. 'To kill an unarmed man,' Tadhg asked, resisting the inclination to punch the man in his red face.

'The dirty *sleeveen* needs killing!' Shaking with rage, the stocky man clenched his hands into claws, and turning from Tadhg, rushed at the object of his hate. The latter, evidently anticipating such a move, jerked himself loose from his captors, and with a lithe leap gained sanctuary behind a startled Tadhg. The fellow smote Cúchulainn on the flank, and the big horse bolted through the ring of men, the '*sleeveen*' clinging like a burr to Tadhg's neck.

Tadhg allowed the horse to run until they were some distance down the road. They were followed by Dónal and the angry shouted threats of the disappointed farmer. Stopping at the side of the road, Tadhg turned in the saddle to gaze into a pair of amused green eyes.

'It's happy I am to share your horse with you,' Tadhg commented sardonically.

His rider looked at him with admiration. He bowed his head gravely. 'Thady Moriarty is always happy to be of service to you, O Noble Fionn, esteemed father of Oisín. it isn't often that a poor, mistreated poet, condemed to a fate more melancholy than that of Fionnuala, rides on the wings of the wind with the great Fionn MacCool himself.' Cupping his hands behind his ear, and staring off into the distance, he said, 'Hark, O Noble Fionn, I hear the distant clamour of Bran and Sceolán, your hounds, on the scent of a lordly stag which has lately drunk of the cool, refreshing waters of the Shannon. Let us hasten ere he is away.'

'My ears tell me it is the bellowing of an angry farmer westwards towards Ballinasloe, not a stag eastwards where flows the Shannon,' Tadhg responded. 'Since I apparantly saved you from a violent end, would you please satisfy my curiosity and tell me what it was all about?'

Thady Moriarty coughed gently. 'T'was just a misunder-standing,' he said disparagingly. 'He mistakenly thought I had something of his. The poor man, he has the Devil's own temper!'

'And what was it he thought you had stolen?' Tadhg continued remorselessly.

Thady patted his hands over his clothing, from the ragged remains of a gentleman's linen shirt to his skintight frieze pantaloons, then looking innocently at Tadhg, declared. 'I have nothing, a chara, as you are witness. Myles O'Larkin was mistaken entirely.'

Tadhg playfully pointed the farmer's pistol at Thady. 'Perhaps you have it hidden in your hair,' he suggested.

The poet's eyes brightened. 'Perhaps you are right,' he said eagerly. Again he went through his routine, patting his luxuriant, wavy, dark brown hair, poking his fingers into his ears, and shaking his head vigorously to dislodge anything that might have been hidden there. He shrugged his shoulders in disappointment.

'And what is it that we didn't find?' Tadhg asked.

'The wife of O'Larkin,' Thady replied.

'What?'

Dónal snickered, alternately looking from the outrged Tadhg to the innocent-appearing poet. After his first shocked incredulity, Tadhg reacted angrily. Swinging about in the saddle, he plucked Thady from Cúchulainn's broad back and dropped him roughly to the ground, where he sprawled in the dirt.

'Did you steal that farmer's wife?' Tadhg thundered.

Thady raised his green eyes reprovingly. 'Steal? That's a strong word, a chara. Does the bee steal the nectar from the flower? Does the sun steal the dew from the grass? Does Thady Moriarty steal the wife of O'Larkin?'

The poet's oblique restatement of the question confused Tadhg. He gazed down at the handsome scallywag and frowned. 'Where is O'Larkin's wife?' he asked less belligerently.

Thady shrugged his slender shoulders. 'I certainly don't have her.' His face brightened and he smiled. 'Do you want to search me,' he asked impudently.

Shaking his head in disgust, Tadhg said, 'No, let's not go through that again.'

Gracefully scrambling to his feet, the poet pointed eastward. 'Your two hounds will be sorely disappointed, O Noble Captain, if you come not.' Beating the dust from his clothes, he set off, whistling gaily.

Tadhg glanced at Dónal who was still grinning. He started to say something, then checked himself, slapped Cúchulainn on the rump, and followed the walker down the road.

After some hours of travel, in which Thady kept up with them by trotting briskly at their heels, they stopped a few leagues short of Athlone where they fed on oatcakes and milk provided generously by an old man in a small cottage. Thady thanked their benefactor in several languages, and then pretending to be surprised that the older man spoke only the Irish, eloquently expressed their appreciation of his hospitality in that tongue.

'What languages were those?' Tadhg asked suspiciously, eyeing their ragged companion with interest.

'Greek, Latin, tinker talk.' The green eyes were amused again. 'You never can tell whom you will meet on the road to Parnassus.'

Tadhg was silent. Was Parnassus on the way to Baile Atha Cliath? If so, perhaps they might stop there briefly.

Tell me, O Fionn, where are you bound? And thy servant?' Thady winked at the amused Dónal.

Not quite sure what attitiude to adopt with Thady, who

apparently was some years older than himself, yet whose impudence kept Tadhg off balance, he related the whole story of Cathal and Donough O'Flaherty and their search for Cathal's son. He insisted that Dónal was his friend, not his servant.

In turn Thady informed them that he was born near Cahirconree in the Slieve Mish mountains overlooking Castlemaine Harbour. Distantly related to Cumara FitzGerald, a cousin to the Knight of Kerry, he had recieved a classical education along with the FitzGerald children.

'How can that be?' Tadhg asked. 'Donough Beag was killed for trying to do the same thing in Connemara.'

'*Ná bac le sin!*' Thady exclaimed scornfully. ''Tis little attention we pay to Dublin Castle in West Kerry! We treat our schoolmasters as welcome guests, not as felons. It is a schoolmaster I intended to be before I was forced to travel the far road.'

'What happened?' Dónal asked.

Thady coughed delicately. 'T'was merely that one of *cailiní* was so fond of poetry that she sought my help after school.'

'Like O'Larkin's wife?' Tadhg was sceptical.

The poet sighed. 'Why is it my intentions are always misunderstood? A poet I am, a poet I will always be.'

'How did you become a poet?' Dónal asked, his eyes wide with awe at the unexpected proximity with one so exalted.

Thady stared at Dónal disdainfully, as if the question was an insult. 'I was born a poet,' he replied haughtily. 'Without the gift, one might just as well tend sheep.'

'What gift?' Dónal persisted.

'Why, the gift of words, of course! The true poet loves words like Deirdre loved Naoise; he caresses them like a mother does her babe; he reveres them like the dutiful son does his parents; he moulds them as the sculptor does the clay; he prizes them as the miser does his gold; he creates music with them like the harper does with his harp.'

'Ah, then,' said Dónal pensively, 'I'd better tend sheep.'

Thady was instantly contrite. 'Feel not sad, Dónal. 'Tis God who lavishes his gifts, it is He who makes the swan majestic, the horse swift, the eagle noble, the fox cunning, the ...'

'And the poet garrulous,' Tadhg interrupted. 'If I don't stem this torrent of words we will never get to Dublin.'

'On to Dublin, then,' cried Thady, leaping to his feet.

They continued on the road to Athlone. Although it's garrison was loyal to King James, Siobhán had advised Tadhg to by-pass it since lawless elements among the soldiery wouldn't hesitate to rob them of their horses and weapons.

So, while still a mile from the city, they left the main road at a crossing where stood the remains of an old church as Siobhán had told them. Their new road was little more than a boreen.

They passed several large mansions built of stone, with rich farmlands adjoining, which appeared utterly devoid of life or activity. Tadhg was to learn later that many of these houses had been deserted by their Protestant landlords who had recently fled to England, or North Ulster, where the protestants were in the majority.

As they paused on the banks of the Shannon, Thady pointed towards distant Athlone. 'What do you see there, Dónal?' he asked.

'Towers, walls, a church and a castle.'

'Spoken like a shepard,' Thady said.

'And what is it the born poet sees?' asked Tadhg, sarcastically.

Thady smiled his pleasure at being asked. Then, closing his eyes, he began: 'I see the great dun bull of Cuailgne rushing back to his home in County Louth after he had been stolen by Maeve and Cúchulainn had defeated the hosts of Erin. The Brown Bull has the body of Maeve's white-horned bull, Finn-bhrannach, which he had killed in a furious fight, still impaled on his horns. Thirsty, he stoops to drink, his eyes sparking, smoke eminating from his nostrils. And as he stoops for the life-giving water, one of Maeve's bull's loins drops. And that is what we call it to this day, Ath-Luain, the Ford of the loin.'

Tadhg was so impressed with Thady's vision that he turned to look upstream. But all he saw was what Dónal had seen. 'I had better tend sheep too,' he confessed.

Looking at the Shannon, broad and swollen from the rain, he despaired of fording it, thinking they may have to go to Athlone after all. While they sat on their horses, a young boy approached shyly. His head was uncovered, disclosing an unruly poll of carroty-red hair. He wore a rough shirt of saffron-yellow, with kilt of the same vivid hue. Skinny legs and feet were bare despite the coldness of the day. Tadhg greeted him affably in Irish, and when the boy responded, asked him if they could ford the river safely.

The lad scrutinised them closely, eyes lighting at the sight of their swords and pistols. 'Are you going to fight for King James?' he inquired, an eager look on his freckled countenance.

From his tone, Tadhg deduced that he was an avid adherent of the King. So he nodded his head solemnly, and repeated the question.

Paying no attention to Tadhg's query, the boy smiled happily. 'I'm going to be a soldier and fight King William too,' he said.

'That's good, King James will dance with joy,' said Tadhg, impatiently. 'Now, tell us where the ford is so we can cross the river.'

The boy eyed him cannily. 'If you'll take me across I'll show you the way.'

'But then how will you get back?' asked Dónal Óg.

A scornful glance at Dónal was the only indication that the boy had heard the question. Dónal repeated it.

'I'm not coming back,' the boy replied stubbornly. 'I'm going to be a soldier and fight for King James.' Dónal eyed the boy, from the red hair at the tips of his toes, blue with cold. 'I'm strong, and I can ride a horse.'

Dónal laughed. 'Why, your feet won't reach the stirrups.'

The boy's eyes flashed passionately. 'I don't need stirrups, I just dig my toes into the horse's ribs!'

'That wouldn't be much help if the horse was ticklish. He'd laugh so loud that King Billy would hear him over in England.'

Tadhg was growing impatient. 'Tell me, *mo bhuchaillín rua*,' he said sternly, 'what name is on you, and where do you live?' The boy stared at his toes. Exasperated, Tadhg said, 'I'll box your ears for you if you don't give me a reply,' and glared.

'If I tell you what you want to know, will you take me with you?'

'That all depends,' Tadhg said. He selected a coin from his pocket, holding it up for the boy to see. 'You can have this,' he coaxed, 'if you show us the ford.'

The youth wrinkled his snub nose in disdain. 'I'll get a shilling a day when I'm a soldier.'

'All right, climb aboard,' Tadhg surrendered, reaching down to help the lad on to Cúchulainn broad back. With their guide directing them downstream a short distance, they plunged into the Shannon and crossed over to Westmeath in Leinster. There, wet, cold and hungry, they found a small cabin where they obtained a few farls of oatcake and fresh milk, warming and drying themselves at the fire. Tadhg asked the man of the house if he knew the boy. The farmer, MacAuley, scrutinised the lad carefully, but shook his head.

'I know most of the young lads in this barony of Brawny, but not this one. Has he no tongue in his head to tell you his name?'

'He has a tongue to be sure, and a silver one. That's his trouble. He refuses to tell who he is or where he is from.'

MacAuley glared at the boy from beneath his beetling black eyebrows. 'Just give him a taste of the back of your hand. It will teach him to have respect for his elders.'

The object of the discussion looked up apprehensively, cringing as if to ward off a blow, but relaxed when he caught Tadhg's wink. 'Sure I'll beat him within an inch of his life if he doesn't tell me soon. He's only a skinny scarecrow anyway.'

After they had left the farmhouse, with instructions how to get to Ballymore, the lad was silent for a long time as he rode pillion behind Tadhg. Tadhg said nothing, leaving him to speak when he was ready.

Finally, the lad said in a low voice, 'Tadhg, if I tell you my name, will you take me to Dublin?'

'That all depends,' Tadhg said.

'Depends on what?'

'On your answer.'

'All right. My name is Rory MacAuley ...'

'Don't be lying,' Tadhg interrupted angrily. 'That's the name of the farmer back there. I'm sure you're clever enough to think of a better story than that.'

'No,' the boy answered earnestly, 'you'd think me a lying *sleeveen* If I told you the truth. I nearly choked on my bread back there when I learned we were of the same name.'

'It's easy to see why he was named Rory,' Dónal said, 'with that red hair.'

Tadhg reined his horse, turning in the saddle to look sternly at the boy. 'If you are truly a MacAuley, you may be kin to that farmer. I had better take you back there.'

'Please, Tadhg,' Rory begged, 'don't send me back, for I am no kin of his. My father, may God have mercy on him, is out of the barony of Clanawley, in Fermanagh.'

'Then what are you doing so far from home?'

'We were in a creaght. 'Twas the barony of Costello in Mayo where I was born. A month ago my father died near Athlone, of the bloody flux. My father's brother, Nelis, is a mean man with a greater fondness for the poteen than for a poor nephew with no parents.'

'Where is your mother, then,' Tadhg asked gruffly, feeling compassion for the boy.

'She died when I was born.'

Tadhg turned to Dónal Óg. 'What do you think we should do with him?'

Dónal frowned. 'What is this creaght? Can't he go back there?'

Tadhg shook his finger in admonition. 'Shame on you. Don't you remember Donough Beag telling us? Many families, sometimes in large numbers, all kindred, travel freely about the country, pasturing their cattle where they can. These groups are called creaghts. Because they are never long in one place, they anger the Sassanaigh, since they can't collect rent from them. And Sassanaigh without rent are haddock without water.'

'They have no home? They just wander?'

Tadhg nodded. 'When they stop for pasturing, they build huts of wattles and boughs. If they stay for the winter, they cover their huts with turf. They live entirely on what their cattle provide. And most remarkable, when they leave an area, they often have more cattle than when they arrive, even though it isn't calving season.'

'Helping themselves to other people's cattle shouldn't endear themselves to the farmers,' Dónal said.

'Oh, there are strict laws against the creaghts. Whenever they can, the authorities seize the leaders, confiscate their cattle for unpaid taxes, and scatter the other members. Lots of them then become beggars on the road.'

Dónal frowned. 'I don't think it's right to take their cattle from them, but it isn't right for the creaght people to steal other people's cows either.'

'True. That's one reason why the old custom is dying. But our problem is not what to do about the creaghts, it's what we are going to do with Rory here.'

Dónal felt he had little choice. 'You're so anxious about getting to Dublin, a search for his uncle would only delay us. Poor lad, he has no one.'

'I would gather from your forthright manner,' Tadhg said drily, 'that you don't want to send him back.'

"Twould be cruel.'

'It's settled, then. On to Ballymore!'

They arrived in Ballymore in good time, and the weather remaining clear, they pushed on to Mullingar. Weary and sore, the travellers bedded down for the night in an old building.

CHAPTER III

Cáit O'Reilly

Many a fine demesne bordered their road as they got closer and closer to Dublin the next day. They crossed a swollen stream which a countryman told them was named the Boyne. Here were rich farmlands with thick hedges and neat fences.

At Maynooth they stopped at an inn which nestled in the shadow of a huge ruined castle. While Tadhg entered to purchase some food, Dónal guarded the horses. When Tadhg returned, Thady was nowhere to be seen. Although the poet was entertaining, and a constant source of information, Tadgh was uneasy in his presence, having a vague feeling that the Kerryman was secretly laughing at him despite his outwardly deferential attitude. He hoped that he has seen the last of him.

Yet when the food was consumed, and Thady's portion left untouched, Tadgh told Dónal to go and find the poet. In a few minutes, Dónal returned alone, and beckoning to Tadgh so that Rory couldn't hear, informed him that Thady was up to his tricks again, in the rear of the inn. Entering a gateway through a thick stone wall that was evidently part of the old castle, Tadgh walked towards the stables as Dónal had told him. Hearing the murmur of voices, Tadhg stopped in embarrassment.

'Ah, Thady, is it the truth you're telling me? That I'm the most beautiful girl you've seen in all of County Kildare? Or is it now just a *bhlastóg* you're giving me?'

'May my tongue wither at its roots, *a chailín bán*,' Thady's voice reassured her, 'if it isn't true.'

There was the sound of a slight scuffle, and then the girl's half-hearted protest, 'No, Thady, no! Don't do that!'

Angry at the poet, and disgusted at himself for eavesdropping, Tadhg turned to go. Only then was he aware that he was not alone. A stocky fellow, with dung-spattered boots, dressed in the garb of a labourer, probably the stableman, stood glowering beyond the doorway. He was breathing deeply, his eyes narrowed, his mouth set. As Tadhg stood transfixed, the fellow suddenly siezed a hay fork, and with the bellow of an enraged bull, charged toward the stable entrance.

'Thady.' Tadhg shouted in alarm, 'run for your life!'

Seconds later the slender form of the poet burst through an open doorway at the side of the stable, and with the speed of red deer running before the hounds, bounded through the stable-yard, his long hair streaming, a bottle held firmly in his right hand. A few steps behind was his pursuer, the tines of the fork pointed menacingly at Thady's posterior. In a moment, pursued and pursuer, vanished through the gateway.

Shaking his head in amasement, Tadhg returned to Dónal, who, with a broad grin on his face, pointed down the road. 'He's off to Dublin, so there's no need for this good food to go to waste.' They ate quickly and started the last leg of their journey to Baile Atha Cliath, the great city of Dublin. Traversing the fertile and beautiful plain, they passed through Leixlip, St Catherine's and Palmerstown. Crossing the Liffey at Chapelizod, they could see the high towers of Dublin Castle, a good two miles away.

Eventually they came to the city itself, and with mounting excitement, they rode through the narrow streets, Rory sitting behind Tadhg. Passing into the walled city through St James's Gate, their horses plodded over the rough streets, squeezing past the carts and stands of numerous hucksters, hawking their wares on both sides of the road in strident accents unfamiliar to the visitors from the west. There were purveyors of fish, oysters, cockles, mussels, chickens, rabbits, wilted vegetables, wildfowl, breads, pastries, sods of turf, clothes and a score or more diverse products of farms and shops. Some of the hucksters were jocular, some sullen, and some belligerent as the horsemen jostled their wares as the horses forced their passage through the narrow, crowded streets.

Like countrymen from time immemorial, they gazed at the strange and new sights, and at the buildings, some of which, to their amazement, were three storeys high, and constructed of timber. Frequently the upper storeys projected over the street, and faces and forms could be seen at the windows. All strangers, Tadhg thought sadly, with not a familiar face amongst them.

Their chief danger, they soon learned, came from overhead, for it was the custom to dispose of slops (and worse) by dumping them out of the window into the street below.

It was Dónal's curiosity that saved him from being doused. Fortunately he was gazing upwards when a woman suddenly appeared at the window of the building they were passing. Abruptly emptying her bucket, she belatedly called out the warning 'Gardy loo', the Dublin version of 'Gardez l'eau', and

Dónal's hasty action in moving his horse saved him the embarrassing ignominy of being the target of her carelessness.

Passage was further hindered by the sedan chairs, hackneys for hire and carriages traversing the narrow streets. One haughty flunkey, dressed in blue livery adorned with big brass buttons and gold piping, flicked his whip at Tadhg, it coming within an inch of his face. Tadhg's temper flared, but before he could retaliate in any way, the vehicle rumbled by in a cloud of dust, the richly clad man and woman inside gazing arrogantly at Tadhg as they swept by.

The crowds of people, the bustling activity, the dirty, smelly streets, the shops, the strange cries of the hucksters and the 'sturdy beggars' all assaulted Tadhg's senses which were more attuned to the roar of the waves, the slap of the water against the curragh, the tang of the sea, the howling of the wind, the salt spray in his face and the cries of the seabirds.

Tadhg was intrigued by the signs on the shops, private houses, taverns and inns. These signs ranged from animal heads to objects, and when he noticed one in the form of a curragh, he immediately reined his horse. They were on High Street, and the building where the curragh sign was hung was around the corner on Winetavern Street, towards the Liffey. Handing the reins to Dónal, Tadhg dismounted. Entrance was through a narrow gateway into a small courtyard, at the end of which was a door to a dark and dingy old building. Ducking his head because of the low lintel, Tadhg entered a small pothouse where a half-dozen rough-looking men were seated around tables made of old wine barrels.

All conversation ceased as they turned to stare at Tadhg's big body blocking the doorway as he stood blinking, trying to adjust his eyes to the gloom. Presiding over a crude counter, consisting of wooden planks placed across two barrels, was a man so burly of build that Tadhg suspected that he too was constructed of a barrel hidden under his long, dirty coat. His totally bald pate contrasted sharply with the luxuriant moustache and full beard, liberally sprinkled with grey, that sprouted from a wide, full face.

'*Céad míle fáilte,*' he greeted Tadhg.

'One hundred thousand welcomes to you, also,' Tadhg responded. 'I saw the sign of the curragh outside, and being a fisherman, thought to inquire if you would have any rooms for two men and a boy.'

A man behind him guffawed, others laughed and a smile spread over the broad face of the man behind the counter. 'What's so funny?' Tadhg asked angrily.

'Rooms?' the burly man replied, still smiling. 'There are no rooms to be had at Devil's Hook Charlie's. I provide many services, but not rooms. If you want a keg of Holland's, a puncheon of rum, a pipe of Spanish wine or a cask of brandy, yes.' He waved his right arm, which Tadhg saw had been amputated at the elbow and which ended in an iron hook, at his kegs, puncheons, pipes and casks. 'All these, but rooms, no.'

Embarrassed by his mistake, Tadhg muttered, 'I'm sorry that I bothered you,' backing towards the door, being careful not to turn his back on any of the cut-throats seated at the table.

'Wait,' Devil's Hook Charlie called after him, 'you sound like a Galway man. Are you now?'

'From Inishmór,' Tadhg said, stopping.

'Faith, and I'm from Bunamillen on Inishbofin. And what is a stout lad from Inishmór doing in a faraway place like Dublin?'

'Seeking information of Captain Hugh O'Flaherty to tell him that his father, and his uncle Donough, have been slain by the Galls.'

'O'Flaherty, did you say? My great-grandmother was once married to an O'Flaherty. Or was it Burke? Her name was Grace O'Malley, and it was many the time she gave the back of her hand to the English queen Elizabeth. Aye, and she didn't think too much of the O'Flaherty either. After squeezing him out of his best lands and castles, she discarded him to catch another rich husband.' Charlie's broad, leering wink to Tadhg insinuated that the O'Flaherty (or was it Burke?) must have been a poor, dry stick of a man. 'Like my great-grandmother, I was a sailor too, but not as famous as she was.' He glared balefully at his hook. 'Until I had my arm hacked off by a blasted Moor pirate. But it is a room you want?'

Tadhg, still standing in the doorway, nodded.

'Well then, you just go down Nicholas Street past the Tholsel to the Sign of the Harper. Tell Cáit O'Reilly that Somhairle O'Malley sent you. She'll provide you with a room. That is, if you have the gold to pay for it.'

'God give you all a goodnight,' Tadhg said and departed.

Dónal and Rory were waiting with the horses, and together they rode down Nicholas Street until they came to the wooden-beamed, three-storey building that bore the Sign of the Harper.

Cáit O'Reilly eyed them dubiously. 'Sure, and I don't care if the

Pope himself sent you, let alone Charlie O'Malley. Is it he who will pay me if you run off with money owing? And that boy, where did he get that outlandish costume? How long do you intend to stay? I don't allow any drinking or brawling in my house. And none of those street women, mind. Will you be eating your meals here too? I think' (to Tadhg), 'you're too big for the bed. It's cheaper by the week. You be careful with those guns. I don't want any of my other lodgers shot. You have horses, did you say? There's a good stable right down Nicholas Street. The evening meal will be served at seven of the clock. If you don't have a watch, you can see the time on the Tholsel's tower clock. But can you tell time? There's a well for water in the rear. You have to carry your own. I have too much work to do now without catering to the lodgers. What are your names? Do you go to Mass on Sundays like you should? There's a church nearby. We don't have to sneak off to Mass any more now that many of the Protestants have run away ...'

'Cáit, Cáit,' a man's voice bellowed, 'where in the name of God did you hide my bottle this time? I need a wee nip to tide me over until we eat.'

'To the devil with you and your bottle,' she grumbled, running a hand through a mass of unruly brown hair. "Tis my brother, Daniel,' she exclaimed, her blue eyes flashing. 'He gives me more work that all of the lodgers. That's your room at the head of the stairs.'

Her conversational barrage left Tadhg dazed. He wasn't sure until her concluding sentence that they would get lodging. But her reference to payment caused him to take out the little pouch with the coins taken from Sir John's forces, and give her four shillings. 'We will pay you in advance, woman of the house,' he said courteously. 'This is for our room and meals tonight and tomorrow morning. It's only the Good Lord who knows where we'll be by this time tomorrow.'

Examining each coin carefully before dropping it in a pocket - there were many foreign coins, counterfeit as well as genuine, circulating - she appeared satisfied, scuttling down the hallway. Dónal and Rory followed Tadhg up to the designated room. It was very small, and the air was stale. When Tadhg saw the bed, he knew what Cáit had meant. Either the people in Dublin were small, or the bed had been designed to fit the small room.

'At least it's a place to sleep, and it's out of the cold,' he

136

observed philosophically. 'Now we'd better take the horses to the livery stable.'

Dusk had fallen by the time they started back from the stables. As they returned up Nicholas Street to Cáit's, they were startled to see lighted lanterns hanging from many of the houses, providing illumination for the passers-by.

'Isn't it hospitable of them to be putting up lanterns for us,' Dónal commented happily. The Sign of the Harper was one of those with a lantern. They met Cáit in the hallway. 'Thank you kindly for lighting the candle for us,' Tadhg said.

She stared at him blankly. 'Light a candle for you? Where did you get that foolish idea?'

Tadhg pointed to the lantern outside the door.

Cáit laughed uproariously, her full mouth wide open. 'Did you hear that, Daniel? They think the light is for them.' She laughed again, this time bitterly. 'Don't thank me, lads, thank those *amadán* down at the Tholsel. They're the great ones to be spending other people's money. 'Twas two years ago they passed a law forcing every fifth house to have a light in the wintertime.'

Tadhg grinned. 'Well, thank the Lord Mayor then.'

'The Lord Mayor? Sir Michael Creagh? And would the likes of him be speaking to the likes of me?'

'I'll tell him myself then, when I see him.'

She laughed again, but this time in good humour. 'And while you're at it, invite him to dinner. Tell him to wear that nice gold collar given to the Corporation of Dublin by King Charles. Then I'll set out my best gold dishes, with gold forks and spoons, the latest fashion from London. Tadhg, my lad,' she said witheringly, ' you're not the first big man to stay here, nor the first fool, but you are certainly the biggest fool.'

Taking no offence at her remark, Tadhg asked the question that had been bothering him ever since he had arrived. 'And why is it that there are so few Irishmen in this Dublin? Most of the names on the shops not only lack an O or a Mac, but don't even sound Irish. If you didn't know this was Dublin, you'd be thinking you were in some foreign place.'

Cáit nodded. 'Sure, the town was built by the Danes, conquered by the Norman-English who had French names and spoke only French, was colonised by Englishmen from Bristol, and now we have another wave of Frenchmen, the Huguenots.' She wrinkled her nose disdainfully. 'They're all newcomers. Now my father was an O'Reilly, of the old Irish stock. My mother, however, was a MacCottir, descended from the *FionnGhaill* who settled here from Norway long before BrianBorú clobbered the Norsemen at Clontarf, on the other side of the Liffey. But when you mix O'Reilly blood with that of the MacCottirs who intermarried with the Irish for eight hundred years, there isn't much *FionnGhaill* blood left.'

They dined that night with the other lodgers. Most spoke English, some the Irish, and others, to Tadhg's great surprise and delight, spoke French. They were pleased when he haltingly conversed with them in their own language, politely refraining from laughing at his awkward, somewhat archaic French, delivered with an Irish-Spanish accent. He learned that they were weavers, Huguenots, who had come to Ireland after the Revocation of the Edict of Nantes. It took more explanation to learn what a Huguenot was, and Tadhg was mortified and horrified to learn that he was dining with Dissenters, even though they were nice people!

To Tadhg, non-Catholics were the Enemy; they were the Galls, the oppressors, the government, the Usurpers. He had yet to learn that the 'Palace Catholics' in Ireland, those powerful Norman-English, English and yes, even some Gaelic Irish who had willingly bowed their knee to the English kings, had as heavy a foot on the necks of the poor peasantry as any Protestant tyrant.

Most talkative and friendly of the Huguenots was a short, thickset, brown-haired and brown-eyed native of Navarre, named Jacques Le Berge. Sadness overcame him when he spoke of his former home. But with expressive shrugs of his thick shoulders he dismissed his melancholy, and turning to Tadhg, said. 'If you care to improve your French, M. Tadhg, I would be most happy to give you a good grammar I brought with me from France.'

'I could not accept it, *monsieur*,' Tadhg replied graciously, 'as it must be a treasured book if you brought it with you when you were forced to leave most of your other possessions behind.'

'If the book was of little value, it would be a poor gift, would it not?'

'That is true,' Tadhg acknowledged.

'Then, if you will not accept it as a gift, would you take it as a loan?'

Noting the eager expression on Le Berge's face, Tadhg felt that the Huguenot genuinely wanted him to have the book. It was a good compromise. The Frenchman would reap pleasure from the giving, and Tadhg would reap knowledge in the acceptance. He nodded. 'I will be most happy to borrow it, M. Le Berge.'

The Huguenot beamed with pleasure. 'Now, if you will but wait for a moment, I will return.' In a few minutes he was back with the grammar, which he handed to Tadhg, and a bottle of wine. 'We will drink a toast to our French scholar,' he announced, with this bottle of Jurançon, the supreme wine of France. Just by coincidence, of course, it is grown in the region of Pau.'

He skilfully extracted the cork, which he laid on the table. Tadhg promptly picked it up and put it in his pocket. 'Are you establishing a winery, *monsieur*?' Le Berge inquired politely.

'I'm a fisherman,' Tadhg explained lamely. 'Fishermen can always use corks.'

'When you're through with dinner, Tadhg my lad,' Cáit interrupted, 'would you mind taking some food down to Charlie O'Malley's now that you know the way?'

Tadhg told her he'd be glad to do so. Leaving Dónal and Rory at the lodging house, he walked down the dimly lit street. As he entered the dark courtyard of the Sign of the Curragh, he heard the sounds of a struggle, muffled curses, and a stifled shout for help in English. Moving quickly and silently, he approached a milling knot of several men, two of whom were pummelling a third. Putting Charlie's dinner down, he seized the two pummellers by the scruffs of their necks, lifting them, still struggling and kicking, off the ground. Their victim stood up slowly, straightening his clothes, and peered up at his rescuer.

When one of the two dangling assailants kicked Tadhg in the groin, he reared in pain and anger, and crashed their two heads together. He then dropped them to the ground where they sat, dazedly holding their heads in their hands and moaning.

'What goes on here?' Tadhg asked.

'These thugs were trying to rob me,' the intended victim replied in English. 'You arrived just in time. My God,' he said admiringly, 'you must be a modern Hercules the way you plucked these two up!'

'What do you want to do with them?' Tadhg asked.

'Zounds! Let them go,' the man said contemptuously. 'They got far the worst of it. But come, have a drink with me.'

'Thank you, I will. This is where I was coming anyway.'

Retrieving Charlie's dinner, they moved towards the pothouse. When the door was opened and the light fell on them, Tadhg was astonished to see that his companion wore the uniform of a soldier. He had apparently lost his hat in the fight, and his uniform, of white cloth lined with red, was torn and dirty. His lips were bleeding, and his right cheeks bruised. He surveyed Tadhg cheerfully through his left eye, since the other was swollen and closed. His attempt to grin resembled merely a grimace.

'Well, Hercules, let me introduce myself. I am Sergeant Henry Williamson of the Earl of Antrim's regiment, formerly with the King's Guards. I had to leave there because anything orange makes me bilious.'

'I'm Tadhg O'Cuirc, lately of O'Flaherty's regiment,' said Tadhg, suppressing a smile.

'O'Flaherty's? Never heard of it,' the sergeant said, puzzled.

'It was disbanded when Cathal O'Flaherty, the Earl of Connemara, died,' Tadhg replied, thinking Cathal would be pleased with that, it has such a grand sound!

'Well then, if you're free, I'd like to have a stout lad like you in our regiment. But we can discuss that later. Now it's time for that drink.' He turned to Devil's Hook Charlie, listening behind the counter. 'Two rums, barman.'

While Charlie poured the liquor, Tadhg handed him the food from Cáit 's. 'Here's your dinner,' he said.

Charlie beckoned to Tadhg to come closer. 'What happened to the soldier?' he asked in the Irish.

'Two men tried to rob him. I came along and helped beat them off.'

Charlie looked disgusted. 'Don't tell me you helped an Englishman against two of your own countrymen!'

'They couldn't have been Irishmen,' Tadhg said heatedly, 'if it took two of them to beat one Englishman. And long ago I learned from the priest that stealing is a sin. If those two were friends of yours, Somhairle, you're no credit to Inishbofin!'

Charlie shrugged, moving the rum bottle around on the plank with his hook. 'It could be worse,' he observed, 'the soldier could have gone elsewhere to spend his money.'

The subject under discussion, having tossed down his rum, slid his glass to Charlie for a refill. 'Drink up, and have another, Sergeant O'Cuirc,' he said gaily, honouring Tadhg as Tadhg had honoured Cathal. 'I have been admiring your pistol. Can I examine it?'

Tadhg handed him the weapon. 'Ah, a wheellock!' he exclaimed with admiration. Carefully he examined the barrel - which was inlaid with heavy silver in the form of angels with little lambs - and the lockplates, with a corresponding design. He hefted it, then handing it back to Tadhg, said. 'It's a magnificent gun. Quite heavy, but you're the man to carry it. Is it a family heirloom? It's quite old, but a beautiful piece.'

'It was left to me by a dear, departed friend,' Tadhg answered, enjoying the game, 'Sir John Ferguson of Connemara. I'll never forget that last, long look he gave me when he died.' Then, switching to the Irish, he added, 'May he burn in Hell.'

Both men looked questioningly at Tadhg, Charlie because he understood the words but not the reason, and the sergeant because he understood neither. Tadhg didn't bother to explain.

Several drinks later, as the great bell in Christchurch struck nine, they departed, Tadhg accompanying his new friend to the street to make sure that his recent assailants weren't waiting to make a second attempt. He promised the sergeant he would come to see him at the castle.

Lying in bed, by the light of the flickering candle, while they killed as many fleas as they could find in their clothes, Tadhg related the adventures of the night to Dónal and Rory. Already a hero in their eyes, he added new lustre to his image. Despite the smallness of the bed, they slept soundly, and even the rapacious attentions of the Dublin bed-bugs failed to interfere with their slumbers.

CHAPTER IV

The Denunciation

At breakfast, Tadhg again conversed with Le Berge. '*Bonjour*, M. Tadhg,' the Frenchman greeted him politely, 'and where are you off to today?'

'To the Castle,' Tadhg replied, scrutinising the Huguenot's clothing. A broad-brimmed black hat was perched securely on the thick chestnut hair; his sturdy frame was ensconced in a knee-length coat, of the same material as the hat; the well-muscled legs were thrust into boots which turned down at the knees. Brown moustache and beard set off the cheerful face with its wide mouth and gentle brown eyes.

'You must come down to our workshop and watch us at our weaving,' he said. 'Perhaps we can weave a nice cloth to make new clothes for you, as you seem to be growing out of these.'

Tadhg took no offence at the Frenchman's innocent comment, and thanked him, but declined the offer, saying he didn't intend to stay long in Dublin. 'Perhaps,' he added, 'I can take advantage of your kind offer when I come back to Dublin to return your book. I hope to be more fluent then. So until then, *au revoir*.'

Tadhg had arranged with Cáit to leave Rory with her until he could return. She would feed and take care of him in exchange for his helping in the scullery. She insisted over Tadhg's objections on getting Rory some new Dublin clothing to replace the 'wild Irish' garb he wore. Rory agreed to stay only on Tadhg's solemn promise to arrange for his joining of King James's army.

When they had retrieved the horses, Tadhg inquired of the livery stable owner, Luke Johnson, if he knew where the Lady Margaret FitzGerald lived. Luke scratched his graying poll, saying there was a FitzGerald demesne called Kilbrendan out of the city past Bloody Bridge on the Kilmainham Road. He though there was a young lady named Margaret whose parents had died of the plague in London years before and that she lived with an uncle who was the cousin of Sir Michael Creagh, the Lord Mayor. He told Tadhg that he could easily recognise the estate because of two stone posts supporting two massive iron gates with the FitzGerald emblem - a silvery shield with a red St Andrew's cross.

Tadhg had observed Dónal eyeing him speculatively as he made the inquiry. 'You remember the Lady Margaret,' he offered lamely, 'the lady that we rescued from the wreck? I remembered that she lives in Dublin. It might be interesting to see her house.'

'But we must go to the Castle first,' Dónal said, a mischievous twinkle in his eye. 'You have been telling everyone how important it is that we get in touch with Captain O'Flaherty.'

'There's plenty of time for that,' Tadhg replied irritably, frowning at Dónal. 'It shouldn't take long just to go out there and see where she lives.'

As the words tumbled from his mouth, and he was at last openly committed, he was painfully aware that the underlying reason for his willing acceptance of his mission to Dublin was as much to see the Lady Mairéad as it was to get word to Captain O'Flaherty. He had thought of her frequently since they had parted near Galway the previous year. The memory of her golden beauty clung to him as tightly as a burr to a sheep. He realised that it was because of her that he had failed to respond to Eithne's love for him, and that it had been part of his refusal of Siobhán's offer of marriage and a good farm, an opportunity he would gladly have accepted before the rescue. She was at once an obsession and a challenge; she was the will-o'-the-wisp he would follow forever, always out of reach, always beckoning.

After passing numerous luxurious estates, they came to the stone posts and the Fitzgerald coat-of-arms as the liveryman had described. There they sat their horses, gazing with wonder at the spacious lawns, wooded slopes, and winding yew-lined driveway that meandered to the massive, three-storeyed greystone mansion.

Ah, Tadhg mused, 'tis naught like your own little cabin on Inishmór which would be lost a hundred times in that building and never be missed at all.

While they gaped, the gates were opened, and a carriage, drawn by four white horses, and accompanied by six mounted soldiers, came dashing down the long driveway. As the carriage swept through the gates, it passed within a few feet of Tadhg, whose blue eyes were suddenly staring into the startled green eyes of the Lady Mairéad. It was a repetition of the first time he had seen her - only the scene was different. She turned her head to the man sitting beside her, and apparently said something to him, for almost immediately an order was shouted to the coachman to halt the vehicle. With a furious tugging at the reins, the equipage stopped with a protesting squeal of the wheels and the laboured breathing of the horses.

A surge of happiness swept through Tadhg at her recognition of him, and at her courtesy of having the coach stopped for him. He hadn't expected such a delightful possibility. With his heart pounding joyously, the anticipatory smile on his face was quickly dissipated however when he heard the lady shout peremptorily in English to one of the soldiers. 'Arrest that man! He is wanted for the hanging of Justice Montgomery.'

'Be careful, milady,' replied one of the soldiers who wore a sergeant's chevrons on his uniform, identical to that of Sergeant Williamson, 'he will hear you and flee before I can apprehend him.'

'He is an ignorant peasant who speaks and understands no English,' she exclaimed loudly. 'I demand that you arrest him.'

The sergeant, a tall thin man with a vivid sabre scar across his right cheek, rode up to Tadhg.

'The lady is mistaken,' Tadhg said carefully in English. 'I'm not an ignorant peasant as she says, but a farmer from Westmeath named MacAuley. This,' and he pointed to Dónal, 'is my younger brother Rory, a mute. He can hear but cannot speak. Do you understand the Irish, Sergeant?'

The soldier shook his head.

'Be careful,' Tadhg warned Dónal in Irish. 'Don't talk. Just make signs occasionally with your hands.'

The sergeant glared suspiciously. 'What did you say to him?'

'I remarked that it is too bad you don't speak the Irish. It is so much more expressive than the English.'

The sergeant sat, frowning. 'What is the problem there? Why don't you arrest him?' a man's voice asked querulously from the coach.

'There must be some mistake, sir - and milady,' he said, this man does speak English. He claims he is a farmer from Westmeath.'

'That is preposterous. I would know that face and giant body anywhere,' the lady's voice snapped angrily as she peered out of the carriage window, staring intently at Tadhg. 'And the other one with him,' she said, pointing at Dónal, 'he was also at the hanging. Be careful with that big one, for he is a dangerous man.'

The sergeant stared perplexedly at Tadhg, reluctant to mix with 'the dangerous man'. And so far there was no proof that he was not who he claimed to be. The man obviously spoke English, was well mounted, well dressed, and also carried a pistol, which he might be able to use effectively at such short range. Then there was the positive statement of the Lady FitzGerald. He, a mere sergeant, was in no position to tell her if she was right or wrong.

Apologetically he addressed Tadhg. 'Since there is some doubt as to your identity, I will have to ask you to accompany me to the Castle, where it can be determined either way.'

The soldiers had surrounded Tadhg and Dónal, making escape impossible.

'I will go gladly,' said Tadhg cheerfully, 'I had intended to go there this morning anyway, as I have an important communication for the Lord-Lieutenant.'

The sergeant looked at Tadhg with respect. 'What is your name, sir?' he asked courteously.

'William MacAuley, of Brawny, in Westmeath.'

'I'm sure we can clear up this misunderstanding, sir,' the sergeant apologised. 'The Lady FitzGerald has powerful connections, as has Sir Oliver Trent, and there would be hell to pay if I didn't obey them.'

He walked his horse over to the carriage where he conversed briefly with the occupants. Then, with a flip of the whip by the coachman, the vehicle rolled down the road in a cloud of dust. Tadhg, Dónal and the soldiers followed at a sedate pace. Tadhg chatted amiably with the sergeant, learning that he was a native of Dublin named Wilson, had served in the English army for nearly twenty years, and had participated in many campaigns, including fighting Indians in the American colonies. Although a Protestant, his loyalty was to King James, and he expressed great contempt for the Rebels, as he termed them, who had plotted against their rightful sovereign.

Tadhg questioned him about America, wistfully wishing that he could visit there some day. 'It's a huge country,' Sergeant Wilson enthused, 'with fine land for practically nothing. That is, if one has the gumption to take it from the Indians.'

'Who were those people in the carriage,' Tadhg asked innocently.

'The Lady Mairéad FitzGerald and Sir Oliver Trent. She is a descendant of an old family, while he is the nephew of the former dean of Christchurch who used his uncle's connections and influence so well that from practically a penniless pauper he is now one of the most wealthy and powerful men in Dublin. He is the one who requested the detail of soldiers to accompany the carriage because the Lady FitzGerald is a Protestant, and there is strong feeling among the Catholics here because of what happened to King James in England.'

'Is Sir Oliver Trent a Protestant or a Catholic?'

The sergeant smiled cynically. 'Rumour has it that he is about to convert to Catholicism. With so many of the Protestants having fled to England or Ulster, and with King James on his way here from France to take command of the army, Sir Oliver will do what is best for himself. And that means becoming a Catholic. His dead uncle will probably turn over in his grave.'

'What was he doing in the carriage with the Lady Fitzgerald?' Tadhg persisted.

The Sergeant shrugged his soldiers. 'It is said that he is supposed to marry her soon. But she is a Protestant, and not about to become a Catholic. He is too canny to wed her now. It could hurt his chances with the Viceroy with whom he's on friendly terms.'

'Why doesn't she become a Catholic, too?'

'It's a long and involved story, the FitzGeralds were once one of the two most powerful families in Ireland. The Earls of Kildare were FitzGeralds and the Earls of Ormonde were Butlers, both of Norman-English origin. They were both forever contesting for power. When Henry the Eighth broke with Rome, the Butlers for the most part became members of the new Church of England. the FitzGeralds, however, remained Catholic. When Henry and Cardinal Wolsey plotted to have Garrett FitzGerald, the earl of Kildare, thrown into the Tower of London, and then circulated the rumour that the earl had been beheaded, the earl's son, Silken Thomas, angrily rebelled against the king's authority and government in Ireland. Thomas was quickly defeated, and all the male FitzGeralds were executed.'

The sergeant paused, checked his detail of soldiers, then continue. 'The one surviving FitzGerald, a boy named Garrett like his grandfather, was in fosterage, which was common in Ireland in those days. Henry's agents couldn't locate him as he was passed from one Irish Catholic family to another until he was able to escape to the Continent. After old Henry died, young Garrett was allowed to return to England where he was raised at Queen Elizabeth's court, but had to agree to become a Protestant, and renounce his Catholicism in order to inherit all the family property in Ireland. Apparently property triumphed over Popery. He joined the Church of England, and his descendants followed his example.

146

Lady FitzGerald's father was one of these. So she is a Protestant. If she became a Catholic now, just to save her inheritance, it would make her a hypocrite. I don't know too much about her, but I have heard she is a lady of high principles, who would rather lose her property than do something she didn't believe in.'

When the party arrived at the Castle, they stopped at the sentry's gate near Bermingham Tower. While Tadhg and Dónal waited Sergeant Wilson dismounted, and walking over to the guard post he disappeared within. after a few minutes, he emerged with another sergeant who Tadhg recognised as the man he had saved from the footpads the previous night.

My masquerade as MacAuley of Westmeath has ended quickly he thought resignedly. What will I do now?

'Sir,' Sergeant Wilson said, 'I am turning you over to Sergeant Williamson who is in charge of the guard detail tonight. He can take you to Captain Butler, who is the regimental adjutant, where you can make your identify known.' He mounted his horse, and with his detail of soldiers, trotted down the road.

Sergeant Willaimson placed his hands on his hips, looking at Tadhg questioningly. 'I beg your pardon, MacAuley of Westmeath, but you're the spitting image of a friend of mine,; (Emphasising the word friend) 'named Tadhg O Cuirc of Connemara!' Then he moved close to Tadhg, a worried expression on his red face, asking in a low tone, 'What the devil have you been up to now?'

Knowing that his position was perilous, and sensing that he could trust the sergeant, Tadhg quickly explained the circumstances of the deaths of the two Montgomerys, and how the Lady FitzGerald had been involved.

'That's a scurvy trick she's playing on you,' the sergeant said, scowling. 'You saved her life, and in turn she wants to send you to the hangman on Gallows Green. I knew Young Montgomery when he was stationed in London. He was a rake and a rascal. But he was expert with the sword.' The sergeant gazed at Tadhg with astonished admiration. He shook his head. 'And you're the famous bucko who killed him in a duel! When you saved me from these gutter-thieves last night I never dreamed that you were the bold lad who finally gave John Montgomery his comeuppance.'

He frowned, worry replacing admiration. Soberly he asked, 'But what can we do about this dangerous situation? With the Lady Fitzgerald, a friend of Sir Oliver Trent, testifying against you, I doubt if you could successfully pass as MacAuley of Westmeath.

You'd become gallows-bait for sure!'

Pausing, he put his fists over his eyes for concentration for a minute, then removing them, looked at Tadhg triumphantly. 'Ha!' he exclaimed, grinning broadly, 'there is no reaon why a desperate Rapparee ruffian like you couldn't escape from a stupid sergeant who mistook you for a harmless farmer from westmeath. Especially when I wasn't expecting it, and you slugged me and got away.' He pointed to the bruises and lacerations on his face. 'See what you did to me, you murderin' Irish blackguard?'

Tadhg was both pleased and dismayed at the prospect - please that he might be freed of his predicament and that he had a loyal friend - and dismayed at his incompleted mission and putting his friend in jeopardy. 'But I have to get information about Captain Hugh O'Flaherty,' he pleaded, 'and there's a lad named Rory down at Cáit O'Reilly's I'm responsible for.'

'Tell me about your Captain O'Flaherty,' he declared impatiently, 'and don't worry about the lad, I'll take care of him for you.'

'Captain O'Flaherty has to be informed that his father and his Uncle Donough are both dead, that Sir John Ferguson is slain, and that the Castle and lands are vacated. Then, too, we are suppposed to meet a friend, Conor O'Donnell, at the Brazen Head Inn, when he arrives from Connemara.'

'Where do I find Captain O'Flaherty?'

'He was last heard from near a town called Coventry with Lord Dumbarton's Fusiliers.'

The sergeant's eyes lighted and he smiled. 'Lord Dumbarton escaped to France with quite a few troops loyal to King James. It could well be that your Captain O'Flaherty was amongst them. If he got away, he will probably be returning to Ireland, if he hasn't already, because a large force is being raised in France. King James is due to arrive here any day now, and he'll make a short shrift of King William and his Dutchmen. So don't worry, Tadhg, I'll make enquiries of your Captain O'Flaherty, and get your message to him. Conor too.'

'But what about little Rory? Will you take care of him for me? Tell him I'll see him again as soon as I can.' Tadhg took out the last of his coins, thrusting them into Sergeant Williamson's hands. He unbuckled the pistol he had taken from Sir John Ferguson, handing it to the soldier. 'Here, take this old pistol. You admired it so now it's yours.'

'No,' the sergeant protested, 'you'll need it yourself.'

Tadhg smiled. 'To tell you the truth, I don't even know how to fire it. I have neither powder or balls for it. Please tale it, you're doing so much for me.'

Seargeant Willliamson caressed the weapon. He raised his eyes to Tadhg's. 'Don't you worry, I'll take good care of both Rory and this fine pistol. Now it's time for you to be off. I want you to strike me down, then ride hell-bent for the Kilmainham Road. When you can, turn north, for General Hamilton, with two thousand men, is at Drogheda, preparing to go to Ulster to engage the Rebels. Since both of you are mounted, you should have no trouble in getting assigned to one of the regiments of horse. Now slug me hard so it looks authentic.'

You'll get into trouble,' Tadhg protested. 'I can't take advantage of you this way.'

'Damn it!' the sergeant exploded. 'It's the least I can do for you after saving my life last might. Besides, when I show then the damage to my face, my story won't be doubted. The important thing is for you to get out of here fast before the Lady Fitzgerald gets here to attest against you.'

Reluctantly, Tadhg raised a massive first, striking the soldier in the face as gently as he could. Sergeant Williamson went down as if poleaxed. Whirling, Tadhg and Dónal galloped down the crowded, narrow street, scattering the amazed onlookers who had witnessed the incident. They made their way as best they could out past Bloody Bridge again, past the new workhouse completed the year before, and crossed oever the Liffey at Chapelizod. Here they turned north on the first good road they came to. Apparently there was no pursuit.

Dónal pointed to his mouth, saying wistfully, 'Am I allowed to speak again, or am I still your mute brother, Rory?'

Tadhg grinned. 'Now how can you be Rory MacAuley when the Lady FitzGerlad said that you were at the hanging of the judge? I recall seeing Dónal Óg there, but not Rory MacAuley.'

Dónal rolled his eyes, and put his hands to his throat, stroking it gently. "Och, I thought for a while we were going to dance the hornpipe for sure,. 'Tis lucky you met up with that Sergeant last night, and him being here today to save us. 'Twas God's will, surely!'

'In truth, I too felt the hangman's breath down my back,' Tadhg agreed, 'but here we are with our necks still unstretched looking for General Hamilton and his bold boys.'

'And heading for Ulster, wherever that might be.'

'Apparently you didn't pay enough attention to Donough Beag.' Tadhg admonished Dónal. 'Tis the old *Uladh*, the land of the O'Neills, Maguires, O'Donnells and O'Dohertys. But since the great chiefs Hugh O'Neill and Hugh O'Donnell were forced to flee to Spain a hundred years ago, their lands were confiscated by the Crown to be sold and given to Protestant Scots and English. Would you believe, Dónal, thee are entire parishes where neither Gael nor Catholic is to be found? And now more Protestants are going there from other parts of Ireland, fleeing estates they or their ancestors stole from the Gael. It's a sad fate for Ulster, the territory of the Knights of the Red Branch!'

Dónal glanced over his shoulder to see of there were any signs of pursuit. 'It will me a sad fate for us, too, if we don't get far enough from Dublin and that ill-mannered *cailín* of yours, who is trying to get us hanged.' Then, turning to Tadhg, he asked, 'If you had the chance to do it over again, would you rescue her, or leave her tied to the wreck?'

'Faith, and I don't know. But of you had asked me when she denounced us to the soldiers, I surely would have said, "Let the crabs eat her". Now that we're free, and riding to fight the English, I can't decide either way.' He sighed deeply. 'Ah, Dónal, didn't she resemble an angel from Heaven? With her hair the colour of the sun setting over the Western Sea, her eyes more radiant than the dew on the morn of spring. How could I have left such rare loveliness and beauty to the waves and wind and the nasty crawling creatures of the sea?'

Dónal was startled. 'Is it the same person we're talking about? If it is, indeed, the Lady Mairéad that you described, then surely she must be the *leanbh sí*, the fairy sweetheart, for she has you completely enchanted.'

Tadhg laughed gaily. 'Indeed! Isn't it far better to be under the spell of one so lovely than some ugly stráinseach with a wart on her nose, and hair of dried seaweed?'

Dónal grimaced. 'It's queer, indeed, Tadhg, how poorly Eithne Rua, and the Widow O'Coffey and her snug farm, fare with you, and they so fond. But the Lady Mairéad - who would have you swinging from the highest gallows in Dublin - has you in an immortal fluster!'

'True,' Tadhg agreed contritely, 'but right now we are more

concerned with the way to Drogheda than the way to the galllows. We had better ask directions of that farmer in yonder field.'

The countryman was talkative and most willing to give directions, but the more he explained, the more confused Tadhg became. He did learn, however, that they were on the road to *Sord Cholmcille* called Swords by the Sassanaigh, which in turn was on the road to Drogheda. In exchange for the directions, Tadhg told the farmer the latest news from Dublin, that King James was on his way, and would soon sweep Ireland of the hated English, like Brian Boru had swept away the Danes.

'Glory be to God,' the man exclaimed delightedly, and pointing to an ancient yew tree growing by the roadside, asked of Tadhg, 'Did you know that the great Brian stopped there for a cool drink of water on his way to the Battle of Clontarf. And wasn't it my great-great-grandmother's grandmother, God rest her immortal sould, who gave him the drink with her own hands? She used to tell how the high king's long, white hair and beard waved in the wind as he quaffed his drink. And him dead at the end of the day, stabbed in his tent by a fleeing, cowardly Dane! It was a great victory indeed, for many a Dane died that day. But many a Gael, too. Are you off to be joining the army?'

Tadhg, who thought that the old woman who had given Brian his drink, must have lived to be as old as Methuselah, nodded in agreement, and thanking the good man for his directions, dug his heel's into Cúchulainn's flanks. At Swords they stopped to drink at the cool and refeshing well that gave the hamlet its name. The well was reputed to have been blessed by the famed Columcille himself, of blessed memory, a century after St Patrick.

Praising the water, Tadhg sweet-talked a meal of oatcakes from an old woman they met at the well. She was so ancient, so wrinkled and decrepit, that Tadhg wouldn't have been surprised if she has identified herself as the grandmother who had brought the Ard Rí, the venerable Brian, his drink on the day of the battle.

They crossed the River Delvin at Ballbriggan. Arriving at the outskirts of Drogheda in the late afternoon, tired, dirty and hungry, they were amazed to find the area outside the town walls swarming with people, mostly men. Some wore uniforms and were armed with muskets or pikes, but most were without weapons of any kind, and dressed in their everyday clothes whose variety showed that they represented all areas and classes of Ireland. Groups were huddled around small, turf fires preparing their meals; mounted men, singly and in groups, dashed about at breakneck speed; women and children cavorted in the open.

'My soul to the devil!' Donnel exclaimed. 'Did you ever see such a sight? All the people of Ireland must be out there.'

So impressed was Tadhg with the panorama that he let Dónal's comment go unanswered. The last rays of the setting sun, slanting down the steep hillsides of the town, illuminated brightly the towering spires of St Mary's Church, the tiers of houses and the ancient castle. Down the middle of the valley flowed the muddy waters of the River Boyne.

'Well,' said Tadhg finally, still enthralled by the busy scene before him, 'if we're going to get anything to eat tonight we had better ride into town.'

As they threaded their way through the groups of men, they were eyed curiously by some, and enviously by others, who noted the fine horses they rode. As they approached the town walls, they were hailed in Irish by a tall, slender young man in uniform astride a grey horse. His smiling face was amiable, but his sea green eyes showed shrewd appraisal.

'Would you consider selling that horse?' he addressed Tadhg abruptly. 'It's a noble animal, far superior to this crowbait I am compelled to ride.'

'If I were to sell him, could I get another as good?' Tadhg countered. 'For if I couldn't, *a dhuine uasail*, there wouldn't be much purpose in selling. And 'tis surely I need a good horse more than the gold it would bring if I'm going to fight for King James.'

'I guess that means no,' the stranger said ruefully. 'But you say you want to fight for the King? Have you been recruited as yet for any regiment?'

Tadhg shook his head. 'No, we just arrived from Baile Atha Cliath, looking for General Hamilton's troops.'

'You need look no further. I am Cornet Edmund Butler, of Kilcop, with a company of the Earl of Tyrconnell's Regiment of Horse, assigned to accompany General Hamilton. we can use more stout men because the company is far from filled. Would you like to enlist with us?'

'One is as good as another if there is food to be had,' Tadhg remarked indifferently.

'Our troop can offer more than these new ones composed of untrained levies,' the Cornet replied, making an encircling movement with his right arm to take in the masses of men in the area. 'One of the first things a smart soldier should learn is to be assigned to a headquarters unit, or to one of the high command. Now what could be better than for you to become members of the regiment of the Lord Lieutenant himself, the general of all the army in Ireland?'

'Indeed!' exclaimed Tadhg. 'If that isn't the queerest thing? I was supposed to report to the Lord Lieutenant at Dublin Castle, but instead here I am at Drogheda joining his regiment.'

The Cornet glanced sharply at Tadhg. 'What were you supposed to report to him?'

'To get a message to Captain Hugh O'Flaherty concerning the deaths of his father and uncle.'

'I doubt you could have bben able to see to him personally,' Cornet Butler remarked, smiling at Tadhg's naiveté, 'as he receives only those of highest rank.' He leaned forward, whispering confidentially. 'Besides, he left Dublin several days ago to go to Cork to greet King James on his arrival from France. But enough of this idle chatter, we had better get to the town before the gates are closed for the night.'

With Tadhg and Dónal following, they entered the ancient walled town through St Laurence's Gate. Riding to the northern part of Drogheda, they stopped at the ruins of an old abbey where several score men were preparing their evening meal. All were attired as was the cornet - a uniform of red cloth lined with white - the colours of the regiment. Tadhg and Dónal were turned over to a grizzled old soldier who was introduced by Cornet Butler as Cavanagh the quartermaster, who would see to their needs.

'Take care of your horses first, yourselves second,' Cavanagh informed them bluntly. 'Tether them with the other mounts in yonder stable. When they have been fed, watered and tended to, return here.'

'Horses first and men second,' Dónal grumbled. 'What kind of business is that?'

'The business of running an army,' the quartermaster snapped. 'This is a company of horse, and our effectiveness depends upon the fitness of our mounts. If you don't like the rules go and join a foot regiment.'

Cavanagh's explanation seemed reasonable to Tadhg. He motioned to Dónal and they did what they were told. When they returned from their chores, the quartermaster issued them with their evening ration of salt beef, raw potatoes, ammunition bread and some flat beer.

Tadhg accepted the food with such surprise and disappointment that Cavanagh sharply inquired if there was something wrong.

'Indeed!' said Tadhg, 'it's just that my heart is filled with pity for poor King James, for the cornet assured that this was his best regiment, and if this is the way his best regiment eats, it doesn't say much for the King's food.'

"Tis better than an empty belly,' the quartermaster retorted. 'And 'tis a lot better than that what the levies outside of town are eating.' He eyed Tadhg's great size expertly, and changing the subject, said 'I have no uniform that will fit you. If one has to be made it will probably take as much cloth as for two ordinary-sized men. See me in the morning and I will issue you your gear and weapons.'

Tadhg and Dónal joined a group at a fire where they placed their potatoes among the embers to roast. Most of the men were conversing in Irish, but two were speaking English in accents which indicated they were Englishmen. One of the pair, a runty man, with a rasping voice, grudgingly made way at the fire, snickering to his companion, 'Look Charlie, more bogtrotters expecting to become soldiers.'

The runty one's companion, an older, taller man with sharp, foxy features, whispered nervously, 'Be careful what you say, Bob, that one is a big lad who might decide to make mincemeat out of you.'

'Zounds!' the one called Bob declared contemptuously, 'these savages don't understand a civilised language.'

Tadhg controlled his temper, remembering that it was the second time that day that he was considered an ignorant native who spoke no English. He realised that it was an advantage to understand speakers who thought that he didn't.

When the potatoes were baked sufficently to eat, they consumed their rations avidly. Their great hunger and youthful appetites transformed their rough rations, and even the flat beer tasted like ambrosia. While they sat at the fire, a drummer mounted a hill nearby and sounded tattoo. Their beds that night were straw piled on the floors of rude huts erected within the abbey ruins.

CHAPTER V

The Rebels

As they slept, ghosts flitted silently through the ancient town. Irish saints and kings had worshipped centuries before on the site of the abbey. Even Turgenius, the Dane, whom Donough had told them tried to stifle learning in Ireland, had lived in Drogheda for a period. Here, too, English kings had received the submission of some of the Irish chiefs who had demeaned themselves by bending the knee. And it had been in Drogheda that the infamous statute known as Poyning's Law had been enacted by a servile parliament near the end of the fifteenth century. This law was intended by its framers to make all laws passed by the Irish parliament invalid unless also approved by the King's Privy Council in London.

They were awakened before daybreak by the roll of drums. With oaths in Irish and English, the sleepy men left their warm, dry beds to assemble in the courtyard in the cold musty darkness of the March morning. A muster was made, and Tadhg and Dónal's names, along with those of several other recruits, were added to the rolls. A young lieutenant with a high-pitched voice told them to be ready to break camp shortly after breakfast, as they were heading for Ulster to seek the rebels. A loud hurrah greeted the news, for the veterans among the regiment were tired of the inactivity.

While they were assembling, Cornet Butler sought Tadhg, inquiring if their names had been placed on the muster-rolls. Tadhg assured him they had. Gradually the darkness of the morning was erased, disclosing the outlines of the buildings of the old town perched on the hills which seemed to sprout from the river on both sides.

The Cornet looked about curiously. 'I wonder where our new Viceroy was struck down during Cromwell's time? It might have been at this very spot.'

'I don't understand, *a dhuine uasail*,' Tadhg said.

'Haven't you heard the story?'

Tadhg shook his head.

'It was the year 1649 when this town, under the command of Sir Arthur Ashton and a garrison of more than two thousand men was besieged by Cromwell's army. After several fiercely resisted assaults, the Parliamentarians finally broke through the defences of

155

the town. Cromwell personally issued the order to put Sir Arthur, Colonel Warren, Colonel Wade, Sir Edmund Varney and the two thousand members of the garrison to the sword. And to make sure that none of the soft-hearted would disobey his orders, the 'Protector' expressly forbade that any of the garrison be spared.

'An orgy of killing followed to nightfall. The next day those survivors who had fled to other parts of the town were captured. Then the original order was changed. All the officers were killed by being knocked on the head, every common soldier decapitated, and all the rest shipped off the Barbados as slaves. Then this sanguinary, sanctimonious, hymn-singing monster proclaimed that the punishment was a righteous judgement of God on these 'barbarous wretches'. Can anyone fail to understand why we Irish still passionately hate the very name of Cromwell?'

Tadhg nodded vehemently. 'Just the mention of his name makes the hair bristle on the nape of my neck. May he burn for ever in hell! But what about the viceroy?'

'Oh yes,' the Cornet said, his grim look and angry eyes subsiding, 'I get so carried away when I think of the foul deeds of that blood-stained murderer Cromwell. Well, to get back to my story. One of the young officers at the garrison was a Richard Talbot. He was so badly wounded in the battle that he was left for dead among the fallen. Found by friends some time later, he eventually escaped from the town disguised as a woman. He reached France where he became a member of the staff of the then Duke of York. That duke is now King James. I wonder how Cromwell would react if he knew that one who escaped the sword that day would eventually become Lord-Lieutenant, the viceroy of Ireland, under Charles's second son, a Catholic. Fortunately for King James, when he was forced to flee England last January, that his old friend Dick Talbot was able to hold Ireland for him, giving him a foothold in his campaign to regain his throne.

'Sure, and fate can play strange tricks,' Tadhg said. 'It was but a short time ago that Dónal and I were attending a small school in Iar-Chonnacht. Now we are in Leinster, soldiers of the king.'

They were interrupted by a corporal, riding up to Cornet Butler. 'Sir,' he said, 'the major wishes to see you.' He looked at Tadhg and Dónal with disapproval. 'Where are your weapons?' he asked.

'We haven't been given any,' Tadhg said.

'Follow me, then,' he said, leading them to the quartermaster who was issuing sabres and pistols. Receiving theirs, they fell back into line. The horses and riders grew restive as time passed and no orders came to move out.

'I thought that we were supposed to break camp early,' Tadhg said to a burly corporal beside him.

The other man snorted in derision. 'I can see that you are new to the army,' he said, introducing himself in a strong Cork accent as Michael O'Herlihy. 'When they say early, they mean late. It's when they say move late that we start with a moment's notice. That's the way we spend most of our time - waiting,' he added with heavy sarcasm. 'These officers, from general to Cornet, can't seem to make up their minds. Sometimes I think their actions are based on sheer contrariness.'

A ruddy-faced old sergeant walked past the troop, and when he saw Tadhg's great size, he whistled in amazement. 'How come you're in the horse?' he asked. 'You should be in the pike.'

Tadhg was puzzled. 'Why should I be in the pike?' he asked.

'Because you're so big. Pikemen are the biggest, strongest and best soldiers in the regiment. They're selected for their size. Anyone can ride a horse,' he said contemptuously. 'Just look at yon skinny specimen,' and he pointed to the runty soldier who had sneered at Tadhg the night before. 'It's a shame to waste a grand horse under the likes of him.'

The Englishman swore furiously, reaching for his pistol, but before he could draw it, Tadhg reached over and plucked him from his saddle. While the victim squirmed and kicked, blaspheming loudly, Tadhg dangled him in the air, and before dropping him to the ground, said in English, 'Don't be so quick to draw a weapon on a comrade, and be careful of the Irish savages who don't speak civilised languages.'

All the troopers but the foxy-faced friend guffawed. He dismounted and helped his companion back on his horse, warning him that his quick temper would get him into trouble some day. The smaller man, whose name Tadhg learned was Holmes, glared at Tadhg with obvious malice.

The ruddy-faced sergeant who had initiated the rumpus spoke to Tadhg. 'Thanks for the help. If you change your mind and decide to become a pikeman, just ask for Sergeant Gallagher. If there are no vacancies, I'll just make one by shooting one of the smaller men.'

'I wish I was big like you,' Dónal said wistfully. 'They all want you in their units. You could have your choice, surely, of any place in the army.'

'Not quite,' Tadhg said, 'I'm sure that General Hamilton isn't going to ask me to take his place.'

Apparently the general was secure in his position for the present at least, for that moment the order came to move out. The column travelled in files of two, with the troop of horse at the head. Riding in front, proudly bearing the pennant, was Cornet Butler.

Behind the troop came several companies of musketeers, then the pikemen, followed by fusileers, dragoons, more horse troops, more foot and then more horse at the column's rear. At the rear, also, was the baggage train. The column plodded on steadily to the north, occasionally stopping to rest and water the horses, and to let the struggling foot catch up. For the foot there was little rest, for no sooner were they caught up than the order came to move again. Seeing their plight, Dónal agreed that even though horses had priority over humans in the cavalry, it was preferable to being in the infantry.

As they passed through Dundalk, Mannogh MacCabe, a pleasant-faced, soft-spoken man from the area, proudly informed Tadhg and Dónal that the famous warrior Cúchulainn had his patrimony there many centuries earlier at Murtheimne Plain, and the ford where he defeated his old friend, Ferdia, was at nearby Ardee. Tadhg was exultant. Here I am, he thought, hardly a week gone from Moyrus Parish, riding at the head of King James's army, and right where Cúchulainn practised his miraculous feats of arms.

That night, 8 March 1689, they camped short of Newry. At last they had passed into Ulster, the home of the Red Branch Knights. Tents were issued, for a cold rain had set in and there was no shelter available.

Passing through Newry the following day, they came to the vicinity of Loughbrickland where the column halted. They were now in the County Down. After a lengthy interval, Cornet Butler beckoned to Tadhg and Dónal, and to a young corporal named O'Rooney. Leading them away from the others, he stopped.

'I have been ordered by General Hamilton', he told them, 'to scout the area, for he had learned from some of the inhabitants here that a large force of rebels under Lord Montgomery is in the vicinity. As this is Corporal O'Rooney's home area, he will guide us. I selected you, Tadhg, because just seeing you astride your big horse makes me feel more secure. Or maybe', and he smiled broadly, 'if you're killed I'll be on hand to inherit your magnificent horse. You, Dónal, will come with us, because I understand that Tadhg won't stir without you at his side.'

Tadhg disregarded the Cornet's macabre humour. 'That is true,' he said, 'for it was Dónal Óg who first saw me the day I battled the great storm. We have been through thick and thin since.'

'Good. Friendship is a great asset. Never squander it. Lead out, O'Rooney.'

They travelled north along a narrow road that wound its way along the course of a small stream. Whenever they climbed a hill, they would stop short of the crest, where O'Rooney would dismount, creep to the top, and carefully survey the area below.

After they had gone about three miles, with the corporal repeating this manoeuvre about five times, they came to a hill higher than the others. But this time O'Rooney beckoned to the Cornet to join him. The officer watched for a few minutes, then gestured to Tadhg and Dónal. 'How would you like to see the enemy?' he whispered.

Lying prone, Tadhg peered over the ridge. 'My soul to God!' he exclaimed excitedly, 'the whole rebel army is there!'

Cornet Butler smiled. 'Not quite, Tadhg, but there is a great number of them. From the number of regimental and command flags, I'd guess that there must be nearly eight thousand men. General Montgomery is out in force, and looking for a fight.'

Tadhg shook his head in amazement - the sight of so many armed men in one place was beyond his comprehension. 'I wouldn't have believed it if I hadn't seen it with my own eyes. And I'm not sure but what they might be liars.'

'We'd better get back to General Hamilton,' Cornet Butler said.

They mounted their horses, heading swiftly south to their encampment.

Just a short distance from their own forces, they encountered a group of a half-dozen rebels, a scouting party like their own. It was a toss-up as to who was most surprised, but it was Cornet Butler who recovered his wits the fastest. Drawing his sabre, he charged the enemy, his three companions following. In a moment they were among the foe, their onslaught sending four rebels to the earth. Of the pair remaining horsed, one, an officer, aimed his pistol at the cornet, but Dónal Óg, who was the closest, swung his sabre at the man's head, cleaving it in twain, while the remaining foeman took off as if the devil himself was after him. Tadhg and O'Rooney, who started to pursue, were sharply recalled by Cornet

Butler.

'It's too late,' he shouted, 'you will never catch him now. Besides, there might be more rebels nearby.'

The excitement engendered by their first engagement with their hated enemy obliterated any feeling of remorse or guilt in the killing of fellow men. They were, after all, just Sassanaigh, anti-Gael, anti-Catholic, anti-King.

General Hamilton was pleased with the report. Within minutes the column was moving again, the musketeers with their match lit, all units ready for battle. An hour's march brought them to the vicinity of Cladyfort, near Dromore, where they found the foe drawn up in battle order, waiting for them.

While General Hamilton and his staff held a council of war, Cornet Butler talked with Tadhg. 'Out there,' and he pointed in the direction of Cladyfort, 'are the men who benefited most from King James's grandfather, the first James, and from his brother Charles, yet they were the first to rebel against their lawful sovereign when William of Orange landed in England to seize his uncle's throne.' The cornet's scowl reflected his opinion of the perfidious William. 'You see, Tadhg,' he continued, 'Ulster had remained the most Gaelic of all four provinces of Erin until 1606, under the strong leadership of the O'Neills and the O'Donnells. the hereditary chiefs. Now it is no longer Irish, just another English colony, populated by Protestant Scots and English, and the native Irish are persecuted and driven from their native lands.'

'What happened in 1606, *a dhuine uasail*?'

Cornet Butler sighed deeply and said sadly, 'Over in England, the wily Lord Cecil, the secretary of state, who hated the Catholics and was determined to exterminate them in order to confiscate their property, having exposed two plots against King James the first, including the so-called Gunpowder Plot which was actually instigated by the Puritans, adroitly switched the blame to the Catholics. For these successes, he was rewarded with the Order of the Garter, and the office of High Treasurer. Then, more powerful than ever, he turned his evil talents for intrigue to Erin where he arranged a scheme for false charges of treason against O'Neill and O'Donnell in order to grab their ancestral lands. His instrument was the Baron of Howth, Christopher St Lawrence, who invited Rory O'Donnell, Hugh O'Neill and other leading Catholics to a secret conference where he informed them that the English court planned to eradicate them.'

160

Tadhg was shocked. 'Was this true?' he asked.

'Of course not! It was merely Cecil's ruse. But after the conference at which the Irish chiefs had sworn their loyalty to James, St Lawrence falsely accused them of plotting against the king. Then, tricked into believing that they were about to be arrested on the charges, Rory O'Donnell and Hugh O'Neill took up arms to defend themselves. Cecil then promptly declared them rebels against James, and their estates ordered forfeited to the Crown.'

Frowning, Tadhg asked, 'Why are the Irish always so stupid to believe the English lies?'

'Not stupid, Tadhg, just lacking in guile. Honourable men believe other men to be honourable as well. The English are masters of deceit and cunning plots. It has been the history of Ireland ever since Strongbow to be outmanoeuvred by the Sassanaigh. Cardinal Wolsey used the same technique to trap and destroy the FitzGeralds. Apparently they are avid students of the doctrine of that wily Florentine, Niccolo Machiavelli, early in the century, who openly advocated such stratagems of deceit to gain and retain political power.'

'To the devil with your Machiavelli and Lord Cecil,' Tadhg said, 'what happened to O'Donnell and O'Neill?'

'Their estates were confiscated, and they were forced to flee to the Continent along with leaders of the other Gaelic families. But mark this, Tadhg, not only were their lands of Tyrconnell and Tyrone taken, but six entire counties were appropriated by the Crown in one massive theft. Then Cecil, in the name of the king, divided the stolen properties between several English and Scots Presbyterians. In turn, these undertakers arranged for thousands of dour and grubby lowland Scots, and impecunious adventurers and land-seekers from England to settle on the estates of the Irish. These people, mostly Sectarians, Puritans or Presbyterians, whatever you want to call them, had one common characteristic, a violent hatred of Catholics and the Irish nation.

Tadhg glared at the rebel army. 'And now we will retake Ulster for its rightful owners.'

The Cornet nodded. 'Yes. But it won't be easy. Those are a tough people over there, and they're not about to give up their ill-gotten lands without a fight.'

While Tadhg meditated on the perfidy of mankind, the order was given to attack. Troops of horse, companies of musketeers, with every third man armed with a pike, fusileers, cannoneers, all moved out eagerly and boldly as if the enemy wasn't four times as numerous. Being Tadhg's first exposure to war, he watched in fascination from a hill, where his troop was in reserve, as the figures below, like a multitude of marionettes, clashed in mortal combat. Men on horses charged furiously, muskets fired, cannon roared, sabres flashed, drums rolled, bugles called, horses neighed, officers shouted and men died.

The vigour and force of the King's men's attack, the valour and esprit was such, that after a brief interval, the Rebels took to their heels, abandoning the field to the exultant victors. General Hamilton was well pleased with the manner in which his outnumbered, and largely untrained and untried forces, had fought. After the surgeons had gone out on the field to help the wounded, and the priests to give the last rites to the dying, details were selected to bury the dead and collect the booty abandoned by the fleeing enemy.

Later the whole army was assembled and General Hamilton personally thanked them for their courageous conduct in wresting victory from a numerically superior force. 'We will follow them and drive them into the North Sea,' he told the troops. A loud cheer burst from the throats of the men, and within the hour they resumed their march to the North.

Hoping to catch up with the rebels, General Hamilton pushed his troops to the limit, passing through Belfast, Antrim, Ballymena and Ballymoney. They crossed the river Bann, going on to Coleraine, without catching sight of them. Coleraine had strong defences, and not having sufficient heavy artillery to better the fortifications, General Hamilton returned to Ballymoney where he gave his men and animals a much-needed three-day rest.

Tadhg was thankful that he was mounted. He felt sorry for the foot soldiers who plodded faithfully mile after mile, day after day, in dust and mud, in heat and cold, carrying their muskets or long pikes, their heavy bandoliers rattling and their loaded packs bending their weary backs.

On Good Friday, after Mass, Tadhg's troop was ordered out, along with some other of the horse, on information that a large body of the rebels had been seen a short distance away. A mile or so northeast of Ballymoney, they saw a large force driving a considerable number of cattle they had seized in their effort to get supplies for the proposed siege of Coleraine. With Cornet Butler in the lead, his battleflag streaming in the wind, the troop chased the rebels. Abandoning the cattle, the enemy galloped to Coleraine, the gates opening to admit them, then closing again in the faces of the king's men.

On one of their rest days at Ballymoney, Tadhg and Dónal were attracted by a large gathering of men on a hillside. Most of them wore red uniforms with white linings and a red facing. They were listening avidly to a speaker standing astride a culverin, his back to Tadhg and Dónal. Waving in the brisk breeze was a regimental flag having a white centre. with the bloody hand of Ulster around it, and bearing the motto 'Fight for King and Country'. Declaiming in the Gaelic, the speaker's voice rose and fell in a panegyric of the O'Neills, with numerous references to a noble Gordon O'Neill.

'Why, 'tis poetry,' Dónal exclaimed, 'like the rhyming that Thady O'Moriarty described to us.'

Tadhg, who had been staring at the speaker's back, but listening attentively to the melodious voice, nodded. 'It's poetry not only as Thady described, but poetry as Thady delivers.'

Dónal turned to Tadhg, his eyes wide with surprise. 'You mean?'

'It's none other than our travelling companion we left behind in Dublin. In as much as he is wearing a soldier's uniform, he must have compromised his principles about becoming a soldier.' Tadhg listened with admiration, then said, 'He surely has the gift, as he so modestly informed us.'

When Thady was finished, Tadhg shouldered his way through the crowd, strangely happy at seeing the rascal again. As Thady leapt lightly to the ground, Tadhg embraced him.

'Och, it's Fionn MacCool himself, returned to Ulster to take his place at the side of the O'Neills. But where is your faithful servant?' His amused eyes scanned the crowd, and seeing Dónal, beckoned to him to join them.

'We heard your poem,' Dónal said, his eyes shining. 'It was beautiful. But how did you become a soldier? And whose regiment is this with the red uniform?'

''Tis an involved tale, better told over a drop or two of *uisce beatha*.' Thady led the way to a tent standing near a larger one identified by a colonel's flag, which featured a spear with a red cross *patée*. He quickly produced a bottle of whiskey which he handed to Tadhg to start.

'Remember when I left you to chase the Earl of Clanrickard's coach? Well, 'twasn't Clanrickard at all, but Lord Bellew. And what would a Bellew, more English than King James himself, do with an Irish poet? And, more to the point, what would an Irish poet do with a Lord Bellew? Sing the praises of his puddings? My soul from the devil! But milord's coachman told me that Colonel Gordon O'Neill was lodged nearby. Unfortunately, however, the colonel informed me he couldn't afford the luxury of an *file*, as all his money was being used to raise a regiment.'

Thady paused pensively, taking a long swig from the bottle. 'I reasoned that there were other salmon in the river, and with King James expected soon, many other lords and family chiefs were gathering in Dublin. Each day I sought them out, but invariably it was a stout lad to swing a sabre or fire a musket they were wanting, and not an *file* to perpetuate their brave deeds in verse. And then King James arrived from the south with his retinue. Ah, it was grand! Harpers from all four corners of Ireland filled the air with music, pretty *cailíns* strewed his path with green boughs and fragrant flowers, the very mud puddles were filled with gravel so that his royal personage wouldn't be spattered. Such a bowing and scraping you never did see! I could hardly keep from being ill!'

Tadhg frowned. 'It was but proper reverence for Ireland's king,' he rebuked Thady.

'Ireland's king! The poet grimaced. 'When did Ireland choose him? He was forced on us like all the other insults and indignities that London conceives for us. Ireland's king should be an Irishman, not a Gall! Well, anyway, 'twas a grand spectacle. The viceroy strutted ahead of his sovereign with the sword of state, his fat buttocks bursting out of his tight breeches, while betwixt and between them were the Lord Mayor and all of his simpletons from the town council. A bevy of holy friars from every order in the country held aloft a huge cross, three dozen lovely maidens carried bouquets, a score of coaches trundled along with their lords and ladies, while hundreds of brave soldiers poked and prodded the cheering multitude. But the full of the bag was yet to come! As James approached the Castle gate to go to his new apartments, the pipers and four solemn bishops, each hoping to wear a cardinal's red hat, carried a canopy presenting the Blessed Sacrament. When King James saw the Host before him, he fell on his knees and prayed.

Where Thady's expression was sardonic, Dónal's was beatific. 'King James kneeling in the street, saying his prayers,' he said, 'how I wish we had stayed to see it.'

'Why did you leave so suddenly then?' Thady asked. 'I looked all over Dublin for you.'

'We'll tell you some other time,' Tadhg interjected. 'Continue your tale.'

'We all had our chance to pray soon,' Thady continued. 'A Te Deum was struck in honour of King James, and for the first time since Brian Boru defeated the Danes, all the Dublin churches were bulging with Catholics. The presence of a Catholic king, all the bishops, priests, friars and nuns, must have had the poor Protestants shaking in their boots. And speaking of boots, King James put his in his mouth at the big ball in the Castle. The king owes a great debt to Richard Talbot, his viceroy whom he has just elevated to be the Duke of Tyrconnell, but he insulted the duchess by leading out a younger and more beautiful woman. You can always count on James to do the wrong thing.'

'Your Castle gossip is all very interesting,' Tadhg remarked, 'but what is more fascinating to us is how they forced you into this soldier's uniform! I distinctly remember hearing you say that the life of a soldier was worse than herding sheep. And stranger yet, what come that you, a Munsterman, have become *file* for an Ulster O'Neill?'

'As the belly tightens, the conscience loosens. In order to eat - and drink -' and Thady gazed fondly at the whiskey, 'one must have the means thereto. The longer I stayed in Dublin, the hungrier and thirstier I became. A poet? Who needs a poet? Be on your way, poet! So I returned to Gordon O'Neill who at least had been sympathetic. He still couldn't afford the luxury of an *file*, but he did have money to pay his soldiers. We reached a mutually happy and expedient agreement - I would become a warrior-*file*. I have my own tent, as you can seen, and am part of the colonel's personal retinue. As for his being an Ulsterman, he is descended from the ancient Milesian stock through his father, Sir Félim O'Neill of Caledon. So here I am in Ulster.'

CHAPTER VI

The Vision

While bivouacked at Ballymoney, the troop was used frequently to accompany foraging parties which kept the men and horses in food. Tadhg enjoyed these expeditions, both for the opportunity of seeing the Antrim countryside, now discarding its drab winter mantle, and for the pleasure of associating with Cornet Butler, who was a veritable reservoir of both the history and general information of local areas. The latter, without divulging to Tadhg the source of his information, made it his duty to seek out men in the Royalist army who came from the various districts they passed through, thus adding to his store of military intelligence. As he winnowed for kernels of military value, he accumulated in the process much chaff concerning families, fables, local lore, history, fact and fiction. Eventually, when the military data was no longer of use, it faded from memory, but the extraneous matter was retained.

He had related to Tadhg as they skirted Lough Neagh on the way to Ballymena, the story of the Serpent of the Lough which he had learned that day. It seemed that on that historic day when St Patrick had banished the serpents from Ireland, one of them, who was a little hard of hearing, failed to learn of the saint's edict. When Padraig learned that there was still one serpent left, he became mightily angry, and departed for Lough Neagh in a bit of a temper. Now this serpent was a fearful monster, but somewhat stupid, so the saint used guile to persuade him to crawl back into the lake, promising that he could come back to land 'tomorrow'.

'To this very day,' the Cornet informed Tadhg, 'the serpent comes to the surface of the land at dawn to inquire if this is 'tomorrow'. But the answer is always, 'No, it's not tomorrow, it is today', and so 'tomorrow' never comes. And that,' he concluded with a straight face, 'is the morrow of the story.'

On a foraging trip one day they travelled far into the glens of Antrim. The morning was as bright as the brass money being minted in Dublin; the dew was heavy and each blade of grass was adorned with its own sparkling jewel; waterfalls plunged noisily over precipices; the ridges were covered with ash, hazel and alder; brooks gurgled, and the gently rounded crest of Bean Ó Conghaile benignly surveyed the countryside.

'Och, it's lovely here!' exclaimed Tadhg, drinking in the intoxicating charm of the scene. 'I could dwell here happily for ever.'

'Aye, it's no wonder the MacDonnells decided to stay when they came over from the mountains of Scotland to serve as gallowglasses to the O'Neills and O'Donnells.' He waved his arm in a circle to encompass all the land around them. 'These are the holdings of Alexander MacDonnell, third Earl of Antrim.'

'The man who was ordered by the viceroy to take Derry?' asked Tadhg, who had accumulated a choice kernel or two himself. 'And because his troops were Catholics, the Derrymen closed the town gates in their faces, refusing to surrender?'

The cornet nodded. 'That's the one. His father, who died just a few years ago, is buried hereabouts near the mouth of the River Margey, along with his father, his grandfather who was the first earl, and his great-grandfather, the celebrated Somhairle Buí MacDonnell who was such a terror to the English. I have reason for coming this way today,' the Cornet confided to Tadhg, 'although it may be foolhardy to go so far from the camp, but the chance may never come again.'

'What is it?' Tadhg asked, his interest fired by his companion's fervent manner.

'No questions now,' the Cornet teased. 'The pleasure will be the greater when we get there.'

Leaving lofty Bean Ó Conghaile behind them, they travelled steadily until they came to high, serrated cliffs overlooking the Atlantic. Here they turned to the northeast until they reached a promontory projecting like a gigantic thumb into the cold sea. This was Bermore. They halted.

Cornet Butler sat silent for a long time, his eager eyes sweeping the panorama before him - Rathlin Island, the hazy outline of Scotland better than a score of miles across the North Channel, the restless, frothing sea, the nesting seabirds, the desolate shore, and the dark rocks below resisting the eternal onslaught of the surging sea.

Finally he turned to Tadhg, his eyes bright. 'Look closely,' he said, rapture in his voice, pointing towards distant Scotland, 'and you can see lovely Deirdre, with Naoise, her lover and his faithful brothers, Ainnle and Ardan, the Sons of Uisnaigh, returning to Erin from Scotland for the first time since they fled King Conor. See their mixed expressions, joyful at their return, but disconsolate because they are aware of their tragic fate as preordained in the spell that Deirdre put on Naoise. Note how smoothly their curragh skims over the grey waves as if it, too, is eager to be back in Erin. If you observe closely now, you can see them landing happily on the strand, hugged happily by poor innocent Fergus MacRoy who is ignorant of the dire role chosen for him by Connchobar, and ere that sad day when his laments will sound across Ulster.'

His imagination aflame by the Cornet's fancies, Tadhg peered out on the vast expanse of the sea. Yes, there was the curragh and its occupants, gliding like a gull over the waters, and there was a girl with the golden hair and green irises of Deirdre. But her features were those of Lady Margaret FitzGerald. And who was it at her side, at whom she gazed with love and adulation? His hair was black as the raven's wing, his cheeks of ruddy hue, and his body snow-white. It certainly wasn't the slender brown-haired John Montgomery! Nor was the voice addressing the girl, every syllable a caress, that of the faceless man in the Dublin carriage. Strive as he might, Tadhg was unable to distinguish the features of this Deirdre-Mairéad's companion - they remained indistinct as the distant shores of Scotland.

Then the curragh dissolved slowly into the grey mist creeping in from the sea, and the figures of Deirdre-Mairéad and her black-haired companion faded away as the mood created by Edmund Butler dissipated, disappearing into the distant past from which they had emerged until there was naught left but the circling gulls, the only sound their cries and the beat of the waves on the rocky shore.

CHAPTER VII

The Spy

A few days later, a wave of excitement swept through the camp. The king's eldest son, James FitzJames, the Duke of Berwick, had arrived with several staff officers, and was conferring with General Hamilton. Tadhg, who had never seen a King's son before, was highly excited over the prospect, and sat with Edmund Butler and Dónal on a hillock of earth as close as they were allowed to approach the royal presence.

In reply to a question from Tadhg, the cornet explained that the Duke was not a real prince. 'He's a bastard son of King James by Arabella Churchill,' he said.

Tadhg was properly shocked. 'You mean that a Catholic like King James had a child by a woman other than his wedded wife, the queen? How could he possibly do such a sinful thing?'

Cornet Butler laughed so hard the tears streamed down his cheeks. Digging his knuckles into his eyes to wipe away the tears, he said, 'Tadhg, don't you know that a king can do no wrong? And if he can do no wrong, then obviously everything he does is right. And if everything he does is right, then that makes his bastard son right. As to his mother, there are those who would call her a queen, only they would spell it Q U E A N. And that applies to the king's younger bother, Henry FitzJames, the Lord Grand Prior, as well.'

'Another bastard son?' Tadhg's indignation mounted.

Edmund Butler nodded. 'And three sisters. All by Arabella. You can see by the results that James worked hard at his fun. One thing you can give him credit for, however - he never openly flaunted his mistresses at court, like most monarchs do, including his late brother.'

The Cornet held up his left hand, counting on his fingers. 'Let's see. There was Lady Denham, Goditha Price, the Countess of Southesk, Arabella Churchill, of course, and the Countess of Dorchester, the last of his loves. The countess was a chip off the old block, for her father, Sir Charles Sedley, was one of the most notorious rakes in all London.' He pursed his lips. 'I wonder where she is now that James was forced to flee London,' he mused.

'Maybe King William inherited her along with the crown and the royal jewels,' Dónal Óg suggested.

Edmund Butler shook his head. 'Not King William! The

169

countess is a woman, and it is whispered that he has little interest in women, including his queen, one of King James legitimate daughters. But look, there is the Duke of Berwick, emerging from his tent.'

'Why, he is but a youth!' Tadhg exclaimed unbelievingly as the duke strolled towards them, wearing a burnished cuirass, his long auburn hair to flowed on to his shoulders. He emanated an air of arrogance and elegance as he stood talking to General Hamilton, shaking a long forefinger to emphasis the point he was making. The general nodded deferentially, but not enthusiastically, his heavy brows drawn as he listened.

'Of course, he is but a youth,' Cornet Butler said. 'He's only eighteen. Did you expect him to be an old man?'

'No. But from the fact that he commands two hundred men in the Royal Guard, I thought he would be older. And he is a duke.'

'Titles come with one's birth or royal favour, not necessarily because of age or qualifications. If you aspire to high rank, Tadhg, become a favourite of the king. Look at what Richard Talbot the viceroy has accomplished from the time he was left for dead at Drogheda.'

As the duke, the general and the other members of the party stood and talked, Tadhg heard a familiar voice. He raised his head to listen closer. A sandy-haired officer, with a perpetual smile and a fawning manner, who bowed his head in acquiescence to every statement by the king's son, said to the duke, 'I will make a full report to the Lord-Lieutenant as soon as I return to Dublin, my lord.'

Tadhg frowned. 'Who is that officer who just spoke to the duke?'

'He's a new one to me. When you're around headquarters you find more high-ranking officers than you do privates. Why do you ask?'

'I'm trying to identify that voice, *a dhuine uasail*. I'm sure I heard it before, but can't imagine where because I don't remember ever having seen him before.'

'He probably sounds like someone else you know,' the cornet said indifferently.

'No, *a dhuine uasail*,' Dónal Óg protested. 'If Tadhg says he heard that voice before, then he did surely. Tadhg has the best ears in all Erin. He can remember people's voices, and can identify animal and bird sounds. And not only that, but he can imitate them

170

too. And people.'

Tadhg laughed to cover his embarrassment. 'You can see that Dónal is a loyal friend. But I'm sure I heard him speak before - it bothers me not to be able to identify it.' He cocked his head an angle, listening attentively as the group passed. Then he shrugged. '*Arrah*, maybe I'm mistaken.'

'What do you think they were talking about?' Dónal asked Cornet Butler.

'How to capture Coleraine, I suppose.'

If indeed that was the subject of the conversation, there would be no need for it. That night, Major Robert Nangle, a Meath man of the Earl of Tyrconnell's regiment, came to where the troop was quartered in the ruins of an old monastery supposedly founded by St Comgall hundreds of years before. Major Nangle informed the troop commander, Lieutenant Séamus Murray, of the reported exodus of the Rebels from Coleraine, and ordered him to investigate.

Grumbling over being disturbed at night, the men saddled and rode to the River Bann, where they found that the enemy had destroyed the bridge before departing. They forded the river and spent the night under the walls of the town. When General Hamilton arrived in the morning with the rest of the army, the gates of the old town were opened to him. Repairing the bridge, and placing a garrison in Coleraine under Colonel O'Meara, the general then marched his forces towards Strabane where he planned to cross the river to gain access to Derry which lay on the west bank of the Foyle, to the north.

Tadhg's troop was assigned the responsibility of guarding the baggage train which rode at the rear of the column. When they came within a few miles of Strabane, orders came for them to reconnoitre the area for signs of rebels. Tadhg had been riding next to a talkative middle-aged man by the name of Francis Murphy who had once lived in the area. He knew every cabin, bridge, hill, stream and pass and pointed out every place of interest.

'Over there,' he said, indicating a distant hill, 'is where Fionn MacCool is buried. It's many's the time I've seen his tomb. And in that copse of trees yonder is where Diarmid and Grainne hid from Fionn before he died.'

'Faith,' said Tadhg, 'I've heard the story hundreds of times, but never did I hear that the lovers got this far north.'

The Ulsterman bristled. 'Do you doubt me?'

171

'No,' Tadhg replied in good humour, 'it's just that the way the tale is told on Inishmór is that the wandering lovers never got further north than Sligo. But this grave of Fionn MacCool's,' he asked, diplomatically changing the subject, 'where did you say it is?'

'On Windy Hill yonder. Many of the old rocks have fallen in, and it's covered with moss, but there is a little room to crawl around in the chambers.'

As Dónal Óg was detailed as sentry that evening, Tadhg walked alone down a winding boreen that led to Windy Hill, about a mile distant. The weather was crisp, with a hint of rain. When Tadhg reached on the crest of a hill, he stood a while to enjoy the magnificent view. Down below, far to the south, he could see the minute figures of his troop, and the slender form of Dónal mounted on his horse. As he stood there in contemplation, he noticed a sudden movement among the furze on the lower slope to the north. As he watched, he made out the form of a man, who was trying to remain unseen.

Tadhg dropped to the ground, and noting that the man was apparently heading in his direction, retreated towards the ancient stone cairn where local legend had the great Fionn entombed. As the man's footsteps came closer, Tadhg crawled inside. The air was fetid and heavy with mould. Where the rains had penetrated the enclosure, the ground was damp. But it was not the physical discomforts that bothered Tadhg - it was the fear that he was encroaching on the grave of Fionn MacCool, especially in the light of how vindictive the giant had been to poor Diarmuid and Gráinne! What might he do to a mere fisherman who was now trampling on his grave?

As the anguished Tadhg huddled in his damp, confined quarters, apprehensive over angering Fionn, he heard the stranger stop at the entrance where he fumbled with some small rocks. Not knowing what to make of the bizarre situation, but not wishing to annoy the ghosts any more than was necessary, he crawled to the exit. As there was no sign of the recent visitor, Tadhg wriggled through the cairn's opening. He could see the man departing down the slopes of the hill towards the north where the road led to Dunnamanogh. As Tadhg stood, wondering at the strange incident, he saw a small white object protruding from the stones at the entrance.

Stooping to retrieve it, Tadhg found several folded sheets of white foolscap. Smoothing out the folds, he started to read. Addressed to no one, there was no signature, simply the statement, after the date 21 April, 1689: 'Thanks to God this day for our Good Fortune through the blessings of St Paul, St William, St Laurence, St Cornelius, St Venantius and St Luke.' Then followed six long columns of two-digit numbers. The longer Tadhg stared at the mysterious message, the more bewildered he became.

The stranger had disappeared behind the rolling hills. The manner in which the message had been firmly tucked behind the rocks suggested that it had been deliberately left there, not lost.

'My soul to God!' Tadhg muttered aloud. 'I'd better get this information to Cornet Butler as fast as I can.'

He scrambled down the hill, running where he could. As he reached the base of the hill, he passed the sandy-haired major who had been talking to General Hamilton and the Duke of Berwick the day before. He appeared startled as Tadhg, a gigantic apparition, booted past in the gathering dusk, the mysterious papers clutched firmly in his hand.

Cornet Butler was conversing with Major Nangle when Tadhg arrived at the enclosure. 'Pardon me, *a dhuine uasail*,' Tadhg panted, 'but I have something here that is very odd, and might be of some importance.'

The Cornet took the papers from Tadhg, glancing at him curiously. When he had examined the missive, consternation showed on his lean face. Without a word, he handed the papers to Major Nangle, who scanned them hurriedly. 'Where did you get these?' he asked sharply.

'On Windy Hill,' he replied, pointing. He then related the story of how he had gone to visit Fionn MacCool's grave, and how he had observed the mysterious stranger, and the subsequent finding of the foolscap.

Major Nangle's usually cheerful face was grim. With controlled excitement, he declared, 'This information will have to be transmitted to General Hamilton at once. You -' he pointed a finger at Tadhg - 'will come with me.' Quickly mounting their horses, they galloped full speed to Strabane, where after some delay they were admitted to General Hamilton's quarters in a spacious house. On being informed of the circumstances of the finding of the coded message, General Hamilton examined it thoroughly, then sent for the Duke of Berwick.

The duke, accompanied by an aid, flushed of face and smelling of wine, was unhappy at being summoned by a mere general. 'What is it?' he inquired petulantly, 'you're interrupting our game of *l'hombre*.'

Hiding his annoyance, Hamilton said suavely, 'I must apologise, Your Grace, but I have received some coded information which might be of great significance.'

Snatching the proffered papers from the general, the duke's hauteur changed to amazement as he examined the sheets. 'Where did these come from?' he asked excitedly.

General Hamilton gestured towards Tadhg. 'This soldier, of the Earl of Tyrconnell's regiment, obtained them under peculiar circumstances.'

Disdaining to speak to a common soldier, the duke addressed the general. 'Peculiar circumstances? What do you mean?'

General Hamilton, patiently and painstakingly. repeated the story as told to him.

His eyes agleam with excitement, the duke told Hamilton, 'This will have to be turned over to someone familiar with codes and ciphers. Do we have anybody with us who is proficient with these?'

'I will send messengers to all units to inquire, Your Grace.'

'Excellent,' the duke said. 'This material looks like it might be similar to the cipher system my uncle Charles used while still in exile in France. It uses numbers, not words as did my late but not lamented cousin, the Duke of Monmouth, and his traitorous ally, the Duke of Argyle, in their rebellion.' The duke smiled thinly, but his eyes showed triumphant malice. 'We solved their code easily. When foolish Monmouth landed in England, and Argyle in Scotland, they were given a totally unexpected welcome that led them to the executioner's axe.' He tapped the papers with his finger, adding, 'This might be equally of value.'

'Yes, Your Grace,' Hamilton agreed. 'But I'm also concerned about finding the person for whom this message was intended. We must have a spy in our ranks. It would appear that the stranger who brought the message to the cairn knew that it would be picked up. We can safely assume that some arrangements had been made for the spy to contact the man at the cairn, or at least to pick up the message there.'

The duke bristled at the thought of a spy in the Royalists' ranks. He became incensed, his face contorted with fury. He clenched his fists angrily. 'I will personally put the hangman's noose around his neck for this perfidious act against His Majesty the King. Oh, my poor father! He is surrounded by traitors! Supposedly trusted friends, his own daughters, his sons-in-law, men in his army all betray him. My God, who can he trust?'

General Hamilton sat with his chin in his hands, the question unanswered. Finally he spoke. 'The spy could be any of the thousands of men in our army,' he mused. 'Yet there aren't too many who could have been, or should have been, in that vicinity. We can narrow our possibilities in the morning when I check the units camped there.'

The duke nodded, then departed with his aide to continue their game of cards. Major Nangle and Tadhg also left. While they walked to their horses, Tadhg mentioned seeing the sandy-haired major near the base of the hill.

Major Nangle was annoyed. 'What sandy-haired major?' he snapped. 'There must be at least a score of sandy-haired majors in the king's army.'

'I Don't know his name, *a dhuine uasail*,' Tadhg said deferentially. 'He is one of the men who arrived yesterday with the Duke of Berwick. I heard him tell General Hamilton he would report to the Lord-Lieutenant when he returned to Dublin.'

'Oh,' said the major, his voice betraying his disappointment. 'That was Major Trent. You're barking up the wrong tree. It couldn't have been him. Are you sure it was a major, not another rank?'

'It was getting dark,' Tadhg acknowledged, 'and I am not too familiar with the insignia of the various ranks among the officers. I don't want to appear stubborn, *a dhuine uasail*, but I think it was the sandy-haired *taoiseach*. I had a good look at him as we passed.'

Major Nangle turned anxiously to Tadhg. 'You must be careful what you say! Major Trent is a close friend of the Lord-Lieutenant. Unless you are sure and have definite proof, you place yourself in the greatest personal danger if you persist in saying that it was Major Trent you saw. Trent is an Englishman, and these English and Scots lords in the king's retinue despise and distrust us Irish. They stay very close to each other. Say no more about it. I will make discreet inquiries through certain avenues available to me.'

'I will follow your advice, *a dhuine uasail*,' Tadhg said soberly.

Dónal Óg, who was awake and waiting for Tadhg's return, eagerly greeted him. 'Arragh, the troop's all agog about your sudden departure with the major. Some say you are to receive a commendation for something, while others claim you are to be court-martialled as a spy in the morning.'

Tadhg snorted angrily. 'I'll wager a day's pay that the latter view was expressed by that runty little Sassanach Holmes.'

'You're right there,' Dónal admitted. 'But which of the two is it?'

'Does it have to be one or their other? Actually, Dónal, it is neither.' Tadhg told him the story, omitting only the reference to the sandy-haired major.

'Imagine that,' Dónal marvelled, 'a spy right here in our own ranks.'

'What's so surprising about that, *a chara*? This is a large army. Don't forget we had our own traitor Nugent in Cathal's little band of Rapparees. It seems that the world is full of dishonourable men.'

The following morning the drums beat early, and after a hasty breakfast, the troop rode into Strabane. After a brief halt, they were joined by several other units of horse and dispatched towards Clady, a small cluster of cottages set on the grassy slopes of the River Finn, about five miles southwest of Strabane. A large contingent of rebels was reported entrenched there. A messenger was dispatched immediately to General Hamilton with the information.

As the Loyalists descended from the hills to where the river flowed at Cladybridge, they saw a large force of the Williamites hastily building fortifications on the high ground opposite. Cornet Butler, with a detail of troopers including Tadhg and Dónal, cautiously approached the stone-arched bridge over the river. A sporadic hail of musketballs greeted them. They found that the enemy had destroyed the first arch of the bridge, but apparently the untimely arrival of the king's men had prevented the enemy's complete destruction of the bridge.

This intelligence being imparted to General Hamilton, who had hastily arrived at the scene, five companies of musket and one of engineers were ordered to the bridge area. The musketeers were instructed to keep a steady fire on the enemy to keep them from harassing the engineers who were to attempt to repair the damaged span.

The foe responded with their mortars from the Donegal side of the river. Their hasty, inaccurate fire failed to hamper the engineers, but did inflict some casualties among the musketeers.

When rough planks replacing the destroyed sections had been installed, the engineers were withdrawn. Then the foot regiments, which were massed in the hills, were given the order to advance. While the infantry marched in waves towards the bridge, the horse regiments were ordered to ford the river in full view of the enemy.

With General Hamilton and the two French generals, Fusighan and Maumont leading, the cavalry plunged bravely into the river. Like most of the new levies, Tadhg had never faced concentrated cannon and mortar fire before. He felt peculiarly frustrated and angry at a distant enemy he couldn't come personally to grips with. Murderous shells from the mortars burst indiscriminately among the swimming horses and riders, while cannonballs moaned their song of death overhead.

Tadhg's growing frustration at the distant enemy gave way to a nauseous uneasiness, which was in turn succeeded by an immense and uncontrollable fear. Wildly he looked about, wanting to turn and bolt to escape the deadly hail of metal, but he was pushed forward by the relentless waves of men and horses behind him. His hands and legs shook as if with fever, and to his shame and disgust, his breakfast arose unbidden to splash on Cuchulainn's broad back.

When he saw Major Nangle's horse, directly ahead of him, struck by a fragment of a mortar shell, and the major quickly snatched away by the current, war for the first time had a personal meaning for him. O gentle Jesus, he prayed fervently, spare my life. I don't want to die!

Although the crossing of the river took but a few minutes, it seemed interminable. Bent low in the saddle over his horse, his teeth chattering audibly, he was suddenly aware that his bowels were out of control. Humiliated and filled with self-loathing, he realised that Cuchulainn was scrambling up on shore, and that he, Tadhg, had miraculously crossed the river unscathed. Exultant that God had saved him, he followed his companions up the hill, sabre ready.

Despite the superior number of the Williamites, the advantage of the hill, and their protective fortifications, the enemy was so demoralised by the intrepid and resolute charge of the Loyalists that they abandoned their positions before the advancing horse and fled. Their companions on the adjoining slope also took to their heels, pursued by the victorious forces of King James.

Tadhg, Dónal and Corporal O'Rooney, riding close to Cornet Butler, were in the forefront as the Loyalists chased the disorganised, fleeting rebels. With the enemy close at hand,

Tadhg's restored confidence in himself caused him to ride berserk among the Williamites, using his great height and strength to use his sabre with devastating effect. Each victim represented to Tadhg a victory over a hated Sassanach who had oppressed his country. The irony of the situation did not occur to him: most of the victims of his avenging sword were descendants of those Scots and English brought into Ulster by his revered King James own grandfather to occupy the stolen land of the native Irish!

As the pursuing Royalists approached Raphoe, Cornet Butler halted his troop, and stopping in a pass, ordered the men to dismount and rest the horses. Tadhg looked for Dónal Óg. Not finding him, he asked for permission to go and search. He climbed to the crest of the hill, looking back in the direction of Cladybridge. Discerning a pair of riders in the distance, he descended the opposite side of the hill to learn if one of them was Dónal Waiting at the edge of a small wood, he discovered that the two riders were the Englishman Holmes and his inveterate companion Wilkinson.

Holmes reined his mount to a halt, looking insolently at the waiting Tadhg. 'See who has lost his horse,' he declared, his broad Midlands accent dripping with contempt. 'He doesn't act so big now he's afoot.' Leisurely he drew his pistol, inserted a ball in the barrel, deftly fixed the powder in the pan, cocked the weapon and pointed it at Tadhg.

Thinking that the man was joking, Tadhg stood silent. He had no desire to carry on a feud with him.

His lips curled in half-smile, half-sneer, Holmes commented casually, 'One more corpse stretched on the battlefield won't make much difference. But this big one will take more work to bury than the others.'

Wilkinson was aghast. He looked at his friend, his eyes incredulous. 'You don't actually intend to shoot him, do you? Don't be a blasted fool, Bob, he isn't one of the enemy.'

'He's an enemy of mine,' Holmes flared. 'Because he's bigger, he roughed me up and humiliated me in front of the men last week. Now the shoe is on the other foot. With this gun I'm the big man, not he.'

Seeing the hatred in the Englishman's curiously flecked green eyes, and suddenly realising that he was in earnest, Tadhg moved with catlike agility, slapping Holmes's horse sharply on the flank and then throwing himself flat on the ground. The sharp report of the pistol coincided with the reaction of the startled horse as it bolted, and the pistolball buried itself harmlessly in the earth near Tadhg's head.

As Wilkinson gaped, Tadhg rose, yanked him from the saddle and set off in pursuit of the would-be assassin. The tired beast, burdened with Tadhg's weight, tried its valiant best, but Holmes speedily outdistanced his pursuer, vanishing in the direction of Raphoe as the rebels had before him.

Realising that it was dangerous to go too far, since there was no way of knowing where the rebels had halted, Tadhg turned back, disappointed at his failure to catch Holmes. Returning to the pass, he related his story to Cornet Butler, corroborated in every detail by Wilkinson, who was obviously stunned by his companion's violent act.

'When he comes back,' the cornet said grimly, 'he'll be placed under arrest for court-martial.'

'If he comes back,' Tadhg corrected. 'I think the rebels have just gained a new recruit.'

'Don't you think the rebels will kill him?' asked Dónal Óg, who had rejoined the troop while Tadhg was chasing Holmes.

'No, he's a veteran soldier and is wily enough to save his own skin. He'll invent a good story to convince the rebels.'

The rest of the army having caught up and entered Raphoe, the troop joined them. Practically every man had acquired booty of some sort from the fallen enemy. Tadhg had obtained a brace of matching pistols taken from a dead officer. The barrels and lockplates were decorated with intricate silver inlay, and the trigger guards damascened with silver. Their stocks were made from a fine mahogany with conventional scroll design panels. Dónal had procured a beautiful saddle of finest leather and workmanship, and a sword with exquisite hilt, pommel and cuillons.

Although the Royalists had suffered few casualties in the rout of the rebels, one of those few had been Major Nangle, who had drowned in the river crossing. His death left Tadhg in something of a dilemma: should he now tell someone else of the incident with the sandy-haired officer, or should he remain silent as Major Nangle had advised?

CHAPTER VIII

Stupid James

Raphoe was well stocked with provisions, so General Hamilton decided to billet there until a decision could be made on what to do about Derry, where many of the fugitives from the rout at Clady had fled. Others had gone to Enniskillen, and these two towns were now the only ones in Ireland in the hands of the rebels. Major-General Dundee, who had commanded the Williamite Army, had surrendered to General Hamilton at Culmore, near Derry, and had sailed for England.

While they were at Raphoe, a delegation representing Governor Lundy came from Derry to seek terms from General Hamilton for the surrender of that well-fortified city with its strong garrison of more than six thousand men. With the capitulation of Derry, Enniskillen would soon fall, this ending the Williamite rebellion in Ireland. All was propitious for the future of King James!

General Hamilton, a shrewd man, aware that he had no cannon capable of affecting a successful breach in the strong walls of the town, and knowing Derry's great strategic value, offered the enemy generous terms on condition that they would surrender the town at noon the following day. These terms were then agreed upon, whereby the garrison and the inhabitants of the city would be spared their lives with no recrimination, they would retain all their property, and would be promised the protection of King James's government in Ireland. General Hamilton, in turn, promised that his troops would remain at Raphoe until the garrison had marched out. The key to Ulster would fall like a ripe plum the following noon.

Information of the successful negotiations swept through the camp. Immediately the king's soldiers began to celebrate. In a short campaign, the Loyalist forces had swept from Drogheda to Derry, scoring two major victories, and General Hamilton's promise to drive the rebels into the sea would soon be fulfilled!

True, Enniskillen still remained in the hands of the Rebels, but it would be untenable once Derry surrendered. Tadhg and Dónal, having obtained some Spanish wine, entertained some of their select comrades that night. Gone was Tadhg's abject fear and humiliation at Cladybridge. War was exciting! War was rewarding! War was fun! So, *slainte* and *slainte* and *slainte* again!

Come, best of comrades, let's drink to war!

As Tadhg tumbled into his rough bed, warmed with the wine, exhilarated and optimistic for the future, joyous with the news that King James himself would soon arrive to take command of his victorious Irish army, little did he dream that one small event, initiated by stupid James, would radically change the whole course of his life, the future of Ireland, and the history of Europe.

General Hamilton, too, slept well. His campaign to crush the Rebels had been successful beyond his wildest hopes. He had lost but a handful of men in the long march and the skirmishes. Although outnumbered by the Williamites by two to one, and inadequately equipped for a long siege, the last of two rebel strongholds was about to fall without a shot being fired. What more could a grateful king ask?

Yes, what more could a grateful king ask?

But the king in question, a king without a kingdom, James II, was not in a grateful mood. At that moment he was ensconced in Mongavlin Castle between Raphoe and Derry, built by another Stuart, one Sir John, some seventy years previously.

James had arrived in Ireland at Kinsale on 14 March with a French fleet, French officers and troops, provisions and weapons of war. Journeying to Cork, he there met with his Lord-Lieutenant and viceroy, the Earl of Tyrconnell. In grateful recognition of Tyrconnell's successfully holding Ireland, the only one of his previous four kingdoms, for him, he promptly elevated the former fugitive to be Duke of Tyrconnell. In this, his first official act in Erin, he angered many of the Gaelic Irish who regarded Richard Talbot as a pompous opportunist.

With James on his arrival were the Count D'Avaux, ambassador from Louis XIV; General Boisseleau; James FitzJames, the Duke of Berwick; William Herbert, the Duke of Powys; Thomas Cartwright, the Protestant bishop of Chester in England; John Drummond, the Earl of Melfort; Henry FitzJames, the Lord Grand Prior; and lesser French, English, Irish and Scots lords, knights and gentlemen.

There was good news and bad news, but mostly good, the new duke reported to his sovereign. The bad news was that the Irish had practically no artillery except for a few small pieces while the Protestants had plenty; also, the Catholics had few arms; and, most of the officers and non-commissioned officers of James's former army in Ireland had fled to England to support William; he had no money to pay the new army or to buy supplies; the Irish lords were trying to raise regiments but they, too, had little cash to pay the soldiers; the Williamites controlled the north, with the exception of loyal garrisons at Carrickfergus in Antrim and Charlemont in Armagh.

But of good news he had an abundance: here in Munster, the rebels had been forced to give up the castles at Bandon and Castlemartyr which they had seized; General MacCarthy and his troops were in complete control of the entire province; Colonel Padraig Sarsfield had driven the Williamites out of Connaught, and several hundred Protestants were jailed in Galway; Leinster was now entirely free of rebels; he had dispatched Lieutenant-General Hamilton with 2000 men to Ulster; the Irish lords were busy recruiting men for the new regiments; he had issued some 20,000 weapons to the troops. It seemed that Catholic Ireland was supporting James completely.

Journeying to Dublin, James made a triumphal entry, the rest of his party, with the exceptions of General De Rosen and Tyrconnell's arch foe, the Earl of Melfort, hastening north to join General Hamilton. James spent some time in the capital, then he too headed for Ulster. While General Hamilton was conferring with the emissaries from Derry, James had marched through Strabane to St Johnstown where he was invited to use Mongavlin Castle, and word of his arrival was sent to General Hamilton.

In the morning General Hamilton, the FitzJames brothers, Lord Galmoy and others left for the castle at St Johnstown, accompanied by several companies of soldiers, including the one to which Tadhg and Dónal belonged. The general was happy with the report he was going to give his sovereign on the plans to surrender Derry, the FitzJames boys were happy that they were to be reunited with their father, and the soldiers were happy at their selection to call upon King James.

But alas for expectations!

The king was in a vile temper. His apartment at the castle had been draughty, damp and cold; friendly but hungry Irish fleas had supped on his royal blood as he lay in his feather-bed; his dinner of the previous evening had not set too well, distending his belly with gas and causing him much discomfort.

Until James's arrival at Mongavlin Castle, all had been propitious for the campaign in Ireland and the king's attempt to regain his throne. But James had not been called 'Squire James' without reason. Despite his success in reorganising the English navy under Charles II, laying the basis for its future as mistress of the seas, he was not held in high respect for his abilities or intelligence. His work with the navy was the high point in his career; perhaps it would be his only fitting monument.

James had been but a youth when forced to flee England the first time because of the arrest and subsequent execution of his father. The action of the Parliamentarians embittered him; if he ever had any doubt as to the absolute authority of the monarchy, it was obliterated by the fall of the executioner's axe on his royal parent.

After the restoration, when Charles II, who knew the need and art of compromise, occupied the throne until he died a natural death, James was so adamant in his beliefs that he was forced to resign the Admiralty where he had accomplished the reorganisation of the navy because he refused to sign the Test Act passed by Parliament requiring all members of the government to attend Anglican communion as a condition for holding office. Despite the earnest entreaties of Charles, who outwardly embraced the Anglican religion, but whose sympathy with Catholicism was so great that he received the last rites of the Catholic Church on his deathbed, James was obstinate, refusing to compromise in any fashion.

When Charles died in February of 1685, after reigning 24 years, James succeeded him to the throne despite the open hostility of many Protestant leaders. In general, most of his subjects were content with the selection, many of the biggest cities and towns celebrating the event with dancing, drinking and fireworks.

Tactfully suggesting to James that he should be judicious in his actions, not to go too far or too fast, Don Pedro Ronquillo, the ambassador to St James from the King of Spain, was told bluntly, 'Senor Ronquillo, I will either win all, or lose all.' Several years later, when James had 'lost all', Ronquillo was on hand to warmly greet William of Orange when he occupied James's throne.

Having none of the resilience of his brother Charles, firmly believing in the absolute power of the king of England, and lacking the ability to foresee the results of his frequently misguided and arrogant actions, James's course was irrevocably destined for disaster. Typical of him, on his visit to Dungalbin Castle, was that decision, arbitrarily and petulantly made, based on the advice of enthusiastic but ill-informed advisers, which was to lead to the defeat of his cause in Ireland, the eventual subjugation of the Irish nation, and the reshaping of the destinies of the countries of Europe.

James had another failing: an inability to distinguish between good and bad advice, and almost invariably favoured the latter. There were those among his retinue that morning who convinced him that his mere appearance at the walls of Derry would make the garrison and inhabitants open wide the gates, for wasn't he their king?

The fact that these were Protestants and Dissenters of the same breed and brood that had brought about his downfall in England made no impression on him. The fact that negotiations had already been made for surrender on the condition that the Loyalists were to stay away from Derry meant nothing to him. He, the king, alone would decide.

And so he lost no time in informing the discomfited and disappointed Hamilton that he was unhappy with the generous terms offered to the rebels, that he was countermanding them, and that he himself would immediately march on the town, demanding its surrender!

In vain did Hamilton diplomatically explain that the situation demanded the most delicate handling; that the terms agreed upon required that the king's troops remain distant from the city; that many of the firebrands in Derry were unequivocally opposed to surrender; that his army had insufficient artillery for a long siege; that with Derry captured, Ireland was assured for James; that with Ireland secure, James, with the assistance of France, would be in a strong position for a concerted invasion of England itself!

James stared down his long nose at the unfortunate general, his lantern jaw locked stubbornly - all warning signs of his displeasure. Coldly and turned imperiously away, telling Berwick to inform his troop commanders to be ready to march to Derry within the hour.

News of the king's decision swept the camp, causing open division and disagreement among the troops. Many of the men, eager for the booty which would not be available under the terms arranged by Hamilton, were jubilant, while others, eager for the Ulster campaign to end so that they could return to their homes, volubly opposed the change. Tadhg and Dónal, infected with the fever for rougher treatment of the rebels, were openly with the king. But Sergeant Gallagher disagreed. He shook his head ominously. 'I know these people. They are of English and Scots blood like King James, and can be as stubborn as he. Mark my words, no good will come of this!'

As the king had ordered, the troops marched within the hour, quickly covering the ten miles to Derry where word was sent in the name of the king, their sovereign, for the fortified city to surrender at discretion. The approach of James and his forces in violation of the terms of surrender caused consternation and dismay in the ranks of those who had wanted to avoid bloodshed and to yield up the city peaceably. This breach of agreement provided the needed ammunition for the fanatics and diehards, the firebrands Hamilton had alluded to, in their opposition to surrender.

A minister - one George Walker - who hated Catholics with all the rabid fervour of a true religious fanatic, quickly emerged as the leader of the malcontents. He reminded the Rebels of all the tales of atrocities - real, imagined and fabricated - that the Catholics had ever been accused of perpetrating against Protestants. He cited the case of the Viscount of Mountjoy, a Protestant, whose regiment had been quartered in Derry when the agitation for the replacement of James with William had been at its height, but who had remained loyal to James. Tyrconnell, who had used the viscount to calm the Protestants of Ulster, then ordered Mountjoy's troops to Dublin as replacements for those being sent to aid James in England at Hounslow Heath. The departure of these troops to the capital provided the rebellious apprentices in Derry, incited by the Reverend James Gordon, a Presbyterian minister from Glendermot, the opportunity to close the gates in the very faces of the troops of the Earl of Antrim.

The Reverend Walker, with devastating effect, further described how Mountjoy, who had remained loyal to James although a Protestant, had been sent by Tyrconnell on a supposed diplomatic mission to France with Sir Stephen Rice, the Chief Baron, who had secret orders to denounce him as a traitor. Mountjoy had quickly been sent to the Bastille where he now languished.

The wily minister then asked the men of Derry about the terms, solemnly agreed to in the name of the king, which included the proviso that the Royalists might stay away from Derry until noon. 'Isn't that the despised, deposed Catholic king himself outside our walls? Was this the man to whom they were willing to entrust their fortunes and their lives? In the name of that great man of God,

Oliver Cromwell,' he shouted, pounding his hand on his Bible, 'I for one won't trust James Stuart. Succour will be coming soon from King William. Who is with me in holding this city against the infamous James and his Papists?'

His inflammatory utterances spread like wildfire through the town, especially influencing the younger element and the Non-Conformists, who were in the majority. The King's demand for surrender was haughtily and defiantly refused. So angered and irreverent at the king's appearance were they that they fired a cannon at him. Their aim to kill the king was obvious, but their aim with the cannon was a trifle wide of the mark, killing Captain Troy who was riding close to James.

The king, whose courage in the face of fire was well known, retreated hastily from the field, not for fear of his life, but shocked by a welcome so contrary to that which his advisers had led him to expect. He had been led to believe that he would be greeted with open arms - not firearms! Humiliated and indignant, he returned to the castle for further conference with his staff.

CHAPTER IX

Friends Reunited

A notable event occurred on the following day, the arrival of Conor O'Donnell with some of the new troops sent to reinforce the king's army. Great was the joy of Tadhg and Dónal when a soldier in the uniform of the Royal Foot Guards burst into their tent and embraced them wildly. It was Conor!

'When I arrived at the Brazen Head Inn in Dublin some sergeant informed me that you had gone to join General Hamilton. He promised to let me know when the first troops were going north. I must have looked at a million horses before I recognized Cuchulain. It was easy to find his owner. So here I am.'

'Ah, it's grand to see you again, Conor,' Tadhg exclaimed happily. 'We've had many an adventure since we saw you last.'

'It seems like three years, at least,' Dónal added.

'What are the tidings from Connemara? What happened after we left you at O'Flaherty's castle?'

Conor's exuberance gave way to seriousness. 'My brother Seán and his wife Caitlín have moved in with Máire to help with the farm. Since Sir John Ferguson is gone, thanks be to you, Tadhg, there is no rent to pay, and they have decided to stay there for a while. We buried poor Murtagh. Máire took it hard, but she has her brood to care for.'

'How is Eithne?' Tadhg asked.

Conor smiled. 'I'm glad you asked that, a chara, because she wants to know how you are faring. Her father's death was a great blow to her. She blames herself for it, saying it is God's retribution upon her for wanting to defy Murtagh.

She wants to become a nun as penance.'

'Och, the poor cailín,' Tadhg said sadly. 'It was none of her doing that her father died. He hated the English ever since his father was sold into slavery in Cromwell's time. The heavy rent that Sir John extracted for that small farm always infuriated him. And because he loved Cathal and Donough O'Flaherty, it was more than he could bear when the land agent shot Cathal.'

'We told her that, but she insists that she is being punished for planning to oppose him. She refuses to tell her mother what it was.'

With a heavy heart Tadhg recalled how Eithne, had been determined to marry him despite Murtagh's anticipated objections.

But if she chose to withhold her reason it was not for him to interfere. He felt a guilt in her guilt, but remained silent, respecting her decision.

Conor gave Dónal Óg messages from his parents who were worried about him. They wanted him to return home. Then Conor described the funerals of the O'Flaherty brothers and the other Rapparees who had perished in the battle at St. Malachi's. His eyes were moist as he related how the entire countryside had responded, and how Roderick O'Flaherty, the chief of the family, had wept at the graveside. 'There's hardly an Englishman in all of Connaught, for most have fled to Ulster or England to avoid Colonel Sarsfield and his men.'

'If Cathal had but waited a few more weeks, he would still be alive,'

Tadhg lamented. 'His castle and lands would have been restored to him.'

Conor shook his head impatiently. 'No. We didn't know then the great changes that were to take place in Eire. And you must remember that Cathal was more concerned about Donough than he was about himself or his lands. Do you think he would have listened for one moment to the suggestion of waiting for a better time to rescue or avenge Donough? When he learned through Murtagh that Donough had been killed, there was no holding him. No, Tadhg, Cathal avenged Donough and you avenged Cathal. It was the first time since Cromwell that the Gaels had arisen in Connemara to strike a blow against the tyrant. It made our people feel like warriors and men again. As for Cathal getting his lands back, that too is doubtful because he was considered an outlaw by the government in Dublin Castle. The Lord Lieutenant might be a Catholic, but that doesn't make him a Gael. Never forger that, Tadhg.'

They spent several hours happily talking and trading their experiences. While they were conversing, Cornet Butler joined them. Introduced to Conor, he told him what exemplary soldiers Tadhg and Dónal were, and what a good regiment they belonged to.

Seizing the opportunity, Tadhg addressed the officer: 'Faith, and we'd be pleased if Conor could be transferred to this regiment. I promise you that he will make a good soldier.'

The Cornet smiled. 'I'll speak to the adjutant about it in the morning.'

And so it was that the three old friends were together again.

CHAPTER X

The Code

The following day Cornet Butler asked Tadhg if he knew what subject was most discussed by the top-ranking officers.

'How to capture Derry in the shortest time, I suppose.'

'Well, that too, but most of them are spending their spare time trying to solve that mysterious message you intercepted. Each has his own theory. Many have temporarily given up *l'hombre*, dice and tippling trying to solve the mystery.'

'Are they making any progress?'

The Cornet laughed. 'Not yet. And I doubt if any of them will as they have had no experience in ciphers and codes. There is one man, a French officer, who is said to have had some training in France under the famous Rossignol. If anyone can solve it, he can.'

'I would like to watch him working at it,' Tadhg said. 'That message has intrigued me ever since I found it.'

'Perhaps I can arrange a meeting. He might consent to see you since you were the one who found the coded message.'

And arranged it was. That night Tadhg called on Lieutenant Rene de Vimeny in his tent. The lieutenant was delighted to learn that Tadhg spoke some French, for he apologised that his English was only fragmentary. His dark eyes agleam with excitement, he showed Tadhg what he had accomplished. He had taken all the number sequences, and had listed them on a sheet of paper in the frequency which they had appeared.

'First I had to learn what letters in English appear most frequently in common usage.' He shrugged his shoulders eloquently. 'When I asked the question of the English officers, they all had different answers. So I took a book printed in English, a Bible, and listed all the letters used on five pages picked at random. In counting them, I found that the letter E led the list, followed by T, A, O, N, R, I, with X, Q and Z used the least. Do you follow?'

Beaming with pleasure, Lieutenant de Vimeny continued. 'Since E, T, A, et cetera were used most frequently in English, I substituted them for the number combinations most frequently used in the message, hoping that it was but a simple cipher that could be easily solved. Getting nowhere, I tried it in French where the most used letters are E, A, S, I, T, et cetera, down to Z, K and

W, the least used.'

'And did you solve it?' Tadhg asked eagerly.

'Non!' Disappointment showed on the Frenchman's face. 'It made no sense in either language. It was - what's the word in English? - ah yes, gibberish! That's all it was. Then I had the thought that it might be in Irish, but I was unable to find out what letters are most used. Discarding that idea, I tried various combinations, eliminating the three sequences that appeared most often that they might actually be meaningless, just inserted in the message to confuse. Still nothing. So I tried many combinations, and I still have made no progress. I have come to the conclusion that it is in code. But when I tell that to my colonel, he says that I'm just using that as an excuse because I can't solve it in cipher.' He looked dispirited, shrugged his shoulders, and added, 'Perhaps he's right.'

'Pardon, *a dhuine uasail*,' Tadhg said, 'but could I see the original message? I was so excited when I found it that I don't remember much of it.'

Searching among the many pieces of foolscap on the table, Lt. de Vimeny produced a set of several sheets. 'This is only a copy,' he explained, 'the original was kept at General Hamilton's headquarters.' He smiled broadly, showing even, white teeth, 'In fact, this is just one of many copies. Every officer who fancies himself capable of solving it has a copy and is working on it. If you would like to make a copy, and try your luck, you are more than welcome to do so.'

Tadhg was embarrassed. 'I didn't mean to imply that I could solve the code message, sir. It is just that I am intensely interested and intrigued by it because I discovered it.'

The Frenchman pounced on the word 'intrigued' 'Aha,' he said enthusiastically, 'perhaps we can "intrigue" you into becoming a student of codes and ciphers. It is a most fascinating subject. I was fortunate enough to attend the academy founded and developed by Antoine Rossignol, the world's greatest expert in codes and ciphers, who has solved many important secret messages concerning both war and diplomacy. Unfortunately, I was assigned to the forces being sent to Ireland before I became very proficient.' He shrugged his shoulders, expressing his disappointment, then hastening to add, 'I mean no disrespect to your beautiful country, but only at not being able to finish my studies at the academy first.'

He handed Tadhg a stick of a slender, hard, black material. 'Use this for your copying. It comes from England and is called 'black charcoal.' It makes the hands messy, but writes well,' he apologised, 'and is less trouble than a quill which has to be dipped into the ink so often.'

Using the 'black charcoal' Tadhg laboriously copied the message, a long list of two-digit numbers preceded by the statement.

'Thanks this day for our blessings to St Paul, St William, St Laurence, St Cornelius, St Venantius and St Luke.

The numbers were in sets in six separated columns. Carefully Tadhg entered them. After he had copied the first four sets,

```
42 80 30 38 17 10
35 20 10 31 26 50
33 10 20 29 11 30
64 10 50 12 14 20
```

the Frenchman interrupted him, impatiently tapping his forefinger on the list. 'Observe,' he said, 'that three of the six columns have no numbers ending with a zero, and that three of the six do. This can mean that these sets of numbers with zero are meaningless, inserted only to mislead, or that the zero itself has no significance, and that only the accompanying number does.'

Tadhg scanned the list, nodding his head in agreement. Then he wrinkled his forehead as he stared perplexed at the paper before him. 'If there is significance in these number combinations, then why the preface in words involving the saints? Why isn't that, too reduced to numbers if it's part of the message?'

Lieutenant de Vimeny beamed at Tadhg in approval. 'That's a very good question. It shows that you are already becoming interested. But, alas, I am unable to answer it. Undoubtedly it has great significance, and if I had the answer, I might well have the key to the riddle. My theory is that this message is directed to one, or all, or any combination of six agents who have been designated by the names of the good saints. This would save the other agents and we can safely assume that there are others the trouble of decoding the message since it is not meant for them.'

'Do you think that it might be an honest offering of gratitude to the saints? The enemy might be religious even if they are not of the true faith?'

A smile showed on the lieutenant's lean face. 'I had considered that, so I checked it with several of the chaplains. They differ amongst themselves in their interpretation of its application, so they were of little help. What bothers me is the use of the names of such obscure saints as Venantius, William and Cornelius. Here we have three unfamiliar saints rubbing haloes with those of the two Apostles, Luke and Paul, and St Laurence. Answer me that, my Irish friend?'

'I must confess I know little about the saints, *a dhuine uasail*. The only two I recognised were Paul and Luke. But tell me, what is the difference between codes and ciphers?'

'Well, briefly, a message written in cipher can be solved by anyone who knows the key, or works out the key as I have been attempting to do. Nothing else is required but a quill and ink, or a 'black charcoal' and a good supply of paper. But a code depends upon a code-book. Both the person who composes the message and the person who receives it has to refer to the code-book because the code words or letters in the message have to be located in the code-book for their specific meaning. If our message is based on a code, then the numbers can represent a letter, a word, a phrase or a whole sentence. Do you understand?'

'Only vaguely. It's new to me, but I'm beginning to understand. Is one system better than the other? Why two?'

The lieutenant was delighted to have someone show an interest in his favourite subject. He glowed with enthusiasm. 'First, let us discuss codes. These can be solved by great ones like Rossignol and his disciples, but they are much harder, and take longer. If a message is in code, and has a time element, it doesn't help to solve it after the need is over. And codes can be changed. This makes the hard, tedious work need to be accomplished all over again. And then once more it might be too late. On the negative side, however, it is necessary to have the code-book available at all times to decode a message . This is inconvenient in the field like we are here. In addition, if the code-book is captured by the enemy, the key to all the secret messages is in their hands.'

'Then you think that the cipher system is better?'

'Not necessarily. It all depends upon the circumstances. A cipher system is more flexible. One is not limited by words or phrases that have to be in the code-book. With ciphers, every letter in the alphabet can be used so that the message can contain any letter one needs, thus making the choice of words unlimited. And one is not required to carry a dangerous code-book. But on the negative side again, it is usually easier for the expert to solve a cipher message than a good code message.'

Tadhg stared at the list of numbers, but the more he stared the more perplexed he became. 'You say that these numbers can represent letters, words, or even phrases? Then, if it is true, as you said earlier, that certain letters appear more often than others, and should therefore reappear frequently in a message, why haven't you solved it?'

The Frenchman showed his exasperation at the question. 'It is not as simple as you think,' he replied tartly. 'These letters, set up in words, can be transposed according to a set plan or key. This makes it more difficult because the message is no longer in its normal order. Then, to make it doubly difficult, these transposed letters or ciphers can be replaced by some substitute cipher.

What did you say your name was? Tadhg? Spelled T-A-D-H-G? Say we wanted your name expressed in cipher. We'll make it really simple. The first letter, T, is twentieth in the English alphabet, so we will designate it as the number twenty with the A as one, the D as four, the H as eight and the G as seven. So Tadhg becomes twenty, one, four, eight and seven in cipher. But that is too obvious, so we scramble it according to a set key, making it one, eight, twenty, four and seven instead. We can further make it more complicated, but for our purposes now, it is unnecessary.'

Tadhg bowed. 'I salute thee, O master, and apologise for my rash question. I'm firmly convinced that it is far more difficult than I had even dreamed it would be, so I'll finish copying the remaining numbers, and keep it merely as a memento, not as a problem to solve.'

'I didn't mean to discourage you,' de Vimeny said, dismayed, 'I was serious when I suggested that you become interested in solving secret messages. You are endowed with the trait of curiosity, which is one of the necessary attributes.'

Tadhg smiled. 'What are the others? Do I have them, also?'

'You have some. I don't know you well enough to say you have them all. To excel in deciphering, or decoding, in addition to curiosity, one must be intelligent, resourceful, imaginative, and above all, persevering, to the point of stubbornness.'

'I note that you didn't include being egotistical. If I were to claim that I had all those attributes you listed, I certainly would be guilty of having a massive ego.'

The lieutenant gazed at Tadhg speculatively. 'I don't want to resort to flattery in order to induce you to become interested in cryptolgy, but you speak remarkably good French for a man who studies it from a book and has little occasion to use it. This means you have intelligence, a good memory, resourcefulness, and that most valuable asset, perseverance.'

'*Merci Monsieur l'Officer,*' Tadhg replied humbly, 'but I did have some instruction from a shipwrecked mariner who was half French and half Spanish. In all honesty I must admit that his instruction was the foundation for my French.'

Lieutenant de Vimeny smiled happily. 'You have just displayed two more qualities, honesty and modesty, which are not necessary for our purpose, but are essential qualities for a man of character.'

Tadhg gathered up his papers, obviously embarrassed by the frank appraisal of the Frenchman. 'I want to thank you for letting me copy this, and also for your instructions, for your compliments and the pleasure of your company, But now I have taken too much of your time, and I better leave.'

The lieutenant arose. 'I, too, enjoyed talking to you. Be sure to visit me again. And so *au revoir, mon ami.*'

CHAPTER XI

The Act of Repeal

A few days after the debacle at the walls of Derry, the king prepared to leave for Dublin to open the special session of Parliament set for 7 May. Many of the Irish regimental commanders, earls, viscounts and barons, who were to sit in the Parliament also left. Flushed with their military successes, James's army was now bereft of most of its leaders, even General de Rosen accompanying the king to the capital. Command was left with General Moumont, the Frenchman, with General Hamilton as his deputy.

Tadhg was one of about five score men who assembled one morning on Pennyburn Hill in response to a special order for exceptionally tall men. A piece of rope had been tied between two trees at a height, Tadhg was informed, of six feet two inches from the ground. Each man was instructed to walk under the rope. Those whose heads failed to touch the rope were dismissed, the others were to remain. Tadhg was one of a dozen who qualified. These were informed that they were to be the king's personal guards, and were to accompany him to Dublin.

At first Tadhg was dismayed at being parted from Conor and Dónal, but the possibility of seeing the Lady Mairéad FitzGerald again - despite her hostile action of a month ago - altered his view. He apologised to his two companions, saying that he had no alternative but to go, for after all it was the king he was to serve. If they suspected his inner motive, they made no mention of it, but congratulated him on his selection.

These special guards, distinct from His Majesty's First Troop of Guards, commanded by Lord Dover, who also accompanied the king to Dublin, rode close to the king at all times to protect his person. James, still athletic despite his age, rode horseback frequently occasionally taking to a carriage when the roads were good, or when conferences with his staff and advisers were necessary.

Winter's cold grasp had relaxed, and with the advent of spring, the willow and blackthorn had burst into bud, and then within a short time, the bare branches once again were green. In the glens sweet violets contrasted their delicate purple with the rich yellow of the buttercups; the gorse thrived with the gentle rains and the sunshine, weaving its subtle gold into the familiar fabric of the country-side. Along the roads and boreens the hawthorn bloomed, and the daffodils waved their golden crowns in joyful camaraderie to the royal passer-by. To Tadhg it seemed as if nature was energetically seeking to hide the scars caused by the Protestant landowners when they laid the area to waste before fleeing to the sanctuary in Derry.

Once the royal party was out of Protestant Ulster, they were exultantly welcomed by the country people who gathered by the road to wave at the king's entourage as it passed, cheering King James, with young maids dancing and strewing flowers and the old ladies making the sign of the cross and giving the king their blessing. It was a sight to bring tears to the eyes of a sovereign who loved his subjects, but Tadhg never noticed any sign of emotion as James acknowledged, with a bow or a wave of his hand, the adulation of the people. With his prominent jaw out thrust, long nose dominating the saturnine face under the fair hair, he often seemed oblivious of the people and their warm welcome.

Holding King James in awe and respect, Tadhg observed nothing in the king's attitude to change his exalted opinion of him. To Tadhg his arrogance was a natural attribute of one who had been chosen by God to rule and dominate other mortals; his haughty disdain for the opinions of others was a concomitant of his arrogance; his belief in the absolute right of kings was only natural and not to be questioned by lesser mortals. Tadhg easily colligated these characteristics, which had led to James's downfall in his native land, as the normal birthrights of a sovereign.

The royal party arrived in Dublin on 29 April where Tadhg and the other guards were quartered in a two-story building across from Dublin Castle where James had his apartment. On 7 May, with the flag of Ireland proudly flying over the ancient bastion, the guards accompanied the king, dressed in his royal robes, and a newly designed and constructed crown on his head, to King's Inns where the Parliament sat. Members of the Commons joined the Peers to hear James address both houses from his throne. After he informed the hushed audience of the reasons for calling this special session of Parliament, he retired, followed by his attendants.

Then Lord Gosworth, the Chancellor of Ireland, instructed the Commons to retire to select a Speaker. Without much ado, the members returned shortly, having chosen Sir Richard Nagle. He was a man of high repute and competence who had extensive legislative experience both in Ireland and England.

With the King safely escorted to the Castle, and no particular duty assigned, Tadhg returned to the King's Inns where he was admitted to the packed gallery. Despite the many lofty aims of the Parliament, its chief reason for meeting was the Repeal of the Acts of Settlement, by which, over the years, the old families had been dispossessed of their lands in Ireland, Old Irish and Norman-Irish alike. With most of the Protestants who had sat in the previous Parliament fled to England, it was a foregone conclusion that the Act of Repeal would carry.

Tadhg sat spellbound during the stirring debate. He was amazed to learn that of the fifty-four Peers represented in the Parliament, six were Protestant Church leaders who vigorously, and sometimes violently, opposed the Act of Repeal. Sir Arthur Forbes, the Earl of Granard, an avid Presbyterian and former follower of the King, was one of these, ably assisted by the Earl of Longford and the Protestant Bishop of Meath.

The bold bishop, looking out into the ranks of the predominantly Catholic Peers - where sat representatives of some of the oldest Gaelic families in the country, MacCarthys, O'Briens, Maguires, MacElligotts, MacDonnells, O'Donovans, MacMahons, MacGuinnesses and O'Neills, mixed with Norman-Irish like Burkes, Powers, Sarsfields, Purcells, Butlers, Dillons, and English-Irish Catholics like the Talbots, Dungans, Luttrells and Dowdalls - openly and contemptuously referred to their fathers and grandfathers, and even themselves as rebels and criminals.

It was a tribute to the fair-mindedness of the Peers that they restrained themselves from the vicious diatribes of the bishop and his colleagues. Behind the scenes, certain English lords, although Catholics, who had fled England with James, such as the Duke of Powys, also opposed the Act of Repeal. They tried to persuade James to use his influence, but the king, who secretly opposed repeal, realised that he owed more to the Duke of Tyrconnelll who was one of its chief proponents, and to the Irish lords who were raising regiments and fighting on his behalf, than to the handful of exiled English lords who were seeking to block repeal.

As expected, when the final vote came, the hated Acts of Settlement and Explanation were repealed, thereby restoring to those Catholics their land taken from them since the year 1641 in the various wars and conquests by soldiers, adventurers, opportunists, court favourites and exploiters.

However, in fairness to those persons who had innocently purchased lands from the Cromwellian soldiers, the various adventurers, or the officers who had benefited in the war year of 1649, a provision was made in the Act of Repeal to reimburse them for their losses. This remuneration was to come from sale of lands that had belonged to various Protestants whose ancestors had owned them since before the time of James's father, Charles I, in 1641, or afterwards, but who now were in rebellion against James, their lawful sovereign, and who were thus attained.

The Parliament was scrupulously fair to the Protestant bishops by leaving the ecclesiastical lands in their possession, and restoring to the Catholic prelates such tithes as were annexed to their station. The parochial priests were awarded the tithes of their Catholic parishioners, while the Protestant ministers were allowed the tithes of their own.

After passage of the Act, with the happy Catholic members of Parliament celebrating the planned restoration of their estates, and their vindication in resisting the tyrannical and oppressive governments in Ireland, Tadhg thought of Cathal and Donough O'Flaherty, both now resting in their graves, who would not benefit. Cathal had given more than lip service to his opposition to the occupying forces and the legal theft of his hereditary estates. He and his band of Rapparees had openly opposed with the force of arms the representatives of Charles II in Ireland, thereby putting prices on their heads. Donough had spent most of his life exiled in France.

While most of Dublin roistered, Tadhg repaired to Christ Church to pray for the souls of Cathal and Donough, Murtagh Blake, and the other Rapparees who had died on the winding road before St Malachi's.

CHAPTER XII

Lady Mairéad

At his first opportunity, Tadhg visited with sergeant Williamson, who was happy to see him safe and a soldier. The sergeant explained that Tadhg's 'escape' had caused no problems but a reprimand for being careless. Several witnesses had testified that the two 'wild Irish' had attacked the unsuspecting sergeant, beaten him and escaped. For some unexplained reason, the Lady Mairéad Fitzgerald had not pressed any probe of the affair, nor did she attend the investigation. So the matter was quietly dropped.

He did have some meagre information on Hugh O'Flaherty. One of the Irish officers who had returned with King James said he had met a Captain Hugh O'Flaherty who had escaped England to France, but that was all that he knew.

Sergeant Williamson's joy at seeing Tadhg again couldn't begin to compare with that of Rory MacAuley's, who was delirious with delight. Tadhg barely recognised the lad in the Dublin clothes which Cáit had provided for him. His scrawny frame had filled out, his hair was cut short, and only the freckled face, the carroty hair and the impish grin reminded Tadhg of the ragtag and bobtail *buachaillín* they had picked up at the crossing of the Shannon. Rory's happiness was cut short when Tadhg explained that his visit was only temporary, and that he would have to return to the army at Derry.

'Take me with you,' the boy begged, tears in his eyes. 'I can help fight for King James.'

'Don't you like it here?' Tadhg asked gently. 'Cáit is like a mother to you.'

The boy nodded through his tears. 'She's very good to me,' he agreed reluctantly, 'but I want to be with you.'

Tadhg explained as best he could the rough and dangerous life outside the walls of Derry, with the enemy hurling cannonballs and mortar shells, the cold and the damp, the coarse and monotonous meals. 'It's no place for a boy. The war will be over when Derry falls, and I'll come and get you,' he promised. 'In the meantime you stay here and take good care of Cáit . She needs someone to help her around the place .'

Rory dried his eyes and nodded. He understood what Tadhg meant. Cáit's brother was usually drunk or out with his cronies, leaving the burden to fall on his overworked sister. Despite the adversities, Cáit was philosophical about her situation, accepting it as the will of God. She had an understanding with a blacksmith named Fiachra O'Byrne over on St Patrick's Well Lane who was the sole support of his aged parents, but the years passed and the old folks clung tenaciously to life like they did to their son. Until they died, there was little chance for the son to marry.

Whenever he was free, Tadhg would ride out to the vicinity of the Fitzgerald place, smoke his short-stemmed clay pipe (he had recently started smoking), and hope he might get a glimpse of Lady Mairéad. Being a special guard to the king, he had little fear of retribution for his acts at Kilkieran. Twice he had observed a carriage leaving the house, but could not see the occupants, and although disappointed, took some consolation from the possibility she had been within, and that he had been close to her.

He recognised that his obsession and preoccupation with the high-born lady was irrational. And he was aware that many a lovely *cailín* and many a beautiful woman, in meeting him, showed more than a casual interest. He was courteous, but reserved; his diffidence angered some, intrigued others. To the latter, his disinterest made then more determined in pursuit of him, but to no avail. To his male companions, other than Conor and Dónal his lack of response to the interest and response of these women made him the butt of much ribald comment, some of which went to the point of questioning his manhood. His great strength and reputation as a swordsman were well known.

One cool evening, shortly after the passage of the Act of Repeal, he was seated in his favourite spot across the road from the Fitzgerald mansion, when he heard boisterous shouting and singing on the road from Dublin. He smiled when he saw a group of soldiers approaching. From their manner, they evidently had drink taken. They paused briefly before the gates where one of them swaggered up to the gateman, demanding admission.

The guard eyed them sourly. 'For what purpose?' he asked.

Grinning, the soldier turned to his companions. 'Tell him, men.'

'Ireland has been given back to the Catholics, and those Geraldines in there are Protestant supporters of King William,' one of the soldiers shouted. 'We're going to take our land back.'

The guard, recognising that the men were drunk, but not realizing that they were in virulent mood, insolently inquired if property had ever belonged to any of their families, and inferred that their only patrimony was a bottle of whiskey, and a place to sleep by the side of the ditch. He then ordered them to be gone, or he would have the lot of them arrested for trespassing.

The soldier at the gate angrily drew his pistol, and before the guard could move, shot him in the chest. Brandishing his weapon, the soldier climbed the barred gate, calling to his companions to follow. Immediately a half dozen or so scrambled after him, entering the roadway beyond.

Scarcely believing his eyes, Tadhg sat stunned momentarily at the sudden assault and slaying of the guard. Jumping to his feet, he hastened to the gate where he grabbed at the stragglers still trying to climb the gate to enter the yard. He succeeded in hauling down three of them who immediately drew their swords and advanced on him in drunken fury. Retreating before their charge, Tadhg glanced desperately about him. Observing an espalier constructed with stout poles, he wrenched one loose, and swinging it in a wide arc, managed in knocking two of his assailants senseless. The third, seeing that the odds were drastically changed, took to his heels down the road. Still carrying his cudgel, Tadhg climbed the gates, running up the main driveway after the other soldiers who had already disappeared from sight.

Either by ruse or by force they had gained access to the house, leaving the door wide open. All was confusion within, with screaming of women, firing of guns, the hoarse shouting of drunken soldiers, and the overturning of furniture. Some of the invaders had already found loot, cramming silver candlesticks and other valuables in their pockets, while others had discovered the wine cellar, and were emptying the bottles as if they were competing in a drinking contest.

Most of the clamour came from one large room down a long hallway, and Tadhg made his way hence. The leader of the mob, the one who had slain the guard, stood with his pistol pointed at the grey head of an elderly man whose naturally florid complexion was several hues darker as he sat flushed with anger in a huge chair. Two others were tussling with the Lady Mairéad. One of them, a big, burly man, was trying to hold her face steady so that he could kiss her, while the other pinioned her arms.

Bellowing like an enraged bull, Tadhg brought the end of his cudgel down on the head of the amorous one who dropped as if he were poleaxed. His companion released the girl to reach for his pistol, and as Lady Mairéad fell to the floor in a faint, Tadhg felled him with one blow.

Seeing Tadhg's uniform, but being unable to understand why one of his companions should suddenly go berserk, the ringleader stood undecided for several seconds, staring uncomprehendingly at Tadhg. Then realising that the big soldier with the pole was not one of his group, he swung his weapon away from the man in the chair, pointing it at Tadhg. Before he could discharge it, however, the man in the chair struck the pistol vigorously with his hand, sending it clattering against the wall.

Tadhg stood for a moment to catch his breath after his long run and recent exertions. The soldier, unable to reach his pistol, drew his sabre. With the memory of the Lady Mairéad's struggle with the two men still vivid, Tadhg smiled cruelly, and drawing his Spanish sword, moved towards the other man. Clumsily and desperately swinging his sabre, the soldier did his best to keep Tadhg at a distance. Unlike his previous opponents in sword duel, his present foe was unskilled. Aware of the disparity between them, Tadhg would normally have been ashamed to engage the other, but the cold-blooded murder of the guard at the gate, and the touching of the person of the Lady Mairéad, enraged him to the point where his sense of fair play was completely submerged by his anger.

Flicking the point of his sword at his opponent, Tadhg deliberately and systematically cut the man's face while he avoided the flail-like swing of the heavy sabre. With blood streaming into his eyes, blinding him, the soldier flung aside his weapon, and falling to his knees, begged Tadhg to stop.

'He's had enough punishment,' the elderly man said, putting his hand on Tadhg's sword arm to stay him.

As he looked at the pitiful, moaning, bloody specimen before him, Tadhg's rage subsided, and acknowledging the restraining hand, replaced his sword in its scabbard. He was still breathing heavily.

The household had been sufficiently aroused by the clamour, and armed servants were searching for any of the band who might still be on the premises. Apparently all the others had fled, leaving only the trio in the great room, two battered unconscious by Tadhg's pole, while the third whined, whimpered and implored Tadhg's mercy.

Several women, including Mary Casey, appeared and carried Lady Mairéad to a divan where they fluttered around like

203

distraught hens. The grey-haired man approached Tadhg, hand extended in greeting. 'I am Henry FitzGerald' He said eagerly. 'To whom do we owe this courageous and timely deliverance from these ruffians?'

Aware that the name of O'Cuirc might be odious in that household, Tadhg had presence of mind, as he hesitated momentarily, to say, 'William MacAuley, of Westmeath, now a member of Tyrconnell's Horse.'

As the older man said, with great feeling, 'We owe you a great debt of gratitude, MacAuley,' Tadhg was conscious of the startled, then conspiratorial expression on the face of Mary Casey, who had appeared at his side.

She lowered her eyes demurely and bowed. Then she took Tadhg's arm, steering him to the divan where the Lady Mairéad was now sitting up, although her face was blanched, and she was shaking violently as with fever.

'This is William MacAuley who rescued you,' Mary Casey said loudly, carefully emphasising every syllable. 'He happened to be passing by as the soldiers broke into the estate.'

Lady Mairéad stared uncomprehendingly at Tadhg. 'MacAuley?' She said. 'Why he ...' The maid immediately interrupted her mistress in a most unservantlike manner as she raised the volume of her voice, 'He is the one who beat off the villains who were holding you, and rescued your Uncle Henry from the man with the gun.' Then she lowered her voice, but still looking firmly and directly at Lady Mairéad whose brow was furrowed with bewilderment, said, 'MacAuley is most deserving of your thanks, mi-lady, for he single-handedly attacked the three knaves, and completely routed them.'

Lady Mairéad sat silently for a moment, staring at Tadhg. Then she glanced at Mary Casey, and with a faint smile on her face, aid, 'I do thank you, MacAuley, from the bottom of my heart. It took great courage to do what you did.'

Tadhg knelt, and imitating the courtiers at the Castle, gently kissed the dainty hand held out to him. Lady Mairéad was startled, but did not withdraw her hand. As she gazed at Tadhg, the half-smile still playing at the corners of her mouth, she asked innocently, 'How did it happen that you were passing at such an opportune time?'

Tadhg blushed and lowered his head. Mairéad leaned forward, her voice low so that none but Tadhg could hear her. 'I have seen you several times from my carriage as you sat near the roadside, Tadhg. It was no coincidence that you were here tonight when the attack occurred. But whatever is the reason you have chosen to play the part of my guardian angel, I am humbly appreciative and thankful.'

'It was nothing, *a bhean uasail*,' Tadhg mumbled.

The golden head hung over his as she continued to speak softly.

'I am sorry that I lost my temper last March and informed on you to the soldiers, but it is difficult to reconcile myself to the death of John Montgomery. I was sorry afterwards,' she added contritely,' and I was happy to learn that you had managed to escape. How did you, a stranger in Dublin, contrive it?'

Tadhg was apologetic. 'I cannot tell you, *a bhean uasail*, it would betray a friend.'

'You are an unusual man, Tadhg O'Cuirc - I beg your pardon, MacAuley - and I would be most happy if you were to consider me a friend also.'

Overcome with emotion from her gratitude and kindness as well as proximity, he could but mutter, 'I do, I do.' As he raised his eyes to hers, now filled with compassion, he was smitten anew with an over-powering love for her. He arose hurriedly to hide his feeling, stating that he must take his leave and report the entire incident to the authorities at the Castle.

Henry FitzGerald, his florid face beaming, assured him that he would appear at the Castle the following day, as well as at the Tholsel, for Sir Michael Creagh, the Lord Grand Mayor, was a distant cousin of his. The three soldiers, the only ones apprehended, had been bound hand and foot, and some of the armed servants were going to take them into Dublin to be turned over to the authorities.

When Tadhg finally took his leave, returning to the roadside where he had left Cuchulain, he observed that the body of the slain guard had been removed. The two men he had beaten outside the gate were nowhere to be seen. Whether they had recovered and departed, or whether they had been captured, he did not know.

As he jogged back to quarters, his mind was in a turmoil. Had he, a Catholic, done the right thing in assisting Protestant landowners against poor Irish soldiers? Where were his loyalties? Would he have reacted as he did if the aggression was against any other Protestant but the Lady Mairéad? Was the slaying of the insolent guard morally wrong? Was his rage righteous or merely subterfuge because the victim was Mairéad?

He was spared any indictment of himself or his actions as he dwelled on the memory of her seated upon the divan, the delicate colouring, the subtle shading of the sea-green eyes, the filigree of spun-gold hair, the melodious voice in his ear. 'You are an unusual man,' she had said. She had apologised for her actions in turning him over to the soldiers. She thanked him for his services. He glowed with happiness, and he went to sleep that night in an exalted mood, and with a clear conscience.

Chapter XIII

Palace Politics

The investigation of the attack on the Fitzgerald household was perfunctory, the only problem was the insistence on the part of a bewildered Sir Henry FitzGerald that the soldier who had come to the rescue was named MacAuley, not O'Cuirc. Fortunately for all concerned, he made no connection between this O'Cuirc and the one who had slain Montgomery. Of the assailants, the one who had killed the guard was sentenced to be hanged at Gallows Green, the others were given long prison terms as a warning.

The ringleader of the affair was a former cattle herder whose family had worked on the estate for several hundred years before its acquisition by Henry Fitzgerald. Applying his own interpretation to the Act of Repeal, he had prevailed upon others of a like mind to seize lands and properties from Protestants, even though they were not in rebellion against James, and thereby excluded from attainder. Fortified with poteen, the malcontents decided their campaign would start with the Fitzgeralds with whose estate the ringleader was well acquainted. When the plot was disclosed during the trial, strict proclamations were issued to citizens and soldiers that private appropriation of properties was forbidden under penalty of death.

Tadhg found it difficult emotionally to accept the edict, being steeped in the history of the bloody usurpations of Irish lands and properties by the English, but he recognised rationally that there was a need for law and order, for discipline and control, for fundamentally he possessed a strong sense of justice which found such lawless acts repugnant.

As the session of what was called the 'Patriot Parliament' dragged on, the legislators enthusiastically passed an act in James's presence declaring the indefensible right of the hereditary succession. The act affirmed in strong language the sovereign's right to be commander of the army, the militia and 'strong places' as necessary to the king's natural person within all His Majesty's realms and possessions.

While the act had significance in Ireland where the adherents of James controlled most of country, it had little effect elsewhere. In Scotland, forces loyal to James were defeated in the Battle of Killiecrankie in July 1689 while James's army twiddled its thumbs futiley outside the walls of Derry. Lord Dundee, leader of James's cause in Scotland, was killed at Killiecrankie, and with his death died James's hopes in Scotland. There were many who had urged that the forces at Derry be sent to Scotland to help Dundee, and some token units were sent, but the suggestion went unheeded.

Lord and Lady Tyrconnelll, with their three daughters, each safely married to a marquis, arranged a brilliant social program for the King's stay in Dublin. There were balls and dances, banquets and parties, and even an occasional foxhunt especially organised for the King. James loved to hunt; it was his chief source of recreation. When on the hunt he lost much of his customary aloofness and reserve.

In as much as James frowned on drinking, many of the balls and parties were dull affairs since few had the temerity to drink as much as they would have liked for fear of the king. He didn't enjoy games of chance, and when he did consent to gamble, he played only for small stakes. Among the members of his court, where swearing and profanity were common, James was unique since he was not profane. When in James's presence, members of the court drank tea since James was an inveterate tea drinker even though it had only been recently introduced into Western Europe.

The more that Tadhg saw and heard of the king, the more confused he became. To live 'the life of a king' was to Tadhg the highest objective in life. But here was a king who didn't live up to the accepted standards. James was a peculiar person. Born of a father steeped in Protestantism, James had become a convert to Catholicism. He had been christened in the Church of England by Archbishop Laud, the head of the Anglican church. Laud, later to lose his head like his king, was blamed for leading Charles I to many of the policies and decisions that brought about the downfall of that unfortunate monarch.

It seemed incongruous to Tadhg to learn that Catholic King James's godparents were among the leading Protestants of Europe in 1633. One of these was the Prince of Orange, whose grandson was later to take James's place on the throne of England. The other was the exiled Queen of Bohemia, one of James's aunts. Perhaps it was his diverse ancestry that gave him his complex character for he was one quarter each of Scottish, French, Danish and Italian blood.

While still in Dublin, Tadhg became aware of the rivalries, antagonisms, jealousies and intrigues among the various elements represented in James's Court. Although the king showed his personal preference towards the English and Scots lords, he was caught in the middle by the feud between the Earl of Tyrconnelll and the Earl of Melfort. The latter, John Drummond, younger brother of James Drummond, Earl of Perth, had been secretary of state in Scotland where he had been extremely unpopular. Both the Drummonds, like King James himself, were converts to Catholicism who had fled England. Melfort was as heartily detested in Ireland as he had been in Scotland.

The Comte d'Avaux, King Louis's ambassador to James, recognising the danger to the common cause, wrote to his sovereign requesting that Louis intervene with James to remove the troublesome Melfort. But it wasn't until Tyrconnelll presented to James a petition, signed by many of James's supporters in Ireland, that the king arranged for the transfer of Melfort to France. When he sailed on 4 September, he was succeeded by one of Tyrconnelll's nephews, William Talbot.

Tadhg's exalted ideas of royalty and high born were shattered during his brief exposure to the in-fighting at Dublin Castle, and he longed for the simple life of Inishmór where the battle was against the elements, not fellow human beings.

CHAPTER XIV

Thady's Masterpiece

On 10 June, Tadhg and the other guards were ordered to return to Ireland to their regiments at Derry. The situation in Dublin, as in most of Ireland, being so secure, it was decided that they were no longer needed. The return trip north contrasted sharply with the march three months previously when the enemy lurked behind every hill, where the marches were long and forced and the winter cold and bleak.

Now the dark boglands had erupted into a mass of colour - the purple of the heather, the gold of the ragwort, the white of the bog-cotton. From a distance Tadhg often mistook the blue of the flax fields for lakes, rimmed with the yellow of bog iris, while the fox gloves pointed their long spikes skyward like a host of stationary pikemen. Tadhg rejoiced in the rich profusion of trees, shrubs, flowers and luxuriant green grasses he had never known on Inishmór.

Dónal and Conor welcomed Tadhg back to the ranks. There was not much change in the situation. The enemy remained defiantly in their walled city while the stalemated army of the king squatted out side the walls. Cannon, necessary to batter a breach in the walls, had been requested at the start of the siege. But alas, when the big guns arrived in June, they were entirely inadequate, consisting of one 48-pounder and one 40-pounder, both in poor condition. In addition, there were two culverins, for which there was powder, but no cannonballs, and a few old mortars, the only usable pieces in the lot.

This fiasco of weapons and supplies was to become the rule rather than the exception for the remainder of the campaign in Ireland. All the great promises and expectations of help from King Louis XIV remained only promises and expectations. The Irish were to learn, to their sorrow, that promises were poor substitutes for weapons, ammunition and supplies, and expectation was far from realisation.

In the meanwhile the enemy used their more than two-score cannon, including the eleven foot-long 'Roaring Meg', with great effect from their positions on the walls, and from the steeple of St Columb's Cathedral. In their occasional sorties through the gates, the rebels generally had the best of it due to surprise, and the superiority of concentrated numbers of men in a small space. Before reinforcements could arrive, they would scurry back to the safety of their walls. In one such sortie at Pennyburn Hill, Marshal Rosen's deputy, Lieutenant General Maumont, and his countryman, Major General Pusignan, were killed. Both generals had boldly forced the river in the rout at Cladybridge.

In describing the fight, in which he had participated, Dónal informed Tadhg, with regret in his voice, that the result might have been different if only he, Tadhg, had been there.

'The Rebels were led,' Dónal said, 'by Colonel Adam Murray, one of their favourite heroes. He's about your size, Tadhg. Some claim that he killed General Maumont in hand-to-hand combat, but I don't believe it because I was near the general much of the time before he went down. This Murray is a giant of a man, and a great fighter, but I'm sure you could have cut him down. And without their leader, the Rebels would have fled. 'Tis sad for sure that you weren't here.'

Although pleased with Dónal's faith in him as a warrior, Tadhg himself wasn't as positive that he could have bested the veteran soldier. Perhaps it's best I wasn't there,' Tadhg teased, 'for I might have been forced to hide from the colonel like Fionn MacCool hid in fear from the Scots giant who came over to fight him. Butler says these Murrays up here came from Scotland just like the giant.'

'Sure, and Tadhg doesn't have a clever wife like Fionn who dressed her husband in baby clothes, tricking the giant into believing that the huge Fionn was just their infant son!' Conor smiled wickedly, then winking at Dónal, asked abruptly, 'And how was the Lady Mairéad?'

Tadhg coloured, and he averted his eyes, hastily changing the subject. 'How is Thady? Been promoted to file to General Hamilton?'

Conor snickered. 'He's lucky he didn't have his neck stretched by General Hamilton.'

'What happened? Did he help himself to one of the officers' wives?'

'No, he out did himself this time. He composed a poem about King James messing up the surrender of Derry. Of course, I agree with him wholeheartedly.'

'But there is no proof Thady is the author,' Dónal protested. 'He was accused of it, but denies it.'

'He'd be a complete fool to acknowledge ownership when his

neck is involved,' Conor said. 'And Thady isn't a complete fool.'

Tadhg frowned. 'What was the poem? Was it really so outrageous?'

'I only know the English version,' Conor explained. 'I'm surprised you didn't hear it in Dublin. The whole country is laughing. Thady, denying authorship, himself points out its flaws. He says it is so bad that he deserved to be hanged if he had composed it. Actually, there is nothing to connect Thady with it other than he is a competent poet, and isn't fond of King James. Otherwise General Hamilton would have been obliged to have had him hanged in deference to the king. Colonel O'Neill was forced to deprive Thady of his privileges for fear that he, too, would be associated with the poem.'

'What's your opinion, Conor?' Tadhg asked.

Conor snickered. 'For my money, Thady not only composed the Irish version, which is beautifully and faultlessly done, but the English version as well, for Thady is not as fluent in English as his native language. It was the Irish version that was most widely circulated, but undoubtedly the English rendition reached the ears of the king. Some Irish lord, laughing inside, but with straight face, probably recited it for him, all the time denouncing the spailpín who composed it.'

'It does have the intricate rhyming that Thady explained to us. Remember, Tadhg, on the way to Dublin?'

Tadhg nodded, then turned to Conor. 'Come, a chara, don't keep me waiting all night. Recite it for me.'

Conor cleared his throat ostentatiously, and striking a Thady-like pose began:

In Drogheda Town, near the Boyne's wide mouth,
A place of renown, in old County Louth,
John Hamilton bold, the morn of March Fourth,
His brave soldiers told they'd march to the North,
Poor Ulster to free from the scurvy churls
In hilly Derry, where the broad Foyle curls
Its course to the sea, whence fled our great Earls
O'Donnell, O'Neill, from that infamous
Monarch of England, the first Rí Séamus .

Oh, póg mo thóin, Rí Séamus !

Through lush County Down and Antrim's green glens,
Past murky bogs brown, skirting lofty bens,
Hamilton's brave men King Billy's boys chased
To their Derry den (so quickly they raced)
From ancient Armagh to where Foyle winds,
From Hamilton braw, the Rebels' best minds
Begged generous terms, saying 'Don't blame us
If we place no trust in shifty Rí Séamus .'

Oh, póg mo thóin, Rí Séamus

Surrender agreed (choice terms they had gained),
They all would be freed, property retained;
The Irish would stay at nearby Raphoe
Until at midday when the Rebel foe
Would open the gate to the much-prized town
Despite their great hate of the Stuart Crown,
Then bewail the fate that had let them down,
For they who had bragged, 'James will ne'er tame us,'
Now must yield in the name of Rí Séamus .

Oh, póg mo thóin, Rí Séamus

But alackaday for expectation!
Foul fate has its way to ruin elation.
Hamilton (bless him) had never reckoned
With the childish whim of James the Second.
For then to the site sour Séamus flounced,
Where he, that same night, Hamilton denounced
For the pact (plain spite) which he then renounced.
Wrathful Rebels then roared, 'He'll ne'er claim us,
For we'll never submit to crass Rí Séamus !'

Oh, póg mo thóin, Rí Séamus

James marched to the fort, the pact violated,
Began to exhort (this king they hated)
That they at once yield, and not be misled,
But Roaring Meg pealed their answer instead!
Then hot cannonballs (with the war resumed)
Flew over the walls while the big guns boomed.

'So make ready the palls, for many are doomed,
If we aren't killed, they surely will maim us,
All caused by interfering Rí Séamus .'

Oh, póg mo thóin, Rí Séamus !

Tadhg was both amused and shocked at the impudence of the poem. That it accurately described the fiasco created by Rí Séamus could not be disputed, but its irreverence to the King upset him. Knowing Thady, he had no doubts that he was the author, but the poet's concept of propriety was far different than his. Yet he had an odd sense of pride in the knowledge that he was acquainted with so notorious a person as Thady.

Not only his friends were happy to see Tadhg return to the regiment, but Sergeant Gallagher, too, had missed his protegee. Despite the press of constant drills in the handling of the sabre, musket and pistol, and exercises in cavalry tactics, the sergeant took time to instruct Tadhg personally in the use of the pistol. Although ammunition was in short supply, he invariably 'borrowed' enough powder and balls for Tadhg's pistol practice. The sergeant took great delight in his pupil's rapid progress, crediting Tadhg's remarkable accuracy and proficiency to exceptionally sharp eyes and a steady hand.

In his spare time, when he wasn't studying from the French grammar the Huguenot had given him, or English from an old volume of Donough's, or his pistol practice, Tadhg gloried in strolling or riding through the green glens, over the brooding hills, or along the leafy bands of the Foyle. Sometimes, out of a sense of loyalty rather than preference, Conor or Dónal would accompany him. Thy preferred, however, to spend their time drinking or gambling with their roisterous companions, or consorting with the wenches who frequented the outskirts of the camp. The other soldiers considered Tadhg strange because he rarely joined them in their revelry, and many a snide or ribald remark was made about him and his books, and his avoidance of the camp wenches.

CHAPTER XV

Inside Derry

One sunny afternoon near the end of June, when Tadhg returned to his tent, he found the Englishman, Wilkinson, waiting for him. 'Could I speak to you in private, O'Cuirc?' he asked nervously, glancing about as if he expected someone to be following him.

Tadhg raised his brows in surprise, then nodded his head. He walked several yards distant, followed by Wilkinson. The Englishman was obviously apprehensive, pressing his hands together, and locking and unlocking his long bony fingers.

'I didn't know who to talk to,' he blurted. 'And then I remembered how fairly you treated me the time that Bob tried to kill you.'

'What is it that's bothering you? Tadhg asked kindly.

The foxy-faced man's body shook violently. His face was ashen. Tadhg then realized that the man was in a state of great fear. He put his hand on Wilkinson's shoulder, saying, 'Come now, it can't be that bad.'

Tadhg's gesture and firmness helped to calm the other. He licked his dry lips several times, then spoke. 'This morning, early, a man I never saw before, but wearing the uniform of our regiment, came to me. He said that Bob Holmes wanted to talk to me at an ancient fort about six miles west of the camp. This stranger warned me that I was to tell no one, or I would have my throat cut by one of King William's spies right in our own camp. If I did what I was told, Holmes would see that I was rewarded, and wouldn't be sent to prison when King James is defeated.'

'Who was this soldier?' Tadhg asked, becoming excited at the prospect of facing Holmes again. 'Was he one of ours?'

'I said I never saw him before.'

'Are you willing to tell this to Cornet Butler? After all, if you don't, I will have to inform him myself.'

The Englishman nodded. 'Whatever you think is best.'

The Cornet was extremely interested in the incident, asking Wilkinson numerous questions. The soldier, although still fearful, answered as best he could.

'I have a feeling,' the cornet said, 'that this early morning visitor came from Derry during the dark of the night. He could have been wearing Holmes's old regimental uniform. With all these new recruits of ours in camp, the stranger could stroll around with little fear of detection. The fact that he took this risk means that there is more to this than just some friendly chit-chat between two old comrades in arms. So it might be advisable that we arrange to meet with our erstwhile colleague, Holmes, tonight.'

'But how would this stranger know where and how to find me?' Wilkinson asked.

'No problem at all. If Holmes is in Derry, as most likely he is, he could have observed the location of your company bivouac from the town's high walls, or from the church steeple, with the aid of magnifying glasses, and could have pointed at you out to the man who visited you. Or the stranger could have entered our lines during the night, and merely asked where your company was located. Then, having located the company, he could ask for you. Unfortunately, discipline in camp is very lax. If he wore, as you say, a uniform of the Duke of Tyrconnell's regiment who was to question him?'

'I would like to accompany you on the expedition tonight,' said Tadhg, his face grim. 'It would give me the greatest personal pleasure to capture that sleeveen.'

'I'd better discuss it with Major O'Meara,' Cornet Butler interjected, 'we'll need his permission to leave camp.'

The major listened to the story, his sad, pale blue eyes showing no emotion. When the cornet had finished talking, Major O'Meara stroked his drooping white moustache while he pursed his mouth, lost in thought. Finally, he spoke. 'This isn't really for me to decide, but since Lieutenant Colonel Sheldon is unavailable, and Holmes is a deserter from your troop, I see no harm in your going to the rendezvous with Wilkinson.'

His face taking on the dirty white shade of his uniform lining, the Englishman stammered, 'Mmmm sir? Do I have to go with them?'

The major frowned. 'Of course,' he snapped. 'You're the bait.' He stared at the soldier with suspicion. 'Is there any reason why you shouldn't go along?'

Wilkinson shook as if he had the ague. 'They'll slit my throat as they threatened,' he whined. 'If I go with, they will know I informed on Bob.'

Major O'Meara stared at him with contempt. 'What kind of soldier are you? You face death every time you go into battle.'

'But that's different from having your throat cut cold-bloodedly

216

in your own bed, and with your own eyes seeing your life's blood run down your chest'

The major glared, then turned abruptly to Cornet Butler.' I'll leave the details to you. Dismissed.'

Shortly after, six men left camp, riding west. Cornet Butler led the detail which included Tadhg, Dónal Óg, Conor, Wilkinson and Sergeant Cahir Gallagher. The latter was chosen because he was not only a Donegal native but because he was an experienced soldier, and a valuable addition to the detail.

In reply to Cornet Butler's question if he was acquainted with the area around the old fort Grianán Ailigh - he replied.

'Och, I know the place like the back of my hand. Many's the time I've played on the walls, and drunk from the holy well nearby. Perhaps that's why I'm so saintly.' Roguishly he rolled his eyes heavenward, for the sergeant was well-known in the army for habits no saint would possess.

'Tell us more, St Cahir,' the cornet responded drily.

'Well, the distance is about seven or eight miles since we are going a circuotous route. The old stone fort was built in the remote past, even before, the Milesians arrived. 'Tis a lonely place now, occupied only by wandering sheep, and the spirits of Druids long dead. No wonder your man Holmes picked it for a trysting place.'

'You said there was a holy well nearby?'

'It will be a joy to drink the uisce beatha' - he clapped his hand to his mouth hurriedly - excuse me, I meant the clear water, again, especially after a long, hot ride. My tongue is so dry, I can hardly wait for a drink.'

As they trotted along, Sergeant Gallagher told them that the area was the former territory of the Ard Néill and that Eoghan, son of Niall of the holy St Patrick himself, was reputed to be buried nearby.

The sergeant turned to Wilkinson. 'Since you don't speak our language ,' he explained in English, 'the word tir means 'land' and since this was once the land of Eoghan it became known as Tireoghan, which you English have corrupted into Tyrone, although that name is generally applied to the territory north of here.'

It was growing dark when they climbed Greenan Mountain from the West, having circled around to avoid being detected. In the dusk, the round, stone fort reminded Tadhg of a large cake set upon a table. It was similar to Dun Aengus, not more than a half-mile from his birthplace on Inishmór. They entered through the massive ring of masonry. Tadhg was posted at the entrance so that he could have the honour to capture the man who had tried to kill him. Wilkinson, shaking with fear despite the reassurances of Cornet Butler, was to guard the horses. The others stationed themselves nearby.

Time passed slowly. The outline of the terraced walls faded as night descended like a covering cloak over the land. Heavy clouds rolled in from the Atlantic, obscuring the dim light of the sliver of moon which hung like a lantern over the ancient dwelling place of the Ard Néill. If only Thady were here, Tadhg mused. He would people the deserted circle until one could envision the venerable Padraig, his long, white beard flowing, as he bent over Eoghan for the immersion, exultant in this baptism of the son of Niall of the Nine Hostages who had captured him as a youth in Britain, and had brought him to Erin as a slave. Warriors on the stone walls turned from their constant surveillance of Aileach to watch curiously as their chief abandoned the ancient religion of the Gael for the new.

The night wore on. It was so peaceful that drowsiness slyly overtook Tadhg, and although he blinked his eyes vigorously, fighting to stay awake, he fought a losing battle, and finally dozed. How long he slept he didn't know, but he was awakened by a loud hullabaloo, and the pounding of running feet. Rising quickly, and drawing his sword, he dashed through the entrance.

'Did you catch him?' Sergeant Gallagaher asked excitedly. 'Where is he.?'

'Who?' asked Tadhg, sleepily and stupidly.

'Holmes, of course. Who else.'

'I didn't see him. Where was he?'

The sergeant clapped his hand to his forehead in disgust. 'He ran right past where you were stationed. How could you have possibly missed him?'

Tadhg stood still, shocked at his negligence. Cornet Butler and the thoroughly frightened Wilkinson joined them.

'Where is Holmes?' the cornet asked, his voice quivering with excitement.

Sergeant Gallagher growled deep in his throat. 'The big amadán!'

'What's that?' Cornet Butler asked sharply.

The sergeant didn't answer just pointed an accusing finger at

Tadhg.

Turning to Tadhg, the Cornet stared at him, awaiting an explanation. Tadhg shook his shoulders in dejection. 'I must have fallen asleep,' he admitted sheepishly.

For a long interval there was silence. Then, with his voice reflecting his intense disappointment, Cornet Butler said, 'God preserve us from stupid soldiers who fall asleep on duty.' Then, more to himself than the others, he asked, 'And how do I explain this to Major O'Meara?'

Tadhg would have felt less despondent if the cornet had been angry and upbraided him, but his moderation made Tadhg feel even more disgusted with himself. Through his carelessness, their quarry had escaped. Now there was no way of knowing what information was to have been communicated to Wilkinson, or why the latter had summoned to Griannan Ailigh. As he stood, silently despising himself, he suddenly thought that perhaps the situation could be rectified.

'*A dhuine uasail*,' he suggested respectfully to Cornet Butler, 'can't we ride in the direction of Derry to see if we can catch up to him?'

'Well, at least that's better than just standing here. Let's get the horses and see if we can redeem ourselves.'

Tadhg was pleased that the cornet said 'ourselves' and not 'you'. They mounted their steeds quickly and galloped towards the east. When they were within a mile of Derry, Sergeant Gallagher signalled to stop. Addressing the cornet, he said, 'Sir, since our army surrounds all of Derry but the Shipquay Gate section which projects out into the Foyle, it's possible that our man gets in and out of Derry by boat. It might be wise to search along the river.'

Cornet Butler nodded. 'A good suggestion. If he tries to slip back into town through our land lines, he can be captured any way. That is, if our men are alert. Let's try the river.'

They proceeded to the Foyle, several miles south of Derry, where they examined the river bank, searching in the trees and reeds near the water's edge. As they approached Derry, they came upon a small, stone wharf that jutted out into the river, where a boat with broad, square ends, and a flat bottom, was moored.

'This might be Holmes's craft, sir,' Sergeant Gallagher said excitedly as they moved towards the bank.

Abruptly they were challenged in Irish. '*Cé ata ann?*' and from the darkness several men of the Earl of Clanrickards Regiment confronted them. The detail was led by an ensign who introduced himself as William O'Kelly, of the Clann Eachach O'Kelly of County Derry. Questioned by Cornet Butler about the boat, O'Kelly declared that it hadn't been used for some time. They had been particularly watchful lest it be taken by the Rebels.

Still acutely aware that his carelessness had let Holmes elude the trap that had been set for him, Tadhg was determined to atone for his lapse. Looking at the boat, he had an idea albeit a desperate one. '*A dhuine uasail*,' he addressed Cornet Butler, 'if Holmes might try to slip into Derry by way of the Foyle, why can't I take this craft and approach as closely as possible so that he can't get by in the darkness?'

The Cornet pondered the question for some time. Then he nodded his head. 'Your proposal has some merit. But you had better take Conor and Dónal with you. If nothing else, they can at least keep you awake. The rest of us will patrol the river bank.'

Tadhg coloured with embarrassment, but the officer's tone was humorous rather than malicious. Clambering into the boat, Tadhg took the oars and expertly swinging the boat into the current, they soon were in a position to see Derry, dark and distant along the Foyle's shore about a half-mile away

'It's dangerous to go closer,' Conor whispered, 'we might be seen.'

Taking a long pole, which Sergeant Gallagher had explained, was used to propel the boat through the shallows, Tadhg stuck it firmly in the river muck, and looping the bow line around it, secured the craft firmly.

'What do we do now?' Conor asked.

'Sit and wait. If Holmes is returning by boat, he might not yet have passed. After all, we weren't far behind him, and we came directly to the river whereas he would have had to approach carefully to avoid our patrols. And if he was afoot, since it would be difficult to obtain a horse, it would take him that much longer.'

'What if he doesn't try to return tonight, or comes in to the north of Derry,' Dónal asked.

Tadhg shrugged his shoulders. 'In that case, Dónal Óg, we will have lost him. But he can ill afford to be wandering around the countryside when he knows the whole area will be alerted to look for him. He speaks no Irish and with his Midlands accent, can't pass for an Ulster Protestant. No, I think Sergeant Gallagher's idea was sensible.'

'Besides, the Foyle above Derry is heavily guarded to prevent General Kirke from slipping by,' Conor added. 'It would be doubly difficult, and he would be forced to row against the current too.'

Small wavelets lapped gently against the boat's sides as they waited. In the sedge at the river's edge, little creatures of the night scurried furtively about, and occasionally a dark form overhead flapped its heavy wings as a black hag moved about restlessly, disturbed by their presence on the river. Heavy clouds had obliterated the silver of moon and the peeping stars, and soon a grey, enveloping mist crept silently in from the distant sea, swirling about the watchers, penetrating their uniforms with its bone-chilling dampness. As the fog eddied around them, the distant outlines of Derry's walls disappeared from view and they were alone in the vast void.

'The wrath of God on this fog,' Conor fumed. 'We won't be able to see Holmes even if he should pass this way.'

Tadhg shook his head in the darkness, a futile gesture. No, I think the mist is a good ally. It will make him more confident of getting back to Derry. And because of the fog, he will be obliged to follow the shoreline where we can hear him. And even if we can't see him, neither can he see us.'

The current tugged gently at the restraining pole, seeking to set the craft free to drift on the broad bosom of the river to the sea. As the minutes passed, and the night grew older and colder, Tadhg's confidence also waned, and he began to doubt if their vigil wasn't in vain. As he sat shivering, cursing himself for having fallen asleep at the fort, he became gradually aware of a new sound on the river, like the sound of the movement of a boat through the water, the slap-slap of waves against its prow, and the sucking noise of the placement and withdrawal of a pole.

He touched Conor's knee with his hand, putting his fingers to his lips in a gesture of silence, as he peered through the grey mist. As the sound grew louder, he discerned the shape of a boat, similar to theirs, approaching. There was one lone figure in the centre working the pole. Dónal, also alert to the craft's approach, gently withdrew their anchoring pole from the muck, freeing the boat.

Taking the pole silently from Dónal, Tadhg manoeuvred their craft to block the path of the other boat, whose occupant, concentrating on polling his vessel, was unaware that he had company until he was but a boat's length away. He stopped abruptly, crying out, 'Who goes there?'

Jubilantly, Tadhg recognised the graty accent of their quarry. 'Soldiers of the King,' he replied, gloating.

There was a moment of hesitation. Then, in a voice of mingled fear and suspicion, Holmes asked, 'Which king?'

'There's only one king, you traitor, and that's King James,' Tadhg replied, his voice angry.

In reply, Holmes swung his boat towards the shore. Fearful that their prey might again escape, Tadhg snatched his pole from the water, and grasping it like a pike in a style that even the critical Sergeant Gallagher would approve, thrust it quickly at the surprised Englishman, tumbling him into the water.

Emerging at the surface, spluttering and floundering, he bawled loudly for help, 'Save me, for the love of God, save me, I can't swim.' Then the river closed over him again, silencing his frenzied appeals until he struggled once more to the surface, repeating his piteous calls for assistance. Tadhg dove into the river, and with a few strokes reached the drowning man. Holmes struggled frantically, attempting to wrap his arms around his rescuer, but Tadhg held him firmly at arm's length. Conor, having retrieved the pole, moved the boat to the side of the struggling man.

Dónal Óg reached over the gunnel to grasp Holmes by the collar while Tadhg held on to the boat's edge as Conor poled it to shore. When Holmes felt the bottom under him, he attempted to wrest himself from Dónal's grip, striking wildly at him, but Tadhg quickly reached the flailing Englishman and pulled him to the river bank.

The clamour having apparently been heard in Derry, loud calls of 'Who goes there?' rang across the misty river. Holmes's mouth opened as if to answer, but Tadhg's broad palm closed over it, stifling him.

'Listen, you Judas,' Tadhg hissed ominously, 'one wrong sound out of you, and you're a dead man, and your rotten carcass will float down to the sea for the gulls to eat,'

'It's O'Cuirc,' Holmes squawked hoarsely, his eyes wide with fear.

'Yes, it's O'Cuirc, the man you tried to kill. And now, my pigeon, it's your scrawny neck that's in my hand. One cry out of you, or one hostile move, and I'll happily wring it! Now tell me, and tell me quickly, what is the information you wanted to pass on to Wilkinson tonight?'

'I wanted him to arrange my return to the regiment,' Holmes

replied sullenly.'

'Don't lie to me, you Sassanach traitor,' Tadhg warned, tightening his hands around the Englishman's throat. 'Your life was forfeit, and you wouldn't have risked it. Tell me the truth, or by God, I'll strangle you right now.'

Holmes shook his head violently and Tadhg relaxed his fingers. 'Stop, in God's name,' he sobbed, 'I'll tell you if you only will stop choking me.' He swallowed several times, rubbing his aching neck in an attempt to relieve the pain. 'I was just to deliver a message to him so that it would be passed to Dublin.'

'What is the message?'

Holmes reached into a pocket, bringing forth a soggy piece of paper, handing it to Tadhg.

'It's all wet, and it's dark here,' Tadhg exclaimed impatiently, 'so I can't read it now. What does it say?'

'I don't know. It's written in some kind of code.'

'If you don't know,' Tadhg commented sarcastically, 'how was Wilkinson supposed to get it to the right person in Dublin? Stand on the Thosel steps and yell?'

'It was supposed to have been delivered in a sealed envelope addressed to Liffey Exports, and given to a Lady FitzGerald in Dublin. She knows what to do with it.'

'Who?' Tadhg's voice was hoarse with incredulity and shock. Convinced that his ears had deceived him, he repeated, 'Who?'

'A Lady FitzGerald in Dublin. That's all I know.'

Tadhg sat numbed. The message was to be transmitted to the Lady Mairéad! He looked to Dónal and Conor for support. Their countenances, too, showed their consternation. They stared back at him, eyes bleak, incredulous. It couldn't be, Tadhg thought wildly. It was a trick! A lie!

While Tadhg gazed at his companions, his eyes questioning, his mind unbelieving, Holmes seized the opportunity to squirm from Tadhg's grasp and run for his boat which was lodged among the reeds on the shore. Tadhg was up in a flash, jumping into the boat after him. Both tumbled into the waist-deep water as the boat overturned, Tadhg with his hands around the Englishman's throat. 'You lie! You lie!' he shrieked madly, holding Holmes's head under water. 'You Judas! You traitor! You liar! Tell the truth before I kill you! Tell me you lied about the Lady Mairéad!'

Conor and Dónal plunged into the river, and after struggling with Tadhg for some time before forcing him to relinquish his hold on the Englishman, they succeeded in getting Holmes on the bank. But they were too late. The man was dead. Tadhg followed them, sitting dispirited and disconsolate on the shore, his head in his hands.

'Tadhg,' Conor said compassionately after some minutes, 'we'd better be getting back to Cornet Butler with the Englishman's body and that coded message.'

Tadhg looked up, his eyes blank. 'His body? What do you mean, his body?'

'He is dead, *a mhic*.'

Tadhg stared at Conor uncomprehendingly. Then suddenly the realisation came, and he stared down at his own hands with self-loathing. 'And I killed him in anger.'

Conor looked significantly at Dónal Óg. 'No. He drowned when the boat overturned. Didn't he, Dónal?'

'Yes, Tadhg, he drowned when he tried to escape.'

'Come, now, let's get the body into the boat and get out of here before those Rebels on the walls get curious, and a patrol is sent out to investigate.'

'No,' said Tadhg, slowly but firmly, 'I'm going into Derry to find out more about this message. If it wasn't for me failing twice tonight, Holmes would be alive. He could have been forced to tell.'

'You are going into Derry?' Conor asked incredulously. 'That is madness, Tadhg, you are sure to be caught.'

'Not if I go in the guise of Wilkinson, the man Holmes went out to see.'

'How, in the name of Heaven, do you expect to do that?'

'I think I can mimic him successfully. Besides, that Warwickshire accent is almost unintelligible to other persons.'

Conor shook his head in disgust. 'If you weren't bigger than me, I'd knock you down and drag you back with us. I never thought you were a fool, Tadhg.'

'How will you get into Derry, Tadhg?' Dónal asked, intrigued at Tadhg's plan.

'In the boat,' Tadhg said.

'You'll never make it,' Conor said flatly. 'If our men don't shoot you first, then King Billy's men will surely hang you.'

'The mist will hide me. Besides, the boat will be floating bottom-side up.'

'Bottom-side up?' Conor was dubious.

'Yes. The boat was dry. That means the seams are tight. If I turn this boat over, there will be sufficient air trapped inside to keep me breathing until I get into Derry.'

'So you will keep breathing until the hangman's noose chokes you later!'

Tadhg strode into the water, carrying Holmes's body. 'Come and help me flip the boat over.'

Conor stood adamant. 'I refuse to help you with so insane an idea.'

'I'll help you, Tadhg,' Dónal Óg volunteered eagerly.

They lifted the boat carefully, turning it so that the keel was up, then gently deposited it in the water to capture a maximum amount of air. Tadhg submerged, then raised his head within the interior of the boat. As he thought, there was plenty of air as the craft rode high in the water. He submerged again, joining Dónal outside. 'I'll take Holmes's body with me. It will help make my story more credible. The current will carry the boat down to Derry. Now the two of you go back to Cornet Butler and tell him that I am trying to learn more about this coded message.'

Arrah, said Conor to himself sadly, what you really want to find out in Derry is the connection of Lady FitzGerald to the plot. With tears in his eyes he then splashed out into the river to embrace Tadhg fervently. '*Slán leat, a chara,* and may God go with you,' he said. After Dónal did likewise, Tadhg dived under the boat, and with the body of the Englishman clutched firmly in his hand, propelled the boat out into the current. His two friends watched disconsolately as it disappeared into the distance, swallowed by the mist.

Conor and Dónal stood on the shore, weighted down with an oppressive sadness, before turning to report to Cornet Butler. As they walked, they heard the sporadic fire of musketry, guessing that it was the sentries on the riverbank taking potshots at the drifting boat hiding Tadhg.

When Tadhg heard the shots being fired, he prayed that none of the balls would penetrate the thin hull, allowing air to escape, for then the craft would have only its own buoyancy, putting it too low in the water, making it impossible for Tadhg to remain inside. He was hard pressed to keep his head high in his air chamber as he clung to the seat for support, holding the body of the dead man which at times seemed reluctant to return to Derry. He hoped that he had correctly estimated the current and the approximate distance to the town. If the current carried him too far out into the river, he would drift past the triangular shaped point of land that projected from the walled town like the bow of a boat, and he would be hung up on the Jacobites own boom across the river at the Narrows.

Perhaps Conor was right. It was a mad idea, an irresponsible impulse. What had prompted it? Was it in the interest of King James and of Ireland? Had he been honest with Conor? Or was it his decision made primarily on Holmes's mention of Mairéad FitzGerald? His compulsion to discover the connection, if any, between the message and the Cailín Bán, was so overwhelming that he was now risking his life to resolve it. His confidence in the success of his mission diminished as the minutes passed. He was glad that it was darkening - he couldn't see the accusing eyes of his passenger. Weighing the odds of his returning alive to his comrades, he began to regret his decision. Conor was right, he admitted to himself, he was too prone to leap before looking.

A scraping sound on the boat alerted him as the craft's gentle movement by the current was suddenly arrested. Then he heard voices. 'It's only a small boat,' one said disappointedly.

'Only a small boat? Why its worth its weight in gold,' a deeper voice replied with scorn. 'Colonel Mitchelburn will be most happy to get it. He can use it to get a messenger to General Kirke.'

'Kirke? That coward?' the first voice said. 'I'll wager he's in the pay of King James. If he really wanted to get his ships past that log boom he'd find a way.'

The boathook which was being used to haul the boat along the quayside now turned it over, disclosing Tadhg, who was holding on to the body of Holmes.

'Damn, it isn't two men,' the deep voice exclaimed. Quick, shine that lantern over here!'

The area was suddenly illuminated, and Tadhg could see several men standing on the quay. The man with the lantern peered at Tadhg, then said, 'Come out of there, whoever you are, or I'll shoot.'

'Give me a hand then,' Tadhg said, adopting the accent of Wilkinson. Several hands reached out to him, and he pushed Holmes's body to them. 'This one is dead,' the deep voice said, as Holmes was laid on the rough planks of the quay. Then Tadhg was assisted from the water, and he, too, stood on the quay. The deep-voiced man, who turned out to be sergeant of the guard, listened attentively as Tadhg, who identified himself as Wilkinson, explained how he had met Holmes at Grianan Ailigh at the latter's suggestion. He related how they had been surprised by Jacobite patrol, escaped to the river where they had retrieved the boat, but in the excitement it had overturned. He had rescued the floundering Holmes - not knowing that he was dead - and had drifted downriver to escape the Jacobites on the shore.

'Aye, we heard the firing,' the sergeant said.

A crowd of soldiers and civilians had gathered around them, listening open-mouthed to Tadhg's tall tale. Then the sergeant gruffly ordered one of the soldiers to secure the boat, while he escorted 'Wilkinson' to the officer-of-the-guard. Tadhg noted that the huge iron padlocks on the massive gates of the walled city were as long as his hand but wider. Three big cannons were placed on each side of the gate on the walkway overhead. Now they were silent, but they would be firing again in the morning at the Jacobites across the river.

Walking up Shipquay Street through the town, which he knew as Doire Cathac, the Oakwood of the Warrior, Tadhg stared curiously at his surroundings. The old town was laid out on sloping ground which exposed many of the buildings to the fire from Irish batteries across the Foyle in Captain Strong's apple orchard. Despite the inadequacies and insufficiencies of the Irish siege weapons, the few that possessed distance and destructive power had badly damaged many of the houses, littering the streets with debris.

Familiar with the general plan of Derry, having often seen it from the hills in the Irish camp, Tadhg knew that it was roughly rectangular in shape, about 1,500 feet long and 750 feet wide. There were four main gates: Shipquay Gate, where they had just entered, faced the river, and opposite it, on the far end near the cathedral, was Bishop's Gate. Butcher's Gate, at Butcher Street, and its counterpart across the way, Ferry Gate, were the favourite exits for the Williamites on their frequent sorties.

Tadhg was shocked to learn from the sergeant that there was much conversation between the besieged and the besiegers in the front trenches, and that the Williamites were aware of the distrust and hatred many or the Irish soldiers had for their French allies who were arrogant and contemptuous of their militarily inexperienced proteges. This laxity of discipline, which Cornet Butler had alluded to, helped to encourage the besieged to prolong their resistance.

As they marched up Shipquay Street towards the guardhouse on Orchard Street, they passed an open area in the centre of the town called 'The Diamond' where stood the Town Hall. Tadhg could see the steeple of St Columb's Church, where two big guns had been placed causing great havoc among the Jacobites. Here the famed crimson flag flapped defiantly at the besiegers, informing them that the town still held for William of Orange.

If Tadhg had been a veteran of espionage rather than an impulsive blunderer, the course of history might have been changed that night, and he would have joined the immortal heroes of Eire, from Cúchulainn to Sarsfield, for the principal powder magazine of the fort was located at nearby Rosemary Lane. But alas for destiny, no such niche had been preordained for Tadhg, and he passed by, unaware of his great opportunity.

The sergeant pointed out to Tadhg the locations of some of the eight sakers and twelve demi-culverins placed upon the walls, and to 'Roaring Meg,' the eleven-foot pride of the garrison. They entered the guardhouse at the Double Bastion, where the officer on duty, a young lieutenant named Jackson, with a wispy blonde moustache and watery blue eyes, interrogated Tadhg.

'Speak more slowly,' he interrupted frequently, 'I can barely understand your outlandish accent.'

Tadhg repeated what he had told the sergeant, adding some embellishment. The lieutenant, who apparently had some knowledge of Holmes's mission, questioned Tadhg thoroughly on the fate of the message. Tadhg deemed it wiser to produce the message, rather than deny possession, and then have them discover it later on his person.

'Here it is, sir,' he said, fishing the water-soaked paper from his pocket.

The officer smoothed it under the flickering light of a candle, careful not to smear the ink. Tadhg stood behind him. The message started with a greeting: 'To God we render our grateful appreciation of His many benefits through the intercession of Saint Cyril, Saint Valentine, Saint Walpurga, Saint Luke Saint Pascal and Saint Linus.' Then followed six columns of two-digit numbers.

Excitedly realising that it was similar to the original message he had intercepted at Windy Hill, Tadhg concentrated on memorising the message. He knew it was impossible to remember the numbers.

Aware of Tadhg's close scrutiny, the officer asked sharply, 'What do you make of this?'

'Nothing, sir, I am but a simple soldier. But it is sure a queer-looking thing, isn't it?'

'Did Holmes tell you to whom and where it was to be delivered?'

'He didn't have time to, sir. He had just handed it to me when the patrol came, and I thrust it in my pocket. We raced hard to the river where we got into the boat. We were so excited that the boat turned over. I felt it was dangerous to go back to my regiment in the event I had been recognised. So I came here with the message.'

The lieutenant sighed. 'I suppose you had to leave your horse at the river bank. 'Tis a pity. It would have made such delicious eating. You might just as well rest until morning when Colonel Mitchelburn will want to see you. Too bad Holmes drowned; he was becoming one of our best agents. With his old uniform, he could pass as one of James's most loyal adherents. And how he hated the Irish especially one with whom he had a fight.' The lieutenant laughed, then yawning, took his departure, after informing the sergeant that he could be reached at his quarters on Rosemary Lane.

The guardhouse gradually emptied, and then with the changing of the guard, none was left but Tadhg. He stretched out on the floor, wondering what he could do to find the key to the mysterious code, and the part that the Lady Mairéad had been scheduled to play. Either his story had been believed, or it was felt that he couldn't escape, and there was no need to post a guard over him.

In the corner of the room, its golden tassels drooping forlornly, a captured French regimental flag, with fleur-de-lis, hung on its standard, looking ashamed. Tadhg heard the door open, but being drowsy, paid no attention. He was relaxing, on the verge of slumber, when suddenly a voice addressed him in the Irish, saying 'God bless all here,' and Tadhg automatically responded, also in the Irish, 'And yourself likewise.'

There was a strained silence as Tadhg realised he had been tricked. He sat upright, staring into the semi darkness beyond the guttering candle on the table. In the faint light he saw a woman, a sardonic smile on her face.

'Just to set the record straight, is it O'Wilkinson or Mac Wilkinson' she asked, chuckling.

Tadhg smiled in spite of himself. 'It takes an O,' he acknowledged.

'You have a pleasant smile, even if you are a fool. Did you really think that you could get away with it?'

Tadhg shrugged his shoulders, saying, 'I hoped to.'

The woman leaned forward, staring at him with frank admiration. Then she shook her head sadly. 'It's a pity that such a big, handsome lad like you will have to dance on the gallows tree instead of kicking up your heels in a dance with pretty girl. Ah, there's many a lass here in Derry that would welcome you in bed on a cold night.' Archness replacing sadness on her countenance, she added, 'Or any night.'

Tadhg sat silent, angry at his stupidity in being so easily unmasked. And by a woman!

'Why did you try such a senseless trick?' she asked, resuming her questioning. 'You should have known that someone would see through your ruse. It takes more than an imitation Midlands accent to hide that Irish face of yours. It might have fooled them in the dark of the night, but not in daylight. I'll wager a guinea that your eyes are blue to go with those black locks.'

Tadhg nodded. 'But the sergeant and the lieutenant believed my story,' he offered in self defence.

'That popinjay Jackson? Why, King James could walk in here and tell him that he was King William, and he'd believe him. But why did you do this foolish thing?' she asked, her tone sympathetic. 'And what did you expect to accomplish?'

''Tis easier to answer your last question than your first. 'I hoped to find out the mystery of the coded message, and the code key.'

The woman laughed loudly, filling the room with her merry peals.

'What's so funny?' Tadhg asked trucently.

'You would have to put your head in the mouth of the lion to get it,' she replied. 'The key to the code is in the safest place possible. It's in the personal Bible of the mighty Reverend Walker himself.'

'In the Reverend Walker's Bible?' Tadhg asked incredulously.

'Why not? He gets all his inspiration from the Bible. But you still haven't told me why you attempted such foolhardy venture to come into Londonderry?'

Tadhg hesitated. There was no longer any need for secrecy, but he felt ridiculous. There was no good reason why he shouldn't tell her. 'You probably won't believe it, but my reason for coming here is even more foolish than the mission I attempted to accomplish here.'

'Impossible!'

'Well,' said Tadhg in resignation, 'before Holmes died, he told me that the message was to be delivered to a certain lady in Dublin.'

'And do you know the Lady?'

Tadhg blushed. 'Slightly.'

'Oho, methinks you're in love with the lady. Do you intend to marry her?'

'Marry her?' Tadhg was aghast. 'I'm only a simple fisherman. I can't even talk with her because she is of the aristocracy. No, the chances of my marrying her are as remote as my getting the Reverend Walker's Bible.'

'And yet you risked your life to come here in her behalf?'

'I suppose so,' Tadhg admitted.

The woman looked at Tadhg with incredulity. 'Well, if that isn't the most futile romance since Conor loved Deirdre. Is she of the Popish faith like you?'

'No, she is a member of the Church of Ireland.'

The woman looked at him as if he was a strange animal. She shook her head in amazement. 'And is she pretty?'

Tadhg's eyes brightened like twin candles. 'None more beautiful walks in all the four provinces of Ireland!' he exclaimed raptuously. 'Her hair is the gold of the bog-fir, her eyes the grey-green of the sea, her lips red as the rowanberry, her breast whiter than the snow, her step is light as thistledown, her form ...'

'Enough, enough,' the woman interrupted, chuckling. 'Your obviously unbiased opinion has convinced me. 'She pursed her lips, gazing at him long and thoughtfully. 'Incredible!' she murmured, almost inaudibly. 'For the love of an unobtainable *cailín* he puts his romantic head in a noose!'

She walked to the door, turning to face Tadhg. 'Let it never be said that Meg Murray blighted a romance, or blocked the course of true love, one-sided though it be. Wait here for me, I know where there are some clothes that will fit you.'

Tadhg waited apprehensively. He was numb with despair. She was right, his disguise would never stand the light of day. And if the man who visited Wilkinson in the Irish camp was brought to see him, he would definitely be exposed. It was some time before the woman returned with a pair of breeches and a shirt. 'Here,' she ordered, 'put these on in place of your uniform. There are no boots,' she added drily, 'they already have been eaten.'

231

As Tadhg stood undecided, she turned to him impatiently. 'Don those clothes, man, we haven't got all night! If it's modesty that's bothering you, let me say that I'm a widow twice over. The last one died of the flux a month ago.'

Tadhg moved to a dark corner. He stripped off his uniform, putting on the clothes, which fit him surprisingly well. He wadded his uniform into a bundle which he placed under his arm.

'Better leave that here,' she warned him sharply, 'so none will see it.'

'Ooh,' Tadhg protested, 'uniforms are hard to come by. Half of the King's men still have none. This one was tailored for me because I am oversize, costing King James three pounds and eight shillings.'

'Bah!' she said scornfully. 'You worry about the cost of clothes when we in Londonderry are paying a shilling and sixpence for a pound of horsemeat when we are lucky enough to get it. Or a shilling for a rat. Even a wee mouse costs sixpence. And you worry over a miserly three pounds eight for a uniform!'

Seeing Tadhg's revulsion at the mention of the dogs, she softened. 'You'll eat anything when you're hungry. But it's your neck I'm trying to save. If you want to put the price of three pounds and eight shillings on it, it's your evaluation of your own worth.' She walked around him, inspecting, nodding approval. 'You look grand in Colonel Murray's old shirt and breeches. Both of you are about the same size.'

'Colonel Murray?' Tadhg asked, startled.

'Yes. He's a cousin of my late husband. It's because of this distant kinship that I am tolerated by the guards.' She smiled. 'When I talk too loudly, they call me Roaring Meg, after the big gun. Now I suppose you're wondering why I'm helping you, an enemy.' She came closer to him, and in the light of the candle, he could see that she was a woman in her early thirties, brown of hair and eyes, still bonny-looking despite the ravages of the siege. 'Although I'm legally Meg Murray now, I was born a Patterson up near Rathmullan. My first husband was named Taylor.' She looked at Tadhg boldly. 'Both of my husbands were plain, ordinary men who feared God but no man. A wife was to be treated kindly but sternly because she, too, was one of God's creatures, albeit inferior. They were good husbands in their way, and Christians. May they rest in peace.'

She gazed past Tadhg pensively, alone with her recollections.

Then she again faced him. 'My family had a good income from their estates. As a young woman, I travelled to Dublin and to London, making it difficult for me to settle down later to the humdrum life in the small, provincial town of Kilmacrenan when I married Taylor. From the time that I was a wee lass, I had dreamed of marrying a big, handsome, reckless man who would carry me off on his white steed like the heroes of old. You can readily see that the stories told by our Irish tenants about Deirdre and Naoise, Diarmuid and Gráinne, rubbed off on me.'

She stood silent for a moment, her face wistful. 'My two husbands are gone, but my dreams are still with me. As a sensible, God-fearing Presbyterian, my romantic notions should long have been permanently stifled. I was restless and sleepless tonight, and was down walking along the quay when there was the sudden excitement over a drifting boat. I watched the guard retrieve it. Then, suddenly, out of the river appeared the handsome, young giant of my dreams. Instead of a horse, he had a boat, like a river god. I followed you and the sergeant to the guardhouse, fully expecting to see you denounced as an impostor, for I detected in your speech a suggestion of the lilt of the Gaelic language.'

'You're the only one who noticed it,'Tadhg said.

She nodded. 'I was confused and excited. So when all the others left, I entered the room, and remembering some of the Irish phrases, I trapped you. But in the process, I also trapped myself.' She smiled. 'Here at last was my hero. But not only is he an enemy spy and a Papist, but he is hopelessly in love with another woman. So I have my hero and I haven't. As a loyal, sensible, twice-widowed anti- Papist, I should have immediately denounced you to the sergeant of the guard. But that would mean that I would be condemning you to death, and all my fond and foolish dreams of romantic heroes would die with you.'

She sighed, then continued. 'As I talk to you, the thought of turning in a bold man who risked his life for the woman he loved became so repugnant that I resolved to take a page from your foolish, reckless, romantic book, and risk my neck to save yours. And my dreams.'

She dabbed at her eyes with her handkerchief, wiping away the gathering tears, then said brusquely, 'But enough of this nonsense. We must get you through the lines before daybreak.'

Clutching his uniform under his arm, Tadhg followed her down the dark streets through the rubble, heavy with the stench of decay and death. When they neared Butcher's Gate, she drew him into the shadows. 'Ask for Sergeant MacGillivray,' she whispered. 'Tell him that you're on a mission to General Kirke's camp at Inch with a secret message in a bladder, the 'spy's suppository'. He will understand. It's a method we have used before, including a young boy who was captured by you Irish, but released with the message still intact where it was hidden. Tell him that it is urgent that you be passed through the lines as soon as possible.'

'But what about you?' he protested. 'There will be a great hullaballoo when they discover I'm gone. If someone has seen us together, it will be you who is hanged as a traitor.'

She smiled up at him, and although he couldn't see her eyes in the darkness, he was sure they were twinkling. 'Well, then, if I couldn't dance with you, I'd dance for you. On the gallows.' Then she quickly reached under her skirt, drawing a bulky object wrapped in a piece of dark cloth, and thrust it at him. 'Here, take it. It's the Reverend Walker's Bible you came for.'

As Tadhg stood there dumbly, she pressed close to him in the darkness. 'And now I must have my reward!' She pulled Tadhg's head down, kissing him long and lovingly. Her lips were full and warm. She moved her mouth back and forth on Tadhg's, and Tadhg was acutely aware of the hard thrust of her breasts against him, and recalled the last woman he had kissed, the other widow, Siobhán O'Coffey, at Aughrim. What is it, he thought, that makes me so susceptible to widows? Or widows so susceptible to me?

'Ah,' she murmured, 'I finally have in my arms the handsome hero I dreamed of, even it is but for a moment. I don't believe I can ever marry an ordinary man again. It must have been an act of God that made me sleepless tonight. Too bad that you have to leave so soon.'

Then she thrust him from her, and with her voice choking, said, 'Now be off with you before I come to my senses and turn you over to the guard.'

Tadhg embraced her, kissing her fiercely, before releasing her. 'I owe my life to you, Meg Murray. May God be kind to you, and bring you the man of your dreams.'

She stood silently in the shadows, watching him. Then, with a dab at her eyes, she turned and walked back up the street. Tadhg walked bravely to the gate - where a group of armed soldiers stood talking - elated with the sudden turn of events. If luck remained with him, he would not only return alive to his own lines, but would bring the key to the Rebels' code with him, fulfilling his mission! It would redeem him for his dereliction at Grianán Ailigh.

He boldly asked for Sergeant MacGillivray, who turned out to be a tall Scot with a pronounced Highland accent. Dressed in a kilt, he had a huge claymore at his side. 'What is it you want, mon?' he asked brusquely, eyeing Tadhg's shirt and trousers curiously, as if Tadhg reminded him of someone whom he couldn't quite place. 'And what are you hiding under your arm? Some horsemeat you have brought as a gift?'

Adopting his Midlands accent, Tadhg said, 'I'm supposed to get to General Kirk's camp at Inch with an important message, hidden you know where.' He winked broadly at the Scot, pointing to his posterior with his index finger. 'And I'm carrying an Irish uniform if I have need for it.'

The sergeant grinned. 'Aye, 'tis an odd place to carry a message. As for me, mon, I prefer to carry my messages in my brain. But perhaps you are carrying your message in your brain, too, for there's no accounting for where you Englishmen have your brains.'

Loud guffaws followed the sergeant's snide remark. Apparently the other guards were fellow Scots. Tadhg's temper flared, but the overriding seriousness of his situation kept him under control. However, one insult deserved another.

'If you Scots had our English brains,' he taunted, 'Scotland would be ruling England instead of England ruling Scotland. And isn't James Stuart over there one of your countrymen?'

The shaft struck home. The sergeant bristled. 'James is only one quarter Scot, and that most likely is diluted. I am of the Clan Chatten, from the region of Badenoch. We are all fighting men, we MacGillivrays, MacPhersons, Davidsons, MacIntoshes and Farquarsons. In many a battle has the Clan Chattan defeated you Sasanaigh.'

Suddenly realising that he was talking out of turn since he was now representing the English cause, the sergeant said irritably, 'Better get out of here and through the gate while the Irish yonder are napping at their posts.' His good humour restored, he grinned impishly. 'We go out there occasionally and steal their food while they are sleeping on duty.'

He turned to his men. 'Open the gate and let him through. I don't want Colonel Mitchelburn on me for holding up his couriers.' He outlined to Tadhg the best route to take to get to Alderman Tomkin's orchard where he could put on his Irish uniform to pass through the Irish camp, apparently the procedure used by the Rebel spies.

It was dark and lonely as Tadhg cautiously ventured out across the trenches outside the walls. He crossed himself fervently, then offered up a silent prayer that King James's men wouldn't fire on him before he had a chance to identify himself. Donning his own uniform again, still damp from his immersion in the river, he called out softly in Irish as he approached Jacobites' outposts. Were they asleep? Or were they waiting for him to come closer before firing? It was silent as the grave. His scalp tingled with fear, every nerve was on edge. What a way to die, he thought bitterly, shot by your own comrades, and only a Protestant Bible in your hands. No priest or rosary. Would he be recognised as an Irish soldier and be given proper burial in consecrated ground? Or would he be left to be eaten by the dogs of Derry that brought five shillings and sixpence?

Creeping slowly along, he was suddenly conscious of the sound of voices conversing in the Irish. He shouted to them to hold their fire, that he was a soldier of King James returning from a secret mission, and needed a guide through the lines.

After a spirited discussion, with one voice protesting that it was better to shoot first and investigate afterwards because it was probably a trick by Irish-speaking Rebels, he was ordered to advance slowly with his arms raised. Happy, he did as instructed, and shortly was greeted by a corporal of Colonel Gordon O Neill's Regiment named MacCormack, whom Tadhg knew slightly. He escorted Tadhg to the revetment where other members of the company greeted him curiously. He identified himself to a Lieutenant Michael O'Madden, and briefly explained his mission.

'You were in Derry?' the lieutenant asked, his lean face showing his disbelief. 'And you got out again?'

'That is right, *a dhuine uasail*.'

O'Madden shook his head, still unconvinced, but accepted Tadhg as a member of Tyrconnell's Regiment. He ordered Corporal MacCormack to escort him to his regiment, and verify his authenticity.

Before leaving, Tadhg asked if the Rebels on the walls could hear them from this post.

'If you can shout loud enough,' MacCormack said.

'Sergeant MacGillivray,' Tadhg roared, "Can you hear me?'

'Yes, who is it?'

'A secret agent of King James you just passed through your gate. Now where did you say your brains were?'

A futile barrage of musket shots in Tadhg's direction was the Scot's furious answer. Grinning broadly, he followed the corporal to his own camp where he was greeted rapturously by Conor and Dónal who had been sure they would never see him again. Then Tadhg went to Cornet Butler, who was still awake trying to think of how he could explain the failure of the expedition and the loss of Tadhg to the enemy.

When the Cornet saw Tadhg, he was so happy at finding him alive and well, that he admonished him but mildly for his foolhardy venture into the camp of the Rebels. Tadhg avidly related his adventure, making the officer promise not to mention Meg's name for fear that loose talk would reach the Derry authorities, thus incriminating her in Tadhg's escape. Then he triumphantly drew forth the object given him by Meg, handing it to Cornet Butler after removing the cloth wrapping.

'This is the Reverend Walker's Bible,' he said proudly. 'It contains the key to the rebels' code!'

Cornet Butler's gloom vanished. 'What a prize!' he gloated. It was an old Bible, its cover tattered and dog eared. As the cornet opened it to its flyleaf, a piece of paper fluttered from it. He retrieved it quickly, spreading it near the candle at his bedside.

'Dear O'Wilkinson,' he read aloud,

If you want to be a good spy, don't be so trustful in future missions. Especially with women. You will discover that they, too, can be deceitful at times. You can keep this Good Book since it belonged to my husband who will need it no longer. I knew that if I gave it to you pretending that it was the Reverend Walker's, that you would happily leave Derry at once with your prize. Otherwise that impulsive Irish heart of yours might have induced you to remain to discover that elusive key to the code, the purpose of your rash adventure. I just couldn't bear to see you become gallows bait. This book is my gift to you. It is a good Protestant Bible. Maybe it will lead you from Papism. Maybe it will be helpful in other ways as well. Read it and think. There are keys to Heaven as well as to codes. So farewell, noble hero, who came to me at the wrong time. I'll think of you often on the long, lonely, cold nights. Meg Murray'

Cornet Butler let the letter flutter from his fingers. He looked up to an abashed Tadhg expectantly. 'Well?' he asked.

Tadhg grinned in spite of his embarrassment and

237

disappointment. Then he shrugged his broad shoulders. 'Ach!' he said, 'tis better to be a live fool than a hanged hero.'

Cornet Butler sighed. 'You and your *cailín*. They'll be the death of you yet. And this one tries to make a Presbyterian out of you. But what about that message you said Holmes carried? Let me have it, and perhaps we can salvage some good out of this incredible night.'

'I don't have it. I had to give it to the officer at Derry.' Then noting the Cornet's unhappy countenance, he added quickly, 'But I memorised the beginning: 'To God we render our grateful appreciation for His many benefits through the intercession of Saint Cyril, Saint Valentine, Saint Walpurga, Saint Luke, Saint Pascal and Saint Linus."

The Cornet had Tadhg repeat the message as he scrawled it on a piece of foolscap. 'Is this all?' he asked. 'That isn't much.'

'Like the original message, it consisted of a long list of numbers in six columns. Under the circumstances, I couldn't possibly have memorised it.'

'Without the numbers, it isn't of any value,' the Cornet said glumly. 'I'll give Major O'Meara this portion of it in the morning. Now if you'll promise not to go on any more unauthorised expeditions in the future, I will not mention this episode further. It could be damaging to both of us. For the record, you never went to Derry. You got the first part of the message from Holmes, but unfortunately he snatched it from you, and then drowned in the river. His body, and the message, were not recovered. Tell your two companions to forget the Derry incident. Swear them to secrecy. Understand?'

It was difficult for Tadhg to refrain from telling the Cornet that Holmes had actually mentioned a name in conjunction with the message, but despite his strong affection for Edmund Butler, and his loyalty to king and country, he knew that Lady Mairéad's sex, her youth, and her beauty, would not avail her against the charge of treason to the king. The mere thought of the hangman's knot around that delicate white throat, the terror in the green eyes, and the last cry of fear and anguish as she plunged to her death, was enough to seal his lips forever.

His preoccupation with his personal problems, and the related situation involving Sir Oliver Trent, the friend of Lady Mairéad, and Tadhg's promise to Major Nangle, drowned in the river passage at Cladybridge, was noticed by Cornet Butler, and he asked if there was anything amiss. But Tadhg shook his head, keeping his secrets locked within himself, and the officer did not probe any further.

Returning to Conor and Dónal, he extracted their promise not to ever mention the boat trip to Derry, or mention of Lady Mairéad by Holmes.

He held out the Bible, his face rueful. 'I'll keep this as a reminder to not ever again take anything for granted. I never read the Bible before. It might help to improve my English.'

'That's a Protestant Bible,' Conor said disparagingly. 'Most likely it's full of lies. Besides, it's a sin for a Catholic to read a Protestant Bible.'

'That may be,' Tadhg replied cheerfully, 'but it's my very own. With my English Grammar from Donough and my grammar from the Frenchman in Dublin, and this Bible, I now have three books. Sure, and if I keep it up, I'll soon be having a whole library.'

'With a Protestant Bible, and a Dissenter's grammar,' Dónal teased, 'it's a Protestant minister you'll becoming soon.'

The following day, disturbed by Conor and Dónal's comments, Tadhg called on Father Taafe, the regimental chaplain, for advice.

'Did you say 'reading the Bible' or 'reading a Bible'?' the priest inquired, a sly twinkle in his eyes. 'There's a great difference.'

'I didn't know, Your Reverence,' Tadhg admitted. 'Is there more than one kind of Bible?'

'Dozens. Different versions of the Bible have occurred in various lands, various languages, and at various times. Bibles have appeared in Hebrew, Greek, Latin, English, German, French, Italian, and many other tongues. In fact, there have been so many different versions that the Holy Roman Catholic Church has had to put restrictions on their use by Catholics to make sure that the version is in accordance with the teachings of the Church. An accepted and approved Bible must represent Divine Revelation.'

'Is it wrong, then, for a Catholic to read a Protestant Bible?'

The chaplain nodded his head. 'Yes. Firstly, the Protestant Bibles tend toward interpretations which lead to doctrines of sectarianism, and secondly, if they are written in the vernacular, permission of the Pope must be obtained. The approved Bible of the Holy Catholic Church in the English language is the Douay Bible, published in 1610. It is based on the old Vulgate Bible written in Latin in Fifth Century by Saint Jerome.'

Tadhg was silent for a while. He had learned to admire the rich

239

language of the Bible he had received from Meg Murray. Along with his two other books, it had become a part of the trinity of his most valued possessions.

'What about the one called the King James Bible?' he asked timidly.

The priest smiled. 'That one turned out far different from what was intended. It was actually started by a group of scholars who were ordered to stay close to the approved Protestant version of the time called the 'Bishop's' Bible, which itself was based upon other Dissenter predecessors, including the one called 'Cranmer's Bible'. Preparation of a new version of the Bible takes a long, long time, with much study, research, debate and discussion.'

'I can see that it would,' Tadhg commented.

'Unknown to the strict Church of England officials who were supervising the word,' the priest continued, 'the small number of men left from the original group who completed the final draft, were greatly influenced by the Catholic New Testament completed in Rheims, France, way back in 1582. This Rheims Bible was translated from the old Latin Vulgate Bible I referred to previously. Although the King James Bible is on the forbidden or restricted list of the Holy Catholic Church, it isn't as bad as many other Protestant and Dissenter versions which are prone to gross errors in doctrine.'

'Would it be lesser sin to read the King James Bible than one of the others?' Tadhg asked innocently.

Father Taafe threw back his head and laughed heartily. 'Hundreds of years ago there were scholars who spent their time seriously debating the question of how many angels could stand on the head of a pin. Your question is in the same category. As I am at present only a chaplain concerned with the salvation of the souls of the soldiers of the regiment, I will have to defer your weighty question to the great theologians at Rome. If, and when, I ever get to the Holy See, I will try to obtain an official answer for you.'

Tadhg was thankful that the interview ended on so indecisive a note, and that the priest hadn't inquired as what prompted the questions. He suspected that the priest had been deliberately vague to spare him any embarrassment. He decided, aware of the whimsy of Father Taafe's delay of an official opinion, that he would keep on reading his King James Bible until the chaplain received the official imprimatur from Rome.

CHAPTER XVI

Strategy Backfires

Upon the recommendation of Cornet Butler, Tadhg had been advanced to the rank of Corporal. The Cornet himself had been promoted to lieutenant. Conor and Dónal were pleased with Tadhg's success, both as a soldier and as a student, for he was rapidly becoming fluent in English and French. He practised the latter daily on a French officer attached to the regiment.

General de Rosen returned from Dublin on 20 June, about the same time Tadhg did, again resuming command from General Hamilton who had succeeded the fallen Mamont. Exasperated that Derry still resisted, he vowed that he would demolish it and bury its defenders in its ashes.

Conrad de Rosen had been born in Liviona on the Baltic Sea, and had early become a mercenary soldier in the pay of various European rulers. Now one of Louis' most skilled and experienced generals, he was determined that drastic steps had to be taken. He ordered that several batteries of mortars be moved from Alderman Tomkins' orchard opposite Butcher's Gate on one side of the water to a hill above the bog on the other side of the town. A couple of small cannon, throwing a ball of 21 pounds, were then stationed at a convenient distance from Butchers' Gate.

Despite these improvements, the besieged still stubbornly resisted. De Rosen then ordered that all the Protestants civilians within a ten-mile radius of the town be rounded up and brought before the walls of Derry where they were to be left in the perilous position between the besiegers and the besieged. This was done.

On the morning of 2 July, the shocked defenders of Derry looked out over the walls where they saw the pitiful crowd of miserable men, women and children huddled forlornly outside the town. Their reaction was not what De Rosen anticipated. Defiantly they erected a gallows in plain sight of the King's army, and sent a message to De Rosen informing him that they would hang the twenty Irish prisoners they had captured if the civilians were not released. The messenger also carried a petition signed by the twenty prisoners entreating the general to free the civilians so that they wouldn't be hanged. Among the signatories were Lord Netterville (who had lost the fingers of his right hand); Major Edward Butler, the son of Lord Mountgarret; one of the

241

MacDonnel's, and a D'Arcy.

De Rosen's strategy was twofold: firstly, he believed that the plight of the civilians would induce the starving garrison to surrender; secondly, that if this was not accomplished, at least the defenders would take in their Protestant brethren, adding 2,000 more mouths to be fed from the dwindling stores, and so hasten the day of capitulation.

The Loyalists had learned from a Captain Strenger and a drummer who had deserted a week earlier that the inhabitants were so short of food and water that they were eating dogs, cats, and rats, and were boiling shoes, saddles and other leather objects to make more chewable and palatable.

Of the 30,000 persons who had been in the city at the start of the siege, half had died of flux, fever, other distempers and diseases, and from the weapons of King James's army. Of military supplies, however, there was still a great store, with the Williamites maintaining a continual fire on the Loyalists who had cleared the trenches before the walls, but because of the lack of heavy, hammering cannon, were unable to penetrate the stout fortifications.

When word of De Rosen's action reached James in Dublin, he immediately ordered that the civilians be returned to their homes. Always soft-hearted where his rebellious former English and Scots subjects were concerned, his interference ended an action that could well have ended the siege. The plan actually backfired, helping the Rebels. Anticipating the possibility of withdrawal, they had quietly at night allowed civilians from the town join those outside the walls, at the same time admitting those able-bodied men among them, who were willing, to enter the town and join the garrison.

Although bitter and angry at James's interference, De Rosen had no choice but to allow the civilians to return to their homes. As they passed through the Irish lines, Tadhg was surprised to see Meg Murray among them. He stared towards her as she stared at him coolly, then demurely lowered her eyes, and with hands folded across her breast, walked quietly past him.

James's decision to release the civilians enabled the Rebels to resist longer. Although a fleet under General Kirke had entered the lough on 16 June with a voluminous store of supplies, including food, Kirke refused to risk crashing his ships against the log boom erected in the narrow part of the river between Culmore and Derry.

Designed by French engineers, the boom consisted of huge fir logs linked by iron chains, and reinforced with a thick cable twisted around it. On one side of the river, the boom was anchored to the arch of a stone bridge. Several batteries of culverins and mortars were strategically placed to span the water, and soldiers armed with firelocks lined both sides of the river.

The Irish and the French, camped on Ballyugry Hill, about two miles southwest of Derry, could see the garrison signal frantically daily from the steeple of the cathedral, but Kirke stayed at his anchorage. News of the fleet's departure from England to Ireland had been known as early as 17 May when James had dispatched Lord Dongan, a nephew of Tyrconnell, to Hamilton at Derry with the information. This knowledge had given James's forces time to construct the log boom across the Foyle.

Tadhg was on duty near the end of June when his squad captured a Derryman named MacGimpsy who was attempting to swim the river to reach the fleet with messages for General Kirke. MacGimpsey informed his captors that a Captain Roche had successfully swum from the anchorage to the town on 25 June with information about the stores of food and military supplies, but had been prevented by James's men from returning to the fleet. MacGimpsey was hanged on a high gallows for all in Derry to see so as to discourage similar attempts.

Chapter XVII

The Sortie

One Sunday morning, with Tadhg's company attending Mass, and while the partakers were kneeling during the Liturgy of the Eucharist with their heads lowered, a murmur swept through the ranks, increasing in volume until it became a roar. The startled priest raised his head, as did his entire congregation, and he saw the gates of Derry opening and a great mass of armed men emerge, quickly assuming battle formation.

After an interval of stupefied amazement and confusion, the Irish troops ran for their stacked weapons. Amidst the excited bawling of orders from officers and non-commissioned officers alike, order finally emerged from chaos, and the Loyalists formed to give battle to the advancing foe.

With 'Roaring Meg' booming ominously, a shower of cannon-balls, grenades and mortar shells rained upon the king's men as the Rebels advanced slowly. Companies of horse protected the foot soldiers, musketeers and pikemen. Tadhg could see that their matches were all lighted and could hear the rattling of their bandoliers during the intervals of quiet between the roar of the cannon.

Fortunately for the Jacobites, every sixth man had been ordered to refrain from attending Mass, and to stand by with matches lighted for just such an emergency. Quickly they offered the glowing ends to their anxious comrades. While the Rebels advanced, the Loyalists made ready for them. The Derrymen had the advantage of a rise in the ground outside the walls, but this also meant that their muskets had to be aimed downhill. In the subsequent discharge of their weapons, many of the balls from the older-type guns dropped ineffectually to the ground.

Tadhg stood next to Thady O'Moriarty, who had joined him and Conor and Dónal at Mass. The Kerryman was pale, the barrage of cannonballs and mortar shells scaring away the usual sly humour in his green eyes. It was apparent that the poet was upset to find himself in the position of a combatant - a situation which he had always prudently avoided. Despite the loss of his sinecure after the scandal of the poem aimed at King James, Thady had managed to avoid a definite assignment in O'Neill's Regiment. The colonel had a soft spot in his heart for the rapscallion, and it was whispered in his regiment that he secretly agreed with the sentiment in the poem. It was probably because of this that Thadys's punishment was not more severe. The poet was used as a messenger, and was the undisputed favourite of the regiment.

Although the King's men in the immediate area were outnumbered by the 3,000-man force of the attacking enemy, they rallied so quickly, and charged so fiercely that the Williamites' advance was turned to a retreat. Tadhg could hear their officers ordering them to reform their ranks and attack, which they did bravely, but once again the fierce resistance of the Jacobites caused dismay, and again they retreated.

Ordered by their officers to halt, they reformed reluctantly. Their platoons fired alternately, with the front ranks kneeling while the rear ranks fired over their heads. Then, while the rear ranks reloaded their firelocks and muskets, the front ranks discharged their weapons. Tadhg was amazed to see some of the rebels were armed with ancient halberds, but they never got close enough to use them.

In the hope of forcing the Jacobites back, a company of the enemy horse charged down the hill to where the battle swirled around Tadhg. They were Enniskilleners, arrogant and fierce. A volley of musketry cut down many of them, the horses screaming in pain and fear, while the wounded lay moaning. Smoke drifted gently with each volley, and the pungent odour of the powder permeated the area, an appropriate perfume for the dead and dying.

Thady was unarmed - he had defiantly refused to learn how to use either musket or sabre - and now he was forced to move with the surging mass of men that hemmed him in. He was alongside Tadhg, a most unhappy soldier of the king he despised, when a red-bearded Enniskillener spurred his horse to within a sword's-length of them. Tadhg's musket had just been fired, his pistol was at his belt, it was too late to do anything but stand and stare and await death. The Enniskillener grinned maliciously, and swung his sabre at Tadhg's head. Tadhg was conscious of the man's hand grasping the weapon, the big hand covered with fine, red hairs, the knuckles straining, and he felt his bowels convulsively clutching as death reached out to embrace him. But Thady, too, had seen Tadhg's great danger. With a hoarse shout of rage and defiance, he shoved Tadhg aside, and with his own arms raised in futile protection, took the sabre's blow.

Angered at the loss of his prey, the Enniskillner looked down at the fallen Tadhg, but he had delayed too long. Dónal Óg shot him dead and he slipped slowly from his saddle, then fell heavily to the turf alongside Tadhg and Thady. The poet was holding out his arms, staring uncomprehendingly at the bleeding stumps, while his severed hands, as if in supplication, lay beside him.

'*A Mhúire is trua*,' Tadhg muttered hoarsely, 'he's lost his hands in saving me.'

'And he'll lose his life, too,' Conor shouted at Tadhg angrily, 'if we don't attend to him immediately.'

Quickly Conor tore the lining from his coat, and bound it tightly around Thady's wrists, the spurting blood now slowed by the confining bandages. 'Help me carry him,' Conor ordered Tadhg, his voice sharp with impatience.

Conor's incisiveness penetrated Tadhg's torpor. He took Thady's legs while Conor lifted by the arms, and forced their way to the rear. The third rally by the Williamites had ended as disastrously as had the others. This time there was no turning the men as they broke and ran for the safety of the fort, streaming through the gates as fast as they could run.

Thady's eyes were closed as they carried him, moaning softly, to the makeshift spital in a gentle glade behind the ridge of a hill. His bandages were now soaked with blood which trickled slowly on to his gay uniform. Poor, foolish Thady, Tadhg thought, his eyes glistening with tears, giving up his own life to save mine.

The surgeon, a stocky man with a ruddy complexion, one Cathal Maguire of the Baron of Enniskillen's regiment, nodded with approval when he saw the bandages.

'Well, at least you didn't let him bleed to death,' he greeted them. Deftly removing the bandages, he daubed the stumps with a tarry material, and expertly applied new bandages. 'Better job of surgery than I could do. Nice and clean. Well, he'll never handle a musket again, that's for sure.' He glanced at Thady's uniform. 'One of Gordon O'Neills men, eh? Poor lad, at least he can be buried in his native Ulster if he doesn't make it.'

'He's not an Ulsterman,' Conor hastily corrected him, 'he's from Kerry.'

'Is he going to die then?' Tadhg asked, his heart heavy.

Maguire shrugged. 'He's in the hands of the Chief Surgeon now,' he remarked piously, looking up to Heaven, 'but we'll do the best we can for him. His pulse is slow. His colour is bad. He's lost lots of blood. Pray for his recovery. Perhaps God will have pity on him, even though he's not from Ulster.'

'Why did he do it?' Tadhg asked Conor as they returned to their area. The battle was over as quickly as it had started. The wounded and the dead were being removed. 'Thady never wanted to be a soldier. He didn't even belong to our regiment which was being attacked. Yet he saved my life at the risk of his own.' Tadhg shook his head in wonderment. 'Why, he wasn't even armed!'

'Thady is a proud man,' said Conor. 'If he had been born a hundred years ago or more, he would have been a powerful member of some great lord's household. But he picked the wrong time, and now he's forced to earn his bread like any *spailpín fánach* along the rough road of life. His poem about the king - if it was a poem - was in protest of James's stupid interference in the peaceful surrender of Derry. It would have spared all this bloodshed, including his own. So how could a proud man like that see you, his friend, struck down before his very eyes? You were defenceless at the time. To Thady, it was outrageous injustice. So he protested in the only way he could. Certainly, there was not time to compose an indignant poem.'

'Thady always was fond of Tadhg,' Dónal added, 'ever since he saved him from O'Larkin back in County Galway.'

'Yes, and in Tadhg he sees the personification of Fionn MacCool, the giant; Naoise, the legendary lover; Cúchulainn, the warrior, and Brian Ború, the leader. How could he allow such an idol be killed by an Enniskillener, a hymn-singing, mutton-eating grandson of a London latrine-cleaner? Does that explain it, Tadhg?'

Tadhg shook his head. 'No. He always seemed so selfish, always thinking of Thady first. What he wanted, he took. Including the *cailíns*, married or not.'

'There's no discrepancy there,' Conor commented. 'This Enniskillener was about to take something from Thady. You are his idol. So he reacted.'

They were greeted warmly by Lieutenant Butler, who was happy to see they had survived the Rebels' sortie. A few stragglers had been taken prisoner by the Jacobites. From them it was learned of the desperate straits of the besieged, and their bitterness towards General Kirke for refusing to run the blockade. The prisoners reported that Governor Baker, who had been ill for some time, had died on 30 June. Colonel Mitchelburn had assumed the duties and powers of governor. It was reputed that he was sharing the authority with the Reverend George Walker, the firebrand minister, but it was not clear as to the division of responsibilities.

The ease with which the Williamites had been repulsed boosted the morale of James's forces, but the number of acrimonious councils of war, and the number of couriers dispatched to Dublin demanding delivery of the wall-breaching heavy cannon, increased as the siege wore on.

General Hamilton wisely refrained from saying 'I told you so', but it was apparent to many of the veteran soldiers (and to many of the new ones, too), that James's intervention, his intransigence, and his contravention of the terms of the April surrender offer, had cost him an easy victory. Conor, as usual, was one of those disgusted with the King's actions. Perhaps his constant concern for his sister Máire and her brood contributed to making the life of a soldier so disagreeable to him, and sharpened his desire for the war to end so that he could return to Connemara.

'King James could accomplish the most good for Ireland, and himself, by returning to France, and stop interfering with the plans of his generals,' he argued vehemently with his friends. 'Maybe he would then be in a better position to persuade his cousin Louis to send all those promised supplies, especially the siege guns.' Conor snorted with disgust. 'Why, just the other day the King grumbled that if only we were English soldiers, we would already have brought him the town, stone by stone. Yet he himself refused to allow ships to be sunk in the channel to prevent Kirke's ships from entering the lough. His reason was 'he didn't want to spoil the future commerce of Londonderry.'

Tadhg and Dónal defended James. 'It isn't King James's fault that his cousin doesn't live up to his promises,' Tadhg declared. 'He's doing his best to win the war and free Ireland. Look what he did in Dublin to get the Parliament to return the old estates to the Irish.'

'He could go to France, and live in grand style,' Dónal added. 'But he stays in Ireland instead to help us defeat King William.'

Conor stared at his friends as if they were demented. 'Did you say that James got Parliament to return the confiscated estates of the Irish? Think again! Those estates restored by the Parliament were only those seized after the year 1641. All those that were stolen, from the first landing of Strongbow in 1169 up to the year 1641, were left intact in the hands of the descendants of those who had usurped them. What about the Irish families who owned all those lands? Weren't they entitled to the same treatment that your 'Patriotic Parliament' gave to the others? The members of that Parliament were a gang of opportunities who conveniently took care of themselves. All your Dowdalls, Talbots, Luttrells and their like were there to protect their own interests. And how did they get their lands? By plunder and conquest from native Irish families that didn't have lords or powerful friends of the Parliament to fight for them. And there are many of us who know that your good King James was even opposed to this small sop, that he was secretly against the repeal, but was in no political position to resist it. But I'm not such an *amadán* as to be taken in by all that *raméis!*'

'It isn't nonsense, as you called it,' Tadhg insisted. 'At least it was better than nothing. Besides, a lot of those old families that lost their lands prior to 1641 are no longer around. And aren't the Luttrells, Dowdalls and Talbots fighting for King James?'

Tadhg felt trapped by Conor's arguments. He had no positive answers to the issues presented, and was uncomfortably aware that perhaps Conor was right. But the King was the King, and that was enough. One was loyal to one's King. That is, when the King was a Catholic.

Each day he visited Thady. 'He's going to make it,' Maguire told him cheerfully. 'I'm going to teach him how to play the harp with his toes. A harper is of the more value than a poet anyway.'

But Thady was not amused by the doctor's banter. He was depressed and withdrawn. He sat listlessly staring at his handless arms. His once agile mind was dulled. Even though he was alive, the old Thady was dead. 'What use am I?' he would respond when forced into conversation. 'I'm condemned to being a miserable *bacach* for the rest of my life. It would be have been far better that my head had been severed than my hands.'

'But you're alive,' Tadhg would plead. 'Thank God for that.'

'A small favour, indeed! What good is a clock without hands? Absolutely useless,' he said bitterly, answering his own question.

'But you are a poet, not a clock,' Tadhg protested. 'You don't need hands to compose poetry, do you?'

'I'm a cripple, a burden. When I have healed, the army will say, 'Thank you, Thady O'Moriarty, for the use of your hands. 'Tis goodbye to you, Thady.' Then I'll be forced to become a wandering bocach, begging my bread along the road, and me without hands to put it in my mouth!' He turned away, his eyes sunken and lifeless in his haggard face. Tadhg left him sadly.

CHAPTER XVIII

Slán Leat, Thady

Tadhg worried continuously about Thady. The stumps were healing, and to all outward appearances he was making progress. But his depression was deep-seated. He was bitter at his fate. His personality was so altered that it seemed as if a stranger had taken possession of his body. Where he had once been garrulous, he was now taciturn; where he had been merry, he was sullen. He would answer a direct question, but would never start or prolong a conversation. Most of the time he stared off into the distance, the corners of his mouth turned down, his eyes remote.

What could be done for him? There were few occupations in Ireland for a man without hands. Especially one of Thady's temperament. It was unlikely that he could go back to his native Cahirconroe, for his scandalous affair with his young pupil precluded a sympathetic reception. In fact, he had more than once hinted that he would be shot on sight by her outraged family. It was possible, of course, for him to eke out a meagre existence as a penny balladeer in Dublin, but this perversion of his talents would be as galling to him as the loss of his hands had been.

Tadhg thought of appealing to Gordon O'Neill, but he knew that O'Neill's fortunes rested with the success of the Jacobite cause. This was yet in the future; Thady's need was in the present. It's a terrible thing, Tadhg brooded, that a man with a gift like Thady's should end as a beggar on the road, or in a dark corner of some poor cabin, dependent on someone's charity.

Thady could still compose poetry of course, if he only would, but who could afford a *file* these dark days? He was an anachronism. Unneeded and unwanted. He was an extraordinary man, but who wanted an extraordinary man? What was needed was ordinary men, with hands that could grasp a musket or swing a sabre. Now if Thady only had that gift of that great Ulster *file*, what was his name, who by the power of his poetry could make the lakes and rivers dance or retreat, he could win undying fame by inundating Derry, and all this futile fighting and dying would be ended. But, alas, Thady was not super-extraordinary.

When he thought of Thady being an extraordinary man, Tadhg was disturbed by some elusive memory, a shadowy thought, and his inability to recall it left him frustrated. Then one day as he was reading Meg Murray's Bible, and the image of Meg appeared, the answer came to him. 'I don't believe I can ever marry an ordinary man again,' she declared. Ah then, Tadhg exulted, I will bring you an extraordinary man instead!

Elated over his idea, he discussed it with his two companions. 'I'm sure she has substantial property,' he said, 'because she referred to Irish tenants and her extensive travels. And with two husbands gone, she undoubtedly inherited their properties as well. If we could only persuade her to take Thady.'

'It might be easier persuading her than Thady,' Conor said.

'But she is a Dissenter, and Thady is a Catholic,' Dónal protested.

'Not a devout one,' said Tadhg. 'It might not be the best solution, but it would get him out of this dismal hospital. And Thady does have a special rapport with the ladies.'

Thady's discharge from the army was arranged by Captain Félim O'Shiel, adjutant of Gordon O'Neill's Regiment. So, on 26 July, Tadhg set out with a totally disinterested Thady, but acquiescent Thady, for Kilmacrenan, the small Donegal town where Meg had been living when hostilities had started. Sergeant Gallagher had given Tadhg instructions on how to get there, a few miles north of Letterkenny.

As they trotted along on Cúchulainn's broad back like the day they had first met, with Thady sitting behind him with his handless arms squeezed around Tadhg's middle, Tadhg recalled how gay Thady had been. But now he was silent, there was no laughter on his lips, no amusement in the green eyes. Tadhg had explained the object of the journey, suggesting that they visit Meg Murray, that perhaps a solution to his plight might be reached. Thady had listened quietly, and when Tadhg mentioned they were going to visit a woman, Thady had half-smiled, and held out his arm sardonically in a mock embrace, then abruptly turned them so that the stumps showed plainly.

Tadhg had been forced to turn away, trying to suppress his pity and despair. In the end, Thady agreed to make the trip, at least for the ride, for it would be the first time out of the camp since the tragedy.

As he was assisted up on Cúchulainn, he gazed curiously about him, and Tadhg was heartened. Leaving Derry behind them, they traversed a barren countryside, Irish forage parties had stripped everything edible and flammable. Most of the farms were deserted, the owners either fled to England or to Derry. Some of the Irish countrymen, formerly labourers on the estates, had moved into a few big houses, and they waved gaily at the travellers as they passed.

Darkness overtook them as they approached Letterkenny, and they bedded down for the night in a stable behind a squalid inn. Although Thady was not talkative, he did respond to Tadhg's overtures more cheerfully than for some weeks, and there was little reference to his plight, which Tadhg optimistically assumed showed his interest in their venture.

They continued their journey in the morning. After several hours, they arrived at Kilmacrenan, a collection of crude cabins, clinging precariously to their foundations. The Widow Murray? Take the middle fork to the cross at the top of the hill, and if you come to a wee lake, why, you've gone too far!

The mist was rising from the Derryveagh Mountains as they rode into the yard. Meg Murray's house was a well-built two-storey building, made of Donegal granite, and timbered, like the houses in Dublin. It had a slated roof and numerous windows. A giant yew tree provided shade in the front yard, and Tadhg tethered Cúchulainn to a limb. Followed by Thady, he approached the massive front door. It was reinforced with broad iron bands, and hung on huge iron hinges shaped into halberd heads. Before Tadhg could knock, the door was flung open, and a blunderbuss thrust in his face. The muzzle looked as big as Roaring Meg's to Tadhg, and he recoiled so sharply, he bumped Thady.

Then the weapon was abruptly lowered, and he heard Meg's throaty voice exclaiming joyfully, 'In the name of Oliver Cromwell, it's O'Wilkinson!'

Tadhg smiled broadly, greeting her in the Irish, 'God bless all here,'

'And yourself likewise,' she answered, reversing their roles at Derry.

'Just to get the record straight, is it O'Murray or MacMurray?'

'It's O'MacMurray.' She laughed again. 'Come in, come in. But what brings you here? Another coded message?'

'It's an involved story, better told sitting than standing.'

They followed her into the room. A turf fire was burning cheerfully at the far end, and the aroma of cooking meat hung tantalizingly in the air. Soon they were seated, Thady introduced, and a servant dispatched for wine and glasses. Meg looked at

Tadhg fondly, and at Thady wonderingly. Thady, in turn, scrutinised her carefully, observing the luxuriant brown hair, unrestricted by ribbon or kerchief, and the alert brown eyes that followed Tadhg's every word or gesture.

Tadhg, too, was pleased with Meg's appearance. Dressed in a red jacket of fine cloth with white lace at the end of full sleeves, and a green apron that had two heart-shaped pockets trimmed with fine gold lace, she was a handsome woman, a great improvement over the emaciated, ill-clad, poorly groomed refugee in Derry.

The woman servant returned, putting a bottle of Spanish wine and three slender glasses on the table. Meg poured, handing a glass to Tadhg. Then she looked questioningly at Thady. He nodded. She filled a second glass. Thady put the side of his arm ends tightly on the glass and carefully lifted it to his mouth. With a terse '*Sláinte!*' he let the liquor trickle down his throat. Meg filled a glass for herself, then imitating Thady, using only her wrists as he did, raised the glass to her mouth.

Thady was startled. The green eyes came alive, showing his admiration and appreciation. For the first time since the sortie, they lost their distant bleakness, and a smile transformed his frozen features. Meg noticed the swift change. Why, he's a fine-looking man, she thought, albeit a bit wan. With his long hair cut, and his beard trimmed, and clean clothes to replace the dirty and blood-stained uniform, he could be very attractive.

Tadhg, too, was happily aware of the change in Thady, and Meg's sudden interest. 'Thady,' Tadhg said, 'is one of the rapidly vanishing *filí* of Erin. He was a member of Gordon O'Neill's Regiment until he lost his...'

'Gordon O'Neill?' Meg interrupted. 'That's the name not to be mentioned in this house, for if King William is defeated, your Gordon O'Neill and his clan will take away all my property. I am living here precariously now with the threat of confiscation over my head.'

'While I am your guest, and drinking your wine,' Tadhg remarked diplomatically, 'I will not dispute with you the true ownership of these lands. I wanted to say that Thady saved my life, and by so doing, lost his hands. There are all too few opportunities for a poet with the decline of the great Irish families, and with the loss of his hands, he is further handicapped.'

Meg looked at Thady, compassion in her brown eyes. 'What do you intend to do now?' she asked.

Animated by the wine and his first association with an attractive woman in some months, Thady grinned impishly. 'Marry a rich widow,' he replied.

Where Tadhg was delighted by Thady's response, Meg was taken aback. While she blushed, nonplussed at the bold rejoinder, Thady sipped at his wine again.

'This is an excellent wine, *a bhean uasail*,' Thady said, deliberately addressing her in a form above her social station. 'Isn't it difficult to acquire with a war going on?'

'Smugglers are seldom deterred by little things like war,' Meg said drily, regaining her usual savoir-faire. 'In fact, with normal commerce reduced or non-existent, the smuggling increases.'

Thady contemplated his wine thoughtfully. 'Arrah!' he exclaimed, 'perhaps I can become a smuggler if it is that profitable.'

A sad smuggler, with no hands, Tadhg thought, as all three sat embarrassed by Thady's remark. Then Meg relieved the situation. 'For shame,' she cried, 'a talented poet, I assume you are talented, contemplating wasting himself as a crude smuggler!'

'Thady composed a magnificent poem,' said Tadhg proudly, 'although he denies ownership, about King James and the siege of Derry.'

Meg turned to Thady, her mouth wide open with amazement. 'Are you the author of that? Why, we even heard of it in Derry. Although you didn't make us quite as despicable as King James, you certainly did make us sound like fleeing cowards. But we did like some parts, especially 'We'll never submit to crass King James, and we positively adored the refrain.' She blushed, lowering her eyes demurely as she added, 'Pog mo Thoin, Rí Séamus .'

Thady laughed so vigorously, he almost fell out of his chair. Tadhg was startled and dismayed to hear the vulgar expression from the lips of a woman. Then Meg, too, laughed heartily.

Meg's praise, her bold frankness, and the wine, coupled with the stimulation of an attractive woman, completed Thady's metamorphosis. Once more he became the loquacious, animated, sparkling Thady of old.

Although he did not acknowledge the authorship of the poem, neither did he deny it. Tadhg soon found himself relegated to the role of mere listener, while Thady and Meg discoursed on many subjects, ranging from poetry to the bouquet of fine wines. Thady freely bolstered his theories and opinions with quotations from Latin and Greek. Meg was obviously impressed with his erudition. It was a great revelation to her for her contacts with the Gael had been of conqueror to conquered, of master to menial, with the resulting condescension of an assumed superior to an inferior race.

'You should be a schoolmaster,' Meg declared enthusiastically, her eyes sparkling. 'We need one here who can teach other subjects than sums, thrift and lugubrious hymns.'

'A schoolmaster!' Tadhg exclaimed. 'Now why didn't I think of that?'

Thady glanced from one to the other, his eyes expressing doubt. 'An Irish schoolmaster in the stronghold of Dissenters? 'Tis not likely, my friends.'

Meg bristled. 'I own considerable property in this barony. I have something to say about who the schoolmaster will be.'

Tadhg seized upon the opportunity. 'Thady would need someone to help him. Could he stay here, on your farm, where your servants could assist him?'

Meg gazed at Thady speculatively. 'It might interfere with his goal of marrying a rich widow.'

'Or it might improve my chances,' he replied boldly.

'Do you think you have more chance of becoming an Irish Catholic husband in a Dissenter household than an Irish Catholic schoolmaster in a Dissenter stronghold?' she asked archly.

'All wives by nature are dissenters,' Thady replied, 'Catholic or Presbyterian.'

'Well, if it's hinting at marriage you are, I'm not sure if I would be having a schoolmaster as a husband, or a husband as a schoolmaster.'

''Twould be far better if I were master of the house as well as master of the school,' Thady said, a humourous half-smile on his lean face.

She threw back her head and laughed. 'You're a rare one,' she said.

'You told me in Derry that you could never marry an ordinary man again,' Tadhg reminded her. 'So I brought you an extraordinary one, or rare, as you called him.'

Meg gazed fondly at Tadhg. 'Well, if your heart is still set on marrying a Protestant and upsetting the Pope, I suppose that I could even the score and marry a Catholic, thereby aggravating the Reverend Walker back in Derry. By the way, how are you making out with his Bible?' She laughed again.

'Very well, thank you, despite the fact that I commit a venial sin every time I read it. I still haven't found the page the code is on, however.'

'And for that little joke, you brought me Thady?'

'One Thady is worth Ten Thousand Reverend Walker's Bibles. And, for that matter, one Thady is worth ten thousand Reverend Walkers.'

She nodded. 'You might be surprised, but I agree with you.'

'Well, then, if we are in agreement, I had better be getting back to camp before King James comes looking for me.'

'If he does, I'll run him off the property with my gun. I'll blister hes royal seat so that he won't be able to sit on his throne for a month. Leave Thady here. We can make him master of the school first. As for his becoming master of the house, he'll have to prove his capabilities.'

Tadhg arose. 'I want to thank you again, Meg Murray. When I bade you goodbye the last time, I certainly never expected to see you again. My thanks to God for sending you home.'

'And your Marshal De Rosen.'

Thady walked with Tadhg to where Cúchulainn was tethered. He smiled whimsically. 'Although I prefer to pick my own *cailíns*, Tadhg, I appreciate your help. She's an unusual woman. And if that isn't enough, she has a fine wine cellar, too.'

'*Slán leat*, Thady,' Tadhg said, turning his steed's head to the south. 'May God go with you and keep you.'

'May the wind always be at your back, Fionn MacCool, and let it blow you back to me again some day.'

Tadhg's emotions were mixed, sad to leave Thady, yet happy that he was more like his old self again. He rapidly blinked away his tears, and set Cúchulainn into a fast gallop.

CHAPTER XIX

The Unplucked Plum

Near the end of July, the gallant defenders of Derry, their ranks greatly decimated by death and disease, their food supply reduced to a few horses, and their daily diet of dogs, cats, rats, mice, tallow, salted hides, horses' blood, chick weed and meal reaching the point of exhaustion, requested a parley to send a messenger with instructions to sound out the Jacobites on terms of surrender.

The messenger was given a full meal and wine to drink. His belly full, he described the dire straits of the garrison and the civilians, smacking the lips over the wine, he commented, 'This is far more tasty than our only beverage which is water mixed with ginger and aniseed. And although I wouldn't recommend it for its flavour, a mixture of starch and tallow not only helps to stifle the pangs of hunger, but is also an excellent cure for such distemper as looseness of the bowels. It has helped many of our men to recover from this debilitating malady.'

He readily acknowledged that of the original 7,020 men, representing eight regiments, with 117 companies of 60 men each, plus 341 officers, there were but 4,200 left. The ratio of loss among the civilians was equally as great.

King James was jubilant upon learning that the rebels were ready to negotiate. But alas, his enjoyment was short-lived. General Kirke, who had vacillated for six weeks, finally decided to relieve the town. He dispatched the Mountjoy of Derry, with Captain Michael Browning in command, and the Phoenix of Coleraine, under Captain Douglas Master, to try to breach the log boom.

Convoyed by the frigate Dartmouth, the two ships bravely approached the Narrows, like ducks between two rows of hunters. When the ships were within range, the Irish opened fire from both sides of the river, assisted by the bigger guns at Culmore.

Tadhg and his companions watched with angry amazement as the Mountjoy successfully ran the gauntlet. It seemed as if it had a charmed life. Then it hit the log boom with tremendous force, causing the boom to break under the impact. The recoil, however, caused her to run aground, where a murderous fire from the Irish raked her mercilessly, killing Captain Browning and many of the crew.

Aground on the mud banks, the Mountjoy was a sitting duck. Before preparing to board her, the gleeful Irish fired a tremendous broadside which had been intended to cripple their prize decisively had the opposite effect, for the Mountjoy reeled so heavily under the blow, that it was set free again.

The startled Irish then watched incredulously as the battered ship joined the Phoenix on a successful run through the shattered log boom to Derry. As the vessels approached, pandemonium broke loose within the walls of Derry, with loud huzzahs, and cries of rejoicing mingled with the indiscriminate firing of cannon and hundreds of muskets. Just 105 days after the gates had been slammed and locked in the faces of the arriving troops of the Earl of Antrim, the besieged town was relieved!

On the following day, 31 July, the disappointed, dispirited and defeated Jacobite decamped. The ripe plum had failed to fall. It was now apparent, even to the most optimistic, that it would remain unplucked.

PART III

Leinster

Cast of Characters

*Marshal Schomberg, a French hugenot General in the service of King William of England

*General Peguilin de Lauzun, a favourite of Mary of Modena, detested by all but James and Mary, his queen, chosen to command James' Army in Ireland by King Louis XIV

*General Zurlauben, a second in command to Lauzun, a competent veteran French officer

*Father Petre, confessor to James, an intriguing, officious Jesuit

Mattie Moley, a Dublin criminal, for whom no crime was to heinous

Wally Whiskers, a Liffey gabbard captain

Captain Henry, smuggler, sensualist and English agent

*Captain Tadhg O'Regan, commandant of Charelmont

*James FitzJames, the Duke of Berwick

*Henry FitzJames, the Lord Grand Prior, James' brother

*Pope Alexander VIII, successor to Pope Innocent XI

Henry FitzGerald, uncle to Lady Mairéad FitzGerlad

Luke Johnson, Dublin livery stable owner

*Comte D'Avaux, French ambassador to Ireland

Siav MacClancy, friend of Connor O?

*Edmund Harney, cornet in James' Irish Army

*Father Tadhg MacCarthy, King James' chaplain

Sir Oliver Trent, a protoge of the Viceroy and friend of Lady Mairéad FitzGerald

Seamus O'Lynn

(* denotes historical figures)

CHAPTER I

Marshal Schomberg

Coincident with the relief of Derry and the departure of James's Army, information came through James's agents that a large army of Williamites, under Marshal Schomberg, was sailing for Ireland with the intent of landing at Dublin. James had great respect for the Marshal's military skill for they once had been comrades in arms for Louis XIV against the Duc de Conde.

Faced with the debacle at Derry, and the new threat of a powerful foe on their flanks, the Royalists headed towards the capital by the fastest possible route. Stopping briefly at Charlemont, near Armagh, General Hamilton garrisoned the old fort with a detachment of 300 men under Captain Tadhg O'Regan. The rest of the army marched to Drogheda where James joined them.

An urgent request was issued throughout the country for more men to swell the ranks of the Irish Army. But even as the new recruits rode or marched into Drogheda, others were departing to return to their homes. Conor was one of those sorely tempted to return to Iar-Chonnacht. Disillusioned with James, and torn between his love for his widowed sister and her family, and his affection for his two comrades, it took the combined entreaties of Tadhg and Dónal to keep him from joining the exodus.

Conor was strongly contemptuous of James, agreeing with many of the disgruntled members of the army that James was a chronic loser, and as long as he remained as commander-in-chief, ill fortune would be their lot.

With James's return to the army, the special guard was reinstated. Its members were to remain in the vicinity of the king at all times. Their tents were set up near his, their mess tent was near his, and they followed him wherever he went. Tadhg watched carefully all the men who came in contact with the king, or his chief lieutenants, always on the look-out for the sandy-haired officer he had encountered on Windy Hill. He learned to recognise the most influential members of the royal household, Scots and English all - Lord Dover; the Earl of Melfort; Duke Powys; the Duke of Berwick, and his brother, the Lord Grand Prior; General Dorrington; General Wauchope and Lord Buchan. Not an Irishman in the lot!

Then there were the representatives of France: the Comte D'Avaux, Louis's personal envoy to Ireland; General de Rosen; General Zurlauben, and the Marquis de la Hoguette.

Whenever a new regiment arrived, or was formed, Tadhg made it a point to visit the adjutant and inquire after Captain Hugh O'Flaherty. But his quest was always futile.

General Schomberg, who had landed near Belfast instead of Dublin, quickly succeeded in capturing the Castle of Carrick-fergus. Lieutenant Colonel MacCarthy Mór, having but one barrel of gunpowder for his entire regiment, was forced to surrender after a feeble and futile defence.

With the loss of Carrickfergus, and the gallant but unsuccessful defence of Charlemont by Tadhg O'Regan and his handful of men, all of Ulster was lost to the Jacobites, thus freeing Schomberg to march southward to Dundalk. Word of his approach being known, the king dispatched two detachments, under Lieutenants Butler and Garland, to observe the foe's movements. Conor and Dónal accompanied Lieutenant Butler's unit, taking the road to Slane, and passing through the mountains towards the little hamlet of Ardee, while Lieutenant Garland's unit took the route on the side of Lurgan Race.

After reconnoitering the area thoroughly, Lieutenant Butler returned with the information that Schomberg had stopped to set up camp. He had carefully anchored his left flank on the sea, his centre reached towards Dundalk, and his right extended along Castle Bellew. Conor and Dónal reported to Tadhg the entire Williamite army, exaggerating its size due to their inexperience in estimating large numbers of men spread out in a long arc.

On 11 September, the drums were beaten, and the order was given for the army to march. It moved slowly about eight miles to Ardee, over the green fields of the lush valley, camping on the south side of the River Dee, in an area farmed by one Séamus O'Lynn a tenant of Lord Bellew's.

Since the supply train, lagging behind as usual, had failed to arrive, most of the men were without tents. Autumn's nip was in the night air, but fortunately there was no rain. Tadhg, being part of the king's entourage, was one of the lucky ones with a tent. He wished he could share it with Conor and Dónal, but they were obliged to stay with the regiment.

The following Monday, King James, accompanied by several regiments of horse, rode out to examine the enemy's position at first hand. It never failed to amaze Tadhg, when he was riding behind the king, that but a year and a half before he was a simple fisherman on a remote island in the Atlantic. The King rode a magnificent black horse, his erect body, resplendent in armour, seated royally on an exquisite saddle. He was, if nothing else, an excellent horseman.

Finding no large body of rebels, they returned to camp. The following day, the army moved again, this time to within five miles of Dundalk. The king then set up quarters in a cabin at a little village near Fane Bridge. His army was stretched along the river as far as Allardstown in a good defensive position. On Saturday, the entire army, in two columns, marched boldly up to the Williamites, trying to incite them to battle, but to no avail as the wily Schomberg refused the bait.

When Schomberg's impetuous young officers provoked at the sight of the hated Jacobites tauntingly paraded before them, attacking their outposts and making sallies into their lines urged the general to give the order for battle, he told them to keep their breeches on, and to wait and see what would happen. The marshal, now 75 years old, a veteran of most of the major wars and campaigns in Europe for the last half century, was both wise and experienced. He didn't intend to be stampeded into battle until he was ready, and then only on terms and conditions of his own choosing. To make sure that nothing would occur to upset his strategy, he promptly issued the order that no cannon was to be fired unless the enemy came within musket shot.

After parading before the foe, the Jacobites returned to camp. The weather had turned foul, with heavy beating rains, followed by cold, miserable days, and then more of the dreary, soaking rains. Despite vigorous attempts to drain their trenches, Schomberg's men fought a losing battle against the weather. Lacking dry quarters and having little wood to make fires, or fresh straw for their beds, conditions were ideal for the spread of flux and fevers. Soon scores were dying every day.

Conditions were more favourable for James's Army, with plenty of area to forage in, wood and thatch for huts was plentiful, as was firewood. Fresh food was available from sympathetic country people. There was no shortage of food for the horses.

Morale was good despite the loss of territory in County Sligo where 500 Enniskilliners had crossed the Curlew Mountains, attacking and defeating the Jacobites under Colonel O'Kelly who was captured together with 500 of his men. Another 250 were killed.

Observing Schomberg across the river, riding with uncovered head, King James turned to Tyrconnell, and in tones loud enough for Tadhg to hear, said sadly, 'If it wasn't for the presence of that one man, there wouldn't be much doubt about the outcome of a battle between the two armies. It is ironic to think, that but for the distance of a foot or two, he would have long since be dead and buried instead of being here leading William's Army against me.'

'To what does Your Majesty refer?' Tyrconnell inquired.

The king sat pensive on his horse for some time before replying as he pondered on the queer quirks of fate. 'It was at the siege of Mousson, away back in 1653. Then M de Schomberg and I were on the same side, fighting for Louis against French factions opposing the young King. We were under the leadership of the incomparable Turenne. One morning M.de Schomberg decided to go down to the trenches to reconnoitre. He was accompanied by the Vidame de Laon, a nephew of M de Turenne, in the centre, and M. d'Humiers, on the opposite side.'

James paused, recalling that day thirty-six years before, when he had been an eager young officer serving his cousin, Louis XIV. He shook his head sadly at the contrast to his present situation. Then he resumed his tale. 'Suddenly there was the sound of a single musket shot from one of the enemy. Just one shot, mind you! It could have hit M. de Schomberg. Instead it struck young de Laon next to him, killing him instantly. Thus spared by Providence, M. de Schomberg is now here in Ireland in the pay of my wretched nephew, that ingrate William, opposing my interests.'

'It is most regrettable, Sire,' Tyrconnell commented, 'that the musketeer selected the wrong target. Without the marshal and his experienced Huguenot brethren out there, there would be, as you most wisely observed, little doubt as to which side would triumph.'

As Tadhg watched, the king turned his head to Tyrconnell, nodding in agreement, the long nose and jaw in sharp profile.

As the days passed, Tyrconnell and the impatient French generals, aware that Schomberg's forces were greatly weakened by death, disease and desertion(the latter induced by printed handbills promising immunity that were spread among the ranks of the Rebels), urged the king to attack. After much vacillation, James reluctantly agreed. Accordingly, the entire army was ordered out for battle, marching opposite the Williamites with the intention of turning the enemy's flank on the side of the bog. A wave of optimism swept through the ranks, they were jubilant at the opportunity to finally come to grips with the enemy after months of inactivity and indecision.

Suddenly and inexplicably, the King changed his mind. He reversed the order to attack, and the disappointed army returned despondently to camp. Angry and frustrated, unable to contain himself any longer, General de Rosen told James, with undisguised scorn, 'Sire, if you possessed a hundred kingdoms, you would lose them all!'

The king stared coldly down his long nose at the Livonian. At another, earlier time, such a remark would have cost de Rosen his head. Now, dependent upon Louis's good wishes (and his generals'), James could do no more than glare at the source of the insult.

To those outside the king's retinue, many reasons and much conjecture were advanced as to James refusal to fight. But to those close to the king who were able to analyse his actions objectively, it was apparent that his personality had changed in the last few years. Where he had been resolute, he was now indecisive; although still physically energetic, there were now indications of mental deterioration; always of a phlegmatic temperament, capable of great calmness and decisiveness in the face of adversity, he was now inclined towards apathy.

James's spirit had been broken by many disappointments and disillusionments. His life had been replete with trecheries and treason. His father had died by the executioner's axe. He had been removed from the Admiralty because he had refused to become Anglican; when a male heir was born to Mary of Modena, the Parliament were hostile and suspicious because of her Catholicism. He had also to contend with his devious son-in-law, William, who, despite his protestations to the contrary, had designs on James's throne: he had been desterted by both his Protestant daughters, his departure from England was forced and he had been sorely let down by Louis, whose agreement to help with the troops and munitions had not materialised in the promised quantity. This coupled with the apparent apathy on the part of the Pope and Catholic Spain and the recent fiasco at Derry had all taken their distructive toll.

Thoroughly disgusted, Conor again spoke of going home to Connemara, saying that while cowardly James commanded, the

English Army of Schomberg was safe from attack. 'He didn't want to spill any English blood,' he exploded. 'If those were Irish troops opposite, he wouldn't have hesitated a moment!'

Although bewildered and disappointed at the king's decision, Tadhg defended him. 'He probably had good reasons which you don't know about,' he retorted hotly. 'He's had much military experience and knew that today was not a good day for battle. Besides, he has all those generals on his staff to advise him, so how do you know that they didn't give him the advice which made him change his mind?'

Conor hooted derisively. 'King James take good advice? that is, if the advice was based on solid reasons? Why, if your Lordship,' and he bowed low before Tadhg, his words dripping with sarcasm, 'were to advise him not to put his hand in the fire because it would burn him, he would be sure to do exactly the opposite. Do you know Sergeant Kingsley, the adjutant's assistant? No? Well, he used to be a member of the King's Guards back at St James in London. He personally overheard King James lambaste Lord Halifax and Lord Guilford one day. He informed them in no uncertain terms that he was the king, and made all the decisions; that instead of giving him unwanted advice, that their duties in the Privy Council were not to dissuade him from his royal decisions, but merely to provide him with legal justification for his royal acts. That's the kind of man your King James is!'

'I think you're unfair, listening to idle, foolish gossip,' Tadhg replied, frowning. 'And I agree with the king. He is the king, and if God didn't intend him to be, He wouldn't have made him so. That's what God makes kings for, to rule the rest of us.'

Conor laughed. 'Well, God saw that He made a mistake with James, even if you fail to see it, for He saw to it that James was kicked out. All that he has left now is Ireland, and the way he has handled things up since his arrival, he will lose that before long, surely.'

Tadhg remained stubborn and unconvinced. 'It isn't his fault. You, yourself blamed the French officers for the faulty log boom at Derry, and the failure of the guns to stop the English ships on the Foyle. King James will lead us to victory yet.' Then he added, confidently, 'Just you wait for the men and supplies his cousin Louis is going to send us.'

Conor stared intently at Tadhg, then shook his head in despair. 'You still haven't learned your lesson, *a chara*, that your friend

Meg in Derry tried to teach you. You're too trusting, and you believe anything you want to believe. You don't stop to analyse situations and think them out, you just act on impulse. You let your heart rule your head. Since you're forever prating about the supplies good Cousin Louis is going to send, what happened to those big siege guns he was supposed to send us to batter down to walls of Derry? What happened to the supplies for MacCarthy Mór at Carrickfergus? What about poor Tadhg O'Regan at Charlemont? Where are the promised working muskets for the regiment? Where are the uniforms for those ragged, shoeless men out there who are supposed to be soldiers? Where are the swords, pistols, musketballs, powder and cannonballs we lack? And where is all that money? If Louis is sending gold, why are we getting paid in brass money minted right in Dublin from old gateposts and ancient cannon? Tell me, *a chara*, tell me!'

Tadhg had no answers for Conor's scathing questions, he realised how foolish he would sound if he reiterated the promises of aid. Not wishing to quarrel, he remained silent, his heart loyal to James, but his mind uneasy over the factual presentation of his friend.

Conor reached out his hand to him. 'I don't want to be hard on you , Tadhg,' he pleaded, 'I just don't want you taken in by a lot of nonsense. Ireland's future is at stake. It can't depend upon a lot of unfulfilled promises.'

Despite the inactivity, and grumbling on the part of many of the soldiers for the failure to attack the Williamites, it was a pleasant camp. The brass money, although unpopular with the tradesmen in the towns, who often refused to accept it, was taken gratefully in trade by the country people who swarmed the area with cattle, fowl, and other produce for sale. King James had promised that it was the equivalent of silver money, and would eventually be redeemed for such, so the trusting peasants kept the Jacobite soldiers well fed. Fat geese were sold for eight pence, a beef carcass for ten to twelve shillings, French brandy and wine for one shilling sixpence. For many of the soldiery, coming from areas where they had eked out a bare existence while keeping the Protestant landlord fat, or the owner opulent in Dublin or London, they were having the time of their lives, with meat and wine several times a week where once it would have signalled a great occasion.

But, like all good things in this world, it inevitably ended.

Inexplicably, on 6 October came the order to set fire to the huts and move out. It was one of those irresponsible, but frequent decisions where no thought had been given to the consequences or to the planning. For the wind was blowing in the wrong direction, and the departing army was halt-blinded by the billowing, acrid smoke. Fortunately, the enemy was not alert to take advantage of the situation.

Even more grave and incredible was the fact, that through someone's carelessness, the entire army moved out, and an order to several regiments of horse and foot to accompany the king, had not been delivered. The king was left unattended except for Lord Dover's troop of gentlemen guards and the special unit to which Tadhg was assigned. It wasn't until General Rosen discovered this serious oversight that he ordered the army to halt immediately until the king and his small, inadequate escort could catch up. Again, had the enemy been alert, they might have captured James, thereby ending the war on a most ignominious note.

They camped that night near Ardee. Here the living conditions were horrendous. Continuous rains had bogged the earth, making a quagmire out of the area where the huts and tents were erected. And because of the heavy rains, little dry turf was available for campfires; a scarcity of saws and axes limited the hewing of wood for huts and fires.

The fuel shortage also hindered the thorough cooking of the fresh meat the men were eating. Combined with a lack of salt for curing the meat, this inadequate preparation of the food soon incapacitated large numbers of the soldiers, including Conor and Dónal, with 'country disease'. As part of the kings official family, Tadhg had it much better. Soon the poor food, the cold and wet, and the insanitary conditions, created an ideal climate for an epidemic of the flux which claimed hundreds of victims. Burial squads made their rounds of the camp daily. Large numbers of men, discouraged and disgusted with the demoralising and debilitating conditions, quietly slipped away during the night for their homes.

Without a battle, the Irish army's effective force was drastically reduced through desertion, disease and death. Gone was the high morale of the previous months as the men grumbled in discontent over the foolish abandonment of their comfortable camp for this death trap. Discipline declined as the enlisted men equally blamed all of their officers, since none knew who was really responsible for the order to move. It seemed to many that a deliberate attempt was made to reduce the Irish army to the level of the enemy's.

Sour, sad and stagnant, thus ended the campaign of 1689 which had started with high hopes and enthusiasm in the victorious spring march through Ulster with General Hamilton.

CHAPTER II

The Trap

Early in November the king and his retinue returned to Dublin. The rest of the army followed a week later. Tadhg was quartered in Trinity College, whose Fellows had been summarily dispossessed. Later the regiment of Henry Fitzjames, the Lord Grand Prior, bastard brother of the Duke of Berwick, was also given quarters there.

James named Doctor Michael Moore, a Roman Catholic secular priest, as Provost of the college. With the kings chaplain, the Reverend Tadhg MacCarthy, he helped to limit the thefts and destruction in the ancient buildings. Then he incurred the royal disfavour when he resisted the proposal by the kings confessor, Father Petre, to turn the entire college over to the Jesuits. Doctor Moore then retired to Paris to teach at the University, later to succeed to the Rector's chair there.

Word had arrived from Rome that Pope Innocent XI had died in mid August, to be succeeded by Alexander VIII. Inasmuch as Pope Innocent had opposed James' cause in Ireland because of the growing power of Louis XIV with whom he had feuded, and strangely supported the cause of the Protestant Prince of Orange, strong efforts were now made to have the new Pope steer an opposite course.

At his very first opportunity, Tadhg went to Cáit O'Reilly's. Rory was overjoyed to see Tadhg again, quickly reminding him of his promise to enroll him in King James's army. Embarrassed because the pledge had been made originally to make the departure from Dublin less difficult, Tadhg reluctantly agreed to take Rory with him. Cáit was sad to see the lad leave since she had grown quite fond of him, but Rory's eager pleading was too much to resist. So Tadhg took him back to Trinity College where he smuggled him into his quarters.

Rory was given a job in the kitchen as a scullion, happy in the belief that he was now a soldier in the king's army. 'Now that you're a Fellow at Trinity College, you must learn to read and write,' Tadhg informed him. 'It might be ruinous to the college reputation if it was known that a prominent member, Rory MacAuley, was illiterate.' So Rory was given lessons at night by Tadhg and Conor in reading and writing. A bright boy, he learned quickly and easily, and he soon became avid in his desire for education.

Now that he was back in Dublin, the Lady Mairéad was again much on Tadhg's mind. He was still greatly concerned by the statement by the deserter, Holmes, that the coded message at Derry had been intended for delivery to her. Several times he rode to the area of the demesne where she resided with her uncle, Henry FitzGerald, hoping to speak to her, but his visits were in vain. Worried over the possibilities and implications, he finally decided to discuss the matter with his companions.

They listened sympathetically, then Dónal asked, 'Why don't we just deliver the message to her as intended?'

Conor shook his head violently. 'No, it would be too risky at this late date. Besides, we never knew what the message included, other than the beginning. They would seek out the messengers, and that would lead right to us.'

'But she wouldn't know that until she deciphered or decoded the message,' Tadhg insisted.

'What good would that accomplish?' Conor asked. 'And we don't know if she can decipher or decode.'

Tadhg shrugged his shoulders. 'I just don't know *a chara*. I'm all confused. I can't believe that one so young and naive could be a traitor. And even if she was part of a spy ring, I can't believe that she could be the ringleader or mastermind.'

Conor was gentle when he replied to Tadhg, knowing his friend's feelings for the *cailín*, although he viewed Tadhg's worship and devotion to the Lady Mairéad as a futility, and hoped that in time he would forget her. 'What do you think would happen if we passed on a message to her?' he asked. 'Do you think she might send it on to the mastermind as you called him?'

A flicker of interest showed in Tadhg's eyes, his despondency vanishing. 'She would have to pass it on to someone, surely, why don't we try it? Perhaps we can find out what is behind all this.'

'But who will deliver it,' Dónal asked. 'None of us can because she knows all three.'

'I can,' Rory volunteered, his lively eyes fixed on Tadhg imploringly.

'Why not,' said Tadhg, smiling at the boy. 'He can say that he got it from a soldier at the Sign of the Curragh down near the river.' He addressed himself to the lad. 'Rory, do you think you can convince them that you got the message from a strange soldier, and if they doubt your story, not reveal where you did get the message?'

Rory nodded, his eyes sparkling. 'I can cry really easily,' he replied eagerly. 'And I can make up some whopping stories.'

The conspirators then got paper and pen, and Conor, who had the best handwriting, transcribed the greeting from the message taken from Holmes. He then listed six long lines of fictitious figures. Then wrinkled the paper, and rubbed it with dirt to give it the semblance of much usage, before giving it to Rory. The messenger then rode with Tadhg until they were close to the FitzGerald demesne where he dismounted to walk rest of the way on foot.

A guard had been placed at the twin-towered gate to keep out the king's marauding soldiers. He stopped Rory, who, in an impassioned plea that he had an important message for the Lady Mairéad, finally was allowed to proceed along the winding tree-lined driveway to the house. Here again the lad was stopped, this time by a footman who informed Rory curtly that such a buffoon as he, Rory, could go no further, but not to worry, the note would be delivered to the lady of the house, and forwarded to Liffey Exports.

Rory was hesitant about leaving the message with anyone other than for whom it was intended, but sensing he might get into difficulties if he persisted, reluctantly handed the note to the lackey. 'Be sure to tell her it was at the Sign of the Curragh where I got it from the soldier,' he insisted. The footman scowled, raised a heavy foot which he directed at Rory's backside, but the agile lad was already scooting down the driveway.

Joining Tadhg down the road, they turned back toward the town heading for Devil's Hook Charlie's pothouse. While they were trotting down Kilmainham Road, a messenger, a lanky fellow in livery, came dashing down the road, mounted on a sway-backed grey horse. Tadhg and Rory watched him as he turned north over Bloody Bridge into the new, exclusive Dublin suburb. If they had followed they would have seen him enter the drive to a magnificent estate near the Bluecoat School. The school had been closed by an order of Tyrconnell who ordered the scholars' beds transferred to the Great Hospital at Kilmainham for the use of wounded and sick soldiers.

Apparently the rats were stirring in their nest, for shortly after the FitzGerald servant started his return journey, a coach drawn by six matched white horses emerged furiously from the school estate. It crossed over the Liffey via Bloody Bridge, heading for the old part of Dublin, finally stopping at a squalid pothouse. A dilapidated sign, hanging from rusted iron hinges, depicted an animal, but probably only the artist would have recognised it for what it was supposed to be, a badger.

An elegantly dressed man descended from the carriage, meticulously avoiding the mudholes so as not to soil his fashionable shoes, and entered the low dive called The Badger. In a few minutes he returned with three roughly-dressed blackguards, who tumbled roisterously into the coach. With the coachmen guiding it expertly, it dashed through the narrow, crowded streets to the Sign of the Curragh, where the three toughs climbed out while the carriage and its solitary occupant clattered away down the street, scattering the hawkers, balladsingers and beggars who pursued their activities there.

In the meanwhile, Tadhg had left Cúchulainn with Luke Johnson at the livery while he and Rory hurried to the Sign of the Curragh. Conor and Dónal were already seated, each at one of the empty barrels that served as tables. Charlie greeted Tadhg with a joyous '*Céad míle fáilte*', and was determined to hear all about Tadhg's adventures since his hurried departure from Dublin. But Tadhg's earnest insistence that he listen to him, finally subdued the loquacious O'Malley as Tadhg explained what he wanted to do, and the parts that Dónal, Conor and Rory would play.

Charlie nodded his head, a happy grin on his face. Of the four barrels in the room, two were occupied by Conor and Dónal, and two vacant. While Rory squatted on the floor, Tadhg placed a barrel over him, then he spoke anxiously through the bunghole. 'Will there be enough air in there for you, Rory?'

The lad's muffled reply came in the affirmative.

'Can you hear me all right?' Tadhg asked.

'Yes, Tadhg,' Rory replied.

Tadhg then went to the fourth barrel-table and ordered a rum. Now the stage was set, but would the other actors arrive? The plan which seemed so solid when it was proposed, now appeared full of holes. What if the note hadn't been delivered to the Lady Mairéad? What if she had decided to do nothing about it? Was the servant at the grey house actually from the FitzGerald demesne? And if so, couldn't it have been another matter entirely which sent him on his errand? If the message had by now been delivered to another person, was there any assurance that person would react as they had hoped? Would they take the bait and appear at the Sign of the Curragh?

As if in answer to his questions, the door opened and three men entered. They scanned the room, and when they saw the three soldiers, conversed briefly in inaudible tones. Then they walked directly to the empty barrel-table where Rory was hidden. One of the trio, a squat, pock-marked man of evil countenance, loudly ordered three gins. As he turned his head slowly to scrutinise each of the soldiers in turn, Tadhg saw that he had but one eye. From the appearance of the empty eye socket, the eye had apparently been gouged out in a brawl. The remaining eye carefully examined Tadhg, taking in his great size, the pistol in his belt, his sword in its scabbard, and his *scian* at his waist.

Tadhg was reminded of Balor, the one-eyed god of the ancient Gaels, and shuddered at the man's malignant aura. 'Balor's' companions were both swarthy-complected, wearing jangling silver earrings. They drank their gin and conversed with each other. Balor, his inspection completed, beckoned to Tadhg with a grubby finger, shouting in a loud voice, 'Come join us, matey, and we'll drink a toast to the king!'

'What king?' Tadhg asked suspiciously, using the Warwickshire accents of Wilkinson.

'Why King James, of course. Who else?'

Tadhg scowled at the mention of King James. Balor, observing this, winked his one baleful eye at his companions, then repeated his invitation to Tadhg to join them. While Tadhg walked slowly over to their table, the one-eyed man bawled loudly for four gins. When Charlie set them on the barrel, the host lifted his glass, shouting, 'To the king and good Dutch gin!'

During his toast, he watched Tadhg closely to see his reaction to the coupling of the word 'king' in the same sentence with the word 'Dutch'. Sensing it was a test, Tadhg repeated the toast, emphasising the word 'Dutch' so that it was unmistakeable.

Obviously encouraged, Balor asked Tadhg if he had been in Dublin long, using the accent of the town, displaying a few broken teeth in a wide-open mouth.

'A couple of days,' Tadhg replied in a surly tone.

Balor's one eye roamed around the room. he pointed at Conor and Dónal. 'How come ye soldiers don't sit together? Got the plague?' He squinted at his gin as if to make the question seem

274

innocuous.

'They're both Popish, but one's from Ulster and one's from Munster, so they don't like each other.'

'What about you?'

'I'm English, so they both hate me.'

Balor seemed satisfied. 'You must have seen lots of fighting in your time. Ever get as far as Derry?'

'Londonderry,' Tadhg corrected him, using the name the Sassanaigh gave the old Irish town of Derry when it was settled by Londoners at the start of the century.

'Yez call it Londonderry, heh?'

'That's right,' Tadhg affirmed belligerently.

'No offence, no offence,' the other man apologised hastily. 'Ever carry any messages?'

Tadhg glared at him. 'What business is that of yours?'

Balor reached into the pocket of his grimy coat and produced three gold sovereigns. He bounced them on the barrel-head. When Tadhg looked avariciously at the money, the other man drew an old, blackened *duidín*, crammed it with coarse tobacco, and expertly lighted it with flint and steel. He crammed the short pipestem into his mouth, leaning close to Tadhg.

'These sovereigns are a reward for a soldier who brought a message today. He gave it to a young lad to deliver. If yez has the right answer, these little beauties are yours.' He jangled the coins temptingly under Tadhg's nose.

Tadhg stared long and hard at Balor before answering. He leaned forward so that only Balor could hear him. 'Well, let's say that maybe I had a message for a pretty little lady from an old friend of hers in Londonderry.'

The other man exhaled loudly, his foul breath making Tadhg move back on his seat. He took his pipe from his mouth, and to Tadhg's consternation, tapped the *duidín* on the barrel, the hot dottle falling through the bung-hole. Tadhg sat transfixed, waiting for Rory's loud howl and the upsetting of the barrel. But nothing happened! He breathed easily again.

Picking up the coins lovingly, Balor placed them in front of Tadhg. 'The pretty little lady wants to express her appreciation to you for delivering the message.' He arose, staring regretfully at the sovereigns on the barrel. He looked down at Tadhg, trying to smile, saying jocularly, 'Now that ye are a rich man, stop off at the Badger and buy a drink or two for your old mates.'

As his companions arose, he added contemptuously, 'They serve real gin at the Badger, not this foul home-made swill.' Looking at Charlie, he deliberately spewed a mouthful on the floor.

Charlie reached quickly under the bar, levelling a cocked pistol at Balor, who grinned malevolently but moved towards the doorway with his mates.

Tadhg nodded, pocketing the coins. 'I'll come down to the Badger later, after I finish this drink.'

After the door closed behind them, Tadhg motioned to Dónal to follow them to check their movements. He returned shortly, saying, 'They're headed up the street as fast as if the devil himself is after them.'

Tadhg then lifted the barrel, disclosing a grinning Rory. 'Jesus,' the lad said irreverently, 'I nearly howled when that hot stuff poured down my neck!'

'You're a brave lad and I'm proud of you,' Tadhg said, hugging him. 'I thought you would upset the barrel. If it would have been me, I would have screamed like a *beansí*, and knocked the barrel clear out of the room. Did you hear anything they said before I came to the table?'

Beaming and glowing with Tadhg's praise, Rory smiled. 'I heard them real plain. First they were wondering which one of the soldiers they should talk to, since there were three of them. Then one voice remarked that he would start with 'the big one'. This same voice added, 'Remember, when the Tholsel clock strikes the same hour of nine tonight, meet me at St Audeon's Gate. And you'd better be sober, or I'll cut off your ears and nail them to the gate.' After that there were two voices talking some strange language. Then I heard your voice at the table.'

'Ach,' said Tadhg, 'so they're planning to meet at St Audeon's Gate, are they? Rory, you did wonderful! You're a true soldier of the king.'

'Which king?' Conor asked, a twinkle in his eye.

'The one who provides real gin, not this vile, home-made stuff,' Tadhg replied, laughing.

Devil's Hook Charlie, who failed to see any humour in Tadhg's remark, shook his head in the direction of the door. Then he drew his forefinger slowly across his throat. 'Yon scum, Mattie Moley, is the greatest unhanged cutthroat in all of Dublin. He has powerful connections of some kind otherwise he would have long since been gibbet bait. He seldom comes here because I'll take none of his nonsense.' He glanced at Tadhg appraisingly. 'He must have had some real important business to come to the Sign of the Curragh and give you three gold sovereigns.'

'That he did,' Tadhg agreed, adding, 'It's sharp eyes you have, Somhairle.'

Charlie shrugged his shoulders. 'It's your funeral. Half of the bodies floating in the Liffey come from the Badger. It's not your charming company that Mattie wants, it's to retrieve those three pieces of gold he gave you.'

He eyed Tadhg from head to toe, estimating. 'Of course, it will take more than the three of them to carry your corpse down to the river since you're somewhat large. But there will be many a willing pall-bearer who will help for the promise of a drink or two. However, what's more to the point, is what Mattie wants of you.'

Tadhg's eyes grew troubled. 'I wish that I could tell you, Somhairle *a chara*, but I can't.'

Charlie studied Tadhg's averted face. He made a shrewd stab. 'Something about the pretty little *cailín*, heh?'

'Your ears are as sharp as your eyes, apparently,' Tadhg said.

'They are that. I don't mean to intrude into your personal affairs, Tadhg, but you're dealing with the most vicious, murdering scoundrel in all of Dublin. Since I know Mattie Moley well, I'd be most happy to lend you a hand tonight at nine o'clock.' He looked wistfully at his missing hand, saying apologetically, 'Sure and it's only one hand that I'll have to be offering.'

Tadhg smiled happily, impulsively reaching out to grasp Charlie's shoulder. 'Somhairle O'Máillie, your one hand will be most welcome. Where will we meet you?'

'At Christchurch. That's nearby. We had better all of us get there a little early.'

When the big, bronze bells of Christchurch tolled the hour of nine, the three soldiers of the king and the alehouse proprietor were waiting in the shadows near St Audeon's Gate. Loud singing and boisterous laughter announced the arrival of the two foreign sailors. Apparently Mattie Moley's warning about drinking too much had been disregarded. When a third person joined them, the listening quartet heard a long, abusive volley of invective as Mattie reacted to their violation of his instructions.

The trio then left, followed by Tadhg and his companions to the vicinity of Christchurch where a double waiting game commenced.

A cold rain was falling, chilling the watchers to their very marrow. Finally the object of Mattie's vigil was revealed. A coach, drawn by six matched white horses, with two men in the box, swept around the bend, heading for the front of the cathedral where it stopped. Immediately Mattie Moley and his two henchmen leaped out of the darkness, with the two swarthy sailors swarming over the coach seat, their knives flashing, and within seconds, the two coachmen's lifeless bodies toppled into the street.

Tadhg and his friends were so surprised and shocked at the suddenness and fury of the murderous attack that they stood uncomprehending and immobile for some moments before joining the fray. As Tadhg and Devil's Hook Charlie arrived at the coach, Mattie Moley was opening the door. He had a pistol in his hand, pointing it at the occupants of the coach. A woman screamed shrilly, and with the sound, Charlie slashed out with his artificial hand for Mattie's throat. The sharp hook encircled the assailant's neck before he could pull the trigger, and he fell heavily to the cobblestones, his throat slashed from ear to ear, blood spurting and burbling from the great wound.

With drawn swords, Conor and Dónal engaged the two sailors whose knives were inadequate for the unequal battle. As Conor dispatched one neatly with a thrust through the man's middle, the other wisely took to his heels, disappearing in the darkness.

Tadhg, his hand warily on his sword handle, peered into the coach. In the dim light he found himself staring into the fear-stricken face of the Lady Mairéad FitzGerald. And if this wasn't surprise enough, he saw that her companion, clumsily reaching for his sword which was wedged between his body and the side of the coach, was the sandy-haired officer he had seen at the base of the hill at Fionn MacCool's cairn.

'I beg your pardon, *a bhean uasail*,' he apologised to Lady Mairéad, in English, 'I didn't mean to affright you. It seems to be a habit of mine.'

'What's the meaning of this outrage?' the man blustered, looking alternately at Tadhg and the fear-stricken girl. 'Why did you halt our carriage? Who was that man with the gun?'

Hearing the man speak, Tadhg immediately recalled the voice. He had heard it the first time when he and Dónal had encountered the Lady Mairéad in her coach outside her home, and the second time when the man had appeared near Derry as part of the king's retinue. It was the voice that had troubled him when he had been unable to identify it. Tadhg wondered if the other man had in turn identified him as the soldier he had encountered at the base of the hill in distant Ulster.

Tadhg bowed. 'It was not us, *a dhuine uasail*, who stopped the coach, but three footpads, two of whom will never stop another coach. The third has escaped.'

'Which one?' Lady Mairéad's companion asked.

That's a peculiar question, Tadhg thought. What difference does it make? Aloud, he said, 'A foreign sailor. Another sailor lies dead along with the ringleader of the group, a Dublin thug named Mattie Moley.'

The Lady Mairéad, now over her shock, began to weep piteously, putting her golden head against her companion's chest. The man handed her his handkerchief, giving him an opportunity to gather his wits as he realised the danger in his question.

'You are a soldier?' he inquired, examining Tadhg's uniform.

'Yes. The Duke of Tyrconnell's Regiment. Likewise, my two companions here. The man who really saved you from being shot is Somhairle O'Maille who has an alehouse nearby.'

'I will most certainly commend you to the Viceroy when I see him,' the other man stated. 'As a matter of fact, we were on our way to the Castle when we decided to stop by the church for a moment. Would you please inform the coachmen to drive back to the lady's house? After this episode, she is certainly in no condition to go to the Duke's party tonight.'

'I am sorry, *a dhuine uasail*, but your two coachmen are dead. The sailors got to them as the coach stopped.'

'Oh, those poor men,' the Lady Mairéad exclaimed sorrowfully, and she began to weep harder.

After comforting his companion, the man said formally, 'I am Sir Oliver Trent. I will need someone to drive the carriage back to the Lady FitzGerald's demesne. Could you help us?'

Tadhg looked at Conor, who nodded. 'We will drive the coach, Sir Oliver, if there is some way of getting us back to the college where we are quartered.'

'That can be easily arranged,' Sir Oliver said.

'What about those bodies? Shouldn't the authorities be notified?'

Somhairle O'Maille, who had remained silent, now spoke. 'I will take care of that, Tadhg, *a chara*. You take the pretty little *cailín* back home.'

Tadhg glanced sharply at Charlie, noting the deliberate use of the expression 'pretty little *cailín*', and realised that the pothouse keeper, in his divination, was informing Tadhg that he had successfully put two and two together.

Closing the carriage door, Tadhg joined Conor and Dónal on the driver's seat. As Conor reached for the reins, controlling the restless horses, and made a turn in the narrow street, he laconically remarked 'Is this becoming a habit, our rescuing the Lady Fitz-Gerald?'

"Tis a fine habit,' Tadhg said defensively. 'Are you objecting?'

'Not at all, not at all.' Then he chuckled.

'What's so humorous?' Tadhg inquired, still sensitive.

'Nobody asked us if we knew where the lady lives. She, of course, knows it because you were at her doorstep the time she turned you and Dónal over to the soldiers. But I wonder if that amadán back there will realise it, and question the *cailín*. And now that you have saved her for a third time, will she tell her escort that you are the notorious Tadhg O'Cuirc who killed his second cousin in a duel?'

'It doesn't make too much difference now. I'm no longer the outlaw Rapparee but a corporal in King James's army.'

The coach, stopped for a moment by the guard at the entrance to the FitzGerald demesne, rolled through the massive wrought-iron gates, and up the spacious driveway. The trees, with winter's cold breath upon them, had performed their annual ritual and shed their leaves, standing stark and straight as silent sentinels. Under a covered archway, apparently the front entrance to the mansion, Conor braked the carriage with a flourish. Tadhg leaped to the ground, opened the coach door, and said solemnly, 'You are home, Lady Mairéad.'

Apparently recovered from her weeping, and the shock of the deadly assault on the carriage, she looked questioningly at Tadhg. 'It seems as if I am obligated to you again. By some strange Providence you are always at hand when I need help. It makes me feel ashamed for my action last spring when I denounced you to the soldiers. I want to apologise for it. Was that Dónal Óg and Conor whose voices I heard? Thank them for me, please. The three of you are my guardian angels. Now I must beg to be excused. The events of the night, and the tragic deaths of Sir Oliver's footmen, have greatly upset me. Goodnight, Tadhg.'

The sound of her voice, the obvious gratitude, the tender solicitude in her eyes, the opportunity of seeing and serving her again, overwhelmed Tadhg, and he turned abruptly to join his companions. A servant was aroused to drive the trio in the carriage back to their quarters in the college. As they revelled in the luxury of the elegant interior of the cab, they excitedly discussed the incident at Christchurch.

'Where does Trent fit into the picture?' Conor asked thoughtfully.

'I'm positive that he was the sandy-haired officer I saw at Fionn MacCuil's Hill,' Tadhg exclaimed excitedly. 'If so, he most likely was the one for whom the message was intended, and is really the man we are seeking.'

Conor shook his head. 'You have no proof, only suspicion. His visit to the site might have been as innocent as yours.' His blue eyes were guileless as he asked, 'You are innocent, aren't you?'

'But who could have arranged for Mattie Moley to try and kill him and the Lady Mairéad?' Dónal interrupted, before Tadhg could utter his indignant answer to Conor.

'We don't know if Mattie was going to kill Sir Oliver,' Tadhg stated. 'Obviously somebody arranged the whole affair. And I'm sure it was our message that triggered the whole episode. Don't forget that Mattie and his men showed up at the Sign of the Curragh patently looking for the soldier who gave it to Rory. And it was Mattie again who arranged the attack on the carriage. From the timing, it is apparent that he knew it would be there at that time. I'll wager a sovereign that Sir Oliver is behind it.'

'But why was it necessary to shoot the Lady Mairéad?' Dónal persisted.

'Because she knew for whom the message was intended. If I'm right, and it was for Sir Oliver Trent, then he was in deadly peril if there was a soldier loose in Dublin with an old message that could link him as a spy. So Lady Mairéad would have to be permanently silenced. And me as well when Mattie could arrange it.'

Dónal was shocked. 'Arrah, and what a cold-blooded sleeveen he must be!'

Conor nodded sombrely. 'And Tadhg was probably next on the list. He was supposed to appear at the Badger where he would have had his throat cut, and Mattie would have retrieved his gold sovereigns.'

'The dirty thieving villains,' Dónal said. 'But we put a stop to their plans.'

'Who is this Sir Oliver Trent, outside of his being a second cousin to John Montgomery?'

'Somebody told me last spring. I think it was the sergeant who escorted me to the Castle. A nephew of a former Dean of the Cathedral, Sir Oliver came over from London and has made a fortune in Dublin. Also, he is supposed to be planning on marrying the Lady Mairéad.'

'That's unfortunate,' Conor commented thoughtfully. 'Your suspicions of him might be prompted by jealousy.'

Tadhg nodded. 'I'm aware of that,' he replied despondently. 'It distorts my judgement I want desperately in my heart to believe that he is the spy and that Lady Mairéad is innocent. But I have to be honest with myself and admit that I might suspect and hate him for his relationship with the lady.' He shrugged his shoulders. 'Maybe she is the guilty one and arranged the attack herself. After all the message was delivered to her.'

'But there is no reason why she should have Sir Oliver killed. You yourself believe that he was near Fionn MacCool's grave to get that message. No I just can't see that,' Conor said.

'That's true,' Tadhg said gratefully, happy that Conor concurred with his opinion. 'We will just have to watch him until we learn something more definite and incriminating.'

'Don't you think we ought to inform your friend, Lieutenant Butler, about this? We might be getting in over our head. This Sir Oliver is a powerful man, and if our suspicions are correct, a mighty unscrupulous and dangerous antagonist.'

'No!' Tadhg replied vehemently. 'That would mean implicating the Lady Mairéad. That's the last thing I want to do.'

'All right, *a chara*, whatever you think best. But we will have to be mighty careful ourselves now that Sir Oliver knows that we were involved in saving the Lady Mairéad.'

'One good thing,' Dónal pointed out, 'Mattie Moley won't be able to tell him anything.'

'But that one sailor is still at large,' Conor said. 'Let's hope that Mattie didn't tell him who his employer was.'

CHAPTER III

The Ceremony

Several days later, with those portions of the regiment stationed in Dublin standing formation in the castle yard, Tadhg, Dónal and Conor were called up front and centre, and the colonel of the regiment, the portly Duke of Tyrconnell himself, read a commendation for the trio for 'Upholding the finest traditions of soldiers of the King by their brave action in protecting ,at the risk of their own lives, the persons of his loyal subjects from certain vicious, unlawful assailants on the public streets of Dublin'.

'In addition,' the colonel announced, smiling benevolently, 'Corporal O'Cuirc is hereby promoted to the rank of sergeant and Conor O'Donnell and Dónal O'Devaney to corporal. Let their brave actions be an example to the regiment.'

Participating in the ceremony was Sir Oliver Trent wearing his uniform of a major. Several times Tadhg was aware of Trent's speculative gaze. Tadhg wondered if he was trying to recall where he had seen Tadhg before, if whether he had been informed that Tadhg was the man who had killed his cousin, Montgomery Óg in a duel. Tadhg was uneasy. If Sir Oliver was responsible for the attack on the carriage with the intent of having the woman he was intending to marry murdered, then he was a cold-blooded, ruthless scoundrel and a most dangerous foe.

Off to one side, with a group of ladies, was Mairéad Fitzgerald. She came forward shyly when the ceremony was concluded to personally thank the Connemara men for their brave acts of saving her life and that of Sir Oliver Trent.

Smiling graciously, the green eyes probing, she said in her firm sweet voice, 'I must add to the duke's comments on your brave deed, for I have learned that the man, Mattie Moley, was one of the city's most notorious cutthroats with a long record of violence and murder. It was doubly courageous for you to take on such a monster.'

Her radiant smile melted Tadhg's resolution to stay aloof. He was completely her captive and most willing slave.

Tadhg remaining speechless, she turned to Dónal Óg. 'My, how you have grown since I saw you last. And how handsome you look in your uniform.'

Dónal blushed and stammered so under her praise that his simple, 'Thank you, *a bhean uasail*', seemed like a long conversation. Deliberately or not, she had another slave.

She smiled prettily at Conor, becoming animated by the rapt admiration of his two companions. 'The last time we were all together,' she said, 'only you spoke any English. I am pleased we can all talk in our common tongue now.'

'The common tongue of Ireland is Irish, not English.' Conor retorted tartly.

Seeing the hurt expression on her face, and realising he had been rude, he smiled at her to offset the sharp edge of his remark. 'With the name of FitzGerald, you should speak Irish well, for the Clann Mac Gearalt is an ancient and honourable family despite its Norman-Welsh beginning.'

'I am properly reprimanded!' she replied graciously. 'Perhaps you can teach me Irish some day.'

'Och, that should be Tadhg's job. He's the expert on languages.'

She turned to Tadhg, who stood silent, still overwhelmed by her closeness and friendliness. An elaborate coiffure showed her golden hair to great advantage; her eyes danced with mischief as she peered up at him, asking, 'Oh, has the fisherman now become a teacher?'

Looking into the green eyes, conscious of the exquisite moulding of the oval face, the rich warm mouth, Tadhg was scarcely aware of the question, but stood transfixed, his own blue eyes looking longingly at the lovely woman before him.

'Sure, and he speaks Spanish and French as well as English,' Dónal interposed eagerly, always ready to praise Tadhg. 'And the Irish, of course. You will teach the *bean uasal* Irish, won't you Tadhg?'

While Lady Mairéad looked at Dónal, the spell was broken, and Tadhg found his tongue again. He bowed. 'I would be most happy to,' he replied, formal and stiff.

The girl turned to him with renewed interest. 'Spanish and French, too? You are a most remarkable young man.' A shadow passed over her face fleetingly as she added, 'You excel at many other things as well.' Then she smiled again, the brief reference to tragedy at Kilkieran set aside. 'You have already advanced rapidly in the army. I'm sure that Major Trent will be most happy to help your career.'

Sir Oliver, who had quietly joined them and had listened to the conversation attentively, intending to question the lady later on her acquaintance with the three Irishmen, nodded his head agreeably. 'If you ever need help, don't hesitate to call on me. I would be dishonest of I didn't admit to having some influence in Dublin Castle, especially with the Duke of Tyrconnell. But we must take our leave now, the carriage is waiting.'

CHAPTER IV

Christmas Ball

As the days passed the three companions often discussed whether another attempt would be made on the life of the Lady Mairéad, and what could they do for her safety. They knew that they were in no position to guard her because of their military duties. Besides, what could they give her for a reason. Somhairle O'Máille and his friends along the riverfront were keeping a close lookout for the sailor who escaped. Tadhg wondered if the man had made contact with Sir Oliver to report that the big soldier at the Sign of the Curragh who had received the gold sovereigns was the same one who had helped foil the attack on the carriage. They concluded, in the absence of any further incidents, that Sir Oliver was satisfied that the soldier-messenger was not a threat to him, and that the matter was closed. The missing seaman was still a source of danger to Sir Oliver in that he was privy to the plot to attack the coach.

On Christmas Eve, Tadhg and eleven other soldiers, chosen for their great physiques, were selected as a special honour guard for the king at the ball to be held at the Castle. With another soldier, a member of the Lord Grand Prior's Regiment that was billeted at the college, Tadhg marched happily from St Patrick's Wall Lane to Dame Street and Lord Edward Street to the entrance on Castle Street. As they walked through the narrow streets they jostled, and were jostled in turn by the throngs of merrymakers who were celebrating 'The Night of the Cakes', named for the special cakes spiced with caraway seeds which were made for Christmas Eve.

They were joined at the Castle Gate by the other men of the honour guard who were under the command of a young Cornet, Edmund Harney, of Tyrconnell's Regiment.

When all twelve were assembled, the Cornet marched them over the lowered drawbridge between the two round towers that guarded it, the Gate Towers. Hanging ominously overhead, with its deadly iron dragon's teeth, was the massive portcullis. Two threatening cannon were mounted on a platform outside the gate. As he noted the high, thick walls and the armaments, Tadhg sensed the aura of the vast solid power of the Castle.

He was awed and humbled at this selection to be a guard at the Castle, that ancient and powerful bastion of the alien power that dominated and controlled Ireland. He recalled the stories he had heard of the Castle, thinking especially of the illustrious and indomitable Hugh O'Donnell who had twice escaped from its confines almost a hundred years before.

Ah, how changed you are, Tadhg thought. As a lad and a young man on Inishmór, you often furiously railed against those Irish who allied themselves with the Establishment, the English rulers of Ireland, whose interests were inimical to those of the Gael. Now you yourself are marching into the iniquitous Castle, the stronghold of the anti-Irish, to help protect the dethroned King of England!

All the apartments in the Castle's living quarters were illuminated by candles, so that the whole area seemed aglow with a soft, pervasive light, entirely befitting the celebration of Christ's nativity. Scores of elegantly dressed ladies and gentlemen roamed the corridors and stairways as they awaited the arrival of the King in the Great Hall. And many a feminine eye, covertly admiring the statures of the young guards, looked adversely at the slight, corpulent, or withered gallants who were their escorts, and sighed.

'Sure, and it's Brian Boru's bodyguards themselves who are here tonight,' one beauty commented as they passed.

The Great Hall was brilliantly lighted with hundreds of candles, the bright beams gleamed and glinted, reflected and refracted in the crystal chandeliers recently obtained from France by the Viceroy to make the dingy, dark and decaying old Castle, long neglected, a more fitting residence for a king.

Tadhg was overwhelmed by the magnificence and opulence. What a contrast it was to Christmas Eve on Inishmór, where a stub of a wax candle, found floating in the sea, took the place, for the special holy occasion, of the usual seal-fat candle in a seashell! He estimated that the cost of the candles alone burning in the Great Hall for just one night was a thousand fold greater than the cost of subsistence of one family on Inishmór for an entire year.

The room was gaily decorated with the colours of the king, the Viceroy, Ireland and France. Those English and Scots members of the Royal Household, familiar with the magnificent, rich and ancient trappings and equipment of St James Palace, sneered openly and scornfully at the throne of King James.

When the bells of Christchurch pealed the hour of nine, a fanfare of trumpets, and the rolling beat of a solitary drum, announced the arrival of the King and his party. Dressed in his

287

royal robes of silks and satins, his hair covered with a magnificent wig, he looked taller and less austere to Tadhg than he did in the field with his army. The king entered the room proudly, his step firm, boldly glancing about the vast hall. He was followed by the Viceroy, the Duke of Berwick, and his brother, the Lord Grand Prior. In the retinue were the Comte D'Avaux, the French ambassador to Ireland; Lord Dover; Duke Powys; General Dorington, Brigadier Wauchope; and Father Petre, the king's confessor.

Trailing behind were the Irish nobility, both the Gaelic and the English descended, as if an afterthought of His Majesty, King James, once the King of England, Scotland, Ireland and Wales.

It's a good thing that Conor isn't here, Tadhg reflected, or he would make some caustic comment on the place of the Irish lords at the end of the regal column. When the music began, the King led the dancing with the Lady Tyrconnell as his partner. Again Tadhg was thankful that Conor wasn't present for he disliked the Viceroy as much as he did the King, and likely would have remarked that in order to keep favour with the King, Tyrconnell would gladly loan her to James for pleasures other than dancing!

James, however, unlike his brother Charles, didn't publicly display his mistresses; he tried to keep them discreetly from the public's gaze. Other than this royal prerogative, his morals were unusual for a monarch of his day. He abhorred drunkenness. In fact, when he became king, he announced that anyone who appeared drunk in court would be removed, and if he had a court post, he would lose it. He was equally violently opposed to duelling.

After he succeeded Charles, his moral persuasions, closely linked to his penurious nature, led him to curtail the lavish expenditures of the court being spent on the personal pleasures his brother was so fond of. Also unique was his action in paying the debts incurred by Charles, and putting a limitation on his own expenditures.

Tadhg, ignorant of these facets of James's character, was soon to become bitterly aware of one of them, the King's quick eye for a pretty face, and his royal concept of the rights of a monarch over those of his subjects. As the Duke of Wales, then as King, many women, of high and low degree, maids and married, had gladly shared his bed. He had married Ann Hyde, his first wife, daughter of the Lord Chancellor, when she was already pregnant. Ironically, it was his marriage to Ann, herself a convert to Catholicism, that led to his own conversion, and the start of his downfall in the political intrigues at the Court of St James.

It was an era when ambitious men conveniently overlooked, or even encouraged, their wife's role as mistresses of the king. Many a member of the court owed his high position and properties to his accepting from a generous king a cast-off mistress, and marrying her.

Standing in the first row of four guards directly behind the seated king , Tadhg saw James poke Tyrconnell, and nod his head in the direction of the door. As Tadhg's glance paralleled that of the Viceroy's, he saw with a start that the Lady Mairéad FitzGerald had entered the room. Dressed in a magnificent pink gown, she was radiantly beautiful, dimming the lustre of the other beauties present.

Accompanying her was Sir Oliver Trent, his sandy hair covered with a dark peruke, and his expensive and lavish costume reflecting the high place he occupied in commercial Dublin. Lady Tyrconnell, fanning herself, smiled cynically as she watched the king gaze hungrily at the girl. What a difference just one year makes, she thought, as she recalled that it was on Christmas Eve in 1688 that James fled precipitously from England in a small ship on the turbulent channel to France. It was partially his anxiety over his queen, Mary of Modena, and their infant son, the Prince of Wales, whom he had sent to France previously, that contributed to his decision not to further resist the advance of William and his Dutch troops. Apparently the king's thoughts weren't on Mary tonight.

James, disregarding the Irish soldiers behind him, whispered loudly in French to Tyrconnell, 'What a stunning beauty! Who is she?'

'The Lady Mairéad FitzGerald, Your Majesty.'

'Is that her husband with her?'

Tyrconnell shook his head. 'No, Sire. She is still unmarried, supposedly mourning the man she was going to wed, but who was slain in a duel some time ago.'

James frowned. 'A man who duels deserves to die.' Admiration replaced the frown as he stared unabashed at the girl. 'She is the loveliest thing I've seen since I came to Ireland,' he said admiringly.

The Duke left the comment unanswered, discreetly overlooking the slight to his own three daughters, all married to Viscounts, who were in the room.

His appetite whetted, the king, still conversing in French, told the Viceroy, 'Arrange to have her visit me in my apartment after the ball.' Then scowling, and pretending to be angry, he asked, 'Where have you been hiding her all this time?'

Although the king's spoken French was somewhat different from that which he was familiar, being a mixture of what he had learned from Pedro de Alvarez and another Frenchman from the south of France who had been in his regiment, he understood the gist of it, and realised that the Lady Mairéad should be warned of what was being planned for her. He gestured to Cornet Harney, informing him in whispered Irish that he had to take an emergency trip to the necessary. As unostentatiously as possible, he made his exit through a rear door to a corridor, frantically trying to devise some way of reaching the Lady Mairéad.

Hearing gay feminine laughter in a room nearby, he peered in, where he saw amongst the group of women, apparently the maids and other servants of guests at the ball, Lady Mairéad's maid, Mary Casey, her round face merrily convulsed with laughter. He halted in the open doorway, the women stopping their banter for a moment to stare at the handsome big soldier. He beckoned frantically to Lady Mairéad's servant, whose face lit up with recognition, and leaving the others, joined him at the door.

One of the females, a big, buxom lass, emboldened by the ale she had consumed, shouted vulgarly, 'Bring him in, Mary, he's large enough for all of us to share.'

While the other woman roared, Tadhg declared in a low, passionate tone, 'For the love of God, Mary, come into the corridor with me!'

Sensing from his serious mien and deportment that it was important, she unhesitatingly followed him down the hall for a few feet where they stopped. He was so upset, that he was shaking. 'Your lady is in peril,' he said hoarsely. 'I just overheard the king instruct the Viceroy to arrange for the Lady Mairéad to be brought to his chambers after the ball.'

Mary Casey stared at Tadhg, her eyes wide with fear. 'Oh my God, he can't,' she exclaimed, realising the king's intentions. 'That dear, sweet girl, he just can't do that to her.'

'Something must be done quickly,' Tadhg told her impatiently. 'She must be informed of the plan before the emissary of

Tyrconnell can get to her. You know that if she refuses his royal command, that she will invoke his enmity, and for a Protestant here in Dublin at this time, if could be extremely dangerous for her. She must be warned so that she can safely leave the Castle before the king's message is delivered!

Mary Casey, her face solemn but her eyes blazing with anger, said resolutely, 'I will send a page in to her to have her meet me outside in the corridor. We will leave immediately.'

Tadhg was relieved. 'Thank you,' he said fervently. 'But I must ask one favour: don't tell anyone who your informant was. If the King learned, my life could be forfeit.'

'Not even the Lady Mairéad?'

Tadhg shook his head. 'No. It must remain a secret between the two of us!'

'The blessings of God on you, Tadhg *a rún*,' she said warmly. 'I will say a prayer to the Blessed Virgin for you tonight.'

'Say one for your mistress instead,' Tadhg retorted, 'she is the one who needs it. Now let us get about our business.'

Tadhg returned to his place behind the king's throne, noting that Mary Casey must still be a secret Catholic despite her outward acceptance of the religion of her mistress. Shortly after, a page ventured on to the floor after the music had stopped for an intermission, where he spoke briefly with the Lady Mairéad. The king, who had hardly taken his eyes off the girl, noted this with quiet satisfaction, assuming that it was Tyrconnell's messenger. His eager eyes followed her as she gracefully threaded her way through the crowed room.

It was quite some time before the king was aware that she hadn't returned to the ballroom. In an intense, whispered conversation with the Viceroy, with the king growing more petulant and unhappy by the moment, the dialogue indicated that Tyrconnell's emissary had failed to locate the girl, and that the rendezvous had failed. Watching the king's angry countenance, Tadhg shuddered to think what would happen to him if King James learned that a common soldier had scotched his romantic plans for the night.

All the enjoyment of the ball seemed to have evaporated for the King after his disappointment. He appeared bored and restless. At midnight, he left the Great Room with some of his retinue, and although the party continued without him, the guard detail was dismissed to return to their quarters.

Tadhg was so shocked by the King's predatory amatory designs on Lady Mairéad that he refrained form mentioning the incident to his two close companions. Ignorant of the quaint custom of *le droit de signeur*, Tadhg's faith in the King's perfection began to crumble.

The following morning, Tadhg, Conor and Dónal attended Mass at Christchurch which now, for the first time in many years, was again being used for Catholic services; St Patrick's Cathedral had been converted into a stable for the horses of the cavalry. With distaste, Tadhg observed King James enter with his retinue, and taking his place later at the altar rail, receive the Sacrament of Communion.

Tadhg wondered if the king had confessed to Father Petre his lustful desires of the previous evening. He had been shocked to learn that James had five illegitimate children. This however, he had taken in stride. But the wilful, shameless planned conquest of the Lady Mairéad was something else. She was not an obscure name out of the murky past, she was someone close and dear to him. He found himself glaring with contempt as the king left the church, faithfully followed by the two royal bastards, Lord Berwick and the Lord Grand Prior.

CHAPTER V

Sive MacClancy

As winter waned, there were repeated rumours that the Rebels in the North were about to lay down their arms and surrender their garrisons. As a result, a feeling of false security and high confidence in the future of the king's cause pervaded the city. All segments of the army, from highest officer to lowest private, entered on a round of personal pleasures and activities which were greatly detrimental to the king's (and Ireland's) interests. Discipline became lax as cards, dice, dancing, drinking and wenching became the chief preoccupation of most of the inhabitants of Dublin, civilians as well as military.

Tadhg and Conor were two of the exceptions. Conor had become interested in a young woman from Cahermacclancy in the County Clare who was a cousin of Cornet Thomas Clanchy of Lord Clare's Dragoons. Named Sive MacClancy, she was a slender, pretty, brown-haired and brown-eyed vivacious girl who had come to Dublin at the invitation of her cousin to enjoy a few weeks of pleasure in the capital while the king held court there. The MacClancys lived a little to the north of the MacGormans, Tadhg's maternal kin.

Conor, as the corporal in charge of a detail of troops, had met her and some of her companions, stranded on a little island in a sea of mud on Patrick Street, one extremely rainy day. The soldiers, including Conor, volunteered to take the girls on their horses as far as the Castle, their destination. Both having come from the West of Ireland, a mutual attraction quickly grew between them despite her higher social standing, for the MacClancys had long been hereditary brehons to the powerful O'Briens who ruled Clare. Lord Clare, colonel of Clare's Dragoons, was Daniel O'Brien.

When Tadhg first met her, he told her that his mother had been a MacGorman, but that he had been born on Inishmór.

Her eyes opened wide as she contemplated him. 'Tadhg O'Cuirc? You are quite a celebrity among the MacGormans now,' she informed him avidly. 'All of the West Country has heard of Tadhg O'Cuirc, and how he conquered Montgomery and Sir John Ferguson in sword duels. Because of you the old quarrel between your father and your mother's brother had been resolved, and the two families visit each other again.'

'Thanks be to God,' said Tadhg fervently, 'at least some good has come of the affair. But tell me, if you are a MacClancy, how is it your cousin calls himself Clanchy?'

Sive laughed. 'His grandfather was a merchant who made frequent trips to Dublin and Waterford. So that he wouldn't be at a disadvantage with his English-Irish counterparts, who didn't like the Irish-Irish, he conveniently dropped the 'Mac' part to hide his Irishness. But no matter how hard he tried to disguise his origin, we MacClancys recognise them as our kin.'

After Sive left Dublin to return to Clare, Conor was more restless than ever. Unlike Dónal, who enjoyed the gambling and drinking which comprised much of the merry life of the city, and Tadhg who had found a school where he spent much of his spare time learning Latin and mathematics, Conor enjoyed physical labour such as a farm demanded. Consequently he got a part-time job on the quays. He was concerned over his interest in Sive, and his intention to marry her, which conflicted with his sense of obligation to his widowed sister, Máire and her children.

Tadhg was disappointed with Dónal's perpetual pursuit of pleasure. He was worried that in his wenching he would contact the great pox which was then prevalent in the city among the more promiscuous girls. Back in Ulster, Sergeant Gallagher had vividly described to Tadhg what happened to a man after being infected with the great pox. His description to the deterioration leading to debility, blindness and a premature and painful death, had made a great and lasting impression on Tadhg. Dónal took Tadhg's advice and admonitions good naturedly, promising faithfully to be careful.

'It's those French soldiers, Tadhg, that give the girls the great pox,' he declared ingenuously, 'so I have nothing to do with the *cailíns* who have been with a Frenchman.'

Tadhg's efforts to point out the universality and non-racial affinity of the disease were fruitless, for the frowning disenchantment and dislike of the Irish for their French allies helped to contribute to Dónal's evasion of the issue by his willingness to blame the scourge on the French.

CHAPTER V

The Teacher

With the lax state of training and general inactivity of the army, Tadhg took the opportunity to attend a school several hours a day. The school was unique for that time because it was run by a woman. Three gold sovereigns, given to him by Mattie Moley, who probably writhed in hell at such a monstrous waste of the money, paid his tuition fees for courses in Latin, French and Mathematics.

Before long the teacher took a personal interest in Tadhg as she became aware of his avid interest in learning. She was a large, but well proportioned woman in her late thirties. By name, Eilís Reynolds, she had come to Dublin nearly twenty years before to greet, upon his return from England where he had studied to become a surgeon, the man she was betrothed to wed. A sudden, severe storm in the Channel had been too much for the small vessel; with it foundered Eilís's dreams of the future.

She remained in Dublin with some distant kin, and whenever possible, went down to the claddach where she walked the lonely seashore as she gazed forlornly over the waters for the ship that would never more arrive. Despite the entreaties of her family, she felt she couldn't return to her native hearth in County Leitrim where she would sink into the obscurity of the unmarried woman. Having been well educated by a wise and indulgent father who decided that his daughter should know more than the social graces required to rule a household, she had started a school. Being a good teacher, despite being a woman, she soon had enough pupils to make the school self-sustaining.

The school was on the second floor of an old building on Lord Edward Street near where the River Dodder flowed to join the Liffey. Noxious odours permeated the neighbourhood where the river was practically an open sewer. In complaining about the stench to his teacher, Tadhg discovered that she had great affection for the Dodder, defending it against any criticism which she considered pure calumny.

Their relationship of teacher and pupil changed to that of friends. Eilís was fond of walking, so one bright, sunny day they trudged out into the countryside to trace the Dodder where it meandered through the meadows, tamed after its tumultuous plunge from its birthplace in the distant hills. Here it still ran clear, untouched and unfouled by man.

'You love this little stream,' Tadhg observed. 'You speak of it as another woman does of her sweetheart.'

She smiled a sad smile. Her soft, brown eyes looked up to the remote, lofty slopes of Kippure, the origin of the Dodder. 'If I do, it's because it reminds me of my Boetius. Like the brook that flows at our feet, he was gentle, but at times could be wild and unpredictable as the Dodder in spring flood. He, too, was destined to end in the sea as are these waters below us.'

She turned to Tadhg, her long, brown, wavy hair blowing in the wintry wind, her cheeks flushed red with the bite of the cold. 'I suppose that it seems foolish, but I could never love another man. The sea took my loving heart when it took Boetius. You resemble him greatly, Tadhg, as you have the same blue eyes, the black, curling locks, the clefted chin. However, he wasn't a giant like you; I didn't have to look up into the clouds to gaze into his eyes.'

Her brown orbs, velvety in their shading, gazed steadfastly at Tadhg. 'I think it is your resemblance to him that makes me enjoy talking and walking with you so much. And, alas, being remiss in my obligations to the other pupils.'

When he was free, he often accompanied her to the seashore where they would stroll, hand in hand, without speaking, as she lived within herself. While they traversed the strand, she would stare off into the distance towards England as if she feared that the ship would elude her if she wasn't vigilant. Tadhg pretended that he never saw the tears that gathered in her eyes, or heard the sobs that oft shook her frame. Upon their return to Dublin, her composure restored, she was once again her controlled self. There would never be reference to her emotional flights.

It was Eilís who first induced Tadhg to try composing Gaelic poetry, teaching him the intricate rhyming and syllabic forms which differentiated Irish poetry from the English. She encouraged him after he despaired at his first clumsy attempts, until in deference to her, he composed a short poem about the Dodder in which he caught her intense feeling for the little stream with such understanding that the imagery that he evoked was worthy of a more experienced poet.

Her praise led him to write secret love poems whose subject was the Lady Mairéad. These he kept from his mentor. Although she was friendly to him, she was of the gentry, the MacRannels of

Leitrim, and he was apprehensive that she might react adversely to the thought of a poor fisherman aspiring, even covertly, to the hand of one so exalted as a FitzGerald.

In the Spring, when the time for the army to take the field for the coming campaign grew closer, they walked together for the last time along the seashore. He was aware that her mood was contemplative, but was unprepared for the drastic change. Instead of watching the sea as usual as they strolled along the wild shore, she looked directly at her companion, and instead of her usual silence, she talked.

'Tadhg,' she said, her brow furrowed in concentration, 'I have been giving much thought to your future. When this horrible war is over, I hope that you will go back to Iar-Chonnacht and resume the work that your friend Donough Beag left unfinished.'

When he interupted to say that he was unqualified to teach, she shook her head in disagreement. 'All you need is a little polishing. This can be accomplished at my school before you have to leave. I believe that God intends you to be more than just another fisherman; it would be a shame to have Donough O'Flaherty's sacrifices to be in vain.'

The prospect of being Donough's successor both startled and pleased Tadhg. He thought of Thady in far-off Donegal, starting a school. He remembered the pupils at Kilkieran deprived of education. His life as a soldier was an uncertain one at best. What of his future? He had never given much thought to it. To become a teacher would give direction to his life. 'Thank you *a bhean uasail*,' he said, 'for your suggestion and your confidence in me. The more I think of the idea the more pleased I am. You are right. Ireland needs teachers more than it does fishermen.'

'Good,' she said brusquely, 'that's settled. There is yet another subject I would like to discuss with you, and I hope you won't think I am intruding into your personal affairs.'

Because of his liking and his respect for her, Tadhg assured her, 'I promise I will not be offended. Anything you advise will be taken as a helpful suggestion from a very valued friend.'

She stopped, facing him, holding both his hands, looked up at him, her eyes probing his. 'You must be constantly on your guard for you are extremely attractive to the opposite sex, and there's many a woman who will set her snares for you. In the first instance, your good looks alone will catch the eye of all the *cailíns*. In the second instance, your huge physique and strong sinews will be considered prime assets for any woman who will look at them in the light of plantng and ploughing, masonry work and thatching, all the numerous and needed chores for running a farm. In the third instance, your intelligence and your love of learning will draw you to another type of woman.' She smiled faintly. 'Such as a spinster schoolteacher.'

Surprised at her personal reference, and not knowing what to reply, Tadhg wisely said nothing.

'You are very fortunate,' she continued seriously, ignoring her own comment and his reaction to it, 'for you can afford to be selective. Don't be hasty in falling in love with the first pretty *cailín* who stirs your blood, or accepting the first woman of property who would buy you much as she would buy a prize bull, or hoodwinked by a father with a sharp eye for acquiring a husband for an unmarried daughter.'

She paused, looking out to the sea for a few moments as if debating whether she should carry on with her discourse. Then, facing him again, she said, 'Times are changing in Ireland, Tadhg. As the English succeed in their plan of breaking up the old Irish families and putting their stamp and seal on the land, it leads more and more to the disintegration of the ancient Irish social order. If there is no longer a chief of the Clan, there is no longer any need for the age-old allegiance of the Clan members to the chief. In some ways, I, too, regret the change, for the MacRannels were part of the old order, but I can see the change will help men of ability and vision to rise above their ordained and established stations under the old system. You are one of those who can benefit, Tadhg, and that's why I urge you to wait for the right *cailín*, whoever and wherever she might be!'

Tadhg longed to tell her that he had already made his choice, that he had lost his heart to a golden-haired vision; that for him there could never be another woman, just as she, Eilís, was irrevocably commited to a man long dead. We are both in the same boat, he thought forlornly, hopelessly in love with the unattainable. And what is worse, we recognise the futility while still stubornly and foolishly clinging to it!

'Here,' she said, thrusting her hand into a pocket and withdrawing an object wrapped in a piece of silk, 'is a present for you. It is a poem, in his own hand, by Geoffrey O'Donoghue of the Glens. It was given to Boetius by his uncle who was a Kerryman like O'Donoghue. Perhaps it can inspire you to follow his example.'

She glanced at Tadhg, then continued. 'O'Donoghue died several years ago, bitterly lamenting the passing of the old Gaelic family structure. After Cromwell died, and the Stuart line was restored, the poet had high hopes for the Gaels in Ireland. But Charles quickly disillusioned him by catering to the same old Establishment, ruling from Dublin Castle. O'Donoghue could be baulked but he couldn't be silenced. His bitter disappointment and his infinite anger surge through the poem. Listen:

Surpassing all previous perfidy, they now send this decree
By which the rightful nobility of Erin are wrongfuly
punished,
Their belongings pillaged through shameful artifices called
laws,
And we are dispossessed of our legitimate birthright to Erin.

That's my awkward, literal translation,' she apologised. 'It has none of the rhyme and beauty of the Irish original which you have, only, perhaps, its heartrending, passionate cry.'

Tadhg stared at the manuscript. He was shocked at the sacrifice she was willing to make. He shook his head. 'I couldn't possibly accept such a priceless gift,' he said. 'This must be your most valuable possession!'

She brushed aside his objections. 'My most precious possession is the discovery that Ireland is still producing men like you. Tadhg, you have changed the course of my life through your Donough O'Flaherty, for I have decided to return to Leitrim and start a school for all the other Tadhg's who need teachers. I can see now that my years in Dublin were wasted, selfish years, teaching the children of stupid shopkeepers who are also destined to grow up and become stupid shopkeepers. As you have altered my life, I want to help you change yours. Take this gift in exchange for the gift you have given me, and over the long years let it always remind you of Eilís MacRannal. If this simple present can accomplish that, what greater reward could I have?'

Her brown eyes were pleading now. For a moment he stood undecided, then realising intuitively that there was something more fundamental involved than the offer and the acceptance of a piece of paper, he reached out his hand for it.

He nodded his head, smiling down at her. 'I will read it often, wherever I may be, and the names of Geoffrey O'Donoghue of the

Glens and Eilís Mac Rannel of Leitrim will forever be remembered. Thank you, *a bhean uasail*, for this precious present.'

She smiled in return - albeit a bit wanly - at his use of the formal '*a bhean uasail*', but was thankful to him for keeping a potentially emotional situation under control.

Chapter VI

The Smuggler

The winter season in Dublin should have been a happy one for Tadhg, since he was being paid and fed while furthering his education at a small school, but he was continually worrying about the safety of the Lady Mairéad. The day following the episode at the Castle when he had foiled the king's amatory adventure, a brief note, addressed to him, was delivered at his quarters. It stated simply: 'The *cailín bán* is off to the country to visit her kin and old friends.' The note was unsigned, but Tadhg felt sure that it was from Mary Casey in as much as she should have been the only one aware of the part he had played in the king's discomfiture.

Instead of being relieved that she was out of the king's reach for the time being, he grew more concerned lest the person who had planned the attack on the carriage have a better opportunity to complete his murderous plans with Tadhg and his companions confined to Dublin. But even if he had been free to leave the city, he would have been unable to help her since he didn't have the faintest idea where she had gone.

One evening when he was with Conor and Dónal at the Sign of the Curragh, he fretted and fumed to such an extent over the situation that his friends became alarmed over his state of mind.

'There is no use of your getting so upset about it unless you intend to do something about it,' Conor pointed out. 'If you think that Sir Oliver Trent is the man for whom the spy message was intended, and who planned the attack on the carriage, then let's prove it.'

'That's easy enough to say,' Tadhg said, his agitation and irritation apparent. 'But how?'

Devil's Hook Charlie, who had been listening to the animated discussion, spoke up. 'It's common talk in the alehouse and coffee houses, Tadhg, about the supposedly secret missions to England by King James's agents. But the Lord Deputy might just as well shout the information from the top of the Tholsel, for it seems that everyone in Dublin knows who the agents are and where they are going. Now there is another activity which is also supposed to be secret, but again too many people know about it. That's the smuggling trade.'

Tadhg was exasperated at the change of subject. 'What's that got

301

to do with Sir Oliver Trent and the Lady Mairéad?' he asked irascibly.

'We'll get to that,' Charlie said calmly. He pointed to his kegs and casks. 'How do you think I could stay in business if I had to pay at the Customs House all the duty that King James and the Lord Deputy demand? Why, I would be forced to close tomorrow!'

'Are you admitting that your liquor is smuggled?' Conor asked, winking at Tadhg. 'If you refuse to pay King James his customs tax, how do you expect King James to pay us in turn so that we can come down and drink to help you get rich?'

'With that worthless brass money the king is coining out of old cannon?' He looked sourly at Conor. 'With that kind of money, I'd be happy if you took your trade elsewhere, preferably the Badger. But to answer your question directly would be foolish. Let me say that all over Ireland, in many a secret cove and harbour, French ships, Spanish ships, and even English ships are quietly unloading their cargoes, and not a shilling of duty is paid. It's not only financially beneficial, but a good way for the Irish to deprive the English loving Ormonde family of their centuries-old source of income from their right of custom's duty. Of course, they're not getting it now, the last Duke of Ormonde who died in London two years ago, the former Viceroy, was a great friend of both Charles, but not of Catholic James, but the principle is the same. If you were to go out on the Liffey in the dark of the night, you would see more vessels going up and down the river than in daylight. They go down to Ringsend, or even to Malahide, get their loads, then creep back up the next night. Some of the biggest fortunes in Dublin have been built this way, including that of an upstart young Londoner.'

'Go on, go on,' Conor encouraged him, 'You're leading up to something!'

Charlie calmly filled their glasses with his good hand. 'It is whispered along the quays that every fortnight or so, this young man goes down the river to meet the ships as they come in. He is reputedly the owner of the Liffey Exporting Corporation. It's not for me to say that he's a smuggler, cheating his friend, the king, out of customs money, but he certainly has some friends in high places.'

Tadhg stared contemplatively at Charlie. 'You're hinting that Sir Oliver Trent is a smuggler?'

Charlie shrugged his thick shoulders.

'But what does smuggling have to do with the spy ring?' Dónal asked.

'What if Sir Oliver is catching two salmon with one spear,' Charlie asked.

Conor's eyes lighted as he realised the inference. 'You're suggesting...?'

'That perhaps he meets someone to whom he passes the information he picks up at the coffee-houses.'

'You have a good point,' Conor remarked thoughtfully. 'If Tadhg is correct in his belief that Sir Oliver is the same man he saw in Ulster, and if Sir Oliver is the man responsible for Mattie Moley's murderous attack, then it's very possible that he is a member of the spy ring, and is one way that he transmits important information in England. And that name, Liffey Exports, is famous.'

'The name Holmes mentioned on the river near Derry,' Dónal said excitedly.

Conor looked sharply at Tadhg who was staring with abstraction at the floor. 'Hold it!' he remonstrated. 'If you're getting one of those upside-down-boat-to-Derry ideas into your thick skull, you'd better forget it. Sir Oliver is no fool. We learned at first hand that he is a dangerous man. Any plan to trap him will have to include all of us, not just you alone.'

'All that I was thinking,' Tadhg replied defensively, 'was that I would like to go downriver on one of these expeditions if Charlie can manage to get me aboard one of the vessels.'

'No problem,' Charlie said. 'Just as soon as I hear our friend is stirring for one of his river trips, I'll do the arranging.'

'Only on the condition that Dónal and I will go down by land at the same time,' Conor insisted, 'so that we will be on hand to help you. That means, of course, that we will have to get permission to leave for a few days.'

Happy at the thought of action, Tadhg agreed readily. 'I'll see Sergeant Williamson,' he said. 'He's in charge of all guard details for the regiment.'

Sergeant Williamson was more than happy to accommodate his friend with a special detail for the trio, and in addition, sniffing adventure, decided to assign himself to be the non-commissioned officer in charge of the group which would report to the provost's section at Ringsend.

303

CHAPTER VIII

A Spy Unmasked

Thus it was that several nights later, dressed in seaman's clothes, Tadhg boarded a vessel tied up at Essex Quay. His name was given as MacLeod. There actually was a soldier in Tyrconnell's regiment of that name, and as Tadhg often listened to his broad Scots accent, it made it easy for him to mimic the Highlander. With a dirty eye patch over one eye, and a ring of Conor's reluctantly given golden curls protruding from under the knitted tam-o-shanter pulled down over his black hair, Tadhg was a remarkable, but revolting sight.

At dawn they were at Ringsend, a small fishing village with a few cottages and a dismal inn. It was the most God forsaken, wind swept spot Tadhg had seen since leaving the wild coast of Connemara nearly a year before. As the tide was in, the village was accessible only from the south road. A few large ships were already anchored off shore, while small vessels were busy in transferring their cargoes for return up the Liffey, many of them to elude the customs men.

In charge of the vessel Tadhg was aboard was a heavily-bearded, roly-poly old man called 'Wally the Whiskers', whose flimsy breeches were suspended with a piece of rope. A *duidín* with such an extremely short stem was crammed in the corner of a toothless mouth, that Tadhg was surprised that the old man didn't scorch his nose when the bowl was filled with glowing tobacco. He had welcomed 'MacLeod' since any friend of Charlie's was a friend of his, especially such a stout lad as this who would come in handy with the heavy barrels.

Wally the Whiskers ran the vessel out to sea a way, then anchored it as the sea was calm. Tadhg asked no questions; apparently their ship hadn't yet arrived. At one time six mounted soldiers rode slowly across a sand-spit, with Tadhg recognising Conor, Dónal and Sergeant Williamson among them. Several coaches had arrived at the inn, their occupants dismounting hastily as if their thirst couldn't wait.

After a while, Whiskers took the *duidín* from the mouth, spat to leeward and ordered the anchor raised. A fairly big vessel, of about twenty-tonnes, had come in and anchored about a half mile from shore. Several other vessels joined Whiskers in his move to greet the newcomer.

'What kept you?' shouted Whiskers, as they tied alongside the bigger boat where the master stood at the helm.

'Blasted navy,' the captain roared in stentorian tones. 'I really had to duck and run to get away. They must have thought that I was King Looey and this was a man-of-war.' He laughed at his own joke as he walked to the ship's rail.

'Sure, and they'll be the death of free trade,' Whiskers shouted back indignantly.

'Quit gabbing,' the other man ordered. 'Get your men aboard and let's get this cargo unloaded.'

As the crews scrambled aboard, Whiskers beckoned to Tadhg. 'Get all the cargo that's marked with a big 'T' and put it aboard my vessel. Don't worry about the other crews, they know better than to touch any of it. Move quickly. I want to be loaded as soon as possible.'

While the men were transferring all the casks and crated identified by the 'T', which Tadhg suspected was for 'Trent', Whiskers and the Captain sat in the cabin over a bottle of rum. After several hours of hard work, Tadhg reported to Whiskers that all his cargo was aboard the vessel. As the two captains emerged from the cabin, holding tightly to each other, their uncertain gait could definitely be attributed to something other than the rolling and pitching of the ship.

Whiskers, clutching a bottle of rum, stood at the starboard rail. 'A fine gift, Captain Henry,' he said, preparing to descend the ladder to his own craft, 'a fine gift.'

As Captain Henry tottered, a cargo net, swinging on a boom, lightly brushed his shoulder, tumbling the unsteady master into the sea. All hands froze, staring stupidly at the water where the victim had disappeared. Without a second thought, Tadhg vaulted over the rail, plunging into the sea. As he emerged, he observed Captain Henry floundering on the surface, and with a few short strokes, siezed him from behind, treading water vigorously to keep them both afloat.

One of the men from Whisker's vessel, still aboard the ship, made a quick appraisal and threw the end of a rope to Tadhg who tied it around the struggling captain. In a trice, sputtering and spewing, he was hauled up the side of the vessel. As Tadhg started to climb up the rope ladder which had been belatedly flung over the side, the face of the man who had thrown the rope appeared, motioning violently with his hands for Tadhg to stay down. Obeying, but not understanding, Tadhg saw him fishing around in the water with a boathook.

Finally he manoeuvered the point of the pole to Tadhg, stating laconically in a soft Munster accent, 'You lost your curls!'

A horrified Tadhg promptly placed the sodden seaman's cap, with the attached eye patch and sewn-in blond ringlets of hair, back on his own head. 'That's better,' the Munsterman commented, 'you might have given the captain a fright by turning suddenly from a *buchaillín bán* into a *buchaillín dhubh*, with your bad eye miraculously restored by the salt water.'

'Many thanks, *a chara*,' Tadhg exclaimed fervently as he clambered over the rail. 'You not only saved my curls, but probably saved my life as well.'

The other man looked at him quizzically. 'What happened to your thick Scots talk? Lose it in the sea?'

Tadhg clapped his hand to his mouth. He had better be careful. Two serious errors in a short time. Fortunately the rest of the men aboard the ship, concerned over the accident to the captain, had paid little attention to the fate of his rescuer. Even Whiskers, attracted by the noise, had climbed back aboard from the opposite side where his vessel was tied.

Captain Henry was draped over a barrel on his belly, emitting the salt water he had swallowed and the rum he had consumed. In between eruptions, he cursed the clumsy swab who had knocked him overboard and praised the big Scot who had saved him.

When the excitement had subsided, and the captain was perpendicular again, he insisted on Tadhg's accompanying him to the inn for dinner and drink, exclaiming in his loud voice, 'And I don't mean that damned seawater, either!'

Tadhg was in a quandary! He had hoped that by working on Sir Oliver's cargo, that he could find something incriminating, something that could lead to unmasking him as a spy. If he went with Captain Henry, instead of accompanying Wally the Whiskers, that contact was lost. Yet Captain Henry was an Englishman, landing cargo in a country which was at war with England, travelling back and forth over the sea route that couriers and secret agents were wont to take. Tadhg knew that the smuggling fraternity in general had no scruples concerning patriotism, laws and national interests, but were concerned only with making money on their illicit trade. Perhaps Captain Henry was one of these, a smuggler and nothing more.

There was one advantage, however. This way he could stay at Ringsend where he could check with Conor and Dónal if they had seen Sir Oliver; after all, it was his cargo that had been brought ashore.

Thus it was that Tadhg found himself on a longboat, bound for the inn, with the boisterous Captain Henry, where they partook of a hearty lunch, washed down with numerous draughts of ale.

'This man can see more with his one eye than the rest of those baboons can with two,' the grateful captain bellowed to all within hearing distance. 'If it wasn't for Scotty here, old Captain Henry would be dining on seaweed tonight.'

Suddenly there was a flurry of excitement as the coach, drawn by six white horses, rolled up to the inn. The innkeeper, an ingratiating rogue who had kept Tadhg's cup full at all times, knowing that the grateful captain wouldn't object, personally greeted the new guest, escorting him to his room at the far end of the building. After food and wine were taken to the room, Captain Henry was told to report with his cargo manifests to Sir Oliver Trent.

'Don't leave,' the captain instructed Tadhg, 'my business won't take long. You saved my life, and by God, you're going to be my guest until it's time to sail.' He winked lewdly, 'And tonight my hospitality will include a wench from Dublin for you.'

Tadhg declined the latter offer with effusive thanks. The captain, although incredulous at the idea of a sailor turning down the offer of a woman, shrugged his shoulders. 'Suit yourself,' he said, and left.

Feeling the effects of the ale, Tadhg found the captain's absence a good excuse to leave the inn, ostensibly 'for some fresh air'. He walked rapidly to the provost's post, established in an old cottage near the shore, where he reported to his friends that Sir Oliver had arrived at the inn and was now conferring with Captain Henry. With gusto he described Captain Henry's fall into the sea, and his invitation to be the captain's guest.

Conor was thoughtful. 'It might be more to it than just checking cargo manifest. What kind of a man is this Captain Henry?'

'Loud and jolly, and fond of everything to drink except sea water.'

'Has he blabbed anything?' Sergeant Williamson asked. 'Said anything that would indicate that he's anything other than a smuggler?'

Tadhg shook his head. 'Absolutely nothing, Sergeant. He expressed great anger at the English fleet for trying to intercept him.'

'Well, he might be just an honest smuggler,' Conor commented, 'but it could have been a little embellishment in the event that the English deliberately allowed him to get past.'

'In that case, would it make him a dishonest smuggler?' Dónal asked, an innocent look in his eye.

'It could be that his ship is a source of contact with the Rebels in Ireland for the English government,' Sergeant Williamson suggested. 'It's an open secret in Dublin that the rebels know everything that is going on. Too many of our agents going to England are seized shortly after their arrival there to be coincidental.'

'If Captain Henry is more than he appears to be,' Conor said, 'then Tadhg ought to get back to the inn so that he doesn't miss anything.'

Tadhg arose. 'I think you're right, Conor. My head feels clearer now that I've had some fresh air.'

When he returned to the inn, he learned that Captain Henry had retired to his room to nap. Evidently too much food and liquor had rendered him out of action for the present. Tadhg went to the room obtained for him by the grateful seaman and stretched out on the small bed. His exertions, plus lack of sleep due to the early start down the Liffey, were too much for him, and he was soon sound asleep.

When he woke, it was dark in the room. He descended the stairs to the dining room, where Captain Henry, his health and good spirits apparently mended, was dining in a dark corner with Sir Oliver Trent. When he observed Tadhg enter the room, he called loudly for him to meet his good friend and customer, Sir Oliver Trent.

The captain introduced him as Scotty, the man who had saved his life. Scotty mumbled in his Scots accent that he was delighted to meet the gentleman. Sir Oliver eyed him curiously, a hulking giant with a patch over one eye and a rim of golden curls peeping from under a dirty tam-o-shanter. Tadhg's heart pumped furiously. Had Sir Oliver penetrated his disguise? Was his mimicry authentic? Had any mannerism betrayed him?

After the scrutiny, Sir Oliver turned without further ado to his conversation with the captain. Since he was not invited to sit with them, Tadhg excused himself, taking a seat at another table, close by.

'What's the matter, doesn't your friend want you to eat with him now that he is with His Lordship?' Tadhg turned. It was the serving maid speaking.

Tadhg smiled, his one visible eye crinkling at the corners to give him a more benevolent appearance. 'Aye, lass, I'm too much of a ruffian to dine with such high and mighty men as aristocrats and sea captains.'

'High and mighty?' She snorted with disdain. 'You take that one, now,' and she pointed a long, bony forefinger at Sir Oliver, 'all afternoon he's been reading his Bible in his room, like a regular saint, he was, and making notes.' She leaned over to Tadhg, her eyes flashing. 'And do you know what he and the captain are going to do tonight? They're going to be entertained by some doxies coming from Dublin! It isn't the wicked ones I mind so much,' she continued, her voice rising in pitch, 'it's the wicked hypocrites like him who read their Bibles, then turn around and do everything that Jehovah commanded man not to do!'

Glaring furiously at Tadhg as if he, too, were one of the wicked hypocrites, she asked, 'Do you read your Bible?' When Tadhg nodded in assent, she cried out in the tones of a Jeremiah, 'God will not allow the adulterers and fornicators to escape unpunished! Woe unto them!'

Embarrassed by the topic coming from a woman, and the startled look of the subject of the conversation who was staring at them, Tadhg implored her to keep her voice low, adding, 'What do you mean, making notes?'

'Alright,' she agreed sullenly, 'but it's true! As for your question, I saw him making the notes.' noticing the surprise in Tadhg's face, she explained, 'Several times I had to take writing materials up to him. First some foolscap. Then some quills and ink. Then he had to have some China Drink. Each time I went in, he had his Bible opened in front of him, with sheets of paper spread all around. With writing on it.'

'Could you see what it said?'

She coloured. 'I can't read,' she apologised, then added triumphantly, a gleam in her eyes, 'but I do know writing when I see it.'

For a moment, Tadhg was lost in thought. Although Sir Oliver was a nephew of a former dean of Christchurch, he was not a clergyman; he was fond of gambling and drinking; he was a practitioner of shady deals; he was engaged in the illegal smuggling trade; and if the serving maid's denunciation was true, was not averse to having a wench share his bed. It was so out of character for him to be reading the Bible in the privacy of his room and making notes from it. Was it for a sermon? Was he, by chance, a deacon? And what about his rumoured plans of conversion to Catholicism? The more Tadhg pondered the contradiction, the more strange it became.

'He that keepeth the commandment keepeth his own soul; but he that despiseth his ways shall die,' Tadhg stated piously.

'Proverbs, nineteen,' the woman replied, her eyes shining with fervour. 'Can a man take fire in his bosom, and his clothes not be burned?' she quoted. Looking at Sir Oliver, who was bent over the table in conversation with his companion, she asked, 'Can a man readeth the Bible with honesty, and not with a lying tongue, if he is not going to break God's commandments later?'

'Perhaps it's a heathen Bible,' Tadhg said, adding in a conspiratorial tone, 'do you think you could get it from his room while he is dining so that I can compare it with my true Bible?'

Her eyes gleamed again. 'That I could,' she answered, happy at harassing a heretic. 'If they follow their usual habit, they will stay long at the table.'

'I'll go to my room,' Tadhg said, rising. 'Bring it as quickly as you can.'

Realising that he was taking a great risk, but interested in what Sir Oliver could possibly be doing with a Bible, Tadhg waited. Shortly, he heard a gentle knock on his door. It was his intrigante who hastily thrust a Bible into his hands. 'It was right on his table where he was working,' she whispered. Tadhg thanked her and closed the door, anxious to examine the book.

Sir Oliver's Bible, dog-eared with use and abuse, was a King James version, published in London in 1611, known as the Authorised Version, identical to Tadhg's copy from Meg Murray. He opened it curiously, and as he did so, a sheaf of papers fluttered to the floor. As he hastily stooped to retrieve them, he was startled to discover that they were covered with rows of two-digit numbers, exactly like those in the message he had found at Fionn MacCool's tomb!

His hands shaking with excitement, he spread the sheets of

paper on the bed. Page one started with the usual thanks to the saints, this time to St. Louis, St. Peter, St. Wenceslaus, St. Cyril, St. Luke and St. Vincent. He stared vacantly at the message for a while. Etched sharply in his memory was the original message with its list of holy men, Paul, William, Laurence, Cornelius, Venantius and Luke. This was curious: only St. Luke was repeated in the new message. Why? What was its significance? Then he remembered Lieutenant de Vimeny's interpretation that the saints indicated specific agents. Accordingly, Sir Oliver must be Luke, in as much as he was involved in both messages, old and new.

He wished ardently that de Vimney was present. But there was not time enough to get to Dublin and locate him. What did he say were the attributes needed to solve secret messages? Intelligence, curiosity, imagination and resourcefulness? Ah, yes, and above all, perseverance! It struck him that resourcefulness was called for first. There was some strange link between the coded messages and the Bible for the servant woman had told him that Sir Oliver had been working with the Bible. St. Luke, St. Peter and St. Paul were familiar enough, but why weren't the other nine Apostles included? This was odd.

He took the piece of black charcoal given to hem by Lieutenant de Vimeny to write down the names as he recalled them from the first message, and those of the last one. They included: Paul, William, Laurence, Cornelius, Venantius, Luke twice, Louis, Peter, Wenceslaus, Vincent and Charles. He struggled to recall the names of those saints in the abortive message at Londonderry, and he added these: Cyril, Valentine, Walpurga, Paschal, Linus, and Luke for the third time.

It was an unusual list as many of the familiar saints such as St. Padraig, St. Fiacre, St. Columcille, and St. Finian were not included. But those were Irish saints and this code was a Sassanach one. That explained that. Idly playing with his cowke stick, he entered the names of the Apostles, linking Peter with Paul, and Luke with Luke. Running out of Apostles, and pleased with the alliterative sound, he matched William, Wenceslaus and Walpurga; Cornelius, Cyril and Charles; Venantius, Vincent and Valentine, and Linus, Laurence and Louis.

He stared at the list. That was strange, for of eighteen saints' names, six of them alone began with the letter L, counting the three Lukes. With growing excitement he noted that three began with P, three with W, three with C, and three with V. He noted with satisfaction that he was now curious, one of de Vimeny's list of attribute, this time, intelligence, to discover if this repetition of initial letters was of significance, and if so, of what.

Carefully he wrote down the five letters represented, L, P, W, C and V. If, as deVimeny believed, the saints' names designated different agents, why were they limited to names beginning with just five letters? Why not any of the other numerous saints, such as those beginning with J, or M, or T, of which there were many?

He examined the Bible. But he could find nothing to distinguish it from other Bibles, including his own; no markings, nothing underlined, nothing unusual. Will, if he couldn't be resourceful, what was another one of the needed attributes? Ah, yes, imagination. Tadhg, told himself sternly, use your imagination! He looked at the letters and he looked at the Bible. But his imagination remained blank.

Alright, then, revert to intelligence. What does your intelligence tell you? For one thing, the Bible must be tied intimately to the messages because Sir Oliver was obviously using it for reasons other than religious. But why the Bible? Well, for one thing Bibles were readily available. Secondly, they were easily carried. And thirdly, a Bible certainly wouldn't arouse suspicion.

Exasperated that his Bible was back at his quarters in Dublin, he closed his eyes to recall what it looked like. There was the black vellum cover, and the flyleaf, with the name of William John Murray scrawled across it. The memory of Meg Murray reminded him how she had trapped him with the Irish expression. He grinned. It had worked out well, all except her promise to get him the Reverend George Walker's Bible which she said contained the key to the code.

The key to the code! He sat upright as he repeated the phrase. The key to the code, Tadhg, the key to the code! He pounded his head with his open palm, hoping by some miracle, to find the key thereby. But it remained elusive.

Again he opened the Bible, scanning the pages. There were Genesis, Exodus, and Leviticus and the other books of the Old Testament. Then there were St Matthew, St Mark, St Luke, the same Luke used three times in the messages, down through all the other books of the New Testament to Revelations. Revelations, indeed, Tadhg thought, disgusted with himself, as no revelation came to him.

He shook his head in annoyance. Why didn't the answer come?

It surely must lie here before him. After all, the Bible was printed on pages like any ordinary book. The only thing to distinguish it, other than its holy contents, was that it was broken down into chapter, verse and line. That's all it was, pages, chapters, verses and lines. He stopped. There was an elusive stirring in his whirling brain. His intelligence was trying to tell him something, something connected with page, chapter, verse and line! In large letters he wrote PAGE, CHAPTER, VERSE AND LINE. Again there was that strange stirring, a feeling of having the answer and not having it. He stared at the word 'line'. What did it remind him of? Why, St. Linus to be sure! Linus! And then miraculously, the words Page, Chapter, Verse and Linus turned into Peter, Charles, Vincent and Linus. Again they turned into Paul, Cyril, Valentine and Luke. Just as easily they became Paschal, Cornelius, Venantius and Louis!

He shook with excitement at his discovery But there were only four letters being used of the six. What about W and the use of L twice in each set of six saints? Yes, W, what did it represent? Why, Word, of course, and the two L's? Why not one for Line and one for Letter?

On the verge of discovery, he decided to carefully copy the list of two-digit numbers from the pages prepared by Sir Oliver. He had forgotten about Sir Oliver. What if he should return to his room to discover that the Bible was missing? He copied them quickly on some of the blank sheets of foolscap. It took him some time, but he finally had the list.

Entering the words Page, Chapter, Verse, Line, Word and Letter over the column of the figures in that order Tadhg turned to page 20, the first number on the list but to his consternation found that Chapter 18 was actually on page 21, and there was no verse 40. He took the second line of figures, turning to page 40, but there was no Chapter 35. The next two lines of columns were as unproductive.

Was he on the wrong track after all? Was it strictly coincidence that the initial letters of the saints' names were those of the divisions of the Bible? He thought of deVimney, trying to recall the brief instructions and comments the lieutenant had made. First, there was the substitution of some symbol for the original letter of the message. Then there was a possible scrambling. Was the latter applicable here? But if it was scrambled, how would the person who was supposed to decipher or decode it know the order? Again Tadhg stared at the infuriating columns of numbers before him.

How could they be unscrambled? He re-examined the first page. The saints who were being thanked were listed in order as Louis, Peter, Wenceslaus, Cyril, Luke and Vincent. This was L, P, W, C, L and V. So he scratched out his previous order of P, C, V, L, W and L, and substituted the new sequence.

Hopefully he turned to page 18. There was a Chapter 14 on the page! And a Verse 13! So far so good. But Line 20 was in Verse 5. Something was wrong. Anxiously he scrutinised the rows of numbers in the Line column. There was something peculiar here, for all the numbers ended with zeros. But why? Could it be that they were exactly that and nothing more - just zeros? If so, then Line 20 was really Line 2. And all the numbers in the Word and Letter columns also ended with zeros. If the same reasoning applied, then it was Line 2, not 20; Word 4, instead of 40, and Litter 2 instead of 20!

He turned to Line 2, Word 4, and Letter 2 of Verse 13. The letter was B. Following the same procedure, he did the same with the next row of figures, coming up with an R this time. The next two letters were I and G, spelling the word BRIG. He spent some time on the next row since the numbers 30, 53, 60, 49, 00, and 27, set in their proper sequence, came out as 53, 49, 27, 30, 60 and 00. He was puzzled by the symbol 00, since it obviously couldn't designate a letter unless it had some other significance.

Again he thought of Sir Oliver. Here he was, racing against time to get the message solved so that he could return the Bible and the papers to the other man's room where they would be missed. And now he was confronted with a new obstacle. He reread the designated line, 'And at night he shall divide the spoil.' The 60 indicated the sixth word of the line, 'divide', but the 00 gave no clue as to what letter of the word was involved.

He ran through the attributes needed for decoding. But which one applied here now that he was struck? He decided on intelligence again. So he sat concentrated in thought. But the harder he tried to solve it, the more insurmountable the problem became. Time was running out on him. If Sir Oliver found the Bible missing, he would undoubtedly start a room-to-room search for it. The landlord would cooperate. If Tadhg got the soldiers, Captain Henry would have his sailors. There was but one thing to do, and that was to think clearly.

'Divide' he muttered to himself. He examined the other numbers which had zeros, remembering his conclusion, that the zeros had no significance other than nothingness, had been correct. But this was a double zero, 00! Well, wasn't two times zero still zero? Perhaps it indicated that no letter was meant here. This left the entire word 'divide.' But why alter the pattern with a whole word when the other symbols indicated only a letter? And what could 'brig divide' mean? Suddenly the possibility occurred to him that it meant exactly what it said, divide. So divide he would.

Eagerly he returned to his number combinations, laboriously and carefully working them out. Every time he came to the combination of 53, 49, 27, 30 60 and 00, he divided, and started a new word. Finally the complete message emerged, 'Brig Tyrconnell sails Jan tenth from Waterford with agents MacDermot and Taafe to be landed at night by longboat at cove two miles north of Lands End.'

When he had the last letter, he hastily put the sheets of foolscap back in the Bible, and crossed over to Sir Oliver's room. It was similar to his, but larger. On a table stood quills and ink, and an empty mug. Hearing boisterous voices, he placed the Bible on the table, returning to his own room just in time as heavy feet ascended the stairs. It was Sir Oliver and Captain Henry, accompanied by two giggling girls, apparently the pieces de resistance of the evening's round of pleasure.

Tadhg breathed a sigh of relief even as he worriedly analysed the result of his labours. The message composed by Sir Oliver, obviously intended for transmission to England by Captain Henry, proved conclusively that Sir Oliver was an agent of the English government. But what should he do now? Major Nangle, God rest his soul, had warned him that Sir Oliver had friends in high places. To whom could he go with his information? What would Sir Oliver, now in dalliance with his doxy, do when he discovered that his papers had been messed with? What could this whole affair mean to the Lady Mairéad?

Sick at heart, Tadhg now regretted the course his relentless and vindictive pursuit of Sir Oliver had taken. His elation at his discovery of the code key was more than offset by his concern over the Lady Mairéad. He had always been aware, but reluctant to admit it to himself, that there was more to his motivation for the capture of a traitor than pure patriotism. Ever since he had learned that Sir Oliver had matrimonial intentions towards the Lady FitzGerald, he had been jealous and resentful of him. And jealousy was but one short step from hatred.

He buried his head in his hands. Now that he had ferreted out the truth of Sir Oliver's treasonable activities, he was obligated to disclose them. But how could this be accomplished without entangling Lady Mairéad? The man was a traitor and deserved to be punished for his dishonourable deeds. His eyes strayed to his sword. 'Drawn only in defense of honour. If drawn against Sir Oliver, in whose honour would it be drawn? Would he deny it? Admit it cringingly? React angrily? Be provoked to the point of challenging Tadhg to a duel? And if Sir Oliver died as a result of a duel, would that be enough to end the matter without getting the Lady Mairéad involved?

All the rest of the night, Tadhg wrestled with his problem. He recalled Conor's admonition at the camp near Dundalk when he had told Tadhg that he didn't stop to analyse situations thoroughly. And just a few days previously, Conor had insisted that he and Dónal accompany Tadhg on this expedition so that Tadhg wouldn't do anything foolish on his own. But how could Conor help him now? His friend was tolerant of Tadhg's affection for the Lady Mairéad, but he was doubtful if Conor would be party to suppressing information which might be harmful to the lady if it meant Sir Oliver going free. Conor would not be corrupted by sentiment. Friendship was one thing; truth, honour and obligation another.

Feeling that he was so deeply committed, he finally made his decision. He realised that it could be the wrong one, but he could see no other way out of his dilemma. Taking a fresh sheet of foolscap, whimsically aware that perhaps he should be wearing it instead of writing on it, he composed a coded note to Sir Oliver. Since he no longer had a Bible, the two-digit number combinations made no sense, but it started off with the usual introductory thanks to the Saints. There were enough number combinations to take care of its pointed and pungent intent.

With his course determined, he sat quietly until the slamming of doors, and the shrill voices of the departing girls, indicated that Sir Oliver should be alone at last. He removed his blond wig and eyepatch, placing them on the bed. Then he arose, sword in scabbard, and strode directly to Sir Oliver's room. He knocked loudly on the door.

'Who is it?' the occupant called querulously, his London accent more noticeable than usual in the quiet of early morning.

'Scotty MacLeod. I have a message for you.'

The door opened, and a partially dressed Sir Oliver appeared, clutching to hold up his breeches. He took the folded sheet, glanced at it, noticed its beginning, then peered sharply at Tadhg's accusing blue eyes. Then he walked to his table, saying, 'Come in, my friend, while I read the message.'

Spreading the sheet of paper before him on the table, he turned to his Bible. He frowned. Glancing once more at his visitor, he took the sheets of foolscap from the book. With a slight smile on his face, he opened a desk drawer took out a pistol, cocked it, and pointed it at Tadhg.

'It seems that somebody,' he began sardonically, stressing the word 'somebody', 'has been at my papers. They are certainly not in the same order as they were when I left them. Ah! The saintly serving wench. I saw the two of you plotting. Why don't we save each other's valuable time by your telling me the contents of the message so that I don't have to bother to decode it?' He maintained the slight smile, but the eyes above the pistol were cold and unsmiling, and the hand holding the weapon was perfectly steady.

Abandoning his Scots' accent, Tadhg enunciated his message clearly and accusingly: 'You are a traitorous dog.'

Sir Oliver raised his eyebrows mockingly. 'Any signature?' he inquired.

'Tadhg O'Cuirc.'

'Aha, the supposedly simple fisherman who slew John Montgomery in a duel, one of the heroes the night Mattie Moley was killed, and very likely the big soldier who rushed past me in the twilight near Fionn MacCool's grave on Windy Hill. I should have known. An admirable masquerade, O'Cuirc, I commend you for it.'

'You admit your guilt?' Tadhg's voice expressed his surprise.

'Guilt? No. Participation? Yes.'

'Then you intended to kill the Lady Mairéad that night.'

'Certainly. At that time she appeared to be a threat to my well-being. Fortunately for her, the attack failed. Later I didn't think the circumstances warranted a repeat since the mysterious soldier with the message disappeared from view. I suppose that was you?'

Tadhg nodded, amazed at Sir Oliver's calm and analytical reaction, his eyes in the pistol which pointed at him unwaveringly.

'I often wondered about the interception of this missing message. It certainly created a stir in the camp, didn't it?' He laughed. 'As a matter of fact, I was one of the supposedly eager officers who obtained a copy of it to try to decode it. What a parcel of fools! Then a man for whom the message was intended misses it when a bumbling peasant stumbles on it! But what happens? Within twenty four hours I had a copy of it. Of course, so did a score of other persons. But there was one major difference; I was able to decode it. Incidentally, you did solve this one, didn't you? You did? I must give you credit, O'Cuirc, for being much smarter than I thought. Especially the multiple use of St Luke.'

'I figured that Luke was the agent's name, in this case, you,' Tadhg said, during this time of seemingly friendly conversation of the spy.

Sir Oliver shook his head. 'No. There were other saints whose names began with the letter 'L' such as Louis, Leo, Leander, Lucien, or Lupus, but we had to have one to designate specifically the last column, which was for 'letter', to distinguish it from the other 'L' column for 'Line'.'

'I should never have listened to Major Nangle's advice about not voicing my suspicion of you,' Tadhg declared, dejected at his failure, knowing that Sir Oliver intended to kill him. 'I should have gone to the Viceroy despite your close association with him.'

'Ah, yes, the Viceroy. Charming fellow, isn't he? I can visualise his fat and fatuous face as he listens horrified to my sad story of how one of his soldiers, a hero too, mind you, was killed while trying to rob me in my room. But it is time to terminate this most enjoyable discussion. As you Irish so aptly put it, *Slán leat go deo*!' Smiling sardonically, he raised the pistol slowly, pointing it directly at Tadhg's heart.

'Not so fast, Sir Oliver,' a stern voice spoke from the doorway, and Sergeant Williamson stalked into the room, pistol in his hand. For the first time, Sir Oliver's icy calm departed him, and his eyes showed his anger and disappointment. But he kept his wits about him. 'Arrest this man immediately, Sergeant. He came in here to rob me. Thank God you arrived in time.'

'Yes. Thank God I came in time. But not the way you want it.' He addressed Tadhg, but carefully watched Sir Oliver. 'What caused this?'

Tadhg raised his eyes to the sergeant, a sensation of tremendous relief sweeping over him. ' I discovered a message he was sending to England,' he replied simply. 'I decoded it, then wrote him a message in return. It made him very unhappy.'

'You broke the code?' The sergeant was incredulous.

318

Tadhg nodded. While Sergeant Williamson stared at him admiringly, Sir Oliver spoke. 'Did you hear me sergeant? I command you to put this man under arrest immediately. I am Major Oliver Trent of the King's Army.'

'King William's army,' Sergeant Williamson blazed. He pointed to Sir Oliver's weapon. 'If he points pistols at people who make him unhappy, what does he do when he is really angry?'

'He challenges them to a duel,' Sir Oliver replied, his face again a mask covering his emotions. 'I insist on meeting this man immediately on the field of honour to satisfy his incredible insult to me.'

Once more an incredulous stare showed on the sergeant's broad face. 'You are willing to meet this man, a mere soldier, on the field of honour? I thought you gentlemen fought only among yourselves.'

'His labelling me as a traitor is an insult of such magnitude that it transcends the normal code of honour. I demand satisfaction!'

'That can be arranged, I'm sure,' Sergeant Williamson replied happily. 'Have you a second?'

'Get Captain Henry in the room at the end of the hall. I'm sure that he will act for me.'

Keeping his pistol levelled at Sir Oliver until the latter reluctantly placed the weapon at his feet, the sergeant instructed Tadhg to go to Captain Henry's room and have him report immediately to Sir Oliver.

Captain Henry, angry at being disturbed, came quickly. His usual jocularity vanished when he saw Captain Williamson pointing his pistol at Sir Oliver, and learned that MacLeod, the Scot, was really O'Cuirc, the Irishman.

'You Irish bastard, I would have made short shrift of you aboard my ship, if I had only known'

Sergeant Williamson glared at him with undisguised contempt. 'You rebel bastard,' he paraphrased the captain. 'if you feel so much like fighting, you may take advantage of the custom whereby the seconds also duel. I will give you the opportunity by so challenging you.'

Captain Henry, torn between desire and discretion, looked to Sir Oliver who nodded his head vigorously to assent. 'I accept,' he said reluctantly, his bluster dissipated.

And so it was quickly arranged. The four principals left the inn, going to a field behind the outbuildings. Sir Oliver carried a highly polished mahogany chest. When they halted, he opened the chest to disclose a set of matched duelling pistols. Tadhg, who had expected to fight with swords, was shocked and apprehensive over the change. Sir Oliver brushed aside Sergeant Williamson's objection that Tadhg, being challenged, had the choice of weapons.

'What difference does it make?' he asked irritably. 'O'Cuirc is a soldier. He should know how to handle a pistol.' He then handed the box to his second, saying 'You had batter test these weapons as they have been exposed to the damp sea air.'

Observing Captain Henry's questioning gaze, he added, 'You know, the usual test.'

The sailor reached into the chest, selecting a gun. He loaded to with a charge of powder and a ball. Taking a small wrench from the chest he used it to wind up the wheel, fitting it to the squared end of the spindle. Then he placed the priming powder in the pan cover, and the mechanism holding the flint was bent over it. He pointed the weapon over the sea and fired it. Replacing the weapon in the box which Sir Oliver held out to him, he methodically repeated the process.

He nodded his head in satisfaction. 'They're both in good shape, and apparently the powder is dry.'

Sir Oliver then carefully selected a pistol before offering the chest to Tadhg who took the remaining weapon. It was about sixteen inches long, beautifully inscribed with elaborate scroll designs. Confused over the rapid and unexpected turn of events, Tadhg stood indecisively, the pistol held idly in his hand. 'Come, man, we don't have all day,' Sir Oliver fumed. 'Take the fall and powder.'

After the weapons were loaded, Sir Oliver took the lead in the role of instructor, one which he had evidently acted numerous times before. 'we will walk ten paces from a back-to-back position, then turn about. After a slow count to three, we will fire. Your second can do the honours of counting.'

Sergeant Williamson stood with brows furrowed, deep in thought. 'did you hear me, Sergeant?' Sir Oliver inquired sharply.

'Yes, I heard you, but I'm going to suggest one simple change.' He drew his own pistol from his belt, handing it to Tadhg, and took the duelling pistol from Tadhg's unresisting hand. 'Use this, my friend. You gave it to me. It's in fine shape. I have given it the most loving and tender care. It is a beautiful weapon; have complete confidence in it.'

'This is highly irregular,' Sir Oliver stormed. 'He must use the weapon that matches mine.'

The sergeant smiled grimly. 'We'll accept that on one condition: that you give me the pistol in your hand, and that you take its mate.'

Sir Oliver's face was crimson, his eyes deadly. 'are you implying there is something irregular?' He raised the weapon, but Sergeant Williamson, his sword drawn, moved quickly, touching the blade point to Sir Oliver's middle.

'If you fire,' he said, 'you will be a dead man before I hit the ground.'

While Sir Oliver stood undecided, Tadhg cocked Sir John Ferguson's old gun. The sound broke the deadlock. Lowering his weapon, Sir Oliver said, 'I'll keep this pistol, O'Cuirc can keep his. Let us proceed.'

As they stood back-to-back, Tadhg towered over his opponent. His black locks, no longer hidden by the tam-o-shanter, contrasted sharply with the sandy red of his foe. On signal, they marched ten paces, turned and faced each other. Sergeant Williamson counted slowly and clearly in the cold morning air.

At the count of one they raised their weapons. If I am killed, Tadhg thought, and Captain Henry succeeds in slaying Sergeant Williamson, then none will know their message of their treason. He cursed himself for being a fool, again thinking that it would be more appropriate if he wore the foolscap instead of writing on it.

At the count of two, he acknowledged to himself that Conor was right, that he let his emotions rule his reason. For his stupidity he deserved to die. By his impetuous and ill-reasoned decision, he had placed not only himself but Sergeant Williamson, in jeopardy.

As the count of three rang across the field, he silently gave thanks for the special attention Sergeant Gallagher had given him, and with hand unwavering, fired straight and true at his opponent. As Sir Oliver fell, his white shirt front stained crimson, his pistol still unfired, Captain Henry stared stupidly and uncomprehendingly at his duelling colleague.

Sergeant Williamson ran to Tadhg and embraced him. 'I told you to have faith in that gun. Now let me have it, for it's my turn.'

In a trance, Tadhg approached the pistol chest, offering the remaining weapon to Captain Henry. The latter, his face drained of all colour, his eyes glassy, walked slowly to the dead man. Looking intently at Sir Oliver's body, as if he expected orders, he stood mute. After a short while, he shook his head vigorously, clearing it of shock and indecision, then reached slowly to pick the pistol from Sir Oliver's unresisting fingers.

This time Tadhg counted, and the strangely assorted pair, the gangling captain in his seaman's clothes, and the stalwart sergeant in his uniform, faced each other over their pistols. At the final count, Captain Henry fired first, the ball passing harmlessly over his foe's head. Sergeant Williamson, looking grim, standing as calm as on the fire practice range, pulled the trigger and the captain tumbled grotesquely to the ground.

'That's that,' the sergeant said with satisfaction.

Congratulating him on his success, Tadhg asked why the captain had refused the pistol in the chest, the one that Tadhg was supposed to use.

'I'll show you.' He took the gun, loaded it with powder and ball, and pointing it into the air, pulled the trigger. Nothing happened. He repeated the process, but again it failed to fire.

'But it fired when Captain Henry tested it,' Tadhg insisted.

The sergeant shook his head. 'No, it didn't. Captain Henry fired the other twice. This one has been tampered with to make it defective. That 'testing 'act aroused my suspicion. I saw Sir Oliver press his thumb hard in the other gun when the captain tried to take it. That's why I made you change guns. You observed that Sir Oliver refused to trade duelling pistols when I offered to do so. He knew that this gun wouldn't fire!'

Tadhg blanched. 'He meant to shoot me down while I was armed with a weapon that wouldn't function?'

'That's right. Sir Oliver was not a man to take chances. Why do you think that he offered to duel with you. Why all the big hurry. To avenge his honour? Not likely! He meant to murder you. I would have been next. If I hadn't come to his room when I did, you would have been killed there. But he took that interruption in his stride. Actually, he probably thought that the double duel was even more credible than a shooting in his room.'

'I owe you my life,' Tadhg exclaimed fervently. 'If it wasn't for you, it would be my corpse there instead of his.'

'That evens us up for the one at Devil's Hook Charlie's,' the sergeant said. 'But we must return to Dublin Castle immediately and report what had happened here. You say you interrupted a message and decoded it? Where is it?'

'In my room.'

'We had better get it before it disappears. I wouldn't trust that innkeeper. He might be part of the plot.'

The sergeant returned both pistols to the chest, tucking it firmly underneath his arm. As they walked back to the inn, they met the innkeeper and several others, attracted by the sound of the pistol fire, rushing down to the field. Briefly Sergeant Williamson explained that there had been an affair of honour, and that both principal and his second were dead. He instructed the innkeeper to have Sir Oliver's coachman and servants put the bodies in the coach and be prepared to follow the army guard detail back to Dublin.

They retrieved the code message, the sheets of foolscap, and the Bible from Sir Oliver's room. Then they got Tadhg's breakdown of the code message, and his belongings. Next they went down to the provosts post to inform the guards to man the post while they went to Dublin.

'Where are Conor and Dónal?' Tadhg asked, looking for his friends.

'Dónal got very ill; Conor took him to Dublin for treatment. I was going to your room to tell you when I heard Sir Oliver and you arguing.'

Tadhg was alarmed. 'What is wrong with Dónal?'

'Bloody flux, I think. Don't worry. He'll be all right.'

When they returned to the inn, a surly but thoroughly frightened coachman reported that his master's body was in the carriage, along with that of Captain Henry. Tadhg and the sergeant mounted their horses, wheeled about, and headed towards Dublin, the coach rumbling behind. As they departed, the serving woman who had helped Tadhg was telling all who would listen that she had warned that God would punish those who broke his commandments.

They rode directly to the Castle where Sergeant Williamson informed the officer of the guard that it was imperative that he talk to the adjutant immediately. Lieutenant Thomas Butler, the adjutant, upon learning the import of the incident, declared that the Viceroy himself should handle it. Tadhg and the sergeant were escorted to a room in Tyrconnell's apartment, where, after some delay, the duke, Lieutenant Dominick Sheldon, Major Francis O'Meara and several other officers of the regimental staff entered.

With colonel Sheldon handling the interrogation, Tadhg told the story from the beginning. He described his meeting with a sandy-haired officer near Windy Hill on the evening he found the first message, of Major Nangle's instructions to keep quiet while he conducted an investigation, of the incident of Holmes message at Derry, and the adventure at Ringsend. He refrained from mentioning Lady Mairéad.

'Amazing, most amazing,' the Viceroy said.

Major O'Meara grimaced. 'I was approached by Major Nangle before he was drowned at Cladybridge. I searched all the officers' tents, including Sir Oliver's. I found nothing incriminating only an old bible and some foolscap!'

The staff members then scrutinized the message material as decoded by Tadhg, examined the duelling pistols, and chattered excitedly.

'Won't Taafe and MacDermott be happy to learn they aren't going to have a welcoming party at Land's End,' colonel Sheldon commented. He turned to the Viceroy. 'Should we cancel their trip?'

'By all means. If Trent had the information, others must have it.'

The duke still showed the shock of the disclosures of the treasonable acts of a man who had been so close to him.

'There will have to be a revision our secret agent section,' Colonel Sheldon said, 'to prevent a repetition of this.'

The Viceroy nodded. 'I will leave the matter in your hands. But first we must take care of this Trent situation. The whole affair will have to be handled with the greatest secrecy and diplomacy. If I understand correctly, none but the persons in this room know the true story. It will be of great advantage to us to have the secret of the code. Under no circumstances will anyone divulge this information. The two deaths in Ringsend will have to be attributed to private quarrels between the principals. Is that understood?'

All nodded, including the two enlisted men.

'What about the English ship at Ringsend?' Major O'Meara asked.

'Confiscate it,' the duke replied tersely. 'It was carrying contraband, wasn't it?'

'What about these two men?' Colonel Sheldon indicated Tadhg and Sergeant Williamson.'

'That's a problem,' the Viceroy replied, a frown on his florid face. 'The King abhors duelling, so they will have to be punished.'

Observing the shocked expressions on all their faces, the Viceroy smiled sympathetically. 'I appreciate what these men have done. The decoding of the message by this man, O'Cuirc, was outstanding. But for appearances' sake, there must be some punishment to allay the kings displeasure at their duelling, and to convince the rest of the army and the public that there was nothing more to it.'

'You have a good point there,' Colonel Sheldon said.

The duke continued. 'They will be reduced to privates, and given thirty days in the guardhouse.' As a gasp of dismay swept the room, the duke raised his hand. 'If we are too lenient, it will arouse suspicion. Privately, the sum of twenty-five pounds will be awarded to O'Cuirc, and five pounds to Sergeant Williamson. And when we take the field in the spring, I want them reinstated to their previous ranks, with periodic promotions. After all, 'he said, frowning at the two enlisted men, 'although you have performed an invaluable service to the King, your actions in getting personally involved are subject to condemnation. O'Cuirc should have reported to the sergeant, and the sergeant should have reported it to the adjutant. If Trent had been successful in his designs to kill you, we wouldn't have the code solution, and Taafe and MacDermott would have gone to their deaths.'

'They were indiscreet,' Major O'Meara said.

'That's putting it mildly,' said the duke. 'I will reiterate that nothing of the true facts of this affair will be further mentioned. If I learn of any information leaks, I will know that it came from one of the persons in this room. I warn you: don't arouse my wrath. Is that understood?'

All nodded solemnly.

As the two culprits were taken away to be locked in the guardhouse, Sergeant Williamson turned to Tadhg. 'You're nothing but trouble for me,' he declared with mock indignation. 'Ten months ago you assault me and escape. Now you get me demoted and thrown in he guardhouse.'

'Ah! But look at the good side.'

'Tell me, Tadhg. Make me laugh real hard!'

You won't be losing your money in drinking and gaming for thirty whole days.'

Williamson groaned. 'Is that your idea of something good, not being able to have any fun? Oh, yes I forgot; you're the one who spends his time studying from books and wandering the countryside with the schoolteacher. But seriously, Tadhg, I'd be happy to spend a whole year in the guardhouse, if necessary, for the privilege of helping punish those two traitors. And do you know that in all my time with this regiment, that this was the first time that I have ever been in the private company of the colonel, the duke of Tyrconnell? For a common soldier, that is quite a honour.'

'Actually,' Tadhg remarked, 'we can never be sure that Captain Henry was a part of the plot. He might have carried messages not knowing what they contained, or that they were secret messages.'

'You're being extremely charitable,' the sergeant said wryly. 'He certainly was in on the plan to give you a defective pistol which would have meant murder. for that scurvy trick alone he deserves to die!'

'I suppose so. But thanks to your sharp eyes, the trick didn't work. I'll always remember you in my prayers for having saved my life.'

Their time in the guardhouse passed quickly enough. because they were considered heroes of sorts for having been victors in duels, their guards treated then as special guests, and granted them many privileges. Tadhg spent must of his time studying; ex-Sergeant Williamson played cards and dice, and traded tall tales with other old soldiers. When they rejoined their regiment, they took much ribbing, most of it friendly, but some malicious jibes from those who were envious of their former high rank, or the adulation because of the duels with the two Englishmen.

Tadhg longed to tell Conor and Dónal the true facts, especially Conor, who, Tadhg felt, suspected that there was more to the incident that the official explanation. Conor never questioned Tadhg, unlike Dónal, about Sir Oliver's death, or why Tadhg suddenly abandoned all interest in the mysterious code messages which had precipitated the expedition to Ringsend. It was easy to put Dónal off with evasive answers, and after a while the youth stopped asking questions. He had recovered from his illness, which, thanks to prompt attention and treatment, never reached the bloody flux stage.

Dónal had been quite impressed with his stay in the hospital. 'If you ever get the extreme flux,' he advised Tadhg, just take what they gave me. First you boil the fruit of the blackthorn until it is soft. Strain the remains, add some sugar, then boil it again. Take some burnt claret wine, and mix well with the blackthorn syrup, add some cinnamon and drink it. You'll be better in no time at all.'

Tadhg grimaced. 'I think I'd rather have the flux.'

Instead of being relieved that Sir Oliver's death eliminated the possibility of further attack on the Lady Mairéad, Tadhg was more worried than before. He was most concerned over her reaction to the news that he had slain a second suitor. As the real reason for the duel was suppressed, she would not know that Sir Oliver was not only a traitor to his king and country, but had schemed to have her murdered by Mattie Moley. All she would know would be the official version - that it had been the result of a private quarrel.

Tadhg would have felt much worse if he had known how she had reacted to the news. She had gone to the home of her mother's kin, the O'Hurleys, of the barony of Coshlea in County Limerick, to avoid the unwelcome attention of King James. The shock of the tragedy was great enough in itself, but to have it happen at the hands of Tadhg O'Cuirc was doubly devastating. She interpreted 'private quarrel' as being fought over her. She took to her bed, so despondent, that Mary Casey feared for her life. She ate little, and then only with much coaxing. In her anguish and despair, she even toyed with the idea of conversion to the Catholic faith and becoming a nun.

Where her relatives and friends thought it was grief over the death of Sir Oliver that devastated her for so long a period, it was chiefly self-blame. She felt hat she was responsible for the tragedy. If it hadn't been for her, Tadhg would never have come into contact with Sir Oliver. She had reconciled herself to Tadhg's innocence in the slaying of John Montgomery, having been goaded into it, but she could find no extenuating circumstances for his having killed Oliver Trent. In time she helped relieve her own burden of guilt by putting more on Tadhg.

Her dislike for him hardened into such hatred that she detested the very name of Tadhg. One of the household servants, who had the misfortune of bearing that name, never did understand why she looked at him with such loathing whenever she encountered him. Out of her despondency grew the fixation that the deaths of her two suitors meant that God had never intended that she would be married. She grew distant and cool with any man who gave the slightest indication of paying her court as she adjusted herself to enforced spinsterhood.

CHAPTER IX

Battle Preparations

Spring came and with it a French fleet to Kinsale, where some 7,000 well-trained and well-equipped foot soldiers of eight battalions were landed before marching up to Dublin. They were commanded by M le Comte Peguilin de Lauzun, who had languished for some years in the Bastille for his defiance of Louis XIV on secretly marrying the king's cousin, La Grande Mademoiselle. After being pardoned, he was restored to royal favour and his place at court by accompanying James's Queen, Mary of Modena, and the infant Prince of Wales when they had fled England to France in December of 1688.

An insolent little man, Lauzun was disliked by most of the influential members of the Court at Versailles. In the eyes of Mary of Modena, however, he could do no wrong. because of Mary's fondness for her protégé, he became King James's personal choice to lead his army in Ireland. To this, Louis acquiesced.

Unfortunately for Ireland, the French Minister of War, Louvois, was involved in a bitter personal feud with the Marquis de Seignelay, of the family of Colbert. Because King James and his family were close friends of the Colberts, Louvois vented his pique by curtailing the promised military aid to Ireland, and selecting an inferior commander to lead James's army. Lauzun had little military experience if offensive warfare. He had taken part in sieges and minor operations, which, as many of James's officers complained, failed to qualify him for the important command he now held.

The arrival of the French forces and supplies was a mixed blessing. On the credit side were the food, ammunition, weapons and twelve cannon. On the debit side was the practice of paying the French soldiers with Louis's silver. King James's brass coins, never a solid financial base, began to tumble in value as the French silver coins circulated. While the value of the brass money declined, prices of commodities climbed, making it difficult for enlisted personnel and officers to obtain the essentials.

Army activities increased, as the advent of the new campaign approached, putting an end to the days of idleness for the soldiery. Those without uniforms were authorised to draw red cloth for their regimental coats, pewter buttons, and white cloth for the linings.

Tadhg found it difficult to tell Rory that he couldn't take him with him, and took him back to Cait O'Reilly's again. She greeted Rory affectionately with hugs and kisses.

'Sure, you'd never know he was the same scrawny *buachaillín* you brought here more than a year ago wearing that ragged wild costume of the mountain men.' She stood back to better admire the boy, then hugged him again, tousling the red hair, now cut short. 'Come,' she begged, 'give Cáit a kiss.'

Rory, an affectionate boy, squeezed her tightly in return, planting the 'little kiss' that she requested square on her lips. 'Musha, Cáit *mo chroí*,' he replied seriously, 'I thank you for being such a good mother to a poor orphan.'

A cheerful greeting to Tadhg in French made him turn to behold the smiling face of Le Berge, the Huguenot who had given him the French grammar.

'*Céad míle fáilte.*' Tadhg greeted him in the Irish, 'it's happy I am to see you again. I thought surely that you would have fled the terrible Papists by now.'

Le Berge smiled broadly. 'I'm afraid that the religious persecution is much worse in England than it is here. We Huguenots were treated well under King James. It was the Viceroy, the Duke of Tyrconnell himself, who interceded with the Municipal Council for us last year to save us the need of paying a fine and special fee for readmission under the new charter as freedmen of this city.'

'He has learned we Catholics don't have horns,' Cáit commented.

The Frenchman bowed. 'I was among the first of the Huguenots who accepted the offer of the Muncipal Council to come to Dublin. Since January of 1682 I have been a freeman here, under Charles and James. Among those of us who came from France are butchers, blacksmiths and bakers, cabinet makers and carpenters, worsted-combers and wool combers. And all the weavers, silk weavers and sarge weavers have prospered and are happy. We worship freely at our church like the Catholics do at theirs. They do not bother us or persecute us.'

Tadhg found himself saying, 'Faith, and that's the way it should be,' with honest enthusiasm, something he could never have done back in Connaught where all non-Catholics were considered anti-Christ.

Tadhg, Conor and Dónal took leave of Cáit and Rory, both of

whom dabbed at their eyes, and Le Berge, who repeated his previous invitation to visit him at his shop for a new coat and breeches. Tadhg thanked him, then pointing to his uniform, said with a smile, 'I'll have to wear these clothes for some time, but when we drive King William out of Ireland, I'll come to see you.'

On 20 May, the entire regiment, together for the first time since the previous November, assembled on Oxmanstown Green for review by King James and the Viceroy. The king's tall figure contrasted with the corpulent duke's as they stood in regal finery on a raised platform. When the review was concluded, the regiment rode out of town to the north, camping that night near Gormanstown, the home of Lord Gormanstown, colonel of one of the King's Regiment of Foot. As it was hot, and the road dusty, many of the men took advantage of the small stream nearby to bathe and refresh themselves.

For the next two weeks the regiment camped at several sites in the vicinity of Dundalk. There was plenty of feed for the horses. And the country people, with their Protestant landlords fled, had victuals of all kinds for sale to the troops.

By 19 June, Tyrconnell's Regiment of Horse near Dundalk had been joined by the Royal Regiment of Foot Guards, the Earl of Antrim's Regiment of Foot, His Majesty's First Troop of Guards commanded by the Earl of Dover, His Majesty's Second troop of Guards commanded by his son, the Lord Grand Prior, Lord Dungan's Regiment of Dragoons, the Earl of Louth's Regiment of Foot, the Lord Grand Prior's Regiment of Foot, Colonel Gordon O'Neill's Regiment of Foot, Lord Bellew's Regiment of Foot and eight Battalions of French foot.

There were several alarums, which proved negative, as no sign of the enemy was found. Then on 22 June, a Sunday, a considerable body of Williamites, to the number of 200, encountered a unit of Lord Galmoy's Horse near Newry. The latter were forced to retreat, having suffered some losses. The enemy pursued them, but ran into an ambush of 200 foot soldiers under Lieutenant Colonel FitzGerald. The Rebels in turn were forced to flee after losing three score men. However Lieutenant Colonel Dempsey of Galmoy's Horse suffered wounds from which he died several days later.

With the main body of Williamites reported to be moving nearby, there was a general beating of the drums early in the morning, and the entire Royal army moved back to the small village of Ardee. Most of the residents, being Protestants, had fled. The army moved several times in the next week, finally taking position on the south side of the River Boyne, about two miles from the old city of Drogheda on their right.

About this time the special guard detail for the King was again constituted, since there was some apprehension that roving bands of enemy cavalry might try to seek out the King for capture. Thus Tadhg was in a position to observe the results of the staff work in which James, Lauzun and the other advisers selected the site for the army's inevitable engagement with the enemy. The key was the Boyne which made a sharp curve west of Drogheda at the base of the Heights of Donore where it flowed in a great loop to the southwest before swinging again to the northwest to pass under the Bridge of Slane.

The Royalist forces took their positions on the south side of the river where it meandered gently through the rich vales of County Meath on its way to the sea. Here the river was deep, making the fords dangerous to cross. Behind the steep banks stretched a deep bog. The French engineers started the men building breastworks along the river bank. Behind the first line of defence arose a succession of hills to which the foot soldiers could retreat for fresh stands if the situation required it.

On Monday, 30 June, the first of the enemy was sighted on the hills on the opposite side of the river. Soon, several regiments marched down the slopes to set up camp, but apparently Marshal Schomberg had most of his forces hidden in the valleys beyond. Some of the Royalist cannon, set in advantageous position to protect the ford of Rosnaree, immediately began firing upon the Williamites in their camp, causing some casualties. In retaliation, the enemy then brought some of their big guns and mortars to fire at the Jacobites.

Accompanied by the Duke of Tyrconnell and the Duke of Berwick, General Lauzun rode along the river back to reconnoitre the area. Simultaneously King WIlliam was doing the same on his side. Although surrounded by members of his staff, he was at once recognised by the three Jacobites. Lauzun shouted an order to a French Lieutenant, and several field pieces were quickly brought up and planted along a hedge. The river at this spot was approximately fifty yards wide, making it an easy cannon shot.

It was a dramatic moment. On the skill and accuracy of a man of the ranks, a cannoneer, rested the fate of kings, countries , thousands of men and the whole course of history. Lauzun restrained his excitement as he stood next to the cannoneer, telling him to hold his match until given the order to fire. After several tense minutes, William was seen remounting his horse, making him a perfect target.

'Now!' shouted Lauzun, and the cannoneer fired, but the ball was just a trifle wide of its mark, instantly killing an attendant at William's side. A second cannon was then fired, and although less accurate than the other, hit the bank and ricocheted, slightly grazing William's shoulder in its passage, tearing a piece of the king's coat and bruising his right side.

As the startled Rebels galloped from their vulnerable position, William still erect in the saddle, the disappointed Jacobites stared glumly at their receding backs. Lauzun shrugged. 'Such are the fortunes of war,' he observed philisophically. 'William was born under a lucky star.'

While William was personally taking charge of the impending battle between the two forces, James was in his quarters at Carnstown Castle where he had a magnificent view of much of Northern Meath and Southeast Louth, with the Boyne flowing serenely between. The castle was situated about three miles north of Drogheda on the road to Clogher. It was an inspiring sight of a beautiful part of Ireland, but James was not thinking of Ireland. He was thinking of James. In fact, much of the afternoon was spent in organising a commission to leave for Waterford where its members were to arrange for a ship to carry him to France in the event it was needed.

While James was making provision for his own safety, Conor and Dónal visited Tadhg, who, along with the other special guards, were camped near the summit of a hill which lay close to the little Church of Donroe. James's tent and much of his baggage had been brought to this site as he had been expected to camp there.

Conor stood on the crest of the hill and surveyed the panorama below.

'I find it difficult to believe, a chara,' he remarked to Tadhg, 'that this is our beloved Eire. Look out there,' and he waved his arm in the direction of the hills and valleys opposite, 'and what do you see? Dutch, Danes, English, Scots, Germans, and French Huguenots. Who leads them? A Dutchman named William. And who is his chief general? A Frenchman named Schomberg.

'And who do we find in charge of the Irish army? A deposed

English King who had a Scots grandfather, a French father, an Italian grandmother and a Danish grandmother. Who is his general? An arrogant popinjay of a Frenchman whose only real conquests have been those of the boudoir. Who are King James's advisers? English, Scots and French. Who are the generals of this Irish army? Leaders with good Irish names like Dorrington, Lauzun, Wauchope, Maxwell, Hamilton, Zurlauben and Slater.

Tadhg shook his head, not having a ready answer.

'I'll tell you then. It's the Irish who are going to do the bleeding and the dying. King James is here not for the sake of the Irish who are supporting him, but just to use us to regain his throne. His dear cousin Louis is sending just enough men and materials to keep his arch enemy, William, fighting here rather than in France. Those Catholics down there with the English names are united with the Catholics with Irish names for the first time. Why? To protect their property and estates here in Ireland, not for any love of the Irish or Ireland. Others are professional soldiers, getting paid for the job, and the job happens to be right here. Who cares about poor Ireland?'

'I do!' Tadhg replied fiercely.

'And I,' Dónal echoed.

Conor's eyes softened, his bitterness abated. 'I know that, dear friends. And there are thousands more of us scattered through the ranks who will gladly die for Ireland. But where are the Irish generals?'

'There is Patrick Sarsfield,' Tadhg said. 'Sure and his grandfather wasn't an Italian or a Frenchman or an Englishman; he was Rory O'More of the Rising in 1641.'

'And does General Lauzun ask his advice? Do you see King James inviting old Rory's grandson into his tent for a wee drop? Does that talbot assign him to a position of authority?' Conor always referred to the Duke of Tyrconnell by his family name so that he could apply the appellation of talbot, a hound.

Tadhg had to acknowledge that Sarsfield, beloved by the Irish soldiers, was not given the authority and responsibility for which his experience, ability, and daring leadership called.

If Conor had known what was actually taking place, he would have been more than embittered, he would have been enraged. Whiles he was talking more to his companions, James was conferring with his generals.

'I have analysed our position in relation to William's army,' he began. 'Because we are in a good defensive area, we partially offset the advantage of his bigger, and more experienced professional forces. Too many of our men are untrained and untried levies.'

When Sarsfield declared that the fighting spirit of the Irish, and their love of their country would make them the equal of the mercenaries, James paid no attention, but continued. 'I do not want my army committed to a decisive battle that could destroy it. If the pressure becomes too heavy, we will disengage and retreat to better positions.'

A low murmur swept through the room. Some looked questioningly at the king as if they didn't believe their ears. Sarsfield eyes flashed with anger, and he restrained himself with difficulty.

'Are there any other instructions?' the Duke of Tyrconnell asked.

'Yes. I want the French battalions to be ready to lead the retreat. They are the most experienced, have the best weapons and training, and are better disciplined.'

General Hamilton, cleared his throat, saying, 'Your Majesty, one of the key points in an attempt to cross the river will be the bridge at Slane. I would like your permission at this time to order eight regiments to the vicinity of the bridge.'

The king, who had been piqued at Hamilton ever since the abortive surrender at Derry, irritably snapped, 'Neill O'Neill's regiment of dragoons will be responsible for protecting the bridge. We can't spare any more.'

Hamilton was shocked at the decision, but bowed, and remained silent. Lauzun will be in command. Orders will be issued to each regiment and unit within the half hour. That is all for now.'

CHAPTER X

James-of-the-Fleeing

It was 1 July 1690. To Tadhg, and the rest of the Irish army, awakened before daybreak by the clamorous beating of the drums, it was just another day. When the grey dawn disclosed the Valley of the Boyne - the river a brown ribbon between the green, rolling hills - the curtain was raised on a drama that was to affect the course of history. The players were all set, heroes and villains alike, all they had to do was say their lines and enact their roles.

When their baggage was collected and sent away, a feeling of a portentous decision being made was experienced by the Irish army. They knew a battle was imminent. It would be delayed no longer. Although glad that they would soon grapple with the enemy, many of the Irish were angered to see Tyrconnell's Regiment of Horse in the centre of the line instead of the pride and hope of the Irish army, the regiment of Patrick Sarsfield.

Across the river, behind the trees, the famous Dutch Blue Guards, held the centre for William. Facing this tough and experienced unit, in addition to Tyrconnell's Regiment, were untrained, untested raw Irish recruits, instead of the disciplined, battle-wise French foot.

Suddenly the quiet of the morning was rent by the thunderous roar of Schomberg's fifty cannon and his mortars as they poured a murderous hail of metal on the Irish positions. One of the first victims was Lord Dongan, colonel of a regiment of dragoons.

Tadhg, again assigned to guard King James, stood on the Heights of Donore overlooking the river. He felt uneasy about being part of a battle, but not in it. To his left, five miles away, was the Bridge of Slane, defended by a handful of dragoons, and to his right, much closer, the old town of Drogheda. Between him and the river, on the sloping hills, were the legions of Schomberg. Puffs of smoke, the roar of shells and the bursting of grenades indicated that the battle had started.

King James had arrived at the Heights of Donore from Carnatown Castle where he had spent the night. Now the king and his Viceroy watched the progress of the battle with the aid of magnifying glasses. After a while, the king put down the glasses, and inquired as to his baggage. He was assured that it had all been collected and sent on towards Dublin. Only then, did he pick up

335

the glasses again.

Across the river William, too, surveyed the battlefield, seeking weak spots in James's position. He shook his head in discouragement as he noted the hills where his uncle's troops were entrenched, and the deep stretches of the Boyne. Then, he called excitedly to Schomberg, and pointed to the Bridge of Slane. The Marshal looked. A slow grin spread across his leathery face. In a moment the king ordered a large force to force the bridge.

At the bridge, Sir Neill O'Neill waited apprehensively with his small force of dragoons. He had agreed with Hamilton that at least a half dozen regiments should have been assigned there to protect the flank of the Irish army. His fears were soon realised at the approach of several regiments of horse and foot. First the enemy set up several cannon on the hill. The shells whistled ominously as they crossed the river, exploding with deadly precision among O'Neill's men massed at the approach to the bridge, forcing them to withdraw from the immediate area. Then a regiment of horse thundered across the bridge, followed by several regiments of foot. O'Neill's outnumbered dragoons fought bravely, but in a short, fierce battle were defeated, with O'Neill himself among the slain. The surviving remnants, led by Major Charles MacCarthy, himself wounded, fled to safety on high ground.

William nodded with satisfaction when his glasses showed his troops safely across the Boyne and in a position to menace the Irish left flank, or to attack James from the rear at Duleek. He gave the order to attack. While James stood watching at a safe distance from the carnage, more concerned about the fate of his baggage than his men, William led his troops in an attempt to storm the river on the Irish right.

In charge of the centre, facing the great bulk of the Irish forces across the river where they were protected by their breastworks, and the rolling hills behind them, was Schomberg. After more than a half century as a soldier, it still bothered him to be responsible for sending brave men to their deaths. But the timetable and plan of battle were inexorable. With the bridge of Slane taken, it was time for the centre of the Irish line to be broached. Pitying his men, he nevertheless gave the order, and veteran Dutch Blue Guards marched resolutely into the cool waters of the Boyne in firm ranks of twelve abreast, holding their muskets overhead to keep them dry. Licking their dry lips, and with pounding hearts, not knowing what fate to expect from the entrenched foe awaiting them, they surged forward in disciplined ranks.

Their fate in the form of the incompetent planning of James and Lauzun, the lack of training of the recruits the previous winter, and the defective muskets that would not fire had already been decided. As the Blue Guards stormed ashore, they were not met with a lethal crossfire as they expected, but only sporadic firing of muskets, with many of the volleys passing harmlessly over their heads. From the ineffectual resistance they knew they were facing raw Irish levies, not the expected veteran battalions of M. Zurlauben now held in reserve to cover King James who would have given them an entirely different sort of welcome.

With the Blue Guards safely across the river, other units of the Williamite foot, Swedes, English, Germans and French Huguenots, poured across the Boyne in ever-increasing numbers. Then to the rescue of the threatened Irish foot came Colonel John Parker and his regiment of horse, sweeping through the ranks of the enemy like a gigantic scythe through a wheat field. A huge Irish soldier dashed into the swirling mass of men and horses, and with one powerful stroke of his sabre, slew General Caillimote, commander of the Huguenot battalions.

Leaderless, the Huguenots faltered, but wily General Schomberg, immediately seeing the danger of a rout, spurred his horse forward, and pointing to some of the French troops fighting for James, shouted loudly, 'Allons, messieurs voilá vos persecuteurs!'

Incensed by the memory of their persecutions in France, the Huguenots reformed their shattered ranks. The old Marshal, a veteran of hundreds of battles and skirmishes, forged forward to rally his men. But an Irish soldier, Brian O'Toole, who had once served under Schomberg, recognised him in the melee. Spurring his horse forward, O'Toole fought his way to the marshal's side. Aiming his pistol carefully, he shot him through the throat. O'Toole watched the marshal slide slowly from the saddle as if reluctant that his final embrace be of enemy soil. He probably died as he wished, O'Toole thought, leading his men in a grand charge. But O'Toole had little time for reverie, however, for as the tide of battle slowed and ebbed, his name too was destined to be added to the roll call of the dead.

When Colonel Parker realised that no reinforcements were being sent to his assistance, he loudly cursed Lauzun and Tyrconnell, and greatly outnumbered by the enemy foot all around him, was forced to order his men to turn about and flee. Of his two squadrons, there were only thirty men left alive and unwounded.

Further down the line, the cavalry regiments under the command of the Duke of Berwick were likewise engaged, but again the masses of Williamites were too much for them. Conor and Dónal, their original optimism dissipated by the enemy's successful passage of the Boyne and their assaults on the Irish Army, struggled desperately in the confused fighting under Berwick. A spent musket ball hit Conor in the right shoulder, leaving a bruise but did not penetrate the skin. Bewildered by the turbulent in-fighting, the charges and countercharges, they responded to Lieutenant Butler's commands as well-trained soldiers, and when ordered to retreat, they did so reluctantly.

From his vantage point Tadhg anxiously watched the battle below. Often the clouds of swirling dust and drifting smoke from burning equipment, completely obscured his view. Only the continual angry roar of the cannon, the whine of the mortars, and the incessant rattle of musketry told him a battle was still going on. Worried over Dónal and Conor, it was impossible for him to discern the standards and pennants of Tyrconnell's regiment among the mixed masses of men and horses on the green, grassy slopes of the river.

With his sword in his left hand, as his right arm was immobilised from his wound of the day before, William personally led his regiments of horse across a ford near Oldbridge. His flag, with its device of 'I Will Maintain,' waved proudly in the ranks. Now almost his whole army was across the Boyne and engaging the Irish in battle. He headed quickly to where the main battle was raging. The onslaught of the new troops was disastrous to the surrounded, battered Irish foot and the remnants of horse, and they were systematically cut to pieces. It was difficult to tell friend from foe as both armies wore similar red uniforms. Only identifying marks were the sprigs of green branches stuck in the Williamites' caps and helmets, and the pieces of white paper in those of the Jacobites.

As the battle raged, Lieutenant General Hamilton desperately tried to change its course. At the head of a regiment of foot, he dashed down to the very banks of the river where he led the attack against two of the French Huguenot regiments under Caillimote and Cambron, plunging into the river to encourage his soldiers. But when the Earl of Antrim's regiment failed to follow in support,

338

the undisciplined Irish foot broke and fled.

Undaunted, Hamilton then took charge of one of Colonel Sutherland's regiments of horse, and under his daring leadership and brave example, they forced a German regiment of foot, and one of the English regiments of Sir John Hammer into the very bed of the river. Despite Hamilton's efforts, the English continued to advance. At the head of the squadron of horse, he charged the hated Enniskilleners near Oldbridge, sending them fleeing with great slaughter, but pursuing too far, he ran into the approaching cavalry of King William. Wounded in the skirmish, he was taken prisoner.

Unknown to Hamilton, one of those killed in his attack on the Enniskilleners was the Reverend George Walker, erstwhile hero of Derry, who never did have the chance to enjoy the £5,000 reward from William and Mary for his actions in saving Derry for the English Crown.

When the Irish horse were forced to retreat, they overran their own regiments of foot, who mistakenly thought that they were the enemy. Throwing down their arms, their coats, their caps - anything that might impede them - the foot broke and ran, terror-stricken, for the high ground. Other regiments of foot, infected with the same baseless fear, followed their example, and soon the entire Jacobite Army was in precipitate, headlong retreat, from well-fortified Stonebridge, through the Heights of Donore, and all the way down to the Ford of Donore.

King James, the Duke of Tyrconnell, Marshal Lauzun, and Tadhg O'Cuirc stared stupefied as the Irish army began to disintegrate. When some of the Irish dragoons had earlier cut down some English cavalry, James had loudly exclaimed, 'Oh, spare my English subjects!' Now he watched impassively as his Irish allies died before the onslaught of the Brandenburgers the Danes, the Dutch, the Huguenots, the Scots, the Enniskilliners and the English.

Suddenly Colonel Sarsfield rode up to James and implored the king to let him lead the French guards and the still intact Irish units in a counterattack, but James indignantly refused.

James and Lauzun were observing the battle through their glasses, and as Tadhg watched the king sitting on his horse, he saw him shake his head sadly, his shoulders bent in dejection. Lauzun put down his glasses, turned to the king, and speaking in French too rapid for Tadhg to understand, said something to which James nodded his head in agreement. Lauzun shouted an order to a Major of one of the French battalions which had been assigned to protect the King in the eventuality of retreat. The Cornet in charge of the special guard in turn ordered the guards to be ready to ride to Dublin immediately.

In consternation and disbelief, Tadhg wheeled his horse to follow the departing King James who spurred his horses towards the road to Dublin. They travelled as fast as their mounts would carry them, arriving in Dublin late at night. The king went right to his apartment in the Castle. Tadhg and the Irish guards stayed in the Castle yard.

All night long elements of the broken army straggled into Dublin. Few came in units and few had saved their colours. Many had thrown away their hats and coats and yes, even their shoes to run the faster. And where was the enemy? Still back at the Boyne, unaware of the complete rout of the Jacobite forces. William was well aware that he had won the field of battle, but it wasn't until after that he learned the extent of his victory.

It was M Zurlauben and Patrick Sarsfield who had organised the desperate but effective rearguard action which had prevented a complete rout. Their skilful actions kept the enemy from engulfing the entire fleeing Irish army. Zurlauben's veteran French troops had stopped the enemy's advance with their fierce resistance, then calmly withdrew in good order with their cannon.

Sarsfield and his horse regiment had been stationed far back in the Irish rearguard at the pass of Duleek. This was a major tactical error, for Sarsfield was a dashing cavalry officer who had trained in France. His presence in the centre of the Irish line could well have made a difference in the outcome of that day. When James and Lauzun fled, he had rallied many of the units and saved thousands of men who would otherwise have been captured or killed.

James's stay at the Castle was brief. He had emerged from a meeting with Lady Tyrconnell with angry eyes and a flushed face. Rumour had it that he had complained to Lady Tyrconnell that the cowardly Irish had run, and that the indomitable woman had coolly told him , 'But apparently Your Majesty won the race.'

There was much activity in the Castle before daybreak. James summoned the Lord Mayor, members of the Municipal Council, the Lord Justices and other dignitaries to his chambers where he delivered a petulant attack on the cowardice of the Irish soldiers, declaring that he would never lead them again. To which many of the audience said to themselves, 'Thank God!'

His horse was then brought, and with the Lord Grand Prior, his bastard son Henry Fitzjames, and a small party of retainers, he galloped south, not leaving the saddle until he had covered fifty furious miles. Given a fresh mount, he rode the rest of the day and all the night, arriving in Wexford as the first light of the new day showed in the east. From Wexford a small ship carried him to Kinsale where he had arrived so full of hope just fifteen months previous. Here he boarded the French frigate that was about to sail for France.

And so it was that King James, contemptuously called 'Squire James' by his English subjects, acquired a new sobriquet in Ireland, where he was know henceforward as 'James of the Fleeing'.

PART IV

Munster

Cast of Characters

*Colonel Patrick Sarsfield, grandson of Rory O'More, daring cavalry leader and darling of the Irish

*Lady Honora Sarsfield, his beautiful wife

*Major Roger MacKettigan of Sarsfield's Regiment of Horse

*Captain St Archange, a Frenchman, adjutant of Sarsfield's Regiment

*Brigadier John Wauchope, one of James' English Generals

*General St Ruth, named by Louis XIV in 1691 to command the army in Ireland

*Major General Boisseleau, governor of Limerick in 1690, also a Frenchman

*Colonel Nicholas Purcell

*Colonel Henry Luttrell

*Colonel Simon Luttrell, his brother

*General Maxwell, a traitor

*Colonel Cormac O'Neill

*Colonel Felix O'Neill

*The Duke of Berwick, James' bastard son

*Captain Murtagh O'Brien, aide-de-camp to Sarsfield

*Galloping Hogan, Rapparee chieftan

Aodh O'Madden, second husband to Siobhán O'Coffey

George Cooke, Protestant dealer in hides form Coleraine

Captain Martin Forsythe, aide to General Ginkel

*Baron Jodert de Ginkel, general of William's army in Ireland in 1691

*Marquis D'Usson, a French officer, guilty of dereliction of duty at Athlone

(* denotes historical figures)

CHAPTER 1

'On to Limerick'

King James's hasty departure and denunciation of the Irish, combined with the stream of disorganised refugees from the Boyne pouring into the crowded city, changed the atmosphere of the capital from confusion to complete chaos. The military and political situation remained uncertain.

Rumours were rampant: the fleeing soldiers swore that the Williamites were right at their heels up to the city's gates; the Catholics charged that the Protestant troops of King William were massacring the Catholics; the Protestants claimed that the Catholics were massacring the Protestants; some officers positively stated that Tyrconnell had arranged with William to meet at the Castle to surrender Ireland to him; others boasted that they knew that William had been slain at the Boyne, and that the English army was retreating north to take ship back to England.

But there was one recurrent rumour that grew from a whisper to a roar: the Irish army was to regroup at Limerick. Word spread rapidly from soldier to soldier, and thence to the non-combatants until it seemed that all of Dublin was crying, 'On to Limerick!'

When Lord Kilmallock's Regiment, which had been left to guard the capital while the rest of the army was at the Boyne, suddenly marched out and headed for Limerick, Tadhg decided that he, too, had better leave. He had roamed the streets looking for Dónal Óg and Conor, but none among the remnants of Tyrconnell's horse knew of their whereabouts or fate. Disconsolate and desperate, he decided he would go immediately to Cáit O'Reilly's to get Rory and leave Dublin.

As he entered the boarding-house, great was his surprise and joy to hear Conor and Dónal's voices in conversation with Cáit. In a moment the three friends, with tears of happiness unashamedly streaking their dusty faces, embraced each other, all shouting simultaneously, so that none knew what the other was saying. Rory and Cáit joined them and the old house had never seen so much hugging and kissing as occasioned by this happy reunion.

It was Conor who finally ended the gaiety by soberly reminding them that if they expected to keep their horses from being forcibly taken from Johnson's livery by prowling soldiers, they had better take their leave quickly. Cáit, a Catholic, was apprehensive of what would happen to her when the Protestants again took command of the city, but since she had been so long in Dublin, decided to stay and ride out the coming storm as best she could. So the tears of joy were transformed to tears of sorrow as the three old friends, with Rory behind Tadhg on the big stallion, bade goodbye to Cáit and joined the exodus on the road to Naas.

As they left, they encountered some of the Protestants who had been kept as prisoners in the College, but who were now free and defiantly parading the streets, openly agitating with other citizens to seize the capital for King William. Captain Farlow, who had been imprisoned in the Castle, seeing the Irish soldiery depart, rallied a few others of his persuasion and easily repossessed that bastion of the English authority in Ireland for King William who triumphantly entered the city on 4 July.

At their first opportunity, slowed by the heavy traffic on the old road to Naas caused by the heavy exodus from the city of soldiers and civilians, they traded their experiences since last seeing each other before the fight at Boynewater.

'We,' Conor began, 'took part in the battle, but when the rout started, were swept along by the fleeing foot. It was impossible to turn in that mass of fearful men whose only thought was to escape.' He smiled cynically, adding, 'It wouldn't have helped much if we had succeeded in turning since many or our officers were running the fastest trying to catch up with that Talbot who was out in front of the pack and running well and fast.'

'But not quite as fast as King James,' Tadhg said, his voice showing his anger and disillusionment with his former idol.

Conor glanced at Tadhg, surprised and pleased at the latter's castigation of the cowardly king, but refrained from comment.

'When we got to Dublin,' he continued, 'we went directly to Cáit's, expecting to meet you there. But when you didn't come, and we had no word from you, we concluded that you were accompanying King James south. So we decided we had best leave while we could, taking Rory with us.'

'It was stupid of me not to go to Cáit 's,' Tadhg admitted. 'I roamed the vicinity of the Castle trying to find someone of the regiment that had seen you.'

'Well, thanks to a merciful God, *a chairde*, here we are together again. But what do you do now that the object of your special guard has fled? Revert to Talbot's Regiment?'

'I suppose so. Perhaps I'll learn when we get to Limerick.'

The road was choked with the multitude fleeing from the north. There were soldiers, mostly unarmed; there were entire Catholic families, only a few of whom were riding; there were wives, children, parents and sweethearts of the soldiery, all moving towards Munster to escape William and his ferocious foreigners.

With Rory riding pillion behind Tadhg, the quartet travelled as quickly as conditions would permit towards Limerick. They were fortunate, they still had their horses and weapons. They passed through Naas, stopping for the night outside of Kilcullen where they took turns guarding their mounts and their arms, now eagerly sought by those soldiers who had discarded theirs in their flight. A gun or a sword was advantageous in persuading innkeepers and country people to part with their precious stocks of food and drink when they otherwise were reluctant, even though they were offered payment. With King James fled, the country people no longer placed any value on his brass coins. By the second night they were in Kilkenny, and the third night in Cashel, the ancient home of the Munster kings, where the lofty cathedral stood stark against the night sky.

Late the following morning, the road being dusty, and the sun beating down fiercely, they stopped to bathe in the clear waters of the River Suir, leaving Rory to guard the horses. Luxuriating in the cool and refreshing waters, it was easy to forget the disappointments of the past few days, and to put aside the ever-present fear that at any moment the vanguard of William's army would be upon them. Tadhg was awed and happy to be in County Tipperary, the territory where his O'Cuirc forbears had lived, and where many of his kin still resided.

Their peace and pleasure were interrupted by Rory's shrill cry of 'Help, Tadhg, help!' The startled bathers heard muffled sounds, followed by a loud curse, and a man's voice saying incredulously, 'Why, the blasted little *spailpín* bit me!'

As Tadhg burst over the bank, still naked, scattering the withered gorse blooms as he ran, he saw a man in uniform holding a writhing, struggling Rory, while futilely trying to clasp a hand over the lad's mouth without being bitten again. An extremely tall man, also in uniform and wearing a cuirass, but with uncovered head, was examining Tadhg's horse.

Tadhg was proud of the stallion, many men had coveted it, and many had tried to buy it. So, when he saw the stranger holding Cúchulain by the muzzle, he was enraged to the point of fury. He grabbed the man by the seat of his breeches and nape of the neck, and despite the stranger's height, lifted him off the ground and shook him vigorously. Panting from exertion, Tadhg dropped the man to the earth again, but keeping a firm grasp, turned him around so that he could see his face.

Large eyes, startled and amused, set in an oval and handsome face, looked back at Tadhg. 'What have we here,' he asked, 'Fionn MacCool at his bath? You may release me now,' he directed, 'I am not going to run away.'

The stranger's companion, having released Rory, drew his sword and advanced on Tadhg menacingly, but the other man waved him away. 'No need for weapons, Roger,' he said coolly.

The tall stranger wore a white lace cravat at his throat which Tadhg recognised as the type worn by officers of James's army, especially those who had served on the Continent. His uniform was that of a regiment unfamiliar to Tadhg, but was of fine quality, obviously fashioned by a craftsman more skilled than the quartermaster tailor. The large eyes, set above a finely chiselled nose in an oval face, still looked questioning at Tadhg.

The man addressed as Roger, said to the other in French, 'Who is this wild man, a local peasant?'

Replying in the same language, Tadhg interrupted in an irritable tone, 'No, this wild man is not a local peasant.' Then, switching to the Irish, he added, 'This wild man is from Connemara.'

The tall man laughed at Roger's discomfiture at the 'peasant's' understanding his French. Picking up the Irish, he said to Tadhg, 'Is there a name on you?'

'Tadhg O'Cuirc.'

The other frowned. 'But that's a Munster name, a Tipperary name. You say you're from Connemara?'

'The Aran Islands, actually. From Inishmór.'

The officer nodded. 'And what is an Islandman doing way down here?'

Tadhg gambled on the other's character. 'Running from William, like you are,' he replied impudently.

Anger showed momentarily in the other man's eyes. Then, observing Tadhg's smile, he too smiled, nodding his head. 'You're right, at that,' he acknowledged, 'we are all running from William.'

He looked about him, observing for the first time that Conor and Dónal, now dressed, had quietly joined the group, their hands on their pistols, watching every move. 'We have been outflanked by superior forces, Roger,' he remarked to his companion, 'just like at the Boyne.'

'You were there, *a dhuine uasail*?' Tadhg asked respectfully.

'In a manner of speaking,' the other replied drily. 'I didn't see too much of the affair, unfortunately.'

'Through no fault of yours,' his companion said. Then turning to Tadhg, he asserted, 'Let me introduce my commanding officer, Colonel Padraig Sarsfield. I am Major Roger MacKettigan of his regiment of horse?'

Tadhg gasped, his mouth wide open. 'Patrick Sarsfield, Rory O'More's grandson?'

Colonel Sarsfield smiled. 'See, Roger, I have no fame of my own. It's all my grandfather's.'

Tadhg was penitent. 'I'm sorry, *a dhuine uasail*, for handling you so roughly before. I didn't know who you were, and thought you were stealing my horse.'

Sarsfield looked up at Tadhg with obvious respect. 'I didn't know you were the man who avenged the O'Flahertys. I heard the story when I was on my campaign in Sligo last year. You are quite a hero in Connaught; the people often wondered what had become of you. In fact, some of O'Flaherty's Rapparees joined my regiment. There's a place in it for you, if you wish.' He smiled again, 'And your horse.'

'See, Roger,' Tadhg said, expertly mimicking and paraphrasing Sarsfield, 'I have no fame of my own. It's all my horse's.'

Major MacKettigan, startled and angry at Tadhg's impertinence, started to remonstrate Tadhg, but seeing his colonel's appreciative grin, switched to a compliment instead. 'The words came from his mouth, Patrick, but I'd swear it was you speaking.'

Colonel Sarsfield shook his head. 'You're wrong, Roger, it wasn't O'Cuirc talking, but his talented horse that spoke.' He turned to Tadhg. 'Well, will you join my regiment? Or do I have to ask your horse?'

'We're already in Tyrconnell's Regiment,' Tadhg replied, his voice betraying his disappointment.

'I can see that from your uniform. A transfer can be easily arranged, however.'

'My horse says 'no' unless Conor and Dónal come also,' Tadhg stated audaciously.

'You have an impudent horse. But if I have to take all three of you *spailpíns* in order to enlist this horse in my regiment, I suppose I have no choice. Do you think it can be arranged, Roger?'

MacKettigan smiled. 'If it's agreeable to the horse.'

'Thank you,' Conor said, addressing Sarsfield, 'you have no idea what it means to me to be in a regiment other than the Lord Tyrconnell's, and especially to be in yours.'

Sarsfield flashed an understanding smile; there was no need for explanation. Dónal Óg, who had added several inches in height in the time since leaving Connemara, and was now taller than Conor, joined with Tadhg in thanking the colonel for the opportunity of serving him.

'Well, Roger, now that we have three replacements for the regiment, do you think you can find your way to Kilmallock to notify the Lady Honora of the necessity of getting to Limerick as soon as possible?'

Major MacKettigan appeared distressed. 'It is a difficult choice, Sir. With the possibility of William's horse being nearby, I am reluctant to leave when I might be sorely needed. Yet I am aware of the problem that would be created if Lady Sarsfield were to be captured.'

'Where is Kilmallock,' Tadhg inquired. 'Perhaps we could carry your message for you.'

Sarsfield's large eyes lost their melancholy expression, and he smiled warmly at Tadhg. 'I don't know if the Lady Honora would be piqued at me for sending a sergeant rather that at least a general or a marshal of France, but as I recall, her father, the Earl of Clarickarde, never did get along too well with his neighbour, Sir John Ferguson. Sir John cheated Honora's father of some land on the east side of Lough Corrib occupied by the MacRedmonds who were kin to the Burkes. So she might be honoured by having the conqueror of Sir John act as her escort to Limerick. You avenged her family's honour.'

Tadhg blushed at Sarsfields's banter. 'We would be most happy and honoured to escort the Lady Honora to Limerick,' he said, 'but we don't know where Kilmallock is.'

'I forgot that you were not a Tipperaryman and unacquainted with this region. Just continue on this road through Tipperary to Knocklong where you will then take the road towards Rath Luirc for about ten miles. It is in the County Limerick, and my cousin, Lord Kilmallock, has a castle there. Inform the Lady Honora that she is to proceed at once to Limerick where I have established residence for her. And inform Lady Kilmallock that her husband is leading his regiment to Limerick also. She can act accordingly.'

While Sarsfield was talking about County Limerick, a suppressed memory came surging to Tadhg's conscious mind in the brief message given him in May that 'a certain lady' was in County Limerick, visiting her relatives, the O'Hurleys.

'Do you know of the O'Hurleys of County Limerick?' he asked diffidently.

Sarsfield nodded. 'There are O'Hurleys in the barony of Coshlea which is a little southwest of Kilmallock. Now, before you go, I would like to make two suggestions: Firstly, you might be warmer if you put on your clothes, and it certainly would be more appropriate if you were dressed when you accompany the Lady Honora to Limerick, and secondly,' Sarsfield leaned forward conspiratorially, 'please don't tell anyone that you handled me as easily as a sack of meal. It would ruin old Rory's reputation to have such a puny weakling for a grandson.'

Again Tadhg blushed with embarrassment. 'I promise,' he said.

As Colonel, Sarsfield and Major MacKettigan mounted their horses and rode away to rejoin their regiment which was bivouacked nearby, Tadhg and his three companions continued down the road to Tipperary. Tadhg was in a turmoil. Although he was flattered at his assignment by Sarsfield, the growing idol of the Irish soldiers, he had wanted to stop in the barony of Clanwilliam in Western Tipperary to visit his kin, the O'Cuircs, just a few miles to the south. He now regretted his impulse action in volunteering to go to Kilmallock since he was now obligated to get to the safety of Limerick before the Williamites arrived on the scene. He compromised by promising himself to return to Tipperary after the war ended.

At Emly they turned southwest to Knocklong where they stopped for the night. It was with some difficulty that they obtained food and lodging since the villagers were fearful of strangers, who could be robbers or looting soldiers. They slept in a byre leaving early in the morning.

Shortly, they rode into the village of Kilmallock, which squatted in a valley dominated by a lofty hill. The village, which was walled, and marked by battlements, had many spacious stone houses. Here they learned that the Earl of Kilmallock had a demesne several miles away on the road to Rath Luirc which these people called Charleville. Within the hour they came to the entrance to the Earl's lands. A tidy road, bordered with ancient yews, meandered through the spacious grounds to a huge, three-storey stone building designed to resemble a castle, complete with turrets and battlements. They were received with suspicion by armed servitors, but after a lengthy explanation, were finally ushered into the presence of the Lady Honora Sarsfield.

Daughter of the seventh Earl of Clarickarde, already a fabled beauty when she was wed to Patrick Sarsfield, she was still one of the most beautiful women in Ireland. A coif covered her dark hair, the border made of exquisite Brussels lace, and eyes of deep blue gazed serenely between long lashes. A well-fitted jacket accentuated the contours of her full bosom. Narrow gold lace provided the trim for both the body of the jacket and its sleeves of crimson velvet, while three rows of gold lace illuminated her petticoat made of brown silk. Leather shoes, with gold-edged laces, peeped from the hem of her petticoat.

Tadhg, the spokesman, trembled when he addressed her, awed by her beauty and station. He was aware of a subtle perfume which permeated the room. She was gracious and understanding, and by her friendly smile and gentle manner, managed to calm him to the point where she was able to elicit the information imparted by her husband.

'Very well then, Sergeant O'Cuirc,' she said, nodding, 'we will be ready to leave in a few hours. But pray tell, what is the status of the war? We have heard but the wildest rumours.'

Tadhg was apologetic. 'I don't know too much, but the King is fled to France, General Hamilton was captured at the Boyne, and the Earl of Kilmallock has led his regiment out of Dublin for Limerick where most of the Irish army is reassembling for a new stand against the enemy.'

'But where are William's soldiers? Are they nearby? Some of the young people are out on a hunt. They might not be safe with enemy soldiers nearby.'

'Where they are I do not know, but I assume that they cannot be too far distant, or the General would have come for you himself. I believe he intends to harass them and delay their advance.'

Lady Honora smiled. 'That's just like Patrick.' There was pride and love in her voice when she spoke his name, but she looked as if she was about to cry. Then she summoned a servant, ordering her to prepare a carriage for herself and two maids. Presently she left the room.

Shortly after, a gay, laughing group of young people entered the room, all wearing riding clothes. Tadhg became rigid as he recognised the Lady Mairéad among them. She saw him at the same time, and she stopped, transfixed, her face drained of colour. For a moment she stared at Tadhg, anger distorting the beautiful face, then she took a step forward, and struck him furiously with her horsewhip. Tadhg saw the blow coming, and raising his arm, succeeding in warding off most of its force, but the flexible tip lashed his forehead, laying it open. With sight of the blood, the ladies screamed, and instantly all was pandemonium. As Tadhg held his hand to his forehead, Conor and Dónal moved protectively in front of him.

Attracted by the screaming of the women, and the amazed shouting of the men, the Lady Honora appeared in the corridor where she saw Tadhg trying to stop the bleeding.

'What's the meaning of this?' she demanded. 'Who struck this soldier?'

'It is nothing,' Tadhg replied. 'It's just an accident.'

Lady Honora looked from Tadhg to Mairéad FitzGerald still holding her raised riding crop. 'Is this true?' she asked.

The girl, horrified at the sight of the blood streaming down Tadhg's face, burst into tears. 'It was no accident,' she sobbed, 'I did it deliberately.'

'Why?' The Lady Honora was inexorable.

'Ask him,' Mairéad replied, pointing at Tadhg with her whip.

Lady Sarsfield turned to Tadhg, saying gently, 'Did you insult this young woman?'

'No, *a bhean uasail*, I said nothing to her. It is best that it all be forgotten.'

She looked at him questioning. Receiving no answer, she said wryly. 'As the victim of an apparently unprovoked assault, you are remarkably forgiving. Regardless of the cause, we'd better get that bleeding stopped.'

Sobbing loudly, Lady Mairéad was led from the scene. Seated in the kitchen, Tadhg had cold water compresses applied to his forehead. When the bleeding had subsided, a bandage was wrapped around his head. Conor's amused smile at Tadhg's outlandish appearance turned to contrition when he saw the victim's hurt expression. Dónal Óg still reflected his astonishment, while Rory was close to tears.

Mary Casey appeared in the kitchen while Tadhg was being treated. Her eyes showing her concern, and kneeling at Tadhg's feet, she earnestly beseeched him to forgive her headstrong mistress.

'She is a troubled, confused young woman who has been treated cruelly by life. She lost her parents when just a young girl; and later her two suitors.' The maid took Tadhg's hand impulsively, pressing it tightly to her breast. 'I'm sure you had good reasons for slaying Sir Oliver. I was always worried that she might marry him. T'was God's will, surely, that caused his death. She would think differently of you if she knew about that party at the Castle, but you swore me to secrecy. But in the name of God and the Blessed Mother, please forgive Mairéad FitzGerald for what she has done to you for the cross she bears is heavy.'

Tadhg nodded mutely. Depression lay on him like the morning fog on the meadow. Never in his darkest moments had he anticipated that she would react so violently to him. He could expect disdain, anger, hatred yes, but not physical assault. The impact of her action made him fully aware for the first time of the enormity of the double tragedy, and he perceived himself as she saw him, a wild, jealous, cruel instrument of a capricious and diabolical fate. Being publicly whipped was the climax of his infatuation. He could sink no lower in his self-loathing.

Noting Tadhg's depressed preoccupation, Conor took charge of the situation. He got their horses ready, hurried and harassed the servants to prepare the carriage for the Lady Honora, questioned the coachman as to the best roads, and directed Dónal to stay close to Tadhg and cheer him.

Their route led almost due north through the small hamlet of Holycross. Once they were accosted by a band of Rapparees, part of a larger group led by a local chieftain called 'Galloping Hogan.' Although the prospect of horses, weapons and loot made them drool with delight, the magic name of 'Sarsfield' caused them to cheer instead, and they accompanied the party for some miles until Limerick was in sight.

While Tadhg and Dónal rode with the Rapparees, relating some of their experiences with Cathal O'Flaherty, the Lady Honora beckoned to Conor to join her in the coach. The carriage was suspended on leather straps which caused it to jolt and rock on the rough, rutted roads. As there was no glass, only leather curtains protected the windows. The driver sat high on the front, exposed to the elements.

Leaving his horse with a servant, Conor rode with Lady Honora for some miles, while she questioned him about Mairéad FitzGerald's attack on Tadhg. She listened thoughtfully as Conor told of the initial meeting on the storm-tossed waters off Kilkieran Bay, the subsequent duel with Montgomery Óg, the rescue in Dublin when the coach was attacked by Mattie Moley, and the incident at Ringsend. He made no mention of the spy suspicions, or the code message.

'It's an unusual and sad story,' she commented. 'But what was the cause of the fight with Sir Oliver? Do you think it was over Mairéad FitzGerald?'

'Partially, perhaps, but not the main reason.' Conor spoke guardedly. Tadhg had never explained exactly what had happened, and later reticence, coupled with the strange demotion and detention, and later restoration to his former rank, had indicated to Conor that there was more to the affair than met the eye.

He hesitated, weighing his words carefully. 'I think, perhaps, that the fight had some important military significance. Tadhg never told me, but I learned that he had met with the Viceroy and other high-ranking officers immediately after the incident. He was demoted and sent to the guardhouse for a short term, a punishment hardly commensurate for the crime, if indeed it was a crime, especially when the slain man was a close friend and intimate of the Viceroy himself.'

Lady Sarsfield looked with shrewd eyes at Conor. 'I think you know more than you're telling. But your theory fits your friend's character better than the alternative that he killed Sir Oliver in a jealous feud for the hand of the girl. I'm sure that my husband must know the background of the affair, and that he would not entrust my safety to an irresponsible, hot-headed young man whom he just met. Patrick must have implicit faith in him.'

Conor smiled wanly. 'Tadhg excels in everything he does, but affairs of the heart. Ever since he met the Lady Mairéad on that wrecked ship, he has been her abject slave. Yet none knows better than he that he might just as well wish for the moon. It is unfortunate that he met her again. Her whip lashed his self-respect as well as his skin.'

'We must pity them both, for Margaret has had more than her share of misfortune. Her father, Garrett FitzGerald, came from the Barony of Glenquin in Western Limerick, while her mother, Ann O'Hurley, was of the Barony of Coshlea. Both were of families that were Protestant, not because of religious choice or conviction, but for political expediency to keep their ancestral lands. On the FitzGerald side it goes back to the generation after Silken Thomas. On her mother's, it was after the Battle of Kinsale, and the flight of the Earls.'

Lady Honora smiled. 'The story is told around here how the six O'Hurley brothers put one black pebble among five white ones, and how Margaret's great-grandfather, Sheeda O'Hurley, unluckily drew the black pebble, thus becoming the Protestant and owner-in-name of the estates. The other five brothers, of course, lived on the land as usual, and when they went to Mass, offered up prayers for their brother's lost soul. Margaret inherited the FitzGerald lands on a deed of endowment when her parents died.'

'But the Lady Mairéad seems to be a convinced Protestant,' Conor observed.

The Lady Honora shrugged her delicate shoulders. 'What can you expect? She has been exposed to the Church of Ireland's teaching and preaching ever since she was born. After her parents died, she was taken to Dublin to be raised by her uncle, Henry FitzGerald. Henry never was one to rock the boat: Dublin was a Protestant world, the Viceroys were Protestant, society was Protestant, all the power, authority and money were controlled by Protestants, so why fight it? This is the atmosphere in which Margaret was reared. Right after Christmas she returned here to visit her O'Hurley kin for the first time since she was a little girl. She never explained why.'

Conor's eyes were mischievous as he asked, 'Does she consort openly with her Catholic relatives? Isn't she afraid of degrading herself?'

'Until the Battle of the Boyne, it was beneficial to have Catholic kin. Besides, they respected her convictions. They arranged for her to attend Church of Ireland services in Rath Luirc.'

'What will she do now that the Williamites have regained Dublin?'

'Knowing Margaret, I'd say that she will get back there as fast as she can. She never was quite content here in the country. It must have been something of great import that caused her to come to Coshlea in the first place. She prefers a carriage to a horse, a cobbled street to a muddy road, and shops and society to stables and rural bumpkins.' Lady Honour smiled, adding, 'I can't say that I blame her.'

Sensing that the purpose of the ride in the coach had been

fulfilled, and feeling ill at ease in the intimate presence of one of the great ladies of Ireland, Conor excused himself, and remounting his horse, rejoined Tadhg and Dónal who were riding ahead with the Rapparees.

'Have you decided where we will enter Limerick?' he inquired of Tadhg, relinquishing the role of leader he had temporarily assumed.

'Eamonn O'Ryan, here,' Tadhg replied, pointing to a tall Rapparee riding next to him, 'who lives nearby at Rear Cross, recommends Mungret's Gate, the south entrance. We pick up the Cork Road soon which leads to the one from Tralee just outside of Limerick.'

Tadhg's sense of responsibility as escort for Lady Sarsfield, and the exhilaration of riding with the Rapparee, had restored much of his equanimity, despite the presence of the bandage around his head, a constant reminder of his recent humiliation at the hands of the Lady Mairéad. He laughed when Dónal, in response to O'Ryan's question, gravely declared that the bandage covered a wound received at the Battle of the Boyne.

They were stopped at Mungret's Gate, but again the magic name of Sarsfield quickly cleared the way, and an escort was provided for the lady and her party to the quarters which had been selected for her. They passed the newly built Capuchin Church and Thom Core Castle in Irishtown on the road to Ball's Bridge where they passed over a branch of the Shannon River into Englishtown.

The narrow passageways were crowded as they slowly made their way down Great Street to the sombre stone house between the Augustinian Convent and St Mary's Church where the Lady Honora was to stay. Tadhg had arranged with Honora that Rory would stay with her where he could help around the kitchen.

When the escort party took their leave, they were thanked graciously by Honora, who, with a mischievous smile, observed to Tadhg that his white bandage matched perfectly with his white stallion, and that he ought to wear it always as some of the officers wore their distinctive cravats.

'Sure, and the people of Limerick will be thinking it's a uniform cap of a new regiment,' Dónal commented gaily, 'like those heathens who ride camels in the Holy Land.'

After leaving the Lady Honora, they continued on Great Street past the Castle, leaving the city by Thomond Bridge to report to Sarsfield's Regiment which was bivouacked on the road to Sixmile

Bridge. The transaction was expedited by the adjutant, a French officer named St Archange. Outside of missing the friendship and counsel of Lt. Butler, whom Tadhg hadn't seen since the Boyne, there was not much difference in the two regiments.

Limerick was an old, proud and rich city, second only to Dublin. Consisting of two parts, roughly in the shape of a figure-eight, the town was divided at its narrow waist by a branch of the Shannon which circled around to form King's Island. Occupying the southwest quarter of this island was the high town, or Englishtown. Stone walls , about four feet in thickness, offered the high town some protection above and beyond that supplied by the encircling river.

South of the island, and connected by Ball's Bridge over the Shannon, was the base town, or Irishtown. Here the walls were thicker, having towers at strategic places. Limerick, as it burgeoned, had outgrown its old walls, and in 1690 had as many houses outside as in.

Connecting the city on the Clare, or west side, was six-arched Thomond Bridge. This was the gateway to Kerry, Clare and Connaught, still held by the Jacobites. The area south of the city, was marshy and boggy in spots, offering some protection against the expected assault of the Williamites.

The houses of Englishtown were mostly multi-storey, and built of stone. Great Street ran from Ball's Bridge to the far end at Island Gate with numerous narrow streets or alleys, leading from it. Not far from the quay, was St Mary's Church, the cathedral, which was now being used by the Catholics. A second church, St Munchin's, was located near Thomond Gate, near to the Bishop's House, but being old and decaying, was used by the gunsmiths as a workshop, and a magazine for ammunition.

Opposite St Munchin's, at the north end of the city, was St Dominick's Abbey, where the Franciscan Fathers had constructed a new chapel. On the Shannon, near Ball's Bridge, the Augustinians had their abbey. Here a large suburb had grown outside the walls in the southeast part of the island around the old St Francis' Abbey of the Franciscans. Although largely a ruin, the church portion was still being used by the religious.

At high tide ships up to 200-tons burden could sail up to the Quay which formed the western side of Englishtown. Behind the Quay, near Thomond Bridge, stood the King's Castle, a stout masonry edifice built originally by King John. Several cannon were installed on its massive towers.

Like Englishtown, Irishtown too, had one main thoroughfare, Mungret Street, running its length, with narrow lanes intersecting it, where lived the poor Irish. This street ran from St John's Gate to Ball's Bridge. On its east side was the Citadel, built of stone, with two platforms on which were mounted several small cannon. Nearby stood St John's, the parish church. A chapel started by the Capuchin fathers, but never finished, stood at the southwest corner near Mungret's Gate where the road led to Tralee. There were two other gates in the walls, East Water Gate and West Water Gate, which opened to the countryside, the former for the road to Dublin.

Suburbs nearly completely surrounded the town outside the walls. Unfortunately, these fine new houses, many with cultivated gardens and orchards, had to be razed so that they couldn't be used by the enemy. In addition, the countryside for miles around was burned, and the buildings demolished, so that it would offer little of value to the Williamites.

While the political stew was stirring in its cauldron on this fine day, 10 July, 1690, the day after Tadhg's assignment to his new regiment, he was instructed to report to St Archange, the adjutant.

With disapproval at the unorthodox procedure showing in his swarthy face, the Frenchman addressed Tadhg. 'I don't know what it's all about, but M. le Colonel has ordered me to name you as his junior aide-de-camp, a strange position for one only of a sergeant's rank. He is now at the Castle where he requests your presence immediately. Here is a pass which will gain you admittance.'

Observing Tadhg's incredulous expression, he relaxed his professional military manner momentarily, and with just the trace of a smile on his lips, added, 'Le Colonel de Sarsfield said he needs some solid support to bolster his arguments before the obstinate Council. Oh, yes, he insists that you wear clothes this time, there might be ladies in the vicinity.'

Elated at this privilege of serving the idol of the soldiery, Tadhg hurried all the way to the Castle which stood near Thomond Bridge. Even with the official pass, he found it difficult to get through to the Council room where Sarsfield, Lauzun and Berwick, along with numerous officers and aides, awaited Tyrconnell. Captain Murtagh O'Brien, Sarsfield's regular aide-de-camp, making room for Tadhg behind Sarsfield's chair, informed him in a whisper that he was not to speak at any time, nor to let anyone know that he spoke and understood French.

As they waited, Captain O'Brien identified for Tadhg some of the officers who were seated nearby. 'Those three there, with their heads together, are the two Luttrell brothers, Colonel Henry and Colonel Simon Luttrell, with their close friend, Colonel Nicholas Purcell. They will support Colonel Sarsfield. Simon Purcell is the former governor of Dublin, where he and his regiment helped cover the retreat from the Boyne.'

The captain glanced around the room. 'Over there,' and he indicated a red-faced man in a periwig, 'is General Maxwell, one of Tyrconnell's party. He's an Englishman, and not to be trusted.' O'Brien's face showed his distrust and disgust when he spoke of Maxwell. 'The officer he is talking to is Major General Boisseleau, a good, but not brilliant officer. He is trying to atone for those French officers like Lauzun, Famechon, Hoguette, Merode and others who hid their regimental colours in their pockets and abandoned their troops at the Boyne.'

The Count de Lauzun, unaware of the scornful glance of the aide-de-camp, was busily grating tobacco with an ivory grater. When he had a sufficient quantity grated, he daintily sniffed some of the powdered tobacco into each nostril, then poured the remainder into his silver snuff-box. Elegantly he flipped some of the dust from his sleeve of his beribboned blue satin coat.

Across the room from Lauzun, the Duke of Berwick, who resembled the Stuarts less than he did the Churchills on his mother's side, was engaged in a serious, low-pitched conversation with Brigadier Wauchope, another of the English officers.

Suddenly the hum of voices ceased as the viceroy, the Duke of Tyrconnell, entered the room. His once handsome and animated face was lined and haggard, his eyes dull. He was a caricature of the haughty, energetic man of two years previous when he had organised and saved Ireland for James. His flabby face, his mottled complexion, his uncertain gait, showed the ravages of the years of high living.

When the lord-lieutenant was ceremoniously seated, Sarsfield, anxious for action, addressed him. 'Word has come, my lord, that Dutch William is near Waterford. The decision must be made quickly as to what we are to do with Limerick.'

The Count de Lauzun turned languid eyes on the Irishman. 'What to do with Limerick? What an absurd question! Nothing can be done with this provincial town. These flimsy walls can be battered down with roasted apples.'

'Perhaps William doesn't have any roasted apples in his siege train,' Sarsfield retorted hotly, his usually gentle eyes flashing. He turned to Tyrconnell. 'Most of the men have now rejoined their regiments. Replacements can be recruited in Munster and Connaught. I think we learned a bitter lesson at the Boyne. Or are we going to turn the country over to William on a silver salver?'

Tyrconnell raised his hand. 'My lords,' he admonished, 'restrain yourselves. This is neither the place nor the time for a display of tempers. Let us coolly and calmly examine our position. Colonel Sarsfield claims we have regained most of our men. That I will dispute for I have with me the latest muster of all the regiments, and our strength has been reduced drastically. And in addition, many of the men who have returned, are without weapons. New recruits will have to be trained. With William at Waterford, there will be insufficient time to make soldiers out of them. The bitter lesson we learned at the Boyne is that William has a bigger, more experienced, and better trained army than we do. And as to weapons of war, there is no comparison.'

Noting Wauchope, Maxwell, Lauzun and other English and French officers nodding assent, Tyrconnell continued. 'Here we are, disorganised, demoralised and disarmed, in a small town with practically no defences. Are we prepared for a siege? Certainly not! Remember what happened to us at Derry when we were fresh, strong and comparatively well armed! Look what happened to us at the Boynewater where we had an excellent defensive position! Now we have little ammunition, few cannon, inadequate supplies and no money. And William is stronger than ever, recruiting new forces from Protestant Ireland. And each day he receives more reinforcements and military supplies from England. He controls Ulster, Leinster, and a large part of Munster while we are trapped in this quarter of the country with the richest parts lost to us.'

Sarsfield stood, towering in his great height, and bowing deferentially, but showing his suppressed anger, said to the Viceroy. 'I'm glad you mentioned Derry, my lord, also a little provincial town, with few defences. Perhaps if we had had roasted apples, we might have been the victors instead of a handful of desperate men and women who had inadequate supplies and little money. But they had courage, my lord, and an indomitable will to win. I will concede that we match the Derrymen in the insufficiencies to carry on a siege, but I will not concede that the Irish soldiers are inferior to the Derrymen in courage.'

A low murmur swept through the room as the Irish officers, despairing of victory since the Boyne, confused over the uncertainties of the future, and playing a minor role of command in an army dominated by English, Scots and French generals, responded to the fire kindled by Sarsfield. Several of them leaped to their feet, but a frowning Tyrconnell raised his hand for silence. The clamour subsided.

'Let me ask the colonel a question. With William getting closer every day, where do you think we can get supplies to sustain us until help could arrive from France?'

'We still have Connaught and parts of southwest Munster,' Sarsfield replied.

The Viceroy grimaced, causing Maxwell and Lauzun to smile. Boisseleau sat expressionless. Many of the Irish officers glared. 'Connaught? What can Connaught offer? It's the poorest, least populated part of Ireland. It couldn't sustain a regiment, let alone an army.'

Donough MacCarthy, Earl of Clancarty, and John Burke, Lord of Bophin, representing that part of Western Ireland still in the hands of the Jacobites, arose to speak, but Tyrconnell silenced them.

'Before we waste time debating whether Connaught or South and West Munster,' and he bowed slightly to MacCarthy and Burke, 'can feed and supply our army, let me read you a letter from our sovereign, King James The Second of England, Scotland, Wales and Ireland.' He beckoned to an aide who handed him several sheets of paper, and read from them. The gist of the letter was that, in James's absence, Tyrconnell was responsible for the administration of both civil and military affairs in Ireland. In addition, all high-ranking officers who desired to join James, were to be offered the opportunity of sailing to France aboard the French fleet than waiting in Galway Bay, and that the officers and men of lesser rank were to make their submission to King William, and to obtain for themselves the best terms possible.

There was absolute silence when Tyrconnell finished reading. Tadhg, although shocked at James's proposals, noted the reaction of the officers, noblemen and gentlemen at the King's recommendations. Lauzun and Maxwell were smiling with approval. The two Luttrells and Purcell were greatly agitated, Cuchonaught Maguire stood with mouth agape, Cormac O'Neill was incredulous, and hotheaded young Ulick Burke, Lord Galway, grasped his sword.

Sarsfield, making great effort to control his anger, arose, and by his commanding presence, received the Viceroy's permission to speak. 'My lords,' he began, his voice raspy with emotion, 'that letter was written some time ago when James was awaiting ship at Kinsale. At that time we had no idea most of the Irish Army was intact, anxious to fight again. If the King had been aware of the improved conditions, I am sure that he would not have written it, or would have revoked it. I readily admit that Connaught is the poorest of the four provinces, but it is rich in its devotion to Ireland, and it can sustain the army until new help arrives from France. My lords, I cannot presume to speak for the rest of you, but as for me, I cannot turn my back on Ireland in this hour of danger.'

This time there was loud applause. The pro-Tyrconnell faction sat stony-faced as little knots of men began private discussions and debates. Realising that the meeting was getting out of control, Tyrconnell imperiously called for silence. 'Would I need remind you that I am still Lord Lieutenant of Ireland, and commander-in-chief of the army? I called this session of the council for help and advice, not for contrariness and argument. You have just heard the King's letter in which His Majesty named me as his representative.' He then looked to the king's son, Lord Berwick, for confirmation.

Although the Duke had no love for the Irish faction, and his natural affinity was to the English and Scots lords who were loyal to Tyrconnell, he was acutely aware that the only hope for the restoration of the Stuarts to the throne of England was to keep Ireland safe for his father. His troubled glance swept the room as an expectant hush settled over it. Tyrconnell leaned forward, an expectant smile of corroboration on his face.

The Duke cleared his throat nervously, and then looking to Sarsfield, declared, 'I hold with those who want to continue to fight.'

Tyrconnell's smile vanished. He looked as if his face had been slapped, but he quickly regained his composure. 'My dear Duke,' he said deferentially, 'I agree with you in principle, but not in practice. Colonel Sarsfield speaks of more help from France. Louis has already been more than generous. Yet what results have we obtained for him to reward him for his generosity? It isn't only in Ireland that he is confronted by the armed might of his enemies; this is but one small segment of the battlefield where he is being opposed by the Protestant armies of Europe. It is my firm belief that we should negotiate with William while we still have some strength and bargaining power, not later when we have been defeated again and are weak. I am sure that William will be most happy to avoid further conflict if he can settle for mutually agreeable terms.'

'What do you consider mutually agreeable terms?' Sarsfield asked coldly.

'Let William confirm the Parliament of 1689's revocation of the infamous Act of Settlement. And he must definitely agree to allow the Catholic population to practice their religion freely. These two accomplishments alone would be worthwhile, far better than to fight on futilely, plunging the country into a prolonged war that would drain her of her men and resources.'

Lauzun nodded his head in emphatic agreement. 'As commander of the French forces in Ireland, I have the responsibility for their welfare. I will definitely not sacrifice them for a town that can't be defended and for a cause that is lost.'

'Lost, M. le Count?' Sarsfield asked, looking down from his great height at the little Frenchman. 'Aren't you a bit premature in your judgement?'

'Apparently we do not have unanimity here for either proposal,' Berwick interjected hastily. 'I suggest that we terminate this futile debate and request his Most Catholic Majesty, King Louis XIV for his decision.'

Tyrconnell, alarmed at Berwick's disagreement with his efforts to seek a settlement with William, pressed his argument. 'If King Louis is coerced into further support of our war here, and if by some miracle we were to defeat William in battle, do you naively believe that the English and the Dutch will not send another army to try again? A bigger and better army? This has always been the policy of the rulers of England regarding Ireland.'

Angered by the use of the word 'coerced', and the reference to England's past treatment of the Irish, Berwick glared at Tyrconnell with distaste. 'I think that the Emperor of France can make his own decisions without our making up his mind for him.'

Tyrconnell realised he had gone too far. Although he was the King's deputy, Berwick was his son. He hastened to make amends by nodding his head in agreement. 'You are undoubtedly right, my lord. Since it is Louis' money, the decision also should be his. We must make arrangements immediately to send a messenger to

France.'

Stalemated until the messenger's return, the Lord Lieutenant met daily with the field officers and the leading citizens of Limerick. Depending upon his mood, his suggestions varied from outright submission to William to stout resistance.

At one of these council meetings, finding himself opposed by a majority, Tyrconnell, in his vexation, proposed that all the horses be hamstrung, and all the soldiers be transferred into the garrisoned towns. This suggestion, which was rejected with anger and loathing, convinced many of the officers and the civilian authorities, that the Viceroy was no longer competent to exercise the authority of his office. Consequently, there were several plots hatched to forcibly remove him, but the cooler heads prevailed, and no such desperate action was taken.

Having made a quick return from France, the messenger brought the eagerly awaited reply from Louis: The war was to continue!

It was undoubtedly the intervention of Le Combe D'Avaux, a jubilant Sarsfield told Major MacKettigan, Captain O'Brien, Lieutenant Sergeant Archange and Tadhg, that convinced Louis that the Irish could continue the war. D'Avaux, who had been Louis' envoy to Ireland in 1689, was aware of the true situation in the country. He knew that the Irish soldiers were brave and competent despite the false allegations made against them. He was cognisant that the English and Scots were loyal only to James, and had but a superficial interest in Ireland. But above all, D'Avaux considered Lauzun as dishonourable and dishonest. Openly he told Louis that Sarsfield was a leader of courage and ability, and always loyal to his troops.

Louis, unlike his cousin James, was a shrewd judge of character. He listened to the pros and cons, then made his decision.

Angered at the decree that the war was to be continued because it was contrary to his opinion and advice, and humiliated at the victory of his opponents, the viceroy decided to move to Galway with Lauzun and the bulk of the French forces, where the French were to embark for their return to France.

When word of Tyrconnell's planned departure with the French, and his order that the cannon salvaged from the debacle at the Boyne would accompany them to Galway became known, a wave of rebellion and rage swept the city. A plot was quickly conceived by the 'war party' composed of the two Luttrells, Colonel Purcell,

Colonel Cormac O'Neill, Colonel Felix O'Neill, Lieutenant Colonel Maurice O'Connell and many others.

It was agreed that on the day that the French were to leave the city that a counterfeit order, supposedly made by the Viceroy, would be sent to the Irish forces camped outside the town for them to march into Limerick as if just moving through. The Irish would fill the streets instead, until upon a signal, the beating of a drum, they would occupy the tower and gates and other strong points. The French were to be told peacefully to stack all their arms which were desperately needed by the Irish troops, and then to depart unarmed to Galway.

Unfortunately for the plotters, but perhaps fortunate for the Irish who would have antagonised Louis by such a hostile action, one of the leaders of the plot discussed it with Tyrconnell's natural son, Colonel Mark Talbot, thinking that he was privy to the plot. The bastard son, loyal to his father, reported the details to him immediately.

The Viceroy, realising that he had an explosive situation, used sound judgement. Instead of notifying the principals that their plot had been discovered, or informing the French who were insolent and undisciplined since many of their leaders had fled to France with James, and who would have reacted violently, he ordered the Irish to march into town as planned. He called a meeting of the Military Council, thus separating the leaders from their troops. While the frustrated leaders of the cabal attended the meeting, the French were marched out of Limerick, still armed.

As if to insure the loss of Limerick to the enemy, Tyrconnell, in his animosity, ordered those troops who were guarding the fords over the Shannon at Limerick, to accompany him to Galway, thus enabling the Williamites to take them shortly without a shot being fired.

One of the Viceroy's premeditated insults backfired on him. Major General Boisseleau, whom he had spitefully appointed Governor of Limerick instead of Sarsfield, had considerable engineering experience and military skill. Under his direction, advanced works were built outside the gates wherever possible, including a counterscarp outside of St John's Gate, a hornwork before Mungret Gate at the south end of Irishtown, and the area was circumvallated. Those French troops that had remained, having had experience along that line of defensive works, then demolished all the buildings outside the walls, laying waste to many fine houses, orchards and pleasant gardens to keep them from being used by the enemy.

CHAPTER II

Ballyneety Raid

William, who spent a week in Dublin after his triumphant entry, left on 11 July for the South. Wexford was taken easily. He then marched to Waterford where the garrison agreed to march out rather than offer serious resistance. Turning West, he took Kilkenny and Clonmel, and at his leisure approached the remnants of the Jacobites still defiantly holding out in Limerick. He would have been cheered to learn that the departing French had sneeringly predicted that Limerick would fall in three days. William, himself, thought that it would take two weeks.

On 9 August, the Irish on the walls saw William's army rolling in from the east. The Williamites quickly set up their camp, and then spreading out in the quadrant formed by the near horse shoe-shaped bend of the Shannon, proceeded to dig trenches and to establish fortifications on the solid ground away from the bogs. Moving freely between St Thomas' Island on the north and the area around Irishtown on the south, they occupied Cromwell's Fort, Ireton's Fort and Old Church Fort. Horse units were assigned to the fords of the Shannon where Tyrconnell had obligingly removed the Irish troops guarding them.

Not long after their arrival, the Williamites began hurling cannonballs and bombs into the town, and firing at the Irish on the walls with their muskets. After a while the bombardment ceased, and a drummer approached from the king's camp, accompanied by an officer who summoned the garrison to surrender. Since other fortified cities on the march capitulated after a brief show of force, William was sanguine that Limerick would do the same.

It was not General Boisseleau's nature to yield without a fight, so he informed the king's representatives that the order of the day was 'stout resistance, not surrender'. Almost immediately, the bombardment was restored. Each commander then knew where the other stood.

Boisseleau shook his head as he saw the size of the army opposing him, and exhorted the Irish to work harder at improving the fortification. He ordered that the Irish horse and dragoons be kept on the west side of the Shannon. When Athlone, to the north, was besieged by General Douglas, he dispatched Sarsfield and his regiment to its aid. Colonel Grace defiantly refused to surrender

Athlone, and when Douglas learned that the indomitable grandson of Rory O'More was coming to its succour, he prudently and quickly withdrew from the area to rejoin William at Carriginlish, four miles from Limerick.

In Limerick the defenders were puzzled. William's army hurled cannonballs and firebombs into the city, and there was intermittent small arms fire, but no attempt was made to assault the city. If one person asked another why the delay, the reply was invariably, 'Why, William is waiting for his roasted apples.'

After Mass on Sunday, 10 August, the War Council was summoned to an emergency meeting. A Huguenot soldier, his national pride paramount to his religion, had crept through the Williamite lines to an Irish outpost near the Devil's Tower where he had surrendered himself so that he could join one of the French regiments in Limerick. Information obtained from him solved the mystery why a major assault had not been mounted. William's siege train had not yet arrived from Cashel!

With Tyrconnell and Lauzun in Galway, where they could not interfere, Sarsfield's suggestion that an attack be launched on the siege train met with enthusiastic approval. General Boisseleau thought it an excellent idea, although extremely hazardous. He then ordered that 600 picked men from Luttrell's, Clifford's, Clare's, Dongan's and Neill O'Neill's Dragoon regiments, and Lord Galmoy's and Sarsfield's Horse comprise the force. He bade the commanders use extreme caution to keep the mission a secret.

Sarsfield sent for Galloping Hogan, the local Rapparee chieftain, who knew the country like the back of his hand.

All afternoon they conferred, working out the details of the plan. The Rapparee, short and stocky, his hairy legs bare from ankle to knee, wore a saffron shirt whose short sleeves disclosed his powerful arms. Red breeches, apparently taken from one of the 'Red Sagums'! as the English soldiers were called, completed his costume. Heelless brogues were on his bare feet.

Quick of movement, he had entered Sarsfield's tent before the latter could arise from his chair. Hogan strode forward, and loudly exclaiming, 'For God and Our Lady and Rory O'More,' embraced the startled Sarsfield. Smiling broadly, the latter freed himself from the bearlike embrace. 'You're fifty years too late,' he replied.

Hogan's alert brown eyes crinkled at their weathered corners, fine white lines showing on the brown skin. 'Better late than never, Sir,' he said. 'My father's father started from Nenagh to join Old

Rory, but he never made it. Some say it was the Sassanaigh who stopped him, some say it was the *cailín bán* who became my grandmother, while others claim it was Maurice MacEgan's mountain dew.'

Sarsfield grinned. 'It would have taken more than the English to stop a Hogan, so it must have been the *cailín* or the whiskey.

Bidden to be seated, Hogan's eyes gleamed with pleasure when the reason for the meeting was explained. In a rough way he outlined the best route to take, pointing out the fords, protecting hills and isolated valleys, providing a running commentary on the persons living in the area, friendly and unfriendly. When he arose to take his departure, his face was thoughtful. 'I will meet you at the dark of the moon on the road to keep watch.'

With their horses' hooves muffled, the mystified selected six hundred men rode silently out of Limerick that night over Thomond Bridge. When but a few miles out of the city, they were joined by Galloping Hogan, his rainbow-hued garments replaced by subdued grey. They crossed the river at a ford near Killaloe where they circled southward to gain the protection of Keeper Hill, where they hid among the hazel and sally copses just as dawn broke.

Tadhg, Dónal and Conor, lying in the heather, watched curiously as country people, farmers, sheep herders, and even a woman or two with voluminous capes covering their heads and parts of their faces, singly strolled to where Sarsfield and Hogan waited to confer with them. By the time the sun was directly overhead, the whereabouts of the siege train, moving slowly towards William's camp, was known to Sarsfield. But there was nothing to do now but wait.

As dusk slowly crept across the hills, a message came to Tadhg instructing him to report to Sarsfield. Rory O'More's grandson was already astride his horse, a magnificent bay. His white cravat gleamed on the scarlet cavalry coat he wore over his cuirass, gay plumes drooped from the wide-brimmed hat set jauntily on his head.

'Sergeant O'Cuirc,' he said, greeting Tadhg with a slight smile, 'I want you to ride next to me in the event it becomes necessary to pluck me from the ground again.'

After some minutes of impatient waiting, the scout sent by Hogan to pinpoint the latest position of the siege train arrived to report. The English force, under the command of a Captain Poultney, had stopped to pitch camp at Ballyneety, a small hamlet about seven miles east of William's encampment before Limerick. There were only about a hundred men in the party, no match for the six hundred Jacobites, the scout said.

The informant reported to Sarsfield that the enemy had lined up their wagons at the site of an old ruined castle, and feeling so secure close to their main force, had posted only a half-dozen men as guards. Their horses had been turned out to graze.

Sarsfield was pleased with the information. In addition, a garrulous woman camp follower, the wife of one of the English soldiers, had let it slip, at a smithy run by a man named O'Kennedy, that the password for the siege train was ironically and prophetically, 'Sarsfield'. It was a good omen.

Orders were quickly passed to be prepared to move. Each trooper was made aware of their perilous position, that their lives and mission depended upon complete silence and absolute discipline. Sarsfield, Hogan and Tadhg led the column as it filed down the hills as they put their heads ever deeper into the muzzles of William's cannon. As they crossed the Thurles road, they could see William's campfires in the west blinking cheerfully, and many a man crossed himself and silently offered a prayer for God's help that night.

When the dark walls of the old castle loomed before them, Tadhg motioned to Sarsfield for permission to go first. Gazing speculatively at Tadhg's huge bulk, comforting at such a crucial moment, he nodded acquiescence.

With Tadhg leading, they approached the first sentry, who, roused from his dozing before a fire, sleepily challenged him. 'Sarsfield,' replied Tadhg, and was passed. Next came the colonel himself. When challenged, he joyously responded, 'Sarsfield is the word, and Sarsfield is the man!'

Abruptly the sentry wakened, and with an oath, leaped to his feet. Before he could sound the alarm, however, he was impaled by Hogan's half-pike. In a flash, the Irish swept through the camp, putting many of William's dragoons and musketeers to the sword. The survivors fled ignominiously into the darkness.

Aware that the escapees could alert William's camp, Sarsfield's men worked at fever pitch to destroy the siege train which was much bigger than they had been led to believe. Its loss would be a severe blow to the enemy.

Squads of dragoons dragged the wagons, 170 in all, loaded with supplies, largely ammunition for the accompanying six twenty four pounders, two eighteen pounders, and six mortars, into a gigantic pile. All the guns were then rammed full of powder and their muzzles shoved into the earth. Tadhg worked in furious exultation, his muscles straining as he helped wrestle the heavy guns into position for their destruction.

Others of the party, working rapidly and efficiently under Sarsfield's directions, piled supply of tin boats, intended for bridge pontoons for crossing the Shannon, on top of the pile. When all was completed, the raiders were ordered to ride to the north with the one Williamite lieutenant taken as prisoner, and the five hundred captured horses which had been conveniently left saddled and bridled, with pistols at the pommel.

Tadhg remained behind with Captain Murtagh O'Brien who took some lighted match and ignited a long snake of gunpowder which led to the massive monument to Sarsfield's audacity. They watched with fascination as the flame ran along the powder, then they too, fled into the night after the others.

Suddenly the quiet peace of the summer night erupted as a tremendous explosion lighted the entire countryside and the ground shook. It was sweet music to the fleeing Irish and they exulted as they rode. Intermittently, lesser succeeding blasts punctured the night as the fire spread, until all that was flammable was consumed, and only the twisted, blackened remnants marked the pyre of William's siege train.

Awakened by the din, the country people smiled in the darkness of their humble cabins, gleefully aware of the cause of the disturbance. But if the loyal Irish knew that something was afoot, so did the disloyal Irish, despite Galloping Hogan's vigilance, a well-to-do farmer named Manus O'Donnell had observed the passage of Sarsfield and his men. A Protestant, son of one of the renegade Irish who had changed their religion to keep their properties at Cromwell's time, he immediately saddled his horse to dash through the night to William's camp to report what he had seen.

William was not unduly perturbed by the news. It was only nine of the clock, and he knew that Sarsfield would have to circle wide to his rear to come up to the siege train at Ballyneety. This would take some hours. He immediately ordered that a company of Danish horse ride out to intercept and guide the convoy and the train into camp. He also ordered other companies of horses and dragoons to be prepared to ride north to seek the marauding Jacobites. He then retired to the special portable house which accompanied him in the field.

For some unaccountable reason his order was not carried out as intended. Instead of leaving at nine o'clock, the Danes didn't depart until midnight. They were about a league distant from their goal when the night suddenly exploded ahead of them, the earth shaking with tremendous blast. Cursing loudly, the captain in charge galloped madly to the scene, only to discover the blazing remnants of the siege train, now a mass of useless wreckage, and the successful Jacobites gone off into the dark.

Knowing that the Irish would have to take a long route back, and hoping to intercept them before they reached the Shannon; the Danes set off in pursuit. With their fresh horses and shorter route, they caught up to Tadhg and Captain O'Brien and the tail of the Irish column at Banghir Bridge. After a sharp and short fight in which the Irish lost about a dozen men, and the Danes also suffering casualties, the latter broke off the engagement. Reluctantly they returned to their camp, where William, awakened by the explosions, furiously awaited them.

A different welcome awaited Sarsfield and his triumphant men in Limerick! They were greeted as heroes, and precious stores of claret were opened to show the appreciation of the military and civilians alike for their great exploit. Nothing was too good for them, and forever any man who rode with Sarsfield that night had become immortal in the minds and hearts of the Irish.

CHAPTER III

The Assault

The Irish achievement had more than just military value for it fused the diverse elements who had been at cross purposes in their desire to continue the fight, and for the first time since the Boyne, there was a spirit of unity and common purpose. While William fumed as he impatiently awaited the arrival of a new siege train and supplies this time carefully guarded by a large force, the Irish of Limerick, directed by the French engineers, worked feverishly to strengthen the fortifications.

A week after the sortie at Ballyneety, William's new cannon and mortars having arrived from Waterford, the bombardment of the tortured city increased in ferocity until it seemed inevitable that every building would be levelled and every inhabitant killed. His forty guns, of long range, were strategically located in a semicircle from the north side opposite King's Island to the southwest of Irishtown. Ceaselessly and devastatingly they poured their red-hot cannonballs and bursting shells into their target. Houses collapsed and fires raged while the civilians, assisted by those soldiers who had no guns or ammunition, worked day and night to clear the streets of rubble and to extinguish the blazing fires.

On 22 August the foe commenced to batter the tower on the southeast wall of Irishtown from four cannon they had placed nearby, continuing the next day after they added two more big guns. When the tower was destroyed, they continued to pound the wall around it. Many of the Jacobite troops assigned to the area were killed by the flying fragments of the rock wall. Then, planting six more cannon on a redoubt they had captured between the southeast angle of the walls and Cromwell's Fort, the enemy increased the tempo of the devil's tattoo, playing hotly on the weakened walls.

During the night of 24 August, the Williamites moved their trenches to within fifty yards of the counterscarp, and in the early morning hours of 25 August, the inevitable occurred, a breach about fifteen paces wide appeared with the debris from the wall helping to fill the counterscarp, making the inevitable assault attempt that much easier.

Tadhg and his apprehensive companions, along with the other horse and dragoon regiments, watched helplessly from the area outside the city beyond Thomond Bridge as the merciless hail of destruction poured into Limerick. General Boisseleau had placed Sarsfield and Berwick in command of the cavalry with instructions to stay out of range of the attack until needed.

On the morning of 27 August, a cloudy day with a hint of rain, and with mists obscuring the surrounding hills, the enemy increased the tempo of the cannonading as if they intended to pulverise the old town, and the noise became so horrendous that soldiers and civilians alike were compelled to put their fingers in their ears to protect their eardrums.

As the day lengthened, the sun appeared, the day growing hot and sultry. The Irish replied with more hope than effect from their few old guns. It soon became apparent that much more of the enemy cannon fire was being concentrated on the walls of Irishtown near St John's Gate. Suspecting the foe's intentions to enter the town there, Boisseleau instructed the engineers to plant a big mine in the vicinity. He also ordered his cannoneers to rake the Williamite trenches with heavy fire.

Weakened by the incessant sledge-hammer blows of the two hundred pound shells, an ominous hole appeared in the wall. Continual pounding gradually increased the gap until it was widened to about thirty five feet, large enough for a considerable force of the enemy to enter abreast when the time for the assault arrived.

At two of the clock in the afternoon, the devilish din subsided, and the belching cannon became mute. Clouds of dark smoke and dust drifted slowly over Limerick. In the sudden hush, the muffled beat of a drum from William's camp was soothing to ears long tortured by the roar and concussion of the cannon. The sound of the drum gradually increased until the watchers on the walls could see the drummer, accompanied by an officer, approach the town. As on the first day of William's arrival, the garrison was called upon to surrender. Once more General Boisseleau firmly but courteously rejected the ultimatum, informing William's messenger that he intended vigorously to defend the city.

Taking advantage of the brief respite the Irish had built a fortification behind the breach, and brought up a battery of cannon, posting other guns along the flanks. This fortification created a cul-de-sac at the side of the breach. General Boisseleau sent a messenger to Sarsfield and Berwick, instructing them to send some of their horse to the island near the vicinity of Ball's Bridge.

Sarsfield, realising that a decisive moment was near, called for Sergeant O'Cuirc, ordering him to take several men and go to the building where the Lady Honora was dwelling, and to guard her in the event that the foe took the city.

Tadhg selected Conor and Dónal, and arriving at the house, were informed by Rory that the Lady Sarsfield had gone to Mass at St John's Church in Irishtown, and hadn't returned. Upset by the information, Tadhg and his companions made haste to cross Ball's Bridge where the traffic was so thick that it took considerable time to reach the church, which was less than a quarter-mile from the breach. Worried over Honora Sarsfield, and incensed at the imbecility of conducting church services there at so perilous a time, Tadhg peered into the interior of the church, now jammed with women and children fervently praying that their lives would be spared. But he was unable to recognise the Lady Honora among the multitude.

'What now, *a mhic*?' Dónal asked, nervously watching the activity in the narrow streets, where files of soldiers fought their way towards the fortification.

Tadhg shrugged. 'We'll have to wait until Mass is over,' he replied. He turned to Conor for counsel, but Conor, whose jaw was swollen and hurting from a toothache, and who had refused to let the regimental surgeon pull the offending tooth when he saw the fearsome clawed tool used for such extractions, merely nodded his head in agreement.

Shortly after three o'clock, the booming of three big cannon broke the uneasy silence. The respite was over. Almost immediately, about 600 Williamites leaped from their trenches to the counterscarp. Grotesquely dressed in costumes of red and yellow, they wore capes with noisy jangling bells, and head pieces of fur with pointed crowns.

These fearsome apparitions were William's pride and joy, the Grenadiers, commanded by Henry Hamilton, the third earl of Drogheda who had rejected James to ally himself with William.

Advancing rapidly, the bells discordant, the Grenadiers hurled their deadly weapons with expert precision. Each man was armed with three grenades which were equipped with lighted fuses timed to explode shortly after being thrown.

The lethal effect of the grenades, the suddenness of the onslaught, the direful appearances of the Grenadiers, all combined to drive the Irish back from the counterscarp and through the breach. Many were left dead and dying, bloody evidence of the weapons' terrible destruction.

Shouting triumphantly, their bells jingling a macabre tune, the Grenadiers pursued the startled Irish foot through the breach. An officer, the same Captain Farlow who had taken possession of Dublin Castle when the Irish had fled Dublin after the Boyne, was the first to the breach. Pointing to Limerick with his sword, he shouted, 'Follow me, lads, the town is ours!'

Almost immediately, a musketball stopped him in his tracks, followed by a withering volley into the ranks of the Grenadiers, many of whom had heeded Farlow's call to follow, but unto death, not Limerick! The Williamites were now confined by the fortification that Boisseleau had ordered constructed, and the Irish musketeers, aided by a hidden battery of two cannon at the Augustinian Chapel near Ball's Bridge, poured a deadly fire into their ranks. Soon the breach began to fill with the piled masses of red-and-yellow uniformed bodies. Some, who had suceded in climbing the barricade, were killed in the city streets; the handful who had survived fled back to the safety of their trenches.

But the Irish success was only temporary. The Grenadiers had been merely the point of a massive assault to take the city, and now William committed his army in full strength. In massed, disciplined ranks, the veteran troops advanced confidently against the poorly trained and poorly equipped defenders of the city. In seemingly never ending waves they poured over the counterscarp, now filled with debris from the battered walls. Bravely they charged through the gap, protected by their big guns which hurled cannonballs and bombs in a deadly rain on Limerick.

Noting the precarious situation, Boisseleau dashed into the streets where his own regiment, Lord Sloan's and the Lord Grand Prior's stood waiting, their matches lighted. Without hesitation he ordered them to proceed immediately to the breach. Advancing at quick step, the regiments moved smartly to the walls. At the sight of the enemy, the officers gave the order to fire. Muskets belched their lethal loads, and the hail of bullets swept the close ranks of the Williamites, causing them to falter. Simultaneously two cannon planted at the Citadel, just a short distance from the breach, and two on King's Island, began a merciless fire into the masses of humanity pouring towards the city from William's camp.

From the walls, and along the edges of the fortification, the Irish loaded and reloaded, firing continuously until their gun barrels burned their hands, but the determined, disciplined ranks of William's army surged relentlessly forward despite the fearful carnage of the enfilade, until by sheer numbers alone, more arrived than fell.

Tadhg and his companions, hearing the tumult, and observing some of the Irish soldiers who had been repulsed by the initial charge of the Grenadiers fleeing from the scene, abandoned the safety of the church and ran toward the walls. They shouted at the fear-stricken soldiers and some of the citizens to turn and fight, but they rushed past pell-mell.

For two hours the battle raged, with Tadhg, Conor and Dónal in the midst of it. The Irish foot fought like veterans. When a man fell, a replacement was there to fill the gap. A cacophony of shouts, oaths, moans and grunts, punctuated by the crackle of musket fire, and the deeper roar of the cannon, dominated the scene. The air was thick with smoke, and the acrid odour of gunpowder mingled with the sickening smell of blood.

With their prize so close to attainment, the Williamites, incited by their officers to greater effort, finally removed most of the earthworks and obstructions in their path, and with a loud shout, streamed into the city. It was then that the enraged citizens, watching the gory conflict from the walls and from their houses, entered the fray. Seizing whatever weapons were at hand, they charged the enemy. Women with broken bottles, blacksmiths with their hammers, butchers with knives and cleavers, unarmed soldiers with rocks, and half-grown youths with clubs, fearlessly charged the enemy. One of the women, a nun, her black habit flying, used the butt of a discarded musket with such effect that she cleared a passage where ever she moved.

As the Williamites faltered before the new furies, Boisseleau ordered his reserves into battle. Inspired by the fierce example of the civilians, the Irish troops rallied, and in savage hand-to -hand combat, slowly but steadily forced the enemy soldiers back to the breach. Inconceivable to William that his well-trained professional veterans could not take the city, he sent more of his reserves pouring through the broken walls into the city streets. These met the same fate as their predecessors. The Irish, no longer disorganised and divided, bravely stood, fought and checked William's elite European troops with coolness and courage.

Tadhg, Dónal and Conor, their pistolballs long since gone, fought hand-to-hand along with the other soldiers and civilians, using their sabres to slash and hack at the masses of Williamite soldiers trying to force their way into the streets. It was an eerie feeling for Tadhg, this face-to-face, body-to-body personal contact with the enemy, so different from the exhilarating rapidly moving action on the back of Cuchulain in a cavalry sweep. Here one stood among a mass of grunting, sweating, desperate men fighting for a few yard's advantage, some with eyes wild with fear, some emotionless, but all conscious that death awaited he who failed to be vigilant at all times.

While the battle raged, a huge plume of black smoke arose, the wind carrying it northeast into adjoining Tipperary. To many a fearful countryman and woman, aware of the battle, it was a dark symbol of disaster, signifying that Limerick had fallen, and that the town was burning.

On the contrary, Limerick had not fallen. A jubilant M. Boisseleau, watching the Irish foot, decided it was opportune for the entry of the horse regiments into the fray. He ordered that the sally ports near St John's Gate be opened. The cavalry, which had stood impatiently for three hours, moved vigorously out in double files through a covered way leading to the breach. Quickly dispersing a regiment of Danish horse which blocked their way, they galloped to the breach, taking the enemy in the rear. With their sabres bloodied, they swept through the surprised foe, like reapers through the wheat fields at harvest.

As the discouraged, disorganised English army tried to regroup, the mine buried at the Black Battery was detonated. A deafening explosion drowned the rattle of musket fire and the shouts of the combatants. Most of a regiment of Brandenburgers, tough German mercenaries who had tenaciously clung to their positions, were killed in the mighty blast, their bodies flung high in the air, some to adjacent rooftops.

Taking immediate advantage of the stunned and decimated foe, the Irish foot dashed furiously among the remaining Williamites. In their charge, they swept the foe from the counterscarp, some being pursued to their very trenches. Again the horse and dragoons fell on the fleeing, disordered enemy, and with flashing sabres and loud cheers, drove the Williamites from the field.

A hush settled over the city, even William's cannoneers stood idle at their gun emplacements as both sides watched the remnants of the 10,000-man assault force ignominiously fleeing from the ragtag and bobtail Irish army. Then the silence was suddenly shattered by a tremendous cheer from thousands of Irish throats as the disbelieving defenders, soldiers and civilians alike, realised that they had repulsed the cream of William's army!

Exhausted by his exertions and the oppressive heat, Tadhg paused to catch his breath. Around him lay heaps of the fallen, friend and foe alike, their animosities, prejudices, passions and hates all stilled, united in death.

Here and there was a Grenadier, his tinkling bells stilled; here was a woman, her grey hair one with the grey dust in which she lay in death; there was a stout, bald-headed man, his hand still clutching his bloody cleaver; near the wall lay a grotesque pile of Red Sagums, their life's blood dying their uniforms a richer crimson; interspersed frequently among the fallen were splashes of red, lined with white, the uniforms of the Lord Grand Prior's Regiment, and others of white, lined with red, of Boisseleau's Regiment, the two which had initially stopped the assault; at Tadhg's feet was sprawled the body of a young soldier in the uniform of the Grand Lord Prior's Regiment, his cap showing a flaming city and its accompanying motto, The Fruits of Rebellion, still held proudly in his blood-covered right hand.

But there were the quick as well as the dead. Exulted, excited, exhausted, the soldiers and the citizens surged through the narrow streets, shouting, crying, kissing, embracing. In their midst was the erect form of a young woman in the habit of a nun, the one who had led the vanguard. Her garb was streaked and stained with blood and dirt, and as she turned her eyes, alight with joy, towards Tadhg, the joy gave way to stunned surprise, and then to joy again as they rushed towards each other, with open arms. In a moment he forced his way through the crowd, elbowing aside those who would not move, and reaching out, plucked her from her admirers, and lifting her in a mighty embrace to his breast.

'Tadhg, Tadhg, Tadhg,' she cried, tears coursing through the grime on her face, 'O Mary, I have found him again! He is alive! And I have found him again!' She flung her arms around Tadhg's neck, burying her head in his breast, moving her head back and forth as if she would burrow her way into his heart.

'*Mo chailín rua*,' he muttered happily, 'take it easy now, I'm not going to disappear.'

A ring of spectators formed around them, and even the extraordinary spectacle of a nun in the embrace of a man couldn't hide their admiration as they saw their goddess of battle being embraced by an Irish giant in the uniform of their beloved Sarsfield.

'She must be his sister,' a grimy blacksmith with his hammer explained to the man next to him, a lean man still grasping his butcher's knife in his hand.

'Whatever,' replied the other, with a broad grin, 'she's our sister today!'

As Tadhg held Eithne, he felt one arm tugged gently. It was Dónal Óg, his uniform tattered and bloody, his eyes apprehensive. 'Come quickly,' he squawked hoarsely, 'Conor is wounded, and we must get him to the surgeon.'

Tadhg stood dazed. Eithne found and Conor wounded! All in the space of a few minutes. Then his head cleared, and he spoke to Eithne. 'It's Conor, *a rún*. We must help him. Dónal says he is hurt.'

Immediately the hazel eyes showed alarm. 'Let us go to him at once, then,' she said.

Dónal led them to a pile of bodies. Conor was lying on his back, his eyes closed, his fair head covered with blood. He was unconscious. 'Oh Merciful God,' Tadhg whispered, appalled at the gory sight, 'please don't let him die.'

'Then just don't stand there,' Eithne blazed, 'get him to a doctor!'

'There's a surgeon in front of the church,' a bystander volunteered.

Carrying Conor gently, Tadhg strode down the cluttered street, nimbly stepping over bodies and debris until he arrived at the church. Here the wounded lay on the cobblestones, some moaning, some shrieking, and some, like Conor, quite unconscious. An ensign in the uniform of the Lord Grand Prior's Regiment, unconcerned that his titular commandant was safe in Paris with his father King James, was assisting the surgeon. He introduced himself as Séamus Dunne. He directed Tadhg to bring Conor to the steps of the church with the other seriously wounded. After some anxious moments as Tadhg, Dónal and Eithne watched, the surgeon, Dominick O'Nolan, of the Earl of Clarickarde's Regiment, approached them. He ordered Eithne to wash away the blood from Conor's matted hair, and when this was done, closely examined the scalp.

'Arrah!' he exclaimed gruffly, 'this one doesn't need Dr O'Nolan, he just needs Dr Time.'

'What do you mean, *a dhuine uasail*?' Tadhg asked fearfully, 'Is he going to die?'

'Far from it! The blood on him is somebody else's. He's just got a big lump on his head. Probably hit by a gun butt, the flat of a sabre, or even a brick. He's one of the fortunate ones.'

'Is he suffering very much?' asked Dónal.

The doctor laughed, shaking his head. 'Not at all. He's feeling no pain. He's in the land of dreams. He'll be all right after a while.'

Dónal stared speculatively at Conor. 'If he isn't feeling anything, this would be a good time to pull his aching tooth. Sure, and we could pluck it like pulling a quill from a goose, and he'd never be knowing the difference.'

Eithne gazed at her uncle's still form, her eyes anxious. 'Has he then a bad tooth?' she asked.

'Och, the very devil of an aching tooth. He was almost swooning from the pain of it,' Dónal said, stretching the truth a bit.

Eithne bent over and opened Conor's mouth. 'Which tooth is it?'

Dónal hesitated momentarily, then pointed to a big molar on the right side. He turned to Tadhg. 'Do you have a puller?'

The 'puller' was a piece of leather thong. Tying a sliding loop in one end, Tadhg, after much effort, succeeded in attaching it to the designated tooth. The other end he attached to the barrel of a discarded musket. Standing over the unsuspecting patient, Tadhg gave a sharp jerk.

Instead of the offending tooth coming out, Conor's head was lifted off the ground by the taut leather strap. Disappointed, Tadhg let Conor's head drop slowly back to the earth. He gestured to Dónal. 'You'll have to hold his head down,' he commanded.

Then, with Dónal firmly gripping Conor's head between his knees, Tadhg applied pressure. Tighter and tighter grew the leather thong as Tadhg exerted his great strength. Eithne watched, her forehead wrinkled in a nervous frown. But the stubborn tooth resisted. Tadhg pulled ever harder until it became a contest as to which would give first, the tooth or the leather. Then pop! Success! The miscreant molar dangled at the end of the 'puller'. Almost simultaneously Conor's eyes opened, and with a loud howl leaped to his feet, his hand clasped to his jaw, bounding about as if his feet were in a bed of hot coals.

'My body to the devil,' he exclaimed, half-shout, half-moan, 'what are you two demons trying to do, kill me?'

'It's your aching tooth we pulled,' Dónal said, beaming.

Conor was quiet for a moment, then poked an exploratory

finger into his mouth. Immediately rage contorted his face, and with eyes blazing, and hands clenched into claws, he sprang at the startled Dónal, grabbing the youth by the throat and started to choke him.

'Stop that,' Tadhg protesting, tearing Conor from his victim. 'This is no way to treat a friend who has done you a great service!'

'Great service?' Conor shouted angrily at Tadhg. 'You inhuman fools pulled the wrong tooth!'

As Tadhg and Dónal stared at each other in consternation, Conor noticed his niece for the first time. Forgetting his pain and rage, his eyes softened, and he reached out hungrily for her, crooning, 'Eithne, *mo chroí*, where in the name of God did you come from?'

He hugged and squeezed her, tears of joy mingling with tears of pain. 'Thanks be to God there's an angel here, or it's sure I'd be that it's dead I am and down in Hell with those two cruel devils.' He glared at Tadhg and Dónal.

'Ooh, Conor, 'tis lovely to see you again,' she said warmly. Then, with mischievous eyes, added, 'At least these two devils have restored you from the dead: 'Tis but a few minutes ago we thought we would be burying you.'

Looking about him, Conor became aware for the first time of the bodies of the wounded, and the doctors treating them. He put his hand to his head gingerly. 'Sure, and the way my poor head's aching, these two devil's helpers must have pulled my tooth right through the top of it.' He shook his head gently as if fearful it might fall off. 'It's not sure I am which hurts the most, my pounding head or my throbbing jaw.' He turned to Tadhg, asking calmly, 'What did happen to me?'

'It was Dónal who found you unconscious when the fighting stopped. We thought that you were dying. So we brought you to the surgeon here, but he said it was just a blow to the head and you'd recover.' Tadhg looked apologetic. 'So we thought it was a good time to pull your aching tooth when you wouldn't feel the pain.'

Pointing to the molar still dangling from the leather thong in Tadhg's hand, Conor said accusingly, 'You *amadáns* pulled a good tooth. Now my jaw aches on both sides. If that's what you do as friends, thank God you're not enemies. But let's talk about something more pleasant. You say the battle's over? Did we win?'

'For the moment,' Tadhg said. 'The enemy has withdrawn to lick

383

his wounds. But God knows what William will throw at us tomorrow.'

Conor sighed. 'We all fought like lions today. But we didn't have King James or that Talbot to hinder us.' He turned to his niece, 'But tell me, Eithne, how you happened to be here in Limerick?'

Her smiling face turned sad. 'You remember that when I last saw you after burying my father that I had resolved to become a nun?'

Conor nodded. "Tis a fine thing to dedicate your life to the Church, but I'd hoped that you would stay home with your mother to help her with the younger children.'

Eithne glanced briefly but enigmatically at Tadhg, then turned again to her uncle. 'I made a promise to God, and with me a promise is not made lightly.' She grasped Conor's shoulder affectionately as if to assure him that her family's ties were strong and enduring, but her obligation to God was greater.

'Several months after the funeral of my father, may God have mercy upon his soul, I went to Galway to the novitiate there as a postulant. About three months ago I was transferred here to the Franciscan Convent. But because it lies outside the walls of Englishtown, we all moved when the siege began to a building next to St John's Church in Irishtown where it was thought we'd be safer. This afternoon as I attended Mass, I looked with great pity at the poor, fearful women and children as they prayed to God to be merciful to them, a great cry arose that the Red Sagums were advancing into the city streets. In a trice I found my feet carrying me into the thick of the fight.'

'We saw a nun, but never dreamed that it was you,' Dónal said, looking at Eithne with admiration.

As Eithne spoke, Tadhg remembered vividly the scene at St Malachi's: How her father, seeing Thomas Morton shoot Cathal, reacted instantly in the same resolute manner, with his feet carrying him too into the thick of the fight, and completely disregarding his own safety, bayonet the armed land agent. Poor, brave Murtagh, who had always worried about what he would leave his children, had left to his daughter the greatest possible heritage, his passionate love of justice!

Eithne's eyes again strayed to Tadhg's, the enigmatic smile again playing at the corners of her mouth. He was unable to discern its meaning, although he strove mightily. Was it that she regretted her decision to take the life of the religious? Did she still feel for him strongly as she once did? Was she happy in her vocation? Or did she blame him for the change of course her life had taken?

As he reflected, another nun, a worried but determined expression on her long, ascetic face, forced her way through the crowd. Reaching out a bony hand, she plucked at Eithne's garment. 'Come, Sister,' she greeted her severely, 'the street is no place for you. It is much too dangerous! Besides, it's time for compline.'

As Eithne was led away, unprotesting, Tadhg stood indecisive, at once compelled to run after her, and at the same time rooted to the ground. He wanted to implore her to leave the convent before she took her everlasting vows, and to tell her that he would go away with her as once she had begged of him. But he stood still, no words coming from his mouth. He realised that his sudden feeling was impulsive, not compulsive. Unconsciously he fingered the still not completely healed wound on his forehead caused by the Lady Mairéad's riding crop as he irresolutely watched Eithne and her companion disappear down the street.

Conor interrupted his reveries. 'Well, Sergeant O'Cuirc, have you forgotten that we were to guard the Lady Sarsfield?'

Tadhg whistled in dismay. In the excitement of the battle, Conor's wounding, the reunion with Eithne, and the fiasco with the tooth extraction, he had completely forgotten his mission. 'My soul to God!' he exclaimed, 'I'll be Private O'Cuirc before this day is over if we don't get to her soon.'

Inquiring at the church, they learned that the Lady Honora had returned to Englishtown. Hastening to her dwelling, they found her serene and happy with the great victory of the garrison over the Williamites.

'Colonel Sarsfield sent us to make sure that you were safe,' Tadhg informed her, neglecting to explain, however, that they were more than three hours late.

'Why, I am perfectly safe,' she said, smiling. 'I have Rory here to protect me.' She turned to the lad who was delirious with happiness at her praise. 'The Irish fought magnificently today,' she continued, her eyes beaming. 'This should make the Duke of Tyrconnell ashamed that he ran away to Galway. If you see Colonel Sarsfield, tell him that I miss him greatly, but that he shouldn't worry about me.'

Tadhg duly reported to the adjutant, Lieutenant Sergeant

Archange, that the Lady Sarsfield was safe and happy, repeating her message for her husband, and in this way avoiding any confrontation with the Colonel himself.

CHAPTER IV

The Rains

When it was apparent that the enemy had retired for the night to reassess his position, Boisseleau called a meeting of the military council which had been named by Tyrconnell before he abandoned the town to its fate. Although Berwick was in nominal command of all the Irish forces, having been designated Governor General of all the Irish forces, Boisseleau was Governor of Limerick, and as such, was exercising his authority. Tadhg again was attending the council meeting, sitting next to Captain O'Brien, who spoke no French.

His voice shaking with emotion, Boisseleau declared, 'Rarely have I witnessed such indomitable courage and fierce resistance as this garrison showed today. It should end for once and for all time the base lie that the Irish soldiers turn tail and run when faced with death. Many looked death in the face this afternoon and met it bravely and with dignity. Their bodies are mute but glorious evidence of their sacrifice for their county. But we cannot rest on our laurels, William is a stubborn Dutchman who will mount another and greater assault tomorrow. I realise that the members of the garrison, and all those brave residents of Limerick who helped to turn the tide of battle today, have had practically no rest in weeks, but we must now redouble our efforts to secure the town, and repair as much damage as possible by morning. I want every able-bodied soldier and civilian to get to work immediately, for the streets must be cleared, the fortification at the breach must be rebuilt, ammunition and supplies brought up. And the blessings of God on all of you!'

Berwick arose, his eyes bloodshot from lack of sleep and the smoke of battle. 'My lords and fellows-in-arms, I, too, wish to offer my commendations to the valiant efforts of your men, and the gallant women, who beat back the enemy this day. It justifies the confidence and faith that His Most Christian Majesty, Louis XIV, has placed in us. I also want to thank you on behalf of my father, King James.

'I do not wish to detract in any way from the bravery of all the defenders,' Boisseleau said, 'for they were all magnificent, but I would like to express my heartfelt admiration and appreciation for the soldierly response of the regiments of Lord Slane, of

Boisseleau, and the Lord Grand Prior when the enemy forced the breach. And it is with heavy heart, and deepest regret, that I must report that an old friend and comrade, Lieutenant Colonel de Beaupre, of Boisseleau's regiment was among the fallen after he led the counter-attack in which we captured the top of the breach. He was a brave and devoted soldier.'

As soon as the conference was over, Tadhg joined with the soldiers and citizens to restore the fortifications, remove the dead, and resupply the troops who remained in arms through the night. Food supplies were running short, many of the soldiers subsisting on raw oats which they carried in their pockets. The citizens had it little better except for those who had hoarded food and ate it secretly in the dark of the night. Despite their determination to resist, the members of the garrison and citizenry knew that their military supplies were now minimal, and that their food situation was even more precarious. So they turned from their dependence only on man (and His Most Christian Majesty, the Emperor of France) and fervently appealed to the Most Merciful God and His Saints for help.

While Tadhg slept fitfully that night, after working hard to help rebuild the fortification, thinking of Eithne, and recalling the excitement of the battle, William's men rested well, and his diabolical cannoneers were up early to renew their infernal pounding of the town. The pattern of their firing was much as of the day previous, playing their heavy cannon on the breach, enlarging it some, and trying to destroy the remains of a small tower on the south wall from which the encroached Irish had poured a withering fire on the Williamites trying to enter the breach. Hoping to prevent the Irish from sending supplies from Englishtown to Irishtown, the enemy maintained a hot fire on Ball's Bridge which connected the two sections of the town.

Anxiety mounted as the day advanced. Then, in the afternoon, the firing ceased as on the day before. Again several officers, walking slowly to the steady beat of a drummer wearing the uniform of Cutt's Grenadiers, approached the Irish lines. But this time there was no arrogant demand for surrender, but a request for a truce so that the enemy could gather and bury their dead. A loud cheer went up from Irish throats as they realised that they would have a respite from the tension which gripped the town.

Governor Boisseleau granted them one hour, on the condition that they would not approach closer than twenty paces to the walls.

The Irish, who had reoccupied all the positions from which they had been driven on the previous day, carried the bodies of the Red Sagums to the line agreed upon. There the corpses were gathered by their erstwhile comrades-in-arms, and removed for burial. As customary, the bodies had been stripped of everything of value, many to be planted in the earth as they had arrived on it.

After the truce time expired, the bombardment was resumed until the sun sank in the West and the cannon fire finally ceased.

Dawn came, grey and cold, and the cannonading resumed again as if the cannoneers were anxious to get their gun barrels heated to warm their chilled hands. Once more came the concentration of the cannon balls and the bomb carcasses on the walls at the breach where the gap was eventually widened to at least forty paces. It appeared to an apprehensive Tadhg and his companions as if William planned to march his entire army in abreast. One of the chains supporting the drawbridge between Englishtown and Irishtown was severed by a cannonball. Although it was dangerous to cross thereafter, many persons being killed or wounded by the stones that were dislodged, it was still passable to traffic.

About noon, grey sullen clouds brooded over the city. The first gentle drops of rain that spattered on the upturned faces of the garrison, quickly developed into a drizzle and then a downpour. Then, gaining momentum, apparently encouraged by its success, it became a steady downpour. William was seemingly satisfied to let the elements assault the city, for the day ended without the emergence of his army on the widened breach.

It was still raining the following day. As the rain continued, the area outside the walls, some of it bog, became saturated with little pools forming. The gathering waters became rivulets that first trickled, then growing larger, poured enthusiastically into the enemy's trenches. In William's camp, too, the soldiers huddled in their soggy tents and poorly constructed huts, while their officers fretted at the interruption of their offensive.

During the night of 29 September, the Irish kept firing their few cannon and small shot into the area in front of the breach to discourage any attempt by the enemy to mass troops there. Soldiers of both sides, being but a few feet apart in their respective trenches, talked and joked with each other, a practice not uncommon, but ironical in the light that they would do their best to kill each other when the time came. As the long night waned, the conversation from the English trenches diminished, and although the Irish taunted and insulted them, the Williamites appeared to prefer silence to speech.

When the first light of dawn crept hesitantly across the rain-soaked plain, the Irish on the walls rubbed their eyes in disbelief, the English trenches below them were empty.

But the enemy was not gone completely, for guns at Cromwell's Fort still hurled their unfriendly greetings upon the area of St John's Gate, and some of the more foolhardy of the Irish soldiers, venturing too far from their walls, discovered to their sorrow that there were still occupants in the outlying trenches.

CHAPTER V

Siege Lifted

Tadhg, Conor and Dónal, along with the other Irish soldiers and civilians, had spent that memorable day under cover as much as possible to protect themselves from the chilling rain, worrying over the expected new assault against the town. They would have been less apprehensive, however, if they had been privy to William of Orange's thoughts.

Thus, on the afternoon of 29 September, the King called a council of war. His ammunition much depleted from the weeks of heavy bombardment, and his abortive effort to take the city two days earlier, he was now confronted with the new and serious problems presented by the rains. With trenches flooded, the camp muddy, the powder damp, the incidence of dysentery bound to rise, his offensive would soon sputter to a halt. So he advocated the ending of the siege. There was some resistance, but William insisted that it was time for prudence. To continue would be to risk all. As he was King as well as a commander, there was little doubt what the decision would be. Besides, he was urgently needed at home. Sailing for England, he left the army in command of the Duke of Berwick's uncle, John Churchill, later to become the famed Duke of Marlborough.

Abandoning Limerick, Churchill marched to Cork, besieging that important bastion of South Munster. Because of a shortage of gunpowder, the chronic complaint of Irish garrisons during the war, the governor, General MacElligot was forced to surrender the city. Moving on quickly to Kinsale, Churchill forced that port city to capitulate also. Here the garrison received better terms than their counterparts at Cork, for they were allowed to march out with their baggage and go to Limerick rather than become prisoners of war.

With the loss of Cork and Kinsale, all of Munster but Limerick, Clare and Kerry counties were in the hands of the enemy. Kinsale was a great loss in that it had provided a means of quick sea communication with France. With most of Ireland now secured, Churchill deemed it time to go into winter quarters.

While the enemy lived well during winter and spring, with most of Ireland providing supplies, the Jacobites in contrast subsisted on small amounts of salt beef and potatoes. Grain being scarce, barley and oats, to the amount of half a pint daily, were issued to the soldiers, while an equivalent amount of wheat was given to the officers. This they used to make their own bread.

With Limerick secure despite their dire predictions, Lauzun and Tyrconnell felt it was expedient to go to France to explain their actions to their masters. They took with them the French troops sent to Ireland the previous spring, and the remainder of those twelve field guns which James had used so sparingly at the battle of the Boyne. While Lauzun first hastened to the Court of St Germaine to see James, thence to the Palace at Versailles to report to Louis, the wily Tyrconnell loitered near the coast until he could determine which way the political winds were blowing.

Lauzun told James exactly what he wanted to hear: that the campaign in Ireland was doomed to failure because of the cowardice and poor fighting qualities of the Irish soldiers. James bought his version lock, stock and barrel. Louis, however, was no fool. Knowing that cowards and incompetents could not have made the magnificent defence of Limerick that the Irish did against William, he decided that Lauzun was lying. It was only the anguished appeal of James and his Queen that saved Lauzun from the Bastille!

When word of Lauzun's reception was received by Tyrconnell, his delicate nose told him the wind's direction. He appeared at court, where, to the consternation and indignation of his former ally, Lauzun, he fulfilled the appellation of 'Lying Dick' scornfully applied to him by the English, by advancing those reasons in favour of continuing the hostilities which had been advocated by Sarsfield, and which he had vigorously opposed. He then ardently pleaded for more money, supplies and ammunition to carry on the war. This Louis agreed to do.

Being unaware of Tyrconnell's sudden conversion to their cause, the members of the War Party back in Limerick decided to send their own delegation to France to plead their aims, and seek Tyrconnell's replacement as Viceroy. The latter, before leaving Ireland, had appointed the twenty year old Duke of Berwick to govern the country in his absence, and had created a council of twenty four members to advise the young duke. Of the twelve army representatives on the council, the name of Sarsfield was last on the list. Although the Viceroy could not ignore Sarsfield completely, the deliberate insult was an indicator of Tyrconnell's (and those of his English-oriented advisers) deep-rooted fear of an Irish-led army!

When the War Party's decision became known, the absent Viceroy's friends became alarmed. Among these was Brigadier Maxwell, no friend of the Irish, who sought an audience with Berwick.

'My Lord,' he said anxiously, 'I beg a few minutes of privacy with you.'

The Duke was agreeable. 'Let us retire to my quarters. We can talk while we dine together.'

Later, over a bottle of claret, Maxwell spoke his mind, 'The brothers Luttrell and Colonel Purcell are firebrands that need quenching. If they are included in the commission which is going to Versailles, and I understand they are, I would most urgently recommend that you dispatch a messenger to your father, His Majesty, the King, to have them placed in custody.'

Berwick looked sharply at Maxwell. 'On what grounds?'

'That their acts are inimical to the interests of James's most loyal adherents in Ireland. They insist upon continuing the war when discretion dictates caution and conciliation until our status is confirmed.'

The Duke twiddled his wine glass. He had no real love for Ireland or the Irish. The Irish war was merely another gambit in the master game played across the chessboard of Europe. Although he was jealous of Sarsfield, frequently belittling his military ability, he had sided with him and Boisseleau that Limerick could, and should, be defended. Further, ever since Lauzun had fled at the Battle of the Boyne, he had grave doubts of the Frenchman's military competence and personal courage. Ironically, he failed to indict his own father on the same charges.

He had one trait in common with James, however, the fatal Stuart defect of being a poor judge of character. Failing to see that he was being used, he nodded his head in agreement.

Maxwell was obviously pleased. He smiled. Draining his wine, he asked, 'Who will you send?'

'You,' said Berwick.

The smile vanished. Analysing his position, Maxwell decided he was hoist on his own petard, that he had no alternative but to accept after making so strong a representation. Grim-faced, he informed the Duke. 'I will make immediate preparations for my departure.'

Maxwell himself came closer to being 'quenched' than the firebrands he denounced. On the trip to France, it was only the strenuous intervention by Dr John Maloney, Roman Catholic Bishop of Cork, a member of the delegation, and by Colonel Simon Luttrell, that prevented Simon's brother Henry, and Colonel Nicholas Purcell from having Maxwell thrown overboard into the sea.

When the 'firebrands' appeared at Versailles, Louis heard them patiently. He promised them that he would send a competent general in the spring for the expected summer campaign of 1691. He informed them that the Duke of Tyrconnell was then on his way back to Ireland with money and supplies, and that the war would continue. Their request for Tyrconnell's replacement was denied. To placate his cousin, James, who insisted that he had the highest faith in Tyrconnell's integrity and ability, Louis had agreed to keep the Viceroy.

Compromising adroitly, he refused to incarcerate the Luttrells and Purcell in the Bastille as James wished, and persuaded him albeit reluctantly, to issue letters patent promoting Patrick Sarsfield to Brigadier General, and naming him Earl of Lucan, Viscount Tully, and Baron of Rosbery. This was a sop to Sarsfield for not being named commander of the army.

When Tyrconnell returned to Limerick, he appointed General Dorrington as Governor of the city to replace Boisseleau who was returning to France. He then ordered the release of Lord Riverstown and Judge Daly who had been imprisoned during his absence for corresponding with the enemy, angering many of the officers. With this mischief accomplished, he departed from battered Limerick for the more comfortable unsullied Galway.

During the so crucial months before the resumption of the war, the Viceroy imitated his master at St Germaine, establishing a glamorous court life featured by sumptuous banquets, sprightly balls and joyous entertainment, all paid for by the money Louis had sent for the conduct of the war!

When Sarsfield, appointed by the Duke of Berwick as Governor of Connaught while Tyrconnell was in France, found it necessary to relieve Colonel MacDonnel of command of Galway for communicating with the Williamites, Tyrconnell refused to punish him. In fact, the Viceroy so favoured him, that Berwick could stand his arrogant stupidity no further, and embarked for France to join his father. Thus the Stuart cause in Ireland was abandoned by even the bastard branch.

CHAPTER VI

French Arrive

Winter finally gave way to Spring. Shamrock grew and gorse flowered in the glens, the hedges were bright with hawthorn and the hedgerows were coloured by primroses and violets. There was much bird activity - lapwings, bullfinches, snipes and wagtails were all on the wing.

While nature stirred, so did the army, as hopes for the coming campaign were renewed. Regiments of horse ranged freely around Connaught, and on one daring dash eastward across the Shannon, General Sarsfield captured Birr, within the border of Leinster. Alarmed, the Williamites sent a huge expedition to relieve the town. Sarsfield prudently retired. It was largely Sarsfield's activities that secured the area west of the Shannon, providing a safe bastion for the Irish army, and maintaining a base for supplies, meagre as they were.

At the end of April came the news from France that on the 18th the French had captured the fortress of Mons. Tadhg and the others attended the Te Deum Mass in the Cathedral. Bonfires were lighted, cannon were fired, muskets discharged, and there was dancing in the streets. It was on this occasion that Dónal first met Sheila MacBrady, a refuge from near Cavan. Her mother had died when Sheila was born; her father, one of Sir Neill O'Neill's dragoons, was slain with his colonel at the crossing of the Bridge of Slane. Young Sheila had fled to Limerick in the great exodus of the Catholic civilian population after the Battle of the Boyne.

On 8 May arrived the new French general and supplies that Louis had promised. The squadron of men-of-war sailed into the Shannon, where about 150 officers and like number of cadets, along with 25 surgeons, 300 Loyalist Scots and English, 175 stone masons, twenty cannoneers, and two bombardiers, a curious combination, disembarked, to the loud rejoicing of the garrison and inhabitants of Limerick. It was a living refute of Tyrconnell's scoffing at the promise of additional French assistance.

Although there was neither money nor men beyond the specialists mentioned, a great disappointment indeed, there were twenty pieces of cannon, 16,000 muskets and some lead and ball. For the cavalry there were 800 horses, 12,000 horseshoes, and 5,000 saddles and bridles. In addition, there were miscellaneous supplies, including a large supply of urgently needed biscuit, and enough uniforms, stockings and shoes for 16,000 men.

What brought the most rejoicing, however, was the arrival of General St Ruth, a veteran of the wars in France, Flanders, Germany and Holland. With the most reluctant consent of James, he assumed the military command from Tyrconnell, who retained his civilian authority as Viceroy.

More competent than the rough Rosen, and infinitely superior to the arrogant popinjay, Lauzun, he immediately started to rebuild the army. He shuttled between Limerick, Athlone and Galway, energetically preparing for the inevitable conflict with the Williamites.

In spite of his admirable qualities, the disappointed Irish were soon to learn that he had two characteristics which tended to undo much of the good. One was his insistence on the strictest discipline, hanging soldiers for the slightest breaches, until the ghastly, diurnal spectacle of hanged Irish soldiers suspended from gallows or trees, caused great resentment and anger.

The second, and most serious, was his vanity. Because of his vast military experience, he refused to take advice from inferior officers, especially the Irish. Sensitive to his position as 'Le General' and desiring to be first in all phases, he resented Sarsfield's great popularity with the Irish troops. Because of this jealousy, he emulated Tyrconnell by disregarding his advice and suggestions, and giving him as little responsibility as possible.

CHAPTER VII

Siobhán Again

In June both armies, as if by mutual agreement, headed towards Athlone, the northern anchor in the Limerick Athlone line of defence. Stopping briefly at Ballymore, some eight miles from Athlone where about a thousand men were garrisoned under the command of Colonel Ulick Burke, the Williamites called upon the town to surrender under honourable terms.

The new commander of the English Army, Baron Jodert de Ginkel, then marched his army to Athlone. Of a noble family, Ginkel had the title of Baron van Reede. He had accompanied William from the Netherlands to England in 1688, and had commanded a body of Dutch cavalry at the Boyne.

General Ginkel, a strong advocate of the massive use of artillery, had assembled the most powerful and numerous train of cannons and mortars ever brought to Ireland. He had declared that he didn't intend to be bogged down at Athlone as had been the Williamite Army at Limerick the previous year. Immediately upon arrival at Athlone on 12 June, he began a heavy and concentrated shelling of the town and castle. The Chevalier de Tesse and the Marquis d'Usson commanded Athlone.

Sarsfield's men, ranging afield with the other horse regiments, learned that the Duke of Tyrconnell had arrived at Athlone from Galway where he proceeded to make certain appointments in violation of the division of authority between him and St Ruth. Word of his actions spread rapidly to the other Irish regiments, causing so much anger that the threats of the men against the Viceroy caused him to return hurriedly to Galway. But damage had already been done to St Ruth's position. One of his officers, the Marquis d'Usson, when told to tear down some old works on the western side of the Shannon in Irishtown, scornfully refused to do so, saying that it was his responsibility to defend fortifications, not destroy them.

Tadhg attended several acrimonious councils of war with Sarsfield. Because St Ruth spoke neither English or Irish, all conversations were in French. St Ruth, frustrated by Tyrconnell's interference, and insubordination by the Marquis d'Usson and other French officers, was determined to restore his authority by a great victory.

Cautioned by Sarsfield and others that the Irish Army was still not ready for such a battle, and urged to conduct hit-and-run warfare until such time as the recruits gained battle experience, St Ruth reacted by rejecting their advice completely, and relegating Sarsfield to minor assignments and responsibilities.

Sarsfield was greatly concerned about the enemy crossing the river, to which the Frenchman replied sarcastically, 'M. le General, it is impossible for the enemy to ford the river, and if Ginkel tries, his master should hang him, and if he succeeds, my master should hang me.'

It was at this meeting that Sarsfield, having learned that General Maxwell was in contact with General Ginkel, openly accused him of treachery in the face of the enemy. Because Maxwell was a close friend of Tyrconnell, St Ruth refused to act on the charge. Consequently, he was left in charge of his regiment.

Jealous of Sarsfield's popularity with the soldiers, General St Ruth tried to win them to him by cancelling his order of death by hanging as the penalty for infractions of discipline. This helped, but the Irish dislike of their French commander and his countrymen had reached the point that much greater concessions would be needed to restore their previous cordial relations.

While the Irish forces were torn by dissension, General Ginkel's men were not idle. Their constantly booming guns pounded at the town and the fortifications. Deciding that the process of destruction was too slow, Ginkel ordered his engineers to prepare a strong wooden bridge to be placed over the broken arches of the old bridge over the Shannon leading into the western part of the town. This they accomplished in the dark of the night of 27 June.

The next morning the Irish on the walls were shocked to see some of the Rebel engineers furiously nailing the last planks into place. In the distance they observed the Williamites assembling their forces for a large-scale attack, and the dimensions of the bridge were such that it would have allowed large numbers of men to cross simultaneously. For a stunned minute there was consternation in the Irish ranks at the bridge. Unless something drastic was done quickly, the fall of Athlone was imminent.

Among the men closest to the bridge was Sean O'Carroll, one of Cathal O'Flaherty's Rapparees who had joined the Earl of Boffin's Regiment, and who later related the action to Tadhg.

'We had heard the noise during the night,' he began, 'but it wasn't until dawn that we saw what they were doing. They must have built most of the bridge elsewhere, then dragged it up in the darkness. Some of their carpenters were trying to put the last planks into place when we discovered them. We fired on the carpenters, killing some. But this wasn't enough because whole regiments were massed a short distance away, ready to march, and their infernal cannons were firing at us all the time. We all stood there stupidly and stared at each other, dismayed at the prospect of losing Athlone.'

'Then an old Sergeant, Custume was his name, said to the officer in charge, "Give me ten men and some tools and we'll go out and cut that bridge down." The officer stared at him, and said, 'It's certain death, Sergeant.' And the Sergeant replies, "So it is, sir, but get me the tools." And the officer quickly got him some axes, saws and weapons, and ten men jumped up to volunteer.'

O'Carroll shook his head with awe as he recalled the incident. 'We opened a sally-port, and those eleven men dashed out on the bridge. When the enemy saw what they were trying to do, practically their whole army turned their weapons on them. Cannonballs and bombs were rained on them while their musketeers used them for target practice. After a few minutes a gust of wind blew away the smoke momentarily, and we could see that they were all dead, their bodies scattered about. Then the Rebels began to cheer because some of the beams were still intact. Again we stood there undecided, mouths open. Once more a brave man emerged, a Sergeant Gallagher, of Tyrconnell's Regiment, calling for volunteers.'

'I know him,' Tadhg interrupted excitedly. 'We were at Derry together.'

'A brave man, surely,' O'Carroll said, resuming his story. 'In a flash he had ten more volunteers at his side. As they ran to the bridge, some were picked off by musket fire or shells, but three or four managed to get to the timbers. In the face of a deadly fire they chopped away at the beams, then with their bodies wrested them loose, and threw the timbers into the river below. Only two of them made their return safely. But this time it was our turn to cheer.'

'Was Sergeant Gallagher one of the two?' Tadhg inquired.

O'Carroll shook his head sadly.

'Well,' said Tadhg, 'none of his beloved pikemen could help him there. But he died as a hero for his country. What more could a man ask? I will go immediately to the Church and pray for his soul. And for all the other brave men who died on the bridge.'

On Monday, 30 June, St Ruth's and d'Usson's chickens came home to roost. Having observed that the Jacobites were neglecting the area of the ford inasmuch as their experienced French general had scoffed at the possibility of a successful crossing, Ginkel decided to risk forcing it. Crossing the river at that point was essential because he wanted to occupy those works on the back part of the town that M. d'Usson had haughtily refused to destroy. From that position he felt that he could defend the town against those Irish within the safety of the castle itself.

The Williamites massed near the river, secure in the knowledge of the laxity of their foe on the opposite side. Then the loud, clear tones of a bugle quivered in the summer air, and they began their mass movement over the Shannon. When word of their intent reached Sarsfield, he rode furiously to St Ruth's tent to seek reinforcements for the garrison. Resentful of Sarsfield's request as an implied rebuke, the Frenchman at first refused. After much valuable time was lost he finally relented, and ordered that the regiments be mustered to march to the aid of the town.

Alas, it was too late! The enemy, having crossed the Shannon, mounted the works which had been left as a gift to them, gained control of the town, and eventually the key to the defence, the castle.

As the Williamites pursued the Irish soldiers through the narrow streets, slaying them without quarter, Brigadier General Maxwell, whom Sarsfield had accused, ran out, crying, 'I'm General Maxwell, don't you know me?' Apparently the Williamites did know him, because instead of slaying him like the others, they escorted him to General Mackay to whom he surrendered his sword.

M. d'Usson, having earned the everlasting gratitude of Ginkel, tried to ride toward the town, but meeting the fleeing Irish soldiers who were running for their lives, was trampled underfoot. Carried unconscious to the regimental surgeon, emergency measures saved his life, thereby enabling him to stay in Ireland to cause more mischief.

Losing Athlone because of the monumental arrogance and stupidity of the top command, the bewildered Irish Army marched the following day several miles from Athlone where they camped. Many of the soldiers who had fled in panic, discarding their weapons, began to return shame-faced to their companions. After resting over night, they marched through Ballinasloe to the vicinity of Aughrim.

Sitting his horse on Kilcommedon Hill overlooking the village, and watching the smoke plumes rising slowly in the cool dawn air, Tadhg wondered which cabin was Siobhán O'Coffey's, and whether she had a spare egg for breakfast. At the thought of the egg, he reached into his pocket for a hard dry piece of ammunition bread, his only food. As he munched, he recalled the stormy meeting he had attended the previous day with Sarsfield in General St Ruth's tent.

The Frenchman, angry and chagrined at his loss of Athlone, blamed the defeat on the Irish regiments of Colonel Cormac O'Neill and Colonel Oliver O'Gara which had been in the works where the enemy attacked, and had fled so quickly before the advancing Williamites that there had been inadequate time for reserve to come to their assistance.

'If we are seeking a scapegoat,' Sarsfield began coldly, 'let us place the blame where it properly belongs. If we had guarded the river, Ginkel never would have crossed it. He cleverly exploited a monstrous oversight on our part. And the reason that he crossed was to seize those works which M. d'Usson refused to demolish!'

St Ruth's dark eyes smouldered. But since his recent deprecatory remark about Ginkel was still fresh in the minds of his staff officers, he found it judicious to refrain from comment.

'The Williamites have Athlone,' Sarsfield continued, 'but inasmuch as it is surrounded by bog, we can attack and harass his supply parties, thereby giving our men badly needed military experience, while gaining invaluable time to train them properly.'

But Sarsfield's suggestion had fallen on deaf ears. St Ruth had already determined that he would retrieve his tarnished reputation by a brilliant victory over the foe.

'No,' he said. 'Such tactics will gain us little. We must destroy the enemy.'

An aide set up a map of the area so that all the staff officers could see. 'Here,' said St Ruth, pointing with his forefinger, 'is a dominating height which is called Kilcommedon Hill. We will set up our camp and fortifications there. Then we will entice Ginkel and his men to attack us. Instead of a defensive operation, as it will appear to be, it will be an offensive position in which we will chop the English to pieces.'

'But our men are not ready for a major battle,' Sarsfield insisted.

'They have esprit, as you French say, and they are great natural fighters, but the most important ingredient, training, is needed before they can become an effective military force. We lost a vital battle at Newtown Butler in Ulster because of an erroneous order by an inexperienced officer. A battle we should have won became a disastrous defeat instead. Anything can happen on a battlefield which will change the course of the conflict. Let not the future of Ireland be left to chance.'

But St Ruth was adamant in his decision to fight a major battle. In vain did Sarsfield plead that a largely untrained army, ill equipped and half-starved, should not be forced to face an enemy so superior in experience, numbers and artillery.

'Wife-beater!' Captain O'Brien muttered angrily in a low tone only Tadhg could hear.

Tadhg looked at the captain questioningly. Speaking in Irish, O'Brien whispered that St Ruth had once been rebuked in open court by Louis XIV for wife-beating.

The following day the Irish army crossed over the River Suck to camp in the vicinity of Aughrim. St Ruth immediately ordered the building of breastworks in the centre of his defence line which stretched for about two miles along the base of the hill behind a bog where a small stream meandered. The old ruined castle which Tadhg and Dónal had seen almost two and a half years earlier when they had ridden to Aughrim, provided the anchor for the Irish left wing. This castle, commanding the Pass of Aughrim, was vital for the defence of the Irish forces. St Ruth's right wing was on solid ground, with the Tristane River in front. It was undoubtedly an excellent defensive position that the veteran general had selected.

Unwilling to place the blame for the loss of Athlone where it belonged squarely on his shoulders and that of his aide, d'Usson, St Ruth was determined to find some other shoulders. And as Conor bitterly pointed out to Tadhg later, where do you find a proper whipping-boy who didn't have the ear of Tyrconnell, or King James or King Louis? Why a mere Irishman, of course!

So, on 7 July, before a large part of the Army in a special formation, Lieutenant Colonel Séamus O'Neill, bearing one of the most illustrious names in Ireland, was publicly disgraced by being broken in rank to a private soldier, and ordered to serve as a common musketeer in Colonel Cormac O'Neill's regiment where he formerly was second-in-command.

His crime? St Ruth charged him with 'quitting his post at Athlone, and running away'. None had the position or temerity to remind St Ruth of his own statement about Ginkel: 'His own master should hang him for trying to ford the river, and if he succeeds, my master should hang me.'

Conor was furious about the whole episode. 'The English, Scots and French can do no wrong,' he stormed. 'When they run, like they did at the Boyne, hiding their regimental colours in their pockets, they receive promotions and honours. When an Irishman runs for his life because he has been placed in an untenable position by the stupidity of his superior officers, he is degraded. I'm getting sick right up to here,' he said, putting his finger under his chin, 'and I think I'll go back to Connemara to get away from King James's collection of incompetent fools.'

On 11 July the Rebel army appeared on the hills opposite Kilcommedon. St Ruth, confident that his strategy was sound, called a council of war. Again Sarsfield reiterated his opinion that an open battle with the Williamites was unwise. Because of Sarsfield's great popularity with the troops, St Ruth could not openly demote him for his opposition, but he could humiliate him.

Sarsfield sat in silence while St Ruth announced that the Chevalier de Tesse, who had arrived with him in May, was to be second-in-command, and was in charge of the right wing. Colonel Nicholas Sheldon, whose loyalty was suspect, was placed in charge of the left wing. St Ruth hesitated, rustling some papers, before revealing his choice for the command of the centre of the line, the obvious place for Padraig Sarsfield, whose dashing cavalry charges were his forte. The council members sat breathless until St Ruth, with flushed face, declared that Lord Galmoy would be in charge of the centre. Lord Lucan would be responsible for the horse in reserve, and would remain behind Kilcommedon Hill until called for!

'Wife-beater!' Tadhg exclaimed in anger and disgust, echoing Captain O'Brien. Some of the Irish officers, understanding what he said, looked at him with warning.

Captain O'Brien watched Sarsfield apprehensively, fearful of his reaction. But Lord Lucan's only visible response to St Ruth's implicit insult was a tightening of the jaw muscles. Then Sarsfield, stretching his great frame, and keeping himself under control as he stood up, asked St Ruth what the battle plans were. Thus addressed, the Frenchman was obliged to reply.

'I will issue them as the battle progresses,' he replied tersely. 'What we will do will depend upon the actions of the enemy and the course of the battle.'

'Shouldn't we know in advance in the event that something untoward should occur?' Sarsfield asked.

St Ruth flushed, disregarding the question. 'Messieurs, you know your positions. That will be all.'

From the hills to the east, Ginkel studied the Irish position with the aid of magnifying glasses. He recognised that St Ruth had chosen well. From its strategic position, he suspected that the wily Frenchman had more in mind than just a stout defence, for if that was his sole object, he could have moved his army back to the safety of Limerick. Uneasy about the situation, he refused to join battle.

Early on the morning of 12 August 1691, a heavy pall of grey fog separated the two armies. Some of the superstitious Irish likened it to a winding sheet, seeing it as an omen of death and disaster. Others, having heard wolves howling in the hills, claimed that they had heard the *beansí* wailing.

Despite St Ruth's open attempt to win their favour, the morale of the soldiers was low. Months of poor and inadequate food, the complete cessation of their pay as Tyrconnell squandered Louis' money in fancy living, St Ruth's ill treatment of Sarsfield, and the inexplicable and unnecessary loss of Athlone, all were on the deficit side of the ledger. They were acutely aware that the Irish Army was greatly outnumbered by the foe's twenty-seven regiments of foot, nineteen regiments of horse, and three regiments of dragoons. The enemy's superiority in cannon and mortars was so great that there was no comparison. Only their secure position at Aughrim sustained them.

The day being Sunday, regimental Mass was said in a level place where a brook chattered peacefully through the valley behind Kilcommedon Hill. When general absolution was given the men because of the impending battle, Tadhg was depressed and apprehensive. Then the chaplain raised the consecrated host high for all to see, and in ringing tones led them in a sacred promise to lay down their lives if necessary in defence of their country and their religion. With rapidly beating heart and with tears in his eyes, Tadhg looked to the broad back of Lord Lucan where he stood near the chaplain at the head of the regiment.

As he promised, in unison with the other men, Tadhg's

depression gave way to exultation, and a sense of spiritual kinship with all the members of the regiment overwhelmed him.

When the hanging curtain of fog lifted about noon, the stage was all set for the drama to start. Ginkel decided to probe the Irish defences. After several attempts were repulsed, he called a council of war. He expressed the opinion that the Irish were too firmly entrenched to be dislodged without great casualties; it would be far wiser to wait and catch them in a less formidable place. He suspected St Ruth's designs.

Then General Mackay, a Scots officer who had deserted James for William, stated his views. Less experienced than Ginkel, he was confident that an assault on the Irish positions would succeed. He advocated that an attack be launched on the Irish left, and that the old castle be captured. This would put the Williamites in the position to cross the bog in strength to attack the Irish centre.

Ginkel was sceptical, but as the majority of the council, scornful of the Irish Army, favoured the proposal, he reluctantly ordered that the plan be implemented. He himself would lead the attack on the Pass of Urrachree, the Duke of Wurtemberg the centre of the line near the morass, and General Mackay the Pass of Aughrim.

While Tadhg, Conor and Dónal, along with other horse reserves, fretted behind the crest of the hill, a force of French Huguenots attacked the Irish beyond the Pass of Urrachree. After some initial success against the foot, they were routed in a charge by Tyrconnell's and Sutherland's cavalry, and pinned down between the trapped Huguenots and the Irish foot among the hedges which blunted the attack, then stopped it completely.

Observing the plight of the Huguenots, Ginkel ordered his Dutch and Danish foot to relieve them. They charged up the slope, but the withering fire of the Irish among the hedges and defiles cut them down. Again Ginkel's offensive was stopped.

At the same time Mackay was probing the Irish defences on the right side of the Williamite line. The narrow road through the bog leading from Ballinasloe to Loughrea wound past the old castle and through the village. Bringing up a dozen cannon, Mackay divided his forces into two. One group would attack the castle and the nearby village, seeking to gain the flanks of the Irish lines, while the other group was to ford the little Meelehen River and advance to the ditch at the foot of the hill where they were ordered to hold.

The sun was low on Kilcommedon Hill when the new

Williamite attack started. General Kirk and General Gustavus Hamilton succeeded in getting as far as the ditch behind the old castle before being pinned down. General George Hamilton's regiment, aided by the cannon, then took the lightly-held village. Presently the regiments of foot led by Colonel Herbert and Colonel Earl waded the Meelehen. After meeting some heavy fire at the first ditch, surprisingly they found their way unimpeded. Enthusiastically, in defiance of their orders, they charged up the hill towards the entrenched lines of Major General Dorrington.

Then the waiting Irish snapped shut the trap. Hidden behind hedges and ditches, they opened a murderous crossfire which stopped the advance of the Rebels. At this moment De Tesse ordered a regiment of Irish horse to attack. With their sabres singing a death dirge, they charged among the confused Williamite foot. The demoralised foe fled back down the hill to the bog, leaving both Earl and Herbert among the slain, followed by the jubilant Irish musketeers and pikemen seeking revenge for Athlone and the Boyne.

With their attacks on both the Irish right and centre repulsed with great losses, the Williamites were now in danger of defeat. Only their anchors on the left side of the Irish line still held. Vexed and angry at the unexpected resistance, Mackay ordered his horse regiments to force the Pass at Aughrim. The first squadron rode out to the narrow road where only two horsemen could pass at one time, anxious eyes on the snouts of two cannon projecting threateningly from the ruins of the castle.

Some of the men, survivors of Mackay's defeat at the Pass of Killiecrankie in Scotland just two years previously, were uneasy, they felt that they were being led by Mackay to another similar slaughter. The Highlanders under Lord Dundee had waited for them, just like the Irish were doing now, to emerge from the pass, and had then fallen furiously upon them with their huge and savage claymores, driving them back into the narrow pass where nearly 2,000 of them had been killed or drowned. They had been fortunate in Scotland, however, for with Dundee dead in his own victory, there was no other leader capable of resisting the English, and Scotland was subdued by Mackay for William by the end of summer.

Apprehensively they advanced, expecting a deadly fire from the Irish hidden in the ruins. An ineffective volley greeted them instead. To their surprise and joy, they found that they were facing not bullets, but uniform buttons!

It was the usual story. When Colonel Walter Burke had been sent with two regiments of foot to occupy the castle, he had been promised cannonballs for the two field-pieces, and ammunition for the French firelocks his troops carried. When the barrels were opened, it was found that the cannonballs were of a larger calibre, and the musket ammunition was of an English type that wouldn't fit the French guns. In anger, despair and desperation, the Irish soldiers tore the buttons off their coats, and ramming them into their gun barrels, fired them at the advancing Williamites. The joy of the latter was short-lived, however, when a force of Irish horse, hidden behind the ruins, in a violent and impetuous charge, sent them fleeing back to the bog.

Watching the ebb and flow of the battle from the top of the hill, General St Ruth was jubilant as his forces repelled the foe on every front. Observing the disorganisation of the Williamites, he ordered that half of the horse reserve be brought up. Sarsfield was instructed to stay with the remainder. It was not intended that he would share in the glory.

It was then that St Ruth, his cuirass a-glitter in the bright rays of the setting sun, led the horse regiments down Kilcommodon Hill. Confident of victory, he shouted joyously, 'Le jour est a nous, mes enfants!' As the enemy scattered before them, all was propitious for a glorious Irish victory. But Atropos was waiting with her sharp scissors, it was not for nothing that the winding-sheet mist had appeared that morning!

At that desperate moment for the Williamites, with a massive defeat facing them, a Huguenot artilleryman, watching the inexorable advance of the Irish down the hill, rammed a cannonball down the hot throat of his cannon. With a muttered curse at 'The Hangman' as St Ruth was known in France for his merciless persecution of the Huguenots, he touched a light to the powder. The cannon belched, and the iron ball discharged straight into the mass of charging horsemen.

Atropos' scissors snipped, the ball went unerringly to its target. General St Ruth's exultant smile and joyous shouts vanished abruptly with his head. His decapitated body stayed upright in the saddle for a stride or two, then slowly tottered and slipped to the earth as if seeking its missing member. Shock and dismay swept the front ranks of the Irish as the general's aide-de-camp reined his horse, and dismounting, covered the body with his cloak before

407

reverently lifting it and placing it across the general's mount. Quickly, then, he led the horse and its lifeless burden to the rear. The great, triumphant wave of men and horses halted, like a spent force on the shore.

Lord Galmoy, in charge of the centre, although competent, was no Sarsfield. Where Sarsfield would have continued the charge, he sat his horse temporarily immobilised, letting victory, and the fate of Ireland, slip from his fingers. The experienced De Tesse, second-in-command to St Ruth, in charge of the right wing, was too far from the scene to know what had happened.

At this crucial time, with the scales delicately balanced, treachery raised its ugly and familiar head, tipping the pan in favour of the English. Colonel Henry Luttrell, in command of the several regiments of horse and dragoons, stationed just beyond the village of Aughrim, observed the squadrons of Mackay approaching along the narrow road through the bog. It would have been easy to attack and drive the thin file of Williamites from their precarious path into the surrounding bog, but inexplicably Luttrell ordered his regiments to abandon the solid ground, and ride off towards Loughrea instead. As he rode off on to infamy, Mackay's astonished troops swept unopposed through Aughrim Pass.

When the fleeing Williamites in the centre became suddenly aware that their enemies no longer pursued them, they turned in wonder, thankful for the totally unexpected respite. Ginkel quickly sensed that the course of battle had changed. He immediately rallied his men from their headlong retreat into a new charge on the Irish right flank. Simultaneously, thanks to the perfidious Luttrell, Mackay's horse regiments turned the Irish left flank, and sweeping into the centre of the line, drove the demoralised and bewildered Irish foot before them like sheep to the slaughter.

It was only the approaching dusk and General Sarsfield that saved the entire Jacobite Army from being annihilated. The Williamites cut down the fleeing Irish with no quarter, whole companies of foot perishing before the swinging, merciless sabres as Dutch, Danes, French Huguenots, Germans, Swedes, Scots and English soaked the fields, hills and bogs with Irish blood. The battle continued until darkness mercifully blanketed the battle field.

Lord Lucan, who had waited fretfully behind the hill as ordered, first became aware of the catastrophe when whole regiments of Irish foot poured panic-stricken down the slope. Learning that St

Ruth was dead, and no longer bound by the general's restrictive edicts, he ordered the remaining cavalry reserves to countercharge. With a loud shout, the Irish followed their leader as they swept with swords swirling into the ranks of the foe. And so fiercely did they fight that many otherwise doomed Irish soldiers were able to escape the field of carnage, many of them fleeing into the safety of the bog.

While the other surviving senior officers fled the field as best they could, Sarsfield assumed command of the broken Irish Army. Uniting his horse units with those of Lord Galmoy, he led charge after charge at the head of his troops against the foe.

Inspired by his bravery and leadership, his men performed miracles against the Williamites' superior numbers, and their deadly big cannon which now commanded the battlefield from atop the hill. When night's dark mantle covered the hills and fields and bog, Sarsfield led the Irish survivors southward with the rallying call, 'On to Limerick!'

In that first wild counterattack, with his sabre in his hand, Tadhg tried to force a path through the shouting, milling mass of men and horses to reach a Williamite officer with a plumed helmet who was apparently the regimental commander. Before he could reach him, however, Tadhg was suddenly felled from his horse by a thrust of pike. Placing his hands over his head to protect himself from the wildly kicking horses, he cowered on the blood-soaked earth.

When the tide of battle had ebbed, and the tumult ceased, he found himself among the massed bodies of the wounded, the dying and the dead. He lay quietly as the shadows lengthened on the ravaged slopes of Kilcommodon. His right shoulder throbbed painfully where the pike had penetrated. When there was little sound but the moans of the wounded and their piteous cries for assistance, he dragged himself over the uneven ground to the nearby bog, desperately seeking safe haven.

Although the brown, stinking water was chest-deep, Tadhg struggled through the muck and reeds in his attempt to get as far away from the scene of battle as possible. Sounds of bodies thrashing through the water near him indicated that there were other fugitives seeking sanctity. He clamped his teeth tightly to make the pain of his wound more bearable. He was determined to get as far away from searching Williamites as his diminishing strength would allow. Oddly, his chief concern was not for himself, but for Conor and Dónal.

As the evening chill set him to shivering violently in his wet uniform, the pain in his shoulder increased in intensity. Yet he plodded on through muck and murk until he stumbled on to solid ground. He pitched forward, completely exhausted, his head cradled in his arms.

He slept for some hours until awakened by the light touch of a hand on his body. Reaching out instinctively, he clasped hold of some one's wrist, and pulling at the arm, tumbled its owner close to him, seizing the intruder in a firm grasp. There was no resistance, but a voice said quietly in the Irish, 'Let go of me; I meant no harm.'

Tadhg slowly relaxed his grasp of the man's body, holding, however, firmly to the wrist. He sat up, peering through the darkness at the stranger. There was nothing to distinguish him from thousands of other similarly dressed small farmers but the dangling right sleeve where the arm was missing. It was probably the chief reason for his lack of resistance.

'What were you trying to do, rob or kill me?' Tadhg demanded angrily.

The stranger shook his head. 'No, sergeant, I was just feeling your heart to see if you were alive.'

His answer sounded plausible, but Tadhg was still suspicious. 'And what are you doing prowling in the bog this time of the night? You're not a soldier.'

'Not any more.' Indicating his stub of an arm, he added, 'I left the rest of this at the Boyne water.'

Tadhg was instantly apologetic. 'I am sorry that I was rough with you,' he said, releasing the man's wrist. 'But what are you doing here?'

'This is a little island in the bog where I have hidden my livestock from the thieving soldiers.'

'From the Rebels or from the Irish?' Tadhg's tone was bitter, remembering the army's frugal fare for the past several months.

'From both,' the stranger replied frankly. 'Our starving to death certainly can't help the Irish. But let us not waste time. You are wounded. I felt the crusted blood on your chest. Let me help you to where you will be safe and warm. My wife can look to your wound.'

Tadhg arose clumsily. He was tired and stiff, and his wound throbbed anew with his movement. Leaning on his guide, a tall but slender man, Tadhg was led to a cunningly hidden enclosure where bog myrtle and tall rushes grew in profusion, and a carpet of heather muffled their footsteps. Behind the waving branches Tadhg discerned in the dim light the vague forms of a cow, a horse, several sheep and some chickens. A woman's form was faintly visible where she half-hid between the horse and cow.

'Everything's all right,' the man greeted his wife. 'It's just a wounded Irish soldier, and he needs some help.'

As the woman advanced cautiously, recognition was instantaneous and mutual. 'Tadhg, *a rún*!' she exclaimed with joy, and running to him, embraced him wildly.

'Och, Siobhán Rua,' he said, kissing her soundly on the lips, 'It's grand to see you again.'

Siobhán turned to her astounded husband, her eyes shining. 'It's Tadhg O'Cuirc. The Islandman, remember? The young fisherman I told you about who made me realise that God hadn't deserted me just because I was pock-marked.' Radiant with joy, she turned again to Tadhg. 'This is the man of the house, Aodh O'Madden. We were wed six months ago on the second Sunday after Epiphany. When Aodh lost his arm, he returned to his home nearby. Everything was sour in his mouth; he thought that with but one arm all he could ever be was a beggar on the road, filling his belly as best he could, sleeping in the lonely ditches.'

Striding to her husband's side, she put her arm around him protectively so that both faced Tadhg. 'Seeing his misery, I suddenly realised what you had been trying to tell me, Tadhg, that God in His mercy bestows his bounties in strange ways. Each morning I would look down the boreen, waiting as Tadhg O'Cuirc had told me, for the right day and the right man. It was quite some time after Aodh had been back, and was walking down the boreen one bright day that I knew he was the man I was waiting for.' She smiled fondly at Aodh, adding, 'After that the poor, dear man didn't have a chance.'

Observing that O'Madden was obviously distressed by her frank discussion, Tadhg changed the subject, saying gruffly, 'The man of the house promised me that the woman of the house would look to my wound, but I'll surely bleed to death instead!'

Siobhán clapped her hand to her mouth. 'Sure, and it's the excitement of seeing you again that made me forget.' She was at Tadhg's side in a moment, gently removing the old, rotted cloth of the shirt to disclose the wound, red, swollen and suppurating.

Evidently the point of the pike had hit Tadhg high in the right shoulder, safely distant from heart or lung. Bleeding had all but stopped. Without hesitation, Siobhán reached under her kirtle, tearing off a length of linen which she dexterously applied over the wound, by wrapping it around arm and shoulder.

'Come,' she directed, 'there is little more that I can do now. It's best that you be kept warm by lying down with the sheep.'

While she soothed the frightened and bleating animals, she covered Tadhg with her own cloak. When the sheep finally settled down to sleep, the heat of their bodies gradually brought warmth to Tadhg's cold and benumbed extremities. The night passed slowly as Tadhg slept but fitfully. Aodh and Siobhán, their arms entwined, stoically endured the cold dampness under the skimpy protection of Aodh's cloak.

Just before dawn, a loud trampling noise brought all three to their feet, Tadhg with his hand on his sword, the Toledo blade, as his sabre was left behind where he had fallen at Kilcommodon. Aodh reached for his *scian*, aware that it would be of little value against armed Williamite soldiers. As they stood, with hearts beating rapidly, peering into the darkness, a large, white form emerged indistinctly from the dark bog. All three hurriedly made the sign of the cross. Fearfully Tadhg recalled the time that he and Eithne had been frightened by the Pooka. The memory calmed him somewhat, for it made him realise that the nocturnal visitor could be other than the *síoga*. But fear of the unknown overpowers rationale in the dark of the morning in an area where beings from another world prowl, dance, make love or mischief, while prudent men (and women) should be secure in their cabins. And who knows, perhaps this little island was a *Lís*, a fairy fort?

It was Siobhán, who was standing closest, that recognised it first. 'Why 'tis only a horse!' she exclaimed with relief, 'a white horse.'

With hope and wonder Tadhg approached the animal. The horse whinnied, bobbed its head several times, then gently took hold of Tadhg's arm with its teeth.

'It's Cúchulainn, my horse,' he exclaimed. 'He has come seeking me.' With awe, he caressed the animal's long bony nose. The saddle was still on, the reins dragging in the mud.

'I have heard of a horse following his master like a dog,' Aodh said, amazed, 'But never have I seen it.'

'It's a miracle, surely,' his wife added.

Tadhg stood for some time, his eyes moist, hugging Cúchulainn, who responded by nuzzling his face. Finally Siobhán persuaded Tadhg to return to his bed.

For three days they stayed in their retreat. Occasionally they heard distant shouts, or firing of pistols and muskets as the Williamites searched the area for hiding soldiers. But their little island, which from a distance resembled only rushes and shrubs growing in the bog, remained inviolate. They drank the reeking bog water, and munched on oats and raw potatoes, washed down with the skimpy milk from the cow. They dared not make a fire. Their chief concern was the sound of the animals. Where they could prevent the horses from neighing, it was difficult to control the bleating of the sheep and the mooing of the cow.

On the fourth day, Aodh left the sanctuary to reconnoitre the neighbourhood. Tadhg was embarrassed at being alone with Siobhán for the first time since their night together, of so many ages gone. Although she never alluded to it, the memory was between them like an invisible bond. When she spoke, it was of Aodh, and what a fine man he was. Tadhg, in turn, told her of his wanderings and adventures in the four corners of Ireland. When she asked him of the future, if the Sassanaigh could be driven from the land, he was faced for the first time with doubts.

'I don't know, Siobhán *a rún*. It seems as if there is a curse on Ireland. All went well until King James arrived with his English and French generals. At that time we had driven the Rebels into Derry and Enniskillen, and controlled all the rest of Ireland. Now we have only a small part of Connaught and Munster.'

'But what happened?'

Tadhg shrugged. 'Who knows? To me, there is a curse on Ireland. Others like Conor, believe there are traitors in high places. At crucial times, passes are left unguarded. There is always a shortage of supplies. We never get enough cannon. Or when we have cannon, there are few, if any, balls to fit them. Garrisons are established with only a handful of men and inadequate supplies. When traitors are arrested, the Viceroy turns them loose. At Athlone it was his friend General Maxwell. While the Irish around him were cut down without quarter, Maxwell was captured alive. And so it goes from one misfortune to another.'

'The dirty villains!' Siobhán exclaimed, her face contorted with anger. 'It seems there are too many foreigners in charge of our

413

army and not enough Gaels.'

'You talk like Conor O'Donnell.'

Their conversation was interrupted by Aodh's return. He was grave but excited. Some of the Williamites were still in the village; many who were camped about the countryside, getting ready to leave for a siege of Galway; their cabin was occupied by a Dutch lieutenant of the Blue Guards; the battle had been a great slaughter and defeat of the Irish; many of the bodies lay unburied where they had fallen; it was rumoured that Colonel Gordon O'Neill, whose mother was a Gordon, had been found on the battlefield (where he had been left for dead) by some Scots officers who recognised him from his similarity to his mother, and had been secreted to keep him from being taken prisoner; the dead had been stripped of their clothes and valuables, so that at night the dogs and wolves from miles around feasted on the bloated corpses, and in the day it was the crows who ate their fill; most of the Irish army had escaped, thanks to Patrick Sarsfield; the Irish had fled back to Limerick, where their plight was desperate; by their victory at Aughrim, the Williamites were in position to control practically all of Connaught.

The tidings that the Irish army was still intact, although badly mauled, was enough for Tadhg. He informed the O'Maddens that he would have to leave them and make his way to Limerick.

'But you can't go, your shoulder isn't healed,' Siobhán protested.

'And the countryside is full of English,' Aodh added.

Tadhg sighed. He was despondent at the information Aodh had brought, but was concerned about Conor and Dónal, and the army. 'I know that, *a chara*, but I am an Irish soldier. My place is with my regiment and my country. More than ever each able-bodied man is needed.'

Aodh looked regretfully at his empty sleeve. 'I wish that I could go with you, but a one-armed soldier is of little value. If you insist on going, at least wait until night falls. I will guide you, for this is O'Madden territory.'

The day passed all too slowly for the impatient Tadhg. When night's encompassing mantle covered the bog, whose dark waters were matched by the darkness of the sky, Tadhg took leave of Siobhán. Her eyes brimmed with tears, and she clung to him. 'Arrah,' he growled, 'do you always have to cry when I depart? You act like I will never see you again. I'll stop by on my way home when this war is over to thank you again for taking care of me. If it wasn't for your help, the food, the protection, I never would have survived.'

'Ah, Tadhg, I'm forever saying goodbye. The other time it was you who said "*Slan leat*, but not *slan leat go deo*". And you came back. So now it will be Siobhán who bids you *slan leat*, Tadhg O'Cuirc, but not *slan leat go deo*.'

Impulsively he lifted her head to his and kissed her on the mouth. Her lips were cool, and she touched him lightly, and Tadhg knew that her marriage to Aodh was a success. For a moment she was passive, then she thrust him gently away from her. 'God bless you, Tadhg, and guide you safe.'

Aodh watched the embrace without comment. Then they waded slowly into the bog, the mud sucking at their feet. Tadhg tied the remnants of his boots to his saddle (the soles were long since gone and only the tops remained) and led Cuchaillin behind him. His guide kept his crude brogues on his feet; the bog water would take out the stiffness. When they had emerged from the bog, they were nearly overwhelmed by the stench of the bodies dotting the hillside and plain along the road to Loughrea.

Aodh pointed. "Tis whispered in Aughrim that three old hags, strangers in town, were seen during the battle. Suddenly they changed to crows and flew to the top of the Old Castle, awaiting their chance to feast on the dead.'

Looking about him apprehensively, Tadhg shivered. 'I have heard of them. They are the three old war goddesses, Macha, Bodb and Anann. Long before the battle was decided, they knew it would be a great slaughter.'

With his nostrils clenched between thumb and forefingers, Aodh led their course to the southwest, keeping to the loneliest, most barren hills and boreens where scarcely a cottage was found. Campfires twinkled in the east where the Williamites lay, their bellies full of the flesh of the cows and sheep pillaged from the Irish farmers. Tadhg cursed them under his breath.

An occasional dog barked at them as they scurried by inhabited places. From the camps and billets of the English army scattered along their route they could hear shouting in a half-dozen languages, or muttered oaths, or the cheerful sound of revelry of those fortunate enough to have discovered wine or whiskey in their foraging. The presence of the Williamites on Irish soil angered Tadhg, but his chief torment was the tantalising aroma of roasting meat that drifted to him from the campfires.

Hungry, fearful and cold, he plodded on, his wounded shoulder aching like a sore tooth. When he thought of the source of his wound, he was reminded of that ardent exponent of the pike, Sergeant Gallagher, and was saddened to think he would never hear his cheerful, booming voice again.

When they came upon an occasional patch of green grass, he would stop and let Cúchulainn graze while he would chew on his carefully nurtured small horde of raw barley and potatoes. If there was sound or movement of any kind, they would pause until it ceased.

After night had grudgingly given way to dawn, Aodh took leave of Tadhg. 'You are on Slieve Aughty,' he said, 'where you can hide safely today. To the south,' and he pointed with his good arm, 'is Slieve Bernagh. When night comes again you can travel that far, and once you're there you can practically spit down to Limerick. I'm sorry I can't go with you.' His voice trailed away as he looked at his empty sleeve, a habit he had.

Tadhg embraced him, thanking him for his help and his guidance. 'It is nothing compared to what you did for Siobhán,' Aodh said. 'Her neighbours have told me, some of them with sly glances, what a changed woman she was after the giant young stranger from Connemara visited her. When she speaks of you, as she has many times, a glow comes over her. She is a fine woman, Tadhg O'Cuirc, and it's happy I am that I married her.'

With that, he turned abruptly and left Tadhg alone on the mountain. From his craggy perch, he watched Aodh descend until he disappeared into the distance. The hours dragged, but the sun shone frequently, warming Tadhg as he fitfully dozed in his soft bed of heather. He thought often of Dónal Óg and Conor and Padraig Sarsfield. Were they alive and safe? What of the Irish army? Would it rally to fight again? And what of poor Ireland desperately trying to arise, only to be beaten prostrate and bleeding again?

From his lofty lair he saw the English foraging parties as they methodically combed the countryside for provender and plunder. Dark plumes of smoke ascended from cottages they had pillaged and then burned. On the roads small knots of dispossessed country people wandered seeking food and shelter.

Grieving at the plight of the innocent victims of the war, Tadhg writhed at his helplessness, aware that he could do nothing for them, and apprehensive as to any future help from the defeated

Irish army.

When night came again triumphantly from out of the east, pushing the last resisting pockets of day out over the Atlantic to the west, Tadhg resumed his journey. Here there were no campfires of the enemy. Apparently it was within striking distance of the Irish horse, and therefore neutral country. Yet Tadhg traversed the area carefully in fear of suddenly stumbling into an enemy party.

As Aodh had predicted, he reached the foothills of Slieve Bernagh before dawn. Finding a secluded place to hide, he lay quietly all day, conserving his strength. He tied Cúchulainn's reins to his ankle to keep the horse from straying. Late in the afternoon his good luck ran out, and the clouds opened, dumping a cold, penetrating rain over the mountains, leaving him wet, cold and miserable in his tattered garments.

The rain was still pouring when darkness arrived, and he descended from Slieve Bernagh. But perhaps it was a blessing in disguise for few patrols would venture forth in such dirty weather. Tadhg and his horse travelled the wet fields, the edges of the bogs, and the ditches at the side of the roads as they plodded on towards Limerick. They halted often, with Tadhg caressing Cúchulainn's velvet flank, or whispering confidently in his ear, to keep him quiet. The horse responded by nuzzling Tadhg gently as if he in turn wanted to reassure his master.

The first, faint rays of dawn were in the eastern sky when they neared the reedy shores of Lough Doon. Cúchulainn's pace quickened at the smell of fresh water. Splashing into the shallows, Tadhg let the reins loose to allow the horse to drink. While his mount thrust his muzzle eagerly into the cool water, Tadhg became aware of a faint sound, which as he listened intently, gradually became the muffled beat of horses' hooves, the creaking of saddles, the hushed conversation of men, and the laboured breathing of the animals.

Tadhg stiffened in the saddle, drawing the reins up short on the surprised and discomfited Cúchulainn. In the dim light a cavalcade of horsemen swept around the bend of the lake shore, and quickly disappeared behind a grove of trees. Apparently they hadn't seen him. After a few minutes, Tadhg cautiously followed. A hubbub from beyond the trees made Tadhg stop and look. They had started to make camp. An officer was bawling orders, and the soldiers methodically went about their assigned duties. Some hobbled the

417

horses, others were gathering wood for a fire, the cooks started preparing the food, and two who were supposed to be sentries were more interested in their coming breakfast than in being on the alert. They were Williamites, and from their accent, apparently Enniskilleners, fanatic Protestants all. They had been among the first to declare for William. Although routed in all skirmishes and battles with the forces of General Hamilton at the beginning of the war, they arrogantly boasted of the defeat and slaughter of the Irish order under Lord Boffin at Newton-Butler when a wrong order given by a confused officer caused the Irish to turn completely about and march to the rear rather than march merely to the right. Of all the forces fighting the Irish, Tadhg hated the Enniskilleners the most.

As Tadhg watched, the fire kindled, and soon the aroma of cooking meat wafted maddeningly to his nostrils. He was acutely aware that it was dangerous to stay there, any minute Cúchulainn might whinny, or one of the sentries come upon him, but the smell of the food kept him spellbound. Then two men approached with shovels, and as Tadhg waited, they stopped short of him and started to dig a long, narrow trench. Grunting and swearing as they worked, they threw the soil to the rear. When they had completed their task and withdrew, the puzzled Tadhg saw the officer walk towards him. He was whistling jauntily, and from his actions had not seen Tadhg. The man certainly showed no alarm, but where was he going? He had discarded his headpiece, but wore a tunic with gold curlicues and gaudy epaulettes.

When the officer stopped at the trench, unbuckling his belt and letting it drop to the ground with his pistol and sword, the mystery was solved. He had come to answer the call of nature! Tadhg grinned as the other man dropped his pantaloons and squatted over the trench. As the hated Enniskillener was so close, Tadhg could no longer resist the urge for revenge. He reached out from behind the thick tree trunk, quickly grasping the man by the throat. The officer struggled furiously, kicking and writhing, vainly trying to tear Tadhg's merciless hands from his throat. Faint, guttural sounds came from his tortured throat as he tried to shout a warning, but none heard.

His convulsive movements lessening, the Williamite fought a losing battle for his life. Then he became limp. After some moments, his anger and hate dissipated, Tadhg dropped the lifeless body to the earth. He stared dispassionately at the round face, now florid, the cold, icy blue eyes, the protruding tongue. The Enniskillener was not tall, but was big of torso. Impulsively Tadhg rolled the body over, taking the tunic, and putting it on himself. It was short and a tight fit, but was wearable.

When Tadhg buckled the belt, with the weapons, and turned to leave, the memory of all the unburied Irish bodies on Kilcommodon Hill inexplicably came to his mind. He looked down at the corpse. His hatred of Enniskilleners surged again. Then a malicious grin spread over his face. What could be more appropriate, he thought, for an Enniskillener's grave than a latrine! With macabre humour, he rolled the body into the ditch.

In a moment he was astride Cúchulainn, determined to leave further temptation behind. He knew that the soldiers, although uneasy at their officer's absence, would wait some time before invading his privacy. Once discovered, it would be unlikely they would seek to find the perpetrator of the deed since Irish patrols could be in the vicinity. Skirting the edge of the lake, he was soon once more on his way to Limerick.

In an hour he was at O'Briensbridge, where, a year earlier, he had ridden with Sarsfield on his way to Ballyneety. The Shannon rolled peacefully on its eternal quest of the distant sea; the sun peeked over the crest of Slievekimalta, called Keeper Hill, where Sarsfield's men had hidden; smoke curled gracefully from scores of campfires of the Jacobite Army squatting on the hospitable plains before Limerick. In such a peaceful setting, the distant hill of Kilcommodon, with its abandoned, decaying corpses seemed to Tadhg a grotesque figment of a bad dream.

Meeting a troop of Galmoy's horse, Tadhg learned that his regiment, what was left of it, was encamped near Sixmilebridge. He informed the lieutenant of the enemy patrol at Lough Doon. Then, giving Cúchulainn his head, the big white stallion stretched his legs for the first time since the battle. Within the hour, Tadhg was at the camp, and in a few short minutes, wildly embracing Conor and Dónal, who, amidst alternate fits of crying and laughing, informed him that they had attended a requiem mass for him, and the other dead of Aughrim, that very morning at St Mary's Church in Limerick!

Inevitably they arrived at the big question, what happened to you and where have you been? 'I was right behind you during the charge,' Dónal said, 'and then,' he snapped his fingers, 'you disappeared just like that. There was nothing that I could do.'

Tadhg grinned. 'Remember Sergeant Gallagher? The one who instructed us in the use of the pike? Well, it was a thrust of pike that knocked me off my horse. I'm a believer now!'

Conor stared at Cuchaillin, nibbling at the grass. Pointing at the horse, he asked, a puzzled question in his eyes, 'If you were toppled from your mount, how did you retrieve him?'

'That,' said Tadhg, becoming serious, 'was a miracle of God.' He then related how he had escaped from the field where the Rebels had dispatched many of the wounded Irish, and how he had struggled into the safety of the bog. He described his fortuitous meeting with Aodh and Siobhán O'Madden, the miraculous appearance of Cúchulainn, and his nocturnal travels back to the regiment.

'The Gentle Jesus was rewarding Tadhg for his kindness to the Widow O'Coffey,' Dónal exclaimed rapturously. 'Because Tadhg helped her when she was sad and dispirited, she was there to help him in his hour of need.' He was thoughtful a moment, then added. 'From now on I am going to be more considerate of people.'

Conor frowned. 'You're going to be more considerate of others so that they will be considerate of you? If you're going to be kind to others on that selfish basis, you will find, Dónal Óg, that God will not respond. Be kind for kindness' sake, not for your own.'

Clearing his throat nervously, Tadhg asked the question he had been dreading. 'Is Colonel Sarsfield alive and well?'

'No English sword has been fashioned nor cannonball cast that can kill Rory O'More's grandson,' Conor said. 'Of course he's alive and well. If it wasn't for him taking command after that conceited Frenchman was killed, there would be no Irish army left to carry on the fight. He rallied the men, holding back the Sassanaigh until the foot were able to flee safely. Many a man here owes his life and liberty to him today.'

Tadhg sighed happily. 'It's time to report to the adjutant that I am back.'

St Archange, the adjutant, stared with unbelieving eyes as Tadhg, in the gay tunic of the Enniskillener, entered the tent.

'Sergeant O'Cuirc, returned from the dead!' he exclaimed. 'I saw you fall on the field of battle.' Then he smiled broadly, and seizing a pen, dipped it into an open inkwell with a gay flourish, saying, 'Back on the regimental rolls goes your name.' He wrote quickly, then rising, grasped Tadhg by the elbow. 'Come with me,' he directed. 'M. le General will be delighted to see you again.'

M le General, surrounded by a bevy of staff officers, frowned at the interruption, but upon seeing Tadhg, leaped to his feet, and with several swift strides of his long legs, reached Tadhg's side.

Grasping Tadhg's shoulders firmly, to the surprise of the other officers, Sarsfield shook him vigorously, and with twinkling eyes belying his words, said sternly, 'So that's what happened to you, Sergeant O'Cuirc, you have deserted me for the Enniskilleners.' Then noting Tadhg's twinge as his tight grasp brought agonising pain to the injured shoulder, he asked, worriedly, 'What's the matter? Are you ill?'

'My shoulder, sir. A pike wound.'

Sarsfield relaxed his grip at once. 'Why didn't you tell me?' He turned to the other officers. 'Remember when St Padraig baptised Aengus, the King of Munster, and accidentally and unbeknownst stuck the sharp point of his crozier through the King's foot? The King stood unflinchingly until the end of the baptismal ceremony, and when the Saint observed what he had done, he was horrified. "Why didn't you say something?" he asked. And the King replied simply, "I thought it was part of the baptism".'

Tadhg smiled. 'But I'm not a king, sir.'

'Not a king?' Sarsfield pretended incredulity. 'Why all those of the royal line of the Milesians claim to be descendants of kings.'

'Then I must be the King of Aherlow,' Tadhg replied, laughing, 'for that is where the O'Cuircs lived.'

'It is nearly time to eat,' Sarsfield informed his staff members, 'Why don't we resume our operations afterwards?'

As the officers gathered their papers, Tadhg also started to leave. 'Not you, King of Aherlow. We will dine together.'

Tadhg stood aghast. Dine with his commander! It was unprecedented. 'I am overwhelmed by the honour, *a dhuine uasail*,' he said, his voice faltering.

As they dined in Sarsfield's tent, served by an orderly, the general talked. He had lost weight, his face was gaunt from fatigue; his expressive eyes mirrored his concern over the desperate condition of the army. He talked of many things, his hopes, his views, his worries, and Tadhg realised that he needed someone to whom he could pour out his problems. Tadhg listened quietly, and only when Sarsfield sadly referred to the death of his uncle, Colonel Charles Moore, did he interrupt with a question.

'I'm sorry, sir, but I did not know. When did it happen?'

'At Aughrim. Along with many another brave soldier and true

son of Erin. He was Old Rory's son. We suffered a terrible blow there, Tadhg, at Aughrim. It might have been mortal to Ireland's cause. In addition to General St Ruth among the slain were the Lords Dillon and Roche, Brigadiers Maurice O'Connell and Henry O'Neill. There were fourteen Colonels killed: Cúchonaught Maguire, David Burke, Daniel MacCarthy, Felix O'Neill, Ulick Byrne, Walter Nugent, Piers Mulledy, James Talbot, John Massey, Thomas Mahony, Peter Delahide, James Purcell, Oxburgh and Sir John Everard. That's quite a parcel of high-ranking officers.'

'Can they be replaced, sir?'

'Perhaps if we had more time. But that isn't all the bad news. Listed among the missing are many that we know, and some that we assume, have been captured.' He held up his left arm, counting on his fingers with his right. 'Three Burkes, two of them named William, and Colonel John Burke, Lord Boffin, three Butlers, Colonel Thomas Butler of Kilcash, his brother, Lieutenant Colonel John Butler, and Major Edmund Butler.'

'Pardon me, sir,' Tadhg interrupted. 'Did you say Lieutenant Edmund Butler?'

'No, Major Edmund Butler,' Sarsfield continued counting. ' Brigadier Gordon O'Neill, Colonel Cormack O'Neill and Colonel Daniel O'Neill. Then there are Major General Dorrington, Major General John Hamilton, Lord Slane, Lord Kilmaine, Lord Kenmare, Lord Galway, Lord Bellew, Brigadiers Tuite and Barker, and Colonels Edmund O'Madden, O'Connell, Grace and Bellew. But why go on? The list is endless. We left more than five thousand men on the slopes of Kilcommodon, including many almost-impossible-to-replace veteran sergeants. The thirty one colours and the eleven standards we lost indicate the magnitude of our defeat.' His face was wry as he added, 'Not to mention the nine cannon, and practically all our tents and baggage. We escaped with only our skins.'

'And our honour, sir,' Tadhg said gently.

Sarsfield looked up sharply. 'Yes. And our honour. Above all with our honour, although tarnished by men like Henry Luttrell.'

Tadhg looked questioningly at Sarsfield. The general's face was grim. 'Haven't you heard? Oh yes, I forget that you just returned from the dead. Luttrell's conduct at Aughrim was suspect, and yesterday he was arrested by General d'Usson for having proposed surrendering Limerick. He was tried by a court-martial and has been sentenced to be shot.'

'Yet he was one of those who supported you against the Viceroy!' Tadhg was aghast at the revelation.

Sarsfield shook his head sadly. 'An old friend. Our families have long been friends and neighbours near Dublin. That makes his treachery harder to believe!'

'What do we do now, sir?'

'Try to assemble the pieces as best we can. That is, if we are allowed to. The Viceroy has finally returned to Limerick from Galway. Who knows what mischief he can concoct?'

But Tyrconnell's days of mischief were over. He was now but a caricature of the energetic, ambitious and capable lieutenant of James II who had organised Ireland for his monarch. Tadhg was shocked when he saw him: He was corpulent, his face puffy and flushed, his eyes dull. Like Ireland, he was in decline. Discredited, mistrusted and despised, the Viceroy's influence was minimal despite his representing James's authority in Ireland.

As the inhabitants of Limerick and its garrison feverishly prepared for a second siege, and the horse regiments ranged the adjacent areas of Kerry and Clare, Ginkel's Army appeared at Galway. The ancient city of the tribes which had danced gaily to Tyrconnell's tune, was ill-equipped for resistance. The garrison under the command of the Earl of Clanrickarde was small, the few old guns on the wall obsolete, and supplies of food and ammunition short. After long and acrimonious debate between the defenders, it was deemed best to surrender. Thus it was that on 24 August just twelve days after Aughrim, the flag of William III waved over the capital of Connaught. In addition to Limerick, only Sligo to the north still remained in the hands of the Jacobites.

The Irish were bitter over the loss of Galway. If Tyrconnell had spent his time organising for its defence, instead of spending Louis' money for organising balls and fetes, it would have resisted longer, thereby giving a respite to Limerick, where the garrison each day looked longingly to the Shannon for the arrival of the expected French fleet with the much-needed supplies.

Added to the anger was shame. Baldearg O'Donnell, bearer of an illustrious Ulster Irish name, had besmirched the Clan O'Donnell by selling out to Ginkel for a reward of £500 pounds a year instead of coming to the aid of Galway with his force of 4,000 irregulars and Rapparees. To prove his loyalty to his new master, William of Orange, he emphasised his perfidy by joining the English attack on Irish-held Sligo. In rage and despair, Tadhg composed a poem in which he called upon Cuchaillin, the great Ulster warrior to return once more to earth to destroy the infamous 'Redmouth'.

When Conor read the poem, his only comment was, 'I see that the price has gone up.'

'What price?' Tadhg asked.

'Judas Iscariot received only thirty pieces of silver. Judas O'Donnell got five hundred.

Although General Sarsfield didn't accompany them, he was far too busy helping plan the defence of Limerick, elements of his regiment made sorties into the surrounding countryside in the double duty of reconnoitring the enemy and bringing in supplies. On St Laurence's Day, 10 August, Tadhg and his companions returned from a forage trip with a squadron under Captain John MacNamara to the camp area which seethed with excitement. The Viceroy, while in his quarters after returning from his devotions at St Mary's, had an apoplectic seizure, and was not expected to live.

'Och, the poor fellow,' Dónal said. 'Isn't it sad?' 'Yes,' said Conor, 'it's very sad. Sad that it didn't happen two years ago!'

Tadhg was horrified at Conor's bluntness. 'You're the hard man,' he said disapprovingly. 'God will punish you for your cruelty.'

'Cruelty, is it? Well, then I hope God is punishing that Talbot for his cruelty against Ireland. If he hadn't interfered with Sarsfield, if he hadn't taken the cannon and the French out of Limerick a year ago, if he hadn't squandered the money and supplies Louis sent, if he hadn't supported and protected all of those traitors, if he hadn't let St Ruth, the hangman, risk the Irish Army at Aughrim, poor Ireland wouldn't be in the desperate situation it is now.'

But the Viceroy didn't die that night as expected. Rallying, he regained his speech, and although feeble, tried to exercise his authority. Some of the Irish prayed for his recovery; most wished that he would die. Captain O'Brien declared that it was only the Lord Lieutenant's perversity that kept him alive.

Four days later, about midnight, his confessor was hurriedly summoned, and Richard Talbot, the Duke of Tyrconnell, Viceroy of Ireland, having attained the age of 67 years, severed his allegiance to the his earthly king, and in the words of Father Taafe, entered into the Kingdom of God. He was hastily buried in a secret grave at St Munchin's old church outside the castle walls. Thus departed Richard Talbot, who for better or for worse, had played a major role in James Stuart's attempt to regain his crown.

With Tyrconnell's death, the Marquis d'Usson, whose gross negligence had contributed greatly to the loss of Athlone, assumed command of Limerick. As Conor cynically commented, it was a continuation of the same old pattern.

The long-awaited arrival of Ginkel's army occurred on 27 August when it appeared on the eastern side of the Shannon. In some ways it was a repetition of the year before. Only this time it was Ginkel instead of William; he had a larger, better-equipped force; and the Irish Army was smaller, weaker, and inferior to the army of 1690. Within hours the English artillery resumed its interrupted bombardment of the garrison and the inhabitants. It seemed, as one dejected citizen remarked, but yesterday that the English had departed, and here they were again.

Ginkel sent a trumpeter shortly after his arrival to request a cessation of fire so that a message could be delivered to d'Usson. The message was brief and to the point: If Henry Luttrell was put to death for having made friendly overtures to the English, Ginkel's army would revenge the deed on the Irish.

The arrogant demand provoked a stormy session of the small council where many of the members insisted that the ultimatum be rejected, but cooler heads pointed out that Ginkel was known as a cruel man, and with the large number of Irish prisoners he had captured at Aughrim, he could well execute his threat. Luttrell's sentence was consequently commuted to imprisonment until 'King James's pleasure would be known'. As James disliked the prisoner, it was considered a delayed death sentence.

The hellish bombardment continued day and night, but with the rains due to commence, the beleaguered city still resisted, hoping that Ginkel would be forced into winter quarters. With hope eternal, the Irish looked to the future and to the arrival of the French fleet.

Two days after Ginkel's arrival, Tadhg was summoned to Sarsfield's tent. The general's eyes were bloodshot from lack of sleep; deep lines etched into his face. He smiled with pleasure when Tadhg was ushered into his presence.

'Sit down, Sergeant O'Cuirc,' he greeted him graciously. 'I have a special mission for you.'

'I will be most happy to serve you, sir.'

Sarsfield leaned back in his chair, his long legs crossed. 'Do you remember that day we first met? On the road near Tipperary?'

Tadhg nodded.

'You mimicked me so well that poor Roger had difficulty in believing that it was not me that was speaking. Now I need a man who can pass as an Englishman to go into the area held by William's forces to seek certain information. I believe that you are that man.'

'What information, sir?' Tadhg inquired cautiously.

'Phases of surrender terms.'

'Surrender terms?' Tadhg was aghast. He shook his head in disbelief. 'You can't be serious, sir. It was you who consistently opposed the Lord Lieutenant and all the others, including the most recent, Colonel Luttrell, when they proposed to sell out their country. It can't be ...' His voice trailed away. He was too shocked to continue.

Sarsfield's long face was sad as he sat quietly for a few minutes. Tadhg watched him with anxious eyes. Finally the general asked mildly, 'Do you think we should surrender Limerick?'

'No sir!' The reply was instant and emphatic.

'Why not?'

Tadhg's blue eyes bored into Sarsfield's. 'It would be giving up the country to the Sassanaigh again. Every man who had died fighting for Ireland will have died fighting in vain. We would be no better than the Viceroy and the other traitors whom we despised for wanting to surrender.'

'You would recommend that we continue fighting?'

'While we still have a chance, sir.'

Sarsfield paused. Idly playing with the ends of his cravat, he appeared lost in thought. His deep blue eyes were pensive, the oval face a portrait of melancholy. Then he sat back in his chair, folding his arms over his breast.

'In the past, Tadhg, as you know, I have always opposed every suggestion of surrender, and have castigated those who advocated it. In my opinion, these men, and there were many in high places, considered surrendering to William of Orange merely to retain their great estates and high positions. They were not concerned with the welfare of Ireland.'

'That's what Conor O'Donnell says,' Tadhg exclaimed, happy that the general's views coincided with those of his friend. 'He claims,' and Tadhg's face was red with embarrassment, 'that those gentlemen of English and Norman blood will betray the Irish again as they have in the past. Even the repeal of the Acts of Settlement

426

left the old Irish out. It was the Luttrells, the Dungans, the Burkes, the Hamiltons, the Powers, the Butlers, the Lords Bellew and Slane and the like who benefited.'

'And the Sarsfields?' The general's face was sad again.

Tadhg's stubborn honesty overcame his devotion to his idol. 'Yes, sir.'

'Do you recall how you thought I was stealing your horse?'

Tadhg nodded abashedly.

'You didn't think of me then as Patrick Sarsfield but as Rory O'More's grandson. The 'old Irish', you know. Will you honour me now by thinking of me as again Rory of the Hills' grandson?'

'Yes, sir, I will.'

'Good. You must first realise that we are in an extremely precarious position. We lost the flower of the army at Aughrim. We have practically no cannon. Our supplies are at a dangerous level. We are utterly dependent upon the expected French fleet. Do you play cards, sergeant? You do? Well then you do recognise that although we still hold some good cards, none of them are high. So that we have to play them most skilfully. Do you agree?'

'Oui, mon general.'

Sarsfield's eyebrows rose sardonically at Tadhg's use of the French. He continued. 'There is a growing group, and that includes many 'Old Irish', who believe we should come to terms with William whereby the Irish Army could go intact to France where it could be properly re-equipped and trained so that it could return to Ireland when the time was propitious to fight again. This group includes my, and yours, old friend Major MacKettigan. And I assure you that Roger's first and only concern is for his country.'

'I am sorry, *a thiarna*, for having doubted your motives.' Tadhg was contrite.

The general smiled. 'I'm glad to see that the O'Mores and the O'Cuircs agree on something. What I need is someone to look into my opponent's hand and see what cards he has. Because it is an extremely hazardous assignment, it is optional. I will not order you to go. The agent must be someone I can trust. He must be intelligent and resourceful. You fit the bill in these respects. In addition, your talent for mimicry is invaluable. Will you accept?'

'I am not afraid of the danger, sir, but I think you need a shrewder and more experienced man than I, for I am but a common soldier.'

Sarsfield raised his voice. 'Lieutenant St Archange, will you please bring the dossier on Sergeant O'Cuirc?'

The adjutant entered the tent. In his accented English he read from a paper: 'O'Cuirc, Tadhg Tomas. Served with courage and distinction during the campaign in Ulster where he was selected by Lieutenant Butler of Tyrconnell's Regiment for special reconnaissance. Distinguished himself at Dublin in the solution of the enemy's code, and the unmasking of a Williamite spy ring. Escorted Lady Sarsfield and party from Kilmallock to Limerick. Fought bravely at the Battle of the Breach 27 August, 1690, where he helped to rally the forces of the King.'

'Would you say that is the record of a common soldier, sergeant?'

Tadhg evaded a direct answer. 'There's a difference, sir, between using a strong arm in swinging a sabre than in contesting wits with people much smarter than I.'

'If you're not bright, as you imply, how were you able to decipher that code?' St Archange asked.

Tadhg shrugged. 'I had to,' he replied simply.

Sarsfield looked at Tadhg, a quizzical smile playing at the corners of his mouth. 'What do you say, Sergeant O'Cuirc? Don't you think that the opinions of a general and his adjutant outweigh those of just a 'common soldier'?'

Tadhg kept a straight face. 'If you phrase it that way, sir, I have no choice but to defer to your better judgement.'

The general laughed, his tenseness gone now that the issue was resolved. 'A masterly retreat, Sergeant O'Cuirc, before numerically superior forces.'

'It would be stupid of me not to, sir, and you both have convinced me that it is stupid to be stupid.'

St Archange looked sharply at Tadhg. Sarsfield put his hands to his face to hide a grin.

'Essentially what I am seeking, Sergeant, is any information which reflects the views of William or Ginkel on the possibility of the capitulation of the Irish army with honourable terms, including the choice of going to France. Feelers are being made through other channels on this subject, but the information we may receive might not be the true thoughts of the other side. I want to know exactly what cards they hold. I want to know what they are thinking, not what they are pretending. Do you follow me?'

'Yes, sir. But may I inquire what cards do we hold?'

'A fair request. First, the promised French fleet with new sinews of war. Second, the possibility of early rains and a stalemate like last year. Third, the salvage of nearly three quarters of our forces at Aughrim. Fourth, the big stakes in our game are not here in Ireland but in Europe, and an early settlement would free Ginkel and his army to return to the continent. Fifth, Ginkel is a professional soldier who is less concerned about grinding the Irish nation into dust than in concluding a successful campaign. Is that enough?'

Tadhg smiled. 'I think so, sir.'

'If it is settled, I'll turn you over to Lieutenant St Archange. He has the wherewithal to transform you into a blond Briton, a swarthy Spaniard or a dour Derryman, whatever you prefer. He will provide you with money, clothing and the necessary bona fides. The rest is up to you. I wish you the best of luck.'

As Tadhg turned to leave with the adjutant, Sarsfield reached out impulsively and placed his hand on Tadhg's shoulder. 'May God go with you,' he said, and turned abruptly.

With the conference terminated, the machinery was set in motion to fit Tadhg with a new identity, that of a buyer of cattle and hides, from the vicinity of Aylesworth in the English Midlands. A passport and other necessary papers were prepared. His black locks were bleached to brown. Then he was provided with a wig as was the mode. Lord Lucan's barber shaved off his moustache and his beard, and he was given a razor made of good Sheffield steel. He was measured by a tailor for civilian clothes.

Thus altered, he was given a hasty indoctrination in the subject of cattle, hides, with emphasis on markets, prices, values, breeds and drovers. And finally, one of the most difficult, the clandestine accumulation of a supply of gold and silver coins then being circulated in England. The project was known to but a select few, all sworn to secrecy.

Chapter VIII

The Spy

His mind crammed with the requirements of his new role, pleased at the trust placed in him by Sarsfield, and excited over the prospect of adventure, Tadhg left early in the morning via Thomond Bridge into County Clare to avoid the surveillance of spies. Cúchulainn being too conspicuous, and too valuable to lose, Tadhg was mounted on a grey cob which had a penchant for stopping suddenly at the roadside to nibble on clumps of grass. He covered the Shannon at Portumna, on the north end of Lough Derg, and swinging in a wide circle, avoided Birr and Mountmellick, staying at small country inns where he practiced his English on his hosts.

With his heart beating rapidly, he rode into Athy on the third day, determined to test himself in a larger town on a well-travelled road. The inn-keeper, a red-faced, sharp-eyed, balding man named Croasdaile, scrutinised him carefully. Tadhg was worried. Was there a flaw in his disguise? Had he given himself away with some inflection of speech? Was he about to be denounced? Actually, Croasdaile was concerned about what his well-dressed and groomed guest was going to have to say when he found his rough mattress crawling with lice. Some of these Englishmen were extremely fastidious, getting fearfully upset at minor little things like fleas which the Irish traveller took in his stride.

To avoid his host, Tadhg stayed close to his room, fleas and all, and got an early start in the morning. Croasdaile, in turn, equally anxious to shun any contretemps, let the woman-of-the-house serve the meagre breakfast, and collect for the lodging. Both Tadhg and the innkeeper were happy when the traveller departed, each feeling he had successfully outmatched the other.

Tadhg's heart was heavy as he passed the poor cabins of the 'mere' Irish. Once more in the firm grasp of the Anglo-Irish aristocracy, they were again relegated to manual and servile labour. The big mansions and estates, abandoned in the spring of 1689 when Irish fortunes were high, had been reoccupied by their owners. Fields were green, cattle grazed peacefully, carriages of the wealthy rattled by on the roads; it was a far cry from the war-devastated Clare and Kerry.

He swung west at Bagenalstown, travelling as far as Kilkenny

430

where he fell in with one George Cooke, a dealer in hides from Coleraine. A survivor of the siege of Derry, he was violently anti-James, anti-Catholic, anti-Irish. Although Cooke had difficulty in understanding his new friend 'Charles Wilkinson' of Aylesworth, whose Midlands accent was almost as bad as a foreign language, he welcomed Tadhg's company.

In turn, Tadhg was pleased with his companion. By listening and observing, he gained much practical knowledge about livestock to supplement the hasty orientation received at Limerick. Cooke also provided good cover. Difficulties and dangers inherent in Tadhg's contact with Protestant farmers, Williamite soldiers, petty officials, and town authorities were minimised by allowing the friendly, garrulous Ulsterman do most of the talking. Although there were few cattle available for purchase, most of them having been procured by Ginkel's quartermasters, good contacts were established by Cooke and 'Wilkinson' for the following year. The paucity of animals was advantageous to Tadhg; he had no way of disposing of them if he had gotten them.

It was not difficult for Tadhg to induce his colleague to move on to Tipperary where, it was rumoured, cattle would be available at the fair. Tadhg chose Tipperary because of its proximity to Ginkel's camp on the east bank of the Shannon at Limerick. They stopped at an inn, little better than a pothouse, run by a woman named O'Cathal who said she was a widow, despite common knowledge that her husband was with the Irish army. Cooke was unhappy with their accommodations: Their straw beds were alive with lice, wooden noggins called methers were used instead of cups, shells known to Tadhg as sliogain substituted for spoons, and, as forks were not known at all, guests used their own *sceana* to cut their food and convey it to their mouths. But the beer, brewed nearby, was good, and the uisce beatha was excellent. The quality and abundance of the liquor placated the disgruntled Cooke.

Tadhg reluctantly abandoned his hope to visit nearby Aherloe and his kin, realising that it would jeopardise his mission.

In his travels around the countryside, Tadhg was careful to avoid English troops, for fear of meeting natives of Warwickshire who could expose him. He met, instead, the Danes, Scots, Derrymen, Brandenbergers, and French Huguenots who comprised a large proportion of the English army. He listened much, spoke little. Most of the Williamites he met liked the affable young giant, especially those who were offered toasts to the health of good King William in his atrocious English. Tadhg's jovial smile during the toasts belied his feelings, for when he shouted, 'Here's to King William,' he invariably added, under his breath, 'May the devil have his soul!'

Tadhg was acquiring knowledge, but to his disgust, none of it was pertinent to his mission. He gradually came to realise that his avoidance of English contacts greatly lessened his chances of success. He would have to deliberately seek persons who might be close to Ginkel. Weighing the selfish, but sensible prospect of returning alive to Limerick with mission unfulfilled against the danger of greater exposure, but with greater chance of accomplishment, he reluctantly decided on the latter course.

Having an understandable fondness for his own neck, he listened carefully for Midlands accents before taking part in conversations with Englishmen. The night of his decision, he shared a table with a Captain Martin Forsythe, an aide to General Mackay. The captain was normally close-mouthed, but, had the tendency, when he had too much drink taken, to grow confidential, and with tongue loosened, prattle on self-importantly about matters better left unsaid.

A lieutenant of General Hamilton's regiment, sitting at the same table, mentioned the Duke of Tyrconnell. Captain Forsythe leaned forward, his mouth pursed with anger, the fine veins of his nose purple in the light of the guttering candle. 'Tyrconnell? Why the bastard's no better than his master, James Stuart! Lying Dick Talbot, bah!' He turned to Tadhg. 'Do you know who Lying Dick is? You don't? Why, it's none other than James's chief lackey who calls himself Lord Lieutenant of Ireland.' He took a hasty swallow of his drink as his thirst competed with his eagerness to denigrate the Duke of Tyrconnell.

'Save your breath, Captain, Tyrconnell's dead,' the lieutenant advised.

'Buried in St Munchin's churchyard,' Tadhg added.

The lieutenant glanced sharply at Tadhg. 'Why do you say that?' he asked.

For a moment Tadhg felt panic. He cursed himself for his stupid garrulity. 'A man I met in Athy told me,' he said quickly, hoping to cover his blunder. Frowning for a moment as he stared at Tadhg, the lieutenant turned his attention again to Captain Forsythe who was still fuming about Tyrconnell, still referring to him in the present tense.

'Lying Dick has his uses,' the captain conceded. 'He's always willing to offer surrender terms when it's to his own personal advantage. Isn't that true, Lieutenant Benton?'

'We English can always find an Irishman who is willing to sell his country to save his own neck,' the lieutenant remarked cynically. 'Take Henry Luttrell. A year ago when the Irish army was intact, Luttrell was ready to assassinate Tyrconnell for even thinking of ending the war. Today he is alive only because General Ginkel saved his neck when Sarsfield and the other Irish hotheads were going to hang him for making friendly overtures to us.'

Captain Forsythe nodded. 'If it wasn't for Luttrell, you probably wouldn't be here now. If he had attacked with his horse regiments when you were pinned down at the old castle at Aughrim, James Stuart would probably be in St Patrick's Cathedral having a Te Deum sung in his honour as King of Ireland.'

'I wouldn't trust Luttrell,' the lieutenant said, 'If he will betray his own countrymen, he will betray us. I'd hang him. That is, after we used him.'

Captain Forsythe turned bleary eyes on Tadhg. 'You, friend Wilkinson, can do more to end this rebellion than all the Luttrells and Tyrconnells.'

'Me?' Tadhg's surprise was genuine. 'How?'

A crafty smile spread over Forsythe's sallow countenance. 'You're a cattle buyer. You go out in the countryside where you meet the small farmers and peasants. These are the people who are the backbone of the rebellion. If you can persuade them they have little to gain, but much to lose, by continuing to support James Stuart, the rebels' supplies will be cut off, there will be no place to hide, and Irish chief information will be eliminated.' He snapped his fingers, saying, 'The rebellion will end just like that.'

He raised his mug as if offering a toast to his own sagacity. Taking a long swallow, he put his drink on the table, then reached out a long, bony forefinger with which he poked Tadhg's chest to emphasise the points he was expounding.

'The fastest way to end the rebellion,' he declared emphatically, 'is to appeal to the meaner sort of people, for there is much less chance of winning the native lords and Irish chiefs who must desperately depend upon a Jacobite victory to retain what they have.' He smiled cynically. 'The costs of this war must be paid some day, and that payment will have to come from the estates which will be confiscated from all those now in rebellion. You are probably too young to remember that when Charles II was crowned, those Catholic lords who got their lands and properties back were not of the old Irish stock. Only with James Stuart's victory will the O'Neills, MacCarthys, O'Tooles, O'Haras, MacNamaras and O'Rourkes be reinstated. These people will fight to the death before surrendering.'

And the O'Cuircs, Tadhg said to himself, his gorge rising. He felt a wild impulse to draw his pistol and shoot the two Sassanaigh seated with him. Restrain yourself, he admonished, there is more at stake than personal revenge. Sarsfield sent you here to use your brain, not your gun. Any fool could do that!

'Your suggestion has possibilities,' he forced himself to say. 'But how could I, a mere dealer in cattle, put it into effect?'

'Ah,' said the captain happily, pleased at his chance to develop his theme. 'If you, and others like you, travelling through the countryside, could convince the little farmer and tradesmen that their own empty nests will be better filled by serving a good and generous Christian King William than a depraved and deposed Papist James, why Sarsfield and his French allies will soon be laid by the heels.'

Emptying his mug, and calling for another round, which he conveniently allowed Tadhg to do the honours for paying, he let himself be carried away by his own enthusiasm. 'Tomorrow,' he declared in tones of the conspirator, his bleary eyes blinking, 'I will take you to General Mackay himself. If he adopts my suggestion, we'll all be home by Christmas.'

Tadhg hastily demurred, but to no avail. Forsythe, visualising himself as a grand strategist, insisted on the meeting. And thus the next morning, Tadhg rode with trepidation for his tryst with Forsythe. He smiled as he passed the road to Ballyneety. It was getting to be familiar territory. He hoped he would be on time, the trip on his slow horse was taking longer than he expected.

Long before getting to Annacorty, where General Mackay was quartered, he encountered the widely spread camp of the English Army which lay sprawled on the gentle slopes and vales overlooking the Shannon. He rode through the camp, noting the incessant chatter of thousands of men's voices in a half-dozen tongues.

Tadhg paused on the crest of a hill where he could see all of Limerick off to the west. Patches of blue indicated the Shannon as it meandered to divide King's Island before debouching to the west to form its broad estuary. St Mary's and St Munchin's tall spires projected like lances high above the squat buildings huddling alongside. Small dark specks moved slowly on the city's walls. English advance works, bristling with cannon, were strategically placed in the half-circle around King's Island and the smaller Irishtown. Several ships were docked at the quays downstream from Thomond Bridge. Tadhg's heart leaped: could they be part of the expected French fleet?

At Annacorty Tadhg asked for Captain Forsythe. A soldier volunteered to take him to the captain. The Englishman greeted Tadhg nervously. Now sober, he was less confident of his great plan to end the war. He had hoped that Wilkinson would fail to come. But rather than admit that he had been indulging in braggadocio, he led Tadhg to the general's headquarters tent. Halted by a sentry, they were informed that General Mackay had gone to be shaved.

A battered basin suspended on a pole in front of a well-built masonry structure, formerly some well-to-do tradesman's residence, advertised the shop of the barber. The leech, a former London barber-surgeon named Edgar Cutter, labelled Eager Cutter by his colleagues for his fondness for phlebotomies, now was the barber for the senior officers of William's Army.

As Tadhg entered with Forsythe, he could see a turf fire blazing under a huge cauldron at the far end of the room, and several chairs with occupants, each attended by a barber. One of the customers was being shampooed, hot water from the cauldron running from the laver to rinse out the soap. The other customer was recumbent, his face covered with steaming towels. The captain disregarded the one whose face he could see, and addressed himself to the other.

'Good morning, general,' he began deferentially. 'If you have no objections I would like to discuss a proposal with you which could possibly hasten the end of hostilities.'

No objection being forthcoming from the quiet figure in the chair, Forsythe launched his exposition. It was much the same as he had outlined to Tadhg the previous evening, with a few embellishments, in the course of which he introduced Tadhg as a dealer in hides and cattle who would be a key figure in the proposed programme of influencing the lower orders.

When he ceased, there was a brief silence. Then, from under the towel, a muffled voice asked, 'How long would this programme take?'

Cocking his head to catch the muted words, Forsythe frowned. 'Two or three months, Sire.'

'Too long!' The man in the chair sat up, taking the towel from his face. He was frowning, creating deep wrinkles in his broad forehead, and around his dark, smouldering eyes. To Tadhg he seemed to emanate an aura of authority and competence, like Sarsfield.

'Marshal de Ginkel!' Forsythe said, his face reddening. 'I thought it was General Mackay.'

My soul to heaven, Tadhg thought, what have I gotten into now? Here, barely five feet away, is the formidable commander-in-chief of William's Army in Ireland. I'm in a bigger mess now than I was in Derry!

'Your proposal isn't a bad one, Captain,' Ginkel said in his guttural English. 'But it comes much too late. The rains will be on us soon. Remember what happened here last year? The quickest way to end this rebellion is to get those stubborn Irish fools over there to realise that they can't win. Our Most Gracious Sovereign has more important work in the countries of Europe than in these bogs. These Irish diehards are only helping Louis, not themselves or their country. You get your dealer in hides over yonder,' and he waved his hand toward Limerick, 'and have him find out what the average soldier is thinking as he goes to bed at night with his belly only half full while his family is starving.' 'That is what we planned, Sire,' said Forsythe, hastily adopting the General's suggestion as his own.

'I don't trust Luttrell and his crowd,' Ginkel continued. 'They will lie and distort the facts to save their own hides, or in deference to you, sir,' he said to Tadhg sardonically, 'their own skins. They tell me that some of the Irish leaders are entertaining the idea of going to France with their men. If this number is small, and I can't imagine why it should be otherwise, I will be most generous and include such a provision in the terms of surrender. But I must know beforehand. It will be of little advantage to have them surrender here, and then face them again in large numbers in France next campaign. Yes, Captain, get your hide dealer to soften the resistance of the Irish soldiers in the next crucial weeks so we can clear out of this Godforsaken land.'

Forsythe was pleased at the Marshal's response despite his

rejection of the original plan. 'May I convey your thoughts to General Mackay, Sire?' he asked.

'By all means. And reimburse this man commensurate with the number of English, and oh yes, Dutch hides, he saves by sparing me another campaign here next year.'

Elated, the captain led Tadhg back to Mackay's tent. The Scotsman, who had postponed his visit to the barber, received his aide's information sceptically. As a rabid Papist-hater, he preferred to squash the Irish army rather than negotiate with it. He felt that Ginkel was too soft with the Irish. But the Marshal was the commander, he shrugged his shoulders, and instructed Forsythe to make the arrangements.

The swift turn of events, the fortuitous meeting with Ginkel, and danger of his position, left Tadhg limp. It was incredible that he had not been detected. He became increasingly aware that most people take others at face value. Only the analytical, the doubting Thomases like Conor, looked beyond the superficial.

He listened carefully as Forsythe discussed the exponible parts of the programme. In conclusion, the captain said, 'You are not to be a spy; you just lack the talents for one. So how do we discover the true sentiment of the Irish soldier? That's what the marshal wants to know.'

Captain Forsythe paused, his brow wrinkling with worry as he realised that he had talked himself into a task which was growing larger and more difficult every moment.

The Englishman's indecision forced Tadhg to concentrate as he recognised that he was in a position to direct the course of the venture. Forsythe's initial enthusiasm had led him into a cul-de-sac: while Ginkel's alteration of Forsythe's original plan had not been issued as an order, it was a directive. Mackay's instructions made it binding.

As the captain floundered in his mire of uncertainty, Tadhg evaluated the proposal as projected by Ginkel: if the Irish soldiers were offered the opportunity to go to France, how many of them would accept? He recalled Sarsfield's statement that many of the Irish desired to go to France to be trained, armed and built into an effective fighting force for a return to Ireland. But if there were many of this mind, would Ginkel agree to such a term? This was unlikely for he had inferred in his conversation with Forsythe that he would acquiesce only if the number was small.

This issue, then, was important to both Generals. It was the main reason for Sarsfield's consideration of surrender. So Ginkel would have to be misled. But how could this be accomplished?

Growing excited with the opportunity offered him, Tadhg's mind whirled with possibilities. One recurring thought was of his ride to this vicinity with Sarsfield to destroy the siege train. Quickly he devised a plan, contingent, of course, upon Forsythe's acceptance.

'Captain,' he began, 'your original idea of using me among the common people had great merit. Why don't you continue along this line by having me talk to some of the local farmers and tradesmen? Undoubtedly some of them are selling food and supplies to the Irish army by crossing over the Shannon at night. As you said, I wouldn't make a very good spy. If I went over to Limerick and started talking to the Irish soldiers, that is, if any talk English, I'd be strung up on a gibbet faster than you can say King William. For a few well-placed guineas, these smugglers could make a quiet survey among the soldiers, and at the same time sow a little discord by convincing them how invincible the English army is, and how desperate their chances are.'

Forsythe nodded vigorously. 'I have always maintained that you could do your best work among the little people', unconsciously using the Irish expression for the *síoga*, 'and that they would listen to you, a civilian, where they wouldn't to an English soldier.' He beamed; the problem of a minute before was solved.

Provided with five guineas, carefully issued by Forsythe, Tadhg set out for O'Kennedy's smithy near the Thurles Limerick Road, trusting to memory to guide him. The day was brisk, with a cold wind blowing in from the Atlantic. Shivering, Tadhg wrapped his coat about him.

Finally he had to admit to himself that the landscape was totally unfamiliar. Things did look different by daylight. It was necessary to inquire at several cottages before finding anyone who could speak English. A toothless old man with the redundant name of Matthew Matthew directed him to the smithy which was just 'past the cross' on the road toward Cullaun. O'Kennedy, grimy and sweaty, was noncommittal as Tadhg conversed with him about cattle and hides.

Hopefully interpreting the man's taciturnity as an expression of being anti-English, Tadhg suddenly switched to speaking Irish, saying, 'I trust you can be as valuable to Sarsfield today as you and your smithy were the night we rode through on the way to

Ballyneety.'

O'Kennedy looked sharply at Tadhg, suspicious blue eyes peering out from under bristling black brows. He carefully laid down his heavy hammer, stroking his soot-black beard with his right hand as he scrutinised his visitor.

'It's odd,' he said finally, 'to hear a Sassanach like you speak the Gaelic.' He spoke in the same shocked tones he would have had he found the Devil reciting the Lord's Prayer.

Tadhg looked carefully about him, then leaned forward, his face within two hands' span of the other. 'Arrah! It's not a Sassanach I am at all,' he declared feelingly, 'but an envoy of Sarsfield who is placing his life in your hands. I am seeking the Rapparee, Hogan, who guided us a year ago to destroy William's siege train. It was he who told the general it was safe for that dragoon to have his horse's shoe changed here. I pray to God that you are as loyal to Ireland now as you were then, for your country needs your help more than ever!'

O'Kennedy thrust the cooling iron bar into the glowing coals, pumped the bellows vigorously, and then, when the bar end was red-hot, began carefully to shape it with his big hammer. Tadhg waited anxiously. With the iron partially shaped, the smith forced it back into the fire. Only then did he speak.

'This man Hogan I do not know. However, there are several families of that name in the Barony of Upper Ormond where some of the O'Kennedys live. I will send my son up there to inquire for you. Perhaps this Hogan of yours is known in the vicinity.'

Tadhg's sigh of relief was audible. The smith went on with his work. 'If he should be known?' Tadhg inquired, adopting the cautious approach of the smith, 'could I arrange a meeting with him as quickly as possible? I must get an important message to General Sarsfield.'

Again there was no immediate reply as the smith pounded the iron on his anvil, expertly fashioning a horseshoe from the glowing iron bar. When it was replaced in the coals, he said, 'If you should drop by here tonight when it is dark, perhaps I might have word for you. Where are you staying?'

'At an inn near Tipperary. The innkeeper is a woman of the name of O'Cathal.'

The smith nodded. 'I know the place.'

Turning his broad back on Tadhg, he pounded the iron with such finality that Tadhg sensed the meeting was over. Mounting his old cob, he spent several hours in the area, talking cattle and hides with those who spoke English. Several times Tadhg observed a horseman trotting along behind him who never seemed to catch up with him despite his frequent stops.

It's probably someone that O'Kennedy set to watch what I am doing, he thought. Well, I would play it safe too under the circumstances.

Returning to the inn, he found Captain Forsythe anxiously waiting. Tadhg informed him that he had found a good contact who would try to arrange the survey for him. Despite the Englishman's desire for particulars, Tadhg was purposely vague. He advised him not to worry, that the project was in good hands. The captain had misgivings about the assignment being taken from him by a civilian, and the arrangement was a far cry from what Marshal Ginkel had suggested, but Tadhg's aura of confidence and responsibility reassured him. Numerous drinks later, he was convinced that success would crown their joint efforts.

When the pothouse was full of roistering drinkers, mostly soldiers, Tadhg unostentatiously departed, without his companion in intrigue being aware. The sun hung red over the rim of the western sky and Tadhg watched it plunge into the distant sea.

Once the sun was down, the darkness swooped over the land like a hawk on a thrush. As he made a turn into the road towards Cullaun, two horsemen emerged from the shadows. With one on each side of him, they rode wordlessly for a hundred yards or so before turning into a boreen which led to the north. At a signal from one of them, Tadhg followed. He heard a clatter of horses' hooves behind him, and the muted sounds of what seemed a scuffle, but as his companions, riding single file before and behind him, paid no attention, Tadhg said nothing.

After about a half hour riding through the woods, they emerged into a glade. Here they sat their horses for some minutes without a word being spoken. Suddenly a half-dozen horsemen appeared, one of whom rode up to Tadhg and peered into his face. Tadhg recognised Galloping Hogan at once.

'Do you ride only at night?' Tadhg asked impudently. Then, without giving the other man a chance to reply, he added, 'The last time I saw you this close, *a chara*, was when you ran your pike through the sentry at Captain Poultney's camp the night we destroyed the siege train.'

'Arrah! It's the big *spailpín* who rode next to Sarsfield,' Hogan

440

exclaimed with delight. 'I recognise that big broad back that always kept me from seeing ahead. But what are you doing on this side of the Shannon? Expecting another siege train?'

'Not this time,' Tadhg replied soberly. 'It is something far more important.'

Rapidly Tadhg outlined his mission, and the situation that developed. The Rapparee rubbed his hairy chin thoughtfully. Then he spoke, the banter gone from his voice.

"Tis sad I am to hear that Rory O'More's grandson is contemplating surrender. But I know how desperate the situation is, and I can understand how he must feel. If those damned French would only arrive!' He sighed heavily, then looked up to Tadhg. 'Why did you send for me? What do you want me to do?'

'Get word to Sarsfield that Ginkel is willing to include permission to go to France in the surrender terms only if the number of Irish so desiring is small. Tell him that Ginkel is in communication with Henry Luttrell; that he should be careful that Luttrell learns nothing of what he is planning.'

'How do you intend to convince Ginkel that only a small number of Irish will go to France? I'd wager that most of the army is willing.'

Tadhg was impatient. 'I'll have to leave that up to the general, *a chara.* He must have some way of preparing supposedly authentic information which can be gotten to me for the delivery to the English.'

Hogan nodded. 'The general will undoubtedly have a solution. And I suppose you are going to insist that I get word to him before midnight?'

'I'll hang your red pants on St Mary's spire if you don't.'

Hogan rubbed his chin again. 'How much time do we have to get this job done?' he asked.

'I would like to say a week, but my neck tingles every time one of Ginkel's men looks closely at me. I can't avoid a real Warwickshireman forever. My feet tell me to return with you to the Irish lines and safety, but my heart tells me I must complete my assignment for the general. Do you think you could accomplish it in two days?' he asked wistfully.

The Rapparee shrugged his thick shoulders. 'I'll try.'

'One question before we depart,' Tadhg said. 'Why was the meeting place changed from O'Kennedy's?'

Hogan ran his finger across his throat. 'Just in case 'Wilkinson' was a Rapparee hunter, and had half the English army with him.'

After making arrangements to meet two nights hence 'somewhere near O'Kennedy's', they separated. Tadhg's two previous guides led him to the main road again. Here they left him, melting into the shadows. Gaily whistling 'Eileen *a rún*', he started the long ride back. Shortly he noticed a solitary horseman standing quietly at the roadside under a tall tree.

Tadhg halted, his hand on his pistol. The figure stayed motionless, but muffled noises arose from its throat. Riding closer, Tadhg saw that it was Lieutenant Benton, a gag in his mouth, and his hands tied tightly behind him. Tadhg was puzzled why the man hadn't ridden away until he noticed the rope that led from the Englishman's neck up over a stout limb of the tree, and back down to the trunk where it was tied.

Dismounting, Tadhg went first to the tree to loosen the rope, then to the victim, untying his hands and gag. The Englishman glared at Tadhg with malevolent fury. 'Where were you?' he asked.

Tadhg's surprise at the situation was only surpassed by the question. For a moment his brain refused to function. Instead of answering, he countered with a question of his own. 'What are you doing here, trussed like this?'

The lieutenant gently rubbed his throat where the rope had chafed. 'The diabolical devils,' he muttered. 'They could easily have killed me, but preferred to torture me instead. They let me know that I was completely at their mercy. If that horse had moved more than a foot I would have been hanged. God, how I sweated.'

'Who were they?'

'Rapparees most likely.' His voice grew angry again. 'You haven't told where you went.'

'It's none of your business, Tadhg said to himself. Then aloud, 'I was supposed to meet a girl. To try some of this Papist stuff.' He leered lewdly. 'But she didn't show up, and with horsemen on the road, I decided it wasn't safe here.'

While hoping that the explanation would satisfy the lieutenant, the thought came to him: what was the Englishman doing here? Why the urgent repeated question? Had he followed him from the inn? If so, he must be suspicious of me! He felt cold all over, and unconsciously began to stroke his neck.

For a minute there was silence. Finally the other man spoke: 'There's no point in staying here. We had better be going.' He kicked his mount's ribs.

Lieutenant Benton made no further reference to the incident as they rode. Well short of Tipperary, he turned off to go to his camp area, Tadhg continuing on to the inn.

The following day Tadhg went with Cooke, the Derryman, to the vicinity of Cahir to the southwest, deliberately staying away from O'Kennedy's. Cooke was disgruntled with his lodgings, and the scarcity of available cattle and hides in the vicinity. He informed Tadhg that he was returning home the next day. That night at the alehouse, Captain Forsythe was insistent on details, but again Tadhg stalled him with his reply that he expected to have information soon.

He spent the next day in the vicinity, wondering if Lieutenant Benton was spying on him, and praying that Hogan would have something definite for him that night. He was growing increasingly apprehensive. His luck so far was good. But any moment he might meet a man from the Midlands; his disguise might fail; or Lieutenant Benton might unmask him! The thought of capture as a spy, and being hanged so far from his friends, set him on edge and only by remembering how much was at stake could he keep from fleeing and returning to Limerick.

To keep himself occupied, he scouted the area around the inn, finding a rough sheep trail which led over a hill, saving considerable time and distance on the road to the west.

He supped early, and while it was still light, rode to the top of the hill. From his coign of vantage he could watch the inn below and all persons arriving or departing. Taking his short clay pipe from his pocket, he filled it with some of his precious tobacco. The fragrant aroma of the Virginia leaf helped to calm him. He waited until dusk settled over the hill. Then, satisfied he wasn't being followed, descended the hill on the opposite side, setting out in the direction of O'Kennedy's. He got all the way to the smithy before being stopped. There a boy of about twelve years of age scrutinised him carefully, instructed him to dismount, spancelled his horse, then told him to follow.

They walked down a long boreen to an old cabin. Entering, he found Hogan and three of his men waiting. The Rapparee chief greeted him effusively. 'Pádraig sends you his best wishes. He is pleased with what you have accomplished. Oh, yes, he said that you shouldn't worry about your big stallion, he'll take good care of it if you're hanged.'

Tadhg grinned despite his worry. Sarsfield's words of praise made him glow with pleasure. The compliment more than compensated for his fears. He wasted no time: 'what did you bring me in the way of information for my good friend, Captain Forsythe?'

Hogan withdrew some foolscap sheets from his inside coat pocket, and with a flourish, presented them to Tadhg. 'It's too dark to read them here,' he explained, 'so I will tell you their contents. One is a copy of a letter from Sarsfield to the commanders of the other regiments exhorting them to work harder to convince the Irish soldiers of their need to go to France if they should be forced to surrender. In the letter Sarsfield bitterly complains that all too few have indicated a willingness to leave Ireland.'

Hogan chuckled. 'This isn't true, of course, but Pádraig wrote the letter anyway so that the information could be further corroborated by Ginkel's other contacts such as the traitor, Henry Luttrell, who probably is rushing a copy of it to Ginkel right now.

The second item is the supposed result of a secret survey of Lord Lucan's own regiment, the one expected to be most loyal, which indicates that fewer than a quarter of the men will accompany their commander to France.

The third item, prepared by the same member of the regiment, one Dónal O'Devaney, in a secret letter directed to General Ginkel, asking to be remembered as a faithful friend of King William when the war is over.'

Tadhg's happiness vanished. 'Dónal wrote that?' he asked, his jaw slack. 'I can't believe he would do such a terrible thing!'

The Rapparee looked at Tadhg with disgust. 'Of course he wouldn't, you fool! He did it at Pádraig's request. You should know better.'

Filled with contrition, Tadhg, in a choked voice said, 'Forgive me, *a chara*, I never should doubt Dónal. But I have encountered so much duplicity since I left Inishmór that I don't know who to trust at times.'

'Like Captain Forsythe trusts you?'

The shaft went home. 'I suppose that all of us at times must practice deception,' Tadhg said thoughtfully. Then he added in justification: But I am doing it for my country.'

'I know it,' Hogan said, putting an arm around Tadhg. 'I didn't intend to insult you, I just intended to shock you into keeping your wits about you at all times. Learn to know a man's motives, or a woman's for that matter. Now it is more important that you take

444

this material and get back to your Sassanach friends. And may God go with you.'

Leaving the Rapparees in the cabin, Tadhg returned to his horse and the long, lonely ride back. The hour was late and the inn was quiet. He undressed and went to bed.

The next morning he rode into the English camp. Captain Forsythe greeted him with an expectant look. Tadhg nodded his head in return, his face serious. 'What have you got?' the captain asked anxiously.

'Too good to be true,' Tadhg replied handing him the three pages of paper.

Forsythe whistled as he noted the signature. 'Sarsfield himself, eh?' Why do you act so gloomy?'

'I'm worried. It could be a forgery by those bogtrotters I paid the guineas to.'

Captain Forsythe's happiness diminished. He, too, began to look concerned. After gazing pensively at the papers, he said, 'We better show it to General Mackay.'

The general, poring over some maps, was annoyed at the interruption, but agreed to give them a few minutes of his time. Tadhg informed him that he had gone into the countryside, as Captain Forsythe had proposed, where he had talked with a blacksmith named O'Kennedy. The smith had agreed, for the sum of several guineas, to speak to some of the peasantry who smuggled provisions to the Irish army across the river. For a share of the money, they were to acquire information on the feelings of the Irish soldiery as to their future in the event of surrender. Specifically, would they go to France with Sarsfield, or stay in their native land? One of these peasants had gone into the Irish camp where he had talked to a young Irishman with whom he had had dealings in the past, mostly illegal. This man, one O'Devaney, was a clerk in Sarsfield's adjutant's section and had access to correspondence. For future consideration and favourable treatment by the English, he had copied a recent letter circulated by Sarsfield.

'Wilkinson is worried,' Captain Forsythe interjected, 'that he has not been hoodwinked by these Irish, and that these papers are not genuine.'

General Mackay, who had read and examined the letters, shook his head. 'No. These Irish are extremely venal. To save their filthy necks they will betray their own mothers. And as for leaving their beloved Ireland,' he said scornfully, 'they'd rather be dead. From the day of Dermot MacMurrough down to the present, with Lord Riverstown, General Maxwell, Baldearg O'Donnell and Henry Luttrell, we have dealt with these types who would sell out their country. There is little doubt that the letters are authentic. I'll take them to Marshal Ginkel. He is already in contact with some of the more sensible men in the Irish camp on capitulation terms. As for me, if the whole Irish population wanted to go where they could worship their idolatrous religion, I'd say good riddance!'

Although momentarily angered over the Scot's derogatory comments, Tadhg followed Hogan's recent advice to keep his wits about him. He was pleased at the success of his stratagem of casting doubt on the missives he had supplied, for the arrogant Mackay had reacted as he thought he would. But would Ginkel be as trusting?

Tadhg was asked to wait. As he ate with Captain Forsythe in his tent, he compared the plentiful, nourishing food with the starvation portions of the Irish army. After the meal, he decided to follow Captain Forsythe's suggestion that he take advantage of the delay by enjoying the pleasures of the barber. Cutter, the master barber, was busy shaving a customer when Tadhg entered the shop, but one of his assistants, a tall, slender man whose pointed beard and moustache ends made him resemble a Cavalier left over from Charles I's heyday, asked Tadhg to be seated. He then removed Tadhg's hat and wig with a flourish.

In accented English which reminded Tadhg of the Huguenot Le Berge in Dublin, he asked if he wanted his hair cut in the English style or in the Spanish or French mode. Tadhg pondered this for a moment. If he was going to France, why not look like a Frenchman?

'Tell me about the French style,' he said.

The man's dark eyes gleamed with pleasure. 'You should grow a beard and moustache. The beard is cut to a point, so,' he explained pointing to his own. 'Like a stiletto, hein? To penetrate the heart of your inamorata.' He sighed. 'Then the moustache. Aha. Trimmed to taper to points, which we twist upwards, to make more amorous. Just one little kiss and your lover she will swoon in ecstasy.'

'But what of my hair? Is there a French style for that also?'

'Oui, Monsieur,' the barber said condescendingly. He looked at Tadhg's hair critically, then nodded approval. 'A hot crisping iron will make it wave to bring joyous smiles from your sweetheart.

446

And a shoulder-length lovelock for your lover to tie her favours to. But, monsieur, you should allow your beard and moustache to grow.' He shrugged his shoulders deprecatingly. 'A woman doesn't want to be kissed by an inamorato whose face is hairless as an egg.'

Tadhg shook his head. 'No, let's do with what we have. Just cut the hair in the French style.'

'Bon, monsieur, but first we must wash the hair.'

As the barber readied the laver to prepare the suds, Tadhg suddenly sat bolt upright in the chair. The dye! The soapy water would wash out the brown dye!

'No,' he shouted, 'no hair wash!'

The startled barber stared at Tadhg with shocked amazement. So did Cutter and his customer, Lieutenant Benton.

'I do not have enough time,' Tadhg added lamely. 'I must be back soon to meet Captain Forsythe.'

Haughtily, the Frenchman returned to Tadhg's chair, took his scissors from its case among the razors and other appurtenances, and proceeded to cut Tadhg's hair. Snippity-snip-snip-snip sang the scissors, one snip of the hair and three in the air. Indignant at Tadhg's tonsorial faux-pas in making him work with dirty hair (also cheating him of a larger fee), the barber sullenly abstained from conversation, punishing himself more than his customer, for he was by nature extremely garrulous. Tadhg was angry for not thinking beforehand of the danger, and embarrassed of the awkward situation he created with his shout.

When the hair was trimmed to his critical satisfaction, and the lovelock fastidiously fashioned, the barber's indignation had subsided. He took genuine pleasure in his work, especially when the customer gave him leeway in styling. He stood back, cocking his head back and forth, to survey his handiwork. Then he moved closer for a minute scrutiny.

'Voila!' he exclaimed, his eyes close to Tadhg's looking at the hairline. Then he muttered in French, 'What is this? Black hair at the roots? It is very strange. I must look into this.'

Tadhg stiffened. Giving no sign that he had understood the barber, he sat in shocked silence, awaiting the denunciation. His heart thumped madly. He felt paralysed with fear. So the game is up, he thought sadly. I'm caught in the enemy's camp like a herring in a net. My life is forfeit; my work here all in vain. Now Ginkel will never accept purported confidential information supplied by an exposed spy. Oh, Ireland, what have I done to you in my stupidity!

In his anguish and despair he failed to hear the barber say, 'Will that be all , monsieur?'

Only when the man stared directly into his eyes, and repeated the question, did Tadhg realise that he had been miraculously reprieved. He fumbled awkwardly in his purse for coins, and in his relief, gave twice as much as would have been a most generous payment. His hands shook as he spilled the money into the other man's extended palm.

'Merci beaucoup, monsieur,' the barber said, his dark eyes staring covetously into Tadhg's well-filled purse.

'You're more than welcome,' replied Tadhg, who in his gratitude would have gladly thrust the entire contents of the purse into the other's hands. In a daze he donned wig and hat and walked quickly from the building, not even stopping to examine his new French hairdo in the one clouded mirror the shop boasted.

I must be more careful in the future, he told himself fiercely. Another slip like that could lead to my undoing. But why had that barber refrained from unmasking him? What had he meant by saying 'I must look into this?'

He walked around for some time in order to calm his nerves before returning to Forsythe's tent. When he entered, he found Lieutenant Benton with the captain. The Lieutenant stared at Tadhg with a steady unblinking gaze which left his victim disconcerted.

But Forsythe's joviality compensated for the junior officer's cold scrutiny. He greeted Tadhg effusively. 'Welcome, friend Wilkinson,' he crowed, 'our information is correct. An identical letter of Sarsfield's has been received by General Ginkel through channels arranged by Colonel Luttrell. It confirms what you obtained earlier. He is extremely pleased.'

'So much so,' Lieutenant Benton interjected, 'that he has a new mission for you.'

Tadhg's happiness vanished. He wanted to get back to the Irish lines as fast as his old horse could carry him.

'A new missionl?' he asked warily. 'What is it this time?'

'Shipments of cattle and hides from the market at Dublin to Bristol show shortages. Somebody somewhere is apparently stealing them.' Lieutenant Benton looked intently into Tadhg's eyes as if seeking to see into his mind. 'The marshal thinks that you are the very man needed to solve the mysterious thefts.'

Tadhg was so upset by the situation that he stammered, 'Whhhy mmme?'

'You are a dealer in cattle and hides, and you were so successful in the recent clandestine operation with the native Irish, the marshal thinks you can work the same miracle in Dublin.' Lieutenant Benton's emphasis of word 'miracle' increased Tadhg's uneasiness.

Tadhg's thoughts whirled wildly. Dublin! The Lady Mairéad! Perhaps he could see her one last time before leaving Ireland. It was a golden opportunity. He had accomplished the main part of his mission. Perhaps he could learn more in the capital. Dublin Castle had always been the seat of intrigue for the English in Ireland.

Slow up, Tadhg, he warned himself sternly. Don't allow your impulsive enthusiasm to carry you away! The longer you delay your return to Limerick, the greater grow your chances of detection. Have you forgotten your recent scare in Cutter's shop? That barber might be at General Ginkel's tent at this very moment. But you can't decline the marshal's request. To do so would arouse questions and suspicions. Better acquiesce for the time being. You can always change your mind later.

He nodded his head affirmatively. 'When do I start?'

'When do we start?' the Lieutenant corrected him. 'Why, as soon as I can be ready. I think that tomorrow morning will be fine.'

Tadhg was startled anew. 'You are going with me?'

'Yes. I will be your official liaison. You will circulate around cattle markets, but report directly to me.'

Damnation, Tadhg thought. Why couldn't it have been Captain Forsythe instead of this suspicious pest? Well, there was little that could be done about it now.

After arranging with Lieutenant Benton to meet him in the morning in Thurles on the road to Roscrea, he started on the long ride to the inn. As he approached the low bridge over the Mulkear River, he heard the sound of a horse's hooves behind him. Thinking that it was Lieutenant Benton following him again, he led his horse into a copse of oaks and waited. But when the rider came into view, he saw that it was the barber who had cut his hair. He felt relieved; there was something disconcerting about Lieutenant Benton. It was odd that the Frenchman had left the camp area, but perhaps he might be good company on the road. He moved his horse to the road again and waited.

'Bonsoir,' the barber greeted him, tipping his hat politely. 'Then in English, 'Your horse, he moves so fast, I was in despair of overtaking you. But this is, ah, how you say, opportune, no?'

'Opportune for what?' Tadhg was puzzled.

The Frenchman tapped his scalp significantly. 'The black hair. Who you fool? These stupid English, maybe. But you not fool Francois. No.'

'What is wrong with dyeing my hair?'

The Frenchman shrugged his shoulders. 'Nothing, if you're an Englander. But Francois knows hair and skin. You, monsieur, have the colouring of an Irelander. Black hair, blue eyes, white skin. Yet you pretend to be English. After you left I felt suddenly sick.' He rubbed his belly and rolled his eyes. 'I leave the shop, go to Lieutenant Benton, tell him you gave me too much money. He says that you are rich with money from General Ginkel; that you meet with Irish peasants.'

Tadhg was alarmed. 'Did you tell the lieutenant about the black hair?'

'Non. That would defeat my purpose.'

'What is your purpose?'

'For thirty guineas, Monsieur, Francois can have his own shop in Dublin. No more starving working for tight-fisted leech, Cutter. For thirty guineas, Francois keeps your secret.'

'I don't have thirty guineas,' Tadhg replied indignantly. 'And moreover, I'm an Englishman, not Irish.'

Francois sighed. 'Ah, then I would be embarrassed, no, if those soldiers over there were to arrest you, and after some days in the dungeon your hair should grow out brown, not black, and you should be an Englishman after all.' He grinned impudently at Tadhg.

Three soldiers, mounted on horses, watched them idly from across the river. Tadhg's palms grew moist, and his feet grew cold. For the second time that day he feared for his life. Confinement and interrogation would undoubtedly disclose his masquerade, for his beard and moustache, as well as his hair, would be black.

'All right,' he grumbled, sliding from his horse, 'I'll give you your thirty guineas.'

As he fumbled in his pocket for his purse, he saw the three soldiers ride slowly away. Digging ostentatiously deep in the purse, he withdrew his last five guineas, jangling them in his hand as he approached the barber, who watched him warily. When he was within range of Francois's horse, he siezed the bridle close to the bit, and twisted it viciously. Squealing with pain, the enraged horse reared on its hind legs, tumbling the surprised rider to the ground.

Catlike, the Frenchman instantly regained his feet. The smile was gone. His eyes narrowed to angry slits. From his tunic pocket he withdrew a razor. Flicking it open, he faced Tadhg. 'The thirty guineas, monsieur, and no more tricks or I'll cut you into little pieces.'

The soldiers are still close enough to hear a gun shot, Tadhg reasoned, so I can't use my pistol. Drawing his *scian*, he advanced on the barber who held his gleaming razor in his right hand as he crouched in a defensive position. Tadhg used his greater height and longer reach to jab with his knife, but his adversary was fast and agile. When Tadhg would thrust, the Frenchman would slash at his wrists with his deadly blade. Tadhg shuddered as the sharp steel whistled in an arc, barely missing his hand. He had seen horses hamstrung. With his wrist tendons severed, he would be completely helpless.

He looked desperately around him for a broken branch or a stone, but none was near. He had to keep his foe occupied so that the Frenchman couldn't turn and run, or get to his horse, to spread the alarm. So with grim concentration he kept feinting and jabbing, turning in a circle with Francois as the hub.

Suddenly the image of Sergeant Gallagher, his old mentor, and one of the heroes of the battle for the bridge at Athlone, emerged from the hidden recesses of memory. It was near Newry and the sergeant was describing the Battle of Benburb in 1646: 'When the sun was beginning to set, shining right into the eyes of the Sassanaigh, Eoghan Rua ordered his men to attack.'

What was good enough for Eoghan Rua should be good enough for Tadhg, he thought grimly, circling about until the sun was at his back, low over the distant hills. When he observed Francois squinting to counteract the glare of the sun, he suddenly acted. Jabbing with his *scian*, he forced his foe to take a swipe at his hand. Then Tadhg kicked viciously at the Frenchman's wrist with his booted foot.

As the razor flew from the stunned barber's hand, flashing in the sun in its short arc, Tadhg lunged with his *scian*. The Frenchman grunted heavily with the impact as the weapon penetrated deep into his chest. Sinking slowly to the ground, he stared at Tadhg with reproach. 'I had to do it,' Tadhg told him in French, filled with remorse. 'You forced me to kill you.'

Francois sighed and expired. Here was no great villain, Tadhg thought sadly, only a poor, venal barber. Montgomery Óg, Sir John Ferguson, Sir Oliver Trent, and even the traitor, Holmes, had deserved killing. This slaying was so needless.

His reverie ended by his acute sense of danger, Tadhg lifted the Frenchman's body and carried it into a thicket where he hid it from view. Returning to his horse, he picked up Francois's weapon. It was a fine razor. He thrust it into his pocket. He slapped the barber's horse smartly on the flank, causing it to trot down the road in the direction of the camp. Then Tadhg mounted hastily and rode on to the inn.

The following morning he waited for nearly half an hour before Lieutenant Benton joined him. 'A slight delay,' the Englishman said laconically, offering no explanation. They got as far as Mountrath that night. Lying in his bed at the inn, Tadhg knew that the sensible thing to do was to mount his horse, ride all night, and get as close to Irish lines as possible. His obsession with Mairéad FitzGerald, however, outweighed his good sense, and morning found him riding on to Naas, their goal for the second day's journey.

As they passed through Kildare, he remembered how he and Dónal Óg had passed the old Geraldine Castle. He thought fondly of his family on Inishmór, of Máire Blake and her brood, of Siobhán O'Madden, of Alice Reynolds and her school, but most of his thoughts centred on the Lady Mairéad.

Shortly after noon on the third day they passed a small church near Chapelizod which had been used for services by the Catholics when they controlled Dublin. Tadhg had attended Mass there several times.

'It's difficult to change the habit of a lifetime, isn't it?' his companion commented suddenly.

Tadhg turned a puzzled countenance to the lieutenant. 'What habit of a lifetime?'

The Englishman's smile was more malicious than humorous. 'The habit of a Catholic crossing himself when he passes a church.'

Sensing catastrophe, but ignorant of the cause, Tadhg nodded his head, saying, 'Yes. I suppose they do.'

'They?' Lieutenant Benton's smile was that of the cat about to pounce on the mouse. 'Don't you mean I?'

Tadhg's head jerked. 'You're a Catholic?' he asked incredulously.

'Don't act coy,' his companion snapped. 'You're the Catholic. You have crossed yourself twice at church as in the last ten miles. You just did it again a minute ago.'

As Tadhg tensed, the Englishman drew his pistol, pointing it at Tadhg's belly. 'You, my strange friend,' he said softly but ominously, 'need investigating. It was strange when you professed to know that Tyrconnell was buried at St Munchin's before any of the English knew it; it was strange that I was captured by the Rapparees that night while you strolled about unharmed with all that money; it was strange how quickly you made contact with the Irish who apparently wandered in and out of Sarsfield's headquarters; it was strange how a man that resembled you was seen by three soldiers on the road to Thurles where a man's body was found the next morning; it was strange that the dead man was a barber who attended you, and who queried me about you shortly afterwards.

'But strangest of all was how completely you hoodwinked Captain Forsythe, General Mackay and even Marshal Ginkel. Unfortunately for you, whoever you are, I didn't trust you for one minute. That's why I got myself assigned to accompany you while you were to work another miracle.'

'When we get back to General Mackay I'll have you court-martialled for this incredible insult,' Tadhg blustered.

'We're not going back to General Mackay. I am turning you in to the authorities in Dublin Castle. There Major Marty will check your passport and recent passenger lists on ships from England. They will get Warwickshiremen who will test you on your authenticity. And if you play stubborn, they have means of making you talk.' He smiled his thin cruel smile. 'They may even get your parish priest for you.'

What a fool I have been, Tadhg thought, to jeopardise my neck on the wild chance of seeing the Lady Mairéad. A desperate hope arose: Maybe she would help him. After all, it could do no harm to try inasmuch as he was already in dire straits.

'The Lady Mairéad can vouch for me,' he said. 'My father used to represent her father in Warwick in the cattle business. Her residence is just a few miles down the road. Let us stop there. It will save you from making a fool of yourself.'

453

The lieutenant's smug smile faded while he pondered the proposal. 'It will be but a waste of time,' he said.

'Are you afraid you might be proved wrong?' Tadhg countered boldly.

'Nonsense. It would take more than a Popish Irishwoman to convince me.'

Tadhg was properly shocked. 'Popish? She is as Church of Ireland as the Duke of Ormond himself!'

Impressed by 'Wilkinson's' insinuated familiarity with the highborn, and with conviction jarred a little, Lieutenant Benton reluctantly agreed to stop at the FitzGerald's demesne. They took the Kilmainham Road towards Dublin, the Englishman riding a few paces behind, his pistol pointing at Tadhg's back. As they approached the familiar entrance, Tadhg's heart beat rapidly with apprehension and excitement. He was now unsure if placing his fate in the Lady Mairéad's hands was a wise decision. Had it been hope or merely an unadmitted subterfuge to see her one last time before he died?

'This is the entrance,' he said authoritatively as they came into view of the heavy iron gates embellished by the silvery shield with the red St Andrew's Cross. As they turned in, Tadhg saw a solitary, small figure seated on the grass besides the gates.

Mother of God, he whispered to himself, not believing his eyes, it's Rory!

The lad drew a deep breath upon recognition, and his friendly face convulsed with joy, but before he could cry out a welcome greeting, Tadhg shook his head vigorously, and with forefinger jabbing violently to indicate the rider behind, succeeded in preventing an outcry. Seeing Lieutenant Benton's pistol, Rory immediately recognised the situation: joy changed to concern, his smile to a grimace, and his clear blue eyes in the briefest flicker as Tadhg passed informed him that the boy was aware that he was being held prisoner.

Admitted by a reluctant gateman, who stared haughtily at the strange spectacle, they trotted up the long driveway to the house. Yes, the Lady FitzGerald was at home, they were informed by the butler. Who was it who wished to see her? Lieutenant Benton of General Gustavus Hamilton's Regiment and Mr Wilkinson? Would they please be seated?

With heart beating rapidly, Tadhg sat in his stiff-backed chair. It was in this room that he had come to the aid of Lady Mairéad and her uncle. He remembered her expressions of gratitude and his hopes rose again. How could she do other than help him in turn?

The double door opened. Both men arose quickly, bowing to the lady. Lieutenant Benton stared with undisguised admiration. Even Tadhg was unprepared for the impact of her beauty. She had grown taller as she matured; the golden head was carefully coiffured; slightly opened red lips showed their fullness under the patrician nose; her clear skin stretched flawlessly over the delicate bones of her face. As she advanced towards them, the green eyes opened inquiringly, and once again Tadhg's eyes met hers for a moment that seemed an eternity.

She halted abruptly, stared at him with amazement, from boots to jaunty hat held in his hands, on up to his eyes. Surprise, recognition, alarm, dislike, all were mirrored successively in the expressive green orbs. Then she shifted her gaze to Tadhg's companion. 'Lieutenant Benton?' she inquired, her voice carefully controlled.

'Yes, Lady FitzGerald. I regret this intrusion. This man here, my prisoner, claims to be one Wilkinson whose father formerly represented your father in cattle dealing in his native Warwickshire. He says that you are an old acquaintance and can vouch for him.'

A faint, ironic smile curved the red lips. She turned again to Tadhg's pleading gaze, staring steadily at him as if he were an obnoxious bug.

'Mr Wilkinson, is it? Two years ago, as I recall, it was MacAuley. And it wasn't Warwickshire, but a county here in Ireland. Tell the lieutenant, Mr Wilkinson, how you acquired those scars over your eye. Was it a sabre? Or a horse's shoe in battle? Or perhaps it was just a lady's whip?'

Her scornful derision cut Tadhg far more acutely than her whip had. He had been a silly, sentimental fool for daring to hope that her reaction would be otherwise. Despite his humiliation, he felt a perverse satisfaction being in her presence once more. He had the ridiculous thought that it would be comforting to die if only she could be with him.

Lieutenant Benton's last, lingering doubts were now dispelled. He looked at his prisoner contentedly. 'MacAuley, is it? Much more appropriate a name than Wilkinson.'

'That isn't the half of it,' Lady Mairéad added, her tone bitter. 'He was Tadhg O'Cuirc the fisherman when he slew John

455

Montgomery, Sir Thomas's son. He was Tadhg O'Cuirc the Rapparee when he killed Sir John Ferguson. He was Sergeant O'Cuirc of the Irish Army when he shot to death Sir Oliver Trent. You have a most notorious villain here, Lieutenant Benton.'

The lieutenant was dumbfounded. He looked at Tadhg with surprise and a new respect. 'This is all true?'

Tadhg bowed. 'Who can dispute the evidence of so lovely a lady?' He was bitter now; he felt that he deserved better of her than she gave; all happiness at seeing her again was dissipated.

'She can tell you what noble, charitable gentlemen they were. She can tell you how loyal they were to their country and their king. King James, that is. She could tell you, too, of a man named Mattie Moley, a hireling of Sir Oliver. She can tell you of some drunken, murderous Irish soldiers in this room. And she might tell you of a contemptible cur named Holmes whom I killed near Derry who had dealings with her.'

'Mattie Moley, a hireling of Sir Oliver? A man named Holmes? I knew no man named Holmes.' She was puzzled and shocked at Tadhg's disclosures.

'A renegade soldier, *a bhean uasail*,' Tadhg replied, still angry and stinging from her denunciation. 'He took Sir Oliver Trent's place in the spy ring when Sir Oliver returned to London. I intercepted the message. The real Wilkinson,' and he turned to Lieutenant Benton, 'was supposed to bring it here to Lady FitzGerald.'

The Englishman was delighted at the disclosure. He gazed with admiration at the Lady. 'All the time Dublin was held by James, you were working for its deliverance? Your courage and loyalty, milady, are only exceeded by your beauty. My congratulations, Lady FitzGerald, you are to be commended.'

Instead of being pleased at the implications and praise, she was very angry and upset. 'I knew nothing of this man Holmes. I was not involved in any spy ring. And neither was Sir Oliver!'

Lieutenant Benton, slightly crest-fallen at the unexpected reaction, nodded his head. 'It really makes no difference. Our prisoner, here, will be the catch of the war. He undoubtedly will be taken to the Tower of London for a big spectacle.' He smiled happily in anticipation. 'First he will be hanged. Then disembowelled. Then drawn and quartered.' He smirked, adding, 'But being so large, he will probably have to be cut into eighths, not quarters.'

Tadhg, watching Lady Mairéad, saw her eyes express shock, then horror; her face drained of all colour, and with a low moan, she subsided in a heap on the floor. Her maid, Mary Casey, who had listened to the gruesome description with angry distaste, rushed to her side. Lieutenant Benton stood as if paralysed. He gazed at the recumbent form stupidly. Tadhg felt oddly detached. He thought it was a good chance to run, but was constrained to remain, not wishing to add to the Lady Mairéad's troubles by having his blood shed in her house.

After cold compresses were applied to the lady's forehead, she sat up, gazing at Tadhg with contrition. She refused to look at or to speak to Lieutenant Benton, but remained seated on the floor with her head in her hands, repeatedly moaning, 'Oh God, what have I done, what have I done!'

Awkwardly the Englishman made his excuses, and motioning to Tadhg to precede him, they left the room and the house. Retrieving their horses, they were passed through the gate to the road to Dublin. Rory was gone. Tadhg's hopes rose. He wasn't hanged, drawn and eighthed yet! He still had a fighting chance!

Watching Tadhg's every move, Lieutenant Benton was gratified that they had stopped at the demesne because he was now aware that he had captured a dangerous and resourceful spy. Otherwise he might have been careless, permitting the prisoner to escape. Consequently, when two soldiers were encountered, he ordered them to accompany him to the castle. They entered the old, walled city through St James' Gate. The familiar shouts of the hucksters, the importunities of the mendicants, the stench of the Liffey, all recalled to Tadhg his previous, and more pleasant, visits to Dublin.

As they progressed through the narrow streets, with the soldiers cursing at the vagabonds and street urchins who impeded their passage, Tadhg glanced apprehensively about him. He could see the forbidding towers of the Castle in the East. Once within its portals he was a plucked goose. He wondered desperately where Rory had gone. But what could one young boy do to help him in the very heart of the enemy's territory?

They plodded along Thomas Street, High Street, and passed Christ Church where Tadhg defiantly made the Sign of the Cross. His captor grinned, drawing his finger across the throat in a counter gesture. When they approached Cork Hill, and the lengthening shadows of the Castle, Tadhg's heart sank within him.

Lieutenant Benton whistled gaily as they turned into Werburgh

Street. He joyfully pictured the chagrin of Captain Forsythe when he learned that a notorious spy had passed through his hands. Visions of promotion and other rewards for Tadhg's capture captivated him.

Suddenly a loud shouting assailed his ears, and out of Skinner's Row behind him poured a mass of angry, yelling, gesticulating men carrying butchers' knives and cleavers. Simultaneously, up Bride Street and into Werburgh below, from the Coombe, appeared a second column of agitated men clamouring defiantly in French, brandishing stout cudgels.

Before the lieutenant could gather his wits, the two groups met head-on around him and his party, completely engulfing captive and captors. A voice cried out loudly in the Irish, 'Tadhg O'Cuirc, down from your horse, quickly!' Dismounting as ordered, Tadhg was soon submerged in the agitated mass that was reaching to tear the three Englishmen from their mounts. In a moment the struggling tide of men and horses was swept far down the street, carrying with it the frenzied lieutenant and the two mystified soldiers.

Out of the agitated throng a pair of brown eyes under bushy brown brows on a face almost covered with beard peered joyously at Tadhg. It was Devil's Hook Charlie. His barrel chest heaved mightily with his recent exertions.

'Ah, Tadhg lad, it's glad I am to see you again.' And as Tadhg started to speak, Charlie interrupted him. 'Later, lad, later. Follow me now.' He ducked into a doorway, pulling Tadhg after him. There, also smiling broadly, was the Huguenot, Jacques Le Berge, who hastily thrust a cloak of the Irish type over his shoulders, adjusting the mantle to cover Tadhg's head.

Le Berge then told Tadhg to follow him, and leaving Charlie behind them, they once again entered Werburgh, then turning to the right, scurried quickly down Bride Street, and thence to the Coombe, where lived the turbulent weavers. Here were stone houses, modelled after those in their native France, with numerous high gables, and small windows with glass in leaded panes. Tadhg was hustled into one of these, now the home and shop of Le Berge, where the prosperous master weaver rented rooms to a score of apprentices. And there, too, was Rory, overjoyed to see Tadhg again. He flung his arms around him, squeezing with all his young strength.

'Now, *a bhuachaillín rua*,' Tadhg said breathlessly, 'tell me how you happened to be in Dublin waiting for me, and you,' turning to the Frenchman, 'tell me what that hullabaloo on the street was about.'

Le Berge bowed deferentially to Rory. 'The honours are yours, young sir.'

With a sidelong glance at Tadhg, the boy began hesitantly, 'I learned that you were leaving Limerick on some kind of a secret trip, so I followed you. But my legs couldn't keep up with your horse. After you disappeared, I just kept on walking to Baile Atha Cliath. Every day I waited for you to arrive at the Lady Mairéad's. Today you did.'

Tadhg hugged the boy. 'For once I'm glad you disobeyed orders. But I wasn't going to Dublin. It was sheer accident that I came here. And how did you know I would go to the Lady FitzGerald's?'

Rory shrugged his shoulders. 'You always go to the Lady FitzGerald's. Everybody knows that.'

Tadhg was startled. 'Everybody?'

Le Berge guffawed. 'Apparently all of Ireland knows it,' he teased. 'But to answer your question of me. Rory came running to Devil's Hook Charlie's pothouse, saying you were a prisoner of an English officer. Charlie came here after sending word to Butchers' Row that one of their colleagues had been apprehended by the soldiers, and was being brought into the Castle. I in turn alerted the weavers that one of their brethren had been captured. Scouts were posted along the road to alert us of your coming. Voila! Many angry men rushed to the rescue.' He beamed with delight.

Tadhg shook his head in amazement. 'My hopes had been raised when I saw Rory at the gates, but they sank lower and lower as we approached the Castle. This is the second time that I have been rescued while en route there. It is getting to be a habit. But a good one.' He rubbed his neck, and sighed happily. 'It was fortunate that I proposed, and the lieutenant accepted, my suggestion to stop at the Lady Mairéad's. Otherwise Rory wouldn't have seen me.'

Le Berge nodded. 'Oui, Monsieur Tadhg. And the delay gave us time to prepare. Otherwise...' and he too rubbed his neck.

A weaver entered the room, and in French too rapid for Tadhg to follow, reported to his master, gazing curiously at Tadhg in the meanwhile.

When the man departed, Le Berge explained. 'The fight, it is over. Result: one with a broken arm, two butchers with gashed heads from an officer's pistol, and one English soldier dead from a butcher's cleaver.'

'Which one?' Tadhg asked, his voice tense.

The Frenchman shrugged. 'The lieutenant who foolishly struck at the short-tempered butchers with his gun butt.'

'Thank God!' Tadhg exclaimed. 'He was the only one who knew the truth of the situation. He told the soldiers nothing but to accompany him and to guard me closely.'

'What did he tell Mademoiselle FitzGerald?'

Tadhg thought for several moments before replying. 'Not much. She did most of the talking. He learned enough to hang me five times over I think that at the end she was sorry for what she told him. The chances are good that she will not inform the authorities, at least not until it is too late. We can thank Lieutenant Benton for describing in gory detail what would have happened to me in London.'

'How is your French?' Do you think you can pass yourself off as a Huguenot weaver tomorrow? We will try St Audeon's Gate. I don't anticipate any great difficulty. Those two soldiers can't have much information for the Castle authorities since they didn't know who you are, what you were being detained for, or where you had come from. All they know is that there was a street brawl in which a prisoner seized the opportunity to escape.'

'My French is not anywhere as near as good as your English,' Tadhg replied. 'With a little study and imitation of your accent I think I can pass as a weaver.' He frowned. 'But what about the weavers and butchers who took part in the melee? Will they get in trouble for killing the lieutenant?'

'Who knows?' Le Berge said, shrugging his shoulders. 'Usually when they brawl, it is with each other. There is bad blood between them. Just a few months ago some of the weavers were hung on the meat hooks in the shops. The weavers retaliated by chopping off some of the butchers' fingers with their own cleavers. I suspect the authorities will take no action against them. Was the lieutenant a stranger here?'

'I think so, mon ami. But undoubtedly he had papers explaining our mission to Dublin which was to investigate the theft of cattle and hides destined for shipment to England.'

'Have you eaten recently?' Le Berge asked.

'Not since early morning,' Tadhg replied, brightening. 'Worrying about my neck made me forget my stomach.'

'Good. We will dine soon. I know I don't have to ask Rory

460

because growing boys can eat any time. Then we will secrete you in the garret while we prepare identification for you as a Huguenot weaver named, ah, let me see, Ettienne Pierre Vallier. Does that suit you? Good!'

After their meal, Tadhg related to the interested Frenchman his major adventures since leaving Dublin the year before, including some of the details of his mission to the English camp. Out of deference to Le Berge, he omitted the incident with the French barber, who most likely had been a Huguenot.

In turn the weaver described the changed situation since the English again controlled Dublin, and how the Catholics had to attend secret Mass to avoid persecution, and capture of the priests. He shook his head sadly as he contrasted the treatment of the Catholics to the tolerance of the Dissenters when Tyrconnell was viceroy.

The following morning, with Rory mounted behind him on his horse which had been retrieved by the rescuers, Tadhg took his leave of Le Berge. 'I can never repay you, and Devil's Hook Charlie, for what you have done,' Tadhg said, his voice choked with emotion.

'Leave it in the hands of God,' Le Berge said. 'It is He who directs us in our actions. I was but serving Him. Charlie thought it best not to see you in the event he was seen on the street yesterday. He sends his regards and regrets. When I told him of your mission here in Dublin, he laughed uproariously, and said to tell you that had you been successful, you would have destroyed one of his most lucrative business enterprises.'

Accompanied by four weavers, selected for their reliability, they rode from the Coombe up Francis Street, and via Back Street to High Street to the Corn Market. In the 'Large Cage' where beggars, idle boys and idle women were confined until their punishment, often deportation to the Tobacco Islands, was decided, a score or more wretches shouted at them, begging for coins. There, too, stood dreaded Newgate Gaol. They passed ancient St Audeon's Church where Tadhg resisted the impulse to cross himself, and descended to St Audeon's Gate where they stopped by a one-legged watchman.

With the four Huguenots and Tadhg all talking simultaneously in French, the old man became so confused that he angrily waved them through the gate with only the most cursory examination of their papers. There were no soldiers at the gate, a good sign that

461

'Wilkinson's' presence in the city was unknown.

From the gate they passed to the busy quays along the river, which, being at high tide; was active with ships arriving and leaving. At Bloody Bridge, the Frenchmen left them to return to the city through St James' Gate, while Tadhg and Rory crossed over to avoid going near the FitzGerald demesne.

Resuming the identity of 'Wilkinson' the dealer in hides and cattle, Tadhg selected a route which led past Lucan where Sarsfield's estates were now confiscated, up to Mullingar, then southwest to the Shannon, using the ford where he first met Rory, over to Ballinasloe, down to Portumna (regretfully bypassing Aughrim and the O'Maddens because of his haste to return) and on to Tumgraney. There Tadhg learned the depressing news that the English had successfully crossed over the Shannon a few miles north of Limerick the night before. Due to indecision and procrastination on the part of Brigadier Clifford, who was responsible for the river fords in the area, the first few troops to cross were quickly reinforced by dragoons, grenadiers and fusiliers in force.

Disheartened by this new catastrophe, they were forced to travel west to Tulla before dropping down to Sixmilebridge, and thence to Limerick. He was greeted by Sarsfield with a joyous embrace, and quickly made his report.

'Our situation has deteriorated since you departed,' the general informed him grimly. 'First, that spineless idiot Clifford allowed the enemy to cross the river above the city. Last night they threw bridges across to King's Island outside of our northeast walls, something they couldn't accomplish a year ago. So with our desperate situation, your information showing Ginkel willing to include a proviso for going to France is more valuable than ever.'

'But only while he thinks it's a small number, sir,' Tadhg cautioned.

Sarsfield's eyes twinkled. 'Yes, Sergeant O'Cuirc, I accept your counsel unconditionally.' Then as Tadhg reddened with embarrassment, he added, 'We will endeavour to make the amount the best kept secret of the war. It will probably be our sole triumph on a sad day.'

When Tadhg rejoined Conor and Dónal, recounting his adventures, he learned how incensed Sarsfield had been upon learning of Clifford's failure to take immediate action against the English bridgehead over the Shannon. He had urged D'Usson, in

462

command of the Irish forces since Tyrconnell's death, to have Clifford arrested for his dereliction.

When Conor started to talk, Tadhg interrupted quickly, 'Yes, it is the same Clifford who was in charge of the bridge at Athlone that was seized by the enemy. Nearly every time our army suffers a severe reverse or defeat, it's one of the English or French officers who manages to be involved.'

'Congratulations,' Conor said, smiling. 'You're beginning to learn.'

Once the English were on King's Island, they mounted a continual and massive bombardment of the walls of Englishtown at the southern end near Ball's Bridge. The ancient stone wall began to crumple, starting a breach which grew every hour. It was apparent that it wouldn't be long before the foe would attempt to enter the beleaguered city.

As the breach expanded, and the plight of the defenders grew more desperate, the leaders met more and more frequently, trying to reach a decision. The citizens of Limerick, hungry, bombarded and weary, lost their will to resist. Although information had been received that the large supply fleet had left France, there was no word of its fate. A large flotilla of English and Dutch warships was prowling off the Irish coast waiting to intercept the French. The writing was on the wall.

Chapter IX

Day of Decision

In any army camp there are many pairs of ears, and where there are
ears, there are mouths. If the matter of negotiations with Ginkel
was intended to be secret, it certainly failed of its purpose. The day
that Tadhg returned to the regiment, the bivouac area was buzzing
with the rumour that the Irish Army was going to capitulate. Many
an eye was blackened, and many a nose ran crimson when flying
fists prevailed over calm reasoning.

Dónal was wrathful at the possibility of surrender; Conor was
thoughtful,; Tadhg non-committal. When a delegation of Irish
officers including Sarsfield, Brig, Wauchope, Lord Galmoy and
Colonel Purcell, left Limerick to openly confer with Ginkel,
rumour became fact. Although unhappy at the thought of
surrender, most of the soldiers were exhilarated by the prospect of
going to France to prepare and to fight again. Their support of the
negotiations was predicated on the leading role played by Sarsfield
and other Irish officers they trusted.

On 3 October the Treaty of Limerick was signed. Representing
William and England were the Right Honourable Charles Porter,
Knight, and Thomas Coningsby, Esq., Lord justices of Ireland; and
his Excellency, the Baron de Ginkel, the lieutenant-general and
commander-in-chief of the English army. For Ireland were the
Right Honourable Patrick Sarsfield, Earl of Lucan; Percy Viscount
Galmoy; Colonel Nicholas Purcell, Colonel Nicholas Cusack, Sir
Toby Butler, Colonel Garret Dillon, and Colonel John Brown.

The terms, as solemnly agreed to, were generous: the Roman
Catholics were to enjoy such privileges in the exercise of their
religion as were consistent with the laws of Ireland. The residents
of Limerick, and those of the several counties of Limerick, Clare,
Kerry, Cork and Mayo, were to retain and enjoy their estates of
freehold and inheritance, provided they took the oath of allegiance
made by act of parliament in England in the first year of the reign
of their present majesties, when thereunto required.

In addition, all persons, military and civilian, including those
volunteers called Rapparees, were free to go to any country of their
choice, excepting England and Scotland. Ships for passage,
carriages to the ports, supplies for sustenance, would be provided
free of charge. All the emigres could take with them their 'families,

household-stuff, plate and jewels'.

To the tattered, hungry, destitute Irish soldier like Dónal Óg, the latter condition was a hilarious joke, and they made much of it. More beneficial, however, was the authorisation for 900 horses. As a reward to Tadhg, Sarsfield included Tadhg's, Conor's and Dónal's horses among those to be transported. Not many in the enlisted ranks were given this opportunity, for all of the officers and gentlemen competed to have their mounts included.

Ginkel was shrewd enough to authorise the proud Irish army to march out of their garrisons with their arms, baggage, drums beating, matches lighted at both ends, bullet in mouth, and with colours flying.

Once the treaty was signed, a massive tug-of-war to win the allegiance of the soldiers immediately started. Proclamations were issued in Ginkel's name which not only promised full pardon to all those who agreed to serve in the English army, but preferment and favours as well. Those who chose to disband and return to struggle with his own conscience, or, as with so many, the hunger pangs in their lean bellies.

Sides were quickly chosen. On one were Sarsfield and Wauchope, assisted by many of the Irish officers and Catholic clergy, exhorting the men to choose to go to France. On the other, with Ginkel, were strange bedfellows, for among the most active in his behalf were the two former firebrands, Colonel Nicholas Purcell, and his old personal friend, none other than Colonel Henry Luttrell, now freed from prison and from King James's vengeance for his traitorous activities.

On the morning of the day of decision, Conor informed Tadhg that he wanted to speak to him about an important matter.

'What is it, a chara? Are you going to ask Sive MacClancy to accompany you to France?' Tadhg asked jocularly.

'I'm not going to France.'

'What?' Tadhg was thunderstruck, 'repeat that. I thought you said you weren't going with us to France!.'

'I'm not going to France,' Conor repeated, looking steadfastly at Tadhg.

There was silence for a long interval. Tadhg stared at Conor as if his friend had suddenly gone mad. His mind refused to accept what his ears had heard.

It was Conor who finally broke the strained silence. 'Why are you going to France, Tadhg?' he asked.

'To save the Irish army. To be refitted and come back to fight again.'

'Do you really believe that will happen?'

Again Tadhg refused to believe that this was his comrade, Conor O'Donnell, his beloved companion, speaking. His reply was an angry question. 'Don't you?'

Conor shook his head sadly. 'No. Once the army sails it will never come back. It will be another tragic chapter in Ireland's unfortunate support of the curse of the Stuarts. It is high time we purged ourselves of them!'

Tadhg felt trapped. 'But Padraig Sarsfield himself has promised that we will return.'

'Do you honestly think that James Stuart will honour, respect and support Padraig Sarsfield in France any more than he has in Sarsfield's native land? From the beginning, Sarsfield has been shunted into the background by the French and English commanders chosen by King James. Why do you think that James Stuart, a congenital fool, is suddenly going to change for the better? No, Tadhg, once poor Ireland has surrendered, England will be stronger than ever. It will be far easier for the Irish army to leave than to return.'

'But what will you do, Conor?' The question burst painfully from Tadhg's lips.

Conor sighed heavily. 'Go back to Connemara, and help Máire on the farm. She needs a man to help her until Tomas is older.'

'Don't tell Dónal of your decision,' Tadhg begged. 'He is determined to go to France, and will fight anyone who is not of the same mind. It is bad enough that we must part, but we must not part in anger.'

Conor nodded, his face sad. 'That's the reason why I wanted to talk to you first. I've known Dónal since he was a small boy. He's hotheaded, *a chara*, and ofttimes thoughtless. You must promise me that you will always look out for him.'

Tadhg embraced Conor, both of them averting their heads to hide the blinding tears. 'I promise,' Tadhg said, sniffling. 'And if you change your mind, we will both be waiting for you to rejoin the regiment.' He tried to smile. 'Or in a year's time we will greet you again when the Irish army returns in triumph.'

Excitement ran high in the camp until the drums were beat on the day of decision and the regiments began to form on the Clare side of the city. Thomond Bridge rang with the muffled tread of the troops leaving Limerick. English officers walked among the waiting men urging them to remain in Ireland, passing out copies of Ginkel's proclamation. Heated arguments were still taking place between disputants, and Ginkel's agents took advantage to recruit converts.

Finally the troops were called to attention. It was announced that they would march, regiment by regiment, to a point on the broad plain where all those who had decided to go to France would continue marching straight ahead. All those who had chosen to remain would turn sharply to the right and march off.

An expectant hush spread over the plain. It was the moment of decision. Then a bugle sounded shrilly, the drums began to beat, orders were bawled. The Royal Regiment, Sarsfield's had been chosen to march first, because of the loyalty of its men. On one side, sitting their horses apprehensively, were Sarsfield and Wauchope. Opposite were General Ginkel, and the framers of the treaty, Lord Justices Porter and Coningsby.

The order to march was given, and the steady tramp of thousands of feet, many of them bare, stirred up the dust in the fallow field. Tadhg, chosen as colour-bearer for the momentous occasion, had impishly donned the brown wig he had worn on his trip to the Williamite camp. When he came abreast of Ginkel, he turned his head and stared directly at the Dutchman. Ginkel looked at Tadhg momentarily, then his glance drifted. A moment later the marshal's head jerked around as he stared at Tadhg, his forehead furrowed, in concentrated thought. Then Tadhg moved on, never knowing whether Ginkel had recognised the missing 'Wilkinson'.

All eyes were on the colour-bearer as he approached the designated spot. Then, as Tadhg marched ahead, followed by all but seven of the 1,400 men in the regiment, a great roar burst from the men awaiting their turn, growing in volume as the spectators on the walls of Limerick joined in.

Dónal, marching proudly, his eyes on the regimental colour, failed to see Conor leaving the ranks. Only angry muttering, and hurled insults, coupled with oaths, made him suddenly aware that the place next to him was now vacant. His jaws slack, his eyes frightened and disbelieving, he stared at Tadhg's broad back.

As the Irish army shuffled through the dust, the newly arrived French officers of the fleet that had come too late, snickered as the tattered near-naked Irish soldiers marched past, with no shoes or stockings, many without shirts or tunics. Even Tadhg, with his precious boots, his wig, and his Enniskillener jacket, was the object of Gallic taunts and insults.

With heads high, the regiments marched to the cadence of the beating drums, delighting Sarsfield, and infuriating Ginkel. It was apparent that a great majority had decided to follow Sarsfield to France. When the last soldier, (a boy named Rory MacAuley) passed the pivotal point, Ginkel turned angrily, calling for his horse.

Of the 3,000 men who had decided not to go to France, approximately 1,000 who had casually traded their allegiance to the cause of King William and the English army, immediately marched off to one side to receive the first instalment of their reward. In sight of the hungry 'loyal' Irish, the 1,000 'traitors' feasted on roasted meats, freshly baked bread and choice of cheese. After they washed down their bountiful meal with wine and brandy, they were issued tobacco, and lined up to receive two weeks' pay.

To the 'loyal' Irish, subsisting mainly on ammunition bread and peas, without pay for months, not even the worthless brass money, the fragrant aroma of the burning tobacco was the most tempting.

Conor, and 2,000 like him who had refused Ginkel's blandishments and bribes, vanished quickly, heading for home as fast as their feet could carry them. Most of these, like the 'traitors', came from the regiments of Luttrell and Purcell and Clifford, where many of the men followed the treacherous example of their leaders.

When the furious Ginkel, who had believed that few of the Irish would choose for France, tabulated the results, he found that nearly 12,000 preferred foreign service to staying in their native land under a man whom they considered a mere Dutch usurper of his father-in-law's throne.

For once in his life the usually irrepressible Dónal was silent and withdrawn. Conor's defection and desertion, as he saw it, was totally beyond understanding. To him the issue was clear, if you were for Ireland, you were loyal to the Irish army; if the army went to France, you went with it. Momentous decisions of Louis XIV, policies of King James, European power struggles, the position and opinion of newly elected Pope Innocent XII, the growing domination of the seas by the English Navy, the difficulties of a seaborne invasion, the fickleness of allies, the ever-changing alignment of nations, meant nothing to him. Conor had deserted them, deserted the Irish cause, and exchanging his sword for a ploughshare, would cost no English their heads!

The first contingent, about 5,000 men, sailed shortly from Limerick with D'Usson and the Chevalier de Tesse with the squadron of M. de Chateau Renaud. This was the squadron on which the Irish hopes had rested. It had arrived just a few days after the Treaty of Limerick had been signed. Many of the Irish army had urged that the treaty be repudiated, and war be resumed. But Sarsfield and the others had insisted it was a matter of Ireland's honour to live up to the treaty.

Soon a second group under command of Brigadier Wauchope, about 3,000 men, departed for France. Ginkel was now hard pressed to supply the ships he had promised. While the remainder of the Irish army, including Tadhg and Dónal, waited for their transportation, Ginkel's agents seized the opportunity to create unrest among the men. As the regiments were marched to Cork for embarkation, the roads were lined with people from all over Ireland, parents, sweethearts, wives, brothers, sisters, children, endeavouring to go to France with their loved ones as Ginkel had agreed in the treaty, or imploring them to stay home. In the face of this heartbreaking spectacle, even the stoutest heart quailed and firm resolution dissolved, so that the marching ranks began to thin before the assembling areas were reached.

While Sarsfield fretted at the delays, Ginkel, pleased with the growing number of desertions, chose not to hurry to improve the situation. It was now glaringly obvious that few civilians would be transported as promised, and Sarsfield became impatient to sail with the last of the army before winter set in.

Tadhg was among those who now looked forward eagerly to the voyage to France. He was firmly convinced that it meant the rehabilitation of the Irish army. Inasmuch as he spoke French, it promised adventure and a new life. In his bitterness at the Lady Mairéad's contemptuous denunciation, he was impatient to get as far away from her as possible. His only regret was his failure to see his family before departure.

Dónal, however, was having his troubles. Sheila MacBrady begged him not to leave her since there was little chance for her to go with him because of the ship shortage. He was fond of Sheila, much more so than any of the numerous other *cailíns* he had consorted with in affaires d'amour from Derry to Limerick.

"Tis hard for me to say it, and harder for you to hear it, Sheila *a rún*, but right now Ireland is first in my heart. There can be little happiness for any of us until our country is free again. The old landlords are stronger than ever, and with so many Irish losing their estates for fighting in the war and going to France, the whole country will soon be under their trampling feet.'

Knowing from previous arguments that to attack on this flank was futile, she tried another. 'That may well be true, macushla, but have you ever considered that King Louis might make peace with William? Where will that leave old Ireland? Or have you ever thought what could happen to me with all these wild foreign soldiers roaming the roads and boreens?' Carried away with her polemic, she was able to produce a few real tears which coursed down her rosy cheeks.

'Arrah!' Dónal exclaimed brusquely. 'Wipe up those tears. You will be safe enough until I return.'

'Yes,' she replied bitterly. 'I'll be waiting with the barrow to trundle you about, you with your legs shot off by a cannonball. And you can rest in the corner of the hearth where I can feed you three times a day. It's a fine husband you will be!'

The more she argued, the more obstinate he became. Finally she used her last weapon. ''Tis bad enough for you to desert me and run off to a strange land, but what about your baby?'

'My baby?' He was flabbergasted at the implication. 'Are you sure?'

'I think so.'

'Och, Sheila,' he said, his voice tender. 'Why didn't you tell me sooner?'

'I didn't know,' she replied tartly. 'What difference does it make?'

'I told General Sarsfield I was going to France with him. It's a promise I can't break.'

She burst into tears. 'Does General Sarsfield mean more to you than I do? Does your country mean more than your child?'

Dónal's jaw quivered momentarily then tightened. 'It's my honour and my word, Sheila *a rún*,' he said. 'I'll be back soon enough.'

He remained adamant despite her protests and tears. And so, on 22 December, Tadhg, Dónal and Rory went aboard the Le Duc, a 40-gun man-of-war, one of the last half-dozen of the embarkation fleet in Cork Harbour. They stood sadly at the ship's rail watching the rainclouds gather over Slieve Boggeragh, their emotions mixed at the prospect of leaving their native land.

Tadhg recalled how, when he first arrived at Dublin, he had longed to sail aboard a large ship. But now that he was aboard such a vessel, there was little happiness in him. When he thought of Dublin, he thought of the Lady Mairéad. How she must have exulted at the surrender of the Irish army. How pleased she must be with the complete subjection of Ireland to the Anglo-Protestant minority. He tried hard to think ill of her to placate the ache in his heart.

While he mused, Dónal watched the shore where a dozen or so of long boats were bringing the last of the soldiers to the ships. Hoarse shouts of men and shrill cries of women drifted across the water. The tide was favourable, and the French shipmasters were anxious to sail.

Dónal poked Tadhg in the ribs. 'Look, at that crowd of women trying to get into those boats. There must be several hundred of them at least.'

Swearing loudly, and fending the women off with their oars, the French sailors laboured to get the longboats moving. When the boats pulled away from the shore, many of the women waded into the water after them, begging to be taken along. They grabbed desperately at the gunwales as the water deepened, while others clung to the ropes trailing in the sea. Angered, the sailors struck at the clutching fingers, and when this failed to dislodge them, used their heavy knives to hack at the desperate women's hands.

Tadhg and Dónal watched with dismay. Some of the most determined held on until their fingers were chopped off, and those who clung to the lines were cut loose only by severing the ropes. Above the hubbub rose one shrill voice crying, 'Dónal! Dónal, save me!'

'My God in Heaven,' Dónal exclaimed, his eyes mirroring the bleakness of his soul, 'it's Sheila!'

And as they watched, too far away to help, Sheila's brown head bobbed momentarily on the surface, white arms thrashing wildly, then she sank beneath the surface of the oily waters. Before their horror-stricken gaze, she again surfaced, and once more the piteous appeal of 'Dónal!' echoed across the harbour. Then the waters closed over her head.

Several of the Irish soldiers in the boats leaped overboard, for a dozen other women also were drowning before their eyes. But the water was too deep, the tide surging, and some of the would-be rescuers, themselves unable to swim, joined the women in death.

While this doleful scene was being enacted, the French sailors stoically pulled at their oars, heading for the distant ships. In a few minutes, the last men unloaded, the longboats slung in their davits, anchors were hoisted, and the ships put out to sea.

As the women on the shore realised that this was the end of their hopes, a low moaning spread among them, and becoming crescendo, arose on the wind in such a wail of woe and pain and despair that even the hardened French soldiers stared with fear, and crossing themselves, looked anxiously to the wind-filled sails to hurry them from this dolorous shore.

As the Le Duc, her old bones creaking, gained headway as they approached the narrows at Roche's Point, leaving Spike Island behind them in a creamy wake, Dónal stood transfixed staring at the distant shore now rapidly disappearing.

Gaining the open sea, with its fresh breezes, the ship responded like a frisky colt, cavorting in a marine pasture, kicking up its heels gaily. But there was no gaiety in the hearts of the two men from Connemara as they watched the shore of Ireland recede. There was only anguish and the never-to-be-forgotten dirge of the women at Cork.

'Dirige, Domine, Deau meus, in conspectu tuo viam meam,' Tadhg intoned, squeezing Dónal tightly to him.

PART V

France

Cast of Characters

*Marshal Luxembourg, the 'Tapissier de Notre Dame', humpbacked military genius commanding the French Army

Jacques Benoit, captain of a French smuggling ship

Etienne Beauvais, guide to Tadhg at Pau

Mme le Berge, mother of Jacques LeBerge of Dublin

Francoise le Berge, her daughter

Pierre le Berge, brother of Jacques and Francoise

Marie le Berge, Pierre's wife

M de Mazandier, brother of Mme le Berge

Gaston Mazandier, his son

Nicolas Beauvais, fugitive Hugenot minister

Sgt St Clair, persecutor of the le Berge family

Mme Jeanne Le Clerc, seductress extraordinary

Dermot O'Lee, formerly a Rapperee with Cathal O'Flaherty, now a surgeon in the French Army

*M le Barbesieux, Minister of War to Louis XIV

Baron Hugh O'Flaherty, son of Cathal O'Flaherty

Baronne O'Flaherty, his French wife

Sister Margrete, a Sister of Mercy

Eithne Blake, also a Sister of Mercy

*Louis XIV, King of France

(* denotes historical figures)

CHAPTER 1

The Sacrifice

They landed at Brest on 2 January after an uneventful journey. True, Rory was woefully seasick, but so were most of the others aboard; and occasionally an English or dutch man-of-war stalked the French ships, but otherwise their voyage was without incident.

Torn between the excitement of visiting a new and strange land, and the despair at leaving the land of his birth, Tadhg thought frequently of his family far away on the distant Inishmór, of Conor in Connemara, and of the Lady Mairéad in Dublin. Often he leaned against the chest-high rail at the stern of the old Le Duc, staring towards the now-vanished Cork shoreline, wondering on the fate that was carrying him still further away from the little cabin at Kilmurvy.

He wondered about Dónal Óg, who lay silent and withdrawn in his hammock, emerging only to eat his meals. Sheila's tragic death had affected him more than Tadhg would have believed.

An icy wind, driving a sleet storm before it, filled Le Duc's straining sails, nudging the ancient ship, creaking and groaning, toward France at a speed which belied its age. When Le Duc lumbered through the rocky, narrow entrance to the vast harbour at Brest, the ship's rigging was glistening with sleet, and the sailors cursed as they clambered aloft with benumbed fingers to the dangerous task of furling the sails.

Drums were beat as the ship was finally berthed at its quay, and the Irish soldiers scrambled over the icy decks to the gangplank, Only a few curious citizens were venturesome enough to brave the bone-chilling storm to watch the Irish march briskly off the quay, still in the tattered remnants of their uniforms, and up the steep streets of the ancient town to temporary billets in cold, damp stone houses which had been reserved for them.

After a few days in Brest they were marched along the road to St Malo, through countryside which reminded Tadhg of Connaught with its forbidding rocky coastline, poor farms, and robust peasants who, like the Irish, believed in fairies and witches. They stayed a few days near St Malo, that formidable bastion against the English, before moving on to Rouen. Here the land resembled that of Leinster, fertile fields which nourished plump cattle and placid, contented peasants.

Rouen, an ancient town of narrow streets, sprawled along a horseshoe bend in the River Seine, with its magnificent cathedral dominating the entire city, its contrasting towers of St Romain and Le Beurre standing in bold relief.

They were billeted in a stone house - like that in Brest - with straw spread in the floors for bedding. Surveying their quarters Dónal wrinkled his nose in disgust. 'The only difference between living here and Limerick is that I now call you 'Mon Ami' instead of "*a chara*" and the fleas say "Pardon Monsieur" before they bite.'

'Ah, now,' said Tadhg, 'it isn't all that bad. We do get good cider with our meals, and there are no accursed English cannoneers interrupting our slumbers.'

'Perhaps.' Dónal sounded dubious. He looked at Rory 'But what are we going to do with this young spailpín here' These French officers are not going to be as lenient with us as were the Irish'

'He's going to become a drummer. I've already made arrangements with Lieutenant St Archange. If anyone asks his age, say he's sixteen.'

Dónal grinned, and Tadhg was pleased to see it, for the usually blithe lad had been unusually sombre ever since the episode at Cork.

'Rory's ageing fast,' Dónal said. 'At this rate he'll be a old soldier and ready for his pension in five years.' He winked at Tadhg and asked Rory, 'Which side of the drum do you beat in the morning?'

'Why the outside, to be sure,' Rory replied.

'Isn't it the clever one you are now that you're sixteen' Dónal said frowning. 'Well then, if you beat the outside in the morning when do you beat the inside?'

Rory looked up at Dónal slyly; 'Only when it's raining and the outside is wet.'

Suppressing a smile, Tadhg said, 'The young sleeveen is too clever for you, Dónal.' He turned to Rory. 'And you better get down to Sergeant McCalvy, the drum-sergeant, before I skin your hide to make a drum for being so impudent to your elders.'

The Irish regiments were issued new uniforms and weapons, the men received pay for the first time in a year, the meals were regular, and soon a new esprit was born. This in turn made the Irish soldiers more amenable to discipline, an essential requisite for success in battle, which they had lacked.

Slowly a huge fleet of French ships was assembled in the ports

476

along the Breton and Normandy coasts for the invasion of England. The French provinces on the English Channel became one huge staging area.

The remnants of the Irish army were reorganised into eight regiments of foot, three independent companies, and two regiments of horse. At the same time, James appointed Sarsfield as commander of his Second Troop of Irish Guards. The First Troop was commanded by the King's son, the Duke of Bewick.

Tadhg's bilingual talent was of great service when the Gardes de Roi Jacques, as the Irish Guards were called in French, negotiated with the French military and civilians for training and supplies. To the French, Tadhg's ability to converse with them made him less of an ignorant Irish barbarian.

Despite the Irish soldiers' inability to speak the language of the country, they had no difficulty in the universal language of love, and were quickly favourites of the French women from sixteen to sixty. The Irishmen treated the women as equals, in contrast to the superior domineering French males, and their wit, generosity, and gay spirits intrigued the women. Dónal speedily made a conquest, the daughter of a wine dealer, thus retiring Sheila to the darkest recesses of his conscience, hidden but not forgotten.

As winter waned, and Spring softened the countryside, the apple trees blossomed, the beeches budded, and King James himself, accompanied by the Duke of Berwick, arrived at Caen from Versailles on 24 April ready to cross the channel where he confidently expected to be received with shouts of joy by his recently rebellious subjects.

Tadhg and his cohorts eagerly awaited the day when they would board their ships for the invasion of England, the first step in their victorious return home. Messages from Ireland brought the news of the Irish Parliament's rejection of many of the terms of the Treaty of Limerick, and the failure of Ginkel and William to repudiate the Parliament's rebellious actions. Those opportunists who had succumbed to Ginkel's promise of service in the English army quickly learned the fragile substance of an English agreement, for in January of 1692 all Irish Papists in William's army were peremptorily dismissed.

By the middle of May, eighty troop ships were ready to transport the Irish forces under the command of General Sarsfield, and 10,000 French troops commanded by Marshal Bellefonds, from the ports of Brest, Le Havre and Cherbourg. The troop ships were to be protected by two French squadrons, composed of 44 men-of-war waiting in the huge harbour at Brest, and an additional 35 at the great base of Toulon in the Mediterranean.

Tadhg, Dónal and the other Irish guards marched from Rouen to Le Havre on 2 May, wearing their new uniforms, and proudly carrying their fusils, the improved snaphanse flintlock. But the 'Protestant Winds' were blowing, and the ships were unable to leave their harbour. Day after day the adverse winds blew. While James fretted at Caen, and French sea captains cursed, the delighted English, aware of the planned invasion, joined their fleet with that of the Dutch, and prowled the channel like hungry cats waiting for the foolish mice to emerge from their holes.

On 18 May, when the orders came for the ships at Brest to join those from Toulon, some of the Irish troops boarded the transports. The few French men-of-war that put out to sea, unable to join the other squadron, courageously engaged the combined superior force of the English and Dutch, but were easily defeated, many of the ships escaping their tormentors only to be wrecked on the rocky shores of the French coast.

The Irish soldiers, saddened and disappointed, disembarked, and for most it was the closest that they ever got to Ireland again. The Great Invasion was postponed, and although abortive efforts were to be attempted during the next several years, the grandiose return of James II to England was destined to be another of his colossal failures.

'I might have known,' Dónal remarked angrily, 'that anything King James was involved with was doomed to fail.'

He sounded so much like Conor in his denunciation that both he and Tadhg thought guiltily of their former colleague.

'Perhaps Conor was right,' Tadhg commented, 'and we should have remained in Ireland to fight the English.'

Unwilling to forgive Conor for what he considered treachery, and reluctant to admit that their choice was the wrong one, Dónal blustered, 'If only King Louis would dispense with King James and give the command to Sarsfield, I'm sure things would be different'.

Tadhg didn't reply. Doubts as to the wisdom of their course, creeping unbidden into his thoughts, conflicted with his faith in Sarsfield's decision. He shook his head violently as if to rid himself of his heresy, trying resolutely to expel the subject from his mind.

With the invasion abandoned for a year, the Irish units became part of Louis' French army. He was happy to have them, for they would be needed in the coming campaign against the Allies. Louis knew their potential because the Irish Brigade - consisting of the regiments of Viscount Mountcashel (Justin McCarthy's, O'Brien's and Dillon's) - sent to France in the Spring of 1690, in exchange for the French forces then being sent to Ireland, had established an enviable reputation as excellent soldiers.

As Sarsfield's and Berwick's Irish Guards rode towards the Sambre River in late May, Tadhg astride Cúchulainn again, the entire French army was on the move toward the Low Countries where William was assembling a huge force to oppose them.

The Irish soldiers, angry and disappointed at the invasion fiasco, further inflamed by their officers reminding them of the violations of the Treaty of Limerick by the emissaries of William in Ireland, soon were in a nasty mood and spoiling for a fight.

They were to get their opportunity soon enough. The great Marshal Luxembourg, affectionately called the Tapissier de Notre Dame (the Upholsterer of Notre Dame) for his magnificent victory over the Allies on 1 July 1690 the same day as the Battle of the Boyne, when he captured 106 enemy standards that were then hung in the Cathedral of Notre Dame, was in command of the French Army.

Padraig Sarsfield, who had previously served under the command of the hunchbacked genius, who was reputed to be as successful in the boudoir as he was on the battlefield, was pleased at Louis' choice.

The King himself had taken to the field in April. After his forces captured the fortress at Mons, he moved on to Namur which the French took in July. With these two victories easily obtained, Louis prudently returned to his palace at Versailles, never again to take an active part in military affairs, leaving Marshal Luxembourg to engage the superior army of William III.

Outmanoeuvred by the English King, Luxembourg was forced to fight on broken ground near the little village of Steinkirk where the feared and formidable French cavalry were of little value among the ditches and hedges.

With consternation, Tadhg and Dónal watched the French Foot driven from their positions, leaving their cannon behind, chased by the forces of General MacKay whom Tadhg had met in the English camp before Limerick.

It's the Irish campaign all over again, Tadhg thought, sick with shame and disappointment, but this time it's not the untrained, poorly led Irish who the French had taunted for cowardice, it was these same arrogant garlic-eaters who were now showing their heels to the English.

Tadhg was reckoning, however, without the genius of Luxembourg. Here was no De Rosen or Lauzen, the second-raters who had commanded the Irish, but the foremost military leader of the time. Recognising the desperate situation, Luxembourg immediately ordered the foot regiments of the King's Household to march against the advancing enemy.

With complete faith in their commander, and led by the three sons of Luxembourg himself; also, the Prince de Conti; the Duke of Berwick; the king's two natural brothers, the Duke and the Grand Prior de Vendome; Marshal de Villeroy, and many nobles from the Court at Versailles, the regiments marched courageously and resolutely into the face of the English fire.

Despite the fearful carnage, the brave, disciplined ranks marched relentlessly forward, their muskets on their shoulders, until they mingled with the enemy. Using cold steel alone, their swords and bayonets (and their gun butts when needed), they methodically flushed the English from the hedges, hills and ditches until the startled but admiring William had his drums beat the retreat, leaving the field to the victors.

When the Irish Horse Guards finally received the order to pursue the fleeing foe, Tadhg felt as if a great burden had been lifted from him, and all the humiliation and despair accumulated since the defeat at Aughrim was swept away as he and the other Guards, shouting 'Remember Limerick', dashed among the English like a pack of ravenous wolves upon a flock of sheep. Tadhg hoped to encounter General MacKay, but the Scot, although brave, was not a fool, and being familiar with his Bible, was well aware that 'The prudent man looketh well to his going'.

Their sabres bloodied, their confidence restored, and the myth of the invincible English foot demolished, the Irish soldiers acquitted themselves so well at Steinkirk that Luxembourg rode to their bivouac a few days later to personally praise them for their valour.

He told them that they had needed no vindication in his eyes because he had never believed the vicious calumnies directed against them. Then, extolling Sarsfield's leadership at Steinkirk, the Marshal declared that Louis had promoted Lord Lucan to Marchal de Camp in the French Army, a rank equivalent to that of

Major General he had held in the army of James II.

Cheers burst from Irish throats, and caps were flung aloft as the former ragtag and bobtail defenders of Limerick realized that at long last merit was recognised, and that they were no longer under the restrictive and contemptuous control of King James and the sycophants who surrounded him.

In October, with the campaign over, General Sarsfield arranged for Tadhg and Dónal to accompany him to Boulogne, a small town near Versailles, where Lady Honora and his young son, Séamus , were living. The rest of the regiment were billeted at Lille, near Flanders.

The Lady Honora, as beautiful as ever, but obviously agitated welcomed her husband affectionately. She gazed at Tadhg with speculation, remarking that they were a long way from Limerick. Then she whispered something to her husband. Lord Lucan frowned, telling Tadhg and Dónal to stand by, that he might be needing them, and excusing himself, left the room with Honora.

General Sarsfield returned shortly, his melancholy face unusually grave. He tried to smile, but it was a poor effort. 'It's getting to be a habit,' he said, 'that whenever I have a difficult problem, I immediately call upon Sergeant O'Cuirc instead of taking care of it myself.'

'I am always at your service, sir,' Tadhg replied.

'I know that. It's all the more reason why I shouldn't take advantage of your generosity. But I have to confer with Rí Séamus's Council at St, Germaine, and with Marshal Luxembourg at Versailles next week. Yet it is imperative that a message be dispatched to Bordeaux immediately. Will you take it for me?'

'I would be most happy to Mon General. But where is Bordeaux?'

'About four hundred miles from here, on the Garonne River in the southwest of France.'

'Am I permitted to take Dónal with me?'

'Certainly. I will arrange it with the adjutant.'

'What is the message?'

Sarsfield sighed heavily. 'I suppose I had better tell you the whole story. It is not a felicitous one. The lady Honora has just informed me that she has learned that two of her nephews, sons of Colonel David Burke who died at Aughrim, are in serious difficulty. The older one, Ulick, is in the Tower of London, condemned to be hanged. The younger, Manus, is hiding somewhere in Kerry. He will have to be rescued and brought to France. Thus the trip to Bordeaux.'

'And what am I to do?'

'You will carry a message to one Jacques Benoit, the master of a ship at Bordeaux. I could euphemistically call him a merchant, but in truth he is a well known smuggler who disposes of his cargoes in secret coves in the West of Ireland. He was of great service in the last days of the campaign when the sea lanes were closed to us. You will get in touch with him, and deliver a message which I will give you.'

'Would it be improper to ask, sir, what caused the brothers to be placed in such a predicament?'

'No. The Lady Honora thought you should be spared the details, but I think it best that you know. Ulick and Manus went to Dublin Castle to plead for the return of their lands which have been placed in the custody of the crown. While they awaited an appointment with the Viceroy, they were accosted in Dame Street by a drunken English officer. Taunts and insults by the Englishman not having the desired effect, he drew his sword, and in a moment the hot-headed Ulick ran him through.'

'They quickly fled. In desperation they recalled that their mother's cousin, Ita O'Hurley, was related to a family living not far from Dublin. They went there, seeking sanctuary. Their distant cousin had them hide in the stable, promising to arrange for their escape when the hue and cry died, Manus left the stable early the next morning to stretch his legs. When he started to return, he heard the clatter of horsemen. Peering through the foliage, he saw a troop of English horse surround the stable, and in a minute, drag his brother from the building.

'He succeeded in escaping into the wilds of Kerry, sending word to his family at Kinvara. Subsequently the family learned that Ulick was taken to London, found guilty, and condemned to die. Manus swears that it was their kinswoman who informed the castle authorities. There is little we can do for Ulick, but we might be able to save Manus.'

Tadhg had listened intently. When the O'Hurley name was mentioned, he felt a premonition of disaster. In a low voice he asked 'What is the name of the cousin in Dublin, sir'.

Sarsfield looked sadly at Tadhg. Again he sighed heavily. 'Mairéad FitzGerald.'

Tadhg buried his head in his hands, rocking it gently from side to side. Lord Lucan and Dónal sat silently until Tadhg raised his head, and in an even voice asked, 'When do we start, mon general'.

'In the morning. I will prepare the message to be delivered to Benoit, arrange your itinerary, and provide you with money to pay for your meals and lodging.'

It was cold and crisp when they left Boulogne, Tadhg astride Cúchulainn, and Dónal on a grey stallion obtained by Sarsfield. Tadhg was compulsively talkative, touching on numerous subjects, but studiously avoiding any mention of the Lady Mairéad. Their route to Bordeaux was via Orleans, Tours and thence to Angouleme and the Dordogne.

As they traversed the valley of the Loire, Tadhg commented on the well-kept vinyards and the cultivated forested areas which dominated the slopes. They passed many magnificent chateaux, some in ruins, evoking poignant memories of abandoned castles in Ireland.

Peasants, with whom Tadhg conversed, although amazed to see such odd soldiers called Gardes de Roi Jacques, were even more surprised to hear Tadhg speak French. In their delight at this phenomenon, they eagerly shared their simple fare with the travellers. As a result, Tadhg and Dónal enthusiastically discovered the regional wines, Vouvray in the Lire Valley, Medoc in Dordogne and Cognac at Angloueme, the most devastating strong drink taken since leaving Ireland and its *uisce beatha*.

The sun was setting when they arrived at their destination on the sixth day after leaving Boulogne, mud spattered and bone-weary. Putting up their horses at a stable, they found an inn near the quays. It was such a disreputable-looking place that the Irishmen were surprised not to find Devil's Hook Charlie presiding behind the bar. Wriggling her hips, a serving girl escorted them to their room. She smiled at them coquettishly, told them to come below for their dinner, then undulated through the doorway. Dónal was surprised and amused to see Tadhg avidly watching her antics.

'She's more my style than yours,' he remarked, 'for her derriere is obviously better developed than her brain, which should leave you cold. That is, based on past performances.'

'Arrah! You have forgotten that I have been studying geometry in which a figure is a surface bounded by lines and planes. Now if we take a figure - her figure, for example - is there any reason why it shouldn't maintain its function if laid in the horizontal rather than the vertical?'

Dónal glanced sharply at Tadhg. 'You lost me in your reasoning, but not the reason. I don't know any geometry, but have learned from practical experience that curved figures, at least, work best in the horizontal. Does that solve the problem?'

'I'll concede that practical experience is superior to the theoretical,' Tadhg said, laughing, 'so I'll leave the problem's solution to you.'

But there was no solution that night for both of them retired immediately after their meal, getting their much-needed sleep.

The next morning they walked the narrow, crooked streets to the quays which stretched along the banks of the broad Garonne. Jacques Benoit was easy to locate; he obviously was well known at the seaport.

He took off his cap, a round, flat headpiece, also favoured by his many colleagues of the quays, and scratched his smooth, round dome.

'Irish soldiers of King James? Down here in Guyenne?'

'To bring you a message from General Sarsfield,' Tadhg replied, handing him the envelope.

Benoit read it slowly, having difficulty with Sarsfield's writing. When finished, he shrugged his shoulders. 'Why not? If I carry contraband to Ireland, why can't I bring contraband back, especially when Le General promises to reward me so liberally?'

'You will do it, then?'

'Certainement! I'll be ready to sail in a week's time.'

'Why the delay?'

'I'm awaiting a load of wine from Pau. It should be here by then.'

Tadhg became excited at the mention of Pau. 'Pau? Is that near here?'

'To walk, no. To ride, yes. About sixty five leagues.' He squinted at Tadhg, his eyes shrewd. 'A mademoiselle, eh?'

Tadhg shook his head. 'Non. It's the birthplace of a Frenchman now in Dublin who helped save my life last year.'

'A Frenchman in Dublin? Unbelievable! What is his name?'

'Le Berge.'

'Le Berge?' Benoit frowned. 'Aha, that family is notorious.'

'Notorious for what?'

'Infidels! Heretics! Huguenots! They're all members of Religion Prétendu Réformée. Followers of Besançon Hughes. We call them Huguenots.' Benoit waggled his forefinger at Tadhg warningly. 'If

I were you, I'd have nothing to do with them. You could bring down the wrath of the King on your head. As of now the authorities are searching for Nicolas Beauvais, one of their ministers who has refused to abjure. Ah, that one! He will have none to preach heresy to but his fellow galley slaves after they catch him!'

Tadhg was stunned by Benoit's words. He stared at the captain with disbelief. 'You mean that he would be condemned to the galleys merely because he's a Huguenot?'

Benoit replied with a vigorous nod. 'Oui! It will do him good. But enough of this idle chatter.' He leaned forward, his swarthy brow furrowed. 'Armand, the hostler, tells me that you have a beautiful horse. I'd like to see him.'

'Why? He is not for sale. Besides, what would a sea captain do with a horse?'

Benoit smiled. 'I have a little farm. I need good horses.'

Noting Tadhg's look of disgust, he hastened to add, 'Non, I would not have him pull a plough. I am fond of horse racing. Armand says your horse would be a great racer.'

'He's not for sale,' Tadhg responded curtly.

Benoit's moustache drooped. 'It is regrettable, Monsieur. He is a magnificent animal. Ah, you wonder why I say that? I saw him at the stable last night, and decided that I must own him. A lovely great brute of a horse.'

'I am sorry, mon ami,' Tadhg said, feeling more kindly towards the mariner because of his admiration for Cúchulainn. 'That horse means much to me. You are not the first to covet him and be disappointed. But we must depart. Handle the general's mission with delicacy.'

'Parbleu! It is as good as done.'

They left Benoit, returning to the stable to get their mounts for their return to Boulogne. As they passed the cathedral, Tadhg stopped impulsively. Dismounting, he handed the reins to Dónal. Entering the church, he genuflected, kneeled and began to pray. As he said his Pater Noster, he suddenly envisioned Le Berge standing at the altar, his usually serene countenance now greatly agitated, his dark eyes appealing to Tadhg, his lips forming words, but no sound issuing.

Tadhg arose hurriedly, startled by the vision. Joining Dónal, he stood undecided for a moment, then addressed Dónal tersely, 'We are going to Pau.'

'To Pau? Are you disregarding Benoit's warning? And what will General Sarsfield say?'

'Stop sounding like Conor,' Tadhg snapped. 'If you don't want to accompany me, return alone to Boulogne. Le Berge risked his neck for me against the English. Now he is asking me to do something for him. We must go to Pau to find out. Our Lord said: 'Therefore all things whatsoever ye would that men should do to you, do you even so to them.' If I am to believe in Jesus, then I must do as he says.'

Dónal looked reprovingly at Tadhg. 'You don't think that I would ever leave you, do you?'

Tadhg was instantly repentent. 'I'm sorry, *a chara*, for speaking harshly and doubting you.'

'Good. Then we'll go to Pau. But where is it?'

Inquiring at an onion stall at the marketplace, they learned that Pau was in the province of Bearn, to the South. It was suggested that they take the road to Gujan then follow the highway to Pax where they would turn inland to reach Pau.

Their first day's journey was through a sandy wasteland, sparsely inhabited, far different from the lush regions of the North. Impatient and apprehensive at his impulsive action, Tadhg set a punishing pace.

From Pax they hastened to Orthez, from which they could see the distant lofty Pyrenees. Then, following the Gave de Pau, they arrived at the outskirts of the village at the end of the third day.

As they trotted down the dusty, rutted road, two mounted dragoons, idly waiting at a crossroads, called upon them to halt. The Frenchmen stared curiously at their uniforms, then one asked politely, 'Pardon, M. le Sergeant, to what regiment do you belong?'

'Les Gardes du Roi Jacques,' Tadhg replied.

The dragoons, obviously puzzled, but unwilling to acknowledge their ignorance, waved them on.

Being market day, the streets of the village were jammed with bullock-carts and jostling countrymen. Many of the older women wore heavy, dark cloaks like their counterparts in Ireland. The men wore sombre jackets, kneebreeches, and stout boots, spattered with animal dung.

When Tadhg inquired where he could find the Le Berge family, he was met with stony silence. The people gazed with hostility on their uniforms, refusing to answer.

As Tadhg stared back, wondering what he could do, a slender

man in a white waistcoat, and buckles on his shoes, forced his way to the front of the crowd.

'You speak French strangely,' he addressed Tadhg, 'for a soldier in the king's uniform. You must be a mercenary. Would you mind telling me what is your origin?'

'We are Irish soldiers,' Tadhg explained. 'Les Gardes du Roi Jacques.'

'Remarkable! And what would Irish soldiers want with the Le Berges?'

'To pay our respects. Jacques Le Berge, now of Dublin, saved my life last year.'

'More remarkable.' The man gazed at Tadhg, his dark eyes speculative. 'Is there any other way this extraordinary tale can be verified?'

Tadhg stared at him stonily. 'You infer, Monsieur, that I have invented this incident?'

'Show him the grammar book Le Berge gave you,' Dónal suggested.

'A good thought, Dónal.' Tadhg reached into his saddlebag, and rummaging around, produced the dog-eared volume. He handed it to the Frenchman who opened it to the flyleaf. 'Jacques Le Berge, Pau, 17 July, 1672,' he read.

'My pardon, M. le Sergeant,' he said. 'If you will but retire to the inn for a while, I'll see what I can do for you.'

Tadhg and Dónal followed him through the narrow street as the crowd made way for them. They were led to a two-storeyed red-bricked building which stood in the shadow of a massive and forbidding-looking old chateau. Tadhg bought a bottle of Jurançon, which they sat drinking while they waited for the next episode. Several guardsmen, boisterous with drink taken, were singing 'Le Roi Boet!'

It was dark before their guide returned. Apologising for the delay, he led them down the dark street, past the Chateau, and out of the town. No words were spoken, and Tadhg was reminded of his visit to Galloping Hogan. They turned down between a row of acacias, at the end of which was a farmhouse, built of the same red brick as the inn, its steep roof covered with brown tiles.

Their guide knocked on a heavy door, which was opened to a mere slit until the visitors were identified. A boy slipped out to take their horses, and Tadhg and Dónal entered the room. The odour of cooked cabbage permeated the air. The floor was of brick, and by the light from a huge fireplace at the far end, Tadhg could see a half dozen people sitting around a massive table.

They stood as Tadhg approached, and a woman stepped forward to embrace Tadhg in a motherly fashion. 'I am Madame le Berge,' she said, 'and this is my daughter, Françoise; my son Pierre; his wife, Marie; my brother, M de Mazandier, and his son, Gaston.'

Tadhg bowed. 'My name is Tadhg O'Cuirc. My companion is Corporal Dónal O'Devaney. We are soldiers of the Gardes du Roi Jacques.'

A warm smile swept Mme Le Berge's wide face. Observing her stocky stature, and her expressive, dark eyes, Tadhg noted the close resemblance between the mother and the son in Dublin.

'Tell me about Jacques,' she pleaded. 'Is he well? Is he happy?'

'He was when I saw him last about a year ago. He is prospering and free to practise his religion.'

'Bien! That is more than we have here, eh Ettienne?' It was the daughter, Françoise, in contrast to her mother, she was tall and slender. She tossed her chestnut-hued hair defiantly.

'Be careful, Françoise,' her mother said, raising a finger to her lips.

'What can they do, send me to the galleys with Nicolas?'

'You know what they can do to you. Do you want more of that?'

'They can billet those brutal dragoons on us,' her uncle added fearfully. 'You know we can't stand any more of that treatment.'

'It's far better to speak freely and die than be a cowardly slave and live,' Françoise declared fiercely, her lips quivering.

'There are other solutions than death or slavery, so let's not bother our guests with family problems,' her mother admonished her. Then, turning to Tadhg, she asked, 'Have you had dinner?'

'Non, Madame, we haven't had time.'

While Françoise set the table with big bowls of onion soup, boiled cabbage, slabs of yellow cheese, chunks of white bread, slices of cold beef and little honey cakes, Tadhg told the family about Jacques and his flourishing weaving business in Dublin.

'If Nicolas could but join him,' Mme le Berge sighed.

'This Nicolas is the minister whom the authorities are seeking?' Tadhg asked.

Pierre frowned, his eyes suspicious. 'How do you know that, Monsieur?'

'I heard of it in Bordeaux. It was indicated that he was a Le

488

Berge family friend.'

'He is my brother, M le Sergeant,' their guide, Ettienne, remarked quietly. 'The authorities seek him because he refuses to abjure, and cease preaching.'

'What do you mean, 'abjure'?' Tadhg asked.

'To renounce our faith, be converted to Roman Catholicism,' Françoise declared passionately, brandishing a long loaf of bread in her hand like a club. 'That is why my brother Jacques left his family and native land to go to Ireland.'

M. de Mazandier sighed. 'Jacques was one of the courageous ones. Like Francoise and Nicolas. moral courage is a rare quality, Monsieur. Unfortunately few of us have it. So we abjured and became 'New Converts'.

But this is mere lip service. In our minds, in our hearts we are still Reformists. Nicolas refused to abjure, so he is destined to slow death in the service of his king pulling an oar in a stinking galley.'

'If we did not become converts,' his son Gaston added, 'the dragoons would have been foisted on us once more. When they were assigned here after the Revocation of the Edict of Nantes seven years ago, they beat us, robbed us, and raped our women.'

Tadhg was horrified. 'These dragoons? Were they soldiers of the king?'

Françoise snorted. 'Are you a dunce? Certainly they were soldiers of Le Roi Soleil. Ever since that viper, Françoise d'Aubigne, who is now called Mme de Maintenon, once a Protestant herself, and a grand daughter of the Huguenot poet, Agrippa d'Auvigne, crawled into the King's bed, he has been persecuting us more and more.'

'In what way? You seem to have a nice house and farm.'

'I had rather be a doorkeeper in the house of my God than to dwell in the tents of wickedness,' Ettienne quoted. 'In what way have we been persecuted? The church school that I attended at Orthez was ordered closed in the king's name. A Catholic girl I was to marry was put under an edict forbidding it. Most of our churches have been closed. By the royal order we have been banned from the professions of medicine and law and from certain trades. We are harrassed from cradle to death bed.'

'But the King has been deluded by those around him, Ettienne,' Mme Le Berge's brother protested. 'He doesn't know his faithful subjects have suffered this way.'

'If it is done in his name, he must know,' Françoise insisted. 'He has been praised by the Pope for revoking the Edict of Nantes. It is Louis' order that prevents physicians from attending those sick persons who refuse the Sacraments. It is in Louis' name that small children such as Hercule and Pierre Danay and Henri Latour are torn from the arms of their parents to be brought up as Catholics; it is in Louis' name that our people are tortured and executed like Jean-Baptiste Beaupre, and it is on Louis' order that the authorities are searching for Nicolas to silence him.'

This must be a dream, Tadhg thought, a recurrent dream that I have had before. But then it was a Cathal, not a Nicolas, who was being sought by the authorities; it was Oliver Plunkett, Archbishop of Armagh and Primate of Ireland, who was captured and executed, not a Jean-Baptiste; it was small children named Aodh, Brian and Dermot, not Hercule, Pierre and Henri who were forced to be raised in an alien faith.

As Tadhg's indignation and anger grew, he sat with clenched jaw and narrowed eyes staring at his plate. Was there no end to hatred, ignorance, malice and torture? Wasn't this France, the country ruled by his Most Christian Majesty? Wasn't this the land of magnificent cathedrals and thousands of churches? Wasn't this a Catholic country where all should be joyful, nurtured by the love of Jesus Christ for all His children? And hadn't Jesus Christ also been a fugitive sought by the authorities, only to be betrayed, captured and crucified for his beliefs?

What kind of man was this Nicolas Beauvais? Was the religion he preached contrary to the teaching of Jesus? Was he really a threat to king Louis? Were these people in this room really agents of Satan sent to tempt him? Were they truly heretics? Was he endangering his immortal soul by consorting with them?

He turned to Ettienne. 'What can be done to help your brother? All I have is my sword and a few coins. They are at his service.'

Ettienne looked long into Tadhg's eyes. Then he asked. 'You are a Catholic, M. le Sergeant?'

'Certainly. But what does that have to do with Nicolas?'

'You are also a soldier of the king?'

'Yes.'

'Then God help you, for you are either a fool, knave, saint, or madman. You risk unbearable torture and a miserable death for a man you don't even know.'

'Do you think, Ettienne, that we Reformers only have the courage of our convictions' asked Mme le Berge gently. 'Do you think that the thousands of our brethren who have died for their faith were fools, knaves, madmen or saints? Couldn't they have been ordinary children of Christ who suffered as did their saviour? Cannot this Irishman's desire to help Nicolas be divine grace?'

'Perhaps he is an instrument of God,' Françoise said, eyes flashing, 'sent by divine guidance to help Nicolas.'

Tadhg smiled, holding up his hand. 'Whoa, there! I don't think I fit any of those categories, although my old friend, Conor O'Donnell, considered me a fool at times. Perhaps he was right. Perhaps if he was here now he would say it again. I seek neither canonisation nor martyrdom. All I asked was how could I help.'

M de Mazandier pointed to Dónal Óg, asking, 'this young friend hasn't said anything at all. Is her a mute or just a good listener?'

'He speaks very little French,' Tadhg explained.

'Does he know what is being discused? Is he of the same mind as you, or could he cause trouble?'

'He doesn't know as yet, but knowing him as I do, I'm sure he will agree.'

'I have observed ,' M de Mazandier continued , 'that he is of a similar build to Nicolas. Do you think he could be persuaded to let Nicolas borrow his uniform and horse, and accompany you from Pau?'

Tadhg pursed his lips as he considered the proposal. It might work, he thought. Aloud he said, 'I'll ask him.'

Speaking rapidly, Tadhg related the situation, informing Dónal of his offer to help Nicolas, and the suggestion that he exchange clothes with the refugee.

Dónal threw back his head and laughed. 'They want me, a devout Catholic, to exchange places with a Protestant minister? And what do I do if I'm caught at it and sent to the galleys in his place? Say Amen?'

Tadhg was alarmed. You mean you won't help?'

'Of course I will,' he said chuckling. 'You know I have even less sense than you. That's why Conor never liked to leave us alone.'

When the decision was announced, all the persons at the table leaped up, eagerly embracing the Irishmen. When Françoise kissed Dónal, he opened his eyes wide, and returned her kiss so long and thoroughly that her brother tapped Tadhg on the shoulder, murmuring, 'Françoise and Nicolas are betrothed.'

Tadhg gently broke up the embrace, informing Dónal in Irish that he had better save his kisses for some other mademoiselle as this one was reserved for Nicolas.

Dónal grinned. 'So what? You said I was to take his place.'

It was decided that Tadhg and Dónal would return to the inn. Then, early in the morning, they would ride out of town on the road to Oloron. Pierre would meet them near the stone bridge and escort them to where Nicolas and Dónal would trade identities. Then Tadhg and Nicolas would ride to Oloron, where the latter would change clothes again, hide with friends, and return alone to Pau with Dónal's uniform and horse. The plan was contingent upon Nicolas' approval.

Tadhg was silent upon the return to the inn. 'If you're worried about what General Sarsfield would do if he knew what we were planning, stop fretting,' Dónal said, 'I think he would approve of the idea but would not want to be a party to it. I know we're taking a great risk, but let's try to use our brains for a change so that it works out all right.'

Tadhg nodded. 'I hope you're right. But I feel that Conor is looking at me and shaking his head.'

He slept fitfully that night, disturbed at his reckless decision to defy the authorities. In Ireland, at least, when he reacted emotionally, it was in the interest of his country. This time it was for a stranger, just another human being. And likely a heretic! What had prompted him to offer his help? Was he really a fool, a knave or madman or saint? None of the last three for sure and only time would tell if he had been a fool.

They cantered down the muddy road toward Oloron early the next morning, with the sun lighting the vineyards, making long shadows where the sturdy oaks and chestnut trees along the roadside blocked its slanting rays. There was no sign of Pierre when they arrived at the bridge, only a young lad nonchalantly leaning in the stone wall, gazing at the rippling waters below.

As they approached him, he said, without lifting his head, 'keep on riding Monsieur, until you come to the winery. Pierre will meet you there.'

'It's curious they are,' Dónal commented.

'Best for them and best for us'.

Several bullock carts were drawn up at the winery where two men were removing empty barrels from the carts. One of the men was Pierre.

'Tie your horses to the hitching rack,' he whispered, 'and go inside.'

They followed his directions and once inside, with the doors closed, were led to a sheltered area behind the huge vats. In the shadows stood a tall figure with shoulder-length hair. When he raised his head, Tadhg was startled to see the gentlest eyes he had ever seen in a man. Large and brown and steadfast, they dominated the pale face. Now they were gazing at Tadhg with curious expectancy, as he greeted them, 'Bonjour, Messieurs, you have come a long way to help deprive the king of an oarsman.'

'Better that than deprive God of an assistant,' Tadhg replied.

'Merci beaucoup,' Nicolas said, his mouth curving in a broad smile, the brown eyes aglow with pleasure. 'I couldn't have phrased it better myself'

'We must hurry,' Pierre interrupted nervously. 'It is rumoured that the dragoons are going to search all the buildings in the area today. And you know, Nicolas, Sergeant St Clair would like to capture you.'

'What do you have in mind' Tadhg asked the minister.

'I will trade places with your young friend. We will ride to Oloron where we will stay with friends until I can be passed from village to village in the mountains. Eventually I will reach Narbonne to take passage on a ship.'

'And leave France?'

'I have no choice.'

'You would do this for your religion?'

Nicolas shook his head. 'No, not for my religion. For my freedom of conscience.'

'You are a courageous man.'

'Perhaps more perversely stubborn than courageous.'

'Enough of this chatter,' Pierre interrupted. It's growing late.'

A few minutes later, Tadhg and Nicolas mounted the horses and clattered on down the road. Tadhg told his companion how he had first met Le Berge, and was given the French grammar. He described his rescue from Lieutenant Benton, praising Le Berge for his role, and pointing out how the Huguenot had placed his life in jeopardy by helping Tadhg, a Catholic.

'A fine man, Jacques,' Nicolas said. 'It is a pity that he had to leave Pau, especially when Françoise was left unprotected. Perhaps it might not have happened of Jacques had been there.'

'What was that, Monsieur?'

Nicolas' eyes were sad and his shoulders drooped. 'It was during the dragonnade two years ago. A squad of dragoons came to Pau to extirpate all vestiges of the evangelical faith. Our minister Jean-Baptiste was seized, children were taken from their parents, and hundreds were forced into the Catholic churches on penalty of severe punishment.'

'By what authority were these atrocities committed?'

'The revocation of the Edict of Nantes, in 1685 by Louis XIV. Our church services were prohibited, and anyone who attended services, or worshipped God according to our religion, were to be punished, the men to the galleys, the women, confiscation of body and goods. Sergeant Antoine St Clair, who commanded the dragoons, and who was billeted at the Le Berge farmhouse, interpreted this as a licence to possess personally the women's bodies. Among others he took Françoise, then a girl fo fifteen.'

Tadhg was aghast. 'You mean this sergeant raped her? A young defenceless girl?'

'Yes, and as long as he was there - for six months - he took her whenever the mood was on him.'

His eyes blazing with indignation and anger, Tadhg asked, 'But why wasn't something done to stop him?'

Nicolas sighed. 'Many wanted to, but Mme Le Berge counselled against it. She said that the entire town would be cruelly punished like at Montauban. She is a rare and courageous women, Mme Le Berge. Françoise wanted to kill St Clair or herself, but her mother persuaded her to suffer her persecutors as did Jesus Christ.'

'And where is this Sergeant St Clair now?'

'He is back in Pau now that the campaign in the North is over. This is the reason for the urgency in my leaving as soon as possible. You see, M Le Sergeant, I have not been a minister very long. When I took Jean Baptiste's place after he was tortured and slain, Sergeant St Clair publicly vowed that he would return to Pau some day and arrest me. Two years ago he and his men came back. I have been hiding ever since.

'I have been told that you are going to marry Françoise,' Tadhg said, undisguised contempt in his voice. 'Why didn't you do something?'

Nicolas's eyes were sad as he looked at Tadhg. 'By something,' he said gently, 'you infer that I should have killed the Sergeant? Or urged others to kill him? I am a minister of God, M le Sergeant. If I am to teach God's commandments, I must obey them.'

Tadhg was instantly contrite. 'I am sorry, monsieur. I did not think. But I am concerned about Françoise. What is she to do with you gone? Become again the plaything of Sergeant St. Clair?'

Nicolas lowered his head, his shoulders drooped. Tadhg quickly averted his head for fear he might see the tears he sensed were coursing down his companion's cheeks. He cursed himself for being so maladroit. He bit his lips in vexation. What to do? As he stared at Cúchulainn's broad back, the solution came.

'Wait,' he said, checking his horse. 'There is a ship at Bordeaux about to sail to Ireland. I think that you should go there instead of Narbonne.' Tadhg beamed. 'And take Françoise with you.'

'Non,' Nicolas said, his eyes forlorn, 'the dragoons will be watching. That way there is great danger. And Sergeant St. Clair would suspect. He and his men are watching all travellers.'

'I know. I know. They intercepted Dónal and me yesterday. They know that we are here in Pau. All the more reason to go boldly past them.'

The Huguenot eyes gleamed. 'And what about Françoise?'

'We'll have the cooper prepare a special barrel for her and send her off to Bordeaux with the wine shipment for Captain Benoit.'

'Mon Dieu, mon Dieu!' Nicolas was ecstatic. 'It might work. We could save Françoise.' He turned his horse. 'Come, M. le Sergeant, let us return quickly to the winery.'

Pierre was furious when he saw them ride up. 'Are you mad?' he shouted, greatly perturbed. 'The hounds are seeking the hare, and the hare runs back to meet the hounds. You should be on your way to Olorn.'

He was more upset when he learned of the change in the plans. But Nicolas was eloquent and convincing. Even the cooper, Penguilin de Pise, was enthusiastic.

'I will make a little seat,' he said, gesturing with his calloused hands, 'to make her comfortable. There shall be food and water. And false bottom with little wine inside to issue from the bung in case a nosy soldier should want to sample the barrel.'

Pierre agreed reluctantly. 'How long will it take?'

The cooper shrugged. 'A couple of hours at the most. In the meanwhile, start loading the cart for its journey. Save room on the end for our special barrel, Vintage Françoise.'

'What's this all about?' Dónal asked Tadhg, puzzled at the return.

Tadhg rapped his forehead with his knuckle. 'I forgot about you,' he admitted. In French, he explained the problem to Pierre.

'He shall wear Bernaise clothing and accompany me on the

wagon. I need a helper, anyway.'

While De Pise returned to his cooperage, and suitable clothing sought for Dónal, two stout Huguenots wrestled the filled barrels on the wagon by the use of ropes, and Pierre went to notify Françoise to prepare for her journey. Tadhg itched to help with the loading, but was advised not to call undue attention to his presence at the winery. He grew apprehensive as the minutes passed, with no sign of the cooper, or the Le Berges, brother and sister.

Nicolas, hiding in the dark corner behind the vats, was alone with his thoughts.

Finally De Pise returned with his oxcart, several barrels rattling back and forth as the crude vehicle bounced on the rutted road. Simultaneously Pierre and Françoise emerged furtively from the vineyard where they had been awaiting the arrival of the cooper. Quickly then, in the gloom of the old building, Françoise, trembling with excitement, climbed in to her barrel, her dark eyes shining happily.

De Pise showed her the food and water, and then attached broad leather straps to keep her from bouncing and possibly injuring herself. Françoise looked about, apparently for Nicolas, as the cooper secured the lid. Then ropes were tied around the wagon, securing the barrels.

While Pierre and Dónal, now dressed as a Brenaise, took their places on the seat, De Pise turned a spigot to draw a glass of wine from Françoise's barrel for an amused Tadhg.

'*Sláinte, sláinte* and *sláinte* again,' Tadhg said to the invisible Françoise, drinking her health.

Pierre cracked his long whip, the horses lurched forward, and the wagon lumbered off on the road through Pau. Tadhg returned to confer with Nicolas. The Huguenot looked worried.

'Pardon, M le Sergeant,' he began hesitantly, 'I am sure you know what you are doing, but just how are you going to persuade the ship's captain to transport two fugitive Huguenots to Ireland.'

Tadhg smiled. 'It's best that you leave that to me.'

The French man looked questioningly at Tadhg. 'It is something you would prefer that I did not know?'

'Perhaps.' Tadhg was non-committal.

About an hour after the wagon had left, Tadhg and Nicolas mounted their horses, riding boldly towards the village. They had passed the old chateau when they encountered two dragons.

'Bon jour,' Tadhg greeted them.

The soldiers stopped abruptly, staring at their uniforms.

'We are Irish soldiers of King James in the service of France,' Tadhg explained. We're here to fight the English,' he added.

'Bien!' the closest one replied, repressing a laugh at Tadhg's quaint French, then nodding, moved on.

As they passed through Pau, the inhabitants paid little attention to them, although several stopped to stare again at Nicolas after a first cursory glance. They appeared puzzled.

Two more dragoons were stationed at the opposite end of the town at the crossroads. It was the same pair that had been there the previous day. They grinned broadly whin they recognised Tadhg.

'Aha, it's the big Irelander,' one said, 'who speaks French like a Castilian. Bon jour, senor.'

'Buenos Dias, Monsieur.' Tadhg replied.

They dawdled over their lunch (sharp goat's milk cheese with coarse brown bread and a flask of Jurançon) lest they overtake the wine wagon too soon. They planned to rendezvous with Pierre at the inn at Orthez. Then they took a nap under a chestnut tree before resuming their journey.

They were plodding up a sharp rise in the road when they heard the sound of angry voices. When they reached the crest they saw Pierre's wagon halted at the entrance to an old wooden bridge. Two mounted dragoons were blocking the bridge.

'Mon dieu!' Nicolas exclaimed, his face grey, 'It's Sergeant St. Clair.'

While they watched from the hill, Pierre climbed down from the wagon, and gesticulating energetically, approached the barrel where Françoise was hidden. Taking a canteen from one of the dragoons, and turning the spigot, he filled it with wine, then returned it to the dragoon. The other, meanwhile, a stocky man with quick movements, proceeded to tap the sides of the barrels with the stock of his musket.

Tadhg felt his heart beat rapidly as he watched the dragoon methodically work his way around the wagon, tapping as he went. When he reached the barrel where Pierre stood, he thrust out his musket which Pierre pushed aside angrily. After a furious exchange of words, the dragoon pointed his weapon at Pierre who slowly moved away.

The sound of the ensuing rat-a-tat on Françoise's barrel was so obviously different from the dull thuds produced by the others that it was apparent even to the apprehensive observers on the hill.

Lowering his musket, the dragoon drew a knife, cutting the rope that secured the cargo. Then he reached to the top of Françoise's barrel, and with a hearty pull, sent it crashing to the ground.

Angry, bruised and humiliated, Françoise crawled from the sodden wreckage of oak staves and iron hoops, her eyes blazing, her gown soaked with wine. It was then that Tadhg lashed Cúchulainn with the reins, charging furiously down the hill. The stocky dragoon watched Tadhg's approach with a smug smile, pleased to have soldier reinforcement as he stood calmly surveying the fuming Françoise, an amused Dónal, and a crestfallen Pierre. Abruptly the dragoon stooped, and clutching the girl by her long tresses, cruelly yanked her to her feet.

When Françoise spat at him, he released her hair, drew her roughly to him, and while his right hand pinched her buttocks, kissed her hard on the mouth, Françoise clawing at him futilely. Dismounting hastily, Tadhg grabbed the dragoon, forcing him to release the girl.

With a loud snarl, the soldier swung around, his face distorted with rage. Hate-filled green eyes glared at Tadhg. His lips were drawn up tightly over his gums, exposing his teeth like a vicious dog about to bite.

As Tadhg watched him warily, the dragoon's rage slowly subsided. Finally, in an icy tone, he said, 'You have interfered with a soldier of the king. You, too, are under arrest.'

'For what?' asked Tadhg. 'Is it contrary to the laws of France to take a load of wine to the market? If so, the vintners have a bleak future.'

The dragoon stared at Tadhg, his mouth agape. Then he pointed to his chevrons. 'I am sergeant of dragoons. These Huguenots, these blasphemous heretics, were escaping from Pau. I am taking them back to be tried for their crimes against the king.'

Tadhg in turn pointed to his chevrons. 'I am a mareschal des logis, Les Gardes du Jacques. I say these people have committed no crimes. You are not going to return them to Pau!'

Sergeant St, Clair turned to the other dragoon. 'Take his pistol and sword, Phillippe.'

Stepping back, Tadhg drew his sword as he faced the dragoon. 'You advance at your peril, Monsieur.'

The dragoon looked at his sergeant, hesitating.

'Do as I ordered,' St, Clair snapped.

When Phillippe again advanced, Tadhg repeated his warning.

The dragoon, intimidated by Tadhg's size and grim visage, reached for his own pistol. With one quick, forward motion, Tadhg ran him through the belly with his sword. Phillippe grunted like a stricken animal, dropped his weapon, and fell inert on the wine-drenched earth.

Sergeant St, Clair snorted loudly (later compared by Françoise to an angry bull), unsheathed his sword swiftly, and pointed it at Tadhg as if he was a chunk of meat about to be spitted.

'Dónal,' shouted Tadhg in Irish, 'get Françoise and Pierre on the wagon and over the bridge. Take the road to Orthez.'

'We can't leave you here alone, Tadhg,' Dónal protested.

'Don't argue with me, just get moving.'

As the wagon started rumbling over the bridge, Sergeant St, Clair moved forward as if to stop it, but Tadhg barred his way, standing his ground. The dragoon paused, thumbs hooked in his baldric, staring at Tadhg with fury and frustration, trying to control himself. But the sight of the wagon disappearing over the bridge was too much for him. With another angry snort forced violently through flaring nostrils, he advanced on Tadhg with extended sword.

It had been a long time since Tadhg had duelled; his Spanish sword felt light in his hand after the heavier cavalry sabre he had been using. As he parried and thrust, however, his confidence in his skill returned. Sergeant St, Clair was a strong swordsman, a worthy opponent, but he was not a Montgomery óg.

Tadhg studied his foe carefully. The Frenchman was extremely agile, despite his bulk, and there was no question of his strength. But he lacked finesse. Although his lunges were powerful, his timing was poor. Tadhg had just to be patient; his opportunity would come.

As the wary adversaries circled, thrusting and hacking, Sergeant St, Clair began to realise that he was outmatched. As his anger gave way to fear, he wanted desperately to submit to his opponent. His instinct, however, told him that his treatment of Françoise was somehow involved, and that it was a fight to the death.

Circling cautiously, with only the angry clash of the steel and the laboured breaths of the swordsmen audible, Tadhg decided to end the fight quickly before more dragoons arrived. He forced his foe back until the Frenchman was standing in the rutted road where the footing was precarious. Off balance, St, Clair struck at Tadhg wildly. It was over in a moment. A lightning thrust through the throat, and Tadhg was standing over his opponent, gazing curiously at the lump of flesh that had once terrorised Françoise, and had been determined to send Nicolas to the galleys.

Nicolas? Where was Nicolas? Tadhg raised his eyes to the hill where he had left him. He was still there, astride Dónal's horse. Tadhg gestured to come down. Slowly the minister descended the hill. The ascetic face was pale, the luminous brown eyes sadder than ever.

He shook his head as he looked down at the dead dragoons. 'Why did it have to come to this?' he asked, and Tadhg felt that the query was directed more to his God than to his earthly companion. Yet Tadhg was constrained to answer, 'It would have cost Pierre his life, and Françoise her liberty.'

Nicolas looked at him with curious speculation. Under the steady gaze, Tadhg felt inadequate, as if he was at fault. 'It had to be done this way. The violence was his decision. He was a tyrant. He was vicious. He was a menace to you and all the Le Berges.'

'Eye for eye, tooth for tooth,' Nicolas said, his voice soft and low. 'Why must the vengeful maxims of the ancient Israelites always triumph over the preaching of our Lord Jesus?'

Tadhg stood silent. He knew that their conflicting views were irreconcilable. The deaths of the two dragoons were regrettable; the alternative, however, would have been disastrous for all concerned.

Finally Nicolas spoke. 'We must do something with these bodies. We must take them back to Pau for proper burial.'

'That would mean your arrest, and most likely your execution,' Tadhg stated tersely, staring at the minister with amazement.

'I realise that.'

'No,' Tadhg replied, shaking his head, 'I will not have it. There is too much at stake here for you to absolve your conscience at the expense of the others. All of us must bear burdens; this will be yours. Now you remount your horse and start down the road to Orthez. Pierre and Françoise must be informed that the immediate danger is over.'

Nicolas was about to protest, but looking into Tadhg's determined eyes, and noting the clenched jaw, climbed on his horse, and with a slight wave of his hand, left Tadhg with the two dragoons.

I have nothing to bury them with, he thought. Besides, I don't have time. Other dragoons or travellers may come upon the scene.

I must get rid of them to prevent alarm and pursuit. But where?

Then he became aware of the muffled roar of the river under the bridge. Why not the river? It would hide the bodies for some time, perhaps forever. The longer the fate of St Clair and his companion remained unknown, the longer the reason for their disappearance would remain unsolved. Quickly then he carried the bodies to the parapet and eased them over the edge. Two loud splashes and it was done. The hurrying waters sang the funeral dirge; Tadhg's brief prayer committing them to their watery graves was their requiem.

Tadhg mounted Cúchulainn, and leading the two dragoons horses, crossed over the bridge to follow the others. He soon caught up to Nicolas who looked into his eyes briefly, but said nothing. They rode in silence until they overtook the wagon.

Françoise was overjoyed to see them. She reeked of wine, but embraced both of them, loudly thanking God for their deliverance. Pierre was still worried. He looked at the dragoons' horses, then back to Tadhg.

'I'll leave one in the first good pasture we come to,' he explained. 'I'll need the other later. It will take some time before word gets back to Pau.'

'What happened?' Dónal asked Tadhg in the Gaelic.

Tadhg described the fight, his difficulty with Nicolas, and the disposal of the corpses.

'I would have stayed if I thought I was needed,' Dónal said, 'but I knew that you could handle him, and that it was best I keep these two on their way. I tried to tell them they needn't worry about you, but my French was inadequate.'

They stayed in Orthez that night, Morcenx the second night, Gujan the third, and late in the afternoon of the fourth day, arrived at Bordeaux. While the three Bernais went to the inn, Tadhg and Dónal sought out Jacques Benoit. The captain was happy to see them, but was astonished.

'I thought you had returned to General Sarsfield by now,' he greeted them. 'What brings you back to Bordeaux?'

'My conscience bothered me. I was too brusque with you when you wanted to buy Cúchulainn. I never gave you an opportunity to make an offer.'

Benoit stared at Tadhg, his eyes questioning. 'You have something in mind, mon ami? You are serious?'

'I'll be honest with you,' Tadhg said. 'If you meet my price

501

Cúchulainn is yours.'

'Why the sudden change of heart?' Benoit asked, a shrewd look on his face. 'You are taking a poor bargaining position, admitting that you are obviously willing to sell.'

'No. I have a set price. You're the one who has to do the bargaining. It all depends upon how overwhelming is your desire to have my horse.'

'Has he gone lame? Are you trying to peddle him to me?' the captain asked, his voice thick with suspicion.

'No again! Why don't you come to the stable and examine him?'

'A good idea.'

Shortly, Benoit was examining Cúchulainn, leading him around the stable yard, carefully watching every move the horse made. He sighed. 'A little tired, perhaps, from hard riding, but apparently he is in good shape.' He stood back, admiring the animal. Then he turned to Tadhg. 'Well, what are you asking for him?'

Tadhg stood close to Benoit, gazing straight into his eyes. 'I want you to do something which I know you will at first refuse to do. Only your greed for this horse will possibly make you waver and accept my offer. I will not even tell you what it is unless you are willing to admit that your passion to own Cúchulainn is so great that you would in effect sell your soul to the devil to own the horse.'

Benoit was aghast. 'Mon Dieu. Then you are not asking for money?'

'No.'

The captain stared at Cúchulainn. He wet his lips. Then he turned to Tadhg. 'Monsieur, I know that you love your horse. You do not want money for him, yet you are willing to part with him, even though it is most difficult, something that you would not otherwise do. And your price is one so great that I would not normally pay except for my eagerness to possess this horse? In other words, we would both be making most unusual sacrifices in this transaction?'

'Yes,' Tadhg replied, trying not to look at Cúchulainn, lest his determination waver, 'that about covers it.'

'Alright, mon ami. I am hooked. Let us discuss your terms.'

'Passage to Ireland for a man and a woman.'

Benoit laughed gaily, showing his relief. 'Passage on my ship? Ah, that is no problem.' Then, realising that the gravity of Tadhg's proposal clearly indicated that the solution couldn't be that easy, his eyes narrowed and he stared at Tadhg intently. 'Who are these passengers?' he asked, his voice suddenly grim.

'Nicolas Beauvais and Françoise Le Berge.'

The mariner recoiled. 'The Huguenots from Pau?'

Tadhg looked at him steadily. 'Two human beings who urgently need your help.'

Benoit shook his head violently. 'Non! I could lose my ship. And my head. And for these spawn of Satan? These Huguenot dogs who defy the true church? This preacher of heresy? Non, mon ami, your price is too great.' He shivered as with fever.

Tadhg reached out and grasped Benoit's shoulder gently, but firmly. 'In Ireland the Catholics suffer from the Protestants; in France the Protestants suffer from the Catholics. This confuses me for it seems contrary to the teachings of Our Saviour. If Jesus forgave those who persecuted and crucified Him, then what else can Jacques Benoit and Tadhg O'Cuirc do? Nicolas and Françoise are good people. This I swear. They need help to flee their persecutors. Your help and mine.'

Benoit sighed heavily. 'You were right when you said I would have to sell my soul to the devil. You ask the impossible. But you, too, risk your life. And you are willing to sacrifice your magnificent horse for the sake of these miserable people. Have they worked a magic spell over you?'

'Perhaps,' said Tadhg, shrugging his shoulders. 'I have rejected many a rich offer for Cúchulainn, yet now I find myself offering him to you to aid two people I didn't event know existed when I was here a week ago.'

The Frenchman shook his head in wonder. He looked again at the horse, pursing his lips so hard his moustache twisted grotesquely. Then he turned to Tadhg, his eyes crinkling in sudden humour. 'Ma foi, M. le Sergeant, they must have put their spell on both of us. We are a pair of fools, eh, mon ami?'

Although inwardly elated at Benoit's change of mood, Tadhg merely shrugged his shoulders. 'You include yourself, then?' he asked.

'Parbleu! It is no secret that I madly covet your horse. I am not a mere Gasconade. So I will accept Cúchulainn, what an odd name for a horse, in exchange for the passage of 'two human beings who need help' to Ireland. But understand it was not alone my greed for the horse. It was you, too, my friend. If you can make the noble gesture, why can't Jacques Benoit? For the animal alone, I would not have consented. I will take good care of your friends. Agreed?'

His voice breaking with emotion, Tadhg said, 'It is agreed. Knowing that Cúchulainn is in the hands of a good man, not a greedy one, will make it easier for me to part with him.'

Benoit smiled joyously. 'A good greedy man,' he corrected. Then he became serious. 'You will want to tell your friends then? We will sail as son as the Juraçon arrives from Pau.'

When the wine barrels were snug in the hold, Dónal went to the inn to get the travellers . They boarded quietly and unostentatiously, going immediately to Captain Benoit's small cabin. Here the tearful farewells were said, kisses exchanged and eternal friendship made. Then Tadhg, Dónal and Pierre clambered over the ship's side to the jetty, the St Teresa's lines were cast off, and the stout ship started its sixty-mile journey down the Garonne to the sea.

They watched sadly, and when they could no longer read St Teresa - Bordeaux on the high stern, Pierre mounted his wagon-seat, cracked his whip, and with a wave of his hand, started back to Pau.

Tadhg and Dónal retrieved their horses from the stable, and were soon on the north bank of the Garonne, heading for Versailles.

Dónal glanced quizzically at Tadhg. 'Well,' he asked

'Well, what?'

'What are you going to tell General Sarsfield when you come riding in on this old swaybacked nag instead of Cúchulainn?'

Tadhg felt an irrational annoyance at Dónal's question. He knew that it was circumlocution, that Dónal was curious at Tadhg's action in helping the Huguenots, and disposing of the stallion, his prized possession. But he hadn't analyzed his own reasons as yet; he was annoyed with himself for having yielded again to an impulsive gesture, risking his life and Dónal's, yet gratified with the result.

'This swaybacked old nag has the king's mark on him. Some miles short of Versailles I will turn him loose to graze. Even if the lucky farmer who finds him in his pasture is stupid enough to return him to the authorities, I doubt if he can ever be traced to Pau. I will tell the general that Cúchulainn was stolen by cut-throats.

Dónal was shocked. 'You will lie to General Sarsfield?'

'Would you have me tell him the truth,' Tadhg snapped.

Dónal winced at Tadhg's tone. 'I suppose it would be best that he didn't know. Not that he would tell King Louis that one of his Irish soldiers had killed two French dragoons.'

'They deserved killing,' Tadhg scowled, eyes angry.

Dónal didn't refer to the subject again. They abandoned Tadhg's mount near Corbeil, and riding and walking alternately, arrived at Boulogne on the evening of the sixth day. Tadhg immediately reported to Lord Lucan.

'It took you much longer than I expected,' Sarsfield said. 'I was worried that you had decided to leave me and return to Ireland.'

'I was tempted to,' Tadhg admitted. He informed the general that Captain Benoit was pleased to be of service, and God willing, would have Lady Honora's nephew with him on the return voyage. He explained that the reason why they were late was the theft of Cúchulainn while he and Dónal were napping by the side of the road near Verdome.

Sarsfield was indignant and shocked at the loss of the horse, for he also had coveted Cúchulainn. I'll report it at once,' he exploded. 'Those thieving French blackguards must be taught a lesson.'

CHAPTER II

The Wager

With the army in winter quarters, and Tadhg acting as an aide-de-camp to General Sarsfield, (while Dónal jocularly referred to himself as 'aide-de-scamp' to Tadhg) the days passed pleasantly. Food was good and plentiful. Their pay was regular and in the coin of the realm, a far cry from the worthless brass money of James II. Wine was cheap, and entertainment was readily available in nearby Paris, including houses with ladies whose commodity was love. It was a period of ease and contentment for the Connemara men.

One cold day in December, Tadhg was sent with a message for Lady Sarsfield who was visiting a friend, Mme de Fortier, on the rue Beautreillis. He was to accompany Lady Honora back to Boulogne, so he waited for her. When she emerged, she was accompanied by a petite, black-eyed woman wearing a heavy cloak trimmed with rich fur and a matching hat. Her bold scrutiny of Tadhg was as thorough as Captain Benoit's with Cúchulainn. Noting his embarrassment, she laughed gaily, peering at him coquettishly under her long, dark eyelashes.

'You have made a conquest, Tadhg,' Lady Honora told him later, an amused smile on her face. 'Mme le Clerc said she was going to request the king to have you assigned to her service instead of Patrick's, and mine.'

Tadhg was appalled. 'She can't do that, can she, *a bhean uasail*?'

'No.' Lady Sarsfield laughed. 'I was just teasing, but she collects men, especially handsome young ones, like Louis XIV collects inamoratas. Her husband is very old and very rich. You had better watch out lest you become one more item in her collection.'

'Not me,' Tadhg replied, annoyed at the implication he could be acquired like a stallion.

'Still thinking of Mairéad Fitzgerald?' Honora teased.

Tadhg coloured. 'I never think of her,' he lied.

'I'll tell Mme le Clerc the next time I see her that you defied her attempt to charm you. I'll inform her that you prefer golden-haired *cailíns* to black-haired French noblewomen. Do you mind if i bait her?'

'No, *a bhean uasail*,' he replied politely, embarrassed to be the subject of romantic banter, yet flattered by the attention of two beautiful women. 'Just tell her to lavish her affection on her husband.'

Lady Sarsfield giggled. 'This is France, Tadhg, not Ireland. Among the nobility, infidelity is the rule, not the exception. Exhibiting affection for one's spouse in public would be considered in bad taste. Open flirtation, assignations, mistresses and lovers are commonplace.'

Tadhg's face reflected his shock at the revelation. Honora thought she had better put it in perspective. 'The nobility merely follows the pattern set by their sovereign. Although Louis has slowed down considerably, he has had many mistresses. He has gone through scores of beautiful women since he was a youth, including Mme de la Vallier, Mme de Monterpan, Mme de Fontages, even Mme de Maintenon, his present inamorata, and although rumour has it that they are secretly married he has not officially designated her as Queen of France.'

Several weeks later Tadhg accompanied Lady Sarsfield to Paris for her monthly visit to Mme de Fortier. As usual, he repaired to a nearby wine shop to pass time while waiting. As he was enjoying one of the vins du pays, a local wine, a footman garbed in a blue satin livery approached him, stating that Lady Sarsfield would not return to Boulogne until the following day, and his time was his own until then.

Tadhg always enjoyed the quiet atmosphere of the shop. It gave him an opportunity to practise his French, and to sample the vins du pays and cuisine. Dawdling over his drink, he was joined by a soldier in the hose, doublet, boots and cape of one of the king's musketeers. The newcomer started a conversation, and Tadhg was amused by the high-pitched voice, like that of a youth before attaining manhood.

'You're quite young to be a musketeer,' Tadhg said, looking into a pair of black eyes set in an oval face which reminded him of Patrick Sarsfield. Then he added, 'Haven't I met you before? You look familiar.'

'Je crois que non,' the musketeer replied. 'Unless it was here where I come occasionally.'

'Well, perhaps,' Tadhg replied, nettled at his inability to remember.

The musketeer then insisted on buying a bottle of wine for each of them, which he jocularly called 'Les Amoureuses'.

'Les Amoureuses?' Tadhg asked, frowning. 'Doesn't that mean ladies in love? What an odd name for a wine.'

'Ah, some day you will understand, perhaps. Now just let us enjoy ourselves.'

Because of his unexpected free time, his companion's clever conversation and the bonhomie, Tadhg drank more than usual, so that when the musketeer suggested that they visit a bordello, Tadhg was enthusiastically agreeable.

Out on the street, the young soldier led the way, singing bawdy French songs as they meandered to the rue St Honore, stopping at a large private hotel where his companion turned to Tadhg.

'Leave everything to me,' he said. 'I will make all the arrangements and pay the girls. No,' he said firmly when Tadhg remonstrated, 'you can return the favour another time.'

The door was opened by a footman who looked quizzically from one to the other, but the musketeer, in a rapid burst of French in a dialect Tadhg couldn't understand, apparently satisfied him.

'This way, monsieur,' the servant said to Tadhg, leading him up winding stairs into a room whose furniture, including a huge canopied bed, and all the furnishings, were gold-coloured, as well as the bathtub.

Tadhg was uneasy with all the opulence, but was intrigued by the tub. His previous experience had been with wooden vats on those rare occasions he had the opportunity to bath indoors. As he stood staring at the tub, a page entered the room carrying a pail of hot water.

'Undress and get in the tub,' the page indicated. 'Turn that spigot for the cold water, I'll bring the hot.'

Impressed with the arrangements, Tadhg stripped and stepped into the tub. He let the cold water run while the page added hot water. When there was sufficient water, the page, started to rub soap on Tadhg. 'Stop it,' he shouted angrily, pushing at the page, 'I can do that myself.'

As Tadhg stared at the apparently disappointed page directly for the first time he blinked, then asked, 'Do you have a brother who is a musketeer?'

'Non. I have only four sisters. Why?'

'You look almost identical to the soldier who brought me here, same dark hair and oval-shaped face.'

'You must be befuddled from too much wine,' the page replied. 'How could I be a soldier and a page simultaneously?'

'You're probably right,' Tadhg said.

'Certainly. Now finish your bath and I'll call Charlotte.'

'Charlotte? Oh, yes, the girl. The fille de joie.'

When Tadhg finished with his bath, and was vigorously drying himself in the bedroom, there came a knock on the door, and a woman's voice saying, 'Monsieur?'

'Come in, mademoiselle,' Tadhg said, covering himself with the towel.

Conforming to the motif of the room, the girl who entered quickly, was dressed all in gold. Bodice, blouse, skirt, stockings, and slippers were all matched with her long, golden tresses. Gold earrings dangled from petite lobes, while gold bracelets on her arms and gold rings on her fingers completed the ensemble. She pirouetted gracefully, flinging her arms aloft, saying, 'Am I not lovely?'

Tadhg stood still, his mouth agape, stunned by the bizarre magnificence of the room and this beautiful woman. She stamped her foot impatiently. 'What's the matter? Are you deaf?'

'My oath,' stammered Tadhg. 'Some men are tempted by lust, and some by gold. My temptation here is both.'

Charlotte smiled happily. 'You admire girls with golden hair?'

Tadhg nodded vigorously.

'You do not like girls with dark hair?'

'Well, I like them, but...'

'Oh as a sister, eh?'

Tadhg brightened at the suggestion. 'Yes, I have several sisters back in Ireland.'

'You are Irish?' She asked, peering at him demurely from the corners of her dark eyes.

'Oui, Mademoiselle.'

'Come then, and make Irish love to me.'

Tadhg hesitated. She stamped her foot again. 'Come here Cheri!'

When he approached, she snatched the towel from his hand, then stood back coolly appraising him. 'Magnificent, just as I thought,' she said in obvious approval.

'Kiss me,' she demanded. He approached slowly, his face red with embarrassment. As he kissed her, she embraced him, running her finger tips tantalisingly up and down his spine, across his back and shoulders.

'Now undress me,' she ordered.

As Tadhg clumsily started to lift her skirt, she slapped his hand.

'Are you a bull, snorting in the pasture? Or a stallion, squealing for a mare? I am a woman, and this is a love chamber. We have plenty of time, so remove my garments slowly and gently, while you kiss me and fondle me.'

What kind of a bordello is this? Tadhg thought. Usually the girl is in a hurry for the next customer. As if in a dream he removed each garment, kissing her avidly, often fumbling fingers impatiently aided by hers.

She tousled his hair, running her fingers through his long locks, then moved her fingertips gently over his torso, kissing him passionately, murmuring inarticulately the while.

When only her undergarments were left - also in gold - she led him to the bed. 'I can see that you know little of the art of love,' she chided, 'so I will be your teacher.'

'Yes, mon amie,' he mumbled.

'Mon amie?' She laughed uproariously. 'What would you call your Irish sweetheart if you were in bed with her? 'My friend?'

Even Tadhg saw the humour of it. He joined her laughter. 'No, I would call her '*mavourneen*', or '*mo rún*'.

'What do these words mean?'

'My darling, mu pulse, my heart and dear.'

'I like the second one best. I have never been called 'my heart and dear' before. So call me '*mo rún*'. I think it is very fitting. When we are locked in loving embrace, our pulses will beat madly. And our hearts. What is your name?'

'Tadhg.'

'Good. Now Tadhg, *mo rún*, you may remove the last of my clothing.'

They tumbled on to the bed in tight embrace. Several hours later, a discreet knock was heard. 'Who is it?' Charlotte asked, sitting up in bed. 'The refreshments, madame,' a man's voice replied.

'Leave them at the door. I will get them.'

She slipped out of bed, her derriere wriggling as she walked to the door. She returned with a tray which contained cognac, champagne and hors d'oeuvres. Tadhg was aghast. 'I can't afford all this,' he complained.

'Stop worrying, your friend, the soldier, has paid for all of it. Come, eat and drink heartily to keep up your strength for most of the night is still ahead of you.'

'All night?'

'Certainement! You still have so much to learn. Now entwine

me with your strong arms, but be careful not to disturb my hair.'

The pale winter sun streaming through the window awoke Tadhg. He sat upright in the strange bed, not knowing where he was. Then the gold furniture and surroundings, plus the pile of golden garments strewn carelessly on the rug, reminded him that he was in a bordello. His head was splitting, his mouth tasted foul, and he had an overwhelming thirst.

'A hair from the hound that bit me,' he muttered to himself, staggering from the bed, intending to finish the cognac or the champagne. But all the bottles were empty. It must have been a wild night, he thought. His companion was sleeping quietly, her lips curved in a slight smile. Tadhg dressed quietly. Before quitting the room, he returned to the bed to bid Charlotte a silent adieu.

As he stood admiring her, with her arms clutched around a pillow as if to hide from his view her firm breasts, her exquisite tapering thighs gleaming white against the golden bedsheet, he suddenly became aware of an incongruity.

That's odd, he thought, alternately looking from the dark triangle at the junction of her thighs to the golden hair of her head. Both should be the same colour, he muttered. Then, shaking his head in bewilderment, he quietly left the room.

He encountered no one as he walked through the hallway, down the curving staircase, and through several magnificent rooms to the front door, although he heard stirrings in the back part of the house where the servants were starting the day's chores. Awed by the munificence of the mansion, and dazed by his experience, he made his way to the street where a lackey, an old man in a faded coat, was busy sweeping.

'A soldier? So early in the morning? Is the enemy attacking Paris?' he cackled, his toothless mouth twisted into a merry grin.

'Oui, grandpere, and I've been ordered to defend this bordello at all costs.'

'Bordello? What bordello?'

'That one, of course,' said Tadhg, pointing to the building from which he had just emerged.

The old man looked at him pityingly. 'Too much to drink, too much to drink. This is no bordello, brave soldier, but the hotel of M le Clerc.'

M le Clerc?' said Tadhg slowly. 'And is there a Mme le Clerc here as well?'

The old man leered, his rheumy eyes trying hard to reflect his lewd thoughts. 'Ah, that Mme le Clerc! I wish I was forty years younger.'

He peered at Tadhg, shrewd conjecture replacing licentiousness. 'She's a rare one. Beautiful and talented. And what fabulous costumes and wigs she wears for the fetes and balls she loves to give. 'Tis said that the great Jean Racine tried to induce her to act in his dramas.'

'Costumes?' asked Tadhg. 'Wigs?'

The old man snorted, 'All kinds.'

'And does that include soldiers, pages and such?'

'I said all kinds. Why just yesterday I saw her leave in her coach dressed like one of her own footmen. Then, later I saw her in a musketeer's uniform.'

'Merci, grandpere,' Tadhg said, 'you have been very enlightening.'

He hurried to the stable where he had left his horse. Then, after waiting briefly in front of Mme de Fortier's hotel, he went to the rear and inquired for Mme Sarsfield. He was informed that Mme Sarsfield had left the previous evening, and was he, perhaps, the soldier who had failed to appear to escort her?

Angry and humiliated, he rode furiously back to Boulogne.

Lady Honora greeted him graciously. He apologised for his failure to appear, explaining that he had been informed by a footman in livery that Lady Sarsfield was going to stay in Paris overnight.

She looked at him with just the trace of a smile. 'And then what did you do?'

He coloured. 'I stayed in Paris.'

Her smile broadened. 'Was the footman dressed in blue satin, with gold embroidered around the buttonholes and lapels?'

'I think so.'

She chuckled. 'I'm afraid that I lost ten pistoles on a wager.'

Tadhg wanted desperately to ask if the wager was with Mme le Clerc, but was too embarrassed. And besides, he was sure that he knew.

CHAPTER III

The Decision

Winter departed grudgingly in 1693. Soot-stained snow in Paris melted under the pelting rains of spring, leaving the streets ankle-deep with dirty water moving sluggishly to the Seine. Gradually the shade trees along the grimy streets and the elegant boulevards thickened with buds as they stirred under the annual prodding of nature.

King James was also busy in the palace of St Germain-en-Laye near Paris, placed at his disposal by his cousin, Louis XIV. Alas, advancing age brought him neither serenity nor wisdom. Inevitably surrounded by sycophants and scheming scoundrels, James still suffered from the Stuart syndrome of betraying loyal friends to win the support of cynical enemies.

While the Irish troops who had loyally followed him to France in his cause were preparing for the summer campaign against William and the Allies, King James, under the guidance of Charles, Earl of Middleton, a Protestant, was preparing a new declaration for his former subjects in England.

Signed by James on 17 April and published the same day, this infamous document promised a free pardon to all of his former subjects who would not oppose him when he landed in England, and he agreed to protect and defend the Church of England, in all its privileges and possessions, that he would submit to Parliament's decision on the extent and limitations of his royal power, and perfidy of perfidies, he solemnly promised to maintain the Act of Settlement in Ireland.

This incredible proclamation reflected completely the character of James II, selfish, stupid, devious and weak. Sent to England and printed, this amazing Declaration produced hardly a ripple of interest among his erstwhile subjects. Only James's colossal ego, constantly nurtured by his inner court of advisers, led by Middleton, could believe in its acceptance.

But if it had little effect on the English for whom it was intended, it had the opposite effect on the faithful Irish who had bled, lost their possessions, and had become exiles in his cause. What little affection had still existed among the Irish, scattered throughout France, Germany, Spain and Italy, was now eliminated forever. The Proclamation's effect was to make James despised

513

equally by both English and Irish.

When Tadhg heard of it, he was instantly reminded of Conor's oft-stated opinion of King James. 'Conor was right, and we were wrong,' he acknowledged to Dónal, who merely shrugged his shoulders, never one to be overly concerned with ideologies.

Luxemburg, anxious to pick up where he had left off the previous year against the Allies, and encouraged by the defeat he had inflicted on William at Steinkirk, began moving his regiments north in the middle of June. By July they had marched into Belgium, and on 29 July, were encamped on the grassy banks of the Landen, a small river which flowed near the village of Neerwinden, firmly held by William and the Allies.

Awakened early by the insistent beating of drums, Tadhg had a hasty breakfast, then attended Mass under the shade of ancient walnut trees. The *beansí* had wailed during the night, he was informed seriously by Séamus Mac Dermott, portending the death of one of the ranks of Milesius.

Tadhg smiled, but refrained from comment. With so many of the old Gaelic families represented, and a general battle impending, it would be more remarkable if none of the members of the old clans would die. Séamus saw the smile, and pointed his finger at Tadhg. 'Mark my word, O'Cuirc, before this day is over there will be a great wailing and sadness in the Irish camp.'

Tadhg's thoughts were not on the *beansí*, however, but on the similarity of their encampment with their position four years previous, when they were waiting on the banks of the River Foyle outside of Derry. Little thought had he then that he would ever leave Ireland to become a soldier of a French king in foreign lands. Yet here they were facing the enemy again, led this time not by the feeble, erratic King James, but by the greatest commander of the decade, the hunchbacked genius, Marshal Luxembourg.

It was indeed a day that he would never forget!

After a heavy French artillery barrage on the entrenched English, Irish troops led by the Duke of Berwick, fiercely attacked the enemy in the little village of Neerwinden. They were followed by French troops commanded by Montchevreuil. Despite the courage of the attacking forces, the Allies were too firmly dug in, and after great carnage, Louis's troops were forced to retreat, leaving Berwick behind as a captive.

After a short pause for regrouping, the attack on the village was renewed with a fresh division led by the Duke de Bourbon. But again Louis' forces were repulsed with great losses.

Acutely aware that Neerwinden was the key to the Allies' position, Luxembourg was stubbornly determined to take it. This time he prepared more thoroughly by committing the elite of the French Army, including Louis's famed household troops, along with other units, among which were Irish Guards led by General Sarsfield.

As always when confronted by the English who had humiliated the Irish at Derry, the Boyne, Aughrim and Limerick, Tadhg was fired with a fierce exultation so strong it suppressed the fear of death, and life had but one purpose, annihilation of the hated enemy. Now he and Dónal followed closely the big bay horse that Sarsfield was riding as the massive wave of humans and horses swept irresistibly into Neerwinden.

Cannon roared, small arms crackled, and sabres swung as the foes contested savagely in the narrow, village streets and lanes. Cobblestones were slick with gore, and the ancient gutters ran red with blood, a crimson Landen, Tadhg thought, in the wild confusion of the battle.

Overwhelmed by the ferocity of the massive attack, the defenders gave way before the third French assault on their positions, abandoning the battered village to the victorious forces. With this most important key to their position lost, the entire English and Allied defense crumbled as the exultant French and Irish pressed their advantage.

Being regulars, the enemy retreated in good order, although suffering grievous losses, until they reached the banks of the Gette River which blocked their escape. With the victors at their heels, the retreat deteriorated into a rout, and frantically flinging aside their arms and standards, a once disciplined army disintegrated into a struggling mass of desperate individuals trying to save themselves.

Streaming frantically across the few bridges available, and frenziedly wading the fords, the Allies were systematically cut to pieces by their relentless pursuers, with the Irish triumphantly shouting their battlecry, 'Remember Limerick', as they avenged themselves in the bloody fray.

Too bad we couldn't have done this at the Boyne, Tadhg thought regretfully, swinging his sabre at a mustachioed sergeant who confronted him, and as his adversary fell, wryly speculating whether perhaps the sergeant had chased him that day to Duleek as the Irish had fled the Boyne Water on their frantic retreat.

Across the river, Allied officers hastily began setting up defences as they rallied those survivors who had reached the opposite side of the Gette. Some cannon were quickly assembled, and soon the air was filled with cannon and musket fire.

Tadhg's reveries were cut short as he was suddenly knocked off his horse by the impact of a musketball hitting him in the left shoulder. He landed heavily on the blood-soaked turf, staring uncomprehendingly at the growing red circle on his tunic.

With a great effort, he arose clumsily to his feet, steadying himself against his horse. The battle still swirled furiously about him, with scores of English being cut down in their efforts to cross the Gette, others drowning as they were swept away by the clutching waters, their once proud standards now their sodden shrouds.

Despite his own intense pain, Tadhg was aware of the anguished cries of the wounded and dying, their imploring pleas for help, their piteous appeals to God to save them, and the triumphant litany of the Irish as they continued their incessant taunt, 'Remember Limerick'.

Glancing about him, he saw General Sarsfield, just a few feet distant, staring with alarm at Tadhg's rapidly reddening shoulder. Simultaneously, the general spun around, anguish and pain contorting the lean oval face as a musketball struck him above the heart. With a hoarse cry of despair and rage, Tadhg struggled among the tangled confusion of men and horses to the place where the general had fallen.

'Dónal,' Tadhg shouted desperately, hoping for assistance, 'Dónal, where are you?' Oh, merciful God, Tadhg prated, his teeth clenched tight against the pain, give me strength to reach my general. He staggered, then stumbled over the inert body of a fallen Irish soldier, and while on all fours, stared incredulously into the boyish countenance of Dónal Óg!

A cannonball had hit Dónal in the stomach, practically severing him in death, the eyes still opened wide as if savouring the sight of the headlong retreat of the scarlet ranks of the English. Sobbing uncontrollably, Tadhg fell prone across the body of his beloved Dónal, mercifully covering the gaping canyon from which the young life had fled. Tears coursed down Tadhg's cheeks, cutting through the battle grime, while the terror and grief of the moment etched itself irrevocably in his soul.

How long he lay there, Tadhg never did know. Hours later, consciousness and memory returned, he was lying on blood-drenched straw on the ground in a field hospital, a soaked, crimson-stained bandage bound around his chest. A myriad of flies buzzed greedily about him, his shoulders throbbed with pain, and a ruddy, vaguely familiar face loomed anxiously over him.

'Tadhg O'Cuirc! It is Tadhg O'Cuirc, isn't it?' The words were Irish, the voice soft-spoken and cultured, evoking in Tadhg elusive memories. Confused thoughts swept through his head. What had happened? Where was he? And to whom did this concerned visage belong?

Then, suddenly, his last-conscious moments flooded his mind, and the terror and anguish of the discovery of Dónal's body, and the fall of Lord Lucan, wracked him with uncontrollable sobbing, his huge frame shaking with torment.

His visitor watched with alarm mixed with compassion. Gradually the paroxysm of grief lessened, and Tadhg opened tear-filled eyes to gaze at the face above him. He shook his head sadly. 'I remember you now. I can still see as if it was but yesterday the old, soot-blackened chimney that had been Dónal Óg O'Devaney's grandfather's, the only part of the cabin not destroyed by Ensign Montgomery and his troops, and I remember you, Dermot O'Lee, as the prosecutor of the two Montgomerys in far-distant Moyrus Parish.'

Dermot O'Lee, for indeed it was he, smiled at Tadhg. 'And I remember well how you and Montgomery Óg matched swords that day.

'But what of now?' Tadhg asked. 'How is General Sarsfield? I saw him shot off his horse. And Dónal Óg ...?'

'Rory O'More's grandson is seriously wounded,' Dermot replied gravely. 'His wife and son are at his bedside. Father O'Shaughnessy has given him the last rites.' Dermot paused. He, too, vividly remembered the site of the destroyed cabin, and the eager young face of Dónal Óg when Tadhg had defeated the younger Montgomery, that fateful day when Dónal had first made Tadhg his idol. The English had killed Dónal's grandparents in distant Connaught, and now their grandson near an obscure village in Belgium. He sighed heavily.

'Dónal has been buried near the little stream called the Gette,' Dermot said gently. 'I am surgeon for Lord Dillon's Regiment, and was at Neerwinden when I was called to the side of General

Sarsfield. Knowing that he was grievously hurt, I field-dressed his wound, then had him removed to the village of Nuy. I found Dónal a musket's length from the general. Arrangements were made for him to be buried on the side of knoll, facing the west so that he will always be looking in the direction of distant Ireland when the sun sets each evening.'

Dermot dabbed at his eyes. 'When I found Dónal, I knew that you would be close by. Some Irish soldiers informed me that Sergeant O'Cuirc had been wounded. It was not difficult to locate you.'

Tadhg lay quietly. He was physically and emotionally exhausted. His wound, Dónal's death, Sarsfield's uncertain fate, and the meeting with the old Rapparee were too much for him. He closed his eyes and began to pray for Lord Lucan and for Dónal, the living and the dead. Dermot watched for a while, then slowly walked away.

For weeks Tadhg's own fate hung in balance. Loss of blood, inadequate care, a raging fever, and most serious of all, periods of deep depression when Tadhg prayed that God would take him as He had Dónal, made his survival doubtful.

It was only Dermot O'Lee's presence, his demand for frequent changing of the bandage, his gifts of fresh fruit and red meat, and his reiterated insistence to Tadhg that he was in no way responsible for Dónal's death, that slowly weighted the scales toward recovery.

When he found himself brooding over the fate of Dónal and Lord Lucan, he resolutely studied his Trinity, his French grammar, his Derry Bible, and his Geoffrey O'Donoghue poem, returned to him by Dermot O'Lee from his effects, until his melancholy subsided.

One morning Tadhg awoke to find, as he frequently did, Sister Margrete, one of the dedicated Sisters of Charity assigned as nurses, bending solicitously over him, her dark brown eyes showing her concern. Dressed in the full grey gown of her order, her coif falling to her shoulders, and the distinctive large, white cornette that so distinguished them from other nuns, she nervously twisted the beads of her rosary hanging from a belt around her waist.

The daughter of one of the Grivois, German mercenaries in Louis' Army, and a French mother, she had taken eager advantage of M. Vincent's offer to admit the poor and underprivileged to the growing ranks of the Sisters of Charity which previously had been the domain of the wealthy and women of society.

'You are looking much better today, M. le Sergeant,' she greeted him. 'I think you will be well enough to leave us soon.'

Tadhg shook his head. His wound hurt. The stench in the tent made him nauseous. And he had dreamed again of Dónal and their carefree life in Iar-Chonnacht. He felt depressed.

'No, Sister, I heal too slowly. There is no strength in me. I am making no progress.'

'Ma foi! And do you know how long it has taken to build the Cathedral in Cologne? It was begun way back in 1248, and it isn't finished yet! Almost 450 years, and you complain after just a few weeks. You must give God a little more time for he has many others to heal too.' She shook her finger at him in mock anger. 'Ich denke dass Sie eine grosse dumpkopf sind!'

Being compared to a cathedral amused Tadhg. He grinned. After a new bandage was applied to his wound, he felt better.

But it was late August before he was well enough to leave the hospital. It was quite an occasion, for Dermot came with a coach borne by six white horses. Three lackeys in livery rode on the footboards as it clattered and jolted down the rutted roads to Paris. Faded leather curtains offered little protection against the weather, but fortunately the day was warm, and the sun shining.

Dermot didn't answer Tadhg's query as to their destination, or the ownership of the coach. He smiled enigmatically, saying it was to be a surprise. So Tadhg rode in silence, alone with his melancholy thoughts. He knew that Sarsfield had died of his wounds at the house in Nuy where he contracted a fatal fever, leaving Honora and their young son alone in France. But it was Dónal's death which disturbed him the most. He blamed himself for bringing the youth with him. Reprovingly, he recalled the promise he had made to Conor that he would always watch out for Dónal. But Dónal was dead. He, Tadhg, had failed him.

They stopped at a village inn late in the afternoon. Greatly fatigued, Tadhg had to be assisted by the lackeys and Dermot to his bed. A hot meal; onion soup, a tasty ragout made of lamb, and a strange but delicious vegetable; served to him in the four-posted and canopied bed, helped him regain his strength. Finally, he was given a large bowl of verbena tea, 'to make him sleep like a babe', in the words of the solicitous innkeeper's wife.

Whether it was the soft feather bed, the verbena tea, or general exhaustion, Tadhg slept soundly. After a hearty breakfast of eggs cooked in a wine sauce, fresh baked bread, and country ham, Tadhg was almost his old, cheerful self again. As they rattled through the countryside, he questioned Dermot as to their destination, even going so far as to ask if the coach belonged to Mme Le Clerc, but judging by Dermot's perplexed reaction, decided it was not another effort by the inimitable actress of the rue St. Honore.

Paris was drowsing in the late afternoon sun when they entered the ancient capital, passing Charonne La Villette, and followed the Seine to the Rue de l'Arbre-sec in a most fashionable neighbourhood. The jaded horses trotted happily up a cobble-stone driveway, lined with ancient oaks as they neared the end of their journey, halting at the entrance to a magnificent mansion.

Tadhg was helped from the carriage by Dermot O'Lee who spurned the assistance of the footmen. As Tadhg waited, Dermot announced their arrival by loudly pounding a big bronze door knocker. A servant opened one of the two massive doors, on which hung a huge shield featuring two lions grasping a hand, all in deep crimson. Below the lions, at the bottom of the shield, was an eight-oared boat. There was something familiar about the coat-of-arms, but Tadhg was so pre-occupied with the unusual situation, that its significance didn't register.

They were greeted at the entrance to a large drawing room by a handsome man and an elegant, beautiful woman. The man beamed at Tadhg from under a full, powdered wig. His moustache and pointed beard were of a flaming red as vivid as the two lions on the front door. An immaculate white shirt, with ruffles down the centre and on the long cuffs, and embroidered with gold thread at the flaps of the pockets and buttonholes, contrasted with the black pantaloons and stockings he wore. Big silver buckles gleamed on his black shoes.

His companion was clad in a pink, pleated dress with woven patterns of the fleur-de-lis, big ruffles on the sleeves, and long leather gloves with similar ruffles above the wrists. Pink, brocaded slippers on dainty feet peeped from under the ruffled hem of the dress. A jewelled comb in dark, wavy hair made her look nearly as tall as her husband.

Dermot O'Lee turned to Tadhg, his eyes dancing with unrestrained mischievous joy, and announced in French. 'I am most happy to present to you the Baron and Baronne Hugh

O'Flaherty.'

Then he turned to the smiling couple, speaking in Irish, 'Four years late, but still carrying the message to you from Ballynahinch, Sergeant Tadhg O'Cuirc of Inishmór.'

Mouth agape, Tadhg stared at the smiling man before him. The son of Cathal O'Flaherty at last! The same red hair and blue eyes. He should have known immediately, and that shield on the door! How often he had seen it when he was with the Rapparees! Tadhg dropped to one knee, not in deference to a baron, but to the O'Flaherty!

'*A dhuine uasail*,' he stammered in confusion, 'I tried to find you. But something always happened.'

Hugh O'Flaherty smiled, reaching down to grasp Tadhg's hand and lift him to his feet. 'Yes, such minor things as battles, sieges, successful charges, humiliating retreats, Derry, the Boyne Water, Athlone, Aughrim, and Limerick twice. But now you're here at last, and doubly welcome for all your efforts.'

'You know, of course, of your father and Donough...?' Tadhg's voice faltered as he remembered the spreaseagled, beheaded body of Donough on the castle walls.

Hugh nodded, his eyes sad. 'Dermot has told me the details. He also told me of one, Tadhg O'Cuirc, a modern Cúchulainn, who takes on whole armies single-handledly.'

Announcement of dinner being served saved Tadhg an embarrassed reply. With assistance from a haughty butler, garbed in livery as pretentious as that of a marshal of France, and a gaggle of serving wenches, the dinner went smoothly as Hugh presided at the head of a long, polished table constructed of a rich dark, wood. Tadhg marvelled at the elegant napery, the silver bowls, plates, chafing dishes, platters, knives, spoons, and that recently introduced table tool called a fork.

As course after course was served, Tadhg thought wistfully of his youth on Inishmór when hunger pains were barely appeased by the skimpy servings of potatoes and fish. Here there was no end of food! There was rabbit, quail in aspic, lamb tripes, pigeon pie, partridge, pâté de foie gras, numerous wines, apples from Normandy, and delicate fruit pastries.

When dinner was completed, the O'Flahertys and their guests moved back to the drawing room. While a servant filled the baronne's goblet with a sparkling wine, Hugh filled three more from a cut-glass decanter containing a clear liquid. He gave one each to Dermot and Tadhg.

'*Sláinte* and *sláinte* again,' Hugh said, raising his glass.

'*Slán agus saol agat, bean ar do mhéin agat, talamh gon chíos agat, agus bás in Eireann,*' Tadhg recited, downing his drink and discovering to his intense delight that it was *uisce beatha*. 'Where did you get this?' he inquired, smacking his lips with satisfaction.

'Through my smuggling friends,' Hugh replied, 'But I note that your toast ended with 'And death in Erin'. I'm curious, Tadhg, do you think that you will ever return?'

The question startled Tadhg. He looked down into his empty glass as if he expected it to give him his answer. Latent memories, evoked by the lingering aroma of the whiskey, came rushing like the incoming tide. He thought of Pierce MacNamara, the poteenmaker par excellence, whom Tadhg had suspected of being a traitor; he remembered poignantly Dónal's losing bout with Siobhán's whiskey at Aughrim; he recalled the faces of old friends and comrades-at-arms around hundreds of hearths and campfires, joyous with the whiskey taken.

Would he ever go back to Erin? Agus bás in Eireann? Hugh's direct question was a challenge. Just what was he going to do? The answer came immediately. He suddenly felt as if a dense, all-obscuring mist had lifted, he could clearly see the road once more.

He raised his glass, looking directly into Hugh's expectant eyes. 'Yes,' he replied simply. 'Yes, and as soon as possible.'

'Why?' Hugh asked, obviously disappointed. 'There's nothing there for you. William has shattered the Treaty of Limerick into smithereens. New penal laws are being enacted against the Irish. Prices on the heads of Catholic priests have drawn new hordes of jackals. King Billy's rapacious rascals who run the country now are stealing so much that even in Parliament in London there are murmers of protest. Undoubtedly there is a price on your head, too, and there are vindictive men in Dublin Castle who have long memories.'

'You say, *a dhuine uasail*, that there is nothing in Ireland for me. Perhaps. But there is less here in France. Tonight I fulfilled the mission for which I left Connemara. And Erin. I found Cathal O'Flaherty's son as I promised. Now Dónal is dead. Sarsfield is dead. At Limerick I really believed that the glorious Irish army would return from France to free our homeland again. I know now that this will never be. I don't intend to enrich the soil of France or Flanders with any more of my blood for the glory of Louis XIV. If

522

my blood is to be spilled, let it be in, as well as for, Ireland.'

Hugh leaned forward, speaking in urgent tones. 'I can help you here, Tadhg. I am in the service of the Marquis de Barnesieux, the secretary of war for Louis. The *bean a ti*', he smiled at his wife across the room, 'is descended from the lesser nobility, and is very rich. She has several unmarried nieces, also wealthy, who would swoon with delight to have a stalwart, handsome husband like you. French girls dote on Irishmen. With a rich wife, estates, an excellent military background, and my connections with King Louis' ministers, you could build yourself a great career and future here in France.'

Tadhg shook his head regretfully. 'I do appreciate, and thank you, *a dhuine uasail*, for your generous offer and help. But this is a foreign soil. I want to return home. I hunger to see my family and friends again.'

'The land of the Gael? Long before our forefathers got to Eire, they lived here and in Spain. Old Milesius, the venerable patriarch from whom the great Milesian families descended, never even saw Ireland. His bones are interred here somewhere, probably along the Spanish Coast. What can you do in Eire? Trade your religion for a pot of Protestant porridge? Become a Rapparee again, hunted in the hills and bogs by the English? Or worse yet, be betrayed for a few gold pieces by some Irishman you trusted too well? I, too, had great ideals. I was in England serving King James at the time his sister's son, Orange Billy, decided to occupy his uncle's throne. I was wounded near Coventry in the subsequent fighting, but succeeded in getting to France. Through King James I was introduced at Court. And I met Madelon again, 'once more he smiled across the table at his wife, 'whom I had known as a young girl when I first came to France from Connemara years ago to learn the art of the military. So you can see that I have prospered here, but not in Ireland. Especially after the collapse of the Irish army at Limerick in 1691, and the second confiscation of the family estates.'

'If you would like to help me, *a dhuine uasail*, arrange for my release from the army as a wounded soldier. I will find passage to Ireland myself.'

Hugh sighed, then turned to Dermot. 'What do you think, old friend, of our stubborn hero? Should I help him go to his certain death?'

'If I wasn't so old, I would go with him,' Dermot replied sadly.

'He isn't the only disillusioned Irish exile, I have met hundreds more like him who have regretted their decision at Limerick.'

'That may be true, but there are hundreds more back in Ireland who now regret their decision at Limerick not to go with Sarsfield because of the broken promises by the English. But, Tadhg *a mhic*, I know when I'm whipped. *Níl aon tinteán mar do thinteán féin.*' Hugh turned to Madelon, explaining the Irish expression by translating it for her, 'There's no fireside like your own.'

He paused, then smiled. 'Tadhg, you fought fiercely to restore my father's lands to him against those who had taken them. Do you know how the O'Flahertys got them in the first place?'

Tadhg shook his head.

'By the same process. Until several centuries ago, my forefathers lived on the east side of Lough Corrib, not west. Then some of the Welsh-Norman adventurers decided they wanted the O'Flaherty lands. After a few lost battles to superior military forces, my ancestors took the hint, and moving west of the lake, being in turn stronger than the native Irish there, chased them out, and took their lands. For example, the O'Keeleys who lived around Ballynahinch, were run off by the O'Flahertys.'

Seeing Tadhg's shocked expression, Hugh hastened to add, 'I'm telling you this only to make you aware in the future of misplaced loyalties. All of us have an inclination to leap before we look. Don't misunderstand me; I do appreciate the help you gave my father. And perhaps, Irish displacing Irish isn't as bad as English displacing Irish. But enough of this. Getting back to the matter at hand, I'll do what I can to obtain your release, but sometimes it's harder to leave the army than to enter.'

The rest of the evening was spent in talking about Connemara, with Hugh and Dermot recalling the days of their youth in happier times. Tadhg's exploits had been previously related by Dermot, and the only mention of them was Hugh's request of Tadhg to tell him about the ambush, and the death of his father. He listened quietly, and his only comment, when Tadhg finished, was to cross himself, and say softly, 'He died as he lived, true to his principles. May he rest in eternal peace.'

Arrangements had been made for the two guests to stay overnight and leave the next morning. Tadhg slept well, feeling at peace with himself for the first time since Dónal's death. After a leisurely breakfast, Tadhg thanked the baronne for her hospitality, and apologised for rejecting the opportunity to become a cousin of hers by marriage.

Amused by Tadhg's quaint French, she assured him that she was not offended, and that he was welcome to visit them at any time. Hugh walked to the coach with his guests, informing Tadhg that he would start that day to seek his release.

'Slán leat, Cúchulainn,' he said, 'and if you change your mind, let me know.'

Tadhg shook his head. 'I'm more determined than ever, *a dhuine uasail*, I feel like a whole man again since I made the decision.'

The coachman flicked his whip at the six horses, and the coach clattered on its way towards the rue de l'Arbre-sac. But instead of turning north, as Tadhg expected, they turned south. He raised quizzical eyes to Dermot who laughed impishly, and said, 'I have another surprise for you.'

After a half-hour's ride, the coach stopped at the entrance to a driveway, the way barred by two huge, closed gates. An ancient concierge tottered from the small gatehouse to confer briefly with the coachman. Then the gates were opened for the coach to pass through. Tadhg and Dermot alighted from the coach, entering an old three-storey stone building through a wide door with a beautiful stained glass panel depicting a woman with a halo kneeling before the Virgin Mary. They mounted footworn, wooden steps to a vestibule where they were greeted by a short, heavy-set nun in the white cornette of the Sisters of Charity. Her plain visage was transformed by a beautiful smile at the sight of the two visitors.

'Sister Barbe, this is Tadhg O'Cuirc,' Dermot introduced him. Bright, alert brown eyes scrutinised Tadhg conspiratorially as she fingered her heavy rosary beads before replying, 'We are ready, follow me.' They accompanied her down a dimly lighted hallway until she stopped at a door and knocked lightly. A voice from within bade them enter. Seated at a desk at the far end of the room was a woman, her head raised better to view the visitors.

A pale face, sharply framed by huge winged cornette atop her head, and the shoulder-length white coif she wore, looked up expectantly at Tadhg. He stood transfixed, his heart pounding. 'Eithne?' he inquired haltingly. 'Eithne? Is it indeed Eithne Blake?'

'Tadhg *a rún*,' she declared ecstatically, decorum flung to the winds, as she rushed to greet him. He opened wide his arms, engulfing her as she buried her head in his bosom, her cornette disarranged, alternately laughing and sobbing with unrestrained joy.

Sister Barbe looked apprehensively at the open door, concerned lest others should witness this most indecorous behaviour.

Eithne finally withdrew from Tadhg's embrace, stood back at arm's length, her hazel eyes mischievous, and said, 'God save you, honest man.'

Tadhg, pleased at the Irish greeting, replied, 'God save you kindly.'

Smiling fondly at Tadhg, Eithne greeted Dermot, then asked them to be seated.

'Tis a long way from Moyrus Parish we are,' said Tadhg, shaking his head in amazement. 'Dermot, Tadhg and Eithne, all in Paris together.'

'And all speaking French,' Eithne added, 'so that Sister Barbe can participate too in this grand occasion.'

Sister Barbe beamed. 'You can converse in Irish if you like. I'm sure you won't give away any of the secrets of the Sisters of Charity.'

'Thank you, Sister,' Dermot responded. 'It will be more natural if we do speak in the Irish for Irish hearts better express themselves in our native tongue.'

'I'll follow your conversation easily by watching those expressive Irish eyes,' the old nun said.

Tadhg addressed himself to Eithne. 'Yesterday I thought I had the greatest surprise possible when I met Hugh O'Flaherty, but today it's surpassed by finding Eithne Blake again. Tell me, what have you been doing these three years since I saw you last?'

'T'would be to long in the telling, but I can touch on the high spots. After my father died, may he rest in eternal peace, Father O'Conlon, our old Parish Priest, arranged for my passage to France with a group of other Connaught girls destined to enter the Order of Franciscan nuns, also called the Order of Saint Clara. But here I learned of the Sisters of Charity, founded by Father Vincent de Paul, a saint if there ever was one, which is less restrictive. So I entered the order, which ministers to the sick and the poor, aids orphans, teaches school and even nurses the wounded in army hospitals.'

'That I know well,' said Tadhg, 'for they nursed me back to good health. But what do you mean that the order is less restrictive?'

Eithne sighed. 'I'm inclined, as you should know well, to be head-strong at times. Self-disciplined is not one of my virtues.

Father Henri, adviser to the Franciscans nuns, suggested to me after a short novitiate with that order, that one with my temperament might be better off with the Sisters of Charity who have no formal vows. Now I'm assigned here to the Academy where I teach catechism, needlework, and the Crosses of God.'

Tadhg furrowed his brows, perplexed. 'It's an appropriate name for so holy a place as this, but what is it?'

Giggling, Eithne replied. 'The characters of the alphabet, *a chara.*'

'You have no formal vows?' asked Tadhg. 'Isn't that unusual?'

'True, but we are an unusual order. As M. Vincent said, 'As a regular rule, they shall have no monastery but the houses of the sick; any cloister but the streets of the town and hospital rooms; any chapel but their parish church; any enclosure but that of obedience; any grille but the fear of God: any veil but the holiest and most faultless modesty'.

'And have you any news from Ireland? What of Conor, your uncle? And your mother?'

'Both are happy and prospering, thanks be to God. Conor has taken a wife, a girl from the County Clare.'

'Siav Mac Clanchy?'

'Och, and do you know her now?' Eithne was delighted.

'From our days in Dublin. A fine *cailín*, indeed.'

'And what of you, Tadhg? Dermot has given me sketchy details. He told me of your last battle, and about ...' She faltered, her hazel eyes filling with tears.

'About Dónal?' Tadhg sighed heavily, the happiness of the moment fading. Despondency swept over him. Dónal and Eithne were of the same age, had grown up together. But now Dónal, happy, gay, carefree Dónal was dead. Never again would he warm himself at a turf fire, race along the strand of Kilkieran Bay, poach a salmon, or indulge in *uisce beatha.*

'There isn't much to tell, Eithne. I have travelled a long way since leaving Moyrus Parish, but now, thanks to God, I'm going home again.'

Eithne looked accusingly at Dermot. 'You didn't tell me this.'

'I didn't know it until last night. And neither did Tadhg.'

'What are you going to do? Return to Inishmór and be a fisherman again?'

He shook his head vigorously, turning to Dermot. 'That poem you returned to me with my books after I was wounded? It was written by Geoffrey O'Donoghue of the Glens. It was given to me by a great lady in Dublin in memory of Donough Beag who lost his life teaching the poor children of the Gaeltacht. He, too, could have stayed safely here in France. I intend to follow Donough's example.'

Eithne was ecstatic. 'Ah, Tadhg, what a magnificent idea! I, too, hope to return to Iar-Chonnacht. Our Father Superior wants to establish the Order of the Sisters of Charity in Ireland. Some of the other Irish sisters and I would form a cadre.'

Dermot sighed. 'I envy both of you. Those are noble sentiments. But Eithne, it would be foolhardy to attempt to establish a Catholic order of nuns in Ireland now. News from Ireland is bad. Conditions are getting worse, not better. Priests are being hunted as in the old days. It would be a hundredfold more difficult for nuns.'

Eithne looked sharply at Dermot, reflecting her disappointment. 'But what of Tadhg's venture? Isn't it risky also?'

Dermot nodded. 'In most respects, yes. But Tadhg is a man and an experienced soldier. He can quickly set up his school behind a hedge like other hedge schoolmasters, moving to place to place. Besides, Tadhg has made up his stubborn mind to return at all costs. Even Hugh O'Flaherty, with all his eloquence, bribes and blandishments, failed to dissuade him.'

Dermot gazed at Tadhg fondly, then added, 'Och, but he's an obstinate young man. Now that he has made his decision, all of Louis' army couldn't stop him.'

'Tadhg really wants to go back to Ireland to see his Sassanach sweetheart, his Cailín Bán.' Eithne teased, 'That golden-haired heiress he saved from the sea.'

Tadhg was startled. He hadn't thought of Mairéad FitzGerald since the Battle of Landen. Or had he? Was Eithne right? Was this the real reason? No, he told himself firmly, the Lady Mairéad had nothing to do with his decision. He had wanted to teach for quite some time. Donough had planted the seed, and Ailis MacRannal, his teacher in Dublin, had nourished it.

'Lady Mairéad is in Dublin,' Tadhg said diffidently, 'a rich Protestant, more secure than ever. I will be in remote Iar-Chonnacht, a poor, Catholic hedge schoolmaster. Our paths will never cross again this side of Heaven.'

'An ea,' Eithne exclaimed, her eyes twinkling. 'Is it believing you are that Protestants can go to Heaven?'

528

Tadhg coloured. 'It was only a figure of speech. I meant to say that it was impossible that I will ever see Mairéad FitzGerald again.'

'You never know, Tadhg. Who would have believed, five years ago in remote Iar-Chonnacht, that you, Dermot and I would be in Paris. I for one would have said that it was an impossibility.'

The debate was suddenly interrupted by the clang of bells. sister Barbe arose hurriedly. 'It's time we go,' she urged, 'the Mother Superior is very strict.'

'We can find our way out,' Dermot suggested. 'Better rush now.'

'Please come visit me again soon, Tadhg,'Eithne called over her shoulder as she was hustled from the room by Sister Barbe.

Dermot sighed. 'It's regrettable that both of you aren't still back in Ireland, Tadhg. She would have made you a good wife. Despite her religious vocation, I suspect she still has a great affection for you. And would gladly give up her place with the Sisters if marriage was a prospect. Perhaps that is why she is in a order without vows.'

Tadhg didn't reply as he followed Dermot down the dark corridor. He remembered Eithne as he had seen her so long ago. He shook his head sadly. It had come to this. She was now the spouse of Christ.

CHAPTER IV

The Departure

A week later, Tadhg was visited at his billet by Hugh O'Flaherty. After inquiring as to Tadhg's health, he got to the purpose of his trip.

'I have discussed with the Secretary of War, the Marquis de Barbesieux, your desire to leave the service of Louis XIV. He sympathises with your wish, and promises me he will do all he can to facilitate it. Experienced non-commissioned officers such as you - and the marquis is very cognisant of your fine record, and your devotion to His Majesty - are difficult to find. He assures me that you will be released in due time. This might take three or four months. In the meanwhile ...'

'Pardon me, sir, for interrupting you,' Tadhg said, deferentially, 'but I'm impatient to leave for Ireland immediately, not in four months.'

Hugh smiled. 'I know. I know. I have suggested to the marquis a solution that should make all parties happy. I have to send a courier to Ireland soon. To that end, I have recommended to the Secretary of War that you be designated that emissary. To expedite your speedy departure, you could carry a secret coded message to Dublin.'

Tadhg looked a Hugh quizzically. 'And what would prevent me from abandoning the mission once I arrived safely in Ireland?'

His answer was an eloquent shrug of Hugh's shoulders. 'Only your conscience,' High added. 'But a Tadhg O'Cuirc who diligently sought to deliver a message to Hugh O'Flaherty, would not betray a trust. Besides, once the mission was consummated, you would be free. By that time your discharge from the French army would be in effect. And if you ever had occasion to flee Ireland to France, your fine army record would be unblemished.'

Tadhg pondered, Hugh's proposal was sound. It would mean that he could leave soon, receive army pay and payment for his passage, yet have a safe haven if ever he had to leave Ireland. But the plan had one major flaw.

'I had hoped to land somewhere on the West coast,' he told Hugh, 'where I would establish my school. Going to Dublin is out of the way and might be dangerous.'

'A good point,' Hugh acceded. 'Our agent, unfortunately is in

Dublin. If you could land at Cork, you could get a horse for the trip, and have our agent, whose name incidentally is Michael Butler - a versatile cognomen since Butler can be English or Irish, Protestant or Catholic - arrange for your clandestine journey from Dublin to the West. Is this agreeable to you?'

Dublin! A danger and a challenge. The Le Berges, Dublin Castle, Michael Butler, Cáit O'Reilly, Devil's Hook Charlie and Mairéad FitzGerald. Don't forget her. As if he could! Why did her image always rise unbidden? Why did the memory of her cling like a burr on a blanket? Mairéad FitzGerald, the grand lady! How she must gloat now that the Catholic Irish have been completely crushed, and the English flag flying arrogantly over Dublin Castle again. Probably married. To a duke, at least! A duke grown fabulously wealthy with acquisition of forfeited estates of the Catholic Irish forced by King Billy to flee their hereditary lands.

'Is this agreeable to you, Tadhg?' Hugh repeated, interrupting his reverie.

Tadhg nodded. It was a risk, of course, going to Dublin. Undoubtedly there was a price on his head, and a thick dossier in Dublin Castle listing his offences against His Majesty, King William, starting with the two Montgomerys, and ending with Lieutenant Benton.

'Good.' Hugh rubbed his hands, please that his plans were progressing satisfactorily. 'I'll be in touch with you again soon.'

'*A dhuine uasail*,' Tadhg said, hesitantly, 'could you find out where Lady Sarsfield is staying, and arrange a meeting with her for me? I would be eternally ashamed to leave France without bidding her farewell.'

'I'll inquire at Versailles as to her whereabouts, and do my best to set an appointment,' Hugh promised.

Now that he was going home again, hopefully to fulfil his dream of becoming a hedge schoolmaster, Tadhg's normal buoyancy returned and his bouts of melancholy diminished. His thoughts were of his family on Inishmór, of Conor O'Donnell and Máire Blake, of Ailis MacRannal, of Thady O'Moriarty and Meg Murray, of Donough O'Flaherty's old school on Kilkiernan Bay, and reluctantly, but irresistibly of Mairéad Fitzgerald. When his reflexions strayed to Dónal and Sarsfield, he tried not to dwell on their demise, rationalising that they were soldiers, and that death in battle was a natural concomitant.

Before he departed France, Tadhg was determined to see Eithne

Blake as well as Honora Sarsfield. Yet he had do desire to go back to his old regiment for last farewells, preferring not to reopen old wounds by maudlin memories of Dónal and Sarsfield.

Two days later a message came from Hugh to be ready the following day to see Lady Sarsfield. He shaved himself carefully with the razor he had wrested from François the barber, on the road from Thurles, and donned his best uniform. He was ready and waiting a full hour before Hugh arrived in his coach.

Tadhg shook his head in amazement at the sight of Cathal O'Flaherty's son, resplendent in a red tunic with solid silver fleur-de-lis emblazoned across front and back, a fine white linen shirt, white doeskin trousers and red leather boots high enough to cover snugly his sturdy calves. A broadbeamed white hat, sprouting red ostrich feathers, sat jauntily atop a full wig. What a contrast, Tadhg thought, with Hugh's father, remembering vividly his first view of Cathal on the wild shore of Kilkieran Bay, and the rough blue jerkin. coarse linen shirt, drab woollen cloak and heavy-soled buskins. But I too have changed, he mused, surveying his own costume, courtesy of His Most Christian Majesty King Louis XlV.

'We are going to Versailles,' Hugh said, 'where I have to meet with the Secretary of War.'

Tadhg showed his disappointment. 'But I thought we were going to see Lady Sarsfield?'

'As the old Irish proverb says, 'A spur in the head is worth two on the heel',' Hugh explained. 'I have arranged a meeting with Lady Sarsfield also. Honora will be at court today presenting a petition to the King for a pension. She is practically penniless, depending on friends from Ireland for help. And I must confer with the Marquis de Barbesieux. With luck, your commission for your trip will be ready.'

Traffic thickened as they rattled over the Porte Saint-Honore on the road to Versailles. It seemed to Tadhg that half the population of Paris was headed toward the current residence of their sovereign. Coaches, carriages, sedan-chairs, carts, horsemen and pedestrians, all dusty from the road, struggled to keep their places in the endless parade. Tadhg's heart was heavy at the thought that the proud Honora Burke Sarsfield being reduced to begging for a pittance from an alien king.

When the last farmhouse receded into the distance, they entered a dense forest, mostly oak trees which formed a verdant bower. 'This used to be a favourite hunting ground of Louis' father as well as his grandfather,' Hugh explained. 'Louis, too, once a tireless venatic, used to hunt extensively, but he has gradually given it up, preferring the grander hunt for Le Roi Guillaume whom he almost caught at Landen.'

In turn, the forest gave way to the beautiful gardens and majestic castle which Louis had built on the site of the old hunting lodge of his father Louis XIII. The coach pulled up at the entrance court, the lackies leaped down to open the coach doors, and Tadhg and Hugh descended. Tall Swiss guards, clutching heavy halberds, flanked the entranceway.

Hugh, no stranger to Versailles, quickly guided Tadhg through enormous, high-vaulted halls of the palace, whose splendour was the envy of all the monarchs of Europe. Nobles, courtiers, servants and hopeful petitioners thronged the rooms and corridors, some talking animatedly, others silent, absorbed in their personal problems, apprehensive of their chances of success.

They passed the enormous dining hall through whose open doors they observed a horde of servants busily setting tables, turned right down a corridor until Hugh stopped before a heavy door adorned with carved Cupids. He knocked, and a woman's voice invited them to enter. The room being in semi-darkness, Tadhg had difficulty in discerning the form of Honora Sarsfield seated in the corner against the dark background of the partially opened heavy purple drapes which obscured the cheery, brightness of the sunny afternoon. Suddenly the sombre atmosphere and the melancholy reason for his visit overwhelmed Tadhg, and he had a strong impulse to turn and flee. Rising as he entered, the widow peered at them in the gloom, and in the manner of the French court, extended her hand which Hugh gallantly kissed.

When she turned to Tadhg, he began to tremble violently as he had when they had first met in far away Kilmallock. Disregarding her hand, he impulsively stepped forward and swept her to his bosom.

'Och, *a bhean uasail*, I miss him so much,' he murmured, his voice quivering as he strived to keep from sobbing.

'We all do, Tadhg,' she responded in a soft, sad voice. 'Seamus Óg, especially is lost without his father. Despite Father MacLysaght's explanation that it is God's will, Séamus continually asks me why. And I must confess that I, too, ask why, why, why?'

Then she gently disengaged him from his embrace, and holding him at arms length, she gazed steadily at him. Despite the ravages of her grief, manifested by newly-etched fine lines at the corners of her mouth and eyes, her famed beauty was still evident. Her hair, now faintly touched with silver, accentuated the classic structure of her face, and only the tear-reddened eyes detracted from her exquisite loveliness.

Aware that Tadhg was in a highly emotional state, and conscious of her own vulnerability, she quickly and deliberately changed the subject. 'Hugh tells me you are going home. You are very fortunate, I envy you. But do you think your decision is wise? Conditions are very unsettled there, and are getting worse.'

Tadhg managed a wan smile. 'Everyone tells me that, *a bhean uasail*. But what does the future hold for me here in France? Death sooner or later, on some obscure battlefield, in the dusty gutter of a small Flemish village, or among the manure of a farmer's pasture in Namur? Or perhaps lose my limbs, and like an oversize potato with a head, beg for bread on the streets of Paris? No, lady Honora, if I must die, at lease let it be in Eire.'

Her eyes filled with tears. 'I know, Tadhg. How well I know. A soldier's life is one of uncertainty. It seems that only death is the victor. but tell me, when do you leave?'

'We will know shortly,' Hugh intervened 'When we confer with the Minister of War. And what of you, Honora, have you had your audience with the king?'

She nodded. 'Temporarily, at least, I will draw a small pension from the tiers de l'ecomat, some kind of fund that sustains many of the penniless Irish adherents of Rí Séamus . Also there will be an army pension later deriving from Patrick's service for King Louis. It appears that no money will be coming from Ireland unless my father, the earl of Clarickardeee, is successful in his petition to King William for restoration of his possessions. You will remember that he was among those attainted in 1691.'

'I will prod M le Barbesieux when I see him to hurry the pension.' High promised.

They chatted for some time about news from Ireland, conditions in France for the Irish Exiles, their friends and mutual acquaintances, studiously avoiding any mention of Patrick Sarsfield and Dónal Óg, both of whom were uppermost in their thoughts.

When the men arose for departure, Honora smiled conspiratorially, asking Tadhg if he had any last messages for

Mme le Clerc.

'Yes, tell her that I will soon be enjoying the vin du pays, namely *poitín*, and the *cailíns* of Iar-Chonnacht.'

'That's a cryptic communication. Will she understand?'

'If she doesn't, tell her it's an Irish version of Les Amoureuses.'

Honora's eyes twinkled. 'Aha! I suspect I am going to get revenge for the ten pistoles I lost to her.'

The levity helped to soften the heartbreak of their leavetaking.

Slán leat,' Hugh said. I'll see you soon again, Honora.'

'Thank you, Hugh, for you help and many courtesies. And thank you for bringing my old friend Tadhg O'Cuirc to see me.'

'God bless you, *a bhean uasail*,' Tadhg said in the Irish, his eyes brimming with tears.

'God and Mary bless you,' she responded. 'Is it '*slán leat go deo*', goodbye forever, Tadhg?'

Tadhg nodded, 'Unless you come back home, *a bhean uasail*.'

'I would be pleased if you would call me Honora,' she said, looking up at him, eyes pleading.

Tadhg closed his eyes tightly and compressed his lips as he struggled against the wave of emotion that swept over him. Then opening his eyes, he looked down at her. 'This is the first time in my life I have been extremely happy and extremely sad at the same time. *Slán leat*, Honora.' Then he turned abruptly and headed for the door.

Hugh was startled, looking at Honora, and wordlessly she motioned for him to follow Tadhg. He caught up with Tadhg in the corridor, suggesting that they wait in the antechamber where he was to meet M de Barbesieux. Tadhg allowed himself to be led briskly through the long halls until they entered a large room with vaulted ceiling. Bright sunshine streamed un-encumbered through wide windows, permitting a broad view of the magnificent gardens below. Gilt-framed mirrors dominated the walls. Stiff backed chairs, upholstered in damask, and decorated with the inevitable fleur-de-lis, were arranged at precise distances from each other around the room, except for one corner wheres stood a heavy, dark wooden desk, with a comfortable chair.

They seated themselves, each lost in his thoughts. Tadhg felt numb, drained of all emotion. The sad realisation that he would never see Patrick or Honora Sarsfield again on earth depressed him. Their friendship had meant more to him than he realised. He, an obscure fisherman from remote Inishmór, had been an intimate of the great Lord Lucan, the idol of the Irish army, grandson of the celebrated hero, Rory O'More, and of Honora de Burgo Sarsfield, daughter of the Earl of Clarickarde. Her departing request that he call her Honora instead of the formal, *a bhean uasail*, had really touched him.

The strident blare of trumpets from the grand reception hall next to their room interrupted their reveries. 'The audience with the King is over,' Hugh said. 'The Minister of War should be along soon.'

Shortly the door opened, and M le Barbesieux entered. Reflecting the subdued styles now prevalent on the Court as Louis grew more conservative as he aged, the minister was clad in a short, close-fitting brown jacket, tight breeches and dark stockings. A powdered wig covered his head. His costume was in sharp contrast to Hugh's flamboyant raiment. Both Irishmen stood as the Minister of War walked to the desk.

He acknowledged Hugh's introduction of Tadhg, then bade them be seated. From a portfolio he withdrew a number of big, brown envelopes, which he placed on the desk. When ready, he addressed himself to Tadhg.

'M le Sergeant, here are all the papers and documents required for your mission. They included money, a passport for you in the name of Armand Deschamps, a sealed envelope to be delivered to our representative in Dublin, M de Bouteillier (Hugh winced at the Gallicising of Michael Butler's name), a warrant for the issue of an Army horse, which you will turn in at Bordeaux, your port of embarcation, and your army discharge papers, effective at year's end.'

As Tadhg was about to ask what ship he should take, a section of the wall behind the minister moved to disclose a secret door, and a tall man entered the room.

Barbesieux and Hugh immediately dropped to one knee, bowed their heads and waited for the King to speak. Tadhg stood, open-mouthed, so shocked by the presence of Louis XIV that he was unaware of his lese-majesté until he noted the King's frown of displeasure, then hastily emulated the others. The King moved to the chair that his Minister of War had vacated, and seated himself wearily. 'Please arise.' he commanded. All three bowed, then stood erect.

'Three hours of listening to my devoted subjects trying to convince me how destitute they are tires me more than a long day at the hunt. The only solution to the problem of having enough gold to satisfy their needs, real or pretended, is to abolish the army and navy. What say you to that, M le Secretary?'

'Not only would that be glorious news to your petitioners, Your Majesty, but also to King William and the Allies.'

The King nodded gloomily. 'Yes, unless I could convince William to do the same.' He smiled at the absurdity, then added, 'Perhaps you could persuade our friend, Innocent XII, in Rome to intervene for me.'

Barbesieux grimaced. 'I'm afraid he would be as cooperative as his predecessor was with your cousin, King James, when he asked the Pope to appoint Father Peter, his Jesuit confessor, to the council of Cardinals.'

'Well, enough of nonsense,' the King said, turning serious. 'What I want to know is the status of the rogues who man our royal galleys. Those contumacious Grey Sisters, the Sisters of Charity, nagged me again this morning, complaining about what they call the 'inhuman conditions of the holding pens in Marseilles'. It was annoying enough when they were worrying themselves about the knaves' immortal souls, but now they are concerned about the drudges' bodies as well.'

The Secretary shook his head angrily. 'They waste Your Majesty's valuable time and patience. I have already spoken to the General of the Galleys about improving their lot. He has promised to do so. Perhaps if we assigned these interfering Sisters to a stint at the banes de vogue in the galleys for several months, they would stop pestering you with matters that shouldn't concern them.'

'Actually, they don't bother me too much. They save wear and tear on my conscience by their good deeds among the poor and sick. And their valuable help nursing the wounded in the hospitals is saving the lives and limbs of many of our soldiers. Keep after the General so I can have something favourable to report next time.'

The King arose, looked curiously at Tadhg, then asked, 'Who is this young giant? A whole regiment of his size would eat more than all of France could produce in a year.'

'One of Mareschal Sarsfield's protégés. He was seriously wounded at the time and place that Sarsfield fell. Now I am sending him as a courier to Dublin. You remember the Baron O'Flaherty? He is my aide for Irish affairs.'

'Yes, yes, M le Baron. General Sarsfield's death was a sad loss for Ireland's cause - and France. Make sure that his widow gets her remittances promptly.' With a brief nod, he turned and disappeared through the secret door.

Barbesieux resumed his chair, explicit instructions were given to Tadhg, and he was handed the envelopes, and then instructed to wait outside while the minister conducted affairs of state with his aide.

Tadhg bowed politely and left the room. He was still overwhelmed by the mornings events - the sad departure from lady Sarsfield, the imminence of his secret mission and return to Ireland, and now this incredible audience with His Most Christian Majesty, Louis XIV.

When Hugh rejoined him, he shook his head in wonderment, hardly believing the evidence of his eyes and ears. 'Nobody in Ireland will believe me if I tell them I met Louis XIV. I'll be called 'Tadhg, the tall tale teller'.'

On their way back to Paris (Tadhg was to stay with the O'Flahertys overnight), Hugh was exuberant. 'We did it, Tadhg, we did it,' he exulted. 'You're on your way home, travelling in style, and representing the king.' Winking broadly, he asked, 'Now that you're an intimate friend of Louis, do you want to reconsider your decision, and return to France when your mission is accomplished?'

Tadhg looked at Hugh askance. 'An intimate friend? I felt more like a piece of furniture. He talked about me, not to me. But it's just as well, I was so paralysed by his presence, I couldn't have spoken if I tried. And the answer is still 'no'.'

'I was happy to learn that he is going to improve the lot of the galley slaves for I've been to Marseilles and other Navy ports, and the miserable existence those men lead is unbelievable.'

'Then I'm doubly glad they never got Nicolas Beauvais,' Tadhg said.

'Nicolas Beauvais? Who is Nicolas Beauvais?' Hugh asked.

'Come to Ireland, and I'll tell you,'Tadhg replied, smiling at his compromising relationship with the King and the King's enemy.

Hugh glanced sharply at Tadhg. I would gather that it would be best for me not to know Nicolas Beauvais. And to forget that I ever heard of him.'

Tadhg's silence was eloquent.

'It's odd,' Hugh mused, 'how fate and history are intertwined. It is unlikely that Honora will ever return to Ireland. So in time she,

538

too, like Patrick, will be interred in France from whence her de Burgo ancestors came, as did the first Sarsfields.'

The thought of the lovely Honora being embraced by the cold arms of death made Tadhg shiver. He had been thinking of Eithne Blake, and since he was leaving for Bordeaux the following day, it would be his last chance to see her.

'Would you mind stopping at the school of the Blessed Sacrament?. he asked. 'It's somewhere along the rue de l'Arbe-sac. I would like to say goodbye to Eithne Blake. Her father died bravely in the battle at St Malachi's Church.'

'Certainly. I never knew Murtagh, but I have heard from Dermot O'Lee how he avenged my father by slaying Thomas Morton. A most courageous and decent man.'

Hugh rapped on the front partition, instructing the coachman to take them to the academy.

When the coach stopped at the entrance to the school, Tadhg felt the same melancholy that had engulfed him earlier in bidding adieu to Lady Sarsfield. He knocked on the door, and when a sister appeared, asked to see sister Eithne.

'Sister Eithne is no longer with us,' she said.

'Not here?' a disappointed Tadhg asked. 'Then where can I find her?'

'I don't know. She has been recalled to Rheims for reassignment.'

Frustrated, Tadhg returned to the carriage. Hugh volunteered to seek information through church contacts as to her whereabouts, but Tadhg shrugged disappointedly, saying that it would be too late as he had to leave for Bordeaux in the morning.

Dermot O'Lee joined them for dinner. It was a pleasant although nostalgic evening, despite its being a farewell between old friends and new - Dermot and Hugh - as they discussed the coming year's campaign against the Allies, hoping that the smashing victory at Landen could be repeated. They spoke of Ireland with tremulous voices and tears in their eyes, eased somewhat by copious drafts of *uisce beatha*. They consoled themselves with the improved situation of Honora Sarsfield, even though, as Hugh pointed out, the payments came from a special fund originally for the Catholic adherents of King James who had fallen on evil days.

The following morning, 10 September, Tadhg mounted his horse - which had been delivered to Hugh's stables - and with his supplies of pistols safely stowed away under his garments, his official documents in his saddle-bag, he prepared to bid farewell to Hugh and Madelon.

'I would like to request one last favour, sir,' he said. 'There is a young drummer boy named Rory MacAuley with Lord Lucan's Irish Guards. I brought him here from Ireland. Could you arrange for his discharge, and send him back with one of your smuggler friends? Preferably on the West coast, with instructions to find me in the vicinity of Ballynahinch.'

'Ah, yes, Ballynahinch! In the shadow of Beanna Beola.' Hugh sighed, 'Many a happy day did I spend as a young boy on the lake. Remember me, *a chara*, a lonely exile in France, as you walk along its shores, or climb the towering bens. Be assured I'll send your Rory to you.'

'*Slán leat, a dhuine uasail,*' Tadhg said, his voice breaking, 'And to you good lady,' he added turning to Madelon. Abruptly, then, he slapped his horse smartly on the rump, and cantered down the road to the southern end of Paris, and the highway towards Orleans which he hoped to reach before nightfall.

He was sombre as he rode, remembering his other trip to Bordeaux with Dónal Óg. Happy, carefree Dónal Óg! To dispel his melancholic mood, he deliberately concentrated on his course of action once he delivered the message to Butler in Dublin. Probably it would be best to dispose of his horse, and become a tramp, to avoid any undue attention by the Crown authorities. And where would he establish his school? Where could he obtain books and other requirements of the scholars? How would he, the teacher, subsist? These, and related thoughts kept his mind occupied as his horse plodded on.

It was already dusk, and fifteen leagues short of Orleans, when he stopped at an inn, wolfed down his meal, and fell wearily into bed. Early the next morning he rode through Orleans, and not knowing that it was the site of the famed victory of the French, led by Jeanne d'Arc, over the English more than two and a half centuries before, did not tarry. He found the road to Tours, and turned southwest.

Again the distance exceeded his expectation, and he was forced to stop overnight at another village inn. Traffic was light the following morning, mostly farmers taking their crops to market, so he arrived in Tours in time to go to morning Mass, offering prayers for the souls of Dónal and Lord Lucan, at the magnificent cathedral with the lofty twin spires. Spiritually refreshed, he resumed his journey.

The third night found him in Poitiers, the fourth in Cognac, where he sampled the local brandy too liberally, causing him to get a late start the following morning, thus delaying his arrival in Bordeaux until after nightfall. He found an inn much more presentable than the one he and Dónal had stayed at near the edge of town, but was too exhausted to go down to the quays and check on ships.

After breakfast, he mounted his horse for the ride down to the river. He was conscious of a growing excitement as he neared the quays. He was going back home at last! His dedication to the cause of King James, his devotion to Sarsfield, and his infatuation with the exciting life in the army were ended. He was going home again, to family, to friends, and a future based upon the fulfilment of his dream to be a schoolmaster.

His thoughts were interrupted by a loud voice bellowing from the curb of the narrow, winding street, 'M le Sergeant, the Irish Hercules, what are you doing here in Bordeaux? Come to steal your horse back from me?'

Startled, Tadhg turned. It was Jacques Benoit, his weather-beaten visage beaming with pleasure. 'Non, mon ami, nothing so treacherous. I am seeking passage back to Ireland.'

Benoit accompanied Tadhg to Armand's livery stable, talking animatedly all the way. Shortly they were seated in a dingy waterfront cafe, a bottle of wine in front of them.

'How is Cúchulainn? Tadhg asked. 'Getting as fat as a Strasbourg goose? Nearby? Could I see him?'

'When you get back to Ireland, perhaps. He's in County Clare, near Lisdoonvarna.' Jacques shrugged his shoulders. 'If I kept him in France, he would soon be appropriated by one of the thieving soldiers of the King. But what of yourself? And what is one of Louis's brave men going to do in Ireland? Tired of soldiering?'

Tadhg hesitated. How far could he trust the Frenchman? For all he knew, the captain could have returned to port after he and Dónal had left Bordeaux, and turned Nicolas and Françoise over to the French authorities, or he could have had them thrown overboard at sea. It was curious that Jacques had made no mention of them. But perhaps less said of the matter the better it was for all concerned. If the Huguenots had been delivered safely, then a confidential bond existed between himself and Benoit as co-

conspirators in a crime against the king. He decided to be cautiously honest.

'I'm on a secret mission. If you're leaving soon for Ireland, I'd like to sail with you if you could put me ashore at Cork.'

'I leave in two days, mon ami, but I can't go into Cork because the authorities would be too interested in my cargo. I can land you nearby, however.'

'Perfect. And two days time will give me opportunity to have new clothes made to replace this uniform. Now would you recommend a good tailor and a reliable auberge?'

So exhilarated was Tadhg the eve before departure that he was unable to sleep. He tossed and turned, reliving the exciting events of the past week, the sad farewell to Honora Sarsfield, his brief meeting with Louis XIV, his disappointment at missing Eithne Blake, the termination of Sergeant O'Cuirc of Les Gardes du Roi Jacques and the emergence of Tadhg O'Cuirc, Irishman, so that dawn found him wide awake and anxious to go aboard Benoit's ship.

After breakfast, he attended mass at St Andre's, then went to the tailor to get his new clothes. Carrying his newly acquired portmanteau, he walked down to the docks, saying farewell to France.

And so on the afternoon of 17 September, M Armande Deschamps, as listed on the ship's papers, fashionably dressed in his new outfit, he boarded the St Teresa, and was shown to a small, cramped cabin he would be sharing with Captain Benoit. The passenger discreetly remained in his cabin while heavy hawsers were cast off, goodbyes were shouted, and the sturdy ship slowly moved out to catch the surging current of the broad Garonne on its way to the sea.

PART VI

Ireland

Cast of Characters

Baptiste Fortier, mate of the St Teresa

Lt Millett, a junior officer aboard the HMS Oliver Cromwell

Major Thomas Marty, chief of intelligence at Dublin Castle

Una and Thomas O'Grogan, of the travelling people, friends to Tadhg and Mairéad

Lazlo, a gypsy spy at Athlone

Félim O'Brien, manager of Jacques Benoit's farm in County Clare

Cormac O'Quinn, a fisherman of Doolin

Fergus O'Loughlin, friend of Cormac's

Dónal MacGeraghty, a canny horse trader

Eoghan MacClanchy, a Doolin fisherman, brother-in-law to Connor O'Donnell

Donnacha O'Halloran, King of the Galway Claddagh

Nuala O'Halloran, Donnacha's wife

Father Carroll, a Franciscan priest

CHAPTER I

The Betrayal

Fatigued from his long journey and his slumberless night at the inn, Tadhg fell asleep, fully clothed, in his bunk. Hours later he awoke, refreshed but hungry, to find the St Teresa pitching and tossing in the open sea. He made his way past the recumbent, snoring form of Captain Benoit to the deck. Only the dim outline of the helmsman was visible, silhouetted against the growing dawn over the dark mass of Europe behind them. Ahead, to the West, towards Ireland, it was still pitch dark.

He steadied himself against the ship's rail, wet and cold from the salt spray, peering into the blackness. It's as dark as my future, he thought. Was it an omen? Was the growing light in the East, in France, indicative of the easy, secure life that Hugh had promised, and the opaque obscurity to the West symbolic of an uncertain, and perhaps short, future in Ireland? He wrapped his cloak securely about him, suddenly lonely and fearful. No longer could he turn to rely on Dónal Óg's cheerful responses, no longer could he turn to Sarsfield for counsel and guidance. His decisions were now solely his own. The old, impulsive, emotional Tadhg must be supplanted by a new, judicious, cool-headed Tadhg.

To dispel his melancholy, he clambered up the steps to the aft deck to join the helmsman. 'Bonjour,' he said politely.

The sailor stared at him sourly. 'Bonjour,' he replied mimicking Tadhg's accented French, then added, his tone surly, 'What kind of Frenchman are you, M Deschamps? Certainly not like anyone I ever met before.'

'You know my name?' Tadhg was surprised. Despite the wheelman's obvious hostility, he added politely, 'I am from the île de France.'

'Oui! I know your name. I am Baptiste Fortier, the mate of this accursed ship. I make it my business to know what is going on, not like that garrulous fool, Jacques. And you're not from île de France. I have lived in Paris, and am familiar with the île de France patois.'

Tadhg was amused despite the mate's virulence. He smiled, then asked, 'Then what is my origin?'

The mate stabbed with his forefinger towards Ireland, saying viciously, 'From there. You resemble exactly one of those thieving Irish dogs, whelped by a dirty, mangy bitch for a mother, and a mean mongrel for a father, that we have to do business with in that miserable, God forsaken island.'

'Thousands of those Irish dogs are fighting and dying for France while you're getting rich smuggling,' Tadhg replied angrily, his resolution to be calm and deliberate dissipated in one great surge of wrath as he thought of the deaths of Dónal and Lord Lucan, and he grabbed the Frenchman by the throat, lifting him, struggling futilely, from the deck.

Only the wild gyrations of the ship's wheel, and the sudden realisation that the St Teresa was in danger, prompted Tadhg to lower fortier, and to release him from his struggling grasp. Gasping convulsively for breath, the mate instinctively clutched the spinning wheel, bringing the yawing ship back under control.

'Be more careful in the future, M le Mate.' Tadhg said, glaring at Fortier, 'how you talk about Irish dogs. They have sharp teeth and short tempers.'

Turning abruptly, Tadhg returned to the cabin where he found Captain Benoit struggling into his boots. 'You were almost minus one mate,' he said tersely. 'That sea scum, Fortier, has a nasty mouth which I almost shut permanently. He apparently hates us Irish.'

Benoit nodded his head sadly. 'Ever since our last voyage. We were running before a big blow, seeking shelter from the storm. In the Bay of Bantry there is an island, Beare Island, I think the charts call it, which offers protection, so we anchored near Castletownbeare. Shortly, several men in a curragh approached the ship. 'Bonjour,' a big fellow like you, dressed in a priest's cassock, greeted us. 'Bonjour, padre,' I replied. 'You're not forgetting 'tis a holy day,' he says. 'Holy day?' says I. 'It's not on my calender. Pray tell me, Padre, what holy day is it? It's St Spailpín's Day,' says he.'

'St Spailpíns Day?' Tadhg interrupted, chuckling. 'There isn't any St Spailpín.'

'No? It sounds Irish,' Benoit replied. 'I'm saying Mass tonight,' the big fellow shouts, waving his hand towards town. 'I'll be expecting you and your men tonight to fulfil your holy obligations.'

Benoit paused, laughing. 'Well, all of us but Baptiste, who stayed aboard to watch the ship, shoved off in the longboat. Oh, I'll admit we had other spirits on our minds as well as the spirit of

God, and hopefully, some fun and frolic behind a hedge with a buxom *cailín*, but we did intend to go to Mass first.

'Very interesting,' said Tadhg, 'but what does this have to do with Fortier's dislike of the Irish?'

'Don't hurry me. I'm coming to it. We tied the longboat to a small wharf, and hurried into town looking for the church, which was on the far side. We entered, seated ourselves, and waited. But nobody came. Finally, after a half hour or so, I decided to find out what was wrong. At the entrance to a cottage, I met an old woman in a long, black cloak. 'Pardon me, grandmother,' I said in my best Irish, which by the way is nowheres as good as your French,' but what time does Mass start tonight?' 'No Mass tonight,' she cackles.

'But the priest told me there was. For St Spailpín's Day,' says I. The old woman snickered. 'Och, 'tis a *spailpín's* day, to be sure, a *spailpín* named Félim O'Mahoney.'

'Where can I find this rascal?' I asked, growing angry.'

'She cackled again, pointing out to the harbour. And there like a swarm of ants around a drop of grease, were a dozen or so curraghs, busily transferring our cargo. I ran back to the church, getting my men, and dashed down to the wharf to get our long boat. But it was gone! I divided the crew and sent a group in each direction along the shore to find a boat, any boat.'

Benoit shrugged his shoulders in resignation. 'Well, to make a long tail short, as the farmer said, swinging his axe at the cat, we found no boat that night. We went back into town, to a wretched little inn, making the best of a miserable situation by downing great quantities of spirits which you Irish more appropriately call *uisce beatha*, the water of life. I awakened at dawn, stiff and sore from sleeping on the earthen floor, afraid to move my head which felt like a regiment of drummers had been beating on it, and walked down to the dock. There, neatly moored, was our boat. I aroused the men, rowed out to the St Teresa, and there we found Baptiste tied to the foremast, miserably cold and furiously angry.'

'I can now understand his vexation,' Tadhg said. 'I'll apologise to him for my rough treatment.'

'Non.' Benoit said, shaking his head. 'It will do no good. Baptiste is a vengeful fellow. I must warn you to stay clear of him, even though he is the husband of my sister Jeanne. You see, mon ami, this O'Mahony, the leader of the brigands, has the same black hair and blue eyes that you have, and Baptiste will never forgive, so humiliating was the ignominy of his experience. Also, as a partner in our family export business, the theft of the cargo hurt our purse. I'm not sure which rankles him most.'

'But what of you, Jacques, you appear to bear no malice?'

Benoit shrugged his shoulders. 'What good does it do now to be angry? Having the devil of hate gnawing at my guts doesn't hurt that thieving scoundrel, that impious impostor, O'Mahoney. Besides, the impudence of the rascal amuses me. And some other Irishmen will have to pay more for my goods until the loss is recouped. But enough of Baptiste, let us go and fill our bellies with good food.'

His hunger sated, Tadhg climbed to the upper deck. The sun, no longer merely a promise, was mounting in the cloudless sky behind them, lighting their churning wake to create a myriad sparkling gems for the pleasure of the beholder. Here is a treasure, Tadhg mused, that no thief can ever steal from me. France had disappeared from vision; all around them was the vast emptiness of the open sea. Vibrated by the wind, the rigging played an eerie tune like that of a sightless harper plucking carelessly at the strings of his instrument.

Carefully Tadhg made his way forward, the weathered deck canted from the stiff breeze, the ancient, patched sails straining and bellying, the salt spume flying. At the base of the bowsprit he stopped, steadying himself at the rails. Somewhere to the north-west lay Ireland. He was going home again.

Several days passed pleasantly, the fair weather holding as the St Teresa headed steadily westward to avoid the coast-watching English warships. Then, when Captain Benoit felt it was safe, he set their course to north. Tadhg's encounters with the mate were uneventful, but he sensed a suppressed antagonism on the part of Fortier. Remembering Jacques's warning, Tadhg was careful not to turn his back to the mate, or to walk carelessly along the deck where a sudden, vigorous shove could hurl him into the sea.

On the morning of 21 September, with the St Teresa cautiously approaching the Cork Coast, the lookout observed a sail on the horizon. Benoit scrutinised the distant ship through the glass, then, turning to Tadhg, said, 'Whoever she is, the captain probably has already seen us. If it is larger and faster, it will overtake us anyway. If it's slower, it will make no difference.' He turned to the helmsman, 'Hold her steady on her course.'

'Come,' he told Tadhg, 'we'll prepare for them.' He walked swiftly to the ship's stern, and opening a chest , removed a wooden sign which he displayed to Tadhg. It read, 'Sta. Margarita Bilbao.' Then, leaning perilously over the rail, he removed the 'St Teresa Bordeaux' nameplate from the slotted iron framework, and replaced it with the substitute. Next he went forward, and lowering the French flag, raised the flag of Spain.

Tadhg looked at him questioningly. Benoit grinned. 'The subterfuge? My mother was Basque, French, to be sure, from Lourdes, not Bilbao. The dialects are different, but I doubt if there are any expert ears out here.' He shrugged his shoulders. 'Basque is a most unique language, resembling no other European tongue. Practically no one understands it but a native.'

'You changed that nameplate so quickly I suspect this isn't the first time.'

Benoit poked Tadhg in the ribs with his forefinger, and winked slyly.

As the hours passed, it became apparent that the other ship was indeed faster, and was closing in on them. Captain Benoit used his glass frequently. With brows furrowed with anxiety, he said to Tadhg, 'We're in for trouble. It's an English man-of-war.'

Tadhg blanched with sudden fear. In his joy at returning home he had forgotten about the English, and hadn't seriously anticipated the possibility of being apprehended. 'What do we do now?' he asked, a knot forming in his stomach.

The answer was the usual shrug. Then the Frenchman, to allay Tadhg's fears, said, 'Wait and see. Spain and England are allies. It might be that our courses merely coincide, and when they overtake us, we'll just keep on going.'

Their conversation was interrupted by the lookout shouting, 'Land ahead, off the right bow.'

Despite his concern over the English ship, Tadhg was aware that his heart was beating rapidly as he strained his eyes to see his native land again. Sure enough. There was the dim outline of a shore, and if Benoit's navigation was correct, it should be the same coast of County Cork he had left nearly two years previously, filled with high hopes for a triumphant return to free Ireland from the oppressor.

As the shoreline of Ireland grew closer, so did the warship. Tadhg could now discern the cannoners standing behind their guns, the sailors scrambling in the rigging, the lookout high at his post on the foremast, the wheelman and a knot of officers at the helm.

Benoit sighed audibly. 'Just an hour too late. If we had a little more time we could elude them by running into a shallow cove where they couldn't follow because of their greater draught.'

Like a nimble cat in pursuit of a slower mouse, the English ship overtook the smaller St Teresa. Sailing to windward to deprive the French ship of wind and mobility, the man-of-war pulled abreast at about a distance of 100 feet. An officer, in an immaculate white tunic, appeared at the rail with a megaphone. In Spanish he ordered the Sta Margarita to heave to, and await a boarding party.

Benoit replied in a strange language which Tadhg assumed was Basque, but complied with the order. Shortly, a longboat with an officer and a half dozen sailors armed with muskets, tied to the side of the St Teresa. A rope ladder was dropped, and Captain Benoit assisted the officer on to the deck. The sailors followed.

The Englishman, a slender man in his late twenties, stared at Benoit, and then his face lighted with an amused smile. 'M. le Smuggler,' he said in French, 'I thought it was you and your ship, although your new flag,' and he pointed aloft, 'and your new ship's name confused me.'

Chagrined, Benoit smiled back. 'Pardieu! You are Lieutenant Millett of HMS Bristol. You, ah, borrowed several casks of wine from me about a year ago. But you have a different ship, yes?'

Lieutenant Millett nodded. 'Yes, it's the HMS Oliver Cromwell, one of our new frigates. That's why you couldn't outrun us. I thought I recognised the St Teresa, and remembering how delicious your wine was, I suggested to the captain that you probably would be delighted to, ah, loan us several more. Now don't you agree that was a most appropriate suggestion?'

Benoit smiled wryly, but played the Englishman's game. 'If I had known that it was you, I would have altered my course to meet you and make the offer myself.' He returned to his mate, who was standing by, listening avidly. 'Baptiste, have the men got two casks of Jurançon for the Lieutenant?'

'Better make it three,' the Englishman said politely, 'this is a larger ship.'

Tadhg, who had followed the conversation intently, began to relax. A dangerous situation had been averted. As Benoit and the lieutenant conversed idly, Tadhg watched Baptiste and the two crewmen open a hatch, removing three casks of wine. Then the mate disappeared for a few minutes while the wine was lowered to the long boat below. When Baptiste returned, he carried Tadhg's portmanteau. He went directly to the English officer, spoke a few words, then dumped its contents on the deck. Lieutenant Millett bent over, rummaged among the pile of Tadhg's effects, then straightened up, clutching Tadhg's envelopes.

Tadhg and Captain Benoit stood open-mouthed, flabbergasted at Baptiste's action. Then Jacques bellowed like an angry bull, rushed forward, and with one powerful swipe hit his brother-in-law so hard that Baptiste was catapulted across the deck, and in falling, struck his head on the rail where he lay senseless.

The Englishman surveyed the scene calmly, his light blue eyes betraying a slight amusement. Then he turned to his men, and pointing to Tadhg, ordered in English, 'Seize him. He's an Irish spy for the French.'

Tadhg exhaled slowly. He was trapped. God damn that treacherous Baptiste, he thought, and O'Mahony too, for initiating this monstrous chain of events! Here I am a prisoner of the English due to a scoundrel of an Irishman I never met!

Benoit looked sadly at Tadhg. 'I'm sorry, mon ami, but I never dreamed that Baptiste's pique would lead to this. It's hard to believe he would do such a despicable thing.'

'No,' Tadhg replied. 'It's my fault. I should have gone to the cabin and destroyed the documents when the British ship approached. I deserve this for my stupidity.'

As the sailors forced Tadhg into the Longboat, Lieutenant Millett addressed Benoit. 'You are very fortunate, M le Smuggler, that we are in a hurry to get to Dublin, and do not have time to bother with you. For past favours, and appreciation for the wine, I will overlook your interference with the seaman who exposed this spy. We can wink at your smuggling, but not at transporting enemies of the Crown. I trust that you will be more circumspect in the future.' He bowed, and followed Tadhg and his men down the ladder.

Taken aboard the frigate, Tadhg was questioned by the ship's officers. His army discharge as Tadhg O'Cuirc, his false French passport, and the coded messages were carefully examined. He explained that he was tired of fighting for the French against the English, and in exchange for his release, he had agreed to carry a message to a contact, one Charles Wilkinson, in Dublin, whom he was to meet at the entrance to Trinity College. How was he to recognise this Wilkinson, a stranger? He wasn't. Wilkinson was to recognise Tadhg instead, by walking with a decided limp outside the gate.

He was then confined to the brig. A most ignominious return home, he thought bitterly, and what could be more fitting and insulting than to be incarcerated in an English warship named for the despot Oliver Cromwell! His intense joy at his brief view of the Irish coast gave way to despair in the close, damp cell deep in the bowels of the man-of-war. But he had been amply warned of the perils of his venture, so he had none to blame for his plight but himself. There was little solace in his predicament, however, in finding such a convenient scapegoat.

By the time they arrived at Ringsend, Tadhg was totally depressed, and resigned to his fate. He was cognisant of the extraordinary good fortune which had smiled in him ever since he had survived the storm that had claimed Somhairle O Conchobhair and Peadar Laidír. He had tempted death and disaster too often to expect his good luck to be limitless.

At Ringsend he was taken ashore, and at the same old inn where he had his encounter with Major Trent and Captain Henry, he was transferred to the custody of the army under armed guard, and then taken into Dublin where he was imprisoned in a small cell in the second floor of Gunner's Tower. There was little consolation in being informed by the guard that it was the same cell in which Hugh Roe O'Donnell had been imprisoned way back in the reign of Queen Elizabeth.

Like all the 'mere Irish', Tadhg knew of successful escapes from the dreaded Tower, most notable being that of Hugh Roe O'Donnell and Art O'Neill on the eve of the Epiphany in 1591. Captured through the duplicity of false friends he trusted, Hugh was returned to his cell in the Castle, but escaped again later, this time successfully.

The next day Tadhg was taken to the quarters in the Castle used by Major Thomas Marty who was in charge of His Majesty's intelligence operations in Ireland. The major, a slight man, with cold blue eyes peering intently from under a rapidly receding hairline, inspected Tadhg as if he was a strange and nasty insect flushed from under a rock.

'You are Sergeant Tadhg O'Cuirc?' he asked.

'Yes,' Tadhg replied.

'Of the French army?'

'No longer. I completed my service.'

'Are you denying that you are a secret agent of Louis?' Tadhg smiled.

Major Marty's eyes flashed with anger. 'What is so laughable?' he asked, reaching into a desk drawer and brandishing the envelope with the coded message intended for Michael Butler.

'This was among your effects seized on the French ship. It is written in code. Your discharge from the French army is dated 31 December. Your own papers prove that. Do you still insist on denying that you are a French soldier, that you were carrying a coded message? Do you still smile in the face of all of this evidence?'

'I smiled at the grandiose concept of my being a special agent for King Louis. It's difficult for me, a simple fisherman, to conceive of myself as being a spy for a famous and exalted a person as the Emperor of France. But you are right in one respect. Technically I am still a member of the French army. And it is futile to deny that I was carrying the message. But it was merely a convenience to hurry my return to Ireland. It helped pay for my passage.'

'And you don't know what the message contains?'

'No.'

'Have you ever been to Dublin before?'

'Briefly, during the war.'

The major paused, tapping his fingernail on the desk top. 'What about Malahide, Bray, Ringsend? Ever been there before?'

'I was at Ringsend yesterday on my way here.'

'Never before?'

'No.'

Major Marty looked at Tadhg guilelessly. 'Are you sure?'

What is this Englishman up to, Tadhg thought, becoming uneasy at the questioning. 'Yes, I'm sure,' he finally replied.

The major turned to a soldier guarding the door. Bring in Mr Brown,' he ordered.

Shortly the soldier ushered in a tall man with thin, bent shoulder who stood nervously, twisting his long, bony hands. 'Turn around, Mr Brown,' the major directed, 'and see if you recognise this man.'

Brown turned and stared at Tadhg, who vaguely remembered seeing him before. But where? And what was the purpose of this confrontation? The man called Brown nodded his head vigorously, smiling obsequetiously at Major Marty. 'That's him,' he said, licking his lips. 'I never could forget him. That's what I told Lieutenant Worthington yesterday when I saw this man at the inn again. He's the one who killed poor Major Trent. Big and black-haired he was without his wig and dressed like a sailor.'

'Thank you, Mr Brown, for your valuable assistance. You can go now.' The major turned to Tadhg, a mocking half-smile on his face.

Tadhg sighed heavily. Any chance he might have had for escaping hanging was now dissipated. He was now linked to another and more serious crime against the Crown. He could not expect any mercy from the English.

'A simple fisherman, eh? Yet you slew Trent in a duel. And from eye-witnesses' reports, a fair fight with all the amenities observed. What do you know about codes, M Deschamps, or do you prefer O'Cuirc?'

'Very little,' Tadhg said trying to avoid any more traps.

'Why did you quarrel with Major Trent?'

'He insulted my religion.'

'Oh, come now, do you expect me to believe that? Major Trent was serving a Catholic King. He certainly would be more circumspect that to do anything that stupid. And why would he, an officer, stoop to duelling with a mere enlisted man over religion? Isn't it true that you had placed him in deadly peril by discovering that he really was an English agent? And this discovery was involved with coded messages?'

'No,' Tadhg replied stubbornly.

Once more the mocking half-smile.

'Will it be necessary for me to bring the serving wench from the inn? The one who procured Major Trent's bible? The King James version?'

Tadhg remained silent, shocked at the deadly evidence being brought against him. And in such short time. This tormentor is not only sly and cruel, but exceedingly competent and resourceful.

Major Marty chuckled, enjoying Tadhg' discomfiture. 'Not so sure of yourself any more, eh? You see, O'Cuirc, I know of the whole affair. I personally set up that code in London. Major Trent and Captain Henry were part of my intelligence operation. Henry was the courier, carrying the messages between Ireland and England. I was very angry when I learned that two of my men were slain by a Sergeant O'Cuirc and a Sergeant Williamson. I realised that King James's counter-intelligence operatives were cleverer than I thought, and oh, how I prayed for the day when I would catch the responsible parties. Do you believe in the power of prayer, Sergeant? I do, for, lo and behold, my prayers have been answered. Next will be Williamson.'

Oh, God, Tadhg thought, dismayed, how could You do this to me? Deliver me to this man? Are Protestant prayers, then, more powerful than Catholic prayers?

'I don't know why that ass, James Stuart, persists in sending his spies over here. Major Marty said, irritably, interrupting Tadhg's thoughts. 'Why, just last week my men caught Mark Beggett, formerly a sergeant-at-arms to James, dressed in women's clothes. After squeezing every bit of information out of him we hanged him. And now I have you. But I'd rather catch you than twenty Baggetts. Compared to you, O'Cuirc, he was a mere Bagatelle.'

The major laughed, pleased at his own joke. It's too bad that I'll have to send you to London. I'd like to revive the old custom of Good Queen Bess when the heads of the rebellious Irish chiefs were impaled in poles until they rotted away at the main gate of the Castle. It was a good lesson to the mere Irish who might get ideas of revolting against English authority. do you know the little verse that went with the impalings in Queen Bess's time?'

Tadhg shook his head.

'No? Well the quality of the poetry might be open to question, but not the message:

These trunkless heads do plainly show
Each rebel's fatal end
And what a heinous thing it is
The Queen for to offend.'

Major Marty looked at Tadhg appraisingly as if visualising his prisoner's black-thatched noggin, with sightless blue eyes, staring at the properly impressed Dubliners in the street below.

Tadhg shivered. Noting it, his tormentor gloated at Tadhg's obvious distress. 'Yesterday, when you were first brought here, I was going to routinely transfer you the Tower of London as an agent of Louis, but now that we are learning more about you, I think I'll keep you here in Dublin while we investigate you further. In the meantime, I hope that you are enjoying our hospitality.'

Tadhg was interrogated every morning for the next few days. He was asked about the death of Mattie Moley, the Chritsmas Ball given in the Castle for King James, the attack of the drunken soldiers at Kilbrendan (the Fitzgerald estate), the coded message,

Charles Wilkinson, his supposed contact in Dublin, his relationship with Mary Casey (scornfully described as a secret Catholic) and event the razor, seized with his possessions on the St Teresa, inscribed with the name of François Rousseau.

He remained mute to all questions, preferring silence to further disclaimers which could easily be disproved as had been his lie about Ringsend. The allusions to Mary Casey and Kilbrendan greatly disturbed him. What could they have to do with spying, or any crimes against the Crown?

Major Marty, strangely showed no displeasure at Tadhg's refusal to answer. To the contrary, he seemed pleased at his victim's reticence, taking great delight in slyly interjecting a new name or incident among the many innocuous questions asked, and observing Tadhg's worried reactions. He also enjoyed describing in lurid detail how convicted enemies of the Crown were drawn and quartered after being hanged just long enough to suffer intensely, but not enough to die.

On his way back to his cell one morning he passed a female prisoner being escorted to Major Marty's office. Garbed in a long, dark cloak, her hair dishevelled, and her head bowed, Tadhg heard her sobbing and smelled the stench of her clothing. Poor creature, he thought, she must have been jailed a long time to have so pervasive and odour.

He frequently had fanciful visions of sliding down a rope to the Castle grounds, emulating Hugh O'Donnell, or overpowering a guard, seizing his weapon and fighting his way to freedom. But how could he acquire a rope? And what chance had he to escape from the Castle with all the hullabaloo that an attack on a guard would cause?

He recalled happier days in the Castle such as the time when he and Conor and Dónal had been commended in the Castleyard by the Duke of Tyrconnell - God rest his soul - for their repulse of the attack by Mattie Moley on Sir Oliver Trent's coach when they saved the life of Mairéad Fitzgerald. And his selection as a member of the guard for Rí Séamus for the Christmas Eve Ball. He scowled at the recollection of the King's attempted seduction, muttering 'Bad luck to you, King James.' He wondered where Sergeant Williamson was now, his good friend who had arranged the escape from the Castle Gate near Bermingham Tower when he and Dónal had been exposed by Lady Margaret.

On the fifth day of his incarceration, as he brooded in his

cubicle, awaiting his guards to escort him to his daily grilling by Major Marty, there was a large trampling of feet, and shouting and cursing. Suddenly his cell door was opened, and he was ordered out. a burly man with bare feet, tattered clothing and long flowing brown hair was shoved into the cell, and the door slammed shut.

Two warders, armed with muskets ordered Tadhg to march. He was let to the courtyard, out through the Gate Towers, across the drawbridge, and west on Castle Street.

Tadhg was perplexed. 'This isn't the route to Major Marty's office,' he remarked to the guard in front of him. The warder, a flabby-faced pensioner, a former soldier, nodded his head. 'You're right. Major Marty left this morning for urgent business in Cork, and will be gone for several days.'

'Then where are we going now?'

'To Newgate Gaol. A band of Raparees from the Galtee Mountains has been captured. They're being kept in the Castle until they are hanged. Des Voeux, the Chief Constable, ordered you to be transferred to Newgate to make room for the Raparees. Major Marty will be furious when he returns and finds you transferred from the Castle.'

'Why?'

The warder snorted. 'security. Nobody escapes from the Castle, but Newgate is notorious for its laxity. 'Tis rumoured that the gaolers there grow filthy rich from taking bribes.'

'Who is the Des Voeux who ordered me moved?' Tadhg asked, intrigued at a French name among the English staff at the Castle.

'One of those Huguenots who fought for King William at the Boyne. Lost a leg, and was rewarded with a good job at the Castle.'

They marched in silence through Skinners' Row, past the Tholsel, into Nicholas Street, turning left on High Street, near Devil's Hook Charlie's, past St. Audeon's Church, and down High Street to where it became Cornmarket, named like nearby Fishamble and Cook Streets for the chief business carried on there.

Tadhg was depressed at the fate of the Rapparees, reflecting sadly that they could be kinsmen since the Galtees are near the Glen of Aherloe, the hereditary homeland of the O'Cuircs. He was pleased, however, that Major Marty was going to be absent, giving him, Tadhg, a much-needed respite.

Little attention was paid to the trio as they approached notorious Newgate Gaol which straddled the Cornmarket from two massive stone towers, three stories high, rising forty feet from the cobbled pavement to the leads of the roof. A toothed portcullis hung menacingly over the pedestrians and vehicles using the roadway below. A gate-house connected the towers on the second and third floors. In the city wall opposite stood the Watch Tower where a sentry kept surveillance on the prisoners.

The Castle warders relinquished custody of Tadhg to the turnkey who gave them a receipt for their prisoner. The turnkey then demanded of Tadhg four pence per night for lodging, and one shilling and four pence for the 'pennypot', the daily ration of liquor which was mandatory. When Tadhg replied that he had no money, that it all had been confiscated when he was captured, he was hustled off to the felons' room, a fetid dungeon with a stench so unbearable that Tadhg felt stifled and unable to breathe.

In the dim light he looked at his fellow prisoners. Some stared back with glazed eyes, their bodies gaunt from starvation. Several mean-looking fellows eyed Tadhg's fine clothes covetously. One inmate lay motionless on the damp floor, face down, his arms reaching towards the dungeon door.

In answer to Tadhg's curious gaze, a tall man with eyes sunken deeply into his skull, explained laconically. 'It won't do him any good to reach, he's been dead since last night.'

Tadhg recoiled in horror and revulsion, getting as close to the door as possible. He retched convulsively, vomit spewing over his fine Bordeaux clothes. Finally, with nothing more in his stomach to bring up, he lay shaking on the slimy floor as with fever. He closed his eyes to blot out the scene, and curiously, the odour of his own vomit seemed to lessen the vile stink of the wretched chamber. He laid quietly for hours, sick in soul as well as in body, berating himself for not heeding Hugh's advice to stay in France.

It was growing dark in the dungeon when his name was called. He looked up, and a guard beckoned to him. Eagerly he bounded to his feet to follow the guard up a flight of stairs. Never did he dream that ordinary air could smell so beautiful. Next to the space taken up by the windlass used to raise and lower the porticullis, was a room on whose stout door was a sign, 'Gaoler, Newgate Prison'.

He waited patiently while the gaoler voraciously devoured a huge meal of meat and potatoes, washed down with prodigious quantities of ale. Tadhg didn't mind the wait, anything was better than the foul hole below. Finally the gaoler, a grossly fat man whose eyes were so obscured by the rolls of flabby flesh on his round face that Tadhg could not discern their colour, wiped his mouth with his coat sleeve, belched mightily, and looked up at the prisoner.

'You are the man known as Tadhg O'Cuirc?' He asked.

Tadhg nodded.

'Do you know a Dublin weaver whose Christian name is Jacques?'

More questioning? More traps? Were they trying to connect the Huguenot to the death of Lt. Benton? He had better be careful with his answers. 'Why do you ask?' he replied cautiously.

The gaoler scrutinised him through his narrow-slitted eyes. 'A man has left some money, a small amount,' he hastened to add, 'for your keep if you're the right Tadhg O'Cuirc. If you can correctly supply his surname, this money will be applied to your credit.'

Some elusive nuance in the gaoler's tone assured Tadhg that the he could answer safely, that it was not entrapment. 'I once knew a weaver by the name of Jacques Le Berge,' he said.

The gaoler sucked at his teeth, found a trapped morsel, chewed it vigorously, then again addressed Tadhg. 'Don't mention this arrangement to anyone,' he warned. 'You're apparently a very special criminal. Those people over there,' he waved a fat arm in the direction of Dublin Castle, 'are very much interested in your former contacts here in Dublin.'

The conversation concluded, Tadhg was taken to a different cell in the south tower. There were three beds, each occupied by at least three men. The air was foul, reeking of urine, excrement, and unwashed bodies, yet it was a decided improvement over the loathsome cubicle he had just left. Narrow slits in the damp moss-covered stone walls provided the only light and fresh air.

'Welcome to Hell,' he was greeted by a short, stout man with a scraggly grey beard, and long, unkempt hair, who was seated on the dirty floor. 'Unlike myself, you should have no trouble in finding bed space because you are big enough to take care of yourself, and take what you want.'

Tadhg looked about with wonder and disgust. A dozen men, dirty and dissolute, sprawled on the beds and the floor. One group was noisily playing one-and-twenty with a deck of grimy cards. In the corner were several filthy buckets, obviously for toilet purposes.

The stout man watched Tadhg with amusement. 'You might just as well get used to it, for you'll be here a long time,' he advised.

'I'll die first,' Tadhg replied vehemently.

'That you might. All sorts are thrown in here indiscriminately, debtors and felons alike. Some have raging fevers, some have smallpox, some large pox, and occasionally a leper. They're all contagious, so take your pick. Or a cutthroat awaiting transportation to Gallows Green will do you for your trousers or fancy shoes to make him a more presentable corpse.'

'How does one get out of here?' Tadhg asked.

His companion guffawed. 'Apparently you know nothing of the workings of law and justice in our fair city. The basis of the system is money, money and more money. If you steal it, you're a felon and are thrown into Newgate. And whereas money is the cause for becoming a dungeon denizen, it can also be the means of getting out. Likewise, money is absolutely necessary for existence here, in relative comfort, squalor or misery. Otherwise your clothes are stripped from you, and you're thrown into the wretched dungeon below where your only hope is to die quickly.'

Tadhg nodded. 'I know. I was put there until a friend provided for my account.'

'You're very fortunate. Here it costs four pence a night for a bed.'

Tadhg pointed to the beds. 'But there are far more men in here than there are beds. Does each have to pay his four pence?'

'Certainly! I told you that money is the grease that keeps the machinery of justice moving. At the top of the hierarchy are the Aldermen and the great officers of the Corporation of Dublin who have been granted by various kings, the powers of Justice of the Peace, and of Cryer and Terminer. Now doesn't that have a grand ring to it? In turn these fine gentlemen hand over the management of this lucrative department of their offices to clerks who pay their masters a percentage of the fees they receive. The clerks, in turn, own the dram shops which provide the liquor for which we have to pay them, like it or not. The gaoler and his flunkeys get their share of the payments, including the multiple charges for a bed that is supposed to have but one occupant.'

'A fine system, indeed. But what are all these men charged with?'

The stout man laughed derisively. 'anything from being a vagabond to murder. You see, the clerks work hand-in-glove with the constables who make arrests on any serious or frivolous charge they can think of. The clerks have batches of blank warrants, presigned by the Aldermen, and they have the authority to have almost any citizen committed to Newgate until the victim can arrange for the fees needed to obtain their freedom.'

'But what about me? Can I, too, buy my freedom?'

'It all depends. What are you in for?'

'I'm charged with being a spy against the Crown.'

The stout man recoiled as if Tadhg had said he was a leper.

He stared at Tadhg with respect and fear. 'Gadzooks, that's a most serious crime. I doubt if you can possibly buy your way out on that one.' He paused and wrinkled his brow. 'On the other hand, it is well-known that convenient escapes have been arranged for all types of criminals.' He shook his head. 'But a spy? That would cost a king's ransom. Are you a king?' he asked facetiously.

Tadhg shook his head sadly. 'Far from it.'

'Then I'd say your chances are nil. Forgive me, sire, but it would be best that I not be seen talking to you. I'm only in here for debt. I can't afford to jeopardise my situation.'

The stout man retreated precipitously to the far corner, leaving Tadhg to his desperate thoughts. But despite the other man's pessimistic opinion, Tadhg began to feel, for the first time since Baptiste had appeared on deck with Tadhg's portmanteau, that there was a ray of hope. Somehow Jacques Le Berge had learned of his capture, and was willing to risk his own neck to help a friend. And was it just coincidence that the Chief Constable at the Castle who had arranged the transfer to Newgate, was also a Huguenot? Obviously Newgate wasn't as impregnable as the Castle. He would have to bide his time and await developments.

CHAPTER II

High Hopes

Tadhg's optimistic belief that Jacques Le Berge had 'somehow learned of his capture' was true, but so did practically everyone in Dublin. The news that an important Jacobite spy was imprisoned in Dublin Castle was a sensation in the capital, and the cause of consternation in a segment of the Huguenot colony.

Great changes had taken place since the Irish capitulation at Limerick, and the victorious Protestants tightened their grip on the prostrate country. The thousands who had fled their demesnes in the rural areas, and their businesses in the cities when James's army controlled most of Ireland, had triumphantly returned, accompanied by an avaricious horde of adventurers who saw a splendid chance for self-arggrandisement in the disposition of the properties of the defeated Irish.

Typical of the leeches who were to bleed Ireland for generations were the Viceroys appointed by William. The first, Henry Sidney, son of the Earl of Leicester, succeeded Lords Justices Coningsby and Porter who had represented the house of Orange after the Battle of the Boyne, and handled the negotiations at Limerick.

Sidney, whose licentious pursuit of the ladies provided Court gossips with choice morsels even until he reached 70, arrived in Dublin in 1692, at age 51, already amply recompensed by his liege lord with 50,000 choice Irish acres and £2,000 annually for his services at the Boyne.

Sidney had been prominent in Charles II's court where his libertine talents had been most productive. Befriended by James, then Duke of York, and his Duchess, the former Ann Hyde, he received valuable appointments through him. He reciprocated for their kindnesses by trying to destroy the Duchess's reputation. Dismissed, he continued his intrigues against them. When foolish James became king, he characteristically took Sidney back into royal favour, yet the king's protege was among the first to join the plot to dethrone him.

The Treaty of Limerick, as predicted by the cynics, had been violated only six weeks after the signing. Protestant magistrates and sheriffs lost no time in seizing property of the Catholics, who protested futilely, referring to the clause in the treaty which stated that: 'The Roman Catholics of this Kingdom shall enjoy such privileges in the exercise of their religion as are consistent with the laws of Ireland; or as they did enjoy in the reign of King Charles II. And their Majesties, as soon as their affairs will permit them to summon a Parliament in this Kingdom, will endeavour to procure the said Roman Catholics such further security in that particular as may preserve them from any disturbance on account of their said religion.'

Alas for fine words and promises! Since the time of Strongbow, the naive, native Irish who believed in such quaint concepts as truth and honour were outmanoeuvred by the wily English who never allowed such impractical ideals to impede them in their quest to subjugate the Gael and confiscate his property. Much more was accomplished over the centuries in attaining this goal by guile than by the sword!

For their support of their sovereign, James II, 3,921 Irishmen were proscribed after the Treaty of Limerick, some eventually had their property restored after paying large fees to intermediaries, or renouncing their religion, but most of the ancient estates were taken as rewards by Williamite soldiers, or as a Royal commission was to report, 'obscure persons who possessed no property at the time Ireland was reduced, are at present masters of large estates, acquired by intrigue or collusion.'

To further hurry the process of acquiring Irish lands, a proclamation was issued in Dublin by the authorities, offering a quarter of the lands liable to confiscation to those who would point them out. This proclamation was a most useful tool to the plunderers, and was the basis for many of the great estates that were to be enjoyed by the Ascendancy in Ireland for nearly two and a half centuries.

Ironically, even Lord Sidney was considered too lenient by the greedy Irish Protestant rulers of Ireland, and pressure was applied to King William to remove him. This was adroitly accomplished by promoting Sidney to the post of Master General of Ordnance. His successor as Lord Lieutenant was Sir Henry Capel who came to Ireland early in 1693, at first to share authority with Commissioners Wyche and Dunscombe.

Lord Capel, a fanatical Protestant who hated everything Popish, was eagerly welcomed in Dublin Castle. Wyche and Dunscombe were less violent in their opposition to Roman Catholicism, but Capel, who did all in his power to infringe on the rights of

Catholics under the Treaty of Limerick, soon dominated them, and his extreme views generally carried. Although not officially proclaimed Viceroy until 1694, for all practical purposes he became Lord Lieutenant shortly after his arrival.

It was at this unfortunate time that Tadhg chose to return. As a former soldier who chose to go the France, as a Catholic and as an accused spy, his fate was sealed. Now incarcerated in Newgate Gaol, awaiting the foreordained judgement of a hostile society, he was consuming his meagre evening meal, a stew with more water than vegetables and very little meat. While he was eating, a guard entered the cell, and beckoning to Tadhg, handed him a huge bucket and shovel.

'You there,' he shouted jovially, 'have just been elected High Sheriff, and these are the tools of your noble office.'

'Sheriff of what,' Tadhg asked innocently.

'Sheriff of Shit,' the guard guffawed, much to the enjoyment of Tadhg's cellmates. 'Now get busy and empty all these honey buckets in this big one.'

Tadhg retched as he dumped the nauseating contents of the pails into the larger bucket, and then, under the cold eye of the guard, shovelled the slopover as well. 'Breathe through your mouth,' a fellow prisoner advised kindly. Tadhg muttered his thanks, finding that it helped.

The guard then took him to the other cells, including the Chamber, or common sleeping room on the third floor, where men, women and children were all confined together, held fast by iron collars, clinched to an iron bar to prevent their escape. Even the children were thus shackled. Tadhg's revulsion and horror at their miserable state were so great that he barely noticed the unspeakable filth.

When he completed his round of all the rooms and cells but one, which the guard said had only two prisoners, both women, he was led down the dank corridor on the ground floor to a door opening on a small courtyard. The barking and baying of a pack of dogs greeted him.

'Leave the bucket and shovel there near the door,' the guard instructed. 'Now you have another task.' From a huge satchel, he took a fistful of bloody meat, handing it to Tadhg. 'The gaoler keeps his pack of dogs out there in the courtyard. You will feed them every night after you clean the cells. The rear exit from the courtyard is at the opposite end, but don't try to escape, the dogs would tear you to pieces. Besides, the door is locked securely.'

'But how can I feed them then?'

'Go to the half-door there. Open the top part just enough to throw the meat through. And watch your hand if you want to keep it!'

Gingerly, Tadhg approached the door. He opened the upper section a few inches. The barking of the dogs changed to frenzied whines, and several bodies thudded against the door. Dropping several chucks of meat at a time from the satchel, he talked soothingly to the animals who ate ravenously, snapping and snarling.

When the meat was gone, Tadhg closed the half-door. 'The dogs eat better than the prisoners,' he commented.

'If you like horsemeat, yes,' the guard grunted.

Each evening Tadhg performed his revolting chore of removing faecal accumulations from the cells, derided and abused by the other prisoners, then fed the dogs which had become so used to his voice that he was welcomed with eager whines and gentle nuzzling. He began to wonder about the rear door, and if it actually was an exit from the prison. He was puzzled by the apparent contradiction of his relations with the dogs. Would they indeed 'tear him to pieces' now that they had become friendly? It seemed unlikely. What would prevent him from escaping through the courtyard? All he needed was a means of opening the locked door, or a tall ladder to scale the high walls.

Realising that the Crown authorities were painstakingly accumulating a mass of damning evidence against him, and that he would be transported to London Tower as soon as Major Marty concluded his investigation, any attempt to escape would have to be made before the major returned to Dublin.

On the evening of his fifth day in Newgate, Tadhg was eating his meal when a prisoner who had just been admitted to the prison that afternoon, joined him as he sat with his back to the damp wall.

'Even pigs would turn up their noses at this slop,' the stranger said, indicating the watery gruel in his bowl.

Tadhg merely nodded, not feeling in the mood for conversation.

'It might be more tolerable if we had but a bottle of Jurançon to drown the taste of this slop we're eating.'

Tadhg carefully scrutinised the stranger, wondering if he was another agent of the wily Major Marty who was setting a new snare for him. The man was olive-skinned, and his eyes, which gazed steadily and candidly at Tadhg, were an unusual dark brown which reminded Tadhg of the chestnuts of France. His clothes were of good quality, but not fashionable. Tadhg was unable to detect any foreign accent in his Dublin English.

'Why Jurançon?' Tadhg asked cautiously.

'Good wine and good friends,' his companion said stressing the work 'friends', 'are valuable assets in an unpredictable world.'

'Indeed,' Tadhg said, excitement rising, 'obviously I have no Juraçon, but perhaps I might have some good friends? From Pau, perhaps?'

'Yes and most grateful. Françoise, Jacques, Nicolas, Pierre, Ettienne, and of course, Mme Le Berge.'

'Nicolas and Françoise? Then they did arrive here safely?'

'Yes, again, and to show their gratitude for their freedom and happiness, they want to repay their debt by helping yours. We must be exceedingly discreet in our conversation. Listen carefully, because I will not approach you again. I am placing three keys next to your thigh. One, the largest, opens the lock on this cell door. The second largest is for the door to the courtyard where the dogs are kept. The smallest is for the exit at the rear. When the bells of Christchurch ring at midnight, leave this cell, open the door to the courtyard, and wait there until you are joined by another prisoner who is scheduled to flee with you. A sack of meat for the dogs will be at its usual place. Feed them. This is an added precaution to keep them occupied and quiet. Although you are familiar to them, they might be uneasy at the scent of another prisoner. Talk to the dogs quietly as you feed them. Lock all three doors behind you, but don't discard the keys until you are well out of Dublin. You will be provided with two horses outside the gate. Go quickly then, in the name of God, for Lord Capel, the Viceroy, will organise the biggest manhunt on the history of Ireland to recapture you. Flee to the West, for there only do you have a chance to retain your freedom.'

'But what about the sentry in the watch tower?' Tadhg whispered.

'The guard is changed at midnight. His replacement will be delayed long enough for your escape. But you must move quickly.'

His companion arose, and casually walking to the opposite side of the cell, started a conversation with two other prisoners. Tadhg's heat pounded in his chest as he reached slowly for the keys. Were they really there? Could it be a cruel hoax? A diabolical jest?

Cautiously he spread his fingers. His groping hand was rewarded. The keys were really there! He covered then with his hand for a few minutes, comforted by the feel of the cold metal. Then carefully he transferred them to inside his shirt.

'Oh, kind and loving Jesus,' he prayed fervently. 'Forgive me for ever doubting You. May Your mercy forgive me and Your patience bear with me. Amen.'

The hours dragged interminably as Tadhg awaited the sounds of the bells of Christchurch. Around him arose a discordant tune of snores as his cellmates sought temporary solace from their misery in slumber. Excitement gripped him as midnight approached, and a hundred random thoughts raced through his mind. God must have been directing his feet, surely, when he found his way to Cáit O'Reilly's where his benefactor-to-be, Jacques LeBerge, was living four years earlier. Who is this stranger who appeared so mysteriously and providentially today? How had he obtained the keys to the gaol? Who was the prisoner who was to accompany him? Would the dogs raise a clamour? How soon would their absence be discovered? It was apparent now that the honey bucket assignment, humiliating as it was, and the feeding of the dogs, had all been part of the escape plan.

Finally, the clear, welcome sound of the church bells signalled that it was midnight. When the last peel had died, Tadhg walked cautiously and slowly to the cell door. Nobody stirred. Outside, the corridor was dark and silent. Selecting the largest key, Tadhg inserted it into the lock and turned. The bolt moved noiselessly. Apparently the mechanism had been recently oiled. So far, so good! He hoped that the rest of the operation would proceed as efficiently. Slowly he opened the cell door. No squeaking of hinges. Also, well oiled. Keeping the aperture small enough to squeeze through, he stepped out into the corridor. Then locking the door behind him, he made his way down the dark hallway to the second door, which he also unlocked. He then fed the dogs, speaking to them quietly.

With freedom so close he was tempted to depart alone. What if the other prisoner was late? Or was apprehended leaving the cell? Did he, Tadhg, have an obligation to this other man? Why had their benefactors arranged for them to escape together? It did make sense, of course, to combine two escapes into one.

Minutes passed, or at least it seemed so to Tadhg waiting desperately in the darkness. What was the delay? Couldn't the other man get his cell door unlocked? Could he have panicked in the darkness, and gone in the wrong direction? Perhaps already captured and being forced to reveal the escape plan? Tadhg's heart pounded so heavily in his chest he was sure that it could be heard as far away as the Castle, awaking Lord Capel himself.

He decided to recite the Lord's Prayer, and if the other escapee hadn't arrived by the time he had finished, he would leave without him. When he got to 'deliver us from evil' a slight sound in the darkness, and the pervading odour of Newgate clothes close to him indicated that he was no longer alone. Hastily he said 'Amen', crossed himself, then whispered, 'Are you ready?'

A muffled 'Yes' was his answer. 'Come, then,' he said softly, opening the door, 'hold on to my coat, and don't be afraid of the dogs.'

When he felt a hand grasp his coat-tail, he stepped into the courtyard, talking quietly to the dogs. The animals whimpered, and one snapped at Tadhg's leg as he inadvertently stepped on its tail, but they made their way safely to the far door. Tadhg fumbled nervously in the darkness trying to find the keyhole, and in his anxiety, dropped the key. He cursed, angry at himself for his ineptness, then dripped to his knees, frantically running his hands along the packed earth until he found it. Taking great care, he inserted the key, the lock turned, he opened the door and they emerged outside Newgate.

Tadhg expelled the air from his lungs with one vast sigh, then filled them audibly, sucking in the fresh air of freedom. Locking the door as instructed, he looked about him. Dimly in the distance was the 'Black Dog', an ancient inn and ale-house, and to the left was the old fosse, now the city ditch, filled with refuse from the prison and neighbouring houses. His companion, wearing a long, dark cloak with a cowl, looked like a mere stripling. I hope he can ride a horse, Tadhg thought, irritated that he might be impeded when haste was of the utmost importance.

Suddenly a dim figure emerged from the darkness, leading two horses saddled and bridled. Tadhg mounted the closest one, his companion was assisted on to the back of the other, and moments later they clattered through Cutpurse Row to Thomas Street, heading west the same route that he Dónal Óg and Rory had travelled on their arrival in Dublin from Connaught.

CHAPTER III

The Revelation

A mass of dark clouds hung over Dublin with the smell of rain in the air, as the fugitives galloped down Thomas Street to James Street, thence to the Kilmainham Road and the gateway to Maynooth which was on the highway to Athlone and Connemara.

Tadhg was assaulted by a dozen thoughts and impressions as he rode; he felt his confidence returning with the feel of a horse under him for the first time since he left Bordeaux; he observed that his companion was an excellent horseman; easily keeping abreast as they pounded the ancient cobblestones through the quiet streets of the sleeping city, the cowl of the rider's hood bobbing up and down; he wondered how soon their absence would be discovered; he pondered anxiously on the distance to Athlone, and their chances of getting there before dawn; he hoped fervently that his Huguenot friends would not be implicated in his escape; he worried over his lack of money which he would need for food and other necessities; he mused on the identity of his fellow escapee; he thought of his family on Inishmór, and of Conor in Moyrus Parish; he dwelt wistfully on seeing Cúchulainn again on the Frenchman's farm in County Clare.

Most disconcerting, however, was his emotion at passing the twin stones posts with the FitzGerald emblem, a silvery shield with a red St Andrew's Cross, at the entrance to Kilbrendan, and his recollection of the happy hours he had spent lurking nearby, eagerly awaiting a chance to see the Lady Mairéad as she passed in her carriage.

She's sleeping soundly in her warm bed tonight, he thought bitterly, secure in the knowledge that the Protestant government of the Dutchman, King William, had a firm stranglehold on a gasping Ireland, protecting her from the perils and pitfalls of Popery, and the savagery of the 'Wild Irish'. He took pleasure, however, in the thought that she wouldn't be happy to learn that he was free.

They rode steadily, their horses now at a canter, passing through Leixlip, near the junction of the Rye Water with the Liffey. Dogs barked at their passing, some dashing out to nip at the horses' hooves, but they encountered no passing travellers.

A half dozen miles further was Maynooth. When they arrived there, Tadhg remembered the ruins of an old castle, and decided it would be an ideal spot to hide while resting their mounts. He left the road, his companion following. Behind the crumbling walls, he dismounted, and promptly relieved himself. The other rider continued past an old arch, tied the reins to the tree, and disappeared into the darkness.

Tadhg was perplexed. Was this as far as his companion wanted to go, and was leaving on foot? Or was he extremely modest, demanding privacy for emptying his bladder? Apparently it was the latter, for in a few minutes be returned and approached Tadhg. At that moment, the clouds parted, and a shaft of moonlight illuminated the area. As his companion raised the face-obscuring cowl, Tadhg stared incredulously into the equally startled eyes of Margaret FitzGerald!

'Merciful God,' he ejaculated, 'it's the Lady Mairéad!'

'You!' she exclaimed, shaking her head in utter disbelief as if the violent motion would dispel the detested image before her. 'You! Of all the millions of persons in Ireland, it has to be you!'

'It's much less surprising that the likes of me would be escaping from Newgate,' Tadhg replied, still stunned by the disclosure, 'for of all the millions of persons in Ireland, surely the last one I would expect to find there would be the rich and influential Lady FitzGerald.'

Her voice betrayed her hatred and malevolence as she answered. 'It was because of you largely that I was there.' She paused, then added, 'And partly my Uncle Henry, partly my mother's O'Hurley blood, partly King James, partly Lord Capel, and partly that devilish Major Marty at the Castle.'

Tadhg was taken aback at her passionate outburst. 'Well, by your own account then, the blame isn't all mine,' he said defensively. 'And when my friends arranged for my escape with another prisoner, I never dreamed for a moment it would be with a woman, and least of all with you.'

'Nor was I informed that it would be with Tadhg O'Cuirc. I'd rather have died and rotted in that cesspool called Newgate than be forced into your company.' She glared at Tadhg, full of loathing. Then she nodded her head. 'Now I am beginning to understand! You were to be the big surprise that Major Marty promised. You were to be the mortar in the edifice of supposes guilt he was constructing, each building block of which was based on lies and deceit, jealousy and avarice. My desperate predicament all revolved around you. If I never had the gross misfortune to have

570

laid eyes on you, I wouldn't be here now, an escaped prisoner with my very life in jeopardy!'

'If you had never laid eyes on me, you would long since have been drowned in the sea near Inishfúipíní,' Tadhg rejoined testily, nettled at her accusation.

Startled at his harsh tone, she jerked up her head abruptly. 'That's true,' she grudgingly acknowledged, 'but you involved me deeply by killing John Montgomery and Sir Oliver.'

'Montgomery Óg goaded and challenged me to the duel. I won the fight fairly. And Sir Oliver was a traitor to the cause he pretended to serve. He was a secret agent of the English. In fact, he was recruited by your 'devilish Major Marty', and was part of his espionage ring. I unmasked him as an English spy at Ringsend, where he tried to murder me by giving me a deliberately defective duelling pistol for our fight.'

'I don't believe it. It's another of your monstrous lies, like all those false names and identities you adopted. And if it was true, why wasn't it brought out at the time?'

'Because Lord Tyrconnell hoped to make the English believe the fight was a personnel quarrel, and thus they wouldn't suspect that their code was broken. Major Marty told me that God answered his prayers by delivering to him the killer of his trusted and valuable agent, Sir Oliver Trent.'

Lady Margaret lowered her eyes, chewing at her lip, fighting the impulses to cry. 'You make it sound convincing,' she reluctantly admitted. 'I thought you had deliberately provoked him because of jealousy over me. That's why I horsewhipped you at Charleville.' Her eyes filled with tears. 'Will you forgive me?'

Inundated by emotion, all Tadhg could do was to nod assent.

She continued. 'I blamed myself for his death. I hated you and I hated myself. Often I considered taking my own life because I thought it was me that caused the fight at Ringsend.'

'No,' Tadhg said compassionately. 'After you and Sir Oliver turned me over to the soldiers when I first came to Dublin, I encountered him again on Windy Hill in Ulster, but failed to recognize him. It was there that I found a message left for him by another spy. But it wasn't until much later, in Dublin, that I realized that the man in Ulster and the esteemed Sir Oliver Trent were one and the same. And I must apologise to you, also, because I suspected that you were involved in his spy ring, since one of the messages was to be delivered to your house. That's why we composed the code message which Rory Óg took to Kilbrendan. Sir Oliver took the bait. And because you were involved, he arranged with Mattie Moley to assassinate you in your carriage.'

'He what?' she exclaimed, eyes wide open with shocked surprise.

Tadhg explained all the steps in the plan, from the composition of the coded message, his meeting with Mattie at Devil's Hook Charlie's, to the subsequent attack on the carriage which he and his companion interrupted.

'But why would he want to kill me?' she asked unbelieving, unable to grasp the implication.

'Because he was so shaken by the sudden and unexpected appearance of the long missing message at Kilbrendan that he feared exposure. Obviously some strange soldier knew that spy messages for him were to be delivered to your house. Both you and the soldier would have to be eliminated. Mattie tried to lure me to a dive along the river called The Badger. Exposure for Sir Oliver meant disgrace and certain death. In his desperate situation, he didn't hesitate trying to sacrifice you to save his neck.'

'I must sit down,' she said faintly, her hands shaking violently. 'These disclosures are too much for me.'

Tadhg was instantly contrite. 'I'm sorry, my lady, I shouldn't have told you.' He helped her to be seated on a tussock.

'No, Tadhg, it is better that I finally learned the truth. Oliver's duplicity shocks me greatly, but I am beginning to have peace of mind for the first time in years.' She reached out impulsively and took his hand in hers. 'You have been a true friend, saving my life on the ship, from the attack on my carriage, and from those drunken soldiers. In return I have maligned you, exposed you to the authorities, repaying your good deeds with my misdeeds. Again, please forgive me for my selfish, vengeful acts.'

'To forgive you is much easier than you realise, for I, too, had harsh thoughts of you. You mention the Burke Brothers. I'm curious about that episode.'

'They came to me for sanctuary. But unbeknownst to me, my overseer at Kilbrendan secretly informed the Castle authorities. Fortunately, Manus was able to escape. Ulick was not so lucky. But why do you ask?'

'Because in France we believed that it was you who treacherously notified the English. I, too, despised you. So you can see, my lady, how misinformation can work great harm. I am happy to say that I helped arrange for Manus's escape to France.'

'Thank God,' she breathed. 'We wondered as to his fate.'

'There is much yet to tell, Lady Mairéad, but the horses are now rested, and we must take advantage of the few hours of darkness that remain to us.'

As he helped her to her feet, she waved her arm. 'Would you believe that these ruins were once a FitzGerald castle, the stronghold of foolish, impetuous Silken Thomas, son of the Great Earl? Perhaps I should add him to my list, too, for if he hadn't reacted so impulsively to Cardinal Wolsey's plot, the FitzGeralds would be the most powerful family in Ireland still, and I could thumb my nose at Lord Capel.'

Tadhg grinned. 'Or as Thady O'Moriarty would say, 'to hell with Sir Henry.''

Lady Mairéad looked askance at him, shaking her finger.

'I'm sorry,' he hastily apologised, 'I sometimes forget I'm no longer in the Army, among soldiers.'

Tadhg looked about him, 'It was here that the cynical expression, 'the pardon of Maynooth' was originated, for Sir Thomas Skeffington, who breached the castle's walls with cannon, callously slaughtered the survivors despite his promise of pardon to spare their lives.'

'The 'pardon of Maynooth',' she mused. 'It applies to much of Irish history, doesn't it?'

Tadhg nodded. 'The same sort of hypocrisy is being enacted again in the violation of the Treaty of Limerick. But there will be time for talking later. Now it is most important that we put many miles between us and Dublin.'

Quickly mounting their horses, they were on their way west again. Tadhg's mind was in a whirl as he considered the bizarre situation of being a fellow fugitive of the once rich and powerful Lady Margaret FitzGerald. Anxious to learn the details of her amazing downfall, he wondered why he hadn't seen her as he attended to his nightly chores with the honeybuckets. Also, who had arranged for her escape, and had they known of the previous relationship of the two prisoners? They rode steadily, pushing their horses to their utmost, passing over the Boyne, of sad memory, until they neared Kinnegad. Behind them the sky was brightening, and Tadhg reflected painfully that the sun was already illuminating Dónal's grave besides the River Gette. He shivered. Was it the cold morning air, or was his death, too, imminent? Even if their escape was not yet discovered, it could not long remain undisclosed.

He reined his horse to a halt, beckoning to his companion to do likewise. 'I think that we had better leave the main road now that it is dawn,' he advised, 'and hide during the daylight hours. The less we're seen, the safer we'll be. We will need food, and hopefully, a change of clothing. This small road branching off to the southwest should take us into the countryside where we can find a place to rest and conceal ourselves and the horses.'

Lady Margaret nodded, then grinned. 'Yes, Sergeant.'

A cold, gusty wind had sprung up from the west, driving the few remaining clouds back towards Dublin, rustling the oak and ash trees bordering the road, and scattering the fallen leaves like foot soldiers before an onslaught of cavalry. Fields and hedges were a motley display of colour, with the blue of the whortleberries, the pink of the spindle, the purple of bell heather, the red of the holly berries, and the gold of the dwarf furze, reminding Tadhg of the multicoloured costume worn by one of Louis's jesters he had seen at Versailles. He looked hungrily at the *frochan*, the whortleberries, recalling their tantalising flavour when eaten with thick cream.

Their road meandered through the rolling countryside, bypassing Kinnegad, but then unexpectedly swinging back northwest to meet the Galway road again. Remains of an ancient edifice, covered with ivy, squatted forlornly by the roadside. 'Not the best protection,' Tadhg commented critically, 'but it will hide us from view by passers-by.'

Dismounting, they led their horses into an old churchyard. Unkempt graves and tumbled tombstones, covered with the debris of centuries, indicated long disuse. Parts of a large Celtic cross, broken by some unknown vandal, leaned against the ancient monastery wall. Tethering their horses to the heavy stone arm of the cross, they seated themselves against a large standing portion of the masonry.

Tadhg looked at Lady Margaret expectantly. 'I suppose you want to know how I happened to be in Newgate Gaol,' she said. 'I should ask you the same question, but being polite, we'll observe the propriety of ladies being first. Assuming I am still a lady.' Her voice faltered, and tears appeared in the green eyes.

Regaining her composure, she sighed deeply. 'I believe that it started with Ulick and Manus seeking sanctuary at Kilbrendan. Oh, I know that the foundations were already established in my knowing you and Sir Oliver, my keeping Mary Casey when I was long aware that she was a secret Catholic, and my Uncle Henry's penchant for cards and gambling, but the hard fact that it was my estate overseer, and not me, who notified the authorities at the Castle of the Burke brothers hiding on my land was what first brought me to the suspicious attention of Major Marty.'

She paused, shaking her head. 'I still find it difficult to believe that it isn't all a bad dream. Only the Newgate stench of these garments brings me back to reality.

Several weeks after Ulick's death, I was called to the Castle. Major Marty, seemingly apologetic, questioned me about Mary Casey, and why a Catholic priest came secretly to Kilbrendan on Sunday mornings. He asked me about my O'Hurley kin, inferring that they were all Catholics, and their professing to be Church of Ireland members was just a sham, a ruse to keep their lands. He claimed that the O'Hurleys had sided with King James, that one of them had represented Knocklong Castle in James's 1689 Parliament, and that several of my cousins had fought in James's army, including Thomas, who had gone to France with Sarsfield.'

'The Major was well informed,' Tadhg interjected.

'He was indeed,' she replied bitterly. 'And 'inform' is the right word. A distant relative, Patrick O'Hurley of County Clare, a notorious informer, for a price of course, told Major Marty the old story about Sheeda O'Hurley, picking the black pebble, and becoming a nominal Protestant.'

'A 'Porridge Protestant',' Tadhg observed.

She nodded. 'It was about this time that my Uncle Henry died. Appropriately enough, he was at cards, his usual pastime. He laid his head on the table and just died. Like that. His last hand, as usual, his cronies told me, was a losing one.'

Lady Margaret shook her head again, pursing her lips to regain her composure. Then she resumed her tale. 'We had hardly buried him when a horde of creditors descended on me like one of the plagues of locusts in the Old Testament. Unbeknownst to me, Uncle Henry had used the estate money to pay his gambling debts. I had trusted him completely in its management. To pay the creditors, I decided I would have to sell Kilbrendan. Then the next blow fell. My overseer, Jeremy Collier, the same one who had reported the Burke Brothers, went to Major Marty and falsely informed him that I was a secret Catholic like my maid, that I attended Mass in my stables every Sunday, that I had consorted with King James, was a paramour of Sir Henry Sidney when he was here, and was a close companion of one of James's soldiers, a Sergeant O'Cuirc, who had killed Sir Oliver Trent.'

'What incredible treachery!' Tadhg exclaimed, his face contorted with rage. 'What made the scoundrel lie like that?'

She shrugged, her face sad. 'Plain greed. And opportunity. A proclamation had recently been issued offering a quarter of all illegally held estates seized to those' loyal subjects of the king' who reported them to the authorities.' Lady Margaret grimaced. 'So, now that I had been exposed as a secret Catholic my estates were forfeit. Consequently, in due time, Collier will become a one-quarter Lord of Kilbrendan.'

Tadhg was aghast. 'But, my lady, it is incomprehensible to me that this catastrophe could have happened to you. What about your friends? Couldn't they help? After all, that proclamation was designed for presumed enemies of the king, persons who had opposed him in some way. Not even all Catholics have had their estates confiscated. So why you?'

'My friends?' Her voice was bitter. 'When they learned I was under the scrutiny of Major Marty, they avoided me as if I had contacted the Black Plague. And with Kilbrendan about to be seized by the Crown, my creditors became more frantic. Thinking I was about to flee Dublin, they applied to a magistrate for a warrant, and incredible as it sounds, I was seized and thrown into Newgate.' She shuddered, and buried her head in her hands, sobbing violently.

Tadhg put his arm around her shaking shoulders to comfort her. She clung to him until the last paroxysm had subsided. Then, raising her tear-stained face, she resumed her story. 'The little money I had was soon gone, but fortunately some unknown benefactors, probably friends of Mary Casey, Catholics, no doubt, each week provided my keep through the Gaoler, with a little extra for a bribe, to keep me in a room with another woman in relative splendour.'

'Just the two of you?'

'Yes, why?'

'That explains why I didn't see you on my nightly rounds of collecting the waste from the cells. But go on with your story.'

'I tried frantically to be released, but the net was tightening around me. Every few days I was taken to the Castle to be questioned by Major Marty. He accused me of being a paramour of

King James, even having a witness testify that I left the ball on Christmas Eve at the Castle to go to the King's quarters just shortly before the king himself left the party.'

'Yes, I know about that,' Tadhg declared with excitement. 'As a special guard to King James that night, I overheard him talking to Lord Tyrconnell about you. I then informed Mary Casey of his intentions, telling her it was imperative that you leave the Castle at once.'

Her green eyes opened wide with astonishment. 'You were involved in that, too?'

'I called Mary Casey from a room where she was enjoying herself with the other servants, including a big, buxom lass who shouted some ribald witticism at me.'

Lady Margaret nodded her head vigorously. 'That's the one, a big brazen girl. The major called her in, and to my face she lied openly, claiming that I went to visit the king. She mentioned a big soldier, one of the king's guards, who arranged the liaison, whispering to Mary Casey in the corridor. And that was you who really came to warn me.'

'But what of Mary Casey, is she imprisoned also?'

'No, thank God! I was able to warn her of possible involvement, and she fled Dublin.'

'Then it must have been you that I passed in the Castle one day after leaving Major Marty. I was quite surprised to see a female prisoner.'

'Did I look familiar to you,' she asked coyly.

Tadhg coloured. 'To be honest, no. My only impression was that you must have been jailed a long time to smell so badly.'

'A fine compliment, indeed,' she said, glaring at him in mock indignation. 'But I suppose it was at that time when I noticed a change in the major's attitude. His previous deference to me vanished. He became more insulting, and seemed to be gloating. He spoke of a big surprise he had prepared for me. I think he was really convinced I was a Catholic, that I had links to a Jacobite spy, and between us arranged the deaths of Mattie Moley and Oliver.' She nodded slowly. 'Now I can see how all the parts of the puzzle are beginning to fall in place.'

'Some factual, and some false,' Tadhg observed. 'But all leading to your being found guilty, and hanged.'

'My world has completely tumbled down around me,' Mairéad said pensively. 'I never realised there could be so many cruel, dishonest people as I have discovered in the last few months. But enough of me, now you tell me how you landed in Newgate, not that I'm greatly surprised, knowing your propensity for trouble. Where have you been since I saw you last at Charleville?' She blushed with embarrassment as the mention of Charleville conjured up the horsewhipping incident.

'It would take me a week of steady talking just to give you the highlights, my lady. As for being in Newgate, it was because I was transferred from Dublin Castle where I was being held as a spy for Louis XIV.'

'You, a spy for the King of France?' She laughed until the tears came, and Tadhg joined with her, happy to see her change of mood. 'Next you will tell me that the King and you are great friends.'

Tadhg coloured. 'Not quite. But I did meet him once. With Hugh O'Flaherty. You remember his father, the leader of the Raparees?'

'How could I forget?, 'she said, sombre again.

Tadhg then related his meeting with Patrick Sarsfield, the surrender at Limerick, the journey to France, the dashed hopes of returning home with a conquering army. Dónal's and Sarsfield's deaths, finding Hugh O'Flaherty, his brief meeting with King Louis, his decision to return to Ireland, the coded message mission, and his seizure at sea which led to his incarceration in Dublin Castle, and his fortuitous transfer to Newgate.

'Little Dónal is dead?' she said, sobbing, covering her eyes with her hands, 'Oh, how futile! And he idolised you. He would have followed you to the ends of the earth.'

'He's dead because he followed me to France.' Tadhg said, his voice choked. 'If I had only taken Conor's advice, we would have stayed in Ireland, and Dónal would still be alive.'

'Don't blame yourself, Tadhg, I'm sure it was Dónal's decision, for you both believed so passionately in freeing Ireland again. But tell me, how did an accused spy have such powerful friends, that he could bribe officials at Newgate? And you, such an important prisoner?'

'It was the hand of God, surely,' Tadhg said, shaking his head, still amazed at the miracle. He told her how he had first met Jacques LeBerge at Cáit O'Reilly's how Jacques and his weavers saved him from Lieutenant Benton, how he and Dónal had gone to Pau, and how he had conspired against King Louis's soldiers to spirit Françoise and Nicolas out of France.

'It's incredible,' she said, staring at him. 'You, a devout Catholic, risking your neck for a couple of French Protestants you didn't know. Why do you do it?'

Tadhg grinned. 'Conor describes me best. He calls Tadhg the Fool.'

'Then the world needs more fools like you.' she said, admiration in both her words and eyes. 'And do you think it was LeBerge who arranged your escape?'

Tadhg nodded. 'A stranger came to me in my cell. A key word in his conversation was Juraçon, a local wine native to the region of Pau in France where the LeBerges lived. He explained the escape plans gave me the keys to the three locks, and told me I was to have a companion in my escape. But never did I dream it would be the Cailín Bán.'

The Cailín Bán,' she repeated, a tender smile playing on her lips, savouring the sound of the phrase.

'Who made your escape plans?' Tadhg asked. 'And how did you learn the details?'

'A serving wench who brought our meals. She whispered to me that Mary Casey had contrived for me to flee Newgate. I was told to leave the cell, whose door would be unlocked, when the bells of Christchurch struck midnight, and to go to the courtyard on the ground floor where I was to meet a fellow escapee. But never did I suspect that it would be the *Búchaillín Dhubh*!'

It was Tadhg's turned to smile at her use of the Irish for the dark-haired lad. 'But we still don't know for sure who arranged it,' he said. 'There is more than just coincidence. I can understand how Jacques LeBerge and Mary Casey felt about our being imprisoned, and how they had friends to raise the huge sums needed for the bribes, but the intrigue, and the knowledge of how and whom to bribe seems beyond their limited experience. It had to be someone with contacts among the corrupt element in Dublin, someone cunning enough to conceive the plan, someone well versed in skullduggery, someone with a droll sense of humour, and above all, someone who knew of our relationship, precarious as it was.'

Lady Mairéad, noticing Tadhg's unconscious use of the past tense, smiled at its implication. she nodded. 'Yes, I think you're right. It does seem beyond the purview of Mary and Jacques. Someone with a broad background, some charming knowledgeable scoundrel. Do you know anyone who fits that description?'

'Indeed! One man who fits it perfectly. Somhairle O'Mhaille, once of Inishbofin, now better know as Charles O'Malley, of Dublin, or Devil's Hook Charlie.'

'The publican who helped you rescue me from Mattey Moley?'

'The same. He must be chuckling this morning.'

'Are you angry at him for having us escape together?' she said archly.

Tadhg coloured, then blurted, '*A bhean uasail*, despite our dangerous predicament, this is one of the happiest days of my life.'

Impulsively she reached out and took his hand. For a long time they looked into each other's eyes, communicating without words, achieving a contentment and serenity long lacking in the hectic years since they first met on the storm-tossed waters near Kilkieran.

It was Tadhg who finally broke the silence. 'What are your plans, *a bhean uasail*? Where do you intend to go?'

She shrugged. 'To Kilmallock. To the O'Hurleys. I have no other place to hide.'

'It will be the first place Major Marty will look for you,' Tadhg said deferentially.

'But where else can I go? I have no close friends or kin outside Kilmallock or Dublin.'

'To the Gaeltacht. To the mountains of Galway and Mayo.'

'But I speak and understand little Irish.'

'I do. And I will teach you the language of the Gael. The tongue of the O'Hurleys. And the old FitzGeralds.'

She looked at him steadily. 'You are inviting me to go with you?'

'Yes. Will you?'

Her gaze drifted to the West where the bright blue sky was completely free of the clouds of early morning. She was acutely aware that in the event of her capture that her situation was hopeless in that she had tried to escape, and the additional damning fact that she had fled with the notorious Tadhg O'Cuirc would irreparably destroy any claim to innocence. If Major Marty ever had doubts of her guilt, they were now gone. Mischance had placed her in jail at the same time as Tadhg, but well-intentioned friends, not realising the consequences, had arranged the simultaneous escape.

What could the future hold for her? Certainly the power, prestige and opulent life style such as she had enjoyed previously were gone forever. She shuddered at the thought of the bleak existence of the Irish-speaking inhabitants of the lonely and poverty-stricken farms of Connaught, recalling the night she had spent with Conor's sister after her rescue from the sea. But what alternatives had she? At the moment, none. A capricious fate had interlocked her life with Tadhg's. He was a soldier, strong and resourceful. He spoke Irish, and was undoubtedly a hero to the Gaels of the bogs and mountain crags. In addition, he had a great affection for her. But to wander the hills and valleys in an indefinite future with a man not her husband? How could she possibly even consider such a possibility?

Her abstractions were interrupted by Tadhg, who said gently, 'There is no need for a decision now, *a bhean uasail*. It's best that we sleep so that we can travel tonight. You must be exhausted.'

She smiled. 'Any claim I might have had to be called '*a bhean uasail*' vanished once I was thrown into Newgate. Call me Margaret, or Mairéad if you prefer. I'm sure you'd rather have me call you Tadhg than your title of Sergeant.'

Pleased but obviously embarrassed, Tadhg managed a weak, 'Yes, Mairéad.'

She stretched out, using the cowl for a pillow. 'And now I will follow your suggestion that I sleep.' She closed her eyes and soon was slumbering soundly.

Tadhg sat for a while, too awed by the bizarre situation to sleep, tired as he was. He gazed with rapt admiration at his fellow fugitive, marvelling at the strange act of providence which had altered their previous relationship. Mairéad's golden hair, which he remembered so well from his first sight of her lashed to the mast of the ill-fated Protector, was snarled and unkempt, but the oval face, with its flawless, clear skin, long curling lashes, and full lips, was still exquisite; her body had matured, and her breast, rising and falling rhythmically, aroused memories of Madame Le Clerc, recumbent in her golden bed. Leaning over Mairéad, he resisted a wild impulse to kiss her. He shook his head vigorously as if to fling such irresponsible thoughts from his mind. Then he stretched out beside her and promptly fell asleep.

CHAPTER IV

The Love Song

The late afternoon sun was shining in his eyes when he awoke. His companion lay quietly beside him. Incongruously, from the dim recess of memory, arose the image of Sergeant Cavanaugh, the quarter master from the Duke of Tyrconnell's Regiment, and Tadhg recalled his stern admonition, 'Take care of your horses first, and yourselves second.' Guiltily he leaped to his feet to look to the needs of their mounts, but the animals were gone. There were hoof marks, but that was all. He was sure that he had tied them securely, so it was unlikely they had wandered off.

Returning to the wall, he gently shook Mairéad awake. She sat up abruptly, her eyes startled, trying to adjust herself to her strange surroundings and companion.

'Our horses are gone, probably stolen,' he said tersely. 'We had better hurry and go in search of them.'

She blinked and rubbed her eyes. 'But do you think it's wise to disclose ourselves?' she asked.

'We have little choice. Without the horses it will take much longer to reach Iar-Chonnacht, increasing our danger of being captured.'

She blanched at the thought, her eyes wide with fear. Tadhg helped her to her feet, and they hurried to the road where an old man sat on a stone wall. ''Tis a fine day,' he greeted them. 'Aye, indeed it is,' Tadhg replied, adopting his Warwickshire accent, 'but not for us. Our horses were stolen while we were resting yonder.'

''Tis not surprising. I saw some of the wandering people nearby a while ago. By now your horses are probably pulling one of their wagons down a remote road as fast as it can be driven.'

Tadhg shook his head in vexation, with difficulty refraining from cursing. 'You might find them down the road a bit,' the old man volunteered. 'They like to camp around the old well there. 'Tis said that the water first gushed forth at the command of St Etchen. He was the bishop who ordained the young St Columcille. But 'tis unlikely you English would be interested in our Saints.'

Thanking the old man, Tadhg took Mairéad's arm and hurried down the dusty road. About a mile further, around a bend in the road, they saw several covered wagons drawn up in a circle, and a score of people, children and adults, gathered around a blazing fire, eating their meal. All talk ceased as Mairéad and Tadhg approached.

'Good evening,' said Tadhg, maintaining the English accent, 'We were told there is a well nearby, and we would like to refresh ourselves.'

A short, slender, red-haired man eyed Tadhg speculatively.

'The well is behind that small hill over there,' he replied in Irish. Tadhg stared at him blankly, shrugging his shoulders. 'I can't understand you,' he said, 'don't any of you speak English?'

After a brief silence, a young ruddy-faced man spoke. 'I do. He told you that the well is behind the hill over there.' Then he turned to the red-haired man, saying tersely in Irish, 'You'd better hide those two horses, Tomas, these are the two Sassanaigh who were asleep in the old monastery. They're probably snooping around looking for their horses.'

As Tomas sauntered towards a distant clump of trees, Tadhg paused to pat a tow-haired youngster on his head, talking to him in English which the child couldn't understand, while the amused parents stood by, grinning broadly. Then taking Mairéad by the hand, he led her towards the well.

When safely hidden by the hill, Tadhg informed Mairéad of the warning to Tomás, instructing her to stay at the well while he went to reconnoitre. Circling the area, still out of sight of the camp, he made his way to the woods where he found Tomás stooping to remove the hobbles from the horses' legs. Grabbing him by the throat with both hands, Tadhg lifted the astounded Tomás clear of the ground, where he hung nonchalantly unprotesting, staring at Tadhg with an amused smile.

'I could easily disable you with a good kick in the testicles, Fionn MacCool,' he declared impudently, 'but t'would be unfair to the *cailín bán.* 'Twas a fine trick, indeed, pretending not to have the Irish.'

'And 'tis a good thing for you, *mo spailpín fánach*,' said Tadhg, dropping Tomás to the ground, 'that I appreciate a sensible man who appreciates a sensible man. And now I will take custody of the horses.'

'Inagh!' Tomás replied, ''tis fair enough. But I would beg a boon of you, the loan of one of the horses to pull my wagon as far as Ath Luain. Mine just died of the distended belly.'

'And what recompense is there for me, Tomás Rua?'

'Food, drink, sanctuary from the Sassanaigh.'

Taken aback by Tomas's perceptiveness, Tadhg managed a weak, 'Why do you say that?'

'Your hiding and sleeping in the daytime when you should be on the road, pretending to be English when you're obviously as Irish as bog butter, wearing good clothes, but reeking of a foul gaol, recovering your horses yourself rather than getting help from the authorities. Well, *a chara*, have I hit the mark?'

Realising that it would be disadvantageous to acknowledge Tomas's shrewd conjecture, but foolish to deny it, Tadhg chose instead to disregard it.

'I'm not a vengeful man, and we could use some hot food and water to wash with, so I'll be happy to loan you the use of a horse and ride with you to Ath Luain.'

'A good bargain,' Tomás said. 'Now let's return to camp.'

The group around the fire leaped to their feet with surprise when they saw a smiling Tomás and a wary Tadhg approach. Tomás quickly explained that he and Una would travel with them to Ath Luan. Nodding agreement, Tadhg then went to the well where a worried and distraught Mairéad was waiting.

'Thank God!' she exclaimed, throwing her arms around him, 'I thought that they killed you.'

'To the contrary. We have an amicable settlement, and are travelling with them to Athlone.'

'But can you trust them?'

He shrugged. 'I don't know. But I'll be constantly wary. Now let's go and join them, have some hot food for the first time since we left Newgate, and hope for the best.'

She shook her head. 'We have only been out of Newgate since midnight, yet it seems ever so much longer. Where it was difficult at first to believe I was in prison, now I find it difficult to believe I'm not.'

Taking their place at the fire, they were served generous portions of mutton stew, made with peas and leeks, from a three-legged bronze cooking pot right in the fire, accompanied by farrels of a flat oatmeal griddle cake and bilberries washed down with cold buttermilk. Although a far cry from the sumptuous meals at Kilbrendan, it was a great improvement over the fare at Newgate.

Far more rewarding for Margaret than the hot meal was the basin of hot water and piece of soap to wash herself. And despite the vile odour of the soap (made from whale oil) which clung to her, she felt like a woman again. To complete her toilette, Una, the red-haired man's wife, let her use her brush and comb. Tadhg, too, washed with hot water for the first time since his capture. It was a luxuriant experience for them both.

Sitting around the fire that night, they learned that there were four families, each with its own wagon, and all from the same district in Northern County Roscommon; Tomás and Una O'Grogan; Cathal (the ruddy-faced man who spoke English) and Gobnait O'Duffy; Félim and Norah MacManus, and Piers and Sheila O'Cooney. They were all young, children of the old creaght families, like Rory, who now travelled the highways permanently as itinerants. No longer possessing any cattle of their own, they eked out a livelihood by working as farmhands, blacksmithing, mending pots and kettles, racing horses and peat digging.

'And stealing horses,' Tadhg added.

'Aye,' replied Tomas smiling roguishly, 'And even a sheep for your stew tonight.'

Tadhg joined in the laughter, then yawned so loudly that Una decided that it was bedtime. 'You can share our wagon with us,' she said. 'We have only one child, little Robert, and there is plenty of room.'

'Thank you kindly,' Tadhg replied, 'we will be happy to accept your kind offer.'

Mairéad was near panic when Tadhg led her to the wagon where Una had spread a linen sheet over a bed of rushes. 'We can't sleep together,' she hissed through clenched teeth, 'we're not man and wife.'

'You will be perfectly safe, I don't intend to violate you.' He grinned and added, 'I hope your intentions toward me are as honourable.'

She blushed and changed the subject. 'But will we be safe with them? Might they try to kill us to keep our horses?'

'I think we're safer here than in Dublin. Borrowing other people's livestock is a normal part of their nomadic life, but killing people isn't. And I know the sleeping order. Tomás will place Una on the far side, then himself, then his son. I, in turn will place my woman on the far side from them, with me in between. And despite my fatigue, I'll sleep with one ear open, a habit I acquired as a soldier.'

'All right,' she agreed dubiously, 'but I probably won't sleep a wink.'

Tadhg was pleased that she did not remonstrate against the

reference to 'my woman'. He helped her up the ladder to the back of the wagon where she reluctantly stretched out on the improvised bed. The O'Grogans stripped to the buff, as was the custom among the poor Irish, and as Tadhg predicted they took the front of the wagon, with Una the furthest away. Mairéad, after one shocked look at the naked O'Grogans, covered her eyes with her hands, and lay quietly. One by one, the other families also climbed into their wagons, and silence settled over the camp.

Mairéad was restless, tossing and turning. Finally she whispered,'Tadhg, I can't sleep. I need a pillow like I'm used to at home.'

'Put your head on my arm.'

'But you will be uncomfortable.'

'No, I won't.'

Placing her head on his upper arm, she turned on her side and was soon asleep. Tadhg lay quiet, afraid to move lest he disturb her. Elated over their intimacy, Tadhg told himself that he would gladly be uncomfortable all night if necessary to have her that close to him. Eventually his fatigue overcame his excitement, and he, too, slept soundly. Upon waking in the morning, he found Mairéad's head still on his benumbed left arm, and his right arm firmly around her slender waist. A week ago, he mused happily, this would have been only a pleasant dream.

The camp dogs' barking finally awoke her. 'Tadhg?' she whispered.

He reacted without thinking. 'Yes, Mairéad, *a stóir*.'

'Is everything all right?'

All right? What inadequate words, he thought, for the elation he felt, lying here with her in his arms, dependent upon him for help and protection. He smiled happily. 'Yes, everything's fine. It's only the camp dogs barking at a passing badger or hare. Dawn is breaking in the East and soon we will be on our way to Athlone.'

She lay still, making no attempt to free herself from his embrace. At the other end of the wagon, Tomas and Una stirred and soon were descending to start the fire for the morning meal.

In a few minutes the camp was alive, with adults, children and dogs all milling about. After a meagre breakfast of hot bread and cold buttermilk, the horses were brought up, including Tadhg's and Mairéad's, hitched to the wagons, and the entourage headed west. Tadhg and Mairéad, hidden from view in Tomás's wagon, watched the road recede in the distance, their second horse trotting behind, tethered to the rear of the wagon.

Athlone, mused Tadhg. Ath Luain, the Ford of the Loins. Poignant memories swept over him. He remembered, too, the courageous defence of the bridge by Sergeant Custume and his volunteers, and the ignominious Irish defeat by Ginkel due to the arrogance and obstinacy of their French commanders.

As they bounced over the rutted road, Tadhg was reminded of the srar crossed lovers, Diarmaid and Gráinne, fleeing from Fionn MacCool at Tara to Athlone in their chariot. Now he and Mairéad were also fugitives, although Tomas's old wagon was far from being a chariot, and Major Marty had none of the heroic proportions of the fabled leader of the Fianna.

'A pence for your thoughts, Tadhg,' Mairéad said, interrupting his reverie.

'Sold!' he replied. 'In my impoverished state, even a penny is welcome. I was remembering the first time I came by here. It was with Dónal, Thady and Rory. We were going to the Castle in Dublin to find Hugh O'Flaherty, then return home to Kilkieran, a simple journey.'

'Yet you had to go all the way to France to find him. It's still quite a distance to Athlone, so why don't you tell me of all of your adventures to relieve the tedious hours of travel in this miserable cart?'

'Tis long and involved. Your ears will ache.'

'No, for more I learn about what you have done in adversity, military defeats, many disappointments, and life in a strange land, may help me with my defeats, my disappointments, and ridiculous as it may sound, my new life in a strange land, the Gaeltacht.'

Pleased with her request, Tadhg related the major happenings from the time they had first parted near Galway to his seizure aboard the St Teresa. It was late afternoon when he finished. They had passed through Horseleap and Moate, and now approaching Athlone, they could see the three bald-topped hills created when Cúchulainn lopped off their tops with his sword in his furious pursuit of Queen Maeve's beaten army.

They had learned from Tomás that there was to be a fair at Athlone with many families of the creaght people gathering there. There would also be the dark-skinned foreign wandering people, the Romany, and Tadhg was warned to avoid them as they were ill-tempered, were wont to steal anything not watched, and were extremely clannish.

'We'll sell one of our horses at the fair to get some money,' Tadhg told Mairéad. 'We need new clothes, and some cash in hand will remove us from pauper status.'

The cavalcade rumbled over the site of the bridge where the Irish had fought so bravely, but in vain. The old castle, badly battered by Ginkel's cannon, was now empty and desolate. Below, the Shannon flowed listlessly. A wave of sad memories tolled over Tadhg. Defeat, defeat, defeat! Would Eire ever be free again? What was her destiny? Sadly, he described to Mairéad the action at the bridge, praising the bravery and dedication of his old friend, Sergeant Gallagher, Sergeant Custume and the other Irish volunteers.

'But it was so useless,' she said frowning. 'They just threw away their lives. They should have known that King William was bound to win. How much better it would be if they had surrendered and now were alive and well. Men do such stupid things!'

Tadhg stared at her, mouth agape. Then, realising the futility of trying to explain the motivation that inspired men like Gallagher and Custume to sacrifice their lives for their country, to place their idealism over her realism, to exalt selflessness over selfishness, he sadly but wisely refrained from comment.

'We're now in Connaught,' he remarked, changing the subject, as the wagons rolled through the old, cobbled streets of Irishtown. 'Every mile to the West is another mile to freedom.'

They stopped at a plain at the far end of town where a dozen other wagons were gathered. On the opposite side three gaily decorated wagons stood segregated. A group of olive-skinned men, women and children were gathered around a fire preparing dinner.

One of the men, a gaudy yellow blouse and red pantaloons covering his thickset frame, and with an ivory-handled knife stuck in a broad leather belt around his waist, stared avidly from black eyes above an aquiline nose and gleaming white teeth, as Mairéad, her golden tresses flying, descended from the wagon. They were, Tadhg deduced, the ancient wanderers, the Romany people.

After dinner that evening, all of Tomas's group gathered around a central fire. Tadhg, seated with Mairéad, observed the Romany standing back, watching Mairéad. Quickly the whiskey appeared, and soon a man's voice was heard above the din, singing 'Róisín Dubh', an old favourite of the Gaels. Immediately the hubbub subsided, another man joining in the song, then a woman, until all but Tadhg and Mairéad were singing.

588

'Why don't you join in the music?' she asked.

He shook his head. 'My heart is so full of joy that if I opened my mouth to sing, the joy would all spill out and be lost.'

'Are you sure it's joy and not the whiskey?' she asked, smiling.

'one leads to the other,' he replied. 'But hark, that's a new one now, one that I have never heard of before.'

'It's called 'Lillieburlero,' volunteered Una, overhearing Tadhg.

Song followed song, some sad, some gay, including some that Tadhg knew well, like that 'the Battle of Killiekrankie', describing the fight in 1689 at the mountain pass in Scotland; 'The Boyne Water'; 'Roscommon Rose', set to the tune of 'The Yellow Jacket', a popular jig; and 'We Brought the Summer With Us'.

Then Una grasped Tadhg's hand, and tugging at him, made him follow her to the centre of the circle. She raised her free hand for silence, then announced, 'Our giant Fionn McCool, wants to sing a song to his *cailín bán*, Mairéad MacCool.'

Tadhg started at Una, too surprised to be angry. Then the joy that was in his heard (or perhaps it was the whiskey) made him turn to Mairéad, his eyes questioning. Smiling, she nodded. so filled with emotion was Tadhg, that he stood silent for some moments, then falteringly, 'I want to sing '*An Cuimhin Leat an Oiche Ud*.'

Mairéad listened with rapt attention as Tadhg sang to her. She didn't understand the Irish words, but there was no mistaking his feelings as he stared directly at her all through the song. His singing voice was deeper than his speaking voice, and as he sang to her, she was suddenly aware of a tender, emotional response she had never before experienced. When he finished, he returned to her side, still locking his gaze with hers.

They sat in silence for some time, as the singing commenced again. Finally she asked, 'What was the name of that song?'

'*An Cuimhin Leat an Oiche Ud*'. In English it's 'You Remember That Night, Love?' but it should be sung by the cailín, not the lad.'

Her eyes glistened with tears. 'I'll remember this night for the rest of my life,' she replied, her voice tremulous. Then, fearful of betraying her emotional state, she avoided further reference to the incident, asking instead, about the variety of songs being sung.

'There are three classifications,' he explained. 'Lively music is *geantraí*, sorrowful music is *gealtraí*, and music for sleep is *suantraí*. And that should be next if these children are going to get any sleep tonight.'

As if on signal, the music stopped as suddenly as it started, and when Tomás and Una had clambered into the wagon, Tadhg and Mairéad followed. She offered no objection when Tadhg placed his arm under her head for a pillow, and snuggled up next to her. They lay in silence for some time before slumber overtook them, each alone with the thoughts that the night evoked. Mairéad wondered at the tenderness she had felt when Tadhg was singing, and the strange elation she had experienced, certainly different from her feelings for John Montgomery or Oliver Trent. She was concerned lest her growing fondness for Tadhg would interfere with her decision yet to be made for her future course.

In turn, Tadhg was surprised at his audacity in singing the love song to Mairéad. But whiskey usually made him bold. He was happy at her response, but puzzled as to its significance. Aware that she had not yet given him an answer to his offer to take her with him to Kilkieran, he was apprehensive that he might have exceeded prudence and offended her.

In the morning Mairéad decided to stay in camp and wash her hair and clothes, while Tadhg went off to the fair with Tomás and the other creaght men.

'You should get twenty pounds for the horse and saddle,' Tomás estimated. 'The market has been extra good for riding horses because there is a shortage since the war.'

'I'm glad that some good has come of the war,' Tadhg said tartly.

Tomás eyed him covertly. 'You look like you have been a good soldier.' he probed.

'Yes, and now I would be a women if I had been born a girl.'

As Tomás pondered Tadhg's evasive answer, they came to the market place where the fair was held. Scores of men, wisely wearing boots, stood about appraising, bargaining, arguing, while hundreds of livestock mooed, bleated, neighed, defecated and urinated, all in apparent harmony.

Tadhg joined a knot of men with horses to sell to better learn the art of bargaining, and the prices being asked. A stocky, red-faced man, holding ropes that loosely restrained two sway-backed farm horses, eyed Tadhg speculatively, apparently trying to trace the source of an offensive odour that suddenly appeared, not sure if it emanated from the man or the horse.

Politely moving downwind, Tadhg spoke, choosing to adopt the role of an Englishman again. 'tis a handsome pair of animals you have there,' he commented.

'Aye,' the red-faced man agreed, yet suspicious at the obvious dissimulation. Shrewd eyes quickly appraised Tadhg's horse and saddle. 'What price are you asking for the old nag, and scuffed old saddle?' he asked. 'My young son, Liam, wants a saddle horse, an old, broken-down one like yours that won't throw him. I'll give three pounds for the horse, saddle included, because I'm a foolish old man. You can ask these other gentlemen,' and he waved a stout arm at the others, 'if Donagh MacGeraghty isn't the biggest-hearted man in the entire barony of Brawny.'

Tadhg was shocked. Only three pounds! He expected at least twenty. Obviously Tomás was wrong, the market was down, not up. But he had to show MacGeraghty that he was no fool, and could bargain with the best of them. He shook his head. 'I won't take a penny less than seventeen,' he said boldly.

'Seventeen pounds? You must be daft, man.' MacGeraghty's face showed pain and sorrow. Then he sighed. 'the *bean an tí* will probably never speak to me again for squandering my life's savings, but Liam does want a horse badly. At the risk of my marriage, I'll give you thirteen, and one of these fine animals, as you yourself so aptly described them.'

What an *amadán*, Tadhg thought, gloating. It's a sin to cheat the man, but I need the money desperately. And I can give the man's horse to Tomás, so he needn't buy one. 'Make it fifteen, and it's a deal' he said trying to be nonchalant.

MacGeraghty grimaced, sighed sadly, reached into his pocket, and reluctantly counted out the money into Tadhg's palm, handing him the rein of the scrawniest of the two horses.

Tadhg departed quickly, fearful that the *amadán* might change his mind. He found Tomás peering into the mouth of a large horse. Don't bother to buy a horse,' Tadhg told him proudly, 'I have one for you for a gift.'

Tomás scrutinised Tadhg's offering carefully, trying to restrain the laugh that was about to convulse him. Biting his lips, he turned and said, 'If you paid more than three pounds for him, you were cheated.'

Tadhg smiled condescendingly.'I got him and fifteen pounds in exchange for my horse.'

Tomás winced. 'Who from?'

Tadhg pointed out MacGeraghty. 'He needed a saddle horse for his son, Liam.'

'Donagh? The canniest horse-trader here? His son Liam is over in France fighting for King Louis. Little need has he for a horse. Old Donagh will probably sell your mount and saddle for twenty-five before lunch. Well, as St Jerome once remarked to the Pope, never examine the teeth of a horse you're given as a gift. I accept your gracious offer. And I suppose that fifteen pounds is better than having it stolen by the Romany people.

'Or by one, Tomás O'Grogan,' Tadhg said, nettled at his stupidity in selling the horse too cheaply. 'But now where can I find a tailor?'

'Back in the town. On Tailor's Row, near the Protestant Church.'

Tadhg passed a succession of tradesmen's shops - nailmaker, bacon curer, weaver, candlemaker, tanner, saltmaker, bootmaker, baker, wheelwright, joiner, tinsmith, cooper, even a boatbuilder, before reaching the tailor shop of Alan Spenser.

To establish better rapport with the tailor, evidently English in origin, Tadhg adopted his Warwickshire accent. It worked admirably. Master-tailor Spenser was so pleased at the prospect of serving a fellow Englishman that he agreed to have Tadhg's clothes ready by day's end.

Next Tadhg went to several shops where he bought under-clothing, a razor, and a coat. Going back to the fair, he mingled with the crowd until sunset when he returned to Spenser's shop. Donning his new clothes, he felt (and certainly smelled) less conspicuous then in his high styled French costume which he decided to take with him to see if could be washed clean again.

Back at the camp, he hung the old clothes outside of Tomás's tent to air. Tadhg found Mairéad at the fire, helping Una to prepare the evening meal. She had not only laundered her own clothes - for the first time in her life - but she had washed her hair as well. Cascading down her shoulders, the tresses reminded Tadhg again of spun gold. He stood mouth agape, at her loveliness. She glanced up, blushed at his unabashed admiration, then looking at his new attire carefully, nodded her head in approval. He sniffed loudly, she did the same, then both laughed, happy that the stench of Newgate was gone.

Tomás returned in high spirits leading a horse far superior to the one Tadhg had given him. Gleefully, he told how he had shod horses for one of the traders, and in exchange for his labour, Tadhg's gift horse, and two pounds, he had acquired the big horse.

Relieved that Tomás would no longer need his horse, Tadhg

informed him that he and Mairéad would leave in the morning. Tomás asked him to stay a few more days until the fair was over, then they could ride with him as far as Galway. But Tadhg, fearful with the two days already passed, was very worried that the inevitable search parties would be getting too close, and thanked him for his kind offer, but had to decline.

'I'm concerned,' he told Tomás, 'over that big Romano across the way. He's forever staring at Mairéad.'

'Lazlo? He's a bad one! Likes fair-haired women. Quick-tempered and loves to fight. Watch out for him, Tadhg, and that knife he carries.'

CHAPTER V

Old Friends Visited

Again they slept as they had the night before, Mairéad trustfully in Tadhg's embrace, her head on his upper arm. But the physical proximity began to disturb him, and it took great will-power to keep from embracing her. He forced discipline upon himself by thinking of the innocent relationship of his youth when he slept in the same bed with his sisters. It helped, too, to dwell on the celibacy of priests he had known, and how they conquered the temptations of the flesh.

In the morning he discovered that one of the sleeves on his new coat was not sewn securely, overlooked, no doubt, in the haste to complete it. He informed Mairéad that she should be ready to leave when he returned from the tailor's. Spenser greeted him warmly, then on learning the purpose of the visit, boxed the ears of the apprentice who had been responsible.

Stopping at the fair, he bade goodbye to Tomás and the other Roscommon men, then hurriedly returned to camp. Noting his old French clothes were gone from where he had hung them the night before and assuming the Mairéad had moved them, he looked for her among the women, but her golden head was not to be seen. Inquiring of Una, he was informed that Mairéad had gone for a walk alone through the meadow towards a distant wood.

In a hurry to depart, Tadhg set out in impatient search. But there was no sign of her, and he walked the boreen calling her name. He was worried when he got to the woods. This is her decision, he thought sadly, she doesn't want to go with me, and this is her way of telling me. He stood for a minute, dejected and undecided, then making up his mind to at least say goodbye to her, he continued along the boreen among the now nearly naked trees, the fallen leaves crinkling beneath his feet.

A muffled sound caught his ear, and looking to his right, he saw Mairéad being held by Lazlo, one brown arm around her throat, and a hand over her mouth to prevent an outcry. Tadhg drew a deep breath, his jaw muscles tightened and an uncontrollable rage surged within him. His fingered curved like talons as he slowly approached Lazlo and the frightened Mairéad. When Lazlo looked into Tadhg's eyes, he sensed the menace, and sudden fear overtook him. He shoved the girl from him, and leaped back, drawing the knife from his belt.

Seeing the long, sharp blade, Tadhg looked hastily for a weapon. A stout, fallen tree branch lay a few feet away, and he quickly seized it. Advancing on Lazlo, swinging the cudgel menacingly, Tadhg noticed for the first time that the Romano was wearing the Bordeaux coat he had left hanging on Tomás's wagon. The sleeves were several inches too long, hindering the Romano's movements. Lazlo, his dark eyes darting, watched the club's arc then leaped quickly at Tadhg, the knife flashing in the sunlight. Despite his bulk, Tadhg jumped back a pace, and with his cudgel's return arc, knocked the knife from his foe's hand.

Slowly, relentlessly, Tadhg advanced on the helpless Lazlo. Then Mairéad rushed to Tadhg, tugging at his arm, crying piteously, 'No, Tadhg, no. Please no more killings over me. Let him go. Please, Tadhg, for my sake!'

As Tadhg and Mairéad stood staring at leach other, they heard a distant clamour, and the baying of hounds in the distance. The sound grew louder as they listened, until Tadhg realised that the pack was heading their way. Grasping Mairéad's hand, and pausing only long enough to pick up Lazlo's knife, he hurried her along the boreen through the woods.

They ran until Mairéad gasped for breath, begging him to stop. The baying became crescendo, and they could hear Lazlo shouting and cursing, then came loud, anguished screams, then the sounds of the excited dogs, the firing of guns and men calling to each other.

'What is it,' Mairéad asked, her tear-stained face showing alarm.

'The search party,' Tadhg said grimly, 'tracking us with hounds.'

'But they'll catch us,' she gasped.

'The Romano has granted us a respite.'

'What do you mean?'

'The dogs were following scent. Probably from a piece of Newgate clothing. A grotesque misfortune for that lecherous devil who stole my coat from the wagon. The dogs caught him instead of me.'

Mairéad stared at Tadhg, her face drained of colour. 'You mean ...' she faltered.

He nodded. 'Lazlo resisted the dogs, and they probably tore him to pieces. But we must run again. Despite Lazlo's black hair, eventually they will find that they have the wrong man, and they will be after us again.'

Gathering her skirt about her, Mairéad followed Tadhg down the boreen until they emerged at the end of the woods where a narrow road meandered to the south. This they took, half-running, half-walking, until the exhausted Mairéad could go no further.

They rested for a while behind a haystack where Mairéad told Tadhg how she had gone for a walk, and how she had become aware that a man was following her. She had run, but he had overtaken her.

'Did he, ah ...' Tadhg asked, embarrassed.

'No,' she replied tartly, 'he did not. You arrived in time.'

She shook her head, her brow furrowed. 'But why must it be that violence follows me? And you are always involved?'

'A spell must have been placed on us when we were born.' He shrugged his shoulders. 'And the sad part of it is that nothing can be done to alter it. We can struggle, we can resist, but we can't change the fate that has been determined for us.'

'Nonsense,' she retorted, tersely. 'Each of decides his or her own future. Your *geasa* is just a remnant of folklore. Sensible people don't believe such tales.'

'That may be,' Tadhg said stubbornly, 'but there was a *geasa* on Deirdre and Naoise, and on Gráinne and Diarmuid. They knew it, but couldn't do anything to change it.'

'What is more to the point is what do we do now?'

'Continue as best we can. With my new clothes, and yours freshly laundered, 'tis unlikely the dogs can follow our scent.'

Keeping to the small roads, they travelled southwestward, Tadhg hoping to reach Aughrim to again seek sanctuary with Siobhán and Aodh O'Madden. Mairéad's shoes, unfortunately more suited for dancing in Dublin that hiking in Connaught, hurt her feet and their progress was slow. In vexation, Tadhg finally had her mount his back, despite her protestations, and carried her piggyback.

At dusk, Tadhg stopped in a small wood on a sloping hillside, where a tarn nestled at the bottom. 'We'd better seek shelter here,' he advised, 'because the night will be cold, and we dare not show ourselves at any of the farms lest we direct attention to ourselves.'

In the protected hollow where the red deer had often rested, as evidenced by the numerous hairs present, Tadhg laid a bed of green boughs pulled from nearby trees. Then he gathered a layer of moss to go on top of the boughs. Next, he went to the tarn below to gather green rushes. Ceremoniously he placed the rushes over the moss, Mairéad watching him with interest.

'These are the three beds of Fionn MacCool and his fianna.' he explained. 'Not as comfortable as your fine feather bed in Dublin, but far superior to the cold, damp ground.'

Mairéad eyed the bed dubiously, then sighed. 'Since there is little choice, I'll accept the help of Fionn.' She nestled on the rushes, moving about to find a comfortable position. When Tadhg joined her, his weight formed a deep hollow, helping to contain his body heat, making the bed warm and comfortable.

Because it was too early to sleep, and still excited by their narrow escape, they talked for some hours, mostly about Tadhg's travels. Finally, Mairéad's deep and measured breathing indicated that she was asleep. Tadhg lay awake, perturbed over the speed with which they had been traced to Athlone. Probably search teams had been dispatched to all major roads out of Dublin, and persons unseen had noticed their passage. And the old man near Kinnegad could describe them, as well as tell about the stolen horses and the wandering people. Thence, easily traced to Athlone, where he had been injudicious in speaking the Irish and openly appearing in public, hounds had been obtained, and with Newgate clothing to provide the scent, it had been simple enough to locate them. He cursed himself for his stupidity and carelessness, but, as he assured himself, God had mercifully interceded on their behalf, at the same time as punishing Lazlo for his evil, carnal desires.

As he lay thinking of ways to elude pursuit, he heard the sharp crackling sound of a twig breaking nearby. Then another, closer. What is it, he thought in panic, had their pursuers found them already? He lay tensed, all senses alert. Another twig snapped next to him, and suddenly Tadhg was aware of a large, antlered head looming above him, and a pair of big brown eyes staring at him curiously.

Tadhg sat up. It was a stag. Tadhg smiled, thinking of the time when he and Eithne had thought that the cow was the púca. The stag vanished at Tadhg's movement. the noise wakened Mairéad.

'What is it,' she asked, a quiver in her voice.

'Just a curious red deer,' Tadhg replied. 'Go back to sleep.'

The raspy croak of a corncrake, dallying in a nearby grain field before migrating for the winter, awakened Tadhg. The sun had already risen, forming fascinating interstices of light through the branches of the gaunt trees. In the treetops overhead, the abandoned nests of a colony of crows were bared.

He helped her from the bed, and without a backward glance, they were on their way again. Mairéad's feet hurt her, but she declined his offer to carry her, so, at a slower pace, they travelled southwestward. They encountered few people along the road and Tadhg greeted them but did not tarry. By noon they reached the small village of Ballinasloe where they stopped to rest by the side of an old ruined castle of the O'Kellys.

'Tadhg,' Mairéad began pensively, 'I have given much thought to your offer to take me to Iar-Chonnacht, but I think it will be better for me to go to my O'Hurley kinsfolk in Kilmallock.'

Just as I feared, Tadhg thought despondently. This is the parting and this time it is forever. I was foolish to think it could be otherwise. And last night I was so optimistic.

'*A bhean uasail,*' he asked, 'have I offended you in any way?'

She shook her head sadly. 'On the contrary, Tadhg. You have been so thoughtful, so considerate, that it makes it doubly difficult to decline your kind offer. I know that you would be willing to carry me on your back all the way to Galway. But what can I do for you besides being a burden? It isn't fair to you.'

'I would gladly carry you for the rest of our lives if it was necessary.'

'I know that all too well. And I appreciate it. In fact it is one of the reasons why I decided to go to Kilmallock for I have found myself growing fonder of you each day. Too fond. The bonds of affection between us are getting so strong that it will be difficult to sever them. But what can our future be together? Hiding for the rest of our lives in the wilds of Connaught? I'm sorry, but I couldn't take that kind of existence. I'd rather risk capture at Kilmallock where I can live the kind of life I'm used to. But God knows I'd rather die than go back to Newgate.'

Tadhg groaned, covering his face with his hands to hide his anguish. 'Please don't speak of capture or death,' he entreated her. 'Please don't despair. Put your faith in God for I'm sure that He will find a way.'

She shook her head. 'Everything is going wrong,' she said, her voice breaking. 'For a while I was happy, thinking that we were going to remain free, but we were almost captured yesterday. Who knows, maybe they are waiting for us around the turn in the road. No, Tadhg, God has forsaken me. If only my parents hadn't died!' If only uncle Henry didn't have that penchant for gambling! If only my cousins hadn't come to Dublin! If only I had never met you!'

She's blaming me again, Tadhg thought sadly. Despite his hurt, he was gentle when he replied. 'If I hadn't left home to be caught in the great storm, I'd probably be still there. And if we had never met, it still wouldn't have kept the Burke brothers from going to Dublin, not changed your uncle's compulsion to gamble, nor altered Mary Casey's Catholicism, nor prevented Major Marty's arrival at the Castle. Don't dwell on the past; have trust in the future.'

He pointed to the River Suck meandering through the country-side. 'Much water has flowed past here since Dónal óg and I passed through here four years ago. And a lot of things have happened to me. Some sad, some glad. I try to think of the happy ones, and trust God for the future. But we can compromise for the present, Mairéad. I have friends at nearby Aughrim. Let us go there, get something to eat - my stomach is empty - and have a good night's sleep. Then, in the morning if you wish it, you can go south to County Limerick. Agreed?

With her eyes brimming with tears, she reached over and kissed him. 'All right, I can leave my decision until tomorrow.'

Resuming their journey, Tadhg told her of Siobhán and Aodh, but making no mention of his spending the night in the widow's bed. He described the great battle on the hill at Aughrim, and how close the Irish were to victory when mischance cost General St Ruth his head and Ireland her freedom. He related the jealousies which had caused St Ruth to keep Patrick Sarsfield from participating in the battle, and the treachery of Colonel Luttrell in abandoning his position, thereby exposing the Irish infantry and leading to the bloody debacle.

'You speak of Sarsfield with the greatest affection, Tadhg.

Was he really a great general like the Irish claim?'

'Yes, a magnificent general, a devoted patriot, and a most remarkable man. And a true friend to me, as was Lady Sarsfield.'

'Is she as beautiful as she is reputed to be?'

'More so, Tadhg replied with enthusiasm, and he told her of his last visit with the Lady Honora at Versailles.

'Were you in love with her?'

Tadhg blushed. 'Not the same way I love you,' He blurted.

She turned away in confusion and they walked in silence for some time. Then Mairéad said contritely, 'My feet are paining me again. Would you mind carrying me?'

Overjoyed, Tadhg lifted her to his back, happy at being of

service, and relishing the pleasure of physical contact. Playfully she tugged at his earlobes for turning right or left, and it was in a gay mood that they arrived at the top of the hill overlooking the few scattered cabins that constituted the village of Aughrim.

Opposite was Kilcommedon Hill, rich with the Irish blood spilled there. And behind it was the area where Sarsfield and his men had waited and fretted while the fate of Ireland was being decided. Tadhg sighed. The memory was painful. He lowered Mairéad to the ground, and they set out for Siobhán's cabin.

He knocked at the half-door. Then the top opened, and framed in it was the surprised countenance of Siobhán, her red hair streaming down her face, and her blue eyes alight with pleasure. 'Tadhg, *a rún*,' she exclaimed, embracing him eagerly. 'you survived the war after all. We often wondered if you got back to Limerick safely.'

'Thanks be to God, and you and Aodh.'

'And who is that you have with you?' she smiled, peering curiously at Mairéad. 'Your wife?'

'Not yet,' replied Tadhg, smiling. 'But aren't you going to invite us in?'

'Arrah! Come in, come in.'

Siobhán's appraising gaze took in Mairéad, whose unblemished skin was in such sharp contrast to her own pock-marked face, and Tadhg standing proudly beside her.

At that moment, Aodh entered. He rushed to Tadhg to embrace him, using his one good arm and his stump as he grasped Tadhg fondly. Then Tadhg introduced Mairéad. 'This is the Lady Fitzgerald. It would be unfair not to tell you that we are fugitives from Dublin Castle, and that you could bring great harm to yourselves for harbouring us. But we both need food, and hopefully, a night's lodging. We place ourselves at your mercy.'

Aodh looked at him reproachfully. 'You are always welcome here, Tadhg O'Cuirc, a fugitive from the Sassanach army or the Castle. And we are honoured by the presence of the Lady Fitzgerald in our humble cabin.' He turned to Siobhán. '*A bhean an tí*, they are hungry.'

As the two women prepared the meal, Tadhg seated himself at the hearth Aodh had built to replace the primitive central fire and hole-in the-roof smoke escape vent he remembered, and related loud enough for all to hear the more important events which had occurred after he had left them after the Battle of Aughrim. At the disclosure of Dónal's death, Siobhán crossed herself, and with tears streaming down her face said a prayer for the repose of his soul. And when Tadhg told of Mairéad's plan to go to Kilmallock, Aodh counselled against it.

'*A bhean uasail*,' he began deferentially, 'this would be a bad time to go there. The Castle authorities are not stupid, they will expect you to seek asylum with your kinsmen. Not only would you be captured quickly, but you would place your kin in peril for hiding a fugitive. Best hide for a while in the wild fastness of Iar-Chonnacht where Tadhg has friends until the hue and cry has subsided. Then, perhaps, it might be safe to go to the O'Hurleys.'

Mairéad bit her lip in vexation. She recognized the good sense of Aodh's advice, particularly the reference to endangering her cousins, but she couldn't tell them that it didn't solve the problem of her growing attachment to Tadhg. She sighed, deciding to wait to see what might develop.

With a hot meal, a proper toilette, a warm fire, and a roof over her head instead of the open sky, she felt more relaxed and cheerful. She slept that night with Siobhán in her bed, while Tadhg and Aodh slept next to the hearth.

CHAPTER VI

The Claddagh

In the morning Aodh volunteered to take them in his cart as far as Loughrea, from whence they could head northwestwards to cross the Galway Road near Oranmore, and skirting Galway, thence to Kilkieran.

The parting with Siobhán was affectionate and tearful. She abashedly kissed Tadhg on the mouth, hugged Mairéad, telling her she was a fortunate *cailín* indeed to have a friend like Tadhg, and with her eyes brimming with tears, bade them *slán* and a safe journey.

Mairéad was thankful for the ride. She had left her fancy Dublin shoes with Siobhán in exchange for more comfortable brogues, and probably could have walked, but Aodh's presence acted as a buffer between herself and Tadhg while she sorted her conflicting thoughts. Perhaps her decision could be made in Loughrea.

Unbeknownst to Mairéad, however, the decision had already been decided by fate. Aodh left them off at the edge of town, and they started walking. But they hadn't gone far before they saw the familiar wagon of Tomas O'Grogan by the side of the road, the family huddled around the fire having breakfast, and their laundry spread over the hedge to dry

'Tadhg O'Cuirc,' Tomás shouted joyfully, 'they haven't caught you!'

Alarmed, Tadhg put his fingers to his lips to indicate caution. Tomás shook his head, 'There's none else to hear, just Una and Babín.'

'But how did you know where to find us, and how did you learn my name?' asked Tadhg.

'By good fortune. Each of us took a different route to look for you and offer help. And it's best that I was the lucky one for I still have your saddle horse. As for your name, we learned that when the soldiers came to the camp searching for you. After they learned that the man the dogs mangled was not Tadhg O'Cuirc but Lazlo. All of the wandering people of the West know the story of Tadhg and the O'Flahertys. Yet we had you in our midst, even in my wagon, and we knew you not. I was close, however, when I called you Fionn MacCool, another of our favourite giants.'

'But what of the soldiers? Have they returned to Dublin?'

'Indeed not! Right now they are in Galway, suspecting you went there. And I have heard that search parties are being sent in all directions looking for you. It's the most wanted man in Ireland you are.'

'Arrah,' said Tadhg, smiling at Mairéad, 'that's not entirely true for I know one person that doesn't want me.'

'Tadhg,' Una interrupted, her face showing her concern, 'tis happy we are to see you again and safe, but for the love of Mary and Joseph, don't stand there chatting with garrulous Tomás, but take your horse and the *cailín bán*, and get out of here as fast as you can. Head for the coast of Clare, 'tis lonely there, where you can hide from the soldiers. Stay away from the Galway roads.'

Tadhg nodded, and Tomás helped Mairéad up behind him. 'You have been extremely kind, Tomás Rua,' said Tadhg, 'and you will be forever in our hearts.'

With a wave of his hand, Tadhg bade them farewell and took a small road leading west. Several hours later they arrived at Gort on the main Galway - Limerick road, but Tadhg heeded Una's advice, and again struck off for the west. The sun was near setting when they arrived at Kilfenora, where, at a fork in the road, one sign pointed towards Ennistimon, and the other to Lisdoovarna.

'Lisdoovarna!' Tadhg exclaimed with delight. "Tis near where Jacques Benoit has his farm and Cúchulainn.'

'Who are Jacques Benoit and Cúchulainn,' Mairéad asked.

'Jacques is the French smuggling captain I told you about and Cúchulainn is my horse, my lovely horse. I gave him in exchange for passage to Ireland for Nicolas Beauvais and Françoise Le Berge. Jacques won't mind if I borrow Cúchulainn for a short time. But it's too late in the day to locate him now. We had better find refuge for the night.'

Fortunately for the fugitives, Ireland was rich in ruins, and Tadhg quickly found the roofless remains of an old cathedral with their horse tied securely, they bedded down for the night in what had been the chancel, with Tadhg's coat over them to help ward off the chill of the night.

Up at daybreak, they traversed the five miles to Lisdoonvarna in little more than an hour, meeting no one on the road. From a farmer going to his field, Tadhg learned that, yes, a Frenchman did own a farm nearby, on the road to Doolin, it was, and managed by one Félim O'Dea.

By making inquiries, they found the farm, and O'Dea himself, a lean man with piercing blue eyes in an oval face, and a luxuriant shock of white hair. Tadhg decided it would be best to negotiate for the horse rather than just take it lest it cause a ruckus that would result in a second set of pursuers after them.

Dismounting, he approached O'Dea. 'I am a friend of Jacques, and the former owner of Cúchulainn, Captain. Benoit's big white stallion which I gave to him in France two years ago. Now I'd like to borrow the horse for a couple of days. I must warn you that I am desperate, and will take him by force if necessary.'

O'Dea scrutinised him carefully, noting Tadhg's great size, and knife stuck in his belt. 'The only white stallion we have here is named Charlemagne not Cúchulainn. And what makes you think I'd let him go even if he formerly was yours, and you are desperate?'

'My name is Tadhg O'Cuirc, originally from Inishmór not far from here, and lately a sergeant in Lord Lucan's Horse. When Sarsfield died in France, I decided to return home. Now I'm a fugitive from the Sassanaigh at Dublin Castle. If you're a true Gael, as your name implies, you will have compassion for me, and let me borrow the horse.'

O'Dea's hostility vanished at the mention of Tadhg's name.

'Tadhg O'Cuirc! The avenger of the O'Flahertys at St Malachi's! I knew your kin, on your mother's side, the MacGormans of the barony of Ibrickan, just below Doolin's Point. Nothing is too good for Tadhg O'Cuirc. Take the whole farm if you wish, and if Jacques's ship was at Doolin, you could have that as well.'

Pleased at O'Dea's response, but abashed at his exuberance, Tadhg replied, 'Just the horse, please. And no mention of my being here to any English soldiers. I'll arrange for the horse's return. And now, a chara, lead me to Cúchulainn, or as Jacques has renamed him, Charlemagne.'

Cúchulainn was grazing as Tadhg approached. When Tadhg called his name, his ears twitched, and he raised his head, looking eagerly about him. Then he neighed loudly, and joyously charged up to Tadhg, burrowing his head against Tadhg's shoulder.

Delighted with the horse's reaction, Tadhg stood for some time, patting its flank, talking soothingly. It was Mairéad who finally interrupted the joyous reunion. 'Tadhg,' she urged, 'we had better be leaving,'

'Let me get a saddle on him,' O'Dea volunteered. In a few minutes, with directions from O'Dea, they were trotting down the road to Ennistimon, as Tadhg had decided to seek help from his kinsfolk, the MacGormans.

They hadn't gone far, when, from a rise in the road, they saw several mounted soldiers coming towards them. Quickly reversing their route, they galloped until they came to a road leading west, which they took, the soldiers following behind them. Despite the danger, Tadhg was elated to have Cúchulainn under him again.

He was sure the big stallion could outrun their pursuers, but was concerned about Mairéad's mount.

Suddenly the broad expanse of the Atlantic Ocean, was before them, with the Aran Islands like large ships astride the horizon. Nostalgia swept over Tadhg at the first sight of his birthplace in four years. He wished that Cúchulainn was Pegasus, and with one mighty leap, he could be safely home in Kilmurvy. But his horse, alas, having no wings, he was forced to turn south instead, Mairéad right behind him, her golden tresses flying in the wind.

Past Doolin, a small fishing village, they pounded, continuing south until they observed another band of horsemen ahead of them, not a quarter of a mile distant. Reining sharply, Tadhg dismounted, rushing to the cliff edge to see if there was a path to the seashore beneath. To his dismay, there were only pathless vertical cliffs, and the surging waters below.

We're trapped, he thought wildly, but then his fisherman's eye noted that the water was deep green, and that there was little wave action at the base of the cliff. Elation replaced despair as he realized that there was deep water below, and the cliff base was probably undercut.

Returning to Mairéad, he said urgently, 'We'll have to jump our horses into the sea to escape.'

She blanched, shaking her head in fear. 'It's too far down. We'll be killed or drowned.'

'No,' he insisted. 'I saw a horse and rider in a circus in Paris leap into a big, wooden tank from a platform as high as this cliff. It's better to try than to be returned to Major Marty.'

'I'm afraid,' she whimpered, closing her eyes. 'I just can't do it.'

Impatiently, Tadhg yanked her from her horse, lifted her on to Cúchulainn, then climbed into the saddle. Both groups of horsemen were converging on them rapidly, and capture was imminent.

'In the name of God,' he implored her, 'hold on tightly to me,' and swatting Cúchulainn on the rump, they charged to the cliff edge, and without faltering, the big horse unhesitatingly leaped out into the void.

For a few brief moments they seemed suspended in air, and Tadhg was conscious of Mairéad's arms locked around him, and his own legs wrapped tightly around Cúchulainn's flanks. So this is the way a seagull feels when it flies, Tadhg thought, momentarily elated at the phenomenon of flying.

Then they hit the water with a jarring wrench, and were immersed in the cold sea as horse and humans struggled to rise to the surface. When they emerged, sputtering and gasping, they were still firmly on Cúchulainn's broad back, and Tadhg saw what he had expected, a cavern at the cliff base.

With Cúchulainn swimming powerfully, Tadhg guided him to the cave entrance. Two red-breasted mergansers, not accustomed to sharing their quarters with a swimming horse, raucously protested the invasion, and noisily departed.

'I can't believe I'm alive,' Mairéad whispered, her tone reflecting her disbelief, as Cúchulainn's hooves touched bottom, and he scrambled up on a sandbar, shaking himself like a large dog.

Tadhg turned and kissed her full on the mouth. Her lips were cold and tasted of salt, but it was the happiest kiss Tadhg ever had.

'Even I had my doubts,' he said, grinning. 'But, come, let me help you down and give our brave Cúchulainn a well-deserved rest.'

She slid into his arms, clinging to him, crying softly.

'There now, Mairéad, *a ghrá*,' he said gently, 'please don't weep, we're safe now.'

When her sobbing had stopped, he led her to the corner of the cave where the sand was dry. 'Let me have your outer clothing,' he directed, 'and I'll wring out most of the water.'

Mutely, without protest, she undressed, handing him the saggy garments, retaining only her underclothes which slung to her body, revealing the outline of firm breasts, flat stomach, and flaring well-formed thighs. She had lost one of her shoes, and her dainty feet were covered with sand. Tadhg vigorously wrung her wet garments, then stretching them, placed them on Cúchulainn's back. Noticing her questioning gaze, he explained that the horse's body heat would help dry them.

To save her embarrassment at her near-nudity, and to avoid any lustful temptations, he busied himself at the water's edge, peering out of the mouth of the cave, wondering how far the water came in at high tide, and whether it was safe to stay hidden in the cave overnight. As if reading his mind, Mairéad asked, 'What do we do now? How do we get out of here?'

'A good question. Wait for low tide. And hope for some kind of a shore.'

'What if there is none?'

'Then we'll have to swim for it.'

'But I can't swim.'

'Cúchulainn can. He'll carry you.'

'But what of the soldiers above?'

'I'd say that they think we have drowned, or have been smashed against the rocks. They'll go back to their post to report and then some *sleeveen* of an officer will insist they resume their search tomorrow.'

'Then they will be on our tracks again. So what good has all this desperate risk accomplished?'

'It has given us a respite.'

Silence. Then softly, 'Tadhg, what are we going to do when we run out of respites?'

He sighed. 'Just keep our faith in God.'

Before she could reply, Tadhg heard the sound of oars, and a man's voice in the Irish. 'It must have been Mannannan MacLir himself, and his daughter Aine, and they have gone to their castle at the bottom of the sea.'

'Mannannan riding a white horse, and chased by Sassanaigh, Cormac? Not likely.'

'*Mo chorp ón diabhail!* Well, whatever. I'm glad they got away from the soldiers. It was amusing to see the arrogant foreigners peering over the cliff, shaking their heads.'

' 'Tis a pity they were killed. Their bodies will probably rise in a day or two.'

'Be sure to sprinkle the holy water, and light a candle,' Tadhg called out loudly, also using the Irish. Aside, he said to Mairéad in English, 'Hurry and dress. God has granted us our respite.'

'Wirra, and did you hear a voice, Cormac?'

'He did that,' Tadhg said. 'We're in the cave and need help.'

Soon the prow of a curragh poked into the cavern, and a voice said, 'Holy Mary, Mother of God, 'tis alive they are!'

Acknowledging to Cormac and Fergus, the fishermen, that he and the *cailín* were fleeing the soldiers, Tadhg offered to pay them for safe passage from the cave. Fergus insisted that no reward was

607

necessary, that any enemy of the Sassanaigh was a friend of his, and helping friends was reward enough. They had witnessed the spectacular leap from where they had been fishing, and had enjoyed the consternation of the soldiers at the disappearance of their quarry, and their subsequent departure from the cliff. They would be happy to take the cailín and Tadhg to Doolin in the curragh, and let Cúchulainn swim behind. But they'd better hurry as the wind had switched to the west, and was increasing in force.

Assured by Fergus that they could get passage at Doolin in a pucán to take them to Kilkieran Bay, Tadhg decided it would be the best course even if there was the risk of their being seen. So, in a curragh again with Mairéad, reminiscent of their first meeting, and with Cúchulainn following, they left the cave.

'It's fortunate you are,' Cormac said, 'that you weren't at the Cliffs of Moher further down when you were forced to leap.'

'Thanks be to God,' Tadhg agreed, 'for they are higher than the most lofty turret on Dublin Castle. We would have been killed surely.'

They put ashore on the sandy strand at Doolin where Cormac mounted Cúchulainn to return him to O'Dea. Tadhg bade a fond farewell to the stallion, solemnly thanking him for saving them from capture, and explaining there was no place for him on the pucán, but promising to see him again soon. When Cormac departed, Fergus led them to a small shebeen where several men sat drinking poteen. Fergus explained that the *búchaillín dhubh* and the *cailín bán* needed immediate transportation to Kilkieran Bay.

One of the men, sandy-haired and sallow-complected, shook his head. 'The wind is rising, I'll not go out to sea today for all the gold in Galway.' The others nodded in agreement.

Tadhg cursed in vexation. He had sent the horse away too soon and now they were on foot at the very edge of Ireland, with their backs to the sea and no place to run. They were trapped!

Taking his money from his pocket, he held it, saying, 'Let me have a curragh then, I'll go myself.'

'And what does the likes of you, in your fancy clothes, think that he can handle a curragh?' the sandy-haired man asked contemptuously.

'I'm from Inishmór yonder, and have been at sea in storms that would send you hiding under your bed.'

'You blow as hard as the wind,' said the sandy-haired man.

'What name is on you?'

'Tadhg O'Cuirc,' he replied defiantly.

'And would you now be knowing Conor O'Donnell?'

Conor?' Tadhg's expression was pure joy. 'Oh, yes. And Máire Blake. And Sive MacClanchy, Conor's wife.'

'Sive is my sister,' said the sandy-haired man, his face lighting up. 'I'm Eoghan MacClanchy.'

'Och!' Tadhg exclaimed delightedly. 'I should have remembered Siav was from the Barony of Corcomroe. And how is she?'

Eoghan grinned, making a curved motion over his belly with his hand. 'But I'll not be hiding under my bed today now that the great Tadhg O'Cuirc needs passage to see his old friends.'

With Fergus O'Loughlin to accompany them, and the other fishermen promising secrecy, Tadhg and Mairéad boarded Eoghan's fishing pucán. Patched old sails were raised, and the boat's stubby bow was pointed northward. Tadhg had a lump in his throat, and he blinked away tears as he saw Inisheer astride the horizon, the afternoon sun illuminating its low profile. Hidden behind it was Inishmaan, and in turn Inishmór. Five years had passed since he left home. Five years away from his loved ones. Five momentous years. There was his birthplace, so near and yet so far!

The wind was indeed rising. Whitecaps began to curl menacingly, and the pucán to roll. Mairéad huddled on the planking, her teeth clenched, her face pale and tense. 'Twill be all right,' Tadhg soothed her. 'This is a stout ship, and God will watch over us.'

'The Protector was a stout ship too, and much bigger,' she said, her voice tremulous. 'And remember what happened to it.'

'Aye,' said Tadhg, 'it went down to Hell to join Oliver Cromwell for whom it was named.'

'You're a strange man, Tadhg O'Cuirc. You passionately hate a man long since dead, yet you love a mere horse, your Cúchulainn. You can be fierce as you are with Lazlo, and yet so tender with Siobhán. When confronted with extreme emergency you have good judgement, yet for your future you have nothing but trust in God. You're a mass of contradictions. How do you explain yourself?'

He shrugged. 'Sometimes I think the world doesn't actually exist. There is no reality. Everything, everybody, every event exists only in my imagination. There is no Mairéad FitzGerald, no sea, no wind, no Dublin, no Paris, no Major Marty, not pursuit, no yesterday, no tomorrow. They exist only as figments of my imagination. Since I create them, I can control them.'

She looked blank, then shook her head. 'I don't understand.'

He smiled down at her. Don't try. It's just whimsy. Look off to the north. That high point is Black Head, and around the curve of the bay is Ballyvaughan. That's where I was going with Somhairle O'Conchubhair and Peadar Láidir the day of the great wind.

I never did get to Ballyvaughan, although I have been to Dublin and Derry, Louth and Limerick, Coleraine and Cork, yes even to Paris and Pau. I have been blown helter-skelter like a dry leaf, fallen from the tree, at the mercy of the wind. And now we are heading for Kilkieran Bay once more to complete the grand circle.'

The pucán no longer in the protective lee of the Aran Islands, was pitching and tossing violently as the wind increased. Eoghan and Fergus, their faces showing their anxiety, watched the straining canvas as the ship lurched through the heavy seas.

They had reached North Sound, with Inishmór far south of them, when a powerful gust of wind struck the much patched mainsail, tearing it to tatters in a trice. The ship yawed, Eoghan struggled to bring it back under control, swinging the tiller to allow the pucán to run before the wind as the remaining small foresail assumed the burden of moving the ship.

Tadhg walked aft. The course was now due east, no longer northwards towards Kilkieran Bay. 'Where are we going?' he asked anxiously.

'I have no choice but to run before the wind,' Eoghan shouted, 'until I can find a haven somewhere.'

'But we're heading to Galway,' Tadhg protested.

'It can't be helped.'

'For the love of God, Eoghan, the *cailín bán* and I are both fugitives from the Castle in Dublin with a price on our heads. That's why we are fleeing the soldiers and the heart of the search is in Galway.'

'Why didn't you warn me sooner?'

'For secrecy. I didn't think you needed to know.'

Eoghan shook his head in disgust. 'I can hide you in the Claddagh in Galway, then send word to Conor.'

'But will we be safe there?'

'The Claddagh people are clannish and close-mouthed. They have their own king, and little contact with the Galwegians. We mights possibly make to to Oranmore of the wind shifts a little more to the north, but it's far better to risk Galway harbour then to be cast up on the shore and drowned.'

Tadhg rejoined Mairéad who was shivering with fear and cold. Her dress was still damp from her immersion in the sea. He put his báinín over her, and his arms around her shoulders, comforting her. 'Don't worry, Mairéad, *a stóir*, we'll be in a safe harbour in a couple of hours.'

'More hope? Another respite? Or some whimsy? Is there no end to the fear and danger?'

'Not this side of Heaven. But there's nothing wrong with hope and faith. There's little else to cling to in this turbulent world.'

'You cling to hope, I'll cling to you,' she said.

With wind and waves relentlessly driving it eastward, the pucán scudded along like a herring gull. When it was lifted high on the crest of a roller, Tadhg could discern the distant low shore of Iar-Chonnacht to the north, and he felt angry and cheated at the loss of the sail so close to his destination.

When Galway was discernible, Eoghan turned the tiller over to Fergus, and came to squat beside Tadhg. 'I think it best that we wrap the cailín bán in an old sail so that no prying eyes from the town's walls can see her. And you, Tadhg, take my knitted cap. From a distance at least, you will look like a fisherman. When we tie up among the pucáns and the curraghs at the wharf, pick up the sail with the cailín bán, sling it over your shoulder, and quickly follow me. Fergus will see to the security of the pucán.'

When Tadhg informed Mairéad she would have to be carried ashore wrapped in the old sail, she eyed it distastefully. 'Ugh,' she shuddered, 'I'll suffocate in there.'

'It will be sufficiently loose. There will be plenty of air. When we get to the harbour I'll put you and the canvas over my shoulder. Remain silent until I remove the sail.'

Eoghan skillfully manoeuvered the crippled pucán into the harbour. Several large ships were berthed at the quays on the right hand side, and Tadhg could see the fortified walls of the town behind them. To the left were the thatched cottages of the fishermen of the Claddagh, smoke blowing briskly from the chimneys, and the remains of a church and friary destroyed by Cromwell in 1651.

Several other pucáns and a half dozen curraghs arrived at the same time they did, making them less conspicuous. As Fergus lowered the foresail, Eoghan sculled the pucán to berth along the decaying wharf. Then, signalling to Tadhg, he jumped ashore and scurried into the heart of the Claddagh, Tadhg following with his burden over his shoulders.

Eoghan pounded on the door of a cabin. larger than its neighbours, until it was opened by a well-proportioned man, with his arms folded on his chest. 'Tis no need to break the door into smithereens.' he said calmly. Then he peered curiously at Tadhg and his burden. 'What have we here, Fionn MacCool selling fish?'

'No, Donnacha,' said Eoghan impatiently, 'in the name of the holy Patrick and all the other saints, let us in and close the door.'

The door opened quickly, the visitors entered, and the door slammed shut. 'God bless all here,' Tadhg said.

'And you likewise,' Donnacha replied.

'This is Tadhg O'Cuirc,' Eoghan said, 'and inside the sail is a cailín known only to me as Mairéad. They are fleeing Sassanach soldiers, and are fugitives form the Castle at Dublin. I was taking them to my sister's husband, Conor O'Donnell, in Moyrus Parish, an old friend of Tadhg's, when my sail disintegrated, and I was forced to bring them here or be wrecked on the coast. They desperately need sanctuary until they can be safely moved to Iar-Chonnacht.'

Donnacha smiled, pulled a short *duidín* from his pocket, filled it with tobacco, lighted it from an ember at the fire, then said, 'Unroll the sail and let me see your catch.'

Tadhg, who had forgotten about Mairéad, clapped his hand to his forehead in embarrassment, then placing the canvas on the floor, carefully unrolled it until the unhappy, dishevelled form of Mairéad was revealed. He helped her to her feet while she straightened her tresses.

Turning to Donnacha, Tadhg noted for the first time the well-formed head covered with wavy brown hair, serene blue eyes contemplating him from under heavy, dark brows, wide mouth, and a firm chin. a regal bearing, with a air of insouciance about him, Tadhg thought. He put his arm around Mairéad, and turned to Donnchadh. 'This is the Lady Margaret FitzGerald,' he said, introducing her.

'You have made quite a catch at that,' Donnacha said, bowing, his eyes showing admiration.

Mairéad looked inquiringly at Tadhg. 'She doesn't speak the Irish,' Tadhg explained.

'And I have not the English,' Donnacha replied.

Eoghan, obviously more impressed with Mairéad's name and title than her beauty, said to Tadhg, 'Tell the cailín that this is Donnacha O'Halloran, King of the Claddagh. He had absolute authority here, and none will dispute or disobey him.'

Tadhg transmitted Eoghan's words to Mairéad, then said in Irish, 'Faith, and I have met both King James and Louis XIV of France, yet neither of them can compare with Rí Donnacha here for kingly mien and bearing.'

Donnacha laughed, but was obviously pleased. 'That's a fine compliment indeed, coming from one so renowned as Tadhg O' Cuirc. Your part in the ambush at St Malachi's has been told and retold countless times in the cabins of the Gaeltacht. But what brings you to the Claddagh, especially when your companion is the beautiful Lady Fitzgerald?'

'Misadventure, primarily. But if we could be seated near the fire where the Lady Mairéad can dry and warm herself, I will give you the highlights.'

'I'm sorry,' Donnacha apologised, 'I should have suggested it sooner.'

'Donnacha,' Eoghan interrupted, 'with your permission I'd like to leave Tadhg and the cailín with you, while I hurry to inform Conor that Tadhg is here.'

'certainly,' said Donnacha, 'They are welcome to stay here until you return. Arrange with Henry Blake down the road - he's kin to Murtagh Blake - for a horse, and tell him that Donnach sent you.'

Tadhg bade Eoghan adieu, thanking him for his help and wishing him Godspeed until his return. Then he seated himself at the hearth, telling of the shipwreck until the present with Mairéad from the time of the shipwreck until the present, and of his spy mission which had landed him in a cell at the Castle.

'You attract trouble like a wolfhound does fleas,' Donnacha commented admiringly. 'Although I was happy to see Sir John Ferguson receive due retribution, as an O'Halloran whose ancestors were chiefs of Clann Fearghaile near Lough Corrib who suffered from the depredations of the fierce O'Flahertys for centuries. I couldn't get too enthusiastic. But we Gaels can boast of so few recent victories over the hated Sassanaigh that I rejoice with you in your triumphs. I am gratified that Eoghan brought you here for what little help I can offer.'

'One thing you can do, ' Tadhg suggested, 'if it isn't too great an inconvenience, is to give us something to eat as we haven't had food since yesterday morning.'

Donnacha was shocked. 'What a breach of hospitality! Especially after the one compliment you paid me. I'll wager that King James or King Louis never showed you such bad manners. Let me go fetch the *bean an tí* to prepare a meal. She is visiting her sister, Bebhinn, down the hill.'

While Donnacha was gone, Tadhg brought Mairéad up-to-date on developments. 'I wish that I could converse in Irish,' she said wistfully. 'I can sense what is happening, and see the respect and affection all these people show you, from Tomás and Una to King Donnacha, all wanting to help you with no concern fo their own safety, or thoughts of remuneration. If I had true friends like that in Dublin, I never would have been in Newgate.'

Tadhg nodded, 'Although I am poor in earthly goods and future prospects, I am rich in friends.'

Mairéad looked at Tadhg, her eyes mischievous. 'Do you remember that day when you asked me if I wanted to accompany you to Galway? And I delayed the answer? Well, after much thought and deliberation, I have decided that the answer is 'no'.'

They both laughed heartily. Then Mairéad added, 'Seriously, Tadhg, we have been through so much adversity together, and I have been a great burden to you when you would have been better off to abandon me to Major Marty, yet you continuously sacrifice your own interest to help me. Why?'

Tadhg stared into the fire at the gleaming coals and the flickering red and yellow fingers of flame. Then he turned to Mairéad, happy at the opportunity. 'I, too, truly wish you understood the Irish language as my thoughts are in Irish. English and Irish are as different as day and night. Much of the eloquent beauty of the Gaelic is lost in translation. They are like two roads going to the same destination by different routes, with one, the English, going by the flat and level plains, while the other, the Irish soared through mountains and valley's, past precipes, raging rivers and singing streams. Translating Irish into English restricts its fluidity, blurs its beauty. But I will try to express my feelings for you in English. Ever since I first saw you, tied to the mast, I have loved you. How often have I longed to call you '*a stoirín na súile uaithne*', O little treasure of the green eyes, or to murmur, 'Margaret, my darling', or '*a stóir grá geal mo chroí*', bright treasure of my heart. May God forgive me, but in truth I have thought of you more often than of my mother. A thousands nights, in all four provinces of Ireland, and in France , my thoughts were of you. Now the warmth of Donnacha's fire has melted the ice that has long locked my heart, and my love for you comes tumbling forth as the freshets in the spring. Why didn't I abandon you? It would have been abandoning a vital part of me. I might just as easily have abandoned my arms or my legs.'

Startled, she turned to him, eyes tender, started to say something, then checked herself. Finally she said softly. 'each day, Tadhg, finds my defences crumbling. Each day there is a little less of Lady Margaret FitzGerald of Dublin, and more of Mairéad O'Hurley, the *cailír bán*. Each day the bonds between us grow stronger. But the transition is not easy. When I learn to speak Gaelic, maybe I, too, can sit by Donnacha's fire and speak to you from my heart.'

Overwhelmed by the unexpected response, Tadhg gazed into her green eyes, glistening with the trace of tears, but his reply was interrupted by the return of Donnacha and his wife, Nuala, a plump, brown-haired woman whose smile was as big as her bosom. She embraced Mairéad, and like a mother hen with a small chick, immediately took her under her wing. Befitting Donnacha's position as king of the Claddagh, dinner consisted largely of the fruits of the nearby sea: succulent lobster, shellfish, pollock, ling and salted herring with pastries, and the inevitable oat pan bread steaming hot from the hearth. With plenty of ale for a lubricant, the meal was a huge success.

She insisted that Mairéad use the single bedroom while she and Donnacha slept in the alcove, and Tadhg curled up before the fire. It wasn't Versailles, Tadhg mused, but with the familiar pleasant and pungent aroma of the turf fire, a full stomach, and Mairéad nearby, he wouldn't have traded places with Louis himself.

CHAPTER VII

Another Respite

All the following day they anxiously awaited the arrival of Conor and Eoghan, Donnacha and Nuala left occasionally, but Tadhg and Mairéad stayed in the cabin. There was no reference to his emotional outburst and declaration of love for her, yet Tadhg sensed an easing of the tension between them, and a tenderness of word and gesture that had not existed before. As Mairéad pottered around the cabin, helping Nuala with meals or sweeping the hearth, Tadhg felt that the bonds between them were indeed growing stronger.

At nightfall, when there still was no sign of Conor and Eoghan, Tadhg expressed his growing concern to Donnacha. 'Give them time, Tadhg,' the king said soothingly, 'for tis further to Kilkieran that a hurler can hit the ball. If there is no word of them by this time tomorrow, I'll send someone to see what is wrong.'

Tadhg slept poorly that night. Perhaps the Blake farm was being watched by soldiers, and Eoghan couldn't make contact. So, the following morning, when a loud knock on the cabin's front door was heard, he was uncertain to glad or sad. But it was only Fergus whispering conspiratorially with Donnacha. When Fergus departed, Donnacha told Tadhg and Mairéad to wait in the bedchamber, stating that he was going to have visitors and that it would be prudent if they stayed out of sight.

Tadhg, looking at the bed, and Mairéad's golden tresses, had fleeting memories of Mme Le Clerc and her blond wig, lying in the massive bed in Paris. Restrain yourself, Tadhg, he told himself, and banish all ribald and tawdry thoughts. He doubted that his new relationship with Mairéad had progressed to that point of sharing. Mairéad paced the room, showing her anxiety. From the front room came the low murmur of conversation with occasional laughter. Then the front door slammed, and Donnacha called for them to return.

As they stepped through the doorway, the whole room seemed to erupt, and a dozen figures hurled themselves at them. If it wasn't for the fervent hugs and kisses and embraces, Tadhg would have thought that Donnacha had betrayed them, and they had been assaulted by a squad of Major Marty's soldiers. When he finally was able to regain his bearings, and assort the bodies, he distinguished Conor and Sive; a tall, redhaired young man who could be none other than Rory; Máire Blake; a Catholic priest; Eoghan and Fergus, the owners of the house, and a beaming nun in a tri-cornered white cornette.

The nun was radiant with joy. 'Och, Tadhg, what a wonderful surprise to see you here. When I saw you last in France, never did I dream I would see you next in Connaught!'

Tadhg shook his head in amazement. 'Eithne Blake! And what are you doing here? Shouldn't you be teaching the Crosses of God to your saintly students?'

'I have been reassigned. To far-away America to teach the heathen Indian children. With Father Carroll. Come, Father, meet my old and dear friend, Tadhg O'Cuirc.'

'Why he's not ten feet tall and four feet wide like I have been led to expect,' the priest said, eyes twinkling, as he grasped Tadhg's hand.

'And Rory, too, home from France,' Tadhg exclaimed, embracing him. 'Apparently the Irish exodus from France had begun. I was worried about you.'

'I arrived a week ago, thanks to Hugh O'Flaherty and Captain Benoit,' Rory said, bursting with joy to be with Tadhg again.

Then Tadhg turned to Conor, embracing him affectionately. 'Conor, *a chara*, I can't describe how happy I am to see you again. How often have I longed to be with you, and to admit that you were right at Limerick, and I was wrong. If I hadn't been so stubborn and blind, Dónal would be here alive with us today.'

Conor shook his head sadly. 'The way things have worked out, Tadhg, with the English constantly violating the Treaty of Limerick, and the increasing heavy oppression of the Irish people, I'm not sure who was right and who was wrong. We live a hard life and daily it gets harder. You would have been wiser to have stayed in France.'

'I couldn't, Conor. With Dónal Óg and General Sarsfield gone, all was empty there. I had to come back.'

Conor gazed at Tadhg fondly. He sighed. 'You haven't changed a chara. You still think with your heart. You must realise that you can't stay in Ireland. Eoghan informed me that you and Lady Fitzgerald are fugitives from the Castle authorities, and from Donnacha I learned that a thousand pound reward has been placed on your heads. That's quite a fortune. Thousands of people have visions of becoming rich by catching you. And, sorry to say, that includes many a Catholic Gael who would be happy to betray you. Your escape has caused much embarrassment to the Crown, and with all the Gaeltacht laughing, you must be captured at all cost. There is no safe haven for you in all of Ireland.' He shook his head sadly, 'It's hard for me to say it, Tadhg, but you must leave again. Immediately.'

Tadhg was stunned. All the joy of his homecoming vanished. Trust Conor to place it in perspective. He was right. As usual. Even the great and powerful Hugh O'Donnell, after his escape from the Castle, eventually had to flee to Spain where he died. Tadhg covered his face with his hands as if to blot out the reality. Even hope, his usual ally, now deserted him.

Finally he looked up to Conor expectantly, his face bleak. 'What can I do, Conor, what can I do?'

Eithne smiled at him. We have a plan, a stór, a daring one, true, but we think it will work. Father Carroll and I are supposed to leave for Maryland in America on a ship that is berthed at the quay, opposite. They are expecting a priest and a nun as passengers. And a priest and a nun they will get. But the priest will be you and the nun will be the *cailín bán*.

Tadhg stood, open-mouthed, unbelieving. Then as he realised the possibilities, he asked the obvious question. 'That is wonderful for us, but what happens to you and Father Carroll?'

'Och, we will exact a price for our sacrifice. The good father will explain all the details for he is much more fluent in English that I, and the Lady Fitzgerald must know everything.'

The priest beamed, his cherubic face wreathed in a broad smile. 'I don't often get a opportunity like this; to be a martyr - in a small way, of course - to make a convert, and to perform the holy sacrament of marriage to departing emigrants.'

Tadhg and Margaret looked at each other, both obviously perplexed.

'Let me explain,' Father Carroll said. 'It's all very involved. I was chaplain in Lord Dongan's Regiment of Dragoons during the war. When Lord Dongan was killed at the Boyne, his cousin, Walter Nugent took over the regiment. Then Colonel Nugent was killed at Aughrim. Command was then given to Lieutenant Colonel Francis Carroll, a kinsman of mine from near Roscrea. It should have been called Carroll's Regiment, there were so many of us in it.

'Back in 1688, Charles Carroll of Litterluna, who was a cousin of Colonel Francis Carroll, having received a large grant of land, settled in Maryland, one of the English colonies in America. He was then commissioned as Attorney General, and named agent and Receiver General by Lord Baltimore. Inasmuch as Maryland is the only colony that tolerates Catholics, when Charles Carroll needed a priest, a Franciscan, for a new parish, he wrote to his cousin in France, who by fortuitous circumstance, had married Maria Pignatelli, a niece of Pope Innocent XII. We Carrolls like to help each other, so, with such well-place friends, it was no great surprise that I was designated to go to America.

'Charles Carroll also needed some nuns as teachers. The Sisters of Charity have been trying to establish their order in America for some time, and because so few of them speak English, Eithne Blake was chosen because she had some knowledge of that language. I also suspect,' and he glanced roguishly at Eithne, 'that they were glad to get rid of her. When she learned that Carroll's ship, which was to carry us, was also picking up supplies at Galway, she seized upon the opportunity to see her family again.

'She was getting her packing done when Sive's brother burst into Conor's cabin with the happy news that Tadhg O'Cuirc had returned. But the rejoicing turned to ashes when they learned that you were a fugitive.'

'And when we learned that you were accompanied by the *cailín bán*, also a fugitive,' Eithne interrupted, 'it complicated the problem. So, when Uncle Conor insisted that you would have to flee Ireland, both of you, I had the happy inspiration that you could replace Father Carroll and me.'

Mairéad, who had listened to the conversation with mounting excitement, rushed to embrace Eithne, sobbing, 'You're so kind, so considerate. I had given up all hope, the future looked so discouraging, but now all is changed. How can I ever repay you for your sacrifice?'

Eithne smiled mischievously. 'When you learn the price, you might change your mind. Father Carroll is much concerned about your immortal soul. He was shocked to learn that you, an unwed maiden, were consorting around the countryside with a man, Tadhg, without the benefit of holy matrimony. He insists, as a condition to your departure to America, that you must be married first. And because that he wants the privilege of performing the ceremony himself, he also insists that the marriage be between two Catholics.'

As the implication struck Mairéad, she looked at Tadhg, her eyes wide with astonishment. He wondered what her reaction would be: indignation, protest, outrage, derisive laughter, or, miracle of miracles, consent.

It was to be none of these. Mairéad's bewildered gaze swept from Tadhg to Eithne and back again. 'I must sit down,' she said, 'I feel faint.'

Máire Blake, previously silent, frowned at Eithne, then said, 'That's cruel. You are forcing the *cailín* to do something against her will. Marriage is a holy sacrament. Tis a sin to coerce her this way. You should be ashamed of yourself.'

Eithne looked at Máire, reproachfully. 'Now Mother, you know Father Carroll and I would not commit deliberate sins. You should ask the *cailín bán* how she really feels about Tadhg. I'm sure she would surprise you. And if she's foolish enough not to have him, I'll gladly marry him myself and go off to America with him. Now, don't look so shocked. You have long known how I feel about the *buchaillín dhubh*.'

Defiantly, Eithne walked to the hearth where Mairéad was seated, and knelt before her. Speaking softly so that no one else could hear , she said, 'My mother thinks I'm unfair, forcing you to do something abhorrent to you just so that you can escape from Ireland. I disagree, for I have long felt that you were fond of Tadhg, and watching you both this morning only confirmed it. Looks and gestures can often be more eloquent than words. I'm sure that you share his affection for you. It would actually be to my benefit to encourage your refusal for it is no secret that I would gladly relinquish the religious life in making the *buchaillín dhubh* happy if he would take me to wife. As to your becoming a Catholic, I am sure that if the situation was reversed, that he would relinquish his faith to accommodate you, averse as he would normally be because he is such a devout Catholic.'

Mairéad burst into tears, burying her head in Eithne's bosom. 'There now, Mairéad, *a rún*,' she said, stroking her hair, 'let these be tears of joy, not sorrow. But if you choose not to go with Tadhg to America, we will not forsake you, but will do our best to hide you until you are safe. Time is short, however, and there is much yet to be done you are to embark tomorrow at the change of the tide.'

Raising a tear-stained face, Mairéad said, 'Thank you, Eithne for helping me make up my mind. This has all been very sudden, and I have endured much adversity in the past year. You are very understanding and compassionate. I would that I were one hundredth as noble as you are. But my thoughts are clearer now, and I an ready to reach my decision.'

Hand in hand they walked back to the hushed gathering. A tender smile on her face, Mairéad turned and looked directly at Tadhg. 'What is the Irish for 'yes',' she asked.

A half dozen joyous voices cheered in unison. Tadhg stood transfixed, his heart pounding. 'Heavenly Father,' he prayed fervently. 'Thou hast granted my heart's desire. Let me be worthy of Thy gift.'

As the excited babble of voices arose, Donnacha raised his hand for silence. 'Quiet, please. You'll have the soldiers on us. There is much yet to be done and little time to do it. I'm sure that Father Carroll will need some time to talk to the Lady Mairéad on her conversion to Catholicism, and what is expected of her. The wedding will take place here at sunset. Now, inasmuch as our new priest, Father O'Cuirc is a head taller that Father Carroll, a new clerical habit will have to be prepared for him. This I will leave to Nuala and Máire. Eithne and Mairéad are about the same size, so there will be no problem with exchanging garments. And Tadhg will have time to talk to his old friends, Conor, Eithne, Rory and Maire.'

'And what do Fergus and I do?' asked Eoghan.

'Go into town and see what rumours are to be heard. And each of us must remember to be guarded in our speech lest unintentionally we will say something which will bring the search to the Claddagh. It is important that you trust no one.'

While Father Carroll talked to Mairéad, Nuala and Máire measured Tadhg for his clerical habit. Tadhg gave then the last of his horse-sale money for the material, commenting that it was his third set of new clothes in six weeks, enough for a lifetime. Then he, Conor, Sive, Eithne and Rory gathered at the hearth, trading experiences each eagerly contributing to the conversation, while Donnacha listened attentively, puffing on his duidín. When Tadhg described the big battle in which Sarsfield and Dónal had died, Conor went to his knees, offering prayers for their souls.

'Eithne,' Tadhg asked, 'where is this Maryland we are going to?'

'Och, Tadhg little is it I'm knowing except that it's across *An Farraige Mór*,' and she pointed to the Atlantic Ocean. 'We were supposed to go the some wee place called Baltimore, named for a small town in County Cork. But it can't be too far away since it's called the next Parish west of Galway.'

'Tis wishing I am that I could go with you,' Conor said sadly. 'My back is near broken from working that rock-strewn farm, yet the crops are next to nothing at all. And the rent is higher than ever before. There is no future in it.'

Tadhg brightened. 'Ah, Conor, God willing, I can become rich enough to pay for your passage, you and Sive, Máire and the children, and Rory, of course. I was dreading the loneliness of a strange and heathen land.'

'It's forgetting you are that you will have a beautiful bride,' said Donnacha, winking at Conor, 'and you won't have the time or strength to be lonely.'

The afternoon passed pleasantly. Nuala and Máire, busy with needle and thread, fitted and refitted, until Tadhg's vestments were completed, and they stood back and complimented him on what a handsome priest he would make. 'I wish my mother could see me now,' Tadhg said wistfully, surveying himself in his white habit and black mantle and broad-brimmed hat, 'she always wanted me to become a priest.'

Mairéad seated herself next to Tadhg, shyly linking her arm with his. 'Are you content?' he asked softly.

'More than just content, I'm ecstatic. but there is one wish I would make if I could.'

'What is it?' Tadhg asked.

'That Mary Casey could be here now. How happy she would be to see me married as a Catholic. And especially to you, as you always were her favourite. You know, Tadhg, perhaps Major Marty was right amid prophetic when he accused me of being a secret Catholic, for I had no difficulty in accepting Catholicism as Father Carroll explained it. Certainly it is most similar to the Church of Ireland's beliefs. Like a dry seed, planted after many years, it has bloomed, My O'Hurley blood can't be as far below the surface as I thought. Now I feel like I have been on a long journey and have finally come home again.'

Tadhg smiled down at her. 'You have made me very happy.'

'Then at last I have begun to repay you for all that you have done for me, for if all your kindness were beads, I would have enough to make another Rosary like the one Sister Eithne gave me.

'Now I can freely call you *a chushla agus a stóir mo chroí*,' he said tenderly.

'It sounds lovely, but what does it mean?'

'O pulse and treasure of my heart.'

She squeezed his arm. 'That is beautiful. I hope that you never tire of calling me such delightful names.'

Fergus and Eoghan returned from town full of excitement, whiskey and rumours. Of the latter, Tadhg accepted several as plausible. A large contingent of soldiers were combing the countryside of Ibrickan as the fugitives are believe to be hidden by the MacGormans; that a Major from Dublin Castle (most likely Major Marty) was directing the search operations; that the sea near Doolin, now called Aghlin, the horse's leap was being dragged with hooks; and that patrols were stopping travellers on all the road from Athlone to Galway.

The sun, like a huge, molten ball about to plunge hissing into Galway Bay, was low on the horizon when Father Carroll set up an improvised altar, then donning surplice and stole, he heard the confessions of Tadhg and Mairéad, using the bedchamber for a confessional.

At sundown the priest knelt before the altar, silently offering prayers to God, then he arose, made the sign of the cross, and addressed the gatherings:

'This is a solemn and unique occasion. Because of its emergency nature, I will have to take shortcuts in administering the Sacrament of Baptism to Mairéad FitzGerald, and the marriage of Tadhg and Mairéad. Although she has been baptised in the rites of the Church of Ireland, I have deemed it best under the circumstances to give her absolute baptism in her conversion to the Holy Roman Catholic Church, since no abjuration or absolution will then be necessary inasmuch as the sacrament of rebirth washes away all sins.'

With Mairéad kneeling before the priest, touching the Book of Gospels with her right hand, she repeated after Father Carroll, the words of the Profession of Faith. The priest then recited the psalm, 'Have Mercy on Me', and ending with 'Glory Be to the Father'. Smiling, he bade her arise, and as a penance, instructed her to visit the first Catholic church she saw in the new land.

With Rory assisting as the altar boy, Father Carroll then said Mass. After the Gospel, he beckoned to Tadhg and Mairéad to approach him before the altar, and preached the Exhortation Before Marriage, concluding with, 'Nor will God be wanting with your needs; He will pledge you the lifelong support of His graces in the Holy Sacrament of Matrimony which you are now going to receive.'

Everybody then stood. Eithne's head was bowed, tears trickling down her cheeks. The priest turned to Tadhg and asked, 'Tadhg, do you take Mairéad, here present, for your lawful wife according to the rite of our holy mother, the Church?'

This must be a dream, Tadhg thought, not reality, for only in my wildest dreams could I be at the altar with the Lady Mairéad. And to being asked such a foolish question when all the world knows that the answer is yes, a thousand times yes, and for eternity.

'Tadhg,' Father Carroll said frowning, 'do you hear me?'

'Say I do,' Conor whispered urgently from behind him.

As if from a great distance, Tadhg heard himself respond with 'I do.'

Then Father Carroll turned to the bride. 'Mairéad, do you take Tadhg, here present, for your lawful husband according to the rite of our holy mother, the Church?'

Without hesitation, in a clear, loud voice, she said, 'I do.'

'Now join your right hands,' the priest declared. Then, repeating after Father Carroll, Tadhg said, 'I, Tadhg O'Cuirc, take you Mairéad FitzGerald, for my lawful wife, to have and to hold, from this day forward, for better, for worse, for richer, for poorer, in sickness and in health until death do us part.'

Then Mairéad in turn repeated the words, 'I, Mairéad FitzGerald, take you, Tadhg O'Cuirc, for my lawful husband, to have and to hold, from this day forward, for better, for worse, for richer, for poorer, in sickness and in health, until death do us part.'

Father Carroll then confirmed the marriage bond, intoning in Latin, 'Ego coniungo vos in matrionium: In nomine Patris, et Filii, et Spiritis Sancti'.

The audience responded with an enthusiastic 'Amen'.

Donnacha then stepped up and placed a ring on a plate held by Rory. The priest blessed the ring and sprinkled it with holy water. He directed Tadhg to take the ring and place it on Mairéad's finger. Tadhg complied, and repeating after Father Carroll, said 'In the name of the Father, the Son and of the Holy Ghost take this ring as a sign of our wedding vows.'

After more prayers, the priest had the newly-weds kneel and bestowed the nuptial blessing. He then instructed them that they should be faithful to each other, that the man should love his wife, and the wife love her husband, and that they should keep themselves in the fear of the Lord. Then he sprinkled them with holy water and resumed the Mass.

When Mass was over, the women all rushed over to kiss the bride. Eithne embraced Mairéad, and whispered, 'He's yours, now, be good to him.

Conor, in congratulating Tadhg, said loudly, 'Faith, Tadhg, after chasing the poor *cailín* for five years, I thought that you had suddenly changed your mind when you got to the 'I do', and decided instead to embark on the life of celibacy to conform with your new clothes.'

'He'll have to be a celibate for a while longer,' Donnacha said, grinning, 'because for caution's sake all the guests will have to stay here tonight, with the men in one room and the women in another.'

Tadhg's happy smile disappeared, and his mouth dropped open. 'You mean that I have to sleep with the men, too, and not with my bride?'

'Yes, unless you want to share your wedding bed with Nuala, Máire, Sive and Sister Eithne as well.'

'My soul to the devil!' Tadhg said, indignantly.

'And the worst is yet to come,' Conor added.

'What could be worse?' Tadhg asked.

'Once you're aboard that ship tomorrow as Father Carroll, and your bride as Sister Eithne, your celibacy will have to last all the way to America.'

'This is a fate worse than Newgate,' Tadhg said. ''Tis enough to drive a man to drink, surely.'

'Speaking of drink,' Donnacha said, 'there is *uisce beatha* and good stout ale on the table yonder, and if we can't drink to Tadhg's happiness, we can at least drink to his good health.'

When Nuala called them to the wedding feast some time later, Eoghan commented, 'If the amount of whiskey we have drunk to Tadhg's health is an indicator, then surely he must be the healthiest man in all of Ireland.'

'And the unhappiest,' Conor added.

'On the contrary,' said Tadhg. 'I'm still the happiest man in all of Ireland as I have three great gifts: the girl of my heart, the best of friends, and the appreciation of a good joke, even when it's on me.'

'Bebhinn, you have truly prepared a feast fit for a king,' Conor said, surveying the steaming hot broth made from chopped eels; a roasted turbot, caught that morning in Galway Bay, and cooked with a succulent sauce; golden brown smoked salmon from the Corrib River; a chicken baked over the hearth and sliced into a sauce of milk, chopped wild herbs and egg yolks; a well-seasoned roast of beef, served cold; a salad consisting of cabbage, onions, lettuce and carrots, smothered in a spicy sauce; flat loaves of freshly baked oat bread; buttermilk, ale, turnip wine, and a potent beverage made from fermented pear juice.

Tadhg and Mairéad were seated at the head of the table, Donnacha and Nuala at the foot, and the other guests arranged around the sides. 'Give Tadhg the *curadh mir*, the hero's portion,' Donnacha directed Bebhinn who was serving, 'and an equal portion to Mairéad, for 'tis a brave woman indeed who would wed the likes of our islandman with the restless feet. and the ready sword to protect the poor and the oppressed.'

At the conclusion of the meal, a custard, made from fruit and white wine, was served to all but the newly-weds, who were given instead a sponge cake, sprinkled with wine and herbs, whose centre was filled with rich cream flavoured with white wine and chopped lemon and orange rinds.

'It's an old Galway dish called 'Diarmaid's and Gráinne's Well,' Donnacha explained, 'made only for lovers. You must break the top, then serve each other the cream from the centre.'

Amid much hilarity, bride and bridegroom fed each other until the cake was consumed. Then Tadhg, smiling at Mairéad, said,'It is only fitting that we have the Diarmaid-and-Gráinne cake, for I, too, like Diurmuid, had a spell placed on me, and had to flee for my life with the *cailín ban* over much of the same route that the fabled lovers were forced to take in fleeing the wrath of Finn MacCool. But instead of a chariot, we rode in Tomas's cart; instead of the Clan Morna pursuing us, seeking my head, we had the Sassanach soldiers; instead of Finn's savage wolfhound, Bran, we had the pack of dogs. And to help us, we too, had a faithful friend Fergus. But we will not make Diarmaid's mistake of going north to Ben Gulban to be killed by a wild boar, our path is to the west with the setting sun.'

Mairéad then jumped up, and going to the foot of the table, bestowed kisses on Nuala and Donnacha, thanked them for all their courtesies, the wedding feast, and for the ring, which she held up for all to see. Nothing elaborate or expensive as fitting a FitzGerald, it was a simple band with two hands clasping a heart.

'We have welcomed the opportunity to repay old debts,'

Donnacha said. 'First, to Tadhg, who fought bravely for Ireland as both a Rapparee and a soldier with Sarsfield. We who have stayed by the hearth have let him fight our battles for us. And second, to you, Mairéad FitzGerald O'Cuirc, because your forebears, originally Welsh-Norman invaders for the English crown, have consistently defended the Catholic cause in Ireland, and have suffered grievously for it. It is a great honour to have a FitzGerald in the humble abode of the King of the Claddagh.'

The evening passed all too quickly. Underlying Tadhg's happiness was a melancholy awareness that it was likely the last time he would ever see his friends, and his future was fraught with peril. Occasionally Donnacha had to caution his guests to restrain their gaiety lest they attract the attention of the soldiers across the river.

Finally it was time to retire. Amid ribald comments by the men, and much giggling by the women, they curled up in their respective rooms for the night, with Tadhg acutely aware of his bride, so near and yet so far.

They were awakened by Nuala and Máire who had to prepare the morning meal. After they ate, Donnacha explained the schedule: Father Carroll would visit the ship and speak with the captain, then come to the cabin to say Mass as it was Sunday. A half-hour before sailing time, high tide being about 3 p.m., Tadhg and Mairéad, dressed as priest and nun, would leave the cabin accompanied by Donnacha, Nuala and Bebhinn, to avoid attracting undue attention and go directly to the ship. Father Carroll and Eithne would remain hidden in the cabin until nightfall, then return with Conor and his party to Kilkieran until such time as new arrangements could be made to go to America from another port than Galway.

Excitement mounted as the hours passed. Father Carroll finally arrived, beaming, to announce that the ship's captain, a Catholic and friend of Charles Carroll, the vessel's owner, had agreed to accept a substitute priest with no questions asked. The priest gave Tadhg a letter to be given only to Charles Carroll upon arrival in Maryland, explaining the substitution, and telling of Tadhg's exploits in Ireland, and his friendship with Sarsfield who was related to the Carrolls through his mother, an O'Moore. Father Carroll instructed Tadhg to guard the letter at all times, and to destroy it if necessary. Tadhg nodded vigorously, recalling his carelessness aboard the St Teresa. Then Father Carroll dropped a bombshell. He had arranged with the captain to take Rory as a cabin boy!

The lad gulped, licked his suddenly dry lips, and burst into tears. Then ashamed of his unmanly outburst, he ran to Tadhg and buried his red poll in Tadhg's chest. Tadhg, too, was overwhelmed by happiness for the orphan who had adopted him four years before at the Shannon crossing below Athlone.

Then, suddenly, came a loud and persistent knocking at the door. All faces blanched as they stared apprehensively at one another until Donnacha finally went to the door, slowly opening it a mere slit. Fully expecting Major Marty and his soldiers, Tadhg sat paralysed.

After a brief glance, Donnacha swung wide the door. Ten sighs of relief were heard as Cormac O'Quinn from Doolin entered, carrying a small package, and a long, slender object wrapped in a linen case. Cormac walked directly to Tadhg, saying, 'These are for you. From Jacques Benoit.'

'Jacques?' Tadhg's eyes were wide with astonishment. 'Is he in Ireland? And how did you know where to find me?'

Cormac smiled. 'The Frenchman was at his farm when I returned the horse. He was most pleased to learn that you escaped from the English. As for finding you, I merely looked for Eoghan's púcan, tracing it to Galway, where the men down at the quay said that Eoghan was with Donnacha O'Halloran. It was that simple. Captain Benoit gave me these articles, he said that you left them aboard his ship.'

Frowning, Donnacha said, 'I'm glad it's getting close to sailing time, for if Cormac could locate you that easily, the Sassanaigh should too. But what's in the packages, Tadhg?'

'My French grammar, my Geoffrey O'Donohue poem, my Derry Bible, and my French razor. And in this long one, my Spanish sword. It was thoughtful of Jacques to return them.'

'And that's not all,' Cormac added, 'he also sent you your horse.'

'Cúchulainn? My soul to God, why did he do that?'

'He said it was to atone for the unpardonable offence committed by his brother-in-law aboard his ship. And he said he already has some magnificent colts sired by Cúchulainn.'

Tadhg was staggered by the news. He turned to Donnacha. 'What can we do about this new development?'

'The ship is carrying horses,' Father Carroll interjected, 'It can be taken aboard as mine.'

Shaking his head, Tadhg said, 'This is too much for me. Yesterday I had nothing. Today I am a priest with a wife, a horse and a sword.'

'Not to overlook a French razor, an Irish poem, and an English Bible,' Donnacha commented drily. 'But I'd better hurry and get the horse aboard the ship. Cormac, you'd better stay here. Where is the animal?'

'Tethered outside the door.'

While Donnacha was gone, Tadhg donned his clerical vestments, and Eithne dressed Mairéad in an exchange of their clothing. She taught her how to genuflect, make the Sign of the Cross, to recite the rosary, and to say the Lord's Prayer and Hail Mary as Catholics did. She also gave her a small prayer book printed in Latin, which Mairéad couldn't understand, but that she could read with Tadhg's assistance.

As the time for departure neared, Tadhg and Mairéad said their final farewells. Tearfully they thanked each one for their help, and promised to arrange for passage of the Kilkieran group to America as soon as they had money enough.

Eithne kissed Tadhg gently, hardly touching his lips, in more of a gesture than a caress, in apparent renunciation of her former feeling for him now that he was a married man. Her voice choked as she told him, 'Perhaps in America you will finally fulfil your dream of having your own school, and I can be teaching the Crosses of God to Tadhg Óg and little Mairéad as well as Indians.'

Conor embraced Tadhg. '*Slan leat, a chara*. I remember well the day you came in from the sea, and I will remember the day you leave by the sea, for a part of my heart will be going with you.'

In turn Máire, Sive, Cormac, Fergus and Eoghan were embraced and bade farewell. Then Father Carroll took Tadhg's hand. 'Remember, *a mhic*, that for the duration of the voyage Mairéad is a nun, not your wife. This will take great restraint. Be careful that you not betray yourself by careless word or gesture, for although the captain is a Catholic, the rest of the crew is not. And he must not suspect that Mairéad is other than a nun. He will turn his head for the substitution of a different priest, but I doubt if he would knowingly transport two fugitives from the Crown. And now, with the blessing of God upon you, be off to your destiny.'

With tears streaming down their cheeks they left the cabin to walk with Nuala and Bebhinn, while Donnacha walked with Rory, to the quay where the ship was docked. It was an appropriate opportunity to thank the O'Hallorans and Bebhinn for their protection, the wedding feast and the ring.

Tadhg and Mairéad were tense as they walked along the quay, feeling conspicuous in their unfamiliar garb, but the few persons they encountered paid them little attention. As they approached the ship, they were awed by its great size, and the activity on board. Sailors were scuttling about, sails were being raised, and the vessel strained at its hawsers as if, too, was anxious to depart. Donnacha quietly but firmly reminded Rory that Tadhg and Mairéad were fugitives, and any careless remark of familiarity on his part, could mean disclosure, and that for the entire voyage he would have to remain apart from them.

'I know,' Rory replied soberly. 'I love Tadhg, and would rather die than hurt him. He's been my father for more than four years. Don't worry, Donnacha.'

The King smiled at the lad. 'I won't,' he said.

With their hearts pounding, the party approached the gangplank. Several soldiers, conversing with giggling *cailíns*, scrutinised them casually, but the ship's captain, standing at the rail, shouted impatiently, 'Come aboard, Father Carroll, we're about ready to sail.'

As the soldiers hesitated, Donnacha took Tadhg and Mairéad by the arms, and hurried them up the gangplank. They were met by the captain, a tall, gaunt, man with deepset eyes, who looked at his passengers curiously, then escorted them to their cabins.

Turning to Mairéad, he said, 'I hope you brought your sea-legs with you, Sister.'

Mairéad smiled demurely, peering up at the captain from her expressive green eyes, her golden hair completely covered by her white coif, and chided him gently. 'Nuns don't have legs, Captain.'

The seaman coloured, then bowed. 'I apologise, Sister, for my unseemly remark. What I meant was that we have a long voyage ahead of us, and I hope that you will make a good sailor.'

Tadhg was apprehensive. 'How long will it be, Captain?'

'Six weeks, Father, if we have good winds.'

Mairéad looked at Tadhg, a mischievous smile on her face as she clapped hands to her mouth to keep from laughing at his obvious chagrin.

'That will cost you six Our Fathers and six Hail Marys, Sister,' Tadhg reprimanded her sternly. 'But first let us get our baggage stowed safely, and I'll meet you on the deck in a few minutes.'

A short time later, Tadhg was joined by Mairéad on the main deck where he stood by the starboard rail. The ship was larger and newer than the Le Duc on which Tadhg had sailed to France. Three tapering, towering masts reached towards Heaven, with a score of sailors scrambling in the rigging. Other crewmen were now hauling in the huge hawsers mooring the ship to the quay, their movements coordinated with a rousing ditty that they sung with gusto.

Imperceptibly at first, then noticeably, the ship eased away from the dock as wind and tide seized her. Waving goodbye to Donnacha, Nuala and Bebhinn, Tadhg looked sadly at the Claddagh where he could easily discern the peat smoke curling from Donnacha's cabin.

The ship's great sails bellied and strained as it gradually picked up speed, overtaking a smaller sailing vessel on which a man in an English Army officer's uniform stood at the rail. As the larger ship passed, the man below was suddenly aware of two surprised faces staring down at him, one under the huge, white cornette of a Sister of Charity, and the other under the dark, broad brimmed hat of a Franciscan priest. The officer made a derisive gesture, then shouted, 'To hell with the Pope.'

Tadhg turned a startled face to Mairéad. She shook her head in disbelief. Then the mischievous smile appeared again, and she muttered, sotto voce, 'To hell with you, too, Major Marty. And to hell with Cromwell as well.'

Tadhg laughed so hard his belly shook, and tears streamed down his cheeks. Finally he gasped, 'And that profanity, Sister, will cost you twelve Our Fathers and an equal number of Hail Marys, but because I enjoyed your sinful comment so much, I'll say them for you.'

She grinned. 'That's a sin I'm proud of.'

'It's amazing that he didn't recognise us, but I suppose that we are well disguised. By the way, do you know the name of this ship? I asked the captain. You'd never guess it in a million years.'

'I won't live that long, so tell me now.'

'The Respite. Out of Baltimore.'

She pursed her lips, and held up her hand. 'Hold it, Father Carroll, let me say it for you. God has granted us another Respite. And how appropriate, just when we encounter our dear friend from Dublin Castle again.'

They stood at the rail, exhilarated with the realisation that they hadn't been recognised by their pursuer, and that they were finally free. They talked excitedly of their voyage, full of wonder about their future in the New World. And as they conversed, Galway disappeared in the distance, the Respite now moving briskly before a freshening east wind, a broad wake at her stern.

The sun was low in the west, with the sea like molten silver before them, and Tadhg told Mairéad how, many, many years before, Ailill the silversmith, and Dubhaltach the goldsmith, quarrelled and fought over Aine, the daughter of Manannan MacLir, the god of the sea. To end their jealous bickering, Manannan ordered them to practice their arts separately, and to this day Ailill covers the sea with silver in the day, and Dubhaltach spreads his molten gold at night. But, Tadhg explained, because of the magic, you can only see the rivals' offerings to Aine when the sun or moon is shining on the sea.

As they headed west, the Aran Islands loomed larger and larger before them. Tadhg's heart beat faster, and his throat tightened as the familiar shapes of Inis Thiar, Inis Mean, and Inishmór, as he knew them, loomed closer. He was reminded of the great storm, and how the winds of chance had shaped his life, and the lonely graves of his two companions on Kilkieran Bay. He thought of his first meeting with Mairéad on the wrecked Protector, his subsequent travels through Ireland, the tragic deaths of Sarsfield and Dónal Óg, his return from France and capture, culminating in his marriage to Mairéad, and now the wind was blowing him once more towards his starting point at Kilmurvy.

Sensing the turmoil Tadhg was experiencing, Mairéad remained silent, watching the swirling green waters below, and listening to the hiss of the waves cleft by the Respite's sharp prow, the hum of the wind in the rigging, the shouts of the crewmen, and the creaking of the straining sails.

When the Respite was well within North Sound, and Golan Head to the north pointed like a long finger at faraway Baltimore, Tadhg turned to Mairéad, eyes glistening with tears. 'Look, Mairéad, my love, to the south on Inishmór, where the waves are breaking, that's the Strand of Portmurvy where we launched Peadar Laidír's curragh, God have mercy on his soul. Beyond is Kilmurvy where I was born. My mother, my father, my sisters, my brother, are all there. 'Tis better than five years since I left them, and may God forgive me for all the heartaches they have endured, worrying about me, for this is as close as I have been to seeing them again.

And now the wind that blew me away from them, the wind that is blowing us to freedom, is blowing me even further.'

Mairéad looked up to him, tears streaming down her cheeks. 'My heart aches for you, Tadhg, *mo stóir*. How I wish that I could take you in my arms to comfort you, to kiss away the sadness, but God in His mercy in granting us our freedom, has seen to put shackles on us in the religious roles we are playing. So I must constrain. But I do want you to know that the bonds of love between us are indestructible, and I can truthfully say, *mo rún*, that I thank God for the great wind that blew you to me five years ago.'

Tadhg stared down at her, his brow furrowed. 'Perhaps that was His purpose,' he said, thoughtfully, 'because if I hadn't been cast up on Kilkieran Bay, there would not have been anyone to save you from the sea.'

She looked up at him and nodded. 'It was God's will!'

They huddled at the ship's rail until the sun hung at the edge of the western world, the Hy Brasil of the ancient Irish, and Inishmór had faded into the distance. Tadhg sighed, then murmured softly, '*Slan leat go deo, Erin, slan leat go deo.*'

Thus ends the story of Tadhg and Mairéad.